Bridges of Turand

Praise for
Bridges of Turand
Ode to the Heroes
Legends from Turand

Bridges of Turand is the continuing saga of Queen Alexa and King Gregor as they work to protect peace in the land they love. Their love of peace is in danger, and the only way to achieve lasting peace forces them to confront once again the dreaded Sifiq. Their path leads to unexpected answers of questions I had from Song of Turand and Return to Turand. Great book that I'll read more than once.

—CW Review

Sandra Valencia gives us a landscape that, while torn by the ravages of war, remains bound together by the love of the god Val for his people, and the love that Gregor and Alexa share for their god, their people, and each other.

Valencia's writing…is as always: so distinctive that anyone having previously read her work would know it without seeing her name on any page, and those reading her writing for the first time would eagerly do so again.

—Robert E. Blackwell, author

Bridges of Turand

Ode to the Heroes
Legends from Turand

Sandra Valencia

Book Design & Production:
Columbus Publishing Lab
www.ColumbusPublishingLab.com

Copyright © 2022 by
Sandra Valencia
LCCN: 2022923690

Hardcover ISBN: 978-1-63337-707-3
Paperback ISBN: 978-1-63337-708-0
E-Book ISBN: 978-1-63337-709-7

Printed in the United States of America
1 3 5 7 9 10 8 6 4 2

While finishing this book, I could not attend a milestone high school class reunion after exposure to Covid. I had been vaccinated and boosted, but I believe in exercising an abundance of caution. Leading up to the reunion, I was in contact with people I attended school with those many years ago. It was nice.

On another note, it reminded me that I have been blessed with two special friends for much longer than those milestone years. Both now live in states far away, but we have kept our bonds of friendship more like a sacred sisterhood. Each of these two women overcame hardships and challenges. They achieved advanced education and careers that served humanity. Leta has always kept her humor and her faith while keeping her eye and her heart fixed on a future she always believed would be hers. Debra is one of the most intelligent and generous souls I have ever known and has inspired me since the day I first called her friend. I now dedicate Bridges of Turand to Debra Price Jackson and Leta Sekavec Lee.

And, Rosie, I hope you are happy with this newest installment of Legends from Turand.

Introduction

During the long months since Queen Alexa's return to Toraval after her abduction and brutal captivity in the Sifiq Kingdom, King Gregor has closely monitored every phase of her recovery. While his priestess-wife draws on the power of her phenomenal faith to restore her health and perspective, her husband must face the dual obligations of his position in life. Gregor is determined to care for the greatest love he has ever known as she resumes her life. However, ongoing violent raids against isolated coastal villages force Gregor to confront a renewed Sifiq threat.

Gregor walks a fine line as he considers the staggering sacrifices and losses resulting from the Sifiq occupation that Turand ended twenty years earlier. Then, Stefan Sidano had helped him devise plans to eradicate those invaders who had spent years tormenting Turand's people. Following the war that delivered their nation back into the hands of Turand's rightful leaders, Gregor and Stefan vowed never again to allow the Sifiq a second chance to wreak destruction in Turand. Gregor now must decide how to honor his pledge to protect his nation and people while keeping his beloved Alexa safe.

Part 1

The Creator's loom had woven cloth so fine,
And no finer cloth than that of an ancestral line.
The spirit awakened from her long years of rest,
When the Creator breathed over the hilly crest,
There so long she had lain, forgotten and unknown,
Nothing more than a strange name carved into stone.

Then came the little one who suffered a fate same as she.
A third mystic who, too, had plummeted into the sea,
Its waves had trapped her in violent heaves and loud roars
Until leaving that little one washed up on dark, sandy shores.
As the mystic listened, seeking answers to haunted inquiries
Images of lives appeared through the mists of shared memories

With newfound breath, like clouds upon breezes amassing,
The wakened spirit arose to bridge time's quiet, slow passing.
Summoned by calls from the one she had labored to give life,
Her beautiful, sweet child sadly sacrificed within bitter strife.
Two precious spirits united again, their purpose made clear,
Guide this strange new mystic with whom bonds both did share.

Bridges of Turand

Through dreams and her babe born in this strange new land
She would speak to the little one who must understand.
Only this new mystic could hear whispers stirring memories to life
Only she could connect links that might conquer this new strife.
"You must save once again the ancestral cloth; our words, please hear.
Pray listen, little one! Hear us, go forth, and know not fear."

And though filled with questions and sure trepidation,
The mystic set her eyes on the road with determination.
Tho' looming ahead lay her journey, long and mysterious,
Senses warning against failure; her soul proven courageous,
Depending on deep faith pledged to her God above,
She bravely advanced, strengthened by ancestral cloth of love.

The Mystics

Chapter 1

Afternoon sunshine reflected off smoothly carved stone, highlighting the intricate splash of colors inherent in the depths of polished granite. Shades of gray, rose, and brown on a field of ivory defied any sense of pattern. Instead, their randomness created a capricious display of flecks, splotches, and spots that mirrored the many directions of her thoughts.

Alexa breathed in deeply before releasing a shuddering sigh. Her right hand rose until her palm flattened against the cool, hard wall of solid rock. Her face tilted forward. With hot tears tracking down her cheeks, she rested her forehead against lettering engraved on the front of the mausoleum.

"Alexa?" Stefan Sidano's words barely registered above the sounds of branches swaying, birds calling, breezes whispering, and the many voices from the past.

Swallowing against thickness in her throat, she searched for her voice. "I'm fine, Stefan. You mustn't worry. I just needed some time alone."

Gray eyes shone with sympathetic concern as he placed his hands on her shoulders before guiding her to a long bench in front of the massive tomb. "You do know how worried everyone is, don't you?"

Oblivious to teardrops glistening on her cheeks, she nodded. "I appreciate their concern. I know this is difficult for everyone. I just need to manage my grief. Except for you, I'm not sure anyone else could really understand."

The line of Stefan's mouth tightened. The end had come tragically. Inside, mourners gathered, seeking whatever solace they could find within the company of friends, cousins, parents, and siblings. In fact, he thought, the whole of Turand grieved deeply over the loss of a man who had raised himself from a state of contempt to become a hero more beloved than ever with his death.

Stefan himself struggled with loss driving itself like an iron spike into his heart. Still, despite the deep mourning gripping his family and godchildren, he had known he must come to Alexa. No one else could possibly appreciate the sorrow filling her—at least no one currently in Turand. Only one other man alive could fully comprehend, and he had yet to return from his perilous journey. With only the slightest shake of his head, Stefan acknowledged that, for the time being, he was the only one who could offer her the real solace she needed when her emotions were held captive to memories of despair and faith, life and death, hatred and love.

"Take as long as you need. I won't leave you," Stefan said while dealing with his own sorrow. Closing his eyes as she leaned against him, he prayed that Alexa would soon do again as she had done throughout all the years he had known her—that she would turn her burden over to Turand's beloved God Val.

Three Years Earlier

Gazing at Alexa's suddenly thoughtful expression, Gregor could hardly avoid his mind's swift recollection of their first moments together that morning. He had failed to stifle a grin when she had squeaked at the end of a long, luxurious stretch and yawn.

"Your Majesty! Such habits you acquired while you were away," he had teased.

The rosy blush coloring her cheeks had replaced all remnants of gray shadows left by starvation and highlighted the returning plumpness of good health. Gregor's heart had swelled with pleasure at her wide smile as he drew her close to kiss her forehead. "Now that we're happily married again and enjoying a real honeymoon, how does a leisurely breakfast sound before we ride over to the springs to bathe?"

"Mmmm, that sounds delightful. May we stop long enough to enjoy the lilacs before we leave?"

"Whatever your heart desires, beloved," he replied indulgently.

In a teasing mood, Alexa lifted her eyebrows high. "If that's the case, Your Majesty, we may never get downstairs to breakfast, let alone to the hot springs."

Later that morning, Alexa had held lavender lilac blossoms close to her nose. The fragrance's essence had floated throughout her being on gentle waves, soothing her spirit with the velvet sweetness Valiria priestesses had cherished for centuries. Looking on, Gregor had felt immensely glad they had come to Lindaval so she could finally gather the elusive threads of her perspective that had unraveled during her captivity in the Sifiq Kingdom.

Now, however, sitting in the warm, bubbling waters of Lindaval's hot springs, her abrupt change of mood caused him to swallow against rising anxiety. Questions rose in those beautiful emerald eyes. He could see them but could not quite define them. Hesitantly, he said, "Alexa, you're so quiet of a sudden. Are you all right?"

When she looked up, her eyes were wide and solemn. Her lips formed a gentle, almost sad smile. "I was thinking how much I hate leaving tomorrow. Four days here with you have been absolutely wonderful. You must admit, though, that it's still somewhat short of a real honeymoon."

Gregor smiled wryly. "You can't deny that it's a tremendous improvement over our first honeymoon."

Alexa chuckled. "I can't deny that since we never had a honeymoon. Still, after being gone from home for so long and then working so hard on my recovery, I suppose I'm feeling more than a little selfish. You even delayed this honeymoon to be sure of my health. You cannot imagine how much I missed you while I was away. Or how much I needed you. Sometimes, all I wanted was your arms around me. Other times, I would have given anything to have you beside me—to be loving me..." Her voice trailed off, and her eyes closed. She hugged herself tightly as her whole body shuddered.

Casting her gaze around, she beheld lush greenery and trees heavy with summery foliage as if enjoying their beauty for the very first time. With its dancing prisms of light and soothing rush, the cascading waterfall still stirred magic in her breast. How she wanted to linger in this place of perennial spring where she knew love for her husband had truly awakened.

Gregor quickly slid closer and pulled her onto his lap. "Beloved, despite everything you've told me, you're right. How can I begin to imagine everything you endured there? I can assure you of one thing. I missed you every minute you were away. My pain rose much more from my heart and soul than it did from my body."

As she rested her head against his bare shoulder, Alexa breathed in the calm of his presence. "I do know that, Gregor. I *feel* that. For now, there are times when I just don't want to share you. It sounds childish, I know. Queen, Valkana, and mother to six children, but all I want is to have you to myself a while longer. Does that sound so terrible?"

"After all you've suffered? Not at all." He kissed damp, curling tresses. "At this moment, I wish we could stay in Lindaval forever, but you know I cannot. Neither can you." The sigh that escaped her delivered a deep ache to his heart. "I do promise to make extra time for us when we return home to Toraval. I very much need you, too, my love."

⁓

"We've been in this coach for nearly three hours, and you've spoken what? Maybe three times?"

Gregor shifted his gaze from the window to his wife's reproachful eyes. His full mane of hair, now liberally woven with silver, waved as he shook his head. He leaned forward and grasped Alexa's gloved hands. "I'm not ignoring you if that's what you think."

"That wasn't what I meant, but you do make another valid point. You were ignoring me." Her accusing grin held no anger, but her expression was sufficient to prompt feelings of guilt.

"Alexa, I only thought to savor your presence these final hours together before we arrive in Toraval. Nothing more."

"By sitting there and staring out the window in gloomy silence? Gregor, I know I was gone for a year, but just because I still can't read your life force the way I do with other people doesn't mean I don't know you well enough to know when you're hiding something."

"Alexa…"

"Gregor, stop. Now. Do you honestly think I don't know? How can you imagine for one single minute that I haven't known almost from the beginning what you, Nikolai, Stefan, and Victor have in mind? If I've said nothing before now, it's because I knew I needed to focus on my health and having my family together again. I also knew what it meant to you to renew our wedding vows since my homecoming came so close to our anniversary."

He heaved an exasperated sigh. His jaw clenched as a once-forgotten lament returned to torment him. "I didn't want to burden you yet. There are still times when my responsibilities as monarch are almost too much to bear."

"And you see this as one of those times?"

He flinched when he saw tears well in her eyes. "I wanted to shield you as long as I could from what lies ahead. You needed time."

"Gregor, I will never escape what happened in the Sifiq Kingdom. With Val's help, I can only keep it in perspective by comprehending that it happened with purpose. I must go forward now and live life each day with purpose—as I always did. That also means picking myself up when I falter—hopefully through the strength of my faith and with your help because you love me. I must also forge ahead to make life the best it can be for those Val brings into my life. Forging ahead will always include being your wife and your queen when you confront a crisis such as this."

Gregor's face dropped. As its wheels rolled over the road, the coach's steady rocking was beginning to annoy him. He hardly knew what to say to her. "How much do you know, and how much do you only suspect?"

Alexa turned and looked out the window. The passing countryside lay beneath brilliant, late-winter sunshine. Stretches of dark green pines lined most of the road and occasionally thinned as they rode by tidy, well-kept farms. Returning her attention to her waiting husband, she drew in a shaky breath. "Whose idea was this?"

"You haven't answered my questions yet." Again, he shook his head. "Alexa, the truth is that Nikolai brought Stefan and Victor in to discuss the matter with me. He had carefully contemplated details and then articulated points we were all loath to accept. Unfortunately, years of direct experience plus discussions with Raf-Zan forced us to formulate action not one of us wishes to take."

"Is that why you requested the emergency assembly of National Council?"

"How?" He stammered to a stop. Stefan had summoned council representatives only hours before the wedding ceremony to prevent Alexa from learning of the unprecedented action. Stefan's security precautions were exemplary, and Gregor felt sure there had been no failure on the part of his Chief Royal Adviser.

Alexa's left eyebrow lifted. "I am still Valkana. I still perceive many things through the revelations of our Lord Val."

"Of course." Gregor's glanced out the window. When he returned his attention to Alexa, his gaze was straightforward. Her expression was solemn but not angry. Truth had always been his ally whenever they had faced difficult circumstances in the past. Truth, no matter how dreadful, was more crucial now than ever. "You know I can authorize military action by royal decree, but this situation is far too critical to undertake without broad consensus, advice, and support from our provincial governorships. We need to proceed expeditiously, but we must also avoid rash action."

Growing uncomfortable on the hard leather upholstery, Alexa shifted on the seat. "Will you tell me exactly what kind of military action you have in mind?"

Deciding to share only basics for the moment, Gregor said, "We plan to send a diplomatic envoy to assess the situation in Atuliq. We must know if Bin-Lot is still in power and the current stability of his reign. If another leader has usurped Bin-Lot's throne, then we must judge what risks he poses to Turand now and in the future. In the meantime, I've already taken steps to develop strategies to address current military readiness here and prepare for military deployment. Members of National Council will be fully apprised of my concerns and plans. I will do everything in my power to forfend all vulnerable provinces against further incursions like the one that resulted in your abduction or the ones that years ago led to the Sifiq occupation. I will not give the Sifiq a chance to invade again."

"Dearest Val," Alexa gasped, her eyes widening, "you're talking about more than a blockade. You're speaking of taking real war directly to the Sifiq Kingdom."

"Only if absolutely necessary. Alexa, I spent nearly half my life planning to rid Turand of their vile pestilence. I almost lost my life fighting the civil war they instigated. Too many fine Turandans died because of them—including your parents and mine. I swore I would do everything in my power to prevent them from ever again having the opportunity to wreak such havoc in this country. They committed their biggest mistake ever when they encroached on my territory, murdered Royal Guards, and abducted my wife. What they did to you and your companions was unconscionable. I have both moral and civil responsibility as King of Turand to ensure they never again pose any such risk to this nation." ·

Against her will, tears eased from Alexa's eyes. Within the close confines of the royal coach, she slid from her seat to her knees and laid her head on her husband's lap. Pushing aside the hood of her lavender cape, he grimaced bitterly as he ran long fingers through lustrous waves still growing out after being cut short in the Sifiq Kingdom. Reaching down, he grasped her arms and drew her up beside him. She turned on the seat until her face lay against his chest.

"Beloved," Gregor said softly, "you must understand. I would never consider such action if I didn't think it vital to the safety and welfare of our people."

She tried to focus on the sounds of his heartbeat and breathing, then on the clatter of horses' hooves outside the coach and the iron-clad wooden wheels spinning over the paved road leading to Toraval. Instead, the past overwhelmed her. Tortured screams during the Sifiq attack on her home in Zinzan. After her wedding, taunts and jeers from Sifiq soldiers when they thought Gregor wouldn't hear. Arguments with Adrina and Victor while she was a prisoner in Garogan Castle. Moans and cries of wounded and dying men from battles that nearly claimed Gregor's and Victor's lives. Tormented citizens left behind in the Sifiq Kingdom. All combined to form a flood of memories that overflowed in a torrent of tears.

Her husband held her tightly, already expecting the pain his revelation would bring. "Alexa, my love, I am so sorry."

Swallowing hard, she straightened on the seat and reached out to caress the line of his perfectly trimmed beard. "I'm afraid, Gregor. I will not lie to you. I am afraid, but I trust you and your judgment. I know this cannot have been easy for you."

At that moment, they felt the coach roll to an unexpected stop. Gregor quickly looked around as he heard one of the escort riders approach the coach door on the side where Alexa now sat. Alexa reached out and lowered the window, glad to see Captain Tirstan Fratino had fallen back.

Leaning over the pommel of his saddle, he alerted them to a problem. "Your Majesty, there has been an accident ahead. A large wagon is overturned and blocking the road. I've sent someone to check if help is on the way."

Moments later, Tirstan again rapped on the coach's door. This time, he was on foot. Through the still-open window, he spoke in a quiet, urgent voice. "Lady Valkana, a young man is critically injured. A physician was summoned, but it's unlikely he will arrive in time. The family is praying. Would you consider joining them for a blessing? I've only told them you are a priestess in the Order of Val."

"Beloved, you needn't go," Gregor told her gently.

She braved a smile. "This is my purpose, my husband. Wait here. We don't want your presence to overwhelm these people just now."

A footman lowered the steps of the coach and opened the door. Quickly, Tirstan helped Alexa descend. The hood of her lavender cape, drawn fully over her head, hid her face as she and Tirstan hurried toward the side of the road. Several family members surrounded the young man's motionless body, who Alexa estimated to be about Nikolai's age.

A handsome, older man on his knees looked up. Tears poured down tan cheeks. "Lady Valiria," he wept brokenly, not recognizing the queen, "Val is taking my only son. I don't understand. I've lived a faithful life. I always fought for what was right. If I hadn't lost my arm in service to my king, I might have been able to help my son so he wouldn't lie here dying. Why? Tell me why this is happening."

Alexa closed her eyes. Questions like his never had clear answers. Instead of responding, she went to the boy's side and knelt beside him. Floating her hands above him, she reacted to an instantaneous jolt throughout her body that originated from his life force. His was a powerful life force, one that was fighting to live.

"Tirstan," she said softly, "I want these people moved back. I need space to work. Let my husband know that this may take longer than I expected. Also, tell him he should stay inside the carriage for now. You understand."

Long years in service to his queen had given Tirstan a unique ability to communicate with her using a minimal exchange of words. Since it was common for Valiria priestesses to travel under royal patronage, she felt it best to retain that anonymity for the time being. He could inform the king and swiftly return to watch over her.

Someone handed Alexa a blanket from the wagon to kneel on. Sweeping her long cape out around her, she again passed her hands over the broken body of the young man.

"His name?"

The father answered. "He is Gregor Maconti. He was born on the king's birthday, so I named him in honor of our king."

Startled at first, Alexa rolled her eyes heavenward. "Dearest Lord Val, is this why you sent us home via this road instead of our usual route?"

she murmured. Then, louder, she said to the others, "Please pray that this humble priestess will have the strength to do Val's will."

As young Gregor's family began their prayers, the noonday sun's rays created a circle around the priestess, whose arms stretched the length of the injured boy's body. Boughs of tall evergreens lining this section of the road to Toraval swayed in a fresh breeze that carried the faint fragrance of lilacs from Lindaval. Misty light began to form around the woman, who chanted her prayers in a lilting voice that soothed the fears of waiting relatives and bystanders. Soon, brilliantly colored sparks of light darted in all directions close to the priestess and the prone, dying Gregor. Within minutes, the sparks combined into a small dome encompassing the two.

Master Maconti's earlier expression of hopelessness transformed into one of astonishment. He whispered to his heartbroken wife and daughter how he had seen those sacred lights before—during the civil war. Those lights, also known as Val's Healing Graces, had been summoned at the time by two of Turand's last remaining priestesses. The lives of many men, including their own King Gregor, had been saved. Others, like himself, had been spared untold suffering from grievous battle wounds. Perhaps there existed a precious thread of hope for their son.

Almost an hour passed. The multicolored lights of the Healing Graces flickered and faded. The midday sun again shone as it did any other day. Breezes calmed. Evergreens once more scented the air with the clean smell of pine. The priestess slowly raised her head. She breathed a heavy sigh before leaning forward to place her right hand over the young man's heart. She felt its strong, rhythmic beat. The flush of youth had replaced the earlier pallor of death. He would live. She heard Val's message. *He would live.*

Tirstan was beside her instantly. "Milady, let me help you."

"What would I ever do without you, Captain?" she whispered, grateful for his supporting arms lifting her to her feet.

Alexa then turned her attention to the family. "Our Lord Val has chosen to heal your son, but he will need at least a week of rest before he fully recovers. There is an inn nearby where my husband and I planned to stop for midday and rest our horses. It might do well for you to take rooms there so your son might rest a few nights."

As her husband tended to her son and others worked on repairing the overturned wagon, Mrs. Maconti approached Alexa. Tears streamed along the woman's cheeks. "I don't know how to thank you, Lady Valiria. We love him so much. Unfortunately, we must reach Toraval tonight. Gregor must rally long enough to present his application tomorrow to study at the Zinzan Spiritual Center. We must get him there. We promised him this would be the year. We cannot fail him now. Especially not now."

Fatigued, Alexa swayed. At her side in an instant, Tirstan steadied her. "Milady?"

"Captain, I think my husband's presence would be useful now if Mistress Maconti would be kind enough to help me find someplace to sit while you summon him."

Tirstan smiled knowingly. She had not wanted to overwhelm an already distressed family with the presence of their king. However, now that a favorable outcome was at hand, His Majesty could manage the situation while the queen rested.

Minutes later, Alexa glanced upward as her impressively tall husband strode toward the long crate where she sat alongside Mistress Maconti. Rising, she reached out to him. "Gregor, my love, I'm sorry it took so long. A young man's life was in serious jeopardy."

Ignoring stunned onlookers, Gregor pushed her hood back and frowned at how pale she appeared. "Captain Fratino said you were overly fatigued. How do you feel now?"

"A little better. I'll be even better after I have something to eat. For now, I want you to meet the Maconti family. They nearly lost their only son."

Taking him by the hand and explaining along the way, she led him to where the family had gathered around a litter holding their son. Other bystanders, who had come to help, huddled close together. All bowed respectfully to their king and queen. Many appeared embarrassed they had not recognized Alexa as their Valkana.

"Please rise. Who is the boy's father?" Gregor asked.

Master Maconti stepped forward, unconsciously recapturing the proud, erect military posture from his time in service to the Crown. "I am, Your Majesty. I am Leondo Maconti, and I am beyond grateful for the kindness extended to my son by our beloved Valkana. I apologize for impeding your journey. I had no idea…"

Seeing the man's nervousness, Gregor nodded and smiled reassuringly. "Master Maconti, you must not apologize. Queen Alexa tells me that you fought with my army in Garogan Province and that your sacrifice was one that has impeded your life ever since. Your king owes you and others like you a debt impossible to repay. I am grateful that we came when we did. I also understand our Valkana summoned Val's Healing Graces to heal your son. What more can we do to help?"

Master Maconti exchanged disbelieving glances with his wife. "Our horses bolted after wild dogs ran at them. Some nearby farmers caught them and are helping us repair our wagon. We must reach Toraval tonight and try to revive our son long enough tomorrow to present his application to the admission officer visiting from the Zinzan Spiritual Center. We couldn't leave home sooner, and tomorrow is the admission officer's last day in Toraval. Tomorrow may be our son's only opportunity to apply, Sire. He delayed until we had reliable help for me on our farm."

"I see." Gregor nodded thoughtfully. "My wife tells me your son requires rest. I must defer to her advice on this matter and insist for your son's sake."

Responding to pained grimaces on the faces of both parents, he continued with a wry grin, "We are fortunate that my wife holds some influence with the admissions council at Zinzan. I suggest we let her speak with your son when he feels better. She can then review his application. If she feels he is worthy of admission, I'm quite sure she can arrange an exception due to today's unusual circumstances."

"Your Majesty, how do we thank you?"

Grinning broadly, Gregor extended his hand to grasp Master Maconti's shoulder. "Sir, you stood by your king in battle and then, as I understand, named your son in his honor. I see this as a fine way to show my appreciation for such loyalty, don't you?"

Alexa's eyes sparkled as she listened to the conversation between her husband and his former soldier as the two watched several escort troops lift the younger Gregor into the wagon. Their mutual respect had been born years earlier during times of violent upheaval when no one knew how Turand would recover from the throes of Sifiq occupation followed by civil war. However, during those years of recovery and renewed prosperity, Maconti's respect had changed into profound regard for the king.

King Gregor had earned his soldier's trust and never once received a bitter rebuke for the hardships caused by the infirmity of the amputated arm. Knowing that her husband faced turbulent decisions ahead, Alexa appreciated this precious reminder that her husband's wise judgment and courage in the past had built such lasting bonds of loyalty and esteem.

Chapter 2

Nikolai stared through the window of Stefan's office. He had listened attentively to plans for the impending emergency session of National Council. His father wanted a concise list of details for the agenda. Gregor believed approval for their proposals depended on clear comprehension that they desired to avoid armed confrontation if feasible. However, he was also determined to proceed with a robust winning strategy should war become necessary.

After dedicating long hours to studying military tactics, the prince also took time to question General Kohira and other officers who had fought alongside his father about their wartime experiences during the civil war. He reviewed voluminous notes about the many fascinating stories his father had told him through the years. He sorted through every shred of information he had heard or read. Analyzing and then comparing the bits and pieces, Nikolai often returned to the men who had helped his father win victory over Sifiq invaders and the rebel army with additional questions.

Thoughtfully, he turned away from the distant image of soldiers marching through a side gate. "I look forward to Papino Victor's return from Garogan. I have several questions for him. Like it or not, he had direct experience with how Sifiq officers planned attacks. I also think he should speak to younger officers and recruits. One critical concept I learned from listening to Father, General Kohira, and other officers is that war is not some grand, glorious adventure. It is miserable and ugly. They emphasized that over and again."

Stefan rose and approached his godson. Pride etched itself into every feature of the older man's face as he grasped Nikolai's muscular arm. "You are wise beyond your years if you comprehend that before you ever walk onto a battlefield, Nikolai. Come. Sit."

Nikolai settled his tall frame into the same leather chair where his father had sat months earlier to discuss Alexa's strange, mystical visitation while she was still captive in the Sifiq Kingdom. After his godfather sat in the chair beside him, the prince sighed. "Didn't you go to the battlefields once?"

Stefan nodded, his still-golden hair falling across his forehead. His lips drew into a taut line. "I did. Your mother woke up half the palace with her screams one night. She had a vision of your father dying and insisted on going to him."

"Did she say what happened in the vision? Or how Father was hurt? I've heard it was quite the story but never any real details."

"Nikolai…" Stefan's face tensed.

"Papino, please. So much has been kept from me. This new crisis with the Sifiq is taking most of Father's time. He then spends almost every free minute fretting over Mother. I don't fault him one bit. She looks happier each day." Nikolai stopped. "I'm sure Father told you I already know that Victor and Mother were betrothed before he maneuvered her into marriage against her will."

Stefan nodded uncomfortably and said, "He told me. He also said he preferred to discuss this when he could get you, your mother, and Victor together. It might make more sense."

"Papino, he also said I could ask you if I had questions. I'm asking. I'm no longer a child. There's so much I don't understand. Help me with this at least."

Stefan sighed in resignation. "Your mother was already six months pregnant with you when we left for Garogan Province. Tirani went with us. That summer was one of the hottest in memory. We arrived late one evening after days of riding. Your mother went straight to the tent where your father lay dying. He had been pierced through by a sword."

"Really? Was no one with him to protect him?" Nikolai asked.

"Niko, it was war. Your father was escorting wounded soldiers back to camp. Then, as I understand, he dismounted to help free an officer trapped under a fallen horse. That's when…" Stefan hesitated, wondering how to continue.

"Papino, just tell me."

"You know well Victor's prowess with a sword. That's why he's the one who has trained you. At the time, Victor was your father's sworn enemy. Victor hated your father for marrying your mother. They fought. Your father lost."

Nikolai straightened in his chair. "You're saying that Papino Victor deliberately stalked Father on the battlefield and engaged him in a fight to kill him."

"Perceptive. That's exactly what I'm saying. When your mother went to Gregor that night, I stayed beside her. Your father's wound was the most hideous thing I had ever seen. She was unbelievably calm as she cleansed both sides before calling down Val's Healing Graces. She stayed with him for hours while Tirani summoned the Healing Graces for soldiers in the hospital tents. Had your mother not risked everything going to that camp, your father would have died that night."

Nikolai swallowed hard before jumping to his feet and returning to stare out the window. "I don't know what to say. I don't even know what to think."

Stefan rose and walked over to his godson, who was so much taller than he. "Niko, those were troubled times. Far worse than you can imagine. You asked about being on the battlefield. Just being there that night brings back ghastly memories. The sounds of men groaning and crying out in agony. The stench of death from bodies waiting for burial while men already accustomed to that dreadful odor were cooking and eating food around their campfires. The reek of dung wafting down from pens holding horses and other animals. And every stinking smell was magnified by that damned heat. That night was my first exposure to a war-weary camp."

"How is it possible that Father ever reconciled with Victor? How?"

"Nikolai, I think that's part of why your father wanted all of you together to discuss the past. So much more than just that happened. How the three of them accomplished what they have since the war is a testament to their faith." He paused. "And to the three most stubborn people I've ever known."

A knock at the door interrupted a moment of quiet reflection. "Yes?" Stefan responded.

The door edged open, and Alexa peeked in. "Hello, Stefan. Ah, I see my son is indeed still here." Then, to Nikolai, she said, "Have you forgotten? You promised to join me for my two appointments today."

The prince rolled his eyes in chagrin and stood. Generally attentive to the smallest details, he hardly dared believe he had indeed forgotten his commitment to her. "Mother! I'm sorry. Am I very late?"

She smiled teasingly. "Not yet, but we must hurry. The first appointment is in the Timeri State Room. Remember. My legs aren't nearly as long as yours, nor am I as quick as I was a year ago."

"Papino, thank you for your time. It seems I must whisk Mother to this meeting before we both embarrass ourselves with a late arrival." Then, with a wink and a mischievous grin, he swept her into his arms. With the swift, long-legged stride inherited from his father, he carried her toward the designated stateroom, delighting in her giggled protests and eliciting amused glances and chuckles from those they passed in the palace corridors.

"Nikolai!" Gasping on a breathless laugh, Alexa attempted to marshal her features into a more serious expression. "Was that really necessary?"

Standing princely tall and erect, Nikolai cocked his head to one side and peeked at Tirstan. "Captain Fratino, are we late?"

"Your Highness, I believe you have arrived six minutes ahead of the scheduled meeting time. Your mother's guests should arrive shortly." Suppressing a grin, the captain ceremoniously opened one of the double doors for the two to pass through.

Glancing around at the elegant decor of the stateroom, Alexa nodded her pleasure. "Just as I requested."

"I'm not sure I understand. I see the thrones for us and the chairs but why the table set for midday? Will we not join Father and the children as usual?"

"Oh, yes, definitely. You'll see. This is a surprise. I hope it works out the way I planned. I need something happy with everything else that's going on."

At that moment, a knock sounded, and two uniformed guards opened the stateroom doors. Escorted by Captain Fratino, two men entered, one with his wife and three children, the other with a pretty, well-dressed girl of about twelve. "Your Majesty, the Tanna families have arrived as you requested."

"Please rise," Alexa said graciously to everyone who had instantly knelt before their Queen and Crown Prince. Then, turning to her son, she said, "Nikolai, I wish for you to meet the two men who first showed me the far reach of our Lord Val. This is Var-Tan and his brother, Lor-Tan."

Nikolai dipped his head to formally acknowledge the introduction, but questions crept into his eyes. "I am pleased to make your acquaintance. I hope my inquiry causes no offense, but are your names not Sifiq?"

Both men quickly blinked away uneasy reactions before each nodded. "Yes, Your Royal Highness. We came to Turand in our youth as part
of the Sifiq occupation army. We were already dissatisfied with the warlike culture of our homeland, but we were coerced into joining the military. While here, we secretly studied faith in Lord Val and were fortunate
enough to be seriously injured in battle. We were healed when the Valiria
priestess Tirani called on the Healing Graces. We have served Val and the
throne of Turand ever since."

Nikolai gazed intently at the two men. "Amazing. I knew some Sifiq
soldiers had accepted Val, but I believe you are the first I've ever met."

Alexa linked her arm with Nikolai's. "Although Lor-Tan took longer
to recover, Var-Tan was healed immediately. There was a major battle in
northern Garogan Province shortly afterward. He helped care for injured
fighters. Without hesitation. But more about that another time." She
turned to her visitors. "Tell us about you and your families."

Lor-Tan tentatively responded, "Before any introductions, Your
Majesty, we read about your terrible abduction and imprisonment in the
Sifiq Kingdom. We can't tell you how deeply we regret what happened or
how ashamed…"

Nikolai saw his mother's face blanch and interrupted the heartfelt
lament. "Sir, my mother holds you and your brother in high esteem.
Trust me when I say that she knows neither of you could ever approve of
such despicable acts. Her intentions today are much happier. After all she
endured, let us give her that pleasure, shall we?"

The men were more than happy to dispense with the unpleasant
subject. Instead, they explained how they had changed their Sifiq names,
adopting Tanna as a surname to make their origin less obvious. Each had
married. Vartin, as Var-Tan now called himself, happily introduced his
wife, two sons, and daughter. Lortin, a widower, affectionately watched as
his daughter politely responded to the queen's inquiries. He was a proud

father, blessed that his well-educated sister-in-law had nurtured his child along with her brood since his wife's death.

After a few minutes, Nikolai noticed his mother's eyes growing brighter with anticipation. Finally, Alexa asked Vartin and Lortin to remain with Nikolai. In the meantime, their family members were seated. She explained she would return shortly with someone she wanted them to meet.

Exiting quickly, she inhaled deeply before nodding appreciatively at Anlía, who had arrived with Oui-lest and an especially nervous woman. "I can't promise how this will develop, but they're waiting inside. You know you always have a home in Toraval after everything you did to help me and the others."

Mei-sat Tan's bright blue eyes shone with a glaze of tears. "Just to see them and know that they are well is more than I ever hoped for before meeting you. For that alone, I am forever grateful."

"Then let us go inside."

Once the guards opened the doors again, Alexa and Anlía entered, closely followed by their Sifiq companions, now attired in beautiful Turandan gowns instead of the plain, straight sheaths required in their home country.

"Gentlemen, I would like to explain my reason for summoning you to Toraval. As you mentioned earlier, I was away for some time. Fortunately, some Sifiq citizens took pity on strangers and extended a helping hand— at serious personal risk, might I add. I would like to introduce you to one of them. I hope you will welcome her to Turand as I have."

Holding tightly to Oui-lest's hand for reassurance, Mei-sat stepped forward as Anlía moved aside. Drawing in a shaky breath, she forced herself to lift her head and meet the waiting gazes of her sons. What she saw caused her heart to leap within her breast. How utterly handsome they looked without their cropped hair and severe expressions. Their blue eyes shone with light and love for life. She wanted to laugh. She wanted to cry. All she could do was stare and wait.

Vartin squinted and shook his head. "Mother? Is that you?" he asked in shock.

"My son, how very well you look. I..." Mei-sat swallowed hard, forcing herself to restrain tears. "Until I met your Lady Valkana, I spent years believing my two beautiful sons were dead. Then she heard my name and felt what she called my life force. She remembered you and insisted you were both alive."

Suddenly, Vartin and Lortin both rushed to her. Their arms wrapped around her in a tight embrace, driving away the block of grief she had carried for more than two decades. Soon, Anlía and Oui-lest informed them that a midday meal would be served and that they could use the stateroom for the remainder of the afternoon as they revived their family bonds.

Leaving his mother, sister, and Oui-lest just outside the Timeri State Room mopping up rivers of happy tears, Nikolai re-entered the room for a few moments. Regretting his brief interruption of the family's reunion, he was at least able to delay any disagreeable discussion until after their celebration. He experienced newfound appreciation for his father's occasional laments regarding the difficulties that too frequently accompanied royal duty.

⌒

Half an hour later, Alexa reviewed the formal application to study at the Zinzan Spiritual Center. Prince Nikolai observed the young man sitting quietly in front of her desk. Although his mother had not explained her motives for considering the unusual exception, Nikolai knew she must have good cause. As such, his curiosity was piqued, so he studied the candidate with more than passing interest.

Although not nearly as tall as Nikolai or his father, this Gregor Maconti was taller than most Turandans. Broad shoulders and muscular build suggested years of hard work, although the candidate's handsome, suntanned features showed him to be about Nikolai's age. Light brown hair, straight and streaked blond by the sun, framed a square face set with sharply intelligent, confident brown eyes. The prince noted a calm demeanor with what he felt to be a dormant, understated capability.

Setting aside the sheaf of papers and looking up, Alexa smiled. "Master Maconti, your application is impressive. Did anyone help you?"

He returned her smile. "I had two questions about the section on expectations and goals, so I took those to the priest at our nearest temple. Once I clarified my understanding, I completed everything else without assistance, Lady Valkana."

She nodded approval. "Your presentation is quite clear, both in content and appearance. Why have you not applied sooner?"

"Milady," he glanced at Nikolai, curious about the prince's presence and his scrutiny, "as I believe you are aware, my father lost his arm during the civil war. He is a farmer, but we are not landed gentry. He relied heavily on my help, and I would never forsake responsibilities to my family. My love and respect for my father are too great. Father's brother recently died. With my aunt long since gone, my two cousins came to live on our farm. They are strong, able, and happy to help. At last, I am free to pursue the education I've always desired."

Alexa inhaled deeply. She sensed both veracity and intensity in the youth's declaration. "Val blesses your father with a son such as you. What are your plans once you complete your studies at Zinzan? Are you considering the priesthood?"

Maconti met her direct gaze and wondered about the glittering lights dancing in her eyes and the hint of a smile tugging at her mouth. He had fully expected the woman who was Queen of Turand and Valkana to be imposing and intimidating. Instead, she was kind and approachable. He felt easy sharing thoughts he rarely spoke aloud.

"Milady, I believe there are many ways to serve our Lord Val; however, the way of the priesthood is not mine. I do wish to study as much of the old religious texts as I may if I am permitted to go to Zinzan. However, my greater wish is to study history, government, and even politics. I have stripped our small town's library bare of every book available. Even a local nobleman has kindly opened his private library to me."

Alexa exchanged glances with her son as they watched young Gregor Maconti's face begin to glow. The youth spoke of what he had read and how much he would appreciate having someone answer the many questions he had written down in his journals. He demonstrated a flow of thought and passion that both surprised and captivated his queen. Meanwhile, she hoped her son might recognize the potential existing within the eloquence of this simple farmer's son.

Suddenly, Gregor Maconti grew silent. He looked directly at Nikolai. "Your Highness, I apologize. I must sound rather dull and boorish to you, but I do envy your good fortune. Your godfather, Sir Stefan Sidano, is one of my heroes. He is a master statesman. I have read both his writings and what is written of him. To work as he has in even the smallest capacity to serve our nation is my ambition."

Nikolai nodded and managed a wry smile. "My godfather is a very wise man. He is also something of a slave driver when it comes to studies. He is also brilliant. Father says he could never have successfully engineered the victory over the Sifiq without Papino Stefan."

A knock at the door interrupted the discussion. "Yes?"

"Mother? Father sent me. He's waiting with the younger ones. It's time for midday."

"My goodness! I didn't realize the time!" She stood and said, "Master Maconti, may I introduce you to my eldest daughter, Princess Anlía?"

24

Having risen immediately when Alexa stood, the young Maconti executed an elegant bow. "Your Royal Highness, I am honored to meet you." When he straightened, his gaze met curious emerald eyes. Unprepared for the shaft of electricity that shot through his body, he barely managed to conquer the peculiar reaction that threatened to collapse his composure.

Puzzled by his reaction, Anlía blinked and glanced away. "I am pleased to meet you, Master Maconti."

Nikolai instantly noted his mother's odd smile and wondered what she was thinking. "Mother? Father is waiting."

"Yes, Nikolai, of course. Master Maconti, I will consider your application and send word to you tomorrow regarding my decision." She took the lead in guiding everyone from her office. "In the meantime, may I invite you to join us for midday?"

Gregor Maconti's eyebrows lifted in surprise. "Lady Valkana, my family is waiting for me. Your invitation is very kind, but I couldn't possibly trespass further on your time."

"It is my fault that you are delayed, and I'm starving. You young people must certainly be hungry." Alexa then signaled one of her guards and requested that a message be delivered to the Maconti family advising their son would take midday at the palace.

⌐

Leaning back into one of the library sofas with his long legs propped up, Nikolai was almost glad his siblings had already gone to bed and that his father was meeting late with Stefan. He appreciated the chance for a private conversation with his mother after what he considered an unusual day.

"How impossible it seems that you encountered the mother of those two Sifiq soldiers after all these years. It boggles my mind."

Tucking her feet beneath her on the leather couch nearest the fireplace, Alexa watched as logs shifted, causing yellow flames to dance higher behind the mesh screen. "Considering how women are treated there, I was surprised, too. In her favor, she came from a prominent family. She also had two sons serving in the army. When her husband disappeared in battle, she moved into quarters that provided service to the king's palace. Mei-sat was a talented seamstress and, thus, helpful to Oui-lest. She was also just old enough to avoid being of more unpleasant use to Bin-Lot's officers."

"What a loathsome—I can't begin to imagine how those people live as they do." Nikolai closed his eyes and shook his head in disgust. Looking once again at his mother, he wondered how she had survived when he saw the faraway expression in her eyes. "Mother, I'm sorry to tell you this, but I asked Masters Tanna if I might meet with them tomorrow morning."

Her attention focused sharply on him. "Why?"

"I know it won't be pleasant, especially after their reunion today. I plan to ask if they would be willing to meet with General Kohira and me to discuss anything they might remember about Sifiq military tactics. Kohira and I also plan to include Raf-Zan in the discussion—if they agree."

"Oh, Nikolai, does your father know?" Alexa asked, her voice distressed.

"Not yet, but I will inform him. He may want to attend. Raf-Zan's experience would be too valuable to miss. Mother, I will not be guilty of disregarding any potential source of valuable information when the lives of so many Turandans might hang in the balance."

Despite her burgeoning sense of dread, Alexa gazed at her son with respect and admiration. Nikolai not only resembled his father, he sounded like Gregor—both in tone of voice and thought. Although still defining his character, Nikolai had already developed most of the attributes necessary to become a strong leader.

"What if the Tannas don't agree?"

"I will try to convince them, but I expect they'll be willing to help if they can. I trust my instincts." He paused, giving her a wry grin. "I can thank you for that. They have built good lives here, and you just restored to them the one good thing they left behind in the Sifiq Kingdom. Never underestimate what any man will do for a mother he loves."

She chuckled softly. "Does that include you?"

"Especially me," he quipped before sitting up. "Now, on another subject. Where in the world did you find this Gregor Maconti? And that story about his name! One might think there would be hundreds of Gregors named after Father, but he's the first I've ever heard about. How very odd."

Alexa laughed. "I asked his parents to tell him not to mention our encounter on the road unless he and I were alone. On the way home from Lindaval, your father and I were delayed by an overturned wagon blocking the road. I'm still not sure how it all happened, but our Master Maconti was critically injured and…" In her mind's eye, she once again saw young Gregor, near death, lying on the road.

"Nikolai, he was dying. I went to pray with his parents, hoping to offer some comfort. Instead, something powerful in that boy struck me. I felt Val's call to me, telling me to summon the Healing Graces, and so I did. Within an hour, Val healed him. Oh, yes, he needed time to rest. You saw how Gregor still moves slowly. It's because he hasn't yet fully recovered.

"Gregor Maconti lives because of Val's will. We rarely travel via the Samana Road, but your father decided to show me all the recent changes. Think about that. I was there that day because Val knew that young man's life would be in grave danger."

"Will you approve his application to Zinzan?"

Alexa studied her son's face. "You think I shouldn't, don't you?"

"Mother..." Nikolai paused uncomfortably before continuing, "Maconti is obviously an intelligent young man. I didn't read his application, but I trust your judgment regarding its merits. My concern is how well he would fit in at Zinzan. He was properly dressed, and his manners were decent enough. Someone took significant time coaching him, I think. Still, he is a farmer's son. There are matters of culture. Music. Art. Many areas where I think he may find himself uncomfortable simply because..." Nikolai hesitated. "Social class."

Alexa directed a pointed glare at her son. "So, because he is a *farmer's son*, you think him incapable of succeeding at Zinzan."

Nikolai flinched. "Mother, it isn't that..."

"It is *precisely* that. Nikolai, first of all, I have every intention of approving his application. I intended to do so before I ever read it. Reading it only convinced me that my intuition still serves me well and that I had properly understood Val's message. Setting that aside, I'm disappointed in you. I can hardly believe you would mock someone's name, let alone judge their potential based on their status at birth. I thought your father and I taught you better."

"Mother, it isn't that."

"Then help me understand because I don't like what I just heard."

Nikolai had never expected his mother's reaction and found himself searching for an adequate response. Finally, drawing a deep breath, he ventured to answer. "Maconti would be thrown together with the sons and daughters of many nobles at Zinzan. Others who study there are most often from families of landed gentry or other leaders in society. He would have nothing in common with them. And no matter what you think, people would likely scowl once they heard his name."

"Nothing in common," she repeated after him as she rose from her seat and went to stand by the carved mantel. Again, she stared into the fire. "No strong faith. No desire for learning. No love of country. Let me explain some things to you, my young son. Listen well.

"That young man's father left his farm and his pregnant wife to fight bitter battles alongside your father. Together, they fought to free Turand from Sifiq domination and the tyranny that evil, power-thirsty Turandans planned to inflict on an already suffering nation. Gregor Maconti's father watched yours nearly die in one battle. In the next, he lost his arm and had to go home. That is courage and sacrifice you have never witnessed firsthand. If you ever do, you will understand why your father has so much respect for those soldiers who never failed him. When Master Maconti arrived home, his wife gave birth to their only son on your father's birthday. Your father was a hero to his soldiers, and Master Maconti decided to name his son in honor of his hero-king.

"Now. Does your father know this? He does. What was his reaction? He was well pleased. Proud even. Your father saw a man who lost an arm during the war and then struggled for years to provide for his family. Your father saw not a farmer, Nikolai. He saw a soldier—a comrade. Our king saw a fellow Turandan who loved this country enough to sacrifice himself not just during the war but every day and every year since so that both their children could live in a free and secure Turand."

"Mother…"

"I'm not finished," she snapped without turning her attention from the fire. "Nikolai, I love you. More than you can possibly know. That's why you must understand—deep within your soul—what I am telling you. You must never judge anyone, man or woman, based on his or her birth or social status. You must learn to judge a person's character. You've always been kind to palace staff. Always. Have you ever seen them as lesser than you because they work as servants and not professionals or because they aren't nobility?"

Confusion marked Nikolai's expression, and he stammered, "No, Mother, the thought never even occurred to me."

"Why? Why is that? Do you treat them like people? Or are they simply invisible to you because they're just always here, responding to your wants and needs?"

"Mother! What a terrible thing to say! You know how close I've always been to nearly everyone. There are some I don't know very well, but I've known most as long as I can remember. They're like family! Honestly!"

"I'm glad for that. When you look at them or anyone else, remember that each one has feelings the same as you. Each has dreams, aspirations, loves, and sorrows, just like you. You look at Gregor Maconti and see that perhaps he isn't as cultured as other nobility or gentry at Zinzan, so what does he have to commend him? He has powerful faith, Nikolai. He has a thirst for knowledge and the drive to work for it. He also has a passion for life that I see as rare and worth nurturing. Learn to recognize those traits in others, Nikolai, and never waste them."

She paused when teardrops began to glisten on her cheeks. "I suppose this bit of family history must have gotten lost somewhere. The Maraná family was always landed gentry. My mother, though, came from a family of farmers. They were industrious farmers—hardworking and interested in education. Still, just farmers. Right now, had it not been for the farming techniques I learned from my mother's family, I probably would be little more than a pile of bones in the Sifiq Kingdom."

Shamed by something he had forgotten, Nikolai started to go to his mother. From the corner of his eye, movement caught his attention. Adding to his guilt and disgrace, he saw his father's solemn expression and the tilt of his head, signaling him to leave. In the corridor outside the library, Nikolai paused and turned. Despite personal humiliation, the prince smiled as he watched his parents together.

Gregor's rich voice sounded immensely tender as his long fingers rose to cradle Alexa's tear-dampened face. Gently, he kissed her forehead. "Beloved, he is still young. You did well to remind him."

"Gregor, I am not ashamed of who I am. I never was."

"And I have never been ashamed of you or your family connections. Deep down, neither is he."

"I know. I love him so much. It just hurt hearing him say what he said."

"I think he will never again say any such thing. Furthermore, knowing my son as I do, I seriously doubt he will ever even think such a thing again. Instead, he'll spend the night pondering everything you just told him and awaken a wiser man tomorrow."

Nikolai turned to go upstairs when he saw his father gather his mother in a close embrace. He forgot about his disgrace and thought about Victor and his mother being betrothed once. She must have loved him. Moments like this made him wonder why his father came between them. Seeing his parents together, though, left no doubt whatsoever that the two loved each other. Profoundly.

Finally reaching his private chambers, Nikolai undressed and went straight to bed. Lying quietly, he recalled the night in Taprina, where his father's party had stopped on the way home with his mother after her return from the Sifiq Kingdom.

Somehow, he could only remember what she said that night as he carried her inside the inn from the barracks after she had summoned the Healing Graces to the Sifiq captain who had so brutally beaten her. Those words, whispered with such intensity, would forever echo in his memory.

"Nikolai, I love your father as I have loved no one else. No man alive could ever have given me the love or happiness he does. Know that, my son."

31

Chapter 3

Gregor leaned forward as his bearded chin rested on his clasped hands. "It's hard to say how useful their information will be. The Tannas were regular troops twenty years ago, not officers. Much may have changed in that time. Raf-Zan is a naval officer. How he will live up to his oath remains untested."

"I cannot argue your points, Father. After discussions with General Kohira, we still think there can be no harm talking with the Tannas. Kohira believes army tactics don't tend to change much without dramatic changes in leadership. No evidence exists to indicate such changes have occurred. Regarding Raf-Zan, I do believe you and Papino Stefan are clever enough to get him to reveal at least some useful information."

"What do you hope to gain from the Tannas?" Stefan asked as he leaned against a tall bookcase.

"Anything they can remember. What they practiced in drills. How orders were given. Fighting techniques. Troop placements. Any details they recall that they think might be helpful. Maybe we're already aware of what we should know. Maybe there's some oddity that fills in a previously unknown gap. I simply see no harm in checking what might tip a scale in our favor one day."

Gregor nodded thoughtfully. "Your arguments are logical, Nikolai. You've done well consulting with Kohira. Would you ask the Tannas to wait until Victor returns the day after tomorrow? I think his presence at such a meeting would be extremely valuable."

Nikolai's black eyebrows lifted high in surprise. "I didn't expect him back so soon. I'll ask the Tannas to stay."

"Good. Have someone arrange for the balance of their stay since it will be at our request. Stefan, I'll trust you to organize the meeting time and details. Make sure Victor attends and that he understands Raf-Zan will be present. Please keep Nikolai and me informed."

Remaining behind after Nikolai departed, Stefan cast Gregor a doubtful look. "Overall, I believe your son has done an excellent job of thinking through possible gains from this meeting. But Victor?" Stefan's face drew into a pained grimace. "We both know how much he once hated you. That is nothing when it comes to Raf-Zan."

"Time alone fostered that change toward me, Stefan. Time, circumstances, and Alexa. In reality, I think Victor's hatred for me only recently transitioned from a state of suppression and tolerance to…"

When Gregor's voice faded, Stefan saw troubled shadows. He approached the man he loved as a brother. Quietly, he asked, "To what?"

With a swift toss of his head, Gregor replied, "I think Victor no longer despises me as he once did. I no longer hate Victor, although I still manage my memories of seeing his arrow almost kill Alexa and then watching him strike her to the ground. Now I must face Raf-Zan, knowing how he whipped her without mercy and threw her overboard into the sea on a stormy night. For her sake and the sake of my people, I will control my temper."

Unfolding his tall body clad in an elegantly tailored, light gray uniform, Gregor stared out a window at the busy square beyond open palace gates. He watched his wife returning from the temple. He smiled at the throng of people approaching to speak to her. Their adoration soothed his heart at a time when heartache had crept in.

"Stefan, there have been times when I've almost cursed my station. When every beat of my heart and every nerve in my body screamed out in furious protest, I wanted what any man would want. I wanted vengeance for what was done to her. I cannot tell you how many times I wanted to place my hands around Victor's throat and choke the life out of him for the way he hurt her—and me—and for the lives his insane hatred destroyed. In Timeri, that feeling evaporated—forever, I think. He searched until he found her there. He finally earned redemption beyond everything he ever did. He saved her life for her children and Turand. Forgetting that I am king, how does any man thank another for restoring to him his heart, his life, and his soul?"

Stefan walked over to the window and rested his hand against Gregor's shoulder. Even he had no answer to that question. "That leaves the Sifiq captain."

Gregor heaved an exasperated sigh before returning to his desk. "Yes, our notorious and suddenly converted Raf-Zan. My wife perplexes me with her leaps of faith. Had she not stopped me, there was one point where I was ready to rip him apart, one small piece at a time, and I would have considered his agony fair reward for his crimes. You didn't see what he did to her. I can barely imagine how she looked when Victor first found her on that beach. When she told me why she went to Raf-Zan for healing…"

"Faith gives her strength that exceeds our combined comprehension," Stefan remarked.

"Indeed." Gregor glanced up as a clock chimed the hour. "You must excuse me, Stefan. Alexa is expecting me. She asked me to join her to deliver news to the Maconti family of their son's acceptance to Zinzan." The king paused and smiled. "Would you have time to join us?"

"Me? Yes, if you wish, but why?"

"As I understand, this young man, who just happens to be my name-sake, aspires to a career in diplomacy. He already has a hero. You."

Dubious laughter created sparkles in Stefan's gray eyes. "Me? His hero? Interesting. It's a role I relish for my children and godchildren, but it's one I never expected to play for anyone else!"

⌣

Evening shadows grew darker with each extinguished candle. Still, soft blue light allowed him to follow her movements from one side of the temple's altar to the other. Her sublime grace had not faded over the years—not even after all she had suffered during her captivity or the agonizing recovery after her return home. He smiled inwardly, savoring her image as he always had.

Her voice echoed quietly through the deserted worship chamber. "I thought you weren't due back until tomorrow."

"I never was able to sneak up on you." Victor straightened from where he had leaned against the door and walked toward the altar. "You never disappoint me."

She grinned and turned around to hug him. "Your life force is far too vibrant to miss. How are you? And how was Garogan?"

"Garogan is already budding into spring, thank goodness. I'm well. I hurried back because of your husband's urgent summons to all National Council representatives. It seems we may be facing some serious business."

Her smile vanished but quickly reappeared. "So it seems, but that can wait. Did you see DiLeno's parents?"

"I did. They're quite well and delighted with the package you sent. I have a letter they sent—along with several jars of Mistress Taranda's jams. They look forward to seeing you when you feel well enough to visit."

"Oh, now I am excited. Did you not know I'm planning a trip?"

Victor's forehead creased in concern as he placed her long cape around her shoulders. "I did not. Soon? And your husband approves?"

She fastened the front of her cape and turned to leave with Victor by her side. "Anlía leaves in two weeks to begin her studies at Zinzan. Gregor knows how much I want to be with her when she first goes—just to see her settled. I won't stay long, but I need time to reconnect with home." She paused and looked up at the moon. "I think you know what I mean."

Victor sighed and swallowed against the anxiety he always felt whenever she spoke of going to Zinzan. Especially now, despite her resilience, he wasn't confident she was capable of returning to Zinzan so early in her recovery. "Sweetest, are you certain you shouldn't wait a while? You know how much Zinzan always drains you."

"I know, Victor," she said firmly, "but I am changed. Concerning Zinzan, I'm confident I'll be fine. I also go this time because I must." She stopped and turned to face him, her eyes glittering eerily in the moonlight, her aura shimmering around her tall figure. "Just as when you and Gregor took me when I finally faced what happened there, I must go now. Will you not trust me?"

From his office window, Gregor watched as Victor's head sharply dropped. He wondered about the sudden posture of burden that caused Victor's shoulders to slump. In contrast, Alexa's blue-white aura shimmered like a glittering mist in the evening twilight. He immediately recognized the way she stood as a stance of resolve. She had told Victor something she planned to do—something he preferred not to hear. Gregor exhaled a heavy breath and left so he could greet her return to the palace.

෴

After bowing in respectful greeting, Raf-Zan silently paused inside the door of King Gregor's spacious, elegantly furnished office. At his left stood

Captain Fratino. Prince Nikolai waited on his right. The former Sifiq officer, who had immediately renounced his commission and his Sifiq citizenship upon arriving in Toraval, watched the distinguished monarch rise and quietly address the key adviser called Stefan Sidano.

"Gentlemen, come in and be seated. I wish to speak to you before we leave for our meeting," Gregor said without formal greeting. "We have a few points to cover before we attend our conference. I want to ensure everyone knows what to expect."

The king first addressed Fratino. "Captain, I asked you to join us this morning because you've had the longest involvement with Raf-Zan of anyone and because our queen personally requested you to assist him with adapting to Turand's culture. I trust that has not imposed on your other duties."

"Not at all, Your Majesty."

"Good. Now, Prince Nikolai, has everyone else been advised regarding the goals of our later meeting, and will they attend?"

"Yes, Sire. Everything is in order, and everyone is expected to attend as planned."

"Does that include Lord Garogan?" Gregor asked.

"It does," Nikolai replied, the tone of his voice a clear indication of the first time he had ever needed to exercise any authority over his godfather.

Gregor's dark eyes then turned to Raf-Zan. "Raf-Zan, I asked that you not be informed about the nature of this meeting until I had time to consider your situation here. Captain Fratino reports that you have conducted yourself extremely well in your training. He also advises that you've applied extensive time and effort to your studies of our religious beliefs and traditions."

Raf-Zan dipped his head respectfully. "Your Majesty, if I may speak, I presume you suspect I might have done so to learn how to use knowledge of your ways against you. Were I in your position, this is precisely what I would think. Until I have time and opportunity to prove myself, the best I can offer is the word of a man who was once an officer and considered his word a matter of supreme honor. My honor is one thing I did not renounce. I swore an oath to serve the throne of Turand and Turand's god after your wife brought healing to me despite what I did to her. I will never dishonor my word. I swear to you again that I will die rather than fail her or you. Tell me what you need from me, and I will do my best to comply."

Gregor remained standing behind his desk. He felt his toes curling inside his boots. Some small part of him still reacted with the unbridled rage he had felt that day he had lifted Raf-Zan off the floor by the throat. At this moment, though, instinct surged stronger than fury. He could see Raf-Zan was telling the truth. In actuality, he felt that truth inside his bones.

"Raf-Zan, despite the value of your training and your experience, I cannot justify giving you an active commission in either of my military forces. You must understand that doing so would be unfair to my officers who have worked for their commissions and who would also know who you are and what you did. Turandans are forgiving people, but I cannot be sure all would be as forgiving as our Valkana—even should she ask them to do so. Also, a military commission could be dangerous in more ways than the obvious.

"As such, I have devised a reasonable option for your future that allows me to avail myself of your valuable expertise—if you are agreeable—while allowing you to build a future here and prove yourself. I am offering you a position as a royal adviser on military affairs. If you wish, you may retain your title of captain as an honorary rank only. The demands on your time will be heavy, I assure you."

Raf-Zan's expression showed little emotion as he considered the king's proposal. There could be few doubts about the direction of Gregor's plans. Raf-Zan's oath to the Sifiq king had been wrested from him over his mother's body, but he had given his oaths to the monarchs of Turand freely—resulting from healing born of his mother's love.

"Your Majesty, there is one thing I wish to ask."

"Yes?" Gregor said, surprised by the response.

"I understand in Turand that it is customary to have a given name and a surname. My mother was Lyn-mar Zan. Zan added to her name meant she was nothing more than my father's property. From today forward, I would like to be known as Rafzan Lynmar. If that meets your approval, I shall be honored to serve as a royal adviser."

Gregor nodded his assent. "So it shall be, Captain Lynmar. Welcome to my service. Now, in our next meeting, we will discuss plans for approaching the Sifiq king about recent incursions of Turand's sovereign borders. We will also discuss possible military tactics. We intend to advise the Sifiq king that we prefer to exist in peace. However, if he insists on his current course, Turand will declare war on the Sifiq Kingdom."

❧

Inside the reserved meeting salon, blue damask draperies were drawn back at four ceiling-high windows to allow the day's sunlight to brighten the wood-paneled room. Above a long, polished, mahogany table, two pewter chandeliers held multiple glass globes adding extra light from dozens of sturdy candles. Several uniformed attendees already sat with opened leather portfolios. However, a distinguished naval officer and General Ivan Kohira huddled in private conversation around maps displayed on tall easels at the chamber's far end. Lord Victor Garogan stood nearby, listening attentively.

When Gregor's party arrived, the king entered first through doors opened by two palace guards. Nikolai and Stefan followed, with Captain Fratino and Lynmar close behind. Those inside immediately rose and bowed. Gregor quickly glanced around and saw Lord Garogan standing in the far corner. Judging by the hate-filled glare blazing in Victor's hazel eyes, he steeled himself for whatever challenges might lie ahead. Extending a terse greeting, Gregor waited for everyone to take designated seats before quickly calling the conference to order.

"Gentlemen, I will not waste valuable time with banalities. You all know of the raid on our borders last year that resulted in the murders of nine members of the Queen's Royal Guard. During that raid, our Valkana and four Valiria were abducted and transported to the Sifiq Kingdom. As prisoners, they faced abuse that included brutal beatings, attempted rape, forced labor, starvation, and other bitter privations. Unsuccessful at forcing them into submission or execution, the Sifiq king decided to violate our territorial waters again to dump them offshore rather than make civilized arrangements to deliver them home. In recent months, four additional raids against small fishing villages have occurred."

Gregor grew silent. His eyes roved from face to face before his expression fixed into a fearsome mask of resolve. "Years ago, Stefan Sidano and I studied the general mentality of Sifiq leadership. We made it our business to learn everything we could about what they thought and how they governed so we could use their own techniques against them. Eventually, we successfully drove them from Turand.

"During Turand's recovery from years of occupation and war, I kept sight of a solemn vow that I would never again tolerate even the smallest Sifiq violation without response. Today, we begin formulating that response. Tomorrow, you begin drafting military strategies that may prove vital to whatever actions we take. In the meantime, I will convene an emergency session of National Council and explain why it may be necessary for Turand to launch a full-scale invasion of the Sifiq Kingdom."

Allowing time for the magnitude of his father's words to settle, Nikolai said, "Sire, shall I begin?"

Gregor yielded the floor to his son, who was already forewarned of the potential for the conference to turn contentious. "The meeting is yours, Prince Nikolai."

When he stood, Nikolai looked more than ever like his father. Black hair was brushed neatly into flowing waves, and dark brown eyes shone with astute intelligence. Nikolai wore the dark gray uniform of Turand's Crown Prince, his squared shoulders and trim waist adding emphasis to his imposing height.

"Gentlemen, as His Majesty already stated, we are tasked with planning what I see as a twofold military strategy. First, we must augment every possible line of defense against future encroachment by our old enemy. That means identifying our most vulnerable points, especially where the ocean gives them access to our shores and where we need additional fortifications and reinforcement of overall defenses."

He paused, waiting for an end to the predictable affirmations to his statement before venturing ahead. He expected no disputes with the intention, but he glanced at his father. They were both ready for the explosive reaction to some of the means for preparation.

"His Majesty, Sir Sidano, and Lord Garogan had long years of personal experience with the Sifiq who governed Turand under the occupation. Especially after speaking with Mother and her companions about their recent experiences with King Bin-Lot, we see patterns of inflexible behavior that continue to be part of the general Sifiq societal mentality. Whether Bin-Lot remains in power or has been replaced, we have little confidence that the current Sifiq government will be receptive to an amenable solution. Nevertheless, we will attempt a diplomatic mission to negotiate a formal agreement to circumvent our territorial waters. If that fails, we will resort to force. The Sifiq Kingdom must understand. We will tolerate no further incursions on our sovereign territory."

Nikolai lifted his chin slightly in a confident expression as he prepared to continue with what he knew would stir controversy. "We will begin by dividing ourselves into two units. General Ravendro and Admiral Darandra will coordinate plans to defend regions most vulnerable to continuing Sifiq attacks. Admiral Firenzdá and General Kohira will prepare for possible invasion of the Sifiq Kingdom.

"We will avail ourselves of the rare opportunity to glean valuable information from former Sifiq military men willing to answer whatever questions you have. You have here Master Vartin Tanna and his brother, Lortin Tanna. They have lived as Turandan citizens since the civil war. They are former Sifiq regular troops and can provide some insight into how the Sifiq army worked from within. Generals, they are available here in Toraval for only two days to assist you. I suggest you make good use of their time and yours."

The prince drew in a deep breath. "Admiral Firenzdá and Admiral Darandra, let me introduce you and the others to His Majesty's newest Royal Adviser on Military Affairs, Captain Rafzan Lynmar. Captain Lynmar has intimate knowledge…"

"This is an unsupportable abomination!" Victor's features flushed bright red as he furiously shouted, "You don't really expect us to trust this damned bast…"

Any boyish immaturity faded from the prince's face, and the prince appeared and sounded as daunting and authoritative as his father ever had. "Lord Garogan!" Nikolai interrupted sternly. "You may stop now! We are not here to debate my father's advisory decisions. If you cannot control your temper or your comments, then you are free to leave. You may lodge any protests with the King and Queen, who have consulted and agreed on Captain Lynmar's appointment. In the meantime, I will work with those disciplined enough to recognize the importance and value of his experience in this time of crisis. Now, if I may continue."

Surprised by his godson's severe, unwavering response, Victor obstinately set his jaw, knowing he had been summarily dismissed. "You will excuse me, Your Royal Highness," he ground out. Then, receiving only his godson's icy stare, Victor snatched his leather case from the table and stalked out.

Ten minutes later, Alexa looked up as the door to her office abruptly flew open. "I expected you."

Victor stopped abruptly, then slammed the door shut. "You can't be serious!"

"First of all, I will thank you to control your temper. There is no need to slam doors or create such disturbances here. Now, sit down and try to control yourself so we can discuss this matter in a civilized fashion."

Victor stared at her, unable to fathom her apparent calm acceptance of Raf-Zan's elevation to a trusted position in the palace after the man had nearly killed her—and brutally so in the process.

"Victor! I said, sit down! Now! This instant!"

After huffing several heavy breaths, Victor finally slumped into a chair opposite Alexa's desk.

Rising, she came to sit in the chair beside him. "Talk to me."

He shook his head. "What good would it do? How did he convince you?'"

Her smile was slow and pensive. "It was I who convinced him. Victor, you must believe that Val has reached deep into Raf-Zan's soul. It was difficult enough for me to accept, but this isn't the first time our Lord Val has taught me lessons the hard way."

"Why, Sweetest? Why did he let that man beat you nearly to death and then make you heal him? And now this?"

Victor gazed at her, but his vision did not encompass her face, now bright with the blush of restored health. Nor did he see the beautiful green velvet gown that today defined feminine curves instead of hanging loosely on a painfully thin figure. Instead, he saw her as he had found her on the windswept beach that stormy night near the Timeri Lighthouse. Then she had been so fragile—emaciated and beaten nearly to death. He had been terrified to touch her, let alone pick her up—almost fearing she might break. Still, he had carried her to a nearby shack and had warmed her before taking her to a safe haven. He had watched over her and made sure she was properly cared for her until *he* came to revive her will to live.

"Victor?"

He shook off the lapse into memory. He grasped for calm. "I am appalled that your husband trusts this man enough to bring him into his circle of advisers. This could be some sort of trick. I thought he despised him as much as I do."

Alexa reached for Victor's hands. "Have you ever noticed how you avoid saying Gregor's name when we talk? It's usually *your husband* or *the king* or just *he*." Receiving a roll of hazel eyes in response, she smiled. "Anyway, this isn't the first time Gregor has accepted someone into a position of confidence with whom he has what I shall refer to as serious past conflicts. You know he relies heavily on my advice and the logic and needs of certain given circumstances. That is the current case with Raf-Zan."

Agitated, Victor stood and started pacing. "Alexa, I still can't understand. Raf-Zan nearly killed you. If not for *Gregor* taking you to the temple for Val's healing," he said, sarcastically emphasizing Gregor's name, "you likely would have died. How can *Gregor* simply dismiss that and carry on with the man who did that to you? How do I possibly forgive Raf-Zan and work with him? For that matter, how do I forgive your husband for placing you in what must be a terribly uncomfortable and even painful situation?"

"Is that what you think? That Raf-Zan's presence makes me uncomfortable?" she asked, her green eyes beginning to glitter in warning.

"Deny it if you wish, but I know how you feel about the Sifiq. I know how you always felt about them." His tone of voice sounded almost taunting.

Alexa stood, straightening her back as her shoulders squared. "Victor Garogan, I am different. Time and experience have changed me. I am no longer the girl who lost everything except her faith and her fiancé. I have become a woman who knows she can withstand the onslaught of war and kings and survive with her life intact. I love, and I am loved. The only fear I have of the Sifiq is of the ruin they can still cause, but I no longer fear them just because they are Sifiq."

Victor stared at her. Renewed rage still coursed through him. "Alexa, Raf-Zan beat you! I saw the hideous wounds he left on your back! Even with the blessing of the Healing Graces, I know you must still bear the scars! You'll live with that reminder for the rest of your life! How can you just ignore that? Damn it, Alexa! If he really loves you so much, how can that precious husband of yours just ignore that?"

Alexa's gaze froze. Slowly, she walked toward the door and opened it. Outside, she saw Anlía, who had come to discuss final arrangements for their trip to Zinzan. She motioned her daughter inside.

Victor looked puzzled. "I'll leave now."

"No, you will not," Alexa said softly but decisively. "You stay right where you are."

Anlía sensed strain in her mother's manner but smiled at Victor. "Good morning, Papino." Turning to Alexa, "I can come back later, Mother."

"No," Alexa said as she turned. "I want you to unlace the top of my gown in the back and pull down the left shoulder."

"All right," Anlía said. Although surprised by her mother's instructions, she proceeded to untie the ribbon lacing her mother's dress in the

46

back. Then, loosening it enough to open the top of the gown, she pulled the fabric down.

"Victor, I want you to look at my back, next to my left shoulder blade."

Unsure what to expect, Victor approached and leaned close. "What am I looking for?" he asked tartly.

"Marks. Scars. You'll see them."

"I do. The ones where he struck you are fading faster than I would have expected. I'm glad."

"And do you see the old one running along the shoulder blade?"

He frowned and squinted, looking closer. His stomach suddenly pitched and rolled when he finally saw the faint line, and he gasped.

She turned tear-glazed eyes to him. "As you see, his are not the only scars I live with from injuries that nearly ended my life. Still, life has a way of building good from ashes. Remember that. Now, if you'll kindly excuse me, my daughter and I have things to do."

⌒

Brilliant sunshine drenched the morning in golden light and warmed the air with the promise of approaching spring. Fluffy white clouds sailed lazily across blue skies. Tall tree branches quivered and swayed in delicate dances with the slightest of breezes.

How fragrant the air of Toraval and freedom! Since Oui-lest Var had come to Turand, how far away her life in the Sifiq Kingdom felt. Shedding a lifetime of subservience was definitely a process. Still, encouragement she received from everyone she met fortified her spirit and made her glad she had found sufficient courage to flee her homeland.

Oui-lest turned her gaze from the woodlands to the brick walkway and took a deep breath. At the end of the curved path, past a cluster of evergreen shrubs, she noticed a relatively secluded bench on the far side of the temple. Victor sat alone, exuding intense waves of gloom. That was clear from the slump of his shoulders and the droop of his head. She stopped, her breath quickening as her thoughts raced. Why did he look so disheartened? Could she possibly lift his spirits as he once lifted hers? Dare she even try?

Overcoming her reluctance, Oui-lest slowly approached before stopping near the end of the carved wooden bench. Sounds from the busy square faded from her awareness as she focused on his forlorn image. He appeared so lonely, so isolated. For a moment, she considered retreating but couldn't bear turning away and leaving him in such obvious distress.

Her voice sounded barely louder than a whisper. "Victor? Victor, whatever is wrong?"

Long moments passed before he lifted his head and turned to acknowledge her. "Oui-lest," he uttered on a heavy sigh, his voice thick. He turned his face away, unable to think of anything more to say.

Slowly, she rounded the end of the bench and sat beside him. Although still uneasy with the spontaneous way Turandans responded to close acquaintances with touch, she sensed an intense need for comfort emanating from him. Responding almost without thought, she gently laid a gloved hand over his forearm. "Is there anything I can do to help?"

Victor shook his head and emitted a short, cynical laugh. "Hardly. I have an exceptional talent for doing and saying things that..."

"That what?" she prompted patiently. When he shook his head and looked away, she slid her hand down to take his. "I take it you've had a serious disagreement with Alexa."

A short, ironic laugh was his response. "Is it so obvious?"

"I wish I better understood your relationship. I know you said you were once—betrothed—that's the term you used, right?" When he nodded, she continued, "I know that you said the king manipulated her into marriage as part of an agreement to overturn your execution order and release you from prison. You said you were to blame. Later, you rescued Alexa from the palace and took her home, but she decided to stay married to the king rather than divorce him and marry you.

"I must admit that I don't understand the three of you. Plainly, there are walls between you and King Gregor, although he seems less tense than you. He and Alexa are devoted to one another as I never even imagined in any two people. You? I don't understand. Especially right now. Help me, Victor. In Timeri, you said you were at peace with their marriage, but now…"

"It isn't that, Oui-lest," he said, finally turning back to her. "I will always care for Alexa. Always. Because of the past, I also always live with a heavy mantle of guilt. Today, for the first time ever, she found it necessary to remind me of past shame after I refused to make allowances for the changes Raf-Zan is trying to make."

"What he did was reprehensible. You and all of Turand love Alexa. I see why you hated him from the beginning. I know why you don't want to forgive him. I find it hard to understand how she can and even harder to understand how the king accepts him."

"For you, that makes sense. You are new to Turand and our faith. For me? I humiliated myself, especially with Alexa. This morning, I stormed out of a meeting because King Gregor appointed Raf-Zan as a royal adviser. I was enraged by what Raf-Zan did to her and then refused to work with him. Then I went straight to Alexa and did even worse."

Oui-lest studied his features. His eyes held grief she didn't comprehend. Without thinking, she reached out, pushing back a shock of hair that had fallen in front of his eyes. Softly, she asked, "How did you make it worse?"

Victor looked away. His vision retreated to years earlier. He once again stood on Garogan Castle's high walls. Gregor sat astride his horse, skirting the edge of trees on the far side of the stream in front of the castle compound. Ignoring warning shouts, Alexa continued riding across the stream toward her husband and his soldiers.

Victor remembered carefully aiming his first arrow to fly close by her face, hoping to intimidate her into stopping. She didn't react. When her horse's hooves finally landed on dry ground, Gregor had urged his mount forward. Victor's anger exploded, and he aimed his second arrow at the man he hated so much. He had never expected Alexa's mad gallop and lunge that knocked the king from his saddle.

The next few minutes were among the worst of Victor's life. First, soldiers positioned themselves to block the king from view. Then, frantic activity revealed the existence of a crisis. Suddenly, soldiers moved their horses. On that bench outside Toraval's great Temple of Val, Victor felt anew the jolt in his stomach and the erratic beat of his heart. He would never forget watching Gregor stagger to his feet with Alexa, swathed in bloody bandages, lying limp in his arms.

"Victor, are you saying the arrow you intended for Gregor struck Alexa?"

When he turned to look into Oui-lest's stunned blue eyes, he could only imagine what she must think. "That arrow—*my arrow*—almost killed her. In all these years, Oui-lest, she has never mentioned it. Until today, and it was my fault. In my fit of anger, I insulted and condemned her husband by asking how he could possibly allow Raf-Zan to remain in the palace after what he did to her, especially knowing she must carry scars from the beating she took from that man. I said terrible things, Oui-lest."

"What did she say? It's hard to believe she retaliated in anger. Especially against you." Oui-lest looked mortified and confused.

Tears finally slid down Victor's cheeks. "That's just it. She didn't. Anlía had come, so she had her open the top of her dress. She told me to look for the scars on her back. At first, I only saw those left from Raf-Zan's beating. How glad I was to see them fading." His voice cracked as he continued, "She told me to look again. That's when I saw the scar my arrow left. She said his weren't the only scars she lived with as reminders of times she had almost lost her life, but that good often rises from bad. She didn't need to say another word to remind me that her husband had not shut me out of her life. Believe me, Oui-lest, I deserved so much worse. That's when she turned away from me."

Raw pain proved beyond Victor's control. Glad they weren't seated in the open, Oui-lest wrapped an arm around his broad shoulders as she felt tremors shake his body. She placed her cheek against his head, breathing in the clean scent of his dark hair as his face lay against her shoulder. Oui-lest had never known what it was to love someone as Victor loved Alexa. Unlike those early days in Timeri, she now wondered what it might be like to be loved by a man like Victor Garogan.

Chapter 4

S tefan glanced up and smiled gratefully as he accepted the snifter of golden brandy his wife offered him. "Thank you, my dear. These last few days have been trying, to be sure." After sipping the fortifying brandy, he gazed at the woman who had made him so happy. "Your brother?"

"Coping. I am exceedingly glad that he finally managed to put the good of Turand ahead of the past and his personal feelings. Whatever happened between him and Alexa shattered him, but Oui-lest seems to have calmed the tempest."

"For now?"

"For now. Did you find out what happened?" Adrina asked worriedly. Her brother had not been so utterly distraught since the weeks before the civil war. Even his depression following Alexa's disappearance hardly matched the dejection she had seen the day after he stalked out of the meeting after learning of Captain Lynmar's new post on Gregor's staff.

Rising from his chair, Stefan crossed the room to join his wife on the sofa in their drawing room. "Gregor has said nothing yet. He and Nikolai have spent practically every waking hour in meetings with members of National Council. When I wasn't chasing down aides to schedule or reschedule meetings and change the agenda, we worked on presentations to ensure all the details were clear and concise. I have the feeling

Gregor is more than just irritated with Victor while being more protective than ever of Alexa."

"Victor would never do anything to hurt Alexa. You know that."

Stefan leaned forward to kiss Adrina's cheek. "Not intentionally, no. But you didn't see him when he left that conference room. We told him the night before that Lynmar would be there, although Gregor hadn't made the final decision about the advisory post until that morning. Victor was livid and shouting like a madman. I don't think it helped that Nikolai remained so calm and retained absolute control of the situation."

"Gregor didn't step in?"

"No. He didn't say a word, although he was ready to if necessary. I can tell you one thing. He was immensely proud of his son." Stefan grinned. "So was I. Standing up to Victor, under those circumstances, was trial by fire. Niko sailed through unscathed."

"So," Adrina mused, determined to better understand Victor's mood, "we know that Victor went to Alexa's office. Everyone heard when he slammed her door. Things quieted quickly, which should be expected with Alexa. Not long after, Anlía went in. Shortly after that, Victor left and disappeared for hours. He hasn't been the same since." She looked up. "Something happened. You know it did."

Stefan shrugged his shoulders. "The question is what. I imagine he was so angry he said something that upset her. Alexa is not vindictive, but she does have a way of quickly setting matters straight. With the history she and Victor share, it's anyone's guess what happened. We're just going to have to wait until someone tells us."

Seeing Adrina's nod, he set his glass aside on the table and took her hands. "Right now, I'm exhausted and glad for an early evening home. Since our family has already gone to bed, I think I may have just enough energy remaining to take my lovely wife upstairs and make love to her before I pass out for the night. Do I hear any objections?"

With eyelashes fluttering and cheeks blushing, Adrina still looked shy and girlish in some ways. That charm was part of her sweetness that Stefan had cherished throughout the years of their marriage. As they walked arm in arm upstairs, he reflected on the many joys she still delivered to his life.

⌒

Propped up on a mountain of pillows against the intricately carved headboard of their enormous bed, Alexa watched as her husband deposited jeweled rings and his royal medallion in a velvet case on a dressing table. How she cherished such simple pleasures after her long absence. She almost hated breaking the silence.

"How was your meeting with Willem?"

He looked up and cast a tired, amused smile over his shoulder. "Good, fortunately. Willem is a thoughtful, sensible man. I think he lets Katara channel all of the levity in their lives so he can focus on more serious matters."

Alexa laughed lightly. "She is a cheerful foil to his staid nature. They are a handsome couple, but I never fully understood how Willem and Katara made such a happy match."

Gregor chuckled. Finally tucking himself beneath the covers she held invitingly high for him, he pulled Alexa close. "A mystery, to be sure, but they will never be as happy as I am," he said, softly kissing her.

She sighed contentedly. "I almost hate leaving for Zinzan this week, but I've planned to go with Anlía ever since she first mentioned studying there. I still regret missing Nikolai's coronation as Crown Prince."

"That wasn't your fault, and he does understand. You go with Anlía for her sake and yours, even though I shall sorely miss you while you're away."

Alexa placed her palm against his cheek and gazed into those dark eyes that she had constantly dreamed about during her time as a Sifiq prisoner. "You and Nikolai have been masterful with council members this week. I'm so very proud."

Gregor closed his eyes and concentrated on her touch. Dearest Val, he thought, how many nights had he lain in this bed, agonizing over her absence and missing the feel of her hands soothing away the stress of his days? He murmured a response. "Lady Valkana, the firstborn son you gave me is impressive. He is developing into quite the diplomat and already possesses a daunting ability to impose order during trying situations."

"Hmmm," she sighed, "I assume you're referring to Victor's outburst?"

Gregor reluctantly rolled onto his back and stared at shadows on the carved ceiling. "That and various other encounters. Has he talked to you? He asked if you knew. Of course, I said yes and that you were very disturbed."

"No, Nikolai hasn't talked to me. Before you ask, I haven't spoken to Victor since that morning, either."

"My appointment to Lynmar infuriated him."

Alexa sat up and gazed down into her husband's suddenly curious face. "Gregor, this time, Victor made me angry. No! Not angry. He made me furious!"

Pushing himself into a sitting position, Gregor cradled her face between his hands. "Beloved, we've had no time to discuss the details. I've known you to be firm with Victor, but furious? What, exactly, did he say that upset you so?"

Alexa exhaled a tremulous breath as she turned her face to place a kiss against one of his palms. "You already know how incensed he was over Rafzan. When he charged into my office, he wasn't rational. You can't imagine his reaction when I told him that Rafzan is sincere with his newfound faith in Val and that I encouraged your decision to offer him the post."

Emerald eyes revealed a blend of emotions that Gregor had spent days trying to comprehend. Finally, knowing her as he did, he detected disappointment, anger, and resentment. "Tell me what he said."

Casting her eyes downward, she shook her head. "He began by reminding me how afraid I always used to be of the Sifiq—how I feared being around them. He was actually taunting me. Then he started shouting about how Rafzan whipped me and how I would live with the scars for the rest of my life as reminders of how Rafzan nearly killed me."

Looking up, she saw Gregor flinch, so she grasped his hands. "He also started hurling insults against you."

"Me?"

"Yes, you. About how my precious husband could possibly work with that Sifiq after what he did to me. He asked how you could really love me and just ignore what Rafzan had done."

Gregor choked back the lump rising in his throat. He recalled his conversation with Stefan right before finally deciding to offer the advisory position to Captain Lynmar. What had he said? He would do it for Alexa and for Turand. Otherwise…

She saw the shadows that crossed her husband's face. For the very first time since meeting him, she read his life force, feeling his thoughts as clearly as if they were her own. "My love, I understand, and I think no less of you. I love you more than ever for being strong enough to do what is right."

"He doesn't know what I have suffered—or still do at times."

"No, he doesn't. He also doesn't always acknowledge how much suffering he has caused. As much as I will always care for him—as much good as Victor has done for me—he has created tremendous pain and tragedy with his temper. That's how his words struck me that day."

"What did you tell him?"

"I heard Anlía outside my office. She came to work on final trip arrangements. I called her inside and asked her to unlace the top of my gown and open it." Seeing the puzzled expression on Gregor's face, she smiled grimly and continued, "I told him to look for scars. At first, he only saw the ones from the captain's beating. Then I told him to look again for one near my left shoulder blade. When he saw it, he knew exactly what it was. I told him that the captain's scars weren't the only ones I'll carry for a lifetime and that good often comes from bad. I haven't seen him or heard a word from him since."

Gregor inhaled sharply. He could only imagine Victor's reaction. "Beloved, no wonder he's been so reserved—and more cooperative."

Lying back, Alexa settled into the comfort of her pillow and guided her husband onto his. Tucking her arm around him, she snuggled close to savor his warmth. "Since tomorrow is the last day before we leave, I know Anlía is curious about what happened in my office. I also know you promised to talk to Nikolai. I hoped Victor would help us, but that won't be practical now. Considering the current crisis, I think we should tell our oldest two tomorrow. Before Anlía and I leave."

Lifting her hand, Gregor let his lips linger against silken skin. How he dreaded delving again into shame he wished he could forget. "If you think that's best."

"Gregor, trust me. Remember. I'm home now, and we'll be together to tell them. I can remind them how very much I love you. I want you to rest now. What was it you used to tell me? Sleep sweet."

With her gentle caresses stroking through his hair, he began to relax. She was right. The night he mentioned it to Nikolai, the idea of telling their children without her about how they had married had struck terror into his very soul. Now, with her home again, the prospect was less intimidating. Breathing a prayer of gratitude that Alexa was safely home, Gregor fell asleep to the sound of her voice whispering his name.

Alexa sat on the library floor near the hearth of the massive fireplace. There were times when even the slightest chill drove itself quickly into her bones and reminded her of the frigid winter she had spent at the Talafaq labor camp. The warmth of the roaring fire chased the bitter memory from her thoughts, and the sound of opening doors claimed her attention.

"Mother, we brought trays of cheese and fruit. Father said we might be a while."

Grinning up at Nikolai, Alexa chuckled. "You and your father never change. You're always hungry. Where is your sister?"

"Here, Mother," Anlía said. "I have tea for us. Father says he'll have brandy."

"All right, everyone," Alexa said, rising from the floor and watching as Gregor closed the library doors and secured inside latches to avoid unwelcome interruptions. "Let's get comfortable. We have much to discuss."

Always sensitive to his moods, Anlía noticed tension tighten Gregor's features. "Father, are you well?"

His eyebrows lifted high as Gregor sighed heavily. "Yes, but your mother and I are about to share some things with you that will be easy for none of us. The telling will be difficult for us and likely hard for you to hear."

Alexa reached for her husband's hand and drew him to the comfort of the sofa where she now sat. "Anlía, I promised to explain what happened with Victor that day in my office. It is connected to a long and complicated story that began years ago. Nikolai already knows a little, but you're both old enough to hear exactly what happened. I think it's especially important now, considering you're leaving for Zinzan while we face the ongoing Sifiq crisis."

Nikolai turned questioning eyes to his mother. "I did finally talk to Stefan. He explained what happened when you went to..." He stopped, directing an intense gaze at his father. "He told me how Mother traveled to save your life after the battle in Garogan Province."

"Oh, Nikolai, there's so much more than that," Alexa said. "So much more. We had expected Victor to help explain, but this might be best."

Ever-empathetic to the emotions of those she loved, Anlía sensed the powerful emotions churning through her parents. From her father, she felt distress and dread verging on terror. Yet, on the other hand, her mother had obviously achieved peace with whatever had occurred. Her mother, now projecting both confidence and resolve, felt it necessary to clear clouds obscuring the past.

"Tell us, Mother. I see this must be very important."

Alexa smiled in appreciation for her daughter's sensitivity. "Before we start, the one thing I want to emphasize is something I'm certain you both know. Your father and I love each other in ways impossible to express. Keep that in your minds and your hearts while we unravel the story of how we met and came to marry."

"You make it sound terrible," Anlía said, her eyes narrowing inquisitively.

Alexa nodded and glanced at Gregor, who sighed and closed his eyes as memories flooded his mind. "It was not good. I start from the beginning. You know the Sifiq murdered my family in the massacre at Zinzan. What isn't widely known is how I survived the massacre."

Nikolai leaned forward in his chair. "So you were there? How did you escape?"

Alexa inhaled sharply. "It was days before my eighteenth birthday. The Sifiq generally avoided Garogan Province, but they were determined to eradicate all Valiria priestesses. They came after me. Although he left early with a hunting party, Victor had a premonition that something was wrong. He returned to my parents' home just as the Sifiq swarmed in.

"He dragged me to a cellar and barricaded us inside before the Sifiq saw us. He kept me there for two nights and two days. We listened to every sound of that massacre. The screams. All of it. They murdered everyone from the village. When we finally emerged, instead of celebrating my birthday and formally announcing our betrothal, Victor and I reassembled the bodies of my parents, covered all the others, and left for help to bury them."

Tears filled Anlía's eyes, their emerald color shimmering in the candlelight. "Oh, Mother, I knew the tragedy of their deaths, but I never imagined…" She shook her head. "I never knew you and Papino Victor were betrothed. Nikolai, you knew?"

Her brother nodded grimly. "I found out the night Father received Victor's dispatch that he had found Mother alive in Timeri. It was a shock."

"Never have I regretted more not having time to explain something to you, Nikolai," Gregor said, his expression begging his son's compassion.

"Father, Mother needed you most at the time. You needed to leave," Nikolai said, hoping his voice conveyed some measure of reassurance.

Alexa squeezed her husband's hand and continued, "At the time, it was too dangerous for me to travel to live with any of my cousins. Victor's parents were still alive, so they decided it was safest to take me to Garogan Castle. Adrina was there, and Victor's family were people I knew and loved to help me recover.

"Six months later, Victor's parents were killed in a Sifiq attack across the border in Pitrand. Things began to change. Victor began to change. He was frequently gone, supposedly planning a revolt against the Sifiq occupation army and your father."

"Against Father? Why?" Nikolai asked, his forehead creased.

"At the time, many Turandans, mostly those of us in the southern provinces, myself included, believed your father was in league with the Sifiq. We called him the *Dark King of Turand* for more than his appearance.

We thought his heart and soul to be dark and evil with little concern for our people's sufferings.

"During that period, Victor always respected my position as a Valiria priestess, but his political involvement caused him to continuously postpone our wedding plans. Eventually, he didn't return home from one of his so-called rallies. Finally, word came. He was imprisoned in Toraval—awaiting execution."

Nikolai's eyes grew wide with disbelief. "Father? Can that be true?"

Solemnly, Gregor nodded his head. "It is. As you well know, Stefan employs a network of very effective operatives. They discovered Victor embroiled in plans to murder several key members of my staff and assassinate me—as we slept in our beds. This came at a particularly crucial time when Stefan and I were working to deceive the Sifiq by making them think condemned prisoners were being executed. In reality, the executions were carefully planned to look like executions. We then secretly moved people to locations where they could train as soldiers to fight when the time was right.

"I was beyond furious with Victor. Had he openly challenged me, I could have respected him. His plan to attack me in secret? I could accept that as well. That he also planned to murder innocent people in their beds was insupportable."

"And you're sure he plotted such a thing?" Nikolai asked, finding the revelation hard to accept.

When Gregor would have answered, Alexa shook her head. "When I heard the news, I saddled a horse and headed to Toraval. Alone. I said nothing to anyone when I left. At the time, it seemed a miracle that I reached the capital without being captured or killed by Sifiq soldiers. When I arrived, I spent the day in prayer in front of the temple. Although I had a vision there that confounded me, I refused to be deterred from my goal. I loved Victor and would have done almost anything to save his life.

"I donned my Valiria cloak and walked through the palace gates. I then marched into the palace and demanded counsel with the king. I remember your father being as much amused as he was shocked, but I was in no mood for games."

Gregor smiled for the first time that evening. "I recall a young priestess daring every Sifiq soldier in my court to come near her. Never had I witnessed such courage."

"You, my love, failed to see my knees shaking or hear my heart pounding. Still, I refused to fail in my mission, and you did agree to hear me in private."

"So I did. I was intrigued. How could I not be?"

She turned back to their children. "I told your father my reason for coming. I saw his anger, but he said little. Instead, he offered to consider the matter and arranged for me to spend the night in safety at the palace. The next day, he told me the reason for Victor's sentence. I didn't believe him, but he arranged to bring Victor to the palace so I could talk to him. When I asked Victor, he avoided admitting the truth outright, but neither would he deny it. Sadly, I recognized the truth. He had indeed planned to commit the atrocities just as your father said.

"Later, I met with your father. He asked if I still wanted Victor set free. I owed Victor my life. At the time, although sick at heart, I was convinced Victor and I loved one another enough to work through whatever had pushed him to pursue such a dreadful plot. I told your father I would do anything if he would free Victor and ensure his safe return to Garogan Province."

"You included a caveat," Gregor added. "You said anything so long as it didn't interfere with the practice of your faith."

Alexa met his gaze with adoring eyes. "So I did, and you promised a solution that would ensure every opportunity to do so." She continued to the children, "Your father said if I agreed to remain in Toraval and marry him, he would release Victor and send him back to Garogan."

Anlía gasped. "Are you saying Father forced you to marry him?"

Alexa's expression turned thoughtful. "Your Father offered marriage in exchange for Victor's freedom. It was my choice to accept his offer."

"Father, why? Why did you do it?" Nikolai asked.

Gregor swallowed. Hard. "I wish I could give you a good answer. Unfortunately, I don't have one. However, I saw something in your mother that I knew I needed in my life. Just as she was willing to do anything to gain Victor's freedom, I was willing to do anything to keep her with me. Was it honorable on my part? Absolutely not. That has made it the one thing in my life that I most dreaded telling my children. I love each of you so much, and the idea of losing your respect…"

"Nikolai. Anlía. Do you remember my mentioning the vision I had at the temple the first day I came to Toraval?"

"The one that you said confused you so?" Anlía asked in a subdued, trembling voice.

"Yes," Alexa replied. "In that vision, I saw your father. I looked down to see him take my hand. When I entered the palace that first night, the vision had already shown me his face. I then relived the vision the night of our wedding. Heartbroken as I was, the only thing clear to me at that moment was that our marriage was the will of Val.

"It took months to overcome the grief of my separation from Victor. Gradually, though, I also began to see your father for the man he is. Times were so complicated. He and Stefan were concentrating on their schemes to oust the Sifiq from Turand. Finally, I saw what your father was doing and realized he wasn't the selfish tyrant I always believed.

"As far as our marriage, we also had our share of personal conflicts, especially getting to know one another while conquering my resentment. Despite our differences, your father proved himself to be protective and kind in many ways. One special time I remember is the anniversary of the Zinzan massacre."

"Beloved?" Gregor's voice softened with concern.

"It's all right, Gregor. It's important that they understand." Memory carried her back to that chilly day. "I was outside, crying. Your father came to me. He was so concerned, insisting on knowing what had upset me. I told him about the nightmare I used to have about the massacre and how Victor saved me by locking us inside that cellar. I remember telling him how Victor tried to drown out the sounds of killing by singing children's songs to me."

Anlía left her chair and went to her mother. Dropping to her knees, she grasped her mother's hands and kissed them. "How terrible, Mother. I'm so sorry."

Alexa reached out and stroked her fingers through her daughter's hair. "It was terrible, but it happened long ago."

"What did Father say?" Nikolai asked.

"Very little. Instead, he wrapped his arms around me and held me while I cried. More than anything else, that was what I needed at the time. Days later, he took me for my first trip to Lindaval. He said we both needed time away."

"We planned to stay several days. I remember getting up that first morning and watching your mother walk downstairs. How beautiful and rested she looked. After breakfast, I took her outside. She had no idea about the weather anomaly around Lindaval, and all the lilacs enchanted her. I had never seen her so happy."

"I don't think I had ever felt so happy in your presence." Smiling again, she said, "Then we rode to the hot springs. I was completely enchanted! We spent the most glorious afternoon there. I hated to leave."

A slight frown crossed her features. "When we returned, Stefan was waiting with a detachment of Royal Guards. An urgent matter had arisen, requiring your father to return to Toraval that very night. In truth, I felt devastated. He wouldn't let me travel back with him, and there was so much I desperately wanted to discuss with him."

Turning his wife's chin with gentle fingers, Gregor said, "You never told me that before."

"When I finally arrived home, I did ask if we could have time to talk. But, as I recall, Lord Manaran monopolized your time."

"Ah, yes, and then we were robbed of any chance for that discussion."

"Robbed? How so?" Nikolai asked.

Gregor grimaced. "Your mother and Stefan took Lady Manaran and her entourage riding the next morning. That way, I could speak to Lord Manaran without distractions. Regrettably, an armed band from Garogan attacked the guards accompanying your mother's riding party. Victor had planned the raid to abduct your mother and return her to Garogan."

Nikolai leaned forward with his elbow on the arm of his seat. His long fingers rubbed circles against his temple as he stared at Alexa. "He took you back?"

"According to him, he rescued me. Victor had researched ancient laws and religious edicts, discovering our marriage was subject to annulment. Along with Lord Anderon and a Tasan priest, they were preparing documents so I could attest to the circumstances of the marriage. The priest would declare the marriage null and void according to religious law. Garogan provincial lawyers would legalize the annulment. I would then be free to marry Victor."

Nikolai and Anlía exchanged looks that revealed how stunned they were as their parents continued to unravel their past. Anlía asked, "You actually had the chance to end your marriage to Father according to religious standards? If you loved Victor so much, why didn't you?"

"Anlía, your father kept his word and freed Victor. I also considered the marriage vows that I made inside a consecrated chapel to be sacred and binding. A Valiria priestess is bound always by faith and honor to her word. Also, for a while after my return to Garogan, I felt confused. Victor became so upset with me that he locked me in my rooms for days."

"But he should know…"

"Nikolai, he did know how detrimental such isolation is to Valiria. His purpose was to weaken my resolve."

"I don't understand how he could treat you that way if he loved you," Anlía remarked.

"As I said before, times were complicated. Very complicated. Did Victor love me? Yes, I believe he did. At the same time, he was committed to the rebel cause and conspiring with subversives from Tasa Coast and Pitrand. He had also become very ambitious. I represented a prize as Turand's only surviving Valiria priestess. Since I had become queen against my will, he sought to end the royal marriage and marry me. What a cry to rally our people! His lost love and Turand's last Valiria—saved from the corrupt, evil king!

"When I refused cooperation, he locked me away again. Then? I remember dreaming one night. Val showed me scenes from my marriage—images of your father and us together at Lindaval. I also saw your father on his stallion and Victor with his bow. That's when I woke up. That dream made me realize I could never renounce my marriage because I loved your father more than I had ever loved any other person in my entire life. Even if it meant death, I would never betray my husband.

"Later that day, Victor and I argued, and his famous temper surfaced. Several times, he shook me nearly senseless and slapped me. Hard enough to knock me to the floor."

"Mother! He hit you?" Nikolai gasped.

"He did, Nikolai. He wasn't rational. He wasn't the same Victor I had known and loved so dearly. He had changed. I finally realized the change had begun long before he went to Toraval. I had simply refused to see it."

"Dearest Val, we never had any idea," Anlía gasped. "This seems so impossible."

"That was one of the darkest times of my life, Anlía," Gregor said. "Your mother was gone for weeks. Stefan and I had convinced the Sifiq that we could more easily manage the provinces if they thought they had some say in their affairs. Then, just as we had scheduled conferences to plan the first National Council of my reign, your mother disappeared.

"While I dealt with representatives planning for Council, Stefan sought to learn what was happening with your mother. When they confirmed she was at Garogan Castle, I lost all hope. I already knew how much I loved her and fully expected to lose her. I had no doubt Victor had discovered he could annul the marriage. Stefan and I soon questioned why Victor wasn't triumphantly announcing the annulment and his marriage to your mother."

Despite the passage of so many years, memories of the despair he felt then delivered haunted shadows to his eyes. "Once preparations for Council ended, I could wait no longer. I assembled troops and rode to Garogan."

Alexa slid closer to Gregor, craving his closeness as much as he needed hers. "It wasn't long before Victor got so angry with me that he left the castle. While he was away, Lord Anderon visited me. While one of his men beat me, Anderon told me to either agree to the annulment or be hanged as a traitor.

"A day later, after deep meditation and Lord Val's gift of healing sleep, I woke up near midnight. Although I didn't realize it at the time, I was beginning to manifest my gifts as Valkana. I undid locks on my door and sneaked outside. Avoiding sentries and reaching the stables, I saddled a horse and escaped through the back gate.

"By that time, the sun was rising. I was crossing the stream when I looked up and saw your father. I hardly dared believe it. That's when

I heard Victor shout, warning me to stop. I suddenly remembered my dream."

Gregor lifted her hand and tenderly kissed it when she couldn't continue. "Stefan called out a warning as Victor raised his bow and aimed at me. I started toward her, but your mother charged in my direction. She bolted and lunged forward, knocking me out of my saddle."

Nikolai and Anlía left their chairs and sat on the carpeted floor in front of their parents. There could be no doubt the memory had shaken both of them. Alexa's tear-stained face appeared pale. Tears glazed their father's eyes. Both children reached out, touching their parents.

"Stefan helped me reach your mother. She was face-down on the ground. When she leapt from her horse, Victor's arrow struck her in the back and lodged against her shoulder blade. She had also hit her head in the fall. Once we removed the shaft and covered the gash in her head, we departed immediately for Toraval.

"Your mother didn't regain consciousness until days after our return. We were terrified she would die, but Tira and Tirani cared for her day and night. Complicating matters was the drama surrounding National Council. I wanted an exception because of her condition. However, Victor arrived with the Garogan delegation, and the southern provinces adamantly opposed any exception.

"Just when I thought my cause lost and disaster at hand, in walked your mother—weak and trembling but so beautiful. Except when you children were born, I never felt more proud of her. We presided over Council that day and every day thereafter, even the day Victor was expelled."

"Expelled? I've never heard of anyone being expelled from Council."

"He was. With a decree of five years of dishonorable censure."

Nikolai could barely contain his dismay. "Dare I ask why?"

Gregor inhaled a deep breath. "He approached your mother during a break, wanting to talk to her. I heard him raise his voice, but before I could reach them, he slapped her, knocking her to the ground."

"Dearest Val, is there no end to his misdeeds?" Anlía gasped, tightly squeezing her mother's hands.

Nikolai drew in a heavy breath. "I assume he must have created quite a scene when he left. Did you see him again before…?"

"His departure from Toraval was dramatic, to say the very least. Fortunately, your mother was spared witnessing that spectacle. I didn't see him again until we met on the battlefield in Garogan Province."

Anlía shifted puzzled eyes from her father to her brother, and Nikolai's mouth drew into a tight line. "Papino Stefan told me that Victor stalked Father in battle. He was determined to kill him. He found him and engaged him in a fight. He succeeded in running him through with a broadsword."

Tears eased down Anlía's face. "Oh, Father, how? How could he do such a thing? How did you survive?"

When Gregor choked on the words, Nikolai grasped his sister's hands. "Papino Stefan said Mother had a vision days earlier and arrived at the camp some hours after Father's army won the battle. Father was dying. Stefan said the sword had completely pierced his body, and the wound was absolutely hideous. Mother arrived in time to summon the Healing Graces and save Father's life."

"So Val granted you a miracle."

"He did," Alexa answered in a quivering voice. Reaching out, she placed her palm against her son's cheek. "I was pregnant with you, Nikolai. I couldn't bear the thought of losing the man I loved most or you growing up without knowing your father."

Alexa gathered her thoughts. "It's vital that you understand all of this in the context of the times. Victor's family and mine were close, so the massacre at Zinzan also killed people he loved. The sounds and sights we experienced there are far too horrific for words. Then, his parents. My marriage to your father broke him. Something snapped. Victor needed to strike back, but he was never the type to strike blindly. He was brilliant and calculating. Any retaliation would reflect intelligent planning. Mentally and emotionally, he lost all ability to master control of his actions. He lashed out at everyone who got in his way."

"What changed him back?"

Gregor smiled. "Your mother, of course. After I recovered sufficiently from my wound, we immediately planned our next offensive. Lord Zephirás had arrived with reinforcements. We needed to move expeditiously. The next battle was vicious. I happened to turn and see Victor fighting with one of my officers. The officer lunged forward, slicing Victor across his body. Blood spurted everywhere. I knew the wound would prove fatal.

"What could I do? No matter what, I knew your mother would be devastated if he died. I dismounted, jerked off my coat, and bound it to his chest. Someone helped get him on my horse. I then rode with all speed back to our camp where your mother, Tirani, and Katara Zephirás were managing hospital tents.

"Just seeing your mother's face told me I had made the right decision. We carried him to my tent so she could tend to him. I can tell you—that hurt like a hot iron to my gut. But her losing him would have been worse. Even if he died, she had to try to save him.

"After that, Victor improved physically. He learned about Anderon tricking the Garogan militia into fighting with disguised Sifiq soldiers. As he recovered mentally and emotionally, Victor became a voice of reason. His experiences offered essential wisdom as we struggled through tribunals and wrote new laws to carry us through Turand's rebuilding. His planning and organizational skills were exceptional and vastly improved the speed of Turand's recovery.

"And," Gregor added almost reluctantly, "you cannot deny that he has been an exceptional godfather to each of you."

"That's all true, Father, but I cannot understand how you trusted him to give him a chance in the first place."

"Nikolai," Gregor began, noticing fatigue on his wife's face, "our journey from the battleground was made during some of the worst heat in Garogan's recorded history. Your mother suffered a sudden bout of heat sickness. Victor saw her and prevented her from getting worse. He likely saved her from losing you and, perhaps, losing her life. I owed him that debt.

"Afterward, to placate your mother when she was so distressed over returning to Toraval, he promised to accompany me until the war ended. No easy feat, considering how much he despised me. He kept his word."

"And now Timeri," Anlía murmured.

Gregor's voice finally broke. "And now Timeri. Telling you all this is not for you to see Victor in lesser light. On the contrary, we want you to understand the past and how it affects all of us now."

He turned hopeful eyes to Nikolai, "I also cannot bear for you to look at me with disdain and disgust. I admit that manipulating your mother into marriage was far from honorable. Neither was it typical of me. I've never understood myself why I did it. But I did, and I cannot regret it."

Straightening, Alexa pensively smiled. "I believe Val guided your father for his good, my good, and the future of Turand. That's my explanation. It is a truth I accept. What I know for certain is what I've told you already, Nikolai. I could never love any man as much as I love Gregor Toscano. No man could have ever loved me better or made me happier than your father."

Chapter 5

Behind his massive desk, Gregor sat with his head tilted back, eyes closed, and mouth drawn into a taut line. His elbows perched in front of him, and the fingertips of his long hands met to form an open, temple-like structure pointing upward. Studying his father's image from the doorway, Nikolai contemplated the complex issues facing the man with responsibilities for so many. As Turand's king, his decisions affected his people's lives daily. He even held power to dispatch them into life-threatening peril. As husband and father, he cared for his family with love and devotion. Loyalty, constancy, and commitment reflected in everything his father said and did.

"Father," Nikolai regretfully interrupted Gregor's solitude, "Council is ready to resume."

Drawing in several deep breaths, Gregor straightened and met his son's waiting gaze. Nodding and rising from his chair, he joined the prince for a silent walk through palace corridors leading to the assembly hall where so many of Turand's most significant historical events had occurred over the centuries, some during Gregor's own reign. Representatives from the nation's twenty provinces now gathered and prepared to discuss status and recommendations regarding the recent Sifiq incursions into Turand's sovereign territory.

An hour passed as leaders of key regional committees summarized their assessments of new threats posed by the Sifiq and strategies proposed by King Gregor and his advisers to deal with the potential menace. When the last presentations finished, an air of impending history once again permeated the assembly hall. No one desired a return to the war-torn years so many remembered. Still, every man and woman stood firm, determined to preserve what they had fought hard to win and then rebuild. They waited as their king stood to address their assemblage.

The passage of time had enhanced the imposing image of Turand's king. A sound diet and exercise regimen had helped him maintain a muscular physique made more impressive by his unusual height. Thick waves of silvering black hair and precisely trimmed beard framed the still handsome, bronzed face. Black-brown eyes shone brightly with wisdom and intelligence as King Gregor Toscano squared wide shoulders and broadened his stance before drawing breath to address his nation's National Council. He began without preamble.

"Twenty years of peace have not erased from my memory the terrible cost we paid for peace." Gregor's powerful voice carried clearly into every corner of the gallery. "The exceptional progress we achieved must be protected lest we fail the memory and the sacrifice of every man and woman who died in the struggle to win the freedom Turand now treasures. As I stated in earlier sessions, I have absolutely no desire—not even the slightest desire—to plunge our nation headlong into war without first attempting to persuade our old enemy that war is not a desirable option. I value the lives of our people—private citizens and soldiers alike—above all else. As such, I prefer to pursue a peaceful resolution to this issue—to persuade them to avoid our waters and our shores.

"However, I also intend to make the Sifiq understand one thing. They will not find us the same as they once did. We are no longer lost in darkness and mired in chaos. We are a people united in light, in faith, and in purpose. While we prefer to co-exist in peace, we will stand and fight with courage, resolve, and determination to preserve our nation and our way of life. Never again will we allow them to run amok over us to inflict terror and death with impunity. Never!"

Hearty hails of approval erupted in response to the brief, emotion-laden words his father delivered to members of National Council. While council representatives voiced enthusiastic support, Prince Nikolai watched when his father turned a solemn face toward Turand's beloved queen. Pride shone from emerald eyes despite her expression reflecting trepidation that Turand might be marching toward the precipice of war. Joining his parents, the prince exercised one of the most vital lessons learned from his father and Stefan: Stand proud and confident while never letting anyone see any of the concerns or doubts churning within his breast.

⌣

Morning's earliest golden rays invaded between open draperies he had risen and drawn himself. How beautiful the play of light and shadow across ivory curves, he thought, as his long fingers indulged in delighted caresses across her silken smooth skin. In the day's first waking moments, dark eyes beheld the beauty of the beloved wife he had missed to the point of physical pain. As his gaze captured the intense regard in her bewitching emerald irises, he pulled her close. His body shuddered with need. Hers responded in kind.

Gregor's lips touched hers tenderly at first. His kiss swiftly deepened as she responded, her mouth opening in invitation. Such power she wielded over him as he surrendered to her in that intensely intimate connection! Their mouths fused them together, allowing his senses to surge as he tasted their kiss and felt nerves throughout his body stir and fiery blood deliver once-stolen desire. Involuntarily straining toward her, his body quaked with passion when she pressed herself close to him and whispered plaintively, "Gregor, my love, I need you so!"

He lost track of time. He had always treasured loving her but never more so than since her return from the Sifiq Kingdom. Never would he take this precious union for granted, he thought, indulging them both in luxurious caresses and fiercely impassioned kisses and strokes that ended with a passionate explosion that left them both clinging to one another, breathless and sated.

Finally, with teardrops on his cheeks, Gregor lifted her hand to his lips. "My beloved Alexa, have you any idea how much I shall miss you?"

"I won't be gone long. And I shall be far from any seashores," Alexa murmured, content to remain in the secure comfort of his embrace.

"It doesn't matter. I must stay and once again trust you into the care of others." His arm tightened around her as his lips lingered against her forehead. "Times are uncertain. I cannot lose you again. I could never bear it."

"You will not lose me, Gregor. After I escort Anlía to Zinzan and get her settled, I plan to address some formalities and collect some materials I wish to study. Then? It's home again to your arms." She affectionately kissed his eyelids and nose. "Now, will you let me up so I can get dressed?"

He breathed out reluctantly. "I suppose I have no choice."

With a soft laugh, she kissed him again. "You created many of these choices, Your Majesty, when you decided to have six children."

Rolling onto his back, he gave a mighty groan. "So the fault is mine alone? Come to me, my love, and let me remind you that I had willing help creating this royal state of chaos!"

Two nights later, Alexa smiled at the memory of their second round of lovemaking that morning while gazing into the depths of the huge bonfire lighting the camp where they stopped after a day of travel on their journey to Zinzan. Until her year-long captivity by the Sifiq, she had occasionally considered her sentimental side almost a vulnerability akin to weakness. Never again. Life as a prisoner had plunged her soul's awareness to a profound level, making her acutely aware that her life was a series of memories. Those cherished memories had provided a potent source of strength during times of trial and sorrow.

"Excuse my intrusion, Your Majesty. Would you like some supper?"

Alexa blinked several times before smiling back at the face that had changed so dramatically in the short time since their meeting. She still found it difficult to believe he was traveling with her to Zinzan.

"Yes, thank you, Captain Lynmar," she said, accepting the plate of food he offered. Allowing him to offer the blessing, she began eating after being assured her daughter had already eaten and was helping with an injured horse.

"You looked very thoughtful, but you were smiling. A happy memory, perhaps?"

Glad that the roaring fire might easily explain any blush on her cheeks, Alexa smiled. "A happy memory. I was thinking of my husband."

Beginning to eat from his plate, Lynmar sighed. "I hope I might someday reflect on happy memories."

Alexa savored the flavor of fire-roasted vegetables for a few moments. "You have none at all?"

Brown eyebrows lifted high beneath blond hair growing out from his classic, cropped, Sifiq military haircut. "Nothing I consider happy. I now have some pleasant memories as I build friendships here."

Alexa gave him a reassuring smile. "Have patience. Everything worthwhile requires time and patience."

"I tire of my lonely existence. I admit that I envy the relationship you share with His Majesty. I long to share such fond intimacy with another person."

"Again, I counsel patience. My relationship with my husband didn't begin well at all. I prayed for divine guidance. I suggest you do the same."

"I can't imagine the two of you ever in opposition," Lynmar remarked smilingly.

Alexa laughed quietly as she finished her food. "You can't imagine how terrible things once were for us. However, I'm more than satisfied with how our marriage worked out. Have faith, my dear captain, have faith."

As Rafzan gazed at her retreating figure, a soft voice from behind interrupted his doubts. "Mother didn't exaggerate her early problems with Father, although things resolved happily. Val always intended for them to be together."

"Your Highness," Rafzan started to rise.

"Don't get up. May I join you? I'd like to sit and enjoy the fire before going to bed."

"Of course," he said, somewhat disconcerted by her easy manner. He thoughtfully considered their brief conversation when she left less than twenty minutes later. The injured horse. The length of the trip. His appreciation for the king's permission allowing him time to visit the spiritual center at Zinzan. How he kept working en route on assignments to avoid failing the king's trust in him. He imagined the topics meant little to her, but she was attentive. Turandans baffled him.

Following two nights of enjoying lodgings at inns and one in Garogan City, the queen's entourage again made camp at a large clearing. Once everyone settled after the evening meal, Alexa walked around, making her usual rounds with Captain Fratino to speak with her guards. Upon returning to the center bonfire, she saw Anlía holding a large book with Rafzan Lynmar sitting next to her, one hand pointing to an open page, the other pointing skyward.

"The two of you look quite occupied," Alexa observed as she approached, accepting a mug of tea from a camp attendant.

Anlía grinned at her mother. "I've been studying ahead on some of my subjects. Captain Lynmar was pointing out star configurations from my astronomy book. He explained how men at sea use them to navigate. It's fascinating."

"I see," Alexa remarked. "I hope you aren't disturbing the good captain."

"Not at all, Your Majesty," Lynmar replied, barely suppressing a smile. "The princess's thirst for knowledge is admirable. The type of knowledge I can share is likely rare so far inland. I'm honored to contribute to her education."

"Mother, Captain Lynmar is studying the Third Tier in the Great Book of Val. I promised to help him with some of the passages."

"Ah, a fair exchange," Alexa said with a nod, curious about the extent of their conversations. "Morning comes early and with it another day of weary travel. I suggest you both get some sleep."

"We will, Your Majesty. Good night."

"I'll join you soon, Mother." Then, shifting her eyes to the sky, she pointed in a different direction, asking a question Alexa couldn't hear.

True to her word, Anlía pulled open the tent's door flap fifteen minutes later and entered. Setting her heavy book aside, she went to her mother and embraced her. "I thought you might be asleep by now. You look tired."

"I am tired, but I wanted to wait for you."

"I haven't done something wrong, have I?" Anlía asked.

Smiling, Alexa shook her head. "I can't imagine you have. I was just curious about this sudden friendship with Captain Lynmar."

"It's not really sudden. We've spoken several times over the past month or so. We often run into one another at the palace chapel. I see him praying there. Often. At first, I think he almost feared speaking to me. He's always very respectful."

"I just wondered."

"Mother, please don't say anything to him. I know what he did and exactly how horrible it was. He does, too. Quite honestly, I feel the guilt burning inside him. He hasn't said so, but I think that's why he wanted to come to Zinzan. He seeks avenues to heal his soul."

Alexa lovingly caressed her daughter's cheek. "You are a true empath, aren't you? You must be careful to protect yourself, dear one."

"I know, Mother. I learned how to do that long ago. You and Tirani taught me. You mustn't worry needlessly."

"There's nothing a mother does better than worry about her children. I'll remind you of this conversation when you give me grandchildren." They both laughed before tucking themselves in for the night.

⌣

Pearl-gray clouds hung over the streets of Zinzan. Final vestiges of morning rains moved slowly eastward on warming breezes. From posts lining city streets hung baskets of multicolored flowers dripping water from their early showers. Bright red, blue, and green frames trimmed doors and windows on solid buildings constructed from stone faced with white stucco. Central Zinzan vibrated with energy generated by students who had come to study with Turand's finest instructors.

Captain Fratino sat straight in his saddle, his posture erect and proud as he escorted Turand's beloved Valkana to her ancestral home. Sparing a glance to the side, he admired her poise and beauty as she gazed ahead, her lavender cape flowing behind her. The jangle of many harnesses and clopping of hooves on brick streets brought pedestrian traffic to a standstill. Passersby quickly recognized the queen's colors on fluttering banners and reverently bowed as Alexa rode by with Princess Royal Anlía and the Queen's Royal Guard.

The troupe rode a complete circle around the Valiria statue in the center of Zinzan before stopping in front of the school's administration building. Constructed of marble, a short flight of steps led to a colonnade supported by polished columns. This heart of the school was where all arriving students began their education at Zinzan.

As soon as Alexa dismounted, a familiar figure bolted down the steps and caught her in an enthusiastic hug. "Alexa! Welcome!"

"DiLeno! Thank you! How are you? And Tirani and DiRobbi?"

"We're all well. And you? And Gregor and the family?"

"The children and I are well. I fear my husband is suffering much stress at the moment, but Val gives him the strength he needs."

DiLeno nodded. "Thankfully, Val gave him the wife he needs to manage these stressful times. That can wait. Where is our new student?"

So began the whirlwind of formalities of registering Anlía at school, assigning her living quarters, and providing the names of her teachers and her class schedule. Knowing the preference to avoid any semblance of preferential treatment, DiLeno had planned for Alexa and her daughter to spend the night of their arrival at his home. The following day, they would organize her move to quarters where her security detachment could be close at hand.

That evening, DiLeno handed Alexa a glass of golden liqueur. "May I ask a question?"

"Yes, I'm tired. And, yes, he was every bit as bad as you heard. Probably worse."

DiLeno shook his head. "My apologies. I shouldn't have troubled you so soon."

"You are the best kind of friend, DiLeno. You don't just worry in silence." The left side of her mouth lifted in a half-smile. "For a while, I was afraid the old Victor from before the civil war might return. He had that look in his eyes."

"You didn't see him while you were gone. I'm honestly not sure who suffered more, Victor or your husband."

"DiLeno, I have begged Victor to get on with his life. I never wanted to hurt him. You know that. What happened—well, it did. I can't change it, nor do I want to."

"Alexa, I do understand. Victor had his chance. Well, many chances that he squandered when he kept delaying your wedding. You deserve your happiness with Gregor. I told you years ago. Never let anyone make you feel guilty, especially not Victor."

She sipped her drink. "From you, DiLeno, that means the world. Thank you."

"Now. Something else. Tell me about this Rafzan Lynmar."

"You'll be glad when I return to Toraval with him in tow. He will keep Tirani, Anlía, and half your instructors tied up with questions while he reviews every line of the Great Book of Val."

Only years of friendship allowed DiLeno freedom to indulge his curiosity. "Is he really the one?"

Alexa's green eyes met those of her longtime friend. "Yes," she confirmed reluctantly.

"It seems our Lady Valkana's ability to recognize his transformation and forgive is a mighty lesson for all of us."

DiLeno turned before rising from his chair. Greeting his petite wife with a kiss, he said, "Tirani, you're home at last. What kept you?"

Smiling brightly as she embraced Alexa, Tirani replied, "Alexa's Captain Lynmar. I left him with an intensive assignment that should keep him quite busy for the next several days. Five at least."

Alexa laughed as she sat down again on the mint-green sofa in the Tarandá drawing room. "DiLeno, get her a drink. Then let's make a wager. She says several days. I say he'll be back with her in three."

"Impossible. He told me he's working every day on projects for Stefan while making time for studying here. I gave him plenty to keep him busy. What is your wager?"

"Let's see," Alexa laughed. "If I lose, I'll present this year's business summary report to the king."

"Lovely. After what I just gave him? I accept."

"You haven't heard what I want when I win."

Tirani smiled as she lowered herself to her husband's lap. "Milady, tell me your dream." Seconds later, the former lady-in-waiting grinned and shook her head. "I recall all those times His Majesty called you impossible. I believe he was right. At least this is one time I don't have to worry about meeting strange expectations."

Alexa's emerald eyes sparkled with good humor. "Every good road and all fine buildings must begin with solid foundations."

DiLeno scowled comically. "It usually does work better that way. However, I do seem to recall at least one exception in my lifetime."

"Disbeliever! Trust me. Time will work in my favor."

Tirani's dark eyes glittered in challenge. "For once, I think time favors me, Lady Valkana. Now, where is our fair princess?"

"Upstairs planning for tomorrow," Alexa replied. "I believe my famously serene daughter is actually excited."

⌒

Three days later, Alexa inspected changes her daughter had made inside the private living quarters she would occupy while studying at Zinzan. With help from her guards, Anlía had rearranged furnishings and added two bookcases to hold the many books she had brought. A stand with a finely crafted dulcimer stood near a window. Although she expected little time to play, Anlía knew there might be times when the instrument's sweet tones might be the perfect tonic to ease bouts of homesickness and stress related to her coursework. Overall, the small apartment appeared comfortable and secure.

"You've done well, Anlía," Alexa praised. "Have you spent all your time inside, or have you been out to meet anyone?"

"Thank you, Mother," Anlía replied as she gazed at two of her guards on the street below. "I have gone out, but it's not especially pleasant with Royal Guards attached to my skirts."

Alexa chuckled. "Hmmm. Your father's work. I shall speak with Captain Fratino and DiLeno. You should be safe going about your daily routine without a constant escort."

Anlía turned grateful eyes to her mother. "Thank you. I did spend an hour yesterday afternoon with Captain Lynmar. He had some questions about an assignment he was finishing before returning it to Tirani. Oh! I also encountered your Master Maconti! He arrived a week ago. I hope you approve. I invited him to join us for midday tomorrow."

Alexa's eyes widened. "You managed all of that with Royal Guards attached to your skirts?"

Anlía blushed and sighed. "I enjoy helping Captain Lynmar. Perhaps it's part of my calling. Master Maconti was alone and looked pleased to see a familiar face."

Suddenly embracing her daughter, Alexa laughed softly. "I look forward to this construction plan."

Anlía pulled away and stared at her mother in confusion. "What?"

᪤

Days later, while Alexa perused old library journals and maps, Anlía wandered out a side door to sit beside a pretty fountain illuminated by moonlight. The early summer night was warm and balmy. Scented air bore the blended perfume of myriad blooming flowers. Breathing in the nearly intoxicating fragrance, Anlía suddenly reacted to a shuddering jolt of energy shafting down her spine.

Looking up and around, she saw several dark figures hurrying toward a two-story structure not far behind the library. Two of them carried small lanterns. Closing her eyes, she tapped into the energies. Something felt wrong. Getting up, she walked toward the building and watched the figures enter. Within minutes, she heard sounds of arguing.

Without thinking, she entered an open door and fearlessly started up a stairwell toward the sound of commotion. Reaching the second floor, she came upon three young men holding Gregor Maconti while two others were punching him.

"Stop it! Now! I demand that you release him immediately!" Anlía shouted furiously.

One of the attackers turned and laughed. "And who do you think you are?"

"Someone who'll make sure you never do something like this again," she shouted as she grabbed a broomstick and swung it at the young man, hitting the side of his head with a solid thwack.

"Why, you…! Hold him while I get her!" Another attacker then lunged at Anlía, who swiftly sidestepped and tripped him. By that time, her first victim had stumbled to his feet, knocking over one of the lanterns they had carried, spilling lamp oil and causing cleaning supplies to erupt into flames. Terrified assailants violently threw Maconti to the floor as the fire swiftly spread. Thick smoke quickly rose in choking clouds. A fleeing attacker shoved Anlía hard against a wall in his haste to bolt but then tripped and tumbled down the stairs.

"Princess! Get out! Stay on the floor and crawl out!" Maconti coughed and sputtered through the smoky haze.

"Anlía! Anlía! Where are you?" Desperation saturated another voice calling her name.

"Here!" she choked out, reaching toward the sound of her rescuer.

A brilliant flash of fire resulted in furious curses as she saw someone beat back a burst of flames. Stumbling to her side, he dragged her scarf over her face. "I'll get you out."

"Maconti! We have to get him! We can't leave him!"

He turned toward the sound of Gregor Maconti's voice. "Are you hurt?"

"Not much. Just get the princess out!"

"Hurry! Cover your face and follow me! Be quick! Anlía, hold me tight."

Dodging flaring flames and fiery, falling debris, the trio navigated the short distance to the stairwell. "Maconti, you go first. I'll bring the princess down."

Clutching treasure more precious than he ever imagined, Rafzan Lynmar ignored blistering burns on his arm and cheek while cautiously negotiating his way down the now-burning stairway. Reaching the bottom, he saw an arriving fire brigade and a crowd gathering outside. Royal Guards also held three young men who were seen escaping the burning building. Gasping for fresh air and falling heavily to his knees, Lynmar saw his queen's terrified face as she ran to where he held her daughter so protectively.

"Anlía! My sweet love!"

Lynmar's heart lurched inside his chest at the heartbroken sound of fear in a mother's voice. For a fleeting moment, he heard his own mother's voice. "She's safe, Your Majesty. She just needs to breathe fresh air."

Gathering her wits, Alexa breathed in, swiftly whispered a prayer, and called on Val's Healing Graces. Within moments, flashes of lights appeared. Elegantly sweeping her hands over Anlía and then along Lynmar's cheek and arm, she delivered blessed relief and healing.

Lynmar reluctantly surrendered the princess to Royal Guards, who placed her on a litter to carry her to the Tarandá house. Then, not forgetting himself entirely, he looked around. "Your Majesty, the young Maconti was also inside. He needs you."

"Of course." Alexa turned and went to kneel beside her young friend. Then, using the healing abilities gifted to all Valiria, she brought healing to him for the impaired breathing and bruises that had required five young men to inflict.

Once Maconti was taken to the Tarandá home for the night, Alexa rose from the ground. First, she turned to Captain Lynmar. "I sensed something wrong. When I came outside, I saw you running and looked up to see those men racing from the building and smoke pouring out the windows. What happened?"

"All I know is that I was taking a walk when I heard the princess shouting. She sounded distressed, so I called your guards and ran to investigate. When I saw those men running and the smoke, I rushed inside and called out to her. When she answered from upstairs, I ran up to get her. Maconti was there. I guided him ahead while I carried your daughter out."

Alexa closed her eyes for just a moment. Her jaw trembled. Overcome by emotions she might never be able to express, Alexa said, "Rafzan Lynmar, I can never thank you enough. You risked your life saving my daughter and one of this school's students. For now, all I can do is pray that Val will bless you this day and every day forward. I promise that I will always pray for your peace and happiness."

The queen then turned to where DiLeno stood with Captain Fratino and the three captives who had escaped the building. "Master Tarandá, do you know these men?"

"I do, Your Majesty. They're students. One is new. Two are second-years."

Alexa's eyes glittered angrily as her aura began to shimmer around her. Each student's eyes widened in surprise. "Do you know who I am?" When no one responded, she asked again, her voice even more stern, "Do you know who I am?"

Timidly, the new student answered, "You are Lady Valkana and Queen Alexa."

"Thank you for the courtesy of answering my question. Why were you in that building tonight?"

The two-year students glared at their younger companion. He glared back. "There were two others, both three-years, Your Majesty. They threatened me if I didn't help them tonight. They have taunted Master Maconti since he arrived. Something about his name and the fact that he's a farmer. They said he didn't belong with nobles and professionals and should learn his place in society."

"I see. And you are?"

"I am Kleondo Baronto."

"Landed gentry from Pitrand?"

"Yes, Your Majesty."

"Master Baronto, have you ever dined privately at the palace with King Gregor? And have either of your friends from tonight's fiasco?"

"I have not. I believe none of them have."

"Let me inform you that Master Maconti has. He also conducts personal correspondence with Sir Stefan Sidano. I assume you have heard of Sir Sidano."

"Er—uh—yes…" came the stuttering reply.

"You will tell the Captain of my Guard the names of your other two accomplices so we can decide on appropriate discipline for tonight's inexcusable behavior." She glared at the other two students. "The three of you injured a fine young man tonight—one I believe you just referred to as a farmer. For your information, your queen's mother was a farmer girl. Yes, your king knows full well and is unashamed. Also, you nearly killed the king's daughter and injured one of his royal advisers who went to rescue his princess. Had either of the three died, you would have been guilty of wanton murder, including the possible assassination of Princess Royal Anlía."

Drawing a deep breath, she asked DiLeno, "Is there even a jail here?"

"No, Milady, but the cellars near the temple can be locked. They say they're still haunted."

Alexa nodded. "If any of the old ghosts do linger, perhaps they can scare some sense into these young fools. Lock them there. I want their friends to join them."

Inside the Tarandá's drawing room a while later, Alexa sipped brandy from a glass Tirani handed her. Tirani blinked back tears as she studied her Valkana's expression. "I just checked Anlía. She's asleep. Master Maconti was sitting up with a book in his hand. We have never had an incident such as this, Alexa. I am so sorry."

Alexa heaved out a frustrated sigh. "The fault is not yours. Nikolai was worried that Maconti might face some ridicule, but I am shocked it reached this level. The situation is intolerable, but it presents valuable teaching opportunities. I hope with all my heart I have judged Master Maconti's character well and that he possesses the courage to continue his studies here."

A firm voice sounded from the arched doorway. "Lady Valkana, I didn't come here to cower away from fools like I faced tonight. If anything, the fact that they endangered our princess emboldens me. Like my father and my king, I cannot tolerate anyone who would strike an innocent out of hateful ignorance."

Setting aside her glass, Alexa stood and went to the young man who wore one of DiLeno's robes. Tears glazed her eyes as she placed a palm against his stubble-roughened cheek. "You make your Valkana and your Queen proud, Gregor Maconti. You also wear your king's name very well. Thank you."

"There is something you should know—if I may." Light brown eyes implored her.

"Of course. Come. Sit and tell us."

Once he settled beside Alexa on the sofa, Maconti paused, gathering his thoughts. "Princess Anlía showed remarkable courage tonight. She must have seen them forcing me inside." Shyly, he said, "I'm rather strong, so they needed three to hold me while two started beating me.

"Suddenly, the princess burst into the room, ordering them to release me. Of course, they didn't recognize her. One started to seize her. Lightning-fast, she snatched up a broomstick and struck him across the head."

"Anlía?" Alexa asked in utter surprise. "My tranquil, reserved Anlía?"

"Yes, Your Majesty." Maconti grinned. "She was impressive."

"Milady will do. I just never imagined my daughter so angry."

"The situation quickly got out of hand. Someone tipped over lanterns and started the fire. One of them kicked me in the chest, knocking the breath out of me. Another slammed the princess against a wall as he ran toward the stairs. Smoke started billowing everywhere almost instantly."

"You faced life-threatening circumstances, Master Maconti," Tirani said. "You must have been afraid."

"No, Lady Tirani, not afraid. I was too furious. Ignorance, such as I faced tonight, has no place in civilized society. It most certainly has no place among people who claim to follow the teachings of our Lord

Val. That same ignorance endangered Princess Anlía's life when she courageously came to my defense. The man who rescued us also risked his life. Fear disappeared in the face of my anger."

"The Great Book of Val speaks of something called righteous anger. Managed properly, such anger can be put to powerful good. Keep that in mind as we move forward, my dear Gregor," Alexa told her young student. "For now, I think you should return upstairs and get some sleep."

"I shall, Milady. Goodnight." He stopped beneath the arch and turned. "Something I forgot. I had no chance to thank the man who rescued us. I never saw him before."

"I will introduce you. Or perhaps Anlía will. He is a special friend of hers, but I warn you. He has a clouded history."

"Not a farmer, by chance?" Maconti asked with a grin.

"No, not a farmer. A former Sifiq naval captain. Goodnight."

⌒

"You mustn't worry, Mother. I'll be fine. Lieutenant Efinjal has my security detachment well in hand. Gregor Maconti and I are becoming good friends. Lady Tirani and Uncle DiLeno will keep a falcon's eye on me. I promise to write. Go home to Father. He needs you most right now."

Grinning, Alexa kissed her daughter's forehead. How lovely Anlía looked as she stood on the brick sidewalk, dressed in a pale lavender blouse beneath a fitted, dark gray silk vest and matching skirt. "I fear admitting this, but you are becoming as difficult to read as your father. There's a mystery about the life forces you and Nikolai have developed as you've grown older."

"All the better. Everyone needs a few secrets, Lady Valkana. Mine are harmless. I love you. Have a safe journey home. Give my love to Father and the family."

Tirstan Fratino boosted the queen into her saddle and signaled the troupe to depart for the trip back to Toraval. As she guided her horse forward, Alexa looked over her shoulder for a parting glance at the daughter she was leaving behind. Returning her attention to the road ahead, Alexa felt disconcerted by the image of Anlía's glowing features and fingers placed against full, pursed lips.

⌒

"Intriguing method of dealing with the troublemakers. Do you think they will change?" Gregor asked, still fuming over details of the incident in Zinzan that had endangered his beloved Anlía's life.

"I cannot be sure. Tirani and DiLeno will monitor them. However, if any maintain such superior attitudes, they will be expelled. The school cannot and will not tolerate such behavior."

"Assigning them duties as school gardeners and as Maconti's personal servants will certainly provide lessons in humility," Nikolai remarked. "The desire for revenge is also possible."

"Already anticipated and addressed with them," Alexa said. "And their families. The prospect of Zenox Prison wasn't especially appealing. It still looms as a distinct possibility since their escapade involved physical injury to Turand's Princess Royal and one of the king's official advisers."

Gregor shook his head. "We don't need this sort of bloody stupidity right now—especially with noble families involved. Much more serious matters are at hand."

Alexa went to where her husband moodily stared out his office window. With a comforting hand at the small of his back, she rested her face against his arm. "My love, remember. All for a reason. They are young and, yes, stupid. But stupidity in the young often teaches wisdom. Let us pray hard that is the case here."

"You may add that to your ever-lengthening prayer list," he said, leaning sideways to kiss her head. Sighing, he returned to his desk. "In the meantime, I must issue a medal and formal certificate of appreciation to Captain Lynmar before Nikolai and I resume working on plans for the mission to Coloridia."

⸌

Two weeks later, a knock at her office door disturbed Alexa as she hunched over large books, studying old records she had brought back with her from Zinzan. Setting aside the enormous files, she frowned before drawing a deep, cleansing breath. "Come in, Victor."

Slowly opening the door, he peeked around the edge. "You haven't lost your touch," he commented sheepishly.

"Did you expect otherwise?"

"Not really," he answered with a smile tugging the corners of his bow-shaped mouth. "I don't have an appointment, but I wondered if I could beg some of your time."

His expression was almost boyish and reminded her of the Victor from her youth. "Of course. Come in. What's on your mind?"

"Many things. I think Nikolai will be ready to leave within the month for Coloridia. Your son is brilliant, Alexa. Hopefully, if meetings go well there, they can negotiate a guaranteed safe meeting with the Sifiq king. That's a beginning."

"You have more than that on your mind," Alexa remarked, noting a certain agitation as he fidgeted in the chair opposite her desk.

Victor stood and walked over to a small painting of Garogan Castle that hung between two windows. Dismissing past dreams, he turned and smiled. "I need to go home to check on some business with my field managers. Before I leave, I have two important personal matters to take care of. That's why I'm here."

"All right," Alexa said, noticing that Victor's posture no longer slumped in defeat. Instead, he had recovered much of the vitality she always associated with him when they were young. "I'm waiting," she prompted.

"First," he started, "I want to apologize for that day I stormed into your office. I still disagree with your husband on Lynmar, but the choice was not mine to make. I shouldn't have taken my anger out on you, either, despite my inability to understand your support. I hope we can leave it at that."

"That's fair enough. We don't always have to agree on everything. Now, you said there's something else?"

Victor swallowed several times before taking a deep breath. "While you were in Zinzan, I asked Oui-lest to marry me, and she accepted. I would like you to perform the wedding ceremony. That way, I can take her home with me when I return to Garogan."

Alexa's eyes opened wide, and she stood so fast that her chair nearly toppled over. "What?"

"Oui-lest and I are engaged to be married. Alexa, I know you think it's sudden, but something about her touched me the moment I met her in Timeri. She is a beautiful woman—inside and out, and I'm tired of my solitary life. When I'm with her, I no longer feel lonely. I want her as my wife."

"Dearest Val," Alexa gasped, "of all the things I never expected to hear today! Victor, Oui-lest is especially dear to me after everything that happened in the Sifiq Kingdom. I would be furious if you hurt her. Do you love her?"

"Sweetest, of course, I do. I'm not so callous as to ask her to marry me without caring for her."

Alexa shook her head admonishingly. "That's not what I asked. Do you love her? She lived a terrible life in the Sifiq Kingdom. She deserves to be loved the way we Turandans know how to love one another. Can you love her that way?"

Victor approached Alexa and grasped her arms. "Alexa, I love her. Maybe not the way I will always love you, but I think we never love the same way twice. Still, I do love Oui-lest. I look forward to being with her every time I leave the madness of these war meetings with your husband. She makes me feel important again. She makes me feel alive again! I want to dream again! Yes, I love her, and I want to make her happy."

Alexa backed away from Victor and leaned against her desk. Casting her eyes downward, she tried to absorb the impact of his words. Catching her breath, she finally met his waiting gaze. "Do you wish to marry according to the laws of Val?"

He chuckled. "Of course. Why else would I ask you to preside over the ceremony? Oui-lest accepts our faith wholeheartedly."

"Does Adrina know?

"You're the first. I was hoping you might be willing to fit a dinner into your schedule so that I could make the announcement."

"Victor Garogan, time is at a premium these days, but I do owe you. This is going to cost you."

"Sweetest, I will always love you!" he exclaimed, throwing his arms around her just as Gregor walked in with Nikolai.

⤶

"I can hardly believe how lovely you looked," Adrina said admiringly while carefully removing the delicate tiara from Oui-lest's golden hair. The ivory pearls and blue and white flowers had looked perfect with the pastel blue gown Oui-lest chose for her wedding. White lace rosettes adorned a ruffled tier several inches above the hem, and a single, delicate rosette marked the point where the gown's neckline met just above the cleft of her breasts. The fitted bodice and flared skirts highlighted her slim, feminine figure to perfection.

Oui-lest's smile spread and faded continuously. "I never expected such a day in my life. I'm almost afraid of feeling so happy."

Alexa leaned forward and kissed Oui-lest's cheek. "You were a beautiful bride today. Everyone thought so. Now, let's get you ready before your new husband grows impatient."

Working quickly, Adrina and Alexa undid the laces of Oui-lest's gown and undergarments before handing them off to Adrina's lady's maid. The nervous bride felt hands everywhere as a brush floated through her hair and scented cream was smoothed into ivory skin. Never in her life had she known such lavish attention as her friends helped her into the pink satin negligee Alexa had given her as a wedding gift. When they turned her to look in a mirror, she gasped at the image of a woman who looked far too happy to be the Oui-lest Var she had been just a year earlier.

Anxious once they left her alone in the Sidano's luxurious guest suite, Oui-lest leaned over a tall, porcelain vase and inhaled the sweet fragrance of the colorful bouquet on the bedside stand. Beside her, the dark, gleaming wood of the headboard contrasted with the ivory pillows and sheets, all plumped and turned, inviting her to spend her wedding night with her new husband. Her stomach lurched at the mere thought of being alone again with a man, especially Victor.

Instantly, she froze upon hearing the suite's double doors open and close. Soft footfalls approached until she felt Victor close behind her. Her breathing quickened, and her heart beat faster. His warm breath fanned her shoulder as his hands came to rest at her waist. His voice was low and gentle when he said, "My beautiful bride. How proud I felt every time I looked at you today. Are you sure you're not a figment of my imagination?"

Turning, she looked up into hazel eyes that had captivated her so soon after her arrival in Turand. "I'm not certain. I've never felt as I have today."

Smiling, Victor turned away and unbuttoned his long, formal coat. As he began pulling his arms from the sleeves, his new wife discovered the courage to move. "Let me help."

With trembling fingers, she undid buttons and cuff links. As he shed each item, she shyly looked away while neatly folding the garment and placing it on a padded chest at the foot of the bed. When he finally stood unclothed before her, he didn't strut or swagger the way her former husband had. He didn't grab with bruising pressure on delicate arms, nor did he squeeze and pinch until she cried out in pain.

Instead, Victor reached for her, drawing her close. Warm hands gently caressed her face and neck. She felt his damp breath as he whispered into her ear, "Oui-lest, I won't hurt you. I want to love you."

When his mouth covered hers, she couldn't recall if her first husband had ever kissed her. She remembered he had bitten her a few times. Victor's kisses were a new experience as he coaxed her mouth open, drawing fresh, exciting sensations from her very core. As his kisses deepened, she was faintly aware of satin fabric sliding away from her skin and the sense of movement as they came to lie together on the bed.

Memories flashed through her mind. She shuddered and whimpered.

"Oui-lest, you're in Turand now. He won't ever hurt you again. I won't let him. I love you, Oui-lest. Let me love you."

Victor's voice anchored her soul. She had dreamed of him loving her. She circled his neck with her arms. Feeling the strength in his masculine body, Oui-lest dared to surrender to the myriad sensations he was awakening with sweeping caresses so different from anything she had ever experienced in her first marriage.

Oui-lest awoke the following morning with her face against Victor's muscular arm. Her palm lay open on his hair-covered stomach. Heavy eyelids fluttered as she relished lingering physical satisfaction she never knew existed. "Mmmm," she sighed dreamily.

"Mmmm?" Victor murmured teasingly.

Oui-lest forced her eyes open. "Am I supposed to get up?" she mumbled.

With a deep, rumbling chuckle, he turned and dragged her tightly against him. "I'm afraid so, Milady. Your husband is going to need serious nourishment if you expect that much exertion from him on a regular basis. Remember. You married an older man."

Oui-lest placed a lingering kiss over his heart. "I never knew it could be like this. Oh, Victor, I really didn't know."

"He always hurt you, didn't he?"

She closed her eyes and nodded.

Tilting her face toward his, he lightly kissed her. "Lady Garogan, your new husband wants you to know you are now a loved woman. Shall we get up and get dressed so we can have breakfast?"

Chapter 6

A month later, Turand's four finest naval ships waited offshore in Timeri Bay. Two had been outfitted with newly developed cannons that should provide superior tactical advantage in case of any encounters with hostile Sifiq ships. Burly sailors waited beside sturdy boats to row finely attired passengers out to vessels ready to transport them on their diplomatic mission.

Sunny skies and gentle breezes out of the west drew a satisfied sigh from Captain Lynmar. He had recommended the timing of the voyage to avoid the stormy rainy season that typically plagued the coastal region nearest Coloridia's capital of Maraya. Although the Turandan vessels were impressively seaworthy, Lynmar argued there was no reason to risk losing ships or the lives of key government officials with a potential crisis looming ahead.

Stacks of trunks and crates crowded the noisy, bustling wharf. Seagulls screeched, adding to the din of boots clomping over the wood dock and boxes being piled one on top of the other. The smells of salty sea, fish, and working men wafted in the air. Dockworkers rushed back and forth, dodging rolling carts and each other as cargo was staged for stowage onboard waiting ships.

Gregor and his wife stood together, ignoring the surrounding commotion. Their focus fixed on Prince Nikolai. Their oldest son exuded self-confidence. Nikolai had spent countless hours organizing this trip. He had worked with his father and godfather to define his goals, learn everything available about the people he would meet, and develop his agenda. His parents saw a young man who had prepared and practiced to act as his father's envoy in the first step toward avoiding war.

"My son," Gregor said as he inspected Nikolai's dark gray uniform, "I do not expect this task to be easy, but you have my complete confidence. Rely on Stefan as your adviser but trust your instincts. Your mother is convinced Lynmar won't fail you, but I still recommend caution."

Nikolai nodded. "I understand, Father. Rafzan says he expects the Coloridians will give us perhaps ten days to make our case before asking us to leave. They will then consult with their so-called Protectors. I will strive to convince them in less time to expedite consultations with the Protectors so we can move ahead with a direct meeting with the Sifiq."

Stefan placed a hand on Nikolai's arm. "They're ready for us."

Nikolai bent over so his mother could kiss his cheek in farewell. "I know, Mother. I won't forget my prayers. I love you."

She smiled proudly. "May Val watch over you and keep you safe, Niko. Your mother loves you dearly."

Gregor embraced his son. "Prince Nikolai, go with your father's blessings."

With Gregor's arm snugly around Alexa's shoulders, the couple witnessed their firstborn son setting out on his first official mission as Crown Prince of the House of Toscano. His contact with experienced international mediators and ambassadors would test not only the quality of his curriculum but the value of intensive mentoring provided by King Gregor and Stefan Sidano. How they regretted that a crisis of this magnitude had arisen while Nikolai was still so relatively young. Massive sails unfurled, billowed, and grew taut in the breeze, moving the ships out to sea. The king and queen stood watch until the vessels disappeared on the open ocean. Hand in hand, they left the dock to begin a new vigil.

⸺

Nikolai's dark eyes swiftly assessed the lodgings the Coloridians had reserved for his small delegation. Spacious and elegantly appointed with velvet-flocked wall coverings, brocade-covered chairs and settees, and gold-leafed tables, the hotel had been designed to receive guests of high social rank. Staff attended its visitors efficiently without sacrificing exquisite manners. Not one to waste time, the prince appreciated the relatively quick process that delivered the Turandans from the lobby to their secured floor of suites.

Once assured of his suite's security, the prince called in Stefan and Captain Lynmar to review expectations. Everyone had agreed that the importance of this mission could not be overstated. The Coloridians maintained limited diplomatic relations with the Sifiq Kingdom based primarily on Sifiq needs for essential supplies. Typically, the Sifiq would just take such supplies by force, but Coloridia's alliance with the Protectors altered the power balance. Suffering two decisive, humiliating defeats by the Protectors, the Sifiq had agreed to a treaty of non-aggression against any Protector ally.

Nikolai's goal was to obtain Coloridia's agreement for one of their ambassadors to accompany him to and from the Sifiq Kingdom under a guarantee of safety from the Protectors. According to Rafzan Lynmar, the Sifiq wouldn't dare risk a treaty violation with such a guarantee in place. Both the Coloridians and the Protectors should find favor in Turandan efforts to end aggressive acts committed by the Sifiq without resorting to war.

"Rafzan, you still seem terribly vague about these Protectors. Can you give me no more insight on them?"

"I honestly cannot. They are something of a mystery. As I've said before, they remain in the background. I know of no one alive who has seen them. They come from an island nation surrounded by ocean that is nearly impossible to navigate. The captain whose command I won tried. He fell overboard and lost half his crew before I succeeded in turning the ship around and sailing out. I never returned. How they sail baffles me. Old tales of our wars with them say they were giant men. The Sifiq king will not defy them."

"Giants?" Nikolai asked, his eyebrows lifting in surprise. "Well, I have no time for tales of mysterious giants. However, if anyone comes up with any ideas we haven't already covered, let me know. Minister Jemini delivered a message asking to meet at nine-thirty tomorrow morning."

Stefan looked pleased. "It seems we shall have time for dinner tonight and breakfast in the morning. Perhaps your father might take scheduling lessons from these Coloridians."

Nikolai laughed. "I seriously doubt that ever happening, Papino."

Stefan clapped Nikolai on the shoulder and laughed, dispelling some of the tension. "It was a thought."

⌣

"I apologize for disturbing you so late. May I?"

"Please. Come in. I was just reading."

"I can't seem to settle my mind for tomorrow's presentation to Minister Jemini."

Nikolai combed his fingers through already untidy locks of black hair. He gazed at his father's controversial adviser with worried eyes. "How can I be sure I haven't missed some fine detail?"

Rafzan Lynmar, who was surprisingly only eight years older, smiled grim comprehension. Sifiq officers typically lived hard lives. They aged fast and often died young. "Nikolai, your concern is natural. Gaining Coloridian backing is essential to enter negotiations with the Sifiq. Remember. King Gregor and Stefan Sidano meticulously worked out every detail of the complaint with you—Turand's demands for the solution as well. Those demands are not unreasonable. Every nation has the right to demand integrity for the safety of its borders. You must be spokesman for that sovereignty."

Nikolai paced back and forth, his exceptionally tall body and tense energy pervading the sitting room of Lynmar's modest suite. "My senses keep swirling about these Protectors. It troubles me that we have no understanding of who they are and why they remain in the shadows. If only I could meet with them."

"You cannot let what you cannot know distract you from your duty. Nikolai, you must focus on your responsibility as Turand's prince. You are *my* prince now, and I am completely confident you will succeed with tomorrow's task."

Nikolai stopped pacing for a moment. "With no insult intended, for a former Sifiq officer, you are remarkably encouraging."

With barely a hint of a smile, Rafzan said, "Our Lord Val and Turand's people have taught me the value of working with each other instead of competing against one another. We share mutual goals for the good of our people. I won't deny that I also hope change might one day come to the Sifiq Kingdom. But first, my loyalties are to Val and the throne of Turand. Therein lies my current priority."

Nikolai nodded and walked toward the door to leave. He paused near the desk where papers and books lay beneath a lighted oil lamp. A hastily folded page had opened and caught his eye, the handwriting very much resembling his sister's. Dismissing the curious notion, he bade Rafzan goodnight and returned to his own suite.

Alone, Rafzan exhaled a sigh heavy with relief and went to the cluttered desk. Retrieving the letter he had read at least a dozen times, blue eyes gazed at the artistic script forming her signature. Tracing the letters, he whispered, "I dare not love you, Anlía, yet I cannot help myself." Then, refolding the page, he tucked it into a book of poetry she had given him and went to bed.

⌐

Indigo wallpaper with scrolled designs in silver covered the chamber walls where Minister Drenj Jemini sat behind an elevated bench of carved, polished pinewood. Scribes on either side sat at low tables, waiting to record upcoming proceedings between their Minister of State and the visiting Turandans. Banks of arched windows to the left and right of the minister's bench permitted the entry of natural light. The center front and back walls were divided by arched double doors of the same pinewood as the minister's bench.

Jemini's deep-set blue eyes studied the youthful Turandan prince, who had conducted himself with extraordinary composure and confidence. Prince Nikolai related Turand's grievance against the Sifiq Kingdom in an orderly, chronological narrative without excessive emotion while retaining his tone of determination to resolve an untenable situation. The minister's long experience prompted keen awareness of every aspect of the young man's presence—his fine mannerisms, his resonant voice, his refined speech.

Crown Prince Nikolai of Turand had presented a complaint worthy of review, and an assessment would be forthcoming. What sent shivers down Jemini's spine was Nikolai's appearance. He looked unlike any of the other Turandans in his entourage. His height and dark coloring were distinctively different. Too different.

Without revealing the nature of his thoughts, Minister Jemini nodded respectfully. "Prince Nikolai, we appreciate your presentation and the efforts the King of Turand extends toward avoiding war. I adjourn our session for today. After I review the documentation you provided, we will reconvene for further discussions. Does the day after tomorrow meet your convenience?"

Nikolai bowed his head respectfully. "Minister Jemini, I am at your disposal. Thank you."

Over dinner that evening, Nikolai stared morosely into a glass of wine. "I felt like an insect under one of Professor Ligorno's magnifying glasses."

Stefan sat back, wine glass in hand. "You managed yourself extremely well, but I can't deny how hard he studied you. I'm not certain what it was, but something about you disturbed him."

"Disturbed him? How? Why? My presentation was straightforward, with no emotional posturing or threats. I didn't suddenly grow two heads!"

Stefan paused thoughtfully. "No, but perhaps we can puzzle out the reason and set it to our advantage."

"May I comment?" Rafzan asked after several moments.

"Please," Stefan replied. "We're certainly perplexed."

"Turand only resumed relations relatively recently with Coloridia and other nations in this part of the world after rebuilding. Few, if any, have met King Gregor. Prince Nikolai, you are the image of your father, only taller."

"So I've heard a thousand times," Nikolai said impatiently. "How does all that correspond to Jemini's strange reaction today?"

"Your Highness…"

"Nikolai, please. It's just Nikolai when we're alone together or with Papino Stefan."

"Nikolai," Rafzan corrected himself, "our part of the world has its own folklore. As I already told you, the Sifiq and continental nations like Coloridia and its neighbors have legends about the Protectors."

"Ah, yes, the giants," Nikolai sighed, shaking his head in exasperation. He signaled a server for more wine after draining his glass.

"Nikolai, let's say they're just myth. Even myth often has basis in fact. The Sifiq, Coloridians, Turandans? Except for traditional dress, we all look alike. We even share the same basic language. In essence, you cannot tell us apart. You must admit that you, your father, and your siblings look nothing like the rest of your people. Even your sister Anlía stands taller than most adult men."

Stefan leaned forward. "What is it you're suggesting, Lynmar?"

"Coloridians keep close contact with the Protectors. I only wonder if Jemini looked at Nikolai and saw some resemblance to how legend describes the Protectors."

"Because of his height?"

"Not just his height," Rafzan answered. "His coloring. His complexion is a rare shade—one I have never seen in my travels. I don't know if anyone here ever knew King Maxim or his queen, but I've seen their portraits at the palace. Maxim was typical Turandan, but Queen Anlía was not."

Stefan was flooded with memories of the couple who had comforted and loved him after his parents were murdered. Quashing the unwelcome onslaught, he said, "I grew up with them. They were both born in Turand."

Rafzan exhaled heavily. He had touched a raw nerve. "All I suggest is that we be aware of what Jemini sees. If he thinks there's a connection, it may sway his thinking."

Nikolai straightened, enhancing the very image they were discussing. "Do you see this as benefit or detriment?"

"That is the question of the day. The answer, I believe, depends on you. If you continue as confidently as you did today, I believe Minister Jemini will look favorably on your cause."

The following afternoon, Nikolai and Stefan sat inside the private office of Ambassador Laritha. Surprised by the distinguished dignitary's summons, they had rushed to meet the requested appointment. Accustomed to Gregor's tight time management, they were beginning to wonder about Laritha's delayed arrival.

When the frowning ambassador finally entered his office, he closed the door with a bang. "Your Highness, Sir Sidano, I sincerely beg your pardon. It seems some people have little respect for time. I must apologize for what appears to be my lack of respect for yours."

"Not at all, sir," Nikolai responded, intrigued by the elderly statesman's obvious irritation. "Delays are often unavoidable, and we appreciate Coloridia's attention to our plight."

"Yes, of course, but there is still no excuse—well, it's done with. Let's move on. I trust your accommodations are satisfactory." The elderly, white-haired gentleman lowered himself into an enormous chair with a plop.

Both Stefan and Nikolai struggled to maintain impassive expressions in the face of Laritha's odd behavior. "Ambassador Laritha, the hotel accommodations have been excellent thus far. Coloridian hospitality has exceeded our expectations. Thank you for asking."

"Good. Good. You wonder why I summoned you. Of course, you do." He leaned across a desk stacked with neat piles of books and documents. Reaching for one, he pulled it toward him while tilting his head with a firm jerk. "Yes, yes. I wanted to talk to you before tomorrow. Questions Minister Jemini will want to clarify before he finally decides on formal consideration of your request. And perhaps a question of my own. If I may."

"Of course, Your Excellency," Stefan responded again.

"The most recent raids on seaside towns and villages. Injured citizens. Six deaths. Stolen livestock and property. The evidence you collected and presented does appear to be recent and is definitely Sifiq origin. There is no dispute. Jemini will also place strong emphasis on this incident involving the abducted priestesses. He will, however, want to know why this rates so high on your list of complaints."

Recalling his father's strict instructions, Nikolai focused black-brown eyes on the ambassador. "As healers, those priestesses were on a mission of mercy following a ground-quake that killed and injured hundreds in a remote province. During the abduction, the Sifiq murdered nine guards who were escorting the priestesses."

Nikolai's jaw tensed with the memory of his mother's frail condition, knowing she was already well into recovery by the time he saw her. He continued, "During their year of captivity, the priestesses were beaten multiple times and starved. Each one faced attempted rape despite informing the Sifiq that they had taken vows of virtue and that some were already married. Later, they were subjected to cruel, forced labor at camps where they watched Sifiq prisoners being whipped and beaten in fields and then dragged off to die. They lived in deplorable conditions not fit for animals. When King Bin-Lot was finally compelled to return them to Turand, one of the priestesses was beaten again, then dumped into stormy seas. Only through Val's great mercy was she found alive on shore and saved."

Underlying Nikolai's response, Laritha detected intense emotion. "You appear uncommonly disturbed by their story."

Stefan responded quickly. "If I may, Excellency, all Valiria priestesses serve under royal patronage. The priestess in question is Turand's High Priestess Valkana and the prince's close relative. She was tortured for a year and then nearly killed when they brought her home. Her recovery required months. The other priestesses suffered grievously, too. Turand reveres the Valiria."

"Although I'm puzzled why Bin-Lot released them, I better understand your feelings." He set aside the documents and leaned back in his seat. His expression changed as he appeared to study his visitors. "I hope you will indulge an old man's curiosity. Prince Nikolai, are you aware that I met your grandfather on several occasions?"

Clearly surprised, Nikolai responded, "Excellency, I had no idea."

The ambassador swiftly cast his gaze around the room before twitching his head from side to side and looking directly at Nikolai. "When I first met him, I was serving as a diplomatic envoy. We were both young men. My dream at the time was to build my diplomatic career because, frankly, our region was working to end Sifiq aggression, and I knew both endeavors would require ongoing attention. Your grandfather's passion centered on moving Turand toward a broad recovery of traditional values. I later met Maxim twice more, the last when I attended his coronation as king."

"Fascinating. Other than my father and Sir Sidano here, I know perhaps only a handful of others who personally knew Grandfather. All of my grandparents died at the hands of the Sifiq." Although his eyes reflected sadness, Nikolai's voice held steady.

"A tragedy many in Turand share. Because of the Sifiq invasion and occupation, I never had the opportunity to meet your grandmother. I understand you closely resemble your father, so I assume the two of you resemble her. You certainly look nothing like Maxim."

Nikolai's black eyebrows raised high. How to answer, he wondered. "If portraits are any indication, yes, I would say that is an accurate conclusion. My grandmother was born in northwestern Turand. May I ask why the interest?"

Laritha shrugged noncommittally. "As I said, I traveled extensively in Turand during my youth, and I knew your grandfather. Meeting you is something of a surprise since I never met any Turandans quite like you. Shall we attribute the matter to an old man's curiosity and proceed with some advice I'd like to offer for tomorrow?"

During the coach ride back to the hotel, Stefan stared at his brooding godson. Finally breaking tense silence, he said, "I can assure you that you haven't sprouted a second head."

Nikolai rolled his eyes and scowled. "Jemini's scrutiny yesterday was bad enough. Now Laritha's not-so-subtle questions following Rafzan's insane stories about dark, killer giants? Seriously?"

"I thought the dark giants were Protectors," Stefan said, his mouth drawn into a half-smirk.

Frustrated, Nikolai tossed his hands in the air. "Killer giants or Protectors. Does it matter? I suppose it depends on whether or not you're Sifiq. Whatever you do, don't mention this to Rafzan. And no mention of this to Father when we arrive home unless absolutely necessary."

"As you wish, Your Royal Highness," Stefan answered, recognizing how deeply disconcerting the Protectors had become to his godson.

Five days later, Prince Nikolai tilted his face to the sky as his mother so often did and gloried in the warmth of the sun's rays. Salty sea scented the air, and full canvas sails billowed in the breeze. How satisfied he felt to be homeward bound with the Coloridians' assurance that they would carry the Turandan petition to the Protectors for consideration. The second meeting with Minister Jemini had proven little more than a formality. Turand's prince now prayed that the Protectors would guarantee safety for a Coloridian ambassador and escort to accompany him and a negotiating team to the Sifiq Kingdom. There he would issue demands to cease all territorial incursions and aggression against Turand.

⌒

Gregor's left eyebrow lifted inquisitively as Alexa entered his office and locked the door behind her. Rarely did she interrupt him during his workday, but the intensity of her gaze told him something serious must have arisen. He watched as she took a deep breath, crossed the office, and rounded his desk to stand beside him.

"Alexa?"

Lifting both hands to his face, she laced her fingers in his hair, running them backward through the thick locks and creating a feathery effect. "I thought you would want to know. Your son is on his way home."

Dark eyes searched her face. "Are you certain? Does he bring good news?"

Alexa grinned. "News as good as can be expected at this point."

Gregor heaved a sigh. "How can you be sure?"

"Husband, after all these years, you ask a question like that?" she teased.

"Wife," he replied, pulling her onto his lap, "after all these years, you still send my mind reeling in astonishment."

She drew closer and pressed her lips against his. "Mmmm. You taste wonderful."

"Thank you, Your Majesty, for the compliment and the good news. Now, I have work to do."

Alexa diligently began undoing the buttons of his jacket. "Work can wait. I told your aides I needed to consult with you on some important matters and that we were not to be disturbed." Her fingers continued their task while she leaned forward and kissed his neck, delighting in the resulting shudder and tightening of his grip around her waist.

"Alexa!" he gasped when her hot breath teased his sensitive ear. Her intentions were obvious. "Here?"

"Why not? I'm in the mood to celebrate, and I want you. Right now. This very minute."

Having successfully opened his coat, her hands tugged his smooth linen shirt free from his trousers so she could feel his heartbeat beneath her hands. As Alexa's fingers registered that familiar, powerful rhythm, her eyelids fell, and her face transformed into a mask of utter sensuality that stole Gregor's breath.

Shafting through his mind with the lightning speed of an arrow flew that first haunting question. How could he possibly deny her? How long had he lived, believing her lost forever? How many desperate hours had he ridden, fearing she might die before he reached her? Rising with her in his arms, he carried her to the sofa in his office. The answer was simple as they frantically pushed aside offending garments. He could never deny her this union that returned to him the wholeness he had missed and yearned for that year while she had been a Sifiq captive.

On his knees, Gregor paid homage to his beloved wife. He kissed the lips begging for him. His mouth then began to sweep along the gentle curve of her shoulder toward the cushioned swell of her breasts. His hands followed suit, pausing so his fingers could entwine with hers and guide them to touch him as he rose above her on the couch. His great body reacted with a sudden quake to the heat of hers as they joined.

If anything, he had needed her even more than she had wanted him. How could she have possibly known? Gregor indulged her sweet moans and cries. Years had taught him every caress and every movement that pleased her best. She continuously stroked his skin and strained her body against his, heightening his senses in a swelling tide until the inevitable explosion that overpowered him.

Finally gathering his wits, Gregor smiled. His arms tightened around Alexa, who lay curled on top of him. Affectionately, he kissed mussed curls and whispered, "Your Majesty, you are a mess. A magnificent mess, but a mess nevertheless."

"King Gregor, it's all your fault. You are such a magnificent lover."

He laughed. "You are impossible."

"So you've said many times before, my love."

"I really do have work waiting for me."

"I know. We have to plan for Nikolai's return. He completed his first diplomatic assignment. You must prepare for the next."

Gregor closed his eyes, dreading a return to the uncertain reality outside his office. "I think I'd rather stay here on the sofa."

Alexa tenderly kissed him. "I know of no happier place in the world than right here in your arms."

⤿

"Do you see this Ambassador Laritha as a potential ally?" Gregor asked as he paced across his office.

"In session with Coloridia's Minister of State, his conduct appeared neutral. Privately, I'm not sure I'd say the same, especially after he told us that he knew Grandfather."

Gregor stopped abruptly. "He knew my father? How?"

Stefan answered. "The ambassador said he first met King Maxim here in Turand early during his diplomatic career. He also attended your father's coronation. As you know, diplomatic ties were later severed by the Sifiq invasion and subsequent occupation."

"Interesting," Gregor mused. "What did he have to say about Father?"

Nikolai shrugged. "Not much, although I believe he was favorably impressed and respected him."

Stefan nodded. "I would agree. I'm also sure he left much unsaid."

Gregor aimed a puzzled glance at his trusted adviser. "You are an exceptional judge of character, Stefan. That makes me wonder what we should expect next from our Coloridian friends."

The chill of autumn air in Toraval coaxed dark rose color into Anlía's cheeks as Captain Lynmar escorted her from the temple to the palace. How much he appreciated the opportunity to walk with her in the open so he could enjoy both her company and her beauty! How he had missed her while she was away in Zinzan and during his journey abroad! No matter. Doubting the possibility of ever fulfilling newfound dreams of love, he smiled at something she said and resolved to enjoy every minute he could carve out with her before her return to school.

"Your brother was quite the consummate diplomat in Coloridia. You should be proud."

Anlía laughed. "I'm very proud, but he needed help to accomplish this first step. Father, Papino Stefan, and Papino Victor have been coaching him for years." She gave the captain a sly, sideways glance. "I understand your advice was also quite valuable."

Blue eyes sparkled in response to her praise. Shaking his head, he said, "I had little worthwhile to offer, but I sincerely hope my contribution, however small, helped."

"Dear Captain Lynmar, do not discount your merits. I will not stand for you downplaying your worthiness."

Images from a stormy night at sea flashed before his mind's eye. If only he could purge that terrible mistake—but he could not. He had nearly killed her mother out of uncontrollable rage conditioned into his behavior. He felt the sting of hot tears and blinked them back, swallowing the involuntary lump that rose in his throat.

"Captain?" she asked.

Rafzan heard the worried way her voice caressed the word. He remembered the moment he had kissed her in Zinzan. He hadn't meant to. Dearest Val, he had never meant to kiss her. What he had never expected was her response to the kiss. Sensing it was her first kiss, he also felt something far stronger than a simple physical connection. Breaking their bond, he had seen it in her eyes. The shock of it had bored straight through the essence of his soul into a place he had only recently discovered.

Shaking off the moment, he said, "My apology. Just a stray thought." Looking up and glimpsing the cause of his detoured memories, he added, "I must hurry. I meet in half an hour with General Kohira. It was a pleasure seeing you again, Your Highness." Then, respectfully acknowledging Alexa, he trotted up the palace steps, leaving the two women together.

Alexa studied her daughter's face and again lamented her inability to read her daughter's life force. Turning to walk up the steps with Anlía, Alexa asked, "Is it my imagination, or was he decidedly uncomfortable when he saw me approach?"

"Can you blame him? Besides the obvious, he worries about being seen too often talking to Turand's Princess Royal."

"Is there cause to worry?"

Anlía stopped as they reached the top step and turned to look at her mother. "What are you asking, Mother?"

Alexa's gaze was direct but not threatening. "The question is simple. I ask because I'm your mother."

Intuitively, she knew she could always trust her mother. "May we talk? Privately?"

"Should I suggest the temple?"

Anlía smiled and nodded. "An excellent suggestion."

A little later, inside a small chamber reserved for the Valkana's use, mother and daughter first prayed for Val's guidance. Then, drawing on every bit of faith and patience she could muster, Alexa sat back and listened to her daughter.

"I'm not sure how it happened, Mother. I suppose it started with questions he had about passages from the Great Book. He was probing into the core of our faith. Conversations diverged from there. Empathically, I connected to his deeper emotions."

"How much have you discussed his emotions?" Alexa asked, hoping to deal carefully with her daughter's feelings.

"I'm not sure how to answer that. He keeps much in reserve because of his Sifiq culture. On the other hand, his mother's death when he was a child planted a seed in his soul that conversion to Val has allowed to grow and flourish. For that, you have no idea how much he adores you or how much he berates himself for what he did. That's why he comes to Temple daily—to pray every single day for forgiveness."

"Anlía, I have said nothing to your father, but I've known for some time about your communications with Captain Lynmar. Will you be honest and tell me how serious this relationship is?"

Directly meeting her mother's gaze, Anlía sighed. "I could tell you all the things other girls say—that I have a right to live my life or choose who I want to love. I could even say you had already set your path as a Valiria priestess at sixteen and were betrothed to Victor Garogan at seventeen. You were very mature. When I give you my answer, I hope you will see me as the same."

Anlía stood and paced around the room. Walls were covered with gold-on-gold striped paper. Two windows admitted late-morning sunshine filtered through filmy curtains. Her eyes shone when she returned to sit in the large, comfortable chair across from her mother.

"Rafzan has always treated me with respect. I want you to know that, above all else, although he did kiss me. Once. It happened, and it was extraordinary. When I'm with Rafzan, we discuss various topics. Our correspondence covers every subject imaginable. Since coming to Turand, he has discovered music, art, and poetry. Whole new worlds have opened to him. As far as how I feel, I can say that I love him, but is it a lasting love like you and Father have?

"That's where another factor sneaks in to complicate matters. I've also grown fond of Gregor Maconti. We tend to disagree more than Rafzan and I do. Often and intensely. Gregor and I can laugh together and discuss almost anything, but then he deliberately provokes me, whereas Rafzan makes me feel..." Her eyes looked suddenly faraway. "Mother, just being near Rafzan makes me feel the way you look when Father holds you."

"Anlía, first, thank you for trusting me enough to confide in me. I know how private you are, and carrying this around cannot have been easy."

Leaning forward, Anlía tightly grasped her mother's hands. "I always knew I could come to you. I just needed to find the right time."

Taking a deep breath, Alexa ventured ahead. "As I'm sure you understand, a mother's first priority is her child's welfare. From my perspective, Rafzan causes many concerns. Former emotional traumas. Cultural differences. His age difference. Perhaps there's no greater concern than your father."

"Not you?"

Alexa sighed. "I can't deny that I don't have moments when I remember that terrible night on his ship. When he tied me to his ship's mast..." She stopped abruptly. "Rafzan was a different man then—lost in Sifiq rage and madness. Val has since healed Rafzan's soul and shown me the depths of his healing. I hold not a single vestige of hatred or ill will. Unfortunately, I cannot say the same for how others feel. There's still the matter of culture and age. "

"Mother, isn't there a big age difference between you and Father?"

"Yes, but not as much as between you and Rafzan."

"But there was a bigger difference between Father's parents," Anlía remarked.

"True, and by all accounts, they were happy."

"Oh, Mother, the truth is I'm far from certain about anything right now except completing my vows as a Valiria priestess."

Clasping her daughter's hands, Alexa sighed. "I suggest, then, that you take special care with the feelings of these men—especially Rafzan's. Be cautious about how and when you're seen with him. Many will always distrust him. I also suggest that you spend more time getting to know Master Maconti. More importantly, know yourself better, dear one. That is when you will find the right path to the love of your life."

Anlía gazed at her mother. "Will you tell Father?"

Alexa sighed uncomfortably. "Dear one, I'm not in the habit of hiding things from him. Our marriage thrives because we are honest with one another. On the other hand, you trusted me with your confidences inside this sacred temple. As long as you give me no cause for concern, I shall respect your confidence and say nothing to him."

That evening, Alexa flexed her shoulders as Gregor brushed her hair. Running his fingers through some of the curling tresses, he clicked his tongue.

"What?" she asked.

"I do believe I see some strands of gray here," he said as he bent forward, setting her brush on her vanity tray.

"Please don't tell me that. Not tonight." She got up and turned wearily into his embrace.

"Let me guess. You disappeared for quite some time with our daughter. The two of you were late for midday. Crisis?"

"Kiss me. Crisis averted," Alexa replied with a tired smile.

"That doesn't sound altogether comforting."

"It should. Be glad your daughter desires to be a Valiria, and she mostly has her mother's good sense."

"The first part is encouraging. The second worries me because I remember what first brought you to Toraval."

Alexa laughed and dragged him toward their enormous bed. "Although I didn't know it at the time, I came because you were here. Come. Remind me again."

Chapter 7

Nikolai's aide hurried into the prince's office and handed him a large, cold, leather dispatch pouch. "Your Highness, a courier just arrived. He said Lord Karanan sent him directly from Timeri to deliver this."

Thanking the aide before dismissing him, Nikolai first noted the address tag attached by Lord Karanan and then the one to the Crown Prince of Turand bearing Coloridia's official seal. Nikolai's breath caught for an instant before he slowly unbuckled the straps and opened the heavy pouch. Carefully, he removed a thick document packet and broke the wax seal binding the cover page. Within ten minutes, the prince rushed down the hallway to the king's office and pushed the documents across the desk for his father to read.

"Nikolai, please ask DiCarlo to send for Stefan and Lynmar. Also, if Admiral Firenzdá hasn't yet left, ask him to join us." When Nikolai returned, Gregor gave his son an approving smile. "Excellent work, my son. I could not be more proud. Our most difficult task now begins."

Alexa had heard about the arrival of the courier from Timeri. She knew the dispatch must have carried critical news when Gregor sent word requesting delivery of the midday meal to the conference room for him and his advisory team. After notifying the kitchen of new meal arrangements, she decided to brave the cold, wintry day and walk to visit Adrina.

"I can't believe you walked all this way as cold as it is. What will Gregor say when he finds out?" Adrina said sternly as she poured two cups of steaming tea.

"I'm sure he won't be pleased, but I needed to work off some nervous energy. I'm more worried about when Tirstan realizes I'm gone. I sneaked away from my office."

Adrina shook her head in admonishment. "I wonder how long before someone starts hammering down my door."

Alexa looked up with a sheepish grin. "About…" Holding her index finger up, she giggled when a loud, urgent pounding sounded at the main entrance of the Sidano home. "Now?"

Once a thoroughly irritated Captain Fratino received assurances of his queen's safety and a string of apologies, he departed, leaving two guards to accompany her back to the palace after her visit. Adrina served fresh tea and laughingly suggested they restart their visit.

"What do you think this courier business is all about?"

Alexa replied, "I'm certain it's the news they've been awaiting from Coloridia. Gregor even asked Admiral Firenzdá to delay his return to Port Timeri."

"That sounds like positive news," Adrina mused.

"I believe so," Alexa replied. "I still hate the idea of Nikolai going to Atuliq."

"Are there any other options? Stefan doesn't seem to think so."

"Neither does Gregor. For that matter, neither do I. That doesn't make me like the idea of my son being in that soulless pit of despair." Alexa trailed off. "I'm sorry. I came here to cheer myself up."

"I understand, my friend. Perhaps I can give you a bit of good news. I received a letter from Victor yesterday. I had planned to call on you after midday. Oui-lest is with child."

Alexa smiled. "I know. Fine news for a change."

Adrina looked perplexed. "How did you know? Did Oui-lest write to you first?"

"No. I always include her in my morning prayers. I sensed the child."

"Alexa Maraná Toscano! I love you dearly, but this Valkana role is not quite fair to the rest of us. How does your family tolerate you?"

"They hold an unfair advantage. Quite like their father, they seem to prevent me from reading their life forces."

"That could be frightening with Anlía so far from home. She has become quite an exotic beauty." Adrina laughed. "At least Gregor has a detachment of soldiers constantly guarding her. I'm not sure who I should pity most—prospective suitors or Anlía."

Alexa nearly strangled on her tea. "Careful with the sympathy. My husband may need it most."

Adrina nearly dropped her teacup. "That deserves an explanation."

"If only I could," Alexa replied ruefully. "Promises, you know. I need to return to the palace. At least one of us should be with the other children for midday. Thank you for the tea. We shall catch up soon."

～

Gregor rubbed his forehead with his fingertips. Following hours of discussion, his head was starting to ache. So many details needed to be arranged in a relatively short period of time. The hardest decision would be who would comprise the final delegation to travel first to Coloridia, then on to the Sifiq Kingdom. Despite ongoing planning for this contingency, the reality had come with unexpected conditions.

"Father," Nikolai said, "why don't we stop for now? The aides can copy down essential requirements for tomorrow. That way, we won't have to work from scribbled notes. We can start fresh in the morning and clarify the ideas we discussed today."

Gregor gazed thoughtfully at his son. Somehow, Nikolai made him think back on Alexa during the weeks leading up to the civil war. "My son, you are as your mother—a voice of sensibility in a sea of chaos. You're right. We've covered dozens of possibilities and concerns today. We can start sorting through them logically tomorrow after getting some rest."

Inside the library that evening, Gregor stared morosely at flames leaping inside the fireplace while sipping brandy. His wife's fingers kneaded tense muscles in his neck and shoulders, relieving some of the day's stress. Speaking at last, he said, "I really don't want to send Nikolai. I would much rather go myself."

"And do what? Lose your temper if Bin-Lot is still in power?"

"You cannot know how much I want to strangle the life out of that cowardly bastard." Tears eased from the corners of his eyes. "If I weren't responsible for all of Turand…"

Leaning forward, Alexa kissed the top of his head. "Gregor, my love, we must accept the responsibilities and challenges Val gives us. This is all happening as Val means it to happen. Be satisfied that I know your heart and that you would do anything in your power to protect me. Don't let vengeance taint our love. Remember Victor's example of how destructive revenge can be."

Swallowing the last of his brandy, Gregor got up. Going to Alexa, he wound his arms tightly around her. "You are my heart, beloved, and my conscience. You always remind me to guard my soul. I was more dead than alive without you. That's what I remember when I think of Bin-Lot."

Bronzed skin flushed darker. Full lips pressed together, and jaws clenched, restraining the sob that threatened to escape. Remembered grief glazed black-brown eyes. Alexa reached up and stroked tears from the edge of his beard.

"I can't lose you again. My fear now is that he might hurt our son. What am I to do?"

"My beloved husband, come. You're worried, and you're tired. Let me take you to bed."

"Alexa..."

She placed two fingers against his lips. "Tonight, we leave this in Val's care. Then we deal with it tomorrow. Will you trust me on that?"

He managed a faint smile. "I always trust you."

Rising on tiptoes, she exchanged two fingers for a brief kiss. "I love you, Gregor Toscano. Always and forever."

⌇

Early the following morning, Gregor's circle of advisers gathered again. Dividing the Coloridian document packet into sections, they methodically analyzed each. Atuliq was the confirmed meeting site. King Bin-Lot had been notified that, with negotiations pending, all hostile actions against Turand were to be suspended. The Turandan delegation would disembark in Maraya and then sail on Coloridian vessels for Atuliq. One Turandan ship, flying Coloridian colors, could accompany the sailing party, but its crew must remain on board. Nikolai would travel with his advisers and Ambassador Laritha. Although a small personal guard from Turand would be permitted to disembark in Atuliq, primary security would be provided by Coloridia under guarantee by the Protectors.

While the document's provisions weren't ideal, they had been successfully utilized by two other nations to curb past Sifiq aggression. However, Alexa had said Sifiq citizens were beginning to rebel. Gregor questioned if Bin-Lot's current situation hadn't deteriorated to the point of desperation and, if so, how it might affect negotiations. Within two days, the king's courier carried a dispatch to Timeri for the next ship departing for Coloridia. Crown Prince Nikolai would assemble his diplomatic delegation and set sail in three weeks for the Coloridian capital of Maraya.

⌒

"Oui-lest! How beautiful you look! I can't believe Victor let you travel in this cold!" Alexa exclaimed as she welcomed her friend with an affectionate hug.

Oui-lest blushed before returning the embrace. "I feel wonderful, my friend, and I missed you so much. When Victor said he needed to come to Toraval, I begged him to let me come, too. He has pampered me every mile of our journey."

"As he should! Come, dear one. Our men are already off for another interminable meeting. Would you like some tea and cakes?"

"That would be lovely. Adrina will meet us here later if that's all right."

"Perfect! Perhaps we can enjoy midday together. I'll send word to the kitchen, and they can notify the Sidano house."

Inside the library, Oui-lest settled comfortably on a chair Alexa pushed close to the fireplace. "Thank you. The fire feels heavenly."

"I remember being so cold when I was pregnant with Nikolai. He was born in late autumn, but Toraval was especially cold that year. Gregor always kept me warm, but he didn't come home from the war until days before I delivered." Alexa paused, her expression tender. "My dear friend, how are you? Really?"

Blue eyes brimmed with tears when they met Alexa's. "When I decided to come here, I was terrified. Frightened that Turand couldn't possibly be everything you said, but even more terrified of staying in the Sifiq Kingdom. Alexa, in all my life, I never dared to dream a woman could live the life I now live."

"Then you are happy?"

Beautiful lips trembled as Oui-lest's hands rested over her swelling abdomen. "I live in a beautiful home where Victor encourages me to use my artistic talents. He often praises the results. He is gentle and kind with me." Her voice grew very soft. "Alexa, he never hurts me the way my first husband did. When I told him about the baby, I apologized in case the baby might be a girl. He started to cry and held me. He asked why I should apologize and said he couldn't complain because his daughter would surely be as beautiful as her mother."

Alexa smiled through a film of tears and then knelt in front of her friend. "Victor insisted he loves you. Quite honestly, I would not have performed your wedding ceremony otherwise."

Oui-lest placed a palm against Alexa's cheek. "When I think of what my people did to you, it breaks my heart. Still, had you not come, I never would have met you, nor would I have known Val—or my new life."

Within her breast, Alexa's heart skipped a beat. Purpose. Her ordeal had not been in vain. "My suffering is over, Oui-lest. I will not regret it because Val shows me the great good that arises."

⌒

Outside the palace, Nikolai prepared to depart for Timeri beneath overcast skies. Light snow dusted the ground. Thankfully, winter weather was easing into spring. Stefan Sidano would go as Nikolai's senior adviser. Admiral Firenzdá would attend as his military adviser. As valuable as Captain Lynmar's knowledge might be, Gregor had decided not to risk sending him, even if he remained on the Turandan ship anchored offshore from Atuliq. Should the Sifiq learn Lynmar's true identity, they might attempt an abduction or an assassination.

Lord LeAndro Karanan had sent word that he would join their delegation in Timeri. Despite being almost eighty years old, he had written he was strong enough to make at least one final contribution to his country's future. His two sons would remain behind to continue his legacy should he perish in the effort.

Kissing Oui-lest farewell, Victor said, "I shall return soon. Remember, I'm only traveling as far as Coloridia to attend some new business."

Oui-lest gazed at him doubtfully. "Do you promise?"

"He promises," Gregor told Oui-lest with a wink while gripping Victor's shoulder. "Besides, my son will see to it that your husband goes no further."

Victor controlled the urge to shake off the king's hand. "You see, my lovely? You have no reason to worry. Stay here with Adrina and Alexa until I return."

When Oui-lest tearfully joined the other women, Victor muttered, "There was no need for that."

Gregor hid his next words behind a smile. "I know you, Victor. I also recall only too well how Alexa felt when she was pregnant with Nikolai, and I was forced to leave her behind. Spare your wife that burden if you can."

Victor buried a barbed comment within a secluded part of his soul he concealed from the world around him. "I apologize. You're right, of course."

A week later, LeAndro Karanan sat in his drawing room with Stefan, Nikolai, and Victor. A servant interrupted discussions regarding their trip scheduled for departure the following morning. A military messenger had arrived from Timeri's docks with an urgent message for the prince.

Nikolai opened the sealed message from the admiral. Leaping to his feet and shaking his head in disbelief, he uttered a vehement curse. "Unbelievable! Of all days! Why today!"

Stefan stood, his forehead creased with concern. "What is it, Nikolai?"

"Firenzdá needs me at the docks immediately. It seems a Sifiq warship just sailed right into port."

"What?" Victor practically shouted, his face contorting instantly with rage.

"Lord Karanan, I must leave immediately. Do you wish to join me?"

"Absolutely!"

Half an hour later, the prince's guards and Karanan's carriage arrived at the military dock. Turandan soldiers had already come to support naval personnel who had secured the Sifiq vessel. Firenzdá rushed to meet the prince.

"Your Highness, praise Val you came so quickly. Two vessels sailed into our waters, flying Coloridian flags, but our captains immediately recognized the ships' design as Sifiq. The lead ship was escorted to dock. Two of our warships are holding the other offshore, pending your instructions."

"Have you spoken to any of the ship's officers?" Nikolai asked.

"The captain and his first mate requested permission to disembark, which I granted. However, upon recognizing my rank, they demanded my cooperation in resolving a problem. I advised them I would refer the matter to a higher authority." The admiral scowled. "They are the most arrogant, overbearing reprobates I ever had the displeasure of meeting. They are under guard inside the port director's office."

"Thank you, Admiral. Let's see what demands they have for Turand's Crown Prince. In the meantime, keep their ships under tight scrutiny. I do not trust these devils."

Moments later, Nikolai whisked into the port office with the force of gale winds. The eyes of the sleekly uniformed Sifiq captain widened when he noted first the prince's furious expression and then his unusual stature. Then, resorting to his typical intimidating behavior to cover his discomfort, the Sifiq captain said, "I am Captain Kar-Lan of the Sifiq Royal Navy. I expect you are the authority with whom I can discuss demands I carry from my king."

Nikolai scornfully regarded the haughty captain. The officer, who looked about thirty, was of medium height and slender build. With its dangling tassel, his formal uniform headdress was blue that seemed to clash with his ruddy face marked with scars likely obtained in battle. "Captain Kar-Lan, why have you sailed Sifiq vessels into Turandan waters under false pretense?"

Stubbornly, the captain stuck out his chest. "I will only explain myself to someone in authority. I believe I made that clear to Admiral Firenzdá."

Nikolai reached out and placed both hands around Kar-Lan's throat. Picking him up from the floor, he said, "Captain, mind your tongue. You are speaking to Crown Prince Nikolai Toscano of Turand. Now, answer my question."

Victor barely contained a grin as he watched his godson put the supercilious Sifiq in his place. Never had he seen such a display of temper from Nikolai.

With a hand at his bruised neck after Nikolai roughly set him down, Kar-Lan swallowed and quickly bowed his head. "My apologies, Your Highness." The captain warily assessed the prince's companions for the first time. Two middle-aged advisers, an old man, plus two additional armed guards. "We considered it a safer alternative than sailing here under the Sifiq flag."

"So you illegally utilized another nation's flag to invade Turand. For what purpose?"

Kar-Lan lifted his head contemptuously. "I did what was necessary to comply with my king's commands."

"Ah," Nikolai replied, "and your king's commands are?"

"King Bin-Lot ordered us to recover the ship and crew he sent to return Turandan citizens. Once we do that, we will leave."

Nikolai laughed sarcastically. "Just like that. After a year, Bin-Lot decides to send two warships to recover a lost ship he thinks might be in Turand. Your king has much to learn about Turand."

Kar-Lan turned surly. "We have a right to our ship and citizens. I issue that demand to you now. Comply, or face the consequences."

Nikolai's dark eyes opened wide. "You dare threaten me on my own soil, Captain?"

"I dare to warn you that there will be consequences if you fail to meet the demands I just delivered."

"Incredible. Absolutely unbelievable! Captain Kar-Lan, let's go outside for some fresh air. I cannot tolerate another moment being confined inside with the likes of you and your fellow officer. You taint the very air we breathe with your dishonesty and false superiority." To his guards, he said, "Take them outside and keep them secure."

Once outside, another officer quickly ran up to confer with the admiral, who whispered into the prince's ear. Turning to Kar-Lan, Nikolai said, "Captain, it seems your deceit has no bounds. I understand my navy has surrounded a third ship farther from shore. Did your king think we would sit like trusting children just because the Coloridians said they had advised the Sifiq to cease all aggressive activity while diplomatic negotiations were in progress?"

"I don't know what you're talking about," Kar-Lan responded.

"Of course, you don't," Nikolai spat back. "You're lying. No matter. My father and I have no time for Sifiq treachery." Glancing sideways, he said, "Papino Victor, how crucial is your business in Coloridia? Can it be delayed?"

"If necessary, yes. It can wait."

"Thank you. I want you to lead an escort back to Toraval and explain today's events to Father."

Stefan grasped his godson's arm. "Nikolai, what in Val's name are you planning?"

"Something outrageous but something necessary, Papino. I don't want to do it, but Father told me to trust my judgment. That is exactly what I intend to do."

Growing impatient, Kar-Lan shook his head. "Your Highness, I need to arrange the return of our ship and our crew. How soon will you accommodate me?"

Nikolai turned to face the Sifiq captain. "Your insolent demands carry no weight here. First of all, there is no ship to recover. That ship ran aground and broke apart. Most of its crew drowned in the process. Those who didn't? Some renounced their Sifiq citizenship and are now learning to live according to the laws and faith of Turand. Others are prisoners for violating our laws. Either way, they will not be released to you."

"My king demands their return!"

"Your king has no right to demand anything in Turand, nor do you! Furthermore, Admiral Firenzdá already sent word to the local garrison for additional troops. Your crew will be arrested, removed from your ship, and confined until we make satisfactory arrangements for their long-term imprisonment."

"You wouldn't dare."

"I do dare! Also, the admiral sent a skiff to your vessel offshore. The captain has been ordered to abandon his ship. Once the order is delivered, he will have twenty minutes to evacuate his crew. The ship farther out will be signaled to do the same."

"Are you out of your mind? They will never abandon ship! They are Sifiq!"

"For the sake of their crews, I hope you're wrong," Nikolai said, his eyes blazing, his mouth set in a grim line. Stefan and Victor exchanged questioning looks, neither knowing what to expect from their godson.

Troops from the local garrison were already marching up ramps to Kar-Lan's ship. Turandan soldiers quickly overpowered sailors onboard, their superior numbers rapidly subduing the few scuffles breaking out. Incensed, Kar-Lan shouted, "This is an abomination! Get off my ship!"

"Correction. My ship. You delivered that vessel into my territory, and I hereby claim it for Turand. Accordingly, I formally advise you that you, your officers, and your crew are under arrest for violating Turand's territorial waters and illegally docking at Port Timeri under a false flag—while under diplomatic ban, I might add."

"You can't arrest us."

"Captain, the deed is done. You are already under arrest."

"Your Highness, what about the vessels offshore?" Firenzdá interrupted. "The captain at anchor refuses to abandon ship."

"Were you able to signal our vessels further out?" When the admiral nodded in confirmation, Nikolai closed his eyes and drew a shuddering breath. More than ever before, he comprehended his father's comments about the difficulties that often accompanied command decisions. "Use the cannons. Sink their ships. Pick up any survivors."

Three successive, resounding blasts reverberated through the air close to shore. Three more echoed in the distance. Shocked onlookers watched in awe as tall masts cracked and slowly toppled onto the shattered deck of the warship closest to shore. Men shouted and howled, some trapped beneath crushed and broken timbers, others caught in flames spreading from cooking fires and smashed lanterns below. Further out to sea, billowing smoke indicated the Sifiq vessel there had fared no better.

Leaving prisoners, management of the confiscated ship, and sinking vessels in the hands of the admiral's command officers, Nikolai said, "Gentlemen, we begin a long journey tomorrow. I suggest we return to Lord Karanan's house. I could use some rest before dinner."

Contrary to his usual calm nature, Stefan requested a fourth glass of brandy. His face remained pale after the incident at Port Timeri. "Astonishment doesn't begin to describe what I felt out there."

Lord Karanan shook his head. "If anyone ever doubted our prince, those doubts disappeared today. He is his father's son."

Victor's chuckle held admiration. "Absolutely no doubt. Had I not seen it, I'm not sure I would have believed it. Still, it was necessary."

"Do you really think so?" Stefan asked, still stunned by Nikolai's calm decisiveness committing such an uncommonly bold act that ended so many lives.

Victor met his brother-in-law's dismayed stare. "Sadly, yes. Don't think Nikolai is unaffected by what he did. He is hurt. Badly. I saw his father bear that same grief in battle every time he struck down a soldier. It is pain one carries forever, Stefan, so be grateful you're a man of statesmanship. Nikolai removed three deadly ships from Sifiq service today, along with a good many Sifiq soldiers. You heard that Sifiq captain. He intended to inflict *consequences,* one way or another, while he was here. Nikolai's bold action translates to Turandan lives saved."

"Victor's right," Lord Karanan agreed. "It was dreadful but necessary."

Admiral Firenzdá walked over to Stefan and rested a hand on his shoulder. "My friend, our prince will be down soon. Before he comes, I tell you this. Respect him for the courage he demonstrated today. I have the feeling we may need much more of it in the near future."

⌒

"Captain Kar-Lan and Captain Bel-Dar have constantly demanded an audience to protest Nikolai's actions at Port Timeri," Victor advised Gregor after relating the details of the Sifiq arrival at Timeri. Nikolai,

Stefan, and LeAndro Karanan had also sent individual written accounts of the incident.

"I assume they've been nothing short of obnoxious."

Victor huffed out a frustrated breath. "An accurate description, if understated. They certainly weren't the most affable traveling companions I've ever had."

"I do apologize, especially considering Nikolai asked you to delay your business in Coloridia." Gregor was sincerely regretful.

Victor grinned. "I must admit. Witnessing his actions with the Sifiq at Timeri was well worth tolerating those two captains all the way to Toraval. Niko was powerfully decisive, even though I know the action came at heavy personal cost."

"You realize this doesn't bode well for the summit in Atuliq."

"I know. Stefan and I discussed that. Admiral Firenzdá sent his fastest ships out to search for additional Sifiq vessels. None were spotted, and interrogating low-ranking officers produced no further intelligence. We're hoping discussions with the priestesses might provide some insight if they're able to read anything in their life forces. Otherwise, any delays in the return of those vessels might be attributed to winter weather."

"I'll speak with Alexa right away. Thank you for escorting them here. I know it was inconvenient. Prison facilities are ready for the prisoners who arrived with you. Renovations at Zenox are almost complete to house the rest when they arrive. I had hoped never again to have to see the inside of that place."

Victor bit his tongue to avoid agreeing with the king. "By the way, before I go, these officers are adamant about access to Lynmar and his crew. They claim that was their reason for coming—to recover his ship and his crew."

Gregor grimaced. "What have they been told?"

"Nikolai told them much of the crew died when a storm drove the ship aground. He said the rest are either prisoners or have sworn allegiance to Turand. The captains are particularly interested in Captain Raf-Zan."

Days later, Alexa delivered results to her husband. She and three other Valiria had spent hours attending the questioning of Sifiq naval officers who arrived in Toraval with Victor. Even those treated for injuries retained their surly attitudes, especially when the priestesses entered the stark interrogation rooms. Despite harsh examinations, no prisoners were subjected to violence. The priestesses reached out carefully with their senses, occasionally recoiling in reaction to the violent nature of the prisoners and their attitudes toward females. Alexa, who had chosen to wear the Valkana's golden veil, was especially cautious. The men's hateful nature was precisely as she remembered, but the priestesses detected only truth concerning the three ships.

Inside a secure conference room, Gregor stood erect and imposing in his tailored, pearl-gray uniform. Waiting with him were General Kohira, Toravalia's governor, several aides, Captain Fratino, and Alexa, who wore the Valkana's golden veils and gown. When the double doors opened, the two Sifiq captains practically strutted inside, their chests thrust out and their faces drawn into expressions of angry pride. Not waiting for their military escort to announce them, each identified himself.

Unsurprised, Gregor's eyebrows lifted. "I see that Sifiq officers have learned no manners since I dispatched them from my country years ago. I am King Gregor. Be seated."

Kar-Lan complained first. "We were forced to travel under deplorable conditions to this poor excuse of a capital. We've spent days in prison cells waiting to lodge our protests with you over your son's inexcusable actions at the port. I see no reason for etiquette under such circumstances."

"Furthermore," Bel-Dar stated, "we haven't had the courtesy of a single report on the status of our crews. Mine, especially, endured a grievous attack ordered by your son. Besides those killed, many were injured. As their commanding officer, I have every right to know their condition."

"Hmmm," Gregor mumbled as if he were bored, finally sitting and inviting his staff to join him, even if the Sifiq captains preferred to stand.

"Hmmm? Is that all you have to say?" Bel-Dar scoffed, his face reddening as he practically shouted.

Gregor leveled a cutting glare at him. "Captain Bel-Dar, no one shouts at me. Your behavior and Captain Kar-Lan's have been most uncivilized since you walked through that door. If you care to discuss your complaints, then you will speak to me in a reasonable tone. Otherwise, this meeting ends, and you may both return to your cells. Is that clear?"

Bel-Dar looked at Kar-Lan. Their king had related stories about how easily intimidated and manipulated Gregor of Turand had always been. Bin-Lot's father had believed his occupation army had grown greedy and decided to establish its own little kingdom. That had been the explanation as to why the occupation forces never returned. Unrest at home later caused the Sifiq kings to ignore Turand and instead focus on internal strife.

"Your son used some strange weapon to destroy my ship," Bel-Dar declared in a less strident voice.

"I have been advised. I was also told that you were warned and given time to evacuate your crew from your ship. Is that true?"

"What captain abandons his ship based on mere threats?"

"Well, Captain," Gregor drawled, "perhaps next time—if there is a next time—you might want to give serious consideration to such warnings. My son does not make *mere threats*. He learned that from his father."

Bel-Dar stared at Gregor, unsure what to expect next.

"You make no apology for the destruction of Bel-Dar's ship or the one farther out to sea?" Kar-Lan asked.

"None," Gregor declared. "Both violated my territorial waters while sailing under false flags and a diplomatic ban."

"What about my ship?"

"Your ship, Captain, has been confiscated and will be repurposed according to my navy's discretion."

"That is piracy."

"Call it what you will. You are free to say whatever you want from your prison cell."

Bel-Dar clenched his jaw. "We came to recover our lost crew and a lost ship, and this is how you treat us?"

"You came to us under deception, Captain, and with intent to do harm. You were caught before you succeeded in inflicting further damage on my people or my nation. You will pay the penalty."

"We came for Captain Raf-Zan. Bin-Lot intends to punish him."

"Captain Raf-Zan? Who is he?" the Toravalian governor asked.

Alexa replied quietly, "The captain of the ship that brought me and the others back from the Sifiq Kingdom."

"Oh, I see."

Then, addressing the Sifiq, Alexa said, "Captain Kar-Lan, as you have been advised, much of the crew on Raf-Zan's ship perished at sea. Survivors who washed ashore were surrounded by Turandan citizens until Royal Guards arrived. Unfortunately, many were critically injured, several fatally so. That includes your Captain Raf-Zan."

"How do you know so much, woman?" Bel-Dar asked in an acid voice.

Alexa placed a restraining hand on her husband's leg beneath the table. If these men were going to stay in a Turandan prison, there was no need to hide the truth. "I was there. I was one of the priestesses he returned."

Both men looked shocked. Captain Kar-Lan recovered first. He then asked sarcastically, "Is that why you're here? To taunt us?"

"Not at all, Captain. I am here because it is my duty. I am Alexa, Queen of Turand."

Chapter 8

"Ambassador Laritha, I recall meeting you at Maxim's coronation celebrations in Turand," LeAndro Karanan said as he straightened from an elegant bow. "I look forward to renewing our acquaintance."

Coloridia's distinguished statesman searched his memory as he welcomed the Turandan prince's newest adviser. "You do look familiar, sir, but an old man's memory can sometimes be a tricky companion."

"How well I know," Karanan laughed. "In those days, my body was thinner, and my hair was thicker. The obvious truth is I had hair—I believe a rather thick, bright, coppery mane."

Laritha laughed. "Now I remember! You were the nobleman constantly by Maxim's side, always scattering everyone on one task or another!"

Lord Karanan nodded up and down. "That would have been this faithful lord. Maxim and I were the best of friends until—well, until his death."

"I'm sorry. I understand his was an early passing."

"Too early and far too unnecessary." Karanan turned and accepted a glass of wine from a server. "On a brighter note, as his son's godfather, I have continued to serve my old friend while making a fine new friend. Nowadays, I am honored to have the trust of Maxim's grandson."

Laritha noted both keen intelligence and unswerving loyalty in Karanan's expression. "It seems you have built bridges between the generations."

"Fine, strong bridges," Karanan replied. "The kind of bridges that do not easily collapse in the face of winds or floods. Turand has mastered bridge-building."

The ambassador smiled, wondering if the Turandan nobleman was simply being philosophical or if he was issuing a warning. "Yes, of course. We can all use bridges like that. Er—I was surprised that the other adviser—what was his name? Captain Lynmar. That was it. He didn't accompany the prince this time. He constantly shared the prince's shadow the last time."

Lord Karanan sipped his wine. "Captain Lynmar is a personal adviser to King Gregor. As I understand, Lynmar and the prince often work closely together on various projects. King Gregor asked the captain to join Nikolai on the previous mission if the prince had questions related to Lynmar's area of expertise."

"And the king thinks the prince has no further need of Captain Lynmar's expertise?"

Karanan met Laritha's probing question with a shrug and well-disguised disinterest. "Stefan mentioned that Gregor had a more pressing issue when we left that required the captain's attention. Besides, Nikolai is quite competent." The nobleman's eyes sparkled with pride. "He's his father's son. I'm sure we can rely on him for an outstanding performance."

"Agreed. Ah, here comes everyone else. Let's enjoy a fine dinner before embarking tomorrow for the Sifiq Kingdom. I suggest you enjoy. I hear the cuisine in Atuliq is not quite so palatable these days."

That night, Stefan anxiously paced across his suite. "Although I'm glad you told me, that man makes me more and more nervous. Last time, it was Niko's appearance. Now it's Lynmar's absence. What is he after?"

Lord Karanan looked up from the sofa, where he sat with a snifter of brandy. "After the incident in Timeri, the questions concerning Lynmar are fairly obvious. They suspect he's a Sifiq defector. I can't say how the Coloridians view him, but the Sifiq would gladly hunt him down and torture him to death." Karanan took a drink of brandy. "What's this about Nikolai's appearance?"

"When we first presented our formal complaint, the Minister of State found it nearly impossible to stop staring at Niko. To be perfectly honest, I have no idea how Niko maintained his composure. Even I felt uncomfortable."

"He was likely just trying to intimidate a young prince to see if he could upset him."

"No," Stefan disagreed. "It was much more than that. If you had been there, you would have seen it. I was very impressed with how Niko managed his nerves and completed the session. Once we returned to the privacy of his suite, however, I realized how much it disturbed him. Then the ambassador scheduled a private meeting with us, ostensibly to discuss the final hearing before the minister."

"And?"

Stefan shook his head at the puzzling recollection and poured himself a brandy from the decanter on a table beside a window. He pushed aside velvet draperies and briefly looked outside. Turning back to Lord Karanan, he said, "That's the first we heard about Ambassador Laritha ever having visited Turand or having known King Maxim."

"He and I discussed that earlier."

"What struck both Nikolai and me was when he said he had heard how much Niko looks like his father. He went on to say that, having known Maxim, Gregor and Niko must look like Gregor's mother."

"He never met Anlía?"

"Apparently not. It just seemed so peculiar, especially after how the Minister of State reacted."

"Well, you must admit that our prince does make a striking first impression. Like Gregor, he also projects a presence impossible to ignore." Seeing hesitation on Stefan's face, Karanan asked, "What is it you're not saying?"

"We mentioned it to Lynmar."

"From the look on your face, I take it Lynmar said something that further unsettled you."

"It seems there's some prevailing legend in this part of the world about a race of dark-skinned giants."

Karanan suddenly laughed. "We're not talking about our mysterious Protectors, are we?"

"That's exactly what we're discussing. I wish you could have seen Lynmar as he described these people. We had a hard time convincing him that Niko's grandmother was from Turand."

"Ah, the stories people choose to believe," the nobleman sighed dismissively. "Well, I think we need to get to bed. We have an early morning ahead. It seems you and I will need to keep our eyes sharp and our wits sharper in the days to come."

⌣

"Dear wife, whatever are you doing? Planning to open a new school or a cartographer's shop?" Gregor joked as he looked around at the stacks of journals, old books, and many maps piled around his wife's large office.

"There's a suggestion I hadn't considered," she said with a laugh as she straightened and shuffled aside maps she had been studying. "How well do you know the Zemfosa Mountains?"

Dark eyebrows lifted in surprise. "The Zemfosa Mountains? Let me see. A rugged mountain range running parallel to the Fosan Sea and through most of Fosan Province. Let me guess. The dreams are back."

She made a face at him. "Not very good timing, I know, but back with a vengeance."

"So I thought. You were restless last night."

"I'm sorry. You need your rest right now. Perhaps I should move back into my old chambers."

Gregor approached her desk and tucked long fingers beneath her chin, lifting her face. "I spent the worst year of my life believing you were dead. Now that I have you back, you are staying right by my side at night where I can keep watch over you."

Smiling, she received his tenderly bestowed kiss. "The dreams must mean something. I simply don't know what. Yet."

"Alexa, I know you need to decipher them; however, don't lose sight of how much I need you right now. Nikolai should be arriving in Atuliq any time. What happened in Timeri makes me think Bin-Lot has no intention of negotiating in good faith. We must prepare for the absolute worst."

The shadows that crossed Gregor's face brought sadness to her eyes. He was terrified he had sent his son and best friend into a viper's pit, ready victims to confront death at Bin-Lot's hands. Her eyelids fluttered a moment as an ethereal voice whispered inside her mind. Reaching up, she caressed her husband's cheek.

"Gregor, my love, we must pray that Nikolai and Stefan will come home. Papino LeAndro, too. I believe you're right about Bin-Lot's intentions, but we must have faith that our delegation will return safely."

His eyes searched her face, finally locking on the emerald jewels that were the eyes he had adored since first meeting her. "Beloved, if I lose Nikolai because of this…"

"We must trust Val to watch over him. Gregor, we must."

Drawing her into his arms, he clutched her tightly. He understood that her intimate connection with their Lord Val provided her this precious source of hope and confidence. Silently, he prayed to Val—begging him to bring home the son he loved so dearly and thanking him for the wife he cherished above everyone else.

⌇

Rafzan Lynmar turned back the thick wool blanket and smooth linen sheet on the bed inside quarters he let at the building complex near the palace where most unmarried palace aides lived. The kerosene lamp on his bedside table shed golden light across the room. Until recently, other than the bed and nightstand, he had only bothered to add a sturdy armoire, a writing desk with a comfortable chair, and a valet stand for his daily attire. The room had been stark and plain until he had framed and hung several pictures Anlía had sketched for him.

Picking up a tan leather portfolio, he climbed into bed and tucked the blanket snugly around him. Deft fingers undid two buckles securing the large binder he kept for his private papers. Opening the case, he laid aside a protective sheet of plain linen paper he kept on top and leaned back.

Rafzan sighed. He spent several minutes examining the many fine strokes of the pen-and-ink portrait one of her friends at school had drawn. With his eyes closed, his memory completed the drawing with the sparkle in her brown eyes, the soft glow of her cheeks, and the rose color of her lips. Sucking in a sharp breath, he gazed again at the image that transfixed his very soul. Carefully setting aside the folder with her picture in full view, he removed her most recent letter.

My dearest Rafzan,

Thank you again for watching over Niko during his voyage to Coloridia. I know my brother can be a handful, but that is his calling. He must one day fill Father's shoes. The longer you live in Turand, the better you will understand how daunting a prospect that must be. I am made happy that Niko is a strong and good soul—a young man of integrity. One day, I'm sure he will be a fine king, although my heart falters at the mere thought of losing my beloved father.

Dear, dear Rafzan, how I miss our many conversations. Do you remember when you were showing me the stars and explaining how seamen use them for navigation? Some nights, I go outside late and gaze up at them. I see them twinkling merrily. They are so pretty, but sometimes they look so cold and lonely. I often looked at you and loved it when I saw a sparkle in your blue eyes. You have wonderful eyes, you know. Other times, my heart trembled with sadness because you reminded me of the stars. You seemed lonely and lost in cold darkness.

My dear Rafzan, you aren't lost anymore. I won't let you be lost. Not ever again. You are in Turand, a land of love. And you are loved. How do I know? Because I send you mine, of course!

I must go now. Master Maconti has promised to help me with my studies in finance. Who would imagine a priestess needing to master a finance class? Mother says it is necessary, though, should I ever assume responsibility for a Valiria community. I have watched her manage accounts for the temple and this school. I respect her diligence, so I will also learn.

Take care, my dear one. If you look up at the stars, only look at the twinkling ones. One of them might be reflecting my thoughts to you.

Anlia

The next morning, Rafzan rose earlier than usual and dressed for the day. He tucked his precious portfolio inside his armoire, behind a stack of folded linens and clothing. He locked the cabinet and then departed for the Temple of Val for the ritual of prayers that now sustained his daily routine.

Beneath the entrance of the sacred space, vibrating electricity caused the former Sifiq captain's blond hair to stand on end. Rafzan felt energy beneath his feet as if the floor were shifting, yet he knew the ground was firm and steady. Outside, he had heard the bells in the tall carillon towers begin to peal, the sound loud and beautiful, yet also ominous. What robbed him of breath was when he looked upward. In front of the altar, straight ahead, he saw the Valkana's gold-clad figure hovering high above the floor with rays of brilliant light from the temple's crystal pyramid connecting to her body.

⌒

Nikolai stared morosely at the churning sea below, grateful for the heavy woolen cape Lord Karanan had draped around his shoulders before retiring to warmer quarters. Nighttime air was biting cold, and salty droplets of seawater occasionally stung his cheeks. Turand's prince hardly noticed the physical discomfort. He knew no shame. The decision had been set in motion before he ever set foot in the Sifiq Kingdom.

Atuliq. Ambassador Laritha had described Atuliq as being a beautiful, thriving city. However, it relied heavily on its military traffic and the spoils delivered by vessels filled with cargo plundered from faraway nations. Decades earlier, two major wars had redirected most Sifiq military conquests to less prosperous countries, enabling the Sifiq monarchy to maintain relatively high living standards for itself and its military.

What Nikolai and his delegation observed on their arrival contradicted the ambassador's description. The port district was undergoing what appeared to be major reconstruction. Warehouses showed signs of extensive damage. As the passengers disembarked and traveled through the city, even Laritha appeared puzzled by rough roads and derelict districts until they reached the central part of the capital. Even there, the facades of many stone buildings revealed cracks. Other structures sat at odd angles where their foundations had shifted beneath them. Atuliq had obviously endured at least one catastrophic calamity.

From the moment they arrived at their accommodations, the atmosphere felt decidedly bleak. Attendants were efficient but as aloof as Coloridians had been attentive. No one smiled. Minimal conversation occurred among employees. Glancing around, they saw no women anywhere.

Once the guests were escorted to their rooms, the delegation members again noted drab surroundings, although everything was scrupulously clean. No pictures hung on plain, painted walls. Furnishings in each room included a desk and chair, an armoire, a washstand with mirror, and a bed covered with a thick blue quilt, white sheets, and matching pillows. A kerosene lamp sat on the desk for lighting, and an ornate iron stove stood in a corner alongside a rack holding wood for heating the room.

When Nikolai met his godfather and Lord Karanan in the hotel dining room downstairs for dinner, his expression was grimly amused. "Such attractive accommodations. The Sifiq certainly have interesting taste when it comes to interior decor."

Stefan rolled his eyes. "Really? Your rooms must be quite nice. As for mine, I've visited more cheerful mausoleums."

Nikolai and Lord Karanan both chuckled, and Nikolai remarked, "It seems we're all agreed. At least everything is clean. Mother did say they are obsessively clean."

"One positive point out of how many?" Stefan responded sarcastically. He suddenly tilted his head, indicating Ambassador Laritha's arrival.

"Good evening, gentlemen. I apologize for my delay. I was making sure our dinner would be served on time. Have you ordered drinks yet?"

Lord Karanan gave him an amused grin. "Ordered? Drinks? We haven't seen a server since the host seated us. We've been quietly entertaining ourselves."

The ambassador shook his head in dismay. "This makes no sense. I've never had such poor service in Atuliq. Not that I've been here in some time, but this is unacceptable. Excuse me."

When the ambassador returned, a server brought a bottle of wine. The remainder of the evening was much more pleasant. The wine served with dinner proved to be of decent quality. While the menu wasn't as extensive or as delicious as what Nikolai and Stefan had enjoyed in Coloridia, the food was prepared well and satisfied the palate.

Once the meal was served, the ambassador dismissed the server. Then, wine glass in hand, he proposed a toast. "Gentlemen, to the success of our efforts here. I sincerely hope we can avert a war."

"As do we, Excellency," Lord Karanan responded.

While dining, the men discussed what to expect now that Laritha had notified officials of the delegation's arrival. The Coloridian expounded on Bin-Lot's court protocol and his temperament. The ambassador appeared genuinely concerned about the conditions of Atuliq, the deteriorated amenities in the hotel, and what he referred to as a prevailing atmosphere of apprehension.

Over a second bottle of wine, the venerable statesman fixed his eyes directly on Nikolai. "Your Highness, I will be honest with you. I want this negotiation to work because I consider war the worst pestilence ever conceived. My years of diplomatic work right now raise flags of concern. Something is terribly wrong here. Be aware."

Nikolai inclined his head respectfully. "Excellency, I've known that since before we departed Turand. We all have, but we're determined to extend every effort possible to avoid hostilities. If we succeed, all efforts are worthwhile. If we fail, we know we tried. Our people will know we tried on their behalf."

Lord Karanan added, "That is why the people of Turand will stay true to their leaders, no matter what lies ahead."

Ambassador Laritha inhaled a deep breath. "I credit you all for your courage, gentlemen. Very few would brave this devil in his den."

Nikolai smiled. "Some have and survived to tell the story."

"Your priestesses?"

"Yes, even though it wasn't by choice. Still, three came home."

"I recall five were abducted. What about the other two?"

Nikolai shook his head, his eyes darker than ever, his expression unreadable. "We don't know. According to the ones who returned, the others disappeared from the labor camp one night after some Sifiq revolutionaries stole the harvest and burned whatever was left."

"Why didn't those three leave with the rebels?"

"One of them was too sick. The other two refused to leave her. Valiria live by their own code." Nikolai's expression remained impassive.

"It's still a mystery why Bin-Lot sent them back to Turand. I understand he also exiled several Sifiq women. Is that true?"

Stefan nodded. "It is."

"Puzzling. One hears rumors. Stories. One can only wonder."

The next night, Nikolai responded to a knock at his door. "Yes? Who is it?"

"Ambassador Laritha. May I come in?"

Nikolai unlocked the door. In the hallway stood the extra Coloridian security guards his father had insisted on. "Come in. There's only one chair. Please."

"I'm sorry to disturb you so late. My aides are advising Sir Sidano and Lord Karanan. King Bin-Lot has advanced your appearance at his court. He wants you there tomorrow morning at eleven."

"So soon?"

"Yes. I believe he hopes to keep you off balance."

"He will fail to do so," Nikolai replied bluntly, leaning against the armoire. "I have too much at stake for that."

Ambassador Laritha studied the prince for several moments. He saw an intense, fiercely loyal man with a sharp mind. Although untested in many ways, this prince possessed potential to become a formidable leader. His father and his advisers had spared no effort in preparing him for whatever challenges might lie along his path to Turand's throne.

"The truth from me to you. I do not trust Bin-Lot. However, I do believe he will not risk defying the Protectors at this juncture, so I'm confident I can protect you and your people until we leave the Sifiq Kingdom. I will use every threat at my disposal to keep him in line. He knows I'm a man of my word."

Nikolai smiled grimly. "I appreciate your candor, Excellency. We understood the risks when we came."

"I admire and respect that. Now, in strictest confidence—on my oath of honor that I will not reveal to another living being anything you say— truth from you to me."

"Yes?" Nikolai asked, his expression growing cautious.

"Bin-Lot is furious on several points. They all seem to revolve around the return of those three priestesses. Will you please help me understand why he's so angry? Perhaps I can use the information to our advantage."

Nikolai sighed heavily. "First, Bin-Lot will not yet know this. He sent three ships to Turand, supposedly to recover the ship that returned the priestesses and to recover its crew. The ships arrived the day before we departed on this mission."

Laritha looked puzzled. "Wait. The first ship never went back?"

"It arrived during a violent storm and was caught in a whirlwind. It broke apart when it ran aground. Half the crew died before the ship wrecked. The rest washed up on shore. Some died from injuries. Most renounced their Sifiq citizenship. The rest are in prison for crimes against Turand."

"I see. And the ships that just came?"

"Bin-Lot sent them with a demand for the recovery. They arrived, flying Coloridia flags and making an assortment of threats. They also demanded custody of the captain of the wrecked ship."

"What happened?"

"We confiscated the vessel that sailed into dock and arrested the captain and crew. I warned the other captains to abandon their ships and ordered their ships destroyed at sea. Survivors were rescued and arrested."

"You're serious."

"I do not jest about such matters. They were threatening consequences over matters for which we had no control. They violated our territorial waters under false pretenses. What would Coloridia have done?"

"Is your Captain Lynmar Sifiq?"

"Captain Lynmar is a Turandan citizen." Nikolai smiled. "He is one of my father's military advisers."

"I shall accept that answer. For now. One more question. Please. It is very important, and I swear I will never say a word to anyone. I know that something dramatic happened with the priestesses. Bin-Lot would never have sent them back otherwise. He simply would have killed them. I know you said one of them is a close relative, but my sources suggest there's more to the story than that."

Nikolai dragged in a deep breath. He was caught on the edge of a spider's web. Looking into the spider's eyes, he detected a spider, not a devil.

"I am under my king's orders to keep certain information confidential."

"I will not violate your king's orders or your confidence. I cannot possibly help you if you do not help me."

"When you were in Turand, did you ever hear of the mystical traits of the Valiria?"

"I did. Primarily teachers and healers, I believe. I also heard tales that there used to be a high priestess in olden times. I don't recall…"

"Valkana. The high priestess was called Valkana. Although she was essentially a normal person, she had many different special abilities—all blessings from our Lord Val."

"Fairy tales."

"Not fairy tales, Excellency. Shortly before the civil war, Val introduced a new Valkana to Turand for the first time in a century."

"What does that have to do with Bin-Lot?"

"Our Valkana was among the abducted priestesses. Every time she was beaten, catastrophes occurred here. Storms. Ground-quakes. The longer he kept her, the worse the catastrophes became. You see the results yourself."

"You actually believe this, don't you?" Laritha said.

"The Valkana told me herself. You must understand. Valiria priestesses make special vows. They must not lie. You knew Bin-Lot in the past. When the Valkana met him, he was a hefty man, but he had changed by the time she left. He had grabbed her, intending to hurt her. Val himself punished the king for that."

Nikolai shook his head. Hard. He heard a faint voice echoing inside. "You must understand. My father only gave me permission to reveal the fact that Bin-Lot held Turand's High Priestess Valkana as prisoner here in the Sifiq Kingdom."

"But there's more?"

Trusting the strange voice without knowing why, Nikolai said, "What you are not free to reveal is that the High Priestess Valkana is also the Queen of Turand. She is my mother."

Turandan delegates quickly surveyed the Sifiq royal court as they were escorted inside the following morning. Watching their steps, they crossed gleaming tile floors that had cracked or lifted in spots. A carved throne at the center of the far wall boasted a variety of colorful velvet cushions. On either side of the massive chair, several upholstered settees were arranged with small tables. Overhead, chandeliers hung from ceilings that showed extensive repairs to plaster cracks.

When Ambassador Laritha first saw King Bin-Lot, no doubt existed that Nikolai had spoken the truth. Laritha was startled by the changes in the monarch's appearance. The vibrant, rotund man he once knew looked thinner, almost sickly. He carried one arm close to his body, as if the limb pained him greatly. His once florid complexion had lost its brilliance. What hadn't changed were his bellowing voice and pompous attitude.

As soon as formal introductions were completed, the Sifiq king's intentions for the negotiations grew obvious. The tables for the visiting dignitaries had no chairs. The monarch immediately began loudly voicing a list of his perceived issues with Turand, especially his grievance concerning the missing ship he had so benevolently dispatched to return the priestesses stranded in Atuliq. Ignoring protocols agreed to with the Coloridians, he drifted into a rambling diatribe until Ambassador Laritha felt compelled to walk around his table and practically shout to be heard.

"Your Majesty! Please! I must report back to the Protectors! They will not be pleased if I advise them you have given the Turandan delegation no opportunity to respond to your allegations or present their issues!"

Bin-Lot nearly growled at the ambassador. "What about my ship? And Captain Raf-Zan?"

Laritha frowned but looked to Turand's prince for a response. "Your Royal Highness?"

Stepping from behind the table, Nikolai assumed his most daunting posture. Knowing that his tailored uniform fit perfectly, he believed at least his height and physique would gain the surly king's attention. "Your Majesty, as Crown Prince Nikolai Toscano, I shall answer your questions. The ship in question arrived in Turand during a bitter winter storm. After discharging its passengers—in extremely rough seas—it attempted to return to its homeport. Unfortunately, the storm overwhelmed the vessel. Most of its crew perished at sea before the ship eventually wrecked. There were survivors, many critically injured, others fatally so, the ship's captain among them. As for the rest, some chose to renounce their Sifiq citizenship. Those who didn't are prisoners for crimes against the sovereign state of Turand."

"Prisoners. Sovereign state of Turand. What are you talking about, boy?"

"King Bin-Lot, the men on that ship violated our coastal waters while holding Turandan citizens abducted against their will. King Gregor determined that to be a violation of our laws and ordered prison sentences."

"Abominable action! I do not accept your king's decision! I demand release of my men!"

"Your Majesty," Ambassador Laritha reminded Bin-Lot, "you agreed to this negotiation. May we please discuss matters in a more civilized manner? And can we start by bringing chairs for the Turandan delegates?"

Bin-Lot scowled and snapped his fingers. Several women, all with downcast faces and wearing plain white shifts, carried straight-backed wooden chairs to the table where the Turandans stood. Nikolai checked with Stefan and Lord Karanan. His temper was rising. Had it not been for Karanan's advanced age, he would have kept his delegation standing.

Bin-Lot glared at the prince, who stubbornly refused to sit. Something in the young man's presence aggravated him. At the same time, his senses warned him to caution. "You, Prince Nikolai, are little more than a boy. How is it that mighty King Gregor sends you on such an errand? Does he insult the Sifiq king?"

Nikolai tilted his head in a gesture of respect he did not feel. "My father does not play games of insult, Majesty. On the contrary, he considers this matter one of utmost importance. He entrusted it to me, his heir."

Bin-Lot grunted. "If it's so important, why didn't he come himself?"

"As a king yourself, I have no doubt you understand the importance of overseeing the interests of your kingdom and entrusting such critical issues to people you have trained and in whom you have the utmost confidence."

This prince's responses reminded him of someone else. Yes. That damned priestess. Too calm. Too direct. Bin-Lot shivered at the memory. "You are his heir?"

"I am Crown Prince and, as I previously stated, heir to the throne of Turand."

Bin-Lot rose from his throne and approached Nikolai, scrutinizing the military precision of the prince's appearance. "You present yourself well, Prince Nikolai, although you are overly tall for useful military service. Tall men like you are generally clumsy on the battlefield."

Lord Karanan cast a questioning glance at Stefan, both wondering at the odd turn of direction in Bin-Lot's comments.

Remaining calm, Nikolai responded, "You know that I have come to avoid war between the Sifiq Kingdom and Turand. That is my goal, and the conditions required are simple. End all raids on Turand's mainland, and stop all incursions into Turand's territorial waters. With such an agreement honorably accomplished, there will be no need to prove that I am as well-trained a warrior now as my father was when he defeated the Sifiq occupation army over twenty years ago."

Bin-Lot first emitted a sarcastic laugh. Suddenly, he guffawed heartily. "Boy! Arrogant boy! So proud are you! What an amusement!" Turning to Ambassador Laritha, he said, "You never told me these Turandans had such warped humor."

Before Laritha could utter a response, the king turned back to Nikolai. His sallow face suddenly blazed scarlet with fury. "I am not amused. You must have seen the damage left by that bitch who called herself a priestess—a healer and teacher, she insisted. All she left in her wake was disaster. I hate her and every Turandan who walks the face of this world."

Nikolai's eyes turned coal-black and flashed fire. "All the more reason to avoid my nation, Majesty. Your people should never have abducted our priestesses in the first place. You, sir, never should have condoned the abuse and torture of another nation's citizens taken as unwilling prisoners from their own homeland."

"So, the Turandan prince can speak with fire on his tongue. Perhaps you can explain one thing to me. How did that bitch do this? What power did she wield?"

Subduing burgeoning fury, Nikolai raised his head imperiously. Lord Karanan and Stefan both rose from their seats, uncertain of what to expect. "King Bin-Lot," the prince said in an uncompromising tone, "I respectfully request that you cease your references to her as a bitch. She is a close, highly respected member of my family. I suggest that none of your problems would have occurred had your own military never violated my nation's sovereign borders or our people's rights without murdering or abducting them. As far as the priestess Alexa Maraná is concerned, I understand that she gave you ample warning on many occasions to stop your abuse of her sister priestesses and herself. You ignored those warnings. What you suffered was not her power. What you endured was your own fault and the punishment of our Lord Val when he finally lost patience with your treatment of our High Priestess Valkana."

The Sifiq king remained silent, considering both the explanation and the tone of its delivery. At length, he said, "I always thought she was their leader."

"The priestesses consider her a sister guide more than a leader. That isn't the issue right now. The pressing matter is your continuing raids on Turand. They must stop."

Bin-Lot shook his head. "Go home, boy. Bin-Lot does not take orders from children. My naval officers are always free to take what they want whenever they have the chance. And give your cowardly father a message from me. Never send a child, even one with your potential, to waste my time."

Turning to Ambassador Laritha, he said, "I told you what I want— my ship and Raf-Zan back. At least I enjoyed some rare amusement. Things have gotten boring around here. Don't come back."

"Your Highness, it's freezing out here and well after midnight. Go back inside your cabin."

Nikolai didn't bother to look up. "Ambassador, this was all a game to him. From the beginning."

"It was, I'm afraid. I've almost finished my report to Minister Jemini and the Protectors. May I ask a question?"

"Of course."

"Bin-Lot mentioned a Captain Raf-Zan. Apparently, he blames this captain for additional catastrophes in the Sifiq Kingdom. I distinctly recall your Captain Lynmar's given name being Rafzan. That cannot be a coincidence. Is he Sifiq?"

"I told you. Lynmar is a Turandan citizen," Nikolai replied quietly.

Laritha paused thoughtfully. "I'm trying to comprehend this situation for my personal benefit. I know you said your mother is Valkana and that the Valkana has special abilities, especially when it comes to healing. I also recall your saying Raf-Zan was fatally injured when he arrived in Turand. I'm lost beyond that."

Nikolai finally turned to meet the ambassador's curious gaze. "Raf-Zan put two priestesses and several Sifiq women off his ship in lifeboats in turbulent waters. At the last minute, rage overtook him. My mother was already half-dead from abuse and near-starvation. He tied her to a mast and used a whip on her. After that, he threw her overboard.

"Our Lord Val miraculously saved Mother. At the same time, he intensified the storm that eventually destroyed Raf-Zan's ship. Val punished the captain by inflicting a terrible injury on the hand he used to throw Mother into the ocean. His agony was nearly unbearable—to the point he begged for execution—as the injury progressed up his arm, slowly killing him."

"What happened?"

"My mother happened," Nikolai answered, tears of pride brimming in his eyes. "Mother was dying, but once my father reached her, she found the will to live and recover. Weeks later, I met them at an inn on the road home.

"I'm still unclear why, but she went to Raf-Zan in the middle of a freezing winter's night. After everything she suffered—after his atrocity against her—she summoned Val's Healing Graces. Val healed him. My father and I had to carry her back to the inn afterward."

"I don't think I understand."

"No one understands except Mother. She is Valkana. The next morning, healed, the captain vowed to serve Val and swore allegiance to the throne of Turand. Later, he changed his name to Rafzan Lynmar. As far as we're all concerned, the Sifiq Captain Raf-Zan lives no more."

"Nikolai—if I may call you Nikolai." The elder statesman smiled upon receiving the prince's permission. "I cannot see how such a man can change so completely so quickly."

Nikolai sighed. "The ways of Val are mysterious. I trust Mother's abilities to read his life force. She says he now seeks to live according to Val's ways. If my mother can forgive him, then I must."

"All this talk of war! You might avoid it if you surrender Raf-Zan to Bin-Lot. Would your father risk war over a Sifiq officer who nearly killed your mother?"

Nikolai shifted his gaze heavenward before meeting Laritha's eyes once more. "Ambassador, I pray I will someday find a love as strong and enduring as what my parents share. Father trusts my mother's judgment. Completely. He is also sworn to protect Turand's citizens. Every single one of them. As am I. Now, if you'll excuse me, I think I shall heed your advice and retire for the night."

⟵

Lord Karanan and Sir Stefan Sidano flanked Crown Prince Nikolai inside Minister Jemini's private chambers. The Coloridian Minister of State shook his head regretfully. "I'm sorry, gentlemen. Ambassador Laritha's report does conclude that King Bin-Lot was unreceptive to negotiations. We are able only to encourage dialogue, not require it."

"Excellency, the situation has escalated to a crisis. The Protectors have resolved past disputes with the Sifiq. I respectfully request a personal audience with them to outline Turand's stance in order to avoid more extensive hostilities."

Minister Jemini looked up. He couldn't help but wonder, but Essila had stated the Protectors expected the Sifiq and the Turandans to resolve their own problems. "I'm sorry. The Protectors want no further involvement. You must settle this among yourselves."

"I see. Sir Sidano?" Nikolai said, extending his right hand and accepting two sets of sealed documents. "Minister Jemini, Turand thanks

Coloridia and you for your efforts to help us with the Sifiq. Lord Karanan has already settled our accounts, so there are no outstanding debts to require future communication on that count."

The minister nodded. "We had full faith in Turand. There was no need to address that matter so quickly."

"On the contrary, sir," Nikolai replied. "Although we have no desire to sever diplomatic ties, I regret to advise diplomatic contact, as well as trade relations, may likely suffer in the foreseeable future. This exercise with the Sifiq has been little more than a farce. We have detailed our official assessment in this first packet. Feel free to respond at your convenience once you review its contents. The second document is our official notification to Coloridia that, as of now, Turand is in a state of war with the Sifiq Kingdom. Good day."

Ignoring the minister's attempt at further discussion, the three Turandans turned and departed for ships waiting to carry them home.

Part 2

Heavens splitting with streaks of silver fire
Mountains trembling beneath thunder's roar
Winds blowing forth with their mighty ire
Oceans crashing upon the darkened shore.

Bravely defying stormy, angry waves
On those wrath-filled seas, his ship did rise
So heavy was the air beneath its decks
She thought, just a moment under open skies.

The vessel, as if alive, was pitching, rolling,
Rain thrust as daggers 'gainst smooth, dark skin
From sturdy rails, her fearful grip wrenching.
His warning ignored; terrified, she has fallen.

Her wide-eyed gaze cast up in abject fear
On swollen waves his noble ship does rise
Icy waters sting and bite her body warm
Her eyes close in grief; with her, their heir dies.

Bridges of Turand

Above her, shining bright, the Healing Lights
The mystic, she opens her eyes to four more
Weary and so cold, she shivers and shakes
Two lives spared on this distant, far-flung shore.

Dark beauty drawn by sickness and sorrow
The mystic now lost in this strange land
Her eyes now filled with fever and hope
Sacred Blood she fights to save in Turand.

Through prayer and chant, they call the Divine
Those mystics who beckon sacred light
Save her who speaks in words unknown
Because she is two, who must win her fight.

The battle rages, death must not prevail
Tho' life wanes often, her great heart rallies
Their heir, their love, the Sacred Blood
She must live 'til light their baby sees.

Worn and weary, she kisses that sweet face
At last, the battle won, relieved her heart
Trusting Sacred Blood, heir, and bridge
To these mystics fair; in peace, she now can part.

And years would pass, the mem'ry would fade.
Sacred Blood, heir, and bridge mourned as lost
Sacred Blood, heir, and bridge loved as queen
For her, too, her life offered up as the cost.

Sandra Valencia

Sacred Blood come to Turand, again was lost,
Yet courage continued its sacred flow
Two mothers building future bridges
Their love not yielding their mystic glow.

Then Turand's own mystic survived the storm.
Bloody and weak, washed up on its shore
Beloved by the son, the Sacred Blood heir,
The king, he came, her love for life to restore.

Their children rejoiced; Sacred Blood still flowed.
Then came the dreams she dared not ignore
Back to sea and mountains did she go
Seeking dreams with her king now off to war.

Truth so strange lay close to the distant shore
She, who, too, had fallen into stormy seas
Drawn by Spirits who faced perils and fears
So the priestess could share past agonies.

Joy and sorrow marked bridges to the past
Life of great beauty saved from the seas
Mystic life stolen, begged the new mystic's help
Who opened her heart to two Spirits' pleas.

Sacred Blood had the new mystic carried.
This sacred quest she would now pursue.
With Spirits now tied by blest shared love
The mission this priestess would carry through.

Bridges of Turand

Across forest and dale, o'er mountains high,
The priestess, although she could not know
This quest begged of her by Spirits mystic,
Would guard the precious Sacred Blood flow.

True to her promise, she would journey afar,
Amethyst and pearls carried to garner his heart,
Worn by her, celebrating her children, his heirs,
Unknown to her were once gifts from his heart.

Restored to him, jewels to tame his raging storms
Restored to build bridges to heal his grief-filled past
Restored to defend his unknown heir
Restored by Spirits Mystic for love meant to last.

Bridges of Turand

Chapter 9

E arly that morning, Rafzan Lynmar had rushed from the temple entrance toward the altar alongside King Gregor. Despite an expression of dread mingled with fear, the king had shown little surprise when he saw his wife hovering high in the air. When Rafzan's steps faltered, the king's stride had been firm as he hurried toward the front of the temple. Rafzan finally forced himself forward and knelt behind the king, who waited on his knees beneath their high priestess.

The carillon bells continued pealing their sorrowful strain as Toravalian citizens began filling the sacred space. Gradually, the bells quieted. Brilliant rays of light receded into the pyramid's golden sun, and the Valkana descended as King Gregor rose to his feet. Accepting Lynmar's assistance, Gregor steadied the priestess. Beneath fine golden mesh shielding her face, both men saw rivers of shimmering tears flowing down her cheeks.

"Beloved, our son?" Gregor forced a whisper.

"He is safe. They all are. They're coming home. He felt compelled to deliver the declaration of war."

Rafzan thought back, remembering the sorrow on both their faces. In the Sifiq Kingdom, from the Sifiq king to the lowest officers, declarations of war spawned celebrations. How they celebrated violence and bloodshed! How he had preferred life on sailing vessels because they kept him far from the killing fields his own father loved so much. He never before realized that.

⌒

News regarding Bin-Lot's cavalier behavior toward Turand's peace delegation incensed the nation's population, especially following the Timeri incident. Already preparing for impending war, announcement of the official declaration galvanized all sectors of the country as they hastened the stockpiling of matériel to sustain their military and ensure supplies for those at home. Gregor and Stefan had been sufficiently foresighted to expect additional Sifiq threats. While rebuilding Turand, they had never neglected contingency plans should their old enemy resurface.

"I worry that Victor is traveling this far with Oui-lest so late in her pregnancy," Alexa told Gregor as they reviewed palace security plans.

"His message said she feels fine. I'm glad Anlía will travel home with them from Zinzan. Oui-lest can use the company, and I can worry less."

"My husband, she is safe here. I am sure of it."

Gregor frowned. "I don't like having so many Sifiq in prison here. There's always the risk some might escape."

"From Zenox? I seriously doubt it."

"Alexa, one thing. The guards have their orders should the prisoners attempt an escape. Promise you won't interfere."

"Gregor?"

Cocking his head to one side, he gave her a sharp look. "Remember, Alexa. Wherever and whenever I have to deal with the Sifiq, my methods may appear harsh—even cruel. I will use them only when necessary, but there are times when I must deal with the Sifiq in ways they understand.

They taught me that years ago. Promise me now that you will never interfere when I find myself in those circumstances."

Wincing at memories, she nodded. "I promise."

"Good." Gregor huffed a burdened sigh and walked over to an office window to stare gloomily at the bustle of soldiers and military aides rushing around. "I hate this. The very idea of sending my son off to war." He choked on the words.

Alexa refused to cry. She would hold her tears in check. "The two of you had already decided before he left for the Sifiq Kingdom. If Bin-Lot refused cooperation, you were bound by oath to protect the people of this nation. War is the only option, but is there a different way to wage that war?"

Gregor continued staring out the window. "Alexa, I have asked that question a thousand times in a thousand different ways. The answer is always the same. I cannot protect every corner of my borders all the time. The only possible solution is to stop the Sifiq at their origin of power. That translates to invasion. I don't expect it to be quick. I don't expect it to be easy. I detest the very idea of the cost in lives—ours and theirs. Pray Val, tell me before it's too late. Am I doing the right thing?"

When he turned, dark eyes bored into her. Turbulent questions twisted inside his gut. He understood the risks he was taking, but he also knew the dangers of letting the Sifiq continue their raids unopposed. "Alexa?"

"Gregor," she finally said, "we've discussed this. More than anything, I trust your judgment. Beyond that, your planning has been meticulous. Bin-Lot is laughing. He thinks this declaration of war is just posturing—a joke. The last thing in the world he expects is an invasion. You have that in your favor. Nikolai will lead the initial thrust. You follow shortly thereafter. Let there be no doubt. The two of you have a tremendous task ahead of you. Still, you will be defending home. Bin-Lot gave you no choice."

Gregor lifted his hands to cradle her face between his palms. "My beautiful Alexa. I will stop him. I swear it. He made his mistake when he hurt you. If it is the last thing I ever do, I will stop them from ever again threatening Turand."

⤚

"She doesn't believe me when I say she looks beautiful. What do you think, Alexa?"

"I agree with you, Victor. She looks lovely," Alexa said, grinning widely.

"There," Victor said. "You aren't allowed to argue anymore. Alexa is Valiria, and Valiria are not permitted to lie."

Oui-lest blushed and laughed. "I surrender. I only feel as if all of me might burst at any moment." Everyone laughed with her before Victor kissed the top of her head before excusing himself to meet the king at the palace.

Once Adrina served tea, the women settled to chat about the progress of Oui-lest's pregnancy and the trip from Garogan City. All three appreciated the chance to catch up about friends in Garogan and the Sidano and Toscano clans.

Trying to avoid the topic of war, Alexa asked, "Oui-lest, will you stay here until after the baby comes?"

Oui-lest nodded. "Yes, I told Victor I would feel better being close to you and Adrina. Our staff at home is very kind, but I'm not as comfortable with them as I am with you."

"Oh, Oui-lest, I'm sure you just need extra time. You haven't had any problems, have you?"

"No, none. It's just…"

Alexa sensed her anxiety. "Oui-lest, you are now Lady Oui-lest Garogan. Don't forget that. This war is with the Sifiq king and military, not you."

"I know, but I am still Sifiq. I also remember the people I left behind. Not all of them were bad."

Nodding, Alexa said, "I know. I even met some decent men."

"Alexa, I understand why we're going to war. I do. It just frightens me. It really does. I sometimes wake up at night, shaking and sick."

Adrina slid closer to her sister-in-law on the couch. "Oui-lest, we're all frightened. We all know someone leaving with one of the armies. Look at Alexa. Gregor and Nikolai are both going. You and I are fortunate that our husbands are staying here to coordinate war efforts."

Tears started to slide down Oui-lest's cheeks, and she began to stroke her rounded stomach. "I'm afraid, Adrina. I don't know why, but I am afraid."

～

Velvet darkness enveloped the woods outside the palace. Anlía perched on top of the boulder that had witnessed her mother's long-ago flight from a Sifiq soldier and, more recently, her godfather's efforts to encourage her brothers and sisters after her mother's mystical midnight visit while still a Sifiq captive. Gazing up at stars through branches only beginning to don spring buds, she hummed an ancient melody her father used to sing to her when she felt sad. A few minutes later, she heard footsteps crunching through leftover fall leaves.

"Such a beautiful sound filling the night woods, but should you be out here alone?"

Just as she looked around, a cloud bank broke, freeing moonbeams to shine on her face. "Rafzan. I didn't expect you to be walking about so late."

"These woods have become my haven when I need a quiet place to think. Now you've invaded my refuge and sent my thoughts scattering in every direction."

"My apologies, dear Captain Lynmar. I shall be more careful in the future."

"What was that you were humming? It was so sweet and uplifting."

"*Soar Free Upon the Breeze*. A very old song Father used to sing to me. He could always make me feel better with that song. You should hear him sing."

Rafzan leaned against a tree and gazed at her. "You love your father very much."

"I adore Father. I can't imagine life without him." She chuckled at a secret memory. "When I was born, the doctor couldn't come fast enough. Father delivered me."

"Your father?" Rafzan asked incredulously. "A Sifiq man would never consider doing such a thing."

"Father was with mother each time one of us was born. He said such miracles were not to be missed."

Rafzan shook his head. "Your father amazes me. I hardly know my father, nor do I want to. My memory of him is so…"

"So what?" Anlía asked, feeling a jolt from his life force.

"Surely your mother told you." Unsure if she knew, he closed his eyes, shutting out the raw childhood image. "When I was five, I watched my father ram a sword through my mother's heart."

Anlía slid down from her perch and went to him. Resting a palm against the side of his face, she didn't simply see his sorrow. She felt it. "I didn't know you were there. That explains so much."

"Until I came to Turand, my mother was the only person who ever spoke about loving me. My father was determined to fill me with the rage that destroyed her. For years, he succeeded. Anlía, do you understand now why I wrote that your mother saved me?"

"I do. She helped you discover the real Rafzan you were meant to be."

How very beautiful she looked with her eyes reflecting moonlight. The faintest floral scent of what he now knew to be lilac floated around her, teasing his nostrils with intoxicating effect. It didn't matter that she was a little taller than he. Of their own volition, his arms wound around her, pulling her warmth against him, allowing him to glory in the feel of her feminine curves against his hard, masculine body.

Unable to resist, he kissed her. He indulged in the sweetest, most exquisite bond imaginable as his lips tentatively touched hers. Slowly, he increased the pressure, deepening the kiss until the taste of her threatened to undo him completely. Forcing himself to part from her, he traced her tender lower lip with his index finger.

"My sweet Anlía. You are such a dream, but one I'm not sure I dare to dream. Let me savor this moment for now." He kissed her once more before wishing her goodnight and watching protectively as she returned to the palace.

🌩

Rising from her knees, Alexa looked upward one final time at the softly glowing crystal pyramid suspended above the temple's altar. Drawing in a deep breath, she softly said, "Is Gregor still meeting with Nikolai?"

"I think they went to the library. You should join them. I believe they could use your encouragement."

Finally turning around, she said, "I fear I was lost in prayer. How long have you been here?"

Victor gazed thoughtfully at her. "Long enough. I'm worried about you."

"I admit to being a little worried for myself. Sending my son to fight a war is…"

Her trembling lips broke his heart, and he reached out to embrace her. "Your message from the altar this afternoon was inspiring when our people needed it most, but you need to take to heart what you channeled from Lord Val. Sweetest, Nikolai is blessed. Of that, I'm sure."

"Victor," she murmured, "I do trust Val. I just wish I could explain. Your child isn't yet born. You can't know how it feels."

Closing his eyes, Victor choked back the response that nearly crossed his lips. How long had it taken to reconcile himself to the fact that Nikolai was Gregor's son instead of his? Had he ever? Alexa had allowed him years to bond with her son. Yet, in that secret, guarded place inside his heart, he would always think of Niko as his own. After all, had he not saved them both while she still carried Niko?

Dismissing the thought, he said comfortingly, "Go to them. They need you, and you need them."

She hugged him tightly. "Thank you, Victor. You always seem to be around when I need you most."

He nearly choked. "Sweetest, I always have been. I always will be."

Victor watched as she straightened, donned the brave countenance she would show her family, and left. Hearing his name and then glancing around, he noticed Captain Lynmar for the first time, kneeling in a nearby row of pews. "Lynmar."

Lynmar acknowledged the terse greeting while dipping his head respectfully. "If I may. Our queen gracefully carries heavy burdens. I am grateful to Val that she is blessed with a friendship such as yours."

Recalling they were inside Val's sacred temple, Victor tamped down his disdain for the man in front of him. "You do recall…"

"I've forgotten nothing, Lord Garogan. Not a day passes that I don't pray to Val to express my sorrow for what I did to her. You could never revile me for what I did as much as I do myself. Still, she led me to Val's love and forgiveness."

Lynmar rose and sidestepped into the central aisle as he prepared to depart. "I wish to hurry to make sure she returns safely to the palace. Before I go, I accept your hatred because I earned it. Just know that I would gladly lay down my life to protect her or her family. Her forgiveness is an undeserved gift I treasure and never take for granted. May Val bless your evening, Lord Garogan."

Victor stared after Captain Lynmar's retreating figure. The man would have to satisfy himself with Alexa's forgiveness and Gregor's apparent acceptance of his presence. Victor knew too well that he could never erase his memories of Alexa on Timeri's beach that stormy night or her cries of pain and fevered whimpers as he struggled to keep her alive while awaiting Gregor's arrival from Toraval.

Clenching his eyelids shut against tormented thoughts, he reminded himself that those days had also brought the wife who now gave him comfort and delight. She also carried the baby who would continue the Garogan legacy. He found the ability to smile. Oui-lest was a joy. Second love was beautiful, too.

⤸

Spring breezes wafted through the tree branches and stirred the top layer of dried leaves carpeting the ground. With the toe of her boot, Anlía drew a curving line through the damp layer beneath. Upon hearing faint sounds approaching through the dark woods, she turned. "Rafzan."

Furtively looking around to be sure they were alone in the depths of the woodland preserve, Rafzan opened his arms to receive her. Drawing in a deep breath, he sighed. "How beautiful you look in the moonlight," he whispered. "How glad I am to see you tonight."

Tilting her face backward, she gazed into his blue eyes. "How can you imagine I wouldn't come for a private farewell?"

"For that, I am glad." Surrendering to clamoring emotions, he claimed her lips in a tender kiss. "I love you, Anlía. I know I shouldn't, but I do love you."

She kissed him, allowing herself freedom to accept the vibrancy of his exploring tongue and the sensations it evoked. Breathless, she finally broke their connection. "Rafzan, you don't have to go. You're a civilian."

He caressed her face near her temple. "Dear Anlía, I must. I swore loyalty to your parents. Something inside tells me I must go to help protect your father and brother—for your sake as much as theirs. Besides, the Sifiq people need change, and people like my mother still suffer. I owe it to her memory to fight for that change."

Tears glimmered in Anlía's eyes. Then, looking downward, she pushed her hand inside her pocket and withdrew a folded, lace-edged scarf. "I embroidered the lilacs on this a long time ago. Mother taught me how. I want you to have it. Keep it with you to remember me."

Rafzan lifted the silky fabric to his face and inhaled the lilac-scented fragrance, her scent. "As if I could ever forget you," he teased. "Thank you. I'll keep it with me always."

Almost desperately, Rafzan Lynmar then embraced the young woman who had inspired him to dream. With her in his arms, life held fresh meaning as he relished the tightening of her arms around him. Perhaps he would dare to love her if only he could survive returning to his homeland. Reluctantly easing away from her, he allowed himself the luxury of extra seconds to appreciate her extraordinary beauty before indulging in a final parting kiss.

↩

"Beloved, you must promise to be careful while I'm away. Our people will rely on you for leadership in my absence." Gregor's features reflected the grave direction of both his thoughts and emotions as he watched his wife perform her longstanding habit of smoothing the fabric of his shirtsleeves as he dressed for this morning of farewells to his family and departure from home. For a fleeting moment, he thought how most noblemen relied on manservants and valets for the ritual of dressing. How very glad he was to share this intimate task with his wife, especially at times like this.

"You know I'll do my best. I am both Queen and Valkana. My service will be to you, our family, and our people—as Val directs me."

"That's what sometimes concerns me most, especially in light of the growing frequency of these strange dreams you've been having."

His eyebrows lifted questioningly. Alexa's expression alone confirmed his perception of the inner agitation provoked by the continuing dreams that had begun shortly after her trip to the battlefield years earlier to save his life. The dreams had been sporadic and infrequent—until recently. Since her return from the Sifiq Kingdom, they had come more often and with greater intensity. Gregor's concern for her burgeoned despite her assurances that she associated no sense of fear with the dreams, only intense curiosity and something she described as an odd connection of critical importance.

"Gregor, my love, you mustn't worry about me. I am fine. I will be fine. You forget how much Val reveals to me through dreams and visions." She raised her hand to stroke his cheek. "It was through a dream that he awakened me to exactly how much I loved you."

Gregor swallowed and forced a smile. "So you told me." Wrapping her in a tight embrace, he inhaled the lilac fragrance in her hair and savored the feel of her body against his. He had made love to her last night and earlier this morning, knowing that such perfect pleasure might never again be his. Slowly releasing her, he gazed down into the emerald eyes reflecting the soul that made his life whole. She had sent him off to war once before without tears. It appeared she would do the same again, although he could already feel her sorrow and loneliness.

"I love you, Alexa. I think it impossible for any man to love a woman more than I have loved you. No matter what happens, remember that. I will do everything I can to end this war quickly."

Taking a tremulous breath, she smiled. "You are courageous and strong, my husband. Trust in Val so that he might guide you and our armies. Meet our son. Defeat our enemy so they will leave us in peace. Then come home to me."

$\backsim$

Déjà vu. Wagons lined up in the distance, laden with supplies for the week-long trip to Port Timeri and beyond. Horses whickered, and harnesses jangled as they tossed their heads. Colorful banners identified different regiments and fluttered in the breeze. Soldiers stood ready to mount. Having listened to their king's inspiring speech, they now waited for a blessing from their beloved Valkana.

Alexa stepped up to the podium in Toraval's grand square and held her arms out to pray just as she had done years earlier when Gregor prepared to lead his army southward to deal with the insurrection threatening to destroy his nation. This time, her husband would leave with an army and newly invented weapons to reinforce the initial invasion force her son had led from Turand two weeks earlier. She fervently prayed for the safety of Turand's armies, just as she prayed for a quick end to hostilities so that there would be minimal loss of life on all sides. Finally, she prayed that Val would restore Turand to a state of peace.

With the prayer and blessing complete, Alexa waited while her children tearfully hugged their father goodbye. As Alexa finally approached him, her memory reverted to his frantic lovemaking earlier that morning—his sweeping caresses and deep, stirring kisses that even now left vibrating vestiges inside her body. She would not send him away remembering her in tears. Instead, she smiled for him.

Stroking wind-tossed tresses from her face, Gregor smiled. "I hate leaving you with all the responsibility for our children and our country, but I trust no one more. Can you forgive me?"

She nodded, her eyes roving over every cherished feature. "My beloved husband, promise me again you'll be careful. I must have you back. I need you."

"I have every intention of coming home. You must write and tell me if you figure out those dreams of yours." He paused. "Alexa, whatever happens, never forget how much I love you." Bending forward, he kissed her, hoping that he would indeed return to the woman and the nation he was willing to defend with his life.

Chapter 10

"Stefan, I must stay informed. You will send all important dispatches to me via both Lord Manaran and Master Telindra?" Alexa's voice sounded brisk as she pulled on riding gloves while standing at the top of the palace steps and preparing to leave.

Stefan huffed an exasperated sigh. "Of course, but I still fail to understand why you're leaving at such a critical time. Gregor just departed Port Fosan for the Sifiq Kingdom, and we're left to train additional troops, guard our shores, and maintain national morale. In the meantime, you go traipsing off to Val knows where for what? To seek the reason behind some dream?"

"Stefan," Alexa responded patiently, "I would not except my intuition tells me this is the right and proper time. It is necessary. Victor is staying here to help you. DiMarco is young, but his organizational skills are excellent. As a prince, it is his duty and his responsibility to assist you. Also, I sent word to Zinzan requesting Master Maconti be released from classes and sent here. He will come with tutors for him and Anlía so they can also work on official tasks. Both are very capable."

Stefan's gray eyes sparked with dismay and surprise, but he knew better than to argue. Through many years working with Alexa, he had learned to judge her moods and decisions. While he disagreed with the timing of this journey from the capital due to circumstances and safety concerns, dissuading her would be impossible. She had also already arranged to smooth his management of official affairs during her absence.

"How long will you be away?"

"I'm not quite sure. I'll keep you advised." Directing an intense gaze at her husband's closest confidant, Alexa finally smiled. "Stefan, I trust you. Of all people, you should know I would never leave Toraval at a time like this if I didn't believe it absolutely necessary. I have asked this of you before. Long ago. Please, Stefan. Trust me."

Stefan closed his eyes and swallowed—so hard that he felt the spittle land with the weight of a boulder inside the pit of his stomach. Nodding, he looked back at her. "I remember. I trust you. And, Alexa, I will pray for you."

⌐

Alexa sat attentively on the leather sofa in front of a rustic stone fireplace in the country manor of Master Telindra, a well-respected landowner with sprawling farmlands on Fosan Province's southwestern border. A crackling fire dispelled the chill of outside temperatures that defied late springtime. Gray skies lent an eerie feel to the evening and added to the ambiance of mystery surrounding the history and legends of the bordering region the locals called Zemtoval.

"According to Mother, the year mentioned in that journal is remembered for particularly bad spring storms. One was so powerful that the ocean swept far inland and washed away entire villages, including the Valiria Faith Community at Zemtoval. Most of the priestesses escaped. Several returned to help the few survivors of the catastrophe."

"I'm curious, Solton. Why was the area never resettled?"

Solton Telindra shrugged broad shoulders. "Superstition, I suppose. Fear, mostly. That was what? Almost seventy-one years ago? Turand already suffered the ill effects of the fall from faith. People in rural areas tend to cling to faith more than city folk. They saw the storms and tidal wave as punishment—an omen. When tales of spirits and ghosts started, most people avoided Zemtoval altogether."

Alexa sighed heavily. "Ghosts and spirits. I had my share of those at Zinzan, but I understand why they appeared at Zinzan. At Zemtoval, I do not. Do you?"

Her host rose from his brown leather chair and walked to stand in front of the fireplace. Although not a tall man, his well-proportioned body was strong from years of overseeing successful farming operations on his estate. He draped one arm across the mantel and gazed at large logs burning on the grate. "I do not, unless it was the shock of sudden deaths. I'm quite certain the Valiria set to peace any restless spirits. My opinion is that any ghosts or spirits are most likely the results of vivid imaginations magnifying the strange mists that blow down from the flanks of the Zemfosa Mountains. With fog often blowing in off the Fosan Sea just to the north, conditions are ripe for all sorts of strange images to form."

"That makes more sense." Alexa stood and stared thoughtfully into the fire before meeting Telindra's waiting gaze. "I am grateful for the maps. We plan to leave early in the morning, so I shall bid you goodnight. Thank you again for your help."

"Alexa, I hope you find whatever it is you seek. Do promise me one thing—that you'll be careful. My wife may be dead, but I would still hate to face her mother, even at her age, if she thought I let something happen to you."

Alexa chuckled. "Lady Lorinda is as protective as ever. My mother's cousin always was a handful, wasn't she?"

"As was her daughter, but I always loved them both. Goodnight."

The following morning, Alexa shivered and tugged her hood firmly around her face as she waved farewell to Solton Telindra before Tirstan Fratino signaled his troops to head out the winding, tree-lined path to the road leading toward the ocean and the deserted Zemtoval region. If Solton's maps were accurate, the journey should take about three days as long as the weather held.

Alexa murmured a fervent prayer, sensing greater urgency with every mile they traveled as lush countryside thinned into straggling trees along the gray and brown crags of the foothills of the soaring Zemfosa Mountains. The changing scenery prompted a change in mood. Alexa was glad for the company of newly anointed Valiria priestess Jalisa Kaminda. The two priestesses started and ended each day with meditative prayers that fortified them for the strenuous riding and the growing tension in their travel companions.

On the fourth morning after departing the Telindra manor, Tirstan fretted over maps and fumed that they must have missed the road turning toward Zemtoval. Shaking his head in frustration, he cast a disgusted expression skyward. "Master Telindra said three days. We have missed the turn. We must backtrack."

Alexa approached him and placed a reassuring hand on his arm. "We have stopped many times to remove fallen trees and other debris impeding our path. That is why we're delayed. My dear Tirstan, you read maps as well as anyone I know—even perhaps better than Lord Garogan. We will continue."

"Lady Valkana…"

"I will help," she interrupted as those emerald eyes glittered brightly, and blue light began to shimmer and cascade around her figure.

Since the civil war, he had accompanied her on missions all around Turand. He had protected her, prayed with her, and spent untold hours in her company. Yet, despite all that time, the appearance of that iridescent aura still wielded sufficient power to set torrents of shivers rolling down his spine and leave him awestruck. Catching his breath, he nodded. "We leave in ten minutes."

Thankfully, the day and the road were clear. With Captain Fratino and Alexa leading, the troop progressed steadily until Alexa suddenly pulled forward and halted her horse. The captain threw up his hand, signaling a halt, and watched as his high priestess turned her head from side to side. Electrifying tingles lifted the hairs along his neck as he recalled memories of his very first frantic journey with her during the civil war. She had done much the same then, guided by unseen forces that never seemed to fail her.

Seconds passed. Her shimmering aura softened and dissipated. She turned in the saddle and pointed to the right. "The road to Zemtoval is there. The morning is late already. There's a clearing here and a stream. We can rest the horses and eat before continuing. What do you think?"

"Gentlemen," Tirstan called out, "we stop here. Eat and rest your horses. Make sure four sentries are posted at all times. Alert, men! We're close to the ocean. I want no unwelcome surprises."

Alexa grinned. "I appreciate your caution, Captain, but no Sifiq are coming this time."

"I intend to take no chances, Your Majesty," Fratino countered, his voice firm and uncompromising. "If I let something happen to you involving the Sifiq and live to face your husband, I dread to think what he might do to me. Worse than that, I cannot bear to think what I would do to myself."

"Perish the thought. We're safe, Tirstan. Trust me."

As the two priestesses shared the last two sweet cakes packed by Solton's cook, Jalisa lifted questioning eyes to Alexa. "Milady, may I ask you something?"

Alexa's eyebrows lifted. "Of course."

"Do I only imagine recently hearing you ask people you've known a long time to trust you?"

The question from Alexa's young protégé prompted a smile. "You imagine nothing. This journey comes at a most inopportune time and carries me to a very unusual destination. It makes little sense, even to me. However, I've learned to trust the messages our Lord Val sends in visions and dreams. I trust without always understanding until the meaning unravels with time. Do you also have doubts?"

Jalisa looked down as she brushed crumbs from her riding skirt. Pursing her lips together and tilting her head sideways, she sighed. "I do not. When I vowed to serve Val and offer aid to his priestess Valkana, I chose faith as my method of trust. You survived the great persecution for a reason. You also survived Sifiq abduction and imprisonment for a reason. Val highly favors you. I trust you without question, but I do admit that I am certainly curious."

Alexa grinned and hugged the younger woman. "As am I, dear one. As am I."

⤳

Hours later, leading skittish horses, the priestesses trudged along the path hacked by several guards through thick, tangled overgrowth. Hewn stones, laid long ago to pave a road, were now pushed apart by plant roots determined to rise skyward and thwart efforts of passersby wishing to journey to the sea. Weary soldiers and priestesses alike stubbornly shoved aside broken branches, clinging stems, and the sharp ends of chopped saplings.

"Your Majesty! Look!" Captain Fratino called out.

Just ahead of lead soldiers, she saw the road curve toward an open area covered in less dense vegetation. In the distance, late afternoon sunshine cast misty light on what must be the desolate ruins of the ghost village of Zemtoval. Her eyes roved over a scene she faintly recalled from one of the dreams; only then, Zemtoval and the faith center had been bustling with life. That was before the deadly tide had struck. Reaching out with all her senses, she felt no threat, no angry spirits. Drawing in a deep breath, Alexa nodded in satisfaction. Her real search for answers could finally begin.

⌣

"Milady, the men just uncovered a well. The water is clean and sweet. We won't have to search for a stream."

"Some good news. Is everyone settled for the night?"

"We are. I see what Master Telindra meant about the mist on the foothills. It forms little clouds that look like ghosts. No wonder people fear coming here." The captain glanced all around the camp. "All seems quiet. Sentries are posted. You should rest now."

Alexa smiled into the concerned face of the Captain of her Guard. "Don't worry so, Tirstan. I shall retire soon."

"Good."

Looking up, Alexa marveled at the brilliance of the moon and the sparkle of stars scattered across the heavens. For a moment, she wondered if Gregor might be gazing up at the sky at that very moment. A soothing warmth suddenly floated through her veins. She felt his thoughts, his emotions. He was staring at those same stars and thinking of her. There was no doubt, so she smiled, rose from her seat in front of the campfire, and bade Tirstan a silent goodnight.

⌣

"Milady, the tidal wave destroyed the entire town. Most buildings were completely crushed. The center where the Valiria lived fared better because of its stone construction, but the damage is still astonishing." Aided by two soldiers, Tirstan pushed aside a broken support column so they could enter what would have served as a teaching and study center. Extending his arm, he said, "Here, let me help you."

Cautiously stepping over piles of rubble, Alexa entered what had been a spacious salon. There, priestesses of her order had once studied the principles and practices related to their faith while preparing to take solemn vows they would honor throughout their lives. All that remained was a battered shell filled with broken furniture, collapsed shelves, and moldy, rotting books.

"Milady?" Jalisa's quiet voice was hardly more than a whisper and drew a solemn shake of Fratino's head. Long experience with Alexa made him keenly aware of her moods and reactions in unusual settings.

Slowly, Alexa's eyelids closed. Then, with hands outstretched, she turned a circle. "What I seek is not here. Let's proceed to the next building."

Jalisa's eyebrows lifted sharply in question. Before she could speak, Fratino placed a finger against his lips and again shook his head. He understood what the young priestess did not yet know. Something very specific was summoning their Valkana, and her senses needed no interruptions if she were to hear its call.

The next two buildings yielded no more success than the first. Broken furniture, piles of shattered glass, scurrying rats, and decomposing animal remains made entry difficult and dangerous. Water stains reached halfway up the walls. Sections of walls not stained by invading seawater were cracked and peeling, the color of paint or paper indistinguishable after years of exposure to the elements. Patiently, Tirstan Fratino guided the high priestess as she assessed each room and its contents. Silently, he waited while she allowed her senses to probe every corner until she was ready to move on.

Leading her safely outside into fresh air, the captain waited while she looked around the derelict center. "Milady, a suggestion. Only two large structures remain that appear safe enough to enter. Why don't we walk around the grounds first? Perhaps you can get a better feel for what it is you seek."

Nodding agreement, Alexa murmured, "Everyone else can stay here. Tirstan, I want only you to accompany me. You understand me best."

"As you wish." Instructing a lieutenant to keep careful watch, the captain then gently grasped Alexa's arm and asked which direction she wished to go.

Glancing right first, she then turned left toward a steep incline. "There, I think. We shall start there."

The base of the small hill was littered with broken stone benches, smashed statues, and other assorted debris that the tidal wave had deposited in its destructive wake. Alexa studied bits and pieces of statuary and quickly realized they were skirting the edge of a cemetery lying at the top of the hill. Glad to be wearing thick gloves and sturdy boots, she pushed aside chunks of rock, large shells, and even rusted cooking pots until she found the chipped edges of stone steps chiseled into the hillside. With Tirstan's help, she slowly climbed upward to the long-deserted graveyard.

"I don't think the tidal wave reached this high," Alexa remarked. "The grave markers show signs of weathering from age. Winds have tipped some over. But, except for needing a good cleaning, it doesn't look too bad."

With Tirstan securely clinging to her arm, Alexa began walking around the cemetery, which provided the consecrated resting place for members of the Order of Val who had died while in service at Zemtoval. Her voice lifted a sweet, prayerful hymn of praise for their spirits as they paused at stone markers. Although she had known none of these servants to Val, their connection by faith superseded time. Both she and Tirstan physically felt the presence of spirits who were grateful that Val's newest High Priestess Valkana blessed them in song.

As the notes of Alexa's hymn floated away on the afternoon breeze, she stopped at a grave in the cemetery's far corner. Kneeling, she began pulling away the tangle of weeds growing over mounded stones and brushed away layers of leaves that had nearly hidden the flat marker. Then, glancing over her shoulder at Tirstan, she said, "Please help me clear this off."

When the two finally stood, they were covered in dirt, woody stems, and shards of mildewed leaves. Alexa, however, looked pleased that the grave was relatively clean. Stepping back, she closed one eye, intently studying the mound. "Curious. Very curious, don't you think?"

Tirstan's dark brows raised. "I'm not sure what you mean, Milady."

Once again, Alexa knelt beside the marker. Then, removing a glove, she picked up a small stick and, using it and her fingernail, scraped dirt from the carving. "This, Tirstan. This is the beginning. Whoever lies here is part of my answer."

"Who is it?"

"I have no idea. The name is strange to me. It is written Mishkla Krisantal. But when you stand, look at the size of this mound. How large it is!"

Seeing what she meant, he shivered involuntarily. "We should return to camp. We can come back tomorrow if you like."

"No. Wait for me at the steps. I'll stay a while longer. Then we can go down before it gets dark."

Alexa allowed the sounds and scents of Zemtoval's spring afternoon to create a cocoon of peace around her. She needed to shield herself from all of the recent fear and preparations surrounding the war with the Sifiq. Val had a purpose in bringing her here, and she must not fail to learn why.

As all outside worries fell away, rhythms of past life vibrated into her consciousness. The beautiful sailing ship no longer rode the waves beneath sun-kissed skies. Instead, monstrous winds tossed the vessel up and down. She had thought only to breathe fresh air. The inner confines of the craft were closing in on her, making her feel sicker than ever in her condition. Her beloved husband had tried so hard to console her, but he just couldn't understand. A few minutes were all she needed. He wouldn't even notice she was gone. Just a few minutes, but then the mammoth wave had crashed over the bow. Even her great strength had not been enough to clutch that rail without losing her balance.

She was swept overboard. Falling. Falling. Falling. She hit the water and wondered at the miracle of not being struck by the ship as it madly leapt from one giant swell to the next. Suddenly, all turned black until she awoke on a beach beneath a dome of dancing lights with four women dressed in lavender robes kneeling around her.

Tirstan stirred when Alexa's hand came to rest on his shoulder. When he turned, the pale face he saw frightened him. "Milady, you are unwell. Let me help you down."

"You mustn't worry, Tirstan. I'm fine—just somewhat overwhelmed. And, to be perfectly honest, a little weak. I should eat something."

"Thanks be to Val." He hesitated before asking, "Do you know who it is yet?"

Alexa shook her head. "Not yet. What I do know is that Mishkla Krisantal was a woman who came to Turand after falling from a ship during a squall. I think she may have been with child. She must have been on the verge of death when she was found on the beach by four Valiria."

"And?" he asked, seeing the bewildered expression on his queen's face.

"We are somehow connected. I have no idea how that can possibly be. Perhaps it is only that we have both gone overboard into the sea during a storm. But I feel it's something more. Something so much more."

"It can wait, Milady. When you have eaten and rested, you can more easily consider the matter and what next to do."

⌒

Dawn had not yet unfurled its colorful tendrils heralding morning's arrival when Alexa emerged from the small tent she shared with Jalisa. Yet another dream had disturbed several hours of deep sleep. This one had taken her back to that terrible moment she plummeted into raging seas off the Timeri coast. Mishkla—whoever she was—had experienced similar terror, although hers had been magnified because of the baby she carried.

Knowing she would sleep no more that night, Alexa stood and stared into the waning fire. A guard on sentry duty asked if she needed help. Assuring him all was well, she silently walked the perimeter of their camp, pausing several times to thank other sentries for their vigilance.

In the quiet of night, she stopped to listen. In the distance, she heard the ocean rolling up on shore. After morning prayers and breakfast, she could walk to the beach and get a feel for where the Valiria had found and saved their hapless storm victim. Afterward, they would return to the faith center to check the final two buildings.

Hours later, Alexa laughed as she closed her eyes and lifted her face to sunny skies. "Take heart, Captain! At least we have a fine, clear day for a walk along the shore!"

Muttering under his breath that at least he could see no Sifiq vessels for miles, Tirstan Fratino reminded accompanying guards to stand ready for any possible menace. Never far from his mind was the Sifiq incursion that ended the Kisana Mission with his queen's abduction and the murders of nine guardsmen. Glancing around and seeing her suddenly drop to her knees, he broke into a run.

"Your Majesty! Are you all right? Have you hurt yourself?" Then, as he had many times through the years, Tirstan grew instantly silent and watched in fascination.

With long fingers fanned out, Alexa's hands floated small circles inches above the surface of fine-grained taupe sand. Although her eyes were tightly closed, her face turned toward the sea and the rushing sounds of incoming tides. Her fingertips, with nails no longer cracked and broken from forced labor, dipped down the moment the leading edge of foamy seawater rolled up. The water kissed her fingers as if in homage and, stopping short of her feet, slid back to the sea.

"This is where she came ashore. I feel faint traces of her life force as well as the Healing Graces that the Valiria summoned to her aid. Hers was a powerful spirit, one I cannot read, yet I feel its strength and its connection." Alexa stood and slapped her hands together to knock sand away. "I'm at a loss, Tirstan. Let's go back."

After a brief rest and eating the midday meal, Alexa sat to peer at stained pages in a large book Jalisa had pulled from a top shelf in the building they had entered first after their arrival. "It appears to be a documentary archive that includes records of those interred at the cemetery. Unfortunately, some pages are stuck, so I've been trying to dry them in the sun."

"You took a risk going in to look for this, Jalisa, but one I do appreciate. Let me see." With a slow sweep of her hands over thick rag paper, Alexa availed herself of Val's gifts that had intensified since her return from the Sifiq Kingdom. Heeding intuition, she slid a nail between pages near the back of the large volume and gently pried apart the edges until the paper separated.

Laying the book out on a makeshift table, the priestesses studied neatly penned entries. A tranquil smile crossed Alexa's face. "You did well, Jalisa. Here is the entry." She proceeded to read aloud, "Corner

Plot North-One-Right. Mishkla Krisantal. Death following childbirth and injuries after washing onto shore at Zemtoval during a storm. Wife. Mother. Unclear origin. May her spirit rest with Val."

"The child lived?" Jalisa asked in surprise.

"Apparently. There's no indication the baby died," Alexa said, running her index finger across the notation as her stomach lurched in response to this curious shred of information. "Please continue to air this out as much as you can. Especially here, place some dry fabric between the pages to keep them clean and separated. We need to wrap this register carefully before we leave. Now I must see what else I can find."

With Tirstan at her heels, Alexa hurried toward the two structures they had not yet searched. She decided one, a storage facility, was unlikely worth much effort. With its long loggia and broken windows, the second building had probably served as offices and dormitories for priestesses at the center. Clearing a pathway to an arched doorway required efforts from four guards and several horses, but Alexa soon clambered over rubble into what was once a foyer leading to a spacious common room.

As in the previous buildings they had entered, waterlines on the walls showed the tide had filled the rooms more than halfway to the ceilings. Furnishings had been tumbled about and broken, then left to mold and mildew. There had been no practical way to enter the damaged facility, so virtually nothing had been salvaged. Fresh air invading through broken windows and doors eased the stifling effect of lingering mold and accu-mulated debris, making breathing easier. Still, Alexa cautioned everyone to cover their faces as they moved through darkened corridors.

Stopping at an opening where floodwaters had forced a door off its hinges, Alexa pushed her way into an office. Rays of afternoon sun filtered into the dreary room where desk and chairs had long since floated out of well-ordered positions. Books in cases near the floor had been destroyed. Shelves screwed high into the walls were intact. Pensively, Alexa gazed upward. A bound leather satchel captured her attention. Tall as she was, it was just beyond her reach. Looking around, she saw nothing safe to climb on.

Eyeing her dubiously, Tirstan shook his head. "You are taller than I, Milady, but I am stronger than you. I'll give you a boost, but we both may take a tumble."

Alexa's responding grin set the captain's mind at ease. "I'll help you. And I'll grab it quickly."

With his hands locked firmly beneath her boot, Tirstan gave a lift. She felt feather-light as she rose from the floor, grasped the pouch, and then stepped nimbly down again. How often did he have to remind himself of her different nature as Valkana? The satisfied smile on her face amused him as he straightened and dusted himself off. "Now what?"

Clutching the brown leather satchel to her chest, she swayed slightly. "This is what I need. We can return to camp now. I want to look inside but not here."

Seated once again at the makeshift table in camp, Alexa carefully undid the bindings of the timeworn satchel. Inside, she found a few musty documents and an old journal. Shifting the loose papers beneath the book, she opened the journal's cover. It had belonged to the center's senior priestess. As before, Alexa let her intuition guide her until she reached the section of the journal calling to her and then started reading aloud a series of entries.

Our mystery patient is very ill. The Healing Graces delivered her from the brink of death, so she must be a woman of faith. She continues to suffer. I believe she fights more for the life of her baby than her own. We do not understand her language, so we make hand signs and draw pictures. With difficulty, we learned her name is Mishkla Krisantal.

Mishkla has been with us for two months now. Her health improves, and she smiles when her baby moves. Still, she is sad. She points to a ring on her hand and then pictures she draws. She is telling us she misses her husband, I am sure. She is of majestic proportions. I wonder if her husband is the same.

Mishkla grows restless. Her lungs are congested again. We continue with all the herbal treatments we know. The Healing Graces come to her and give relief, but they do not heal her completely. Is it because she does not know Val, or is it because her life is meant to be short? There is such kindness and goodness in her. I feel it. Why has Val delivered this strange woman into our care?

The time for Mishkla's baby is near. I am worried. She communicated to me that, should she die, she wants the child to receive her ring, her necklace, and her jeweled brooch. She has written something in her own language for the child, too. Odd. The necklace is triangular, similar to Val's pyramid. How I wish we better understood one another.

The baby is coming. The timing is good because we have received premonitions of a coming catastrophe. Priestesses are already evacuating the center and sending word to the townspeople. Three others will stay with me to care for Mishkla. We should have just enough time.

Alexa paused, something causing her breath to catch and her heartbeat to quicken. Gathering her thoughts, she lifted the book again and continued.

Mishkla delivered a beautiful daughter with dark hair and eyes. The birth took long because of Mishkla's weakened condition. The joy in her eyes was beautiful to behold as she held her daughter and kissed the baby's face. So many kisses to that little face and those tiny hands. This mother's love is boundless.

We will hurry to get Mishkla and the baby into a wagon that two priests are bringing and then travel to higher ground. Pray Val that we reach safety in time. From our vantage point in the vision, we saw the ocean swallowing everything we knew to be homes and crops. All will be left in devastation.

We have perhaps one more day here. I just checked on my patients before we leave. Dear, sweet Mishkla. I will carry always the expression on her face as she gazed at her baby. She uttered a few stumbling words before she died. "My babe. Care for her. Her name. Call her Anlía. It means Spirit-Bridge."

Alexa let the book drop and gasped. "Great and sacred Val! How can this be?"

Tirstan knelt by Alexa's side. He instantly understood the implications of the journal's passage. "Lady Valkana, come. Walk with me."

Tears glazed Alexa's eyes as she let the captain take her hand and lead her from the table. As they strolled, the words she had just read echoed through her mind. "My husband, Tirstan. Gregor has no idea. He only knows that his mother was an orphan raised by Valiria. He never even knew she had sworn vows as a Valiria until I found her pendant at Lindaval."

"Milady, at least you better understand why you were drawn to this place." Tirstan stopped and thought. "You now comprehend the connection you felt at the gravesite on the hill. You have much more in common than a plunge into stormy seas. The woman buried there is your husband's grandmother and great-grandmother of your children. You gave life to her descendants."

"And we both named daughters Anlía."

"There is that."

A fragrant breeze rushed in from the ocean. Warm, salty air caressed her cheeks and soothed some of the shock of the journal's revelation. Alexa closed her eyes. Gregor's image clarified before her mind's eye. His uncommon height and unusually dark complexion weren't just an anomaly. The size of Mishkla's grave clearly indicated that she had been exceptionally tall, possibly even taller than Gregor. How had the Valiria described the stranger? Yes, *a woman of majestic proportions*. That was a trait Gregor had inherited and passed along to his children.

After a few more minutes of contemplation, Alexa turned to Tirstan. "Let's go back. After some supper, I'd like some quiet time to ponder this."

Tossing restlessly in her sleep, Alexa tugged her blanket closer around her face despite the night's velvet warmth. For a while, meditation carried her far from Zemtoval and across the ocean toward the Sifiq Kingdom, where a Turandan fleet approached. Watching her husband stare out over the bow of a ship, she admired the air of confidence and command he projected. More than ever, she respected Gregor's resolve as he pursued an end to violence the Sifiq king refused to end.

Reluctantly, her spirit departed the inbound flotilla. Her mother's heart courageously crossed Sifiq shores and sought the fortified encampment Prince Nikolai had established west of the capital city of Atuliq. Leaning over maps and talking with his officers, her son looked every inch the consummate, battle-tested leader. Now bearded like his father, he was the very image of the Gregor she had first met in Toraval. Lifting prayerful entreaties to Val to protect both her son and her husband, Alexa indulged in a swift kiss for each of them. She then quickly returned to her sleeping mat in Turand.

She had been back only a short time before the new dream invaded. Or was it a vision? She had been here before. In other dreams or visions. The tall cave carved into the mountainside. Lanterns and candles dispelling the shadows. Rugs covering stone floors. Tapestries hanging over rock walls. The voices. Alexa could hear their voices, but she couldn't understand their words. She never saw their faces. They were dangerous, but she was not afraid.

"Will you go?"

This voice she had heard before. But when? Where?

"Who are you?"

"You called on me when you were in great need. You called on me when *he* was in *his* greatest need. I answered you. I went and stayed with him until you came. I ask you now. Will you go?"

Through the haze of a sleep-heavy brain, Alexa struggled for some sort of clarity. "If I can understand where this place is, I will go."

She felt the unmistakable swirl of spiritual energies surround her. A mystifying mélange of sensations filled her mind with sounds, images, and words. Abruptly, she awoke. Although absolute clarity escaped her, she had asked Solton Telindra for maps to Port Fosan and then planned to call on Lord Manaran following the trip to Zemtoval. How convenient that the trip eastward would carry them around the Zemfosa Mountains. As she waited for morning to break, she tried to recall whose voice had spoken to her and how far Corlozem Pass lay from the main road to Port Fosan.

⌐

The ruddy-faced innkeeper retied the strings of his blue apron and barked out a fresh round of orders to the staff in his employ. While clerks, servers, and maids rushed to their tasks, the man then turned to his unexpected guests. "Your Majesty, please forgive the delay. I want you to feel welcome while we make ready for your party. We rarely receive groups as large as yours."

With a reassuring smile, Alexa said, "Worry not, Master Koliro. I do understand we arrived without notice. My Guard will appreciate whatever accommodations you can provide. We've been traveling several weeks now."

True to his word, the industrious innkeeper soon had hot meals on tables for his queen and her company. In the meantime, with his current guests being regular clients, the innkeeper's wife found alternative lodging at the homes of nearby friends. As quickly as accommodations were vacated, staff moved in to clean.

When Mrs. Koliro guided Alexa and Jalisa to the inn's best suite, the woman's round face glowed with pride and welcome. "Your Majesty, because you requested rooms for your men, we have only this suite left for you and your priestess. There are two beds, though. I hope that will do."

"That is fine, Mrs. Koliro. We have shared a small tent during most of our travels. Clean beds under a real roof are welcome."

Mrs. Koliro's smile brightened. "I hope that I have done right. My maids prepared a bath for you. I thought it might do you well before you go to bed. You can leave any clothes that need washed or mended in this basket by the door. Someone will fetch it and see to it by morning."

Appreciation made Alexa smile. The woman's actions weren't simply because she had a business to operate. Her thoughtfulness rose from basic kindness. Alexa reached out and placed her palm against the hostess's cheek. "May Val's blessings be upon you always for such thoughtfulness, Mrs. Koliro. Thank you, and goodnight."

The warm bath and clean, soft bed relaxed Alexa more than expected. Soon, ushered into deep slumber, her spirit once again soared free.

Without hesitation, she went to her husband, feeling his need. The Sifiq night was as dark and foreboding as any she remembered. He lay awake in the large tent he now shared with son Nikolai. His thoughts were not of the next battle. Instead, he whispered her name and how much he missed her. As was her habit, she ruffled strands of his hair and watched as he shuddered slightly in response. Hopefully, he would feel the kiss her spirit softly bestowed on those lips she so loved.

She heard him whisper, "Alexa? Beloved, you're here, aren't you? I love you, but you must go home. This place hurt you. I cannot let that happen again. I will not let that happen again. Not ever. I swear it. I love you, Alexa."

Alexa smiled and caressed anxiety from his face until his eyes closed in sleep. She then smiled at her son, kissed his sleep-tumbled hair, and returned to Turand and the body that awaited her wandering spirit.

While sipping strong tea the following morning, Alexa's thoughts drifted to the brief moments inside her husband's tent the night before. His burden intensified her sense of urgency to pursue the cave destination from her dream. When Master Koliro appeared to replenish her cup, she smiled and invited him to join her at the table.

"Sir, your hospitality has been excellent. I wish we could stay longer, but Captain Fratino will settle our account and prepare my Guard to leave as soon as we finish breakfast."

"Your Majesty, we are honored to have served you. I hope everything has been to your liking."

"More than satisfactory, I assure you. Your wife is a dear. Now, I must ask you something. You know these parts well, do you not?"

"I do," he said, his forehead wrinkling in question. "I've lived here all my life."

"I have heard of a place in the mountains called Corlozem Pass. Do you know of it?"

The innkeeper's eyebrows lifted high, his eyes opening wide. "Corlozem Pass? I haven't heard that for many years. Corlozem Pass is naught but a legend, Your Majesty. It was supposedly a hidden passage for quick travel from the sea through the mountains to this more traveled road to Port Fosan. Legend now says it's haunted by ghosts and guarded by giants."

Emerald eyes widened and lit up with interest. "Giants?"

Master Koliro chuckled, but he looked uncomfortable. "I know some men who went looking for the pass. Only one ever came back. He was never right in the mind afterward."

Alexa sat back and nodded. "Do you know where it is?"

The innkeeper stared at her. "Your Majesty, it's a legend. Even if it is real, it isn't safe for you to go. Especially not now with King Gregor off to war."

"I go with our Lord Val watching over me. You must have faith, just as I must find this place."

Standing behind her husband, Mrs. Koliro studied the queen's determined expression. "Your Majesty, what you propose is not a safe endeavor. On that, my husband is right. However, if you insist, I have a cousin who lives near where the pass is supposed to be. I can give you directions to his farm and a letter of introduction. He is the only one I know who might be able to help."

By this time, Captain Fratino had appeared to inform Alexa the company was ready to depart. "Mrs. Koliro, how far is your cousin's farm?"

"On horseback? With fair weather, I would say two days at most."

"Will your cousin welcome royal visitors?" Alexa asked.

"My cousin was too young to fight when King Gregor ousted the Sifiq from Turand and then fought the civil war. However, both our families sent soldiers, including two of his brothers and two of mine. We each lost a brother for the cause of Turand's freedom. We grieved their deaths, but we know they rest peacefully with Val. I hope that answers your question."

"It does, dear lady. Please give their names to Jalisa, and I shall offer special prayers for each of them." Returning her attention to Master Koliro, she said, "Before I leave, Captain Fratino will show you the maps we have. Would you kindly look at them to be sure they're accurate?"

"Your Majesty, are you sure about this?" the innkeeper asked, still unnerved by her plan to search for Corlozem Pass.

Resolve drew Alexa's face into a mask of concentration as she adjusted leather riding gloves. "Nothing, sir, will stop me."

⌣

A well-worn path lined with evergreens led toward a rambling stone farm-house with tall chimneys at each end. Several children chased chickens and each other across a neatly tended farmyard. Troughs in front of a nearby barn held water for sturdy draft horses and lowing cattle. Two women carried the ends of an enormous basket of fresh laundry to hang on lines to dry. A man emerged from the door of the house and stopped abruptly. He had spotted Captain Fratino approaching the house with one other soldier.

"Greetings, sir," the captain leaned over the pommel of his saddle to introduce himself. "I am Captain Tirstan Fratino of Her Majesty Queen Alexa's Royal Guard. Can you tell me if this is the farm of Melchan Forsay?"

"It is. I am Samlian, his son." The man stared impatiently. Dressed and ready for a day's ride to bring a doctor for his ailing father, he could imagine no reason queen's guards should be arriving at his doorstep. "My father is sick, and I'm leaving for help. You must excuse me."

"Master Forsay, if your father requires healing, we may be able to offer assistance. We have come far, and our Lady Valkana rides in our company."

Samlian Forsay froze. His light brown hair rippled in the breeze. His broad, tanned face twitched before settling into a mask of disbelief. Hazel eyes finally narrowed. "Our Lady Valkana? Her Majesty Queen Alexa rides with you? Why in Val's name would our queen come to this remote corner of Turand?"

The sounds of hooves and harnesses broke momentary tension. "Captain Fratino, is all well? Is this the Forsay farm?"

"Your Majesty, yes, it is. This is Samlian Forsay, who informs me that Melchan Forsay is ill."

"Master Forsay, perhaps I might offer my assistance."

Dumbfounded, the farmer just stared at her, unable to speak. Before him sat his queen. Although shielded from the sun by a woven, wide-brimmed hat, her sparkling eyes, high cheekbones, and shapely lips created a face that reflected both compassion and approachability. She was a tall woman who carried herself with grace as she dismounted and walked toward him. The stories were true. Their queen was lovely to behold.

"Master Forsay?"

Stuttering, the ordinarily confident Samlian Forsay rediscovered his voice and bowed. "Your Majesty, I would be happy for your help. In truth, I think my father is dying. I was going for help to ease his pains."

"Then I shall go to him. I understand he is a man of faith. Perhaps I can ease his return to our Lord Val." Turning to Tirstan, she said, "Captain, while Master Forsay takes me to his father, will you send Jalisa to the house and find a place for the men? I don't know how long we might be here."

That evening, after two hours with Alexa, Melchan rested quietly in bed under Jalisa's watchful eye. Alexa sat with Samlian and his wife after supper. For the first time in a week, the couple ate together without one or the other being called constantly to Melchan's side.

"The Healing Graces are a blessing, even if they do come only to ease Father's passing," Samlian said quietly. He drank the last from a glass of wine. "I am most grateful to you."

Alexa nodded. "Serving our people this way was part of why I joined the Order of Val. Although death must come to us all, that doesn't mean we must forsake peace."

"Lady Valkana, why are you here? My cousin wrote that you needed our help. We live peacefully, but we are in the middle of nowhere. How could we possibly help you?"

"I had hoped to speak to your father about a most urgent matter—a place I need to find. I…"

"Milady?" Jalisa interrupted. "Master Forsay has awakened. He asks for you and his son."

Samlian and Alexa exchanged puzzled glances and rose from their chairs. Inside the bedchamber, Samlian gestured for Alexa to sit on a wooden chair at his father's bedside while he grasped the back of another chair and affectionately smiled down at the man he would always remember as strong and wise.

"Father, what is it you need?"

Earlier, Samlian had combed long, thin, gray hair away from Melchan's gaunt face. Melchan's light brown eyes shone as, despite his pallor and drawn features, he gazed at his son. "Samlian, listen carefully. I must rely on you to do what I cannot. Our Lord Val trusts me to help our Lady Valkana. Promise that you will complete this mission that I will not live to fulfill."

"Father…"

"Samlian, promise me. I must have your promise." As weak as Melchan was, his voice held notes of strength and stridency.

Sighing sadly, Samlian said, "I promise, Father. I will do whatever you ask."

The old man nodded. "You have always been a fine son, Samlian, and my greatest pride in life. I bless you, your wife, and your children. Now listen." Faded eyes then met Alexa's. "You seek the strangers—the ones who came after their ship wrecked decades ago, leaving them to take refuge in caves just past Corlozem Pass."

Alexa showed no sign of surprise. "It is imperative that I find them, Master Forsay. The mystery has only begun to reveal itself to me, but I'm certain that finding them is essential to Turand's survival."

Melchan Forsay closed his eyes for a moment's rest. "My father and I helped rescue them from their shipwreck. Now, Samlian and I are the only ones they allow near. You will not be welcomed. You must be careful."

"Father," Samlian said worriedly, "how can you send them there? You know how they are!" Suddenly, he turned to face Alexa. "How do you even know about them? We've kept their secret for ages. Even my own wife knows nothing about them."

"Remember. I am Valkana. Val shows me many things in his own way—in his own time."

A frail hand reached for his son's. "I do not expect he will be pleased, Samlian, but face him with all your courage. He respects courage. That is well for you to remember, too, Milady. Do not let him intimidate you."

Alexa smiled. "I have stood my ground before kings and the Sifiq military. Twice. I'm not sure who *he* is, but I am in no mood to let *him* intimidate me. I have neither the luxury nor the time to do so. Our country, our people, and my husband's and son's lives are at stake; otherwise, our Lord Val would not have set me to this task. Have no worry, dear Melchan. I will leave you with your son. Then rest."

Excusing herself to the two men, Alexa walked outside. The evening was pleasant beneath starry skies. Breezes carried the sweet perfume of blooms from fruit trees in nearby orchards. Distant waters danced along their river-bed. Horses whinnied softly in their pens. Moonlight cast silver shadows on mountains standing like sentinels around this small, idyllic valley.

"Your Majesty, is all well?"

"Yes, Tirstan," Alexa said quietly. "Val calls the elder Master Forsay to his eternal rest, but first, he gave him a final task."

"To help you?"

"To help us. More than ever, I believe this mission is as much for the good of all Turand as it is to clarify the past. I'm anxious to understand why. Patience is not always easy when those you love most are in harm's way."

"Lady Valkana? My father! Please come!" Samlian's voice sounded desperate.

Hurriedly returning to Melchan's bedchamber, Alexa immediately went to him and perched on the side of his bed. Grasping his hands and holding them against her heart, she began singing an ancient hymn. The words were sweet and comforting, describing the beauty and security of rest within Val's eternal embrace. As her voice filled the room, the blue-white light of her aura shimmered. Melchan smiled at her and then at his son before softly exhaling his final breath.

Three days later, Samlian carefully inspected four pack animals and the horses Captain Fratino, Alexa, and six guardsmen would ride to Corlozem Pass. Jalisa and the remainder of Alexa's troupe would accompany them as far as the base of the mountain and then wait until Samlian could gauge reactions to their arrival at the cave complex.

"Today's ride will be easy," Samlian said, his expression severe. "By mid-morning tomorrow, we begin a slow, rocky ascent. Riders must be careful until we reach the site where we'll set up camp. The next morning, you, your best horsemen, and Her Majesty follow me up and across the ledges of Corlozem Pass. Good riders should pass with no great difficulty, but one never knows when there might be a rockslide or other calamity. Backing down is perilous."

Fratino met Forsay's glare with a stern air of command. "I understand. My men have trained under rigorous conditions to protect our queen. We are ready."

Grunting in response, Forsay looked around. "And where is our queen?"

"I am here," she said, leaning over her mount's neck.

Samlian Forsay shook his head. Hard. He had not seen her leave the house. How she had reached the horses and mounted without him noticing was impossible. Still, there she was with that enigmatic smile and those shining green eyes. Had this not been his father's dying wish...

That night, Alexa gratefully accepted a cup of hot tea as she warmed herself in front of one of several campfires. Winds sweeping off the mountain carried a chill that quickly insinuated itself beneath her lightweight summer jacket and split riding skirt. Shaking off a shiver, she would definitely roll those up in the morning and switch to warmer clothes before undertaking the climb toward the pass.

When Samlian came to warm his hands by the fire, she asked, "Will you tell me something of what you know about these people?"

His eyebrows lifted quizzically, but Samlian lowered himself to a mat near the fire. "They say little about themselves or where they're from. I know they were stranded after a violent storm. Before the ship drifted back to sea, my father and grandfather helped rescue the few survivors and some of their cargo. That was seventy years ago."

"I didn't realize your father was so old."

"Ninety-one. Anyway, few of the men spoke our language. They were exhausted. Father said all they wanted was to find a place to care for their injured and decide what to do. They were adamant they didn't want to be seen by anyone else because they understood their appearance might stir trouble."

"Their appearance?" Alexa asked.

"Milady, you really don't know, do you?"

"My dreams have shown me their cave, tapestries, and rugs. I have heard their voices. I know nothing more."

Fear shadowed Samlian's face. He heaved a sigh. "They are strange, Milady. As elegant and refined as any gentlemen I've ever seen, and I've seen a few. On the other hand, though few are left, they are fearsome to behold. Their skin is dark—a bronzed tan like none I've ever seen. It's not the cinnamon shade typical of folks from Shamal Province. And they are tall. Almost like giants, Milady."

"Giants, you say? How tall would you say?" she asked, her curiosity swelling.

"Taller than any man I've ever known." He stood and asked her to stand. "You are tall for a Turandan. I know few men as tall as you. They are taller still."

"How much taller?"

Samlian squinted as he studied her. "Perhaps three heads taller than you. They are that much taller. Maybe more. And as muscular and strong as they are tall. That is why it's wise not to anger them."

"Samlian, did your father ever say anything about the storm that caused their shipwreck?"

"Only that it was peculiar in the way the winds kept shifting directions. It seemed they blew for hours in one direction and then changed to blow for hours in the opposite direction. The currents were just as dangerous. Seasoned seafarers spoke of it for years."

"Can you tell me the names of who we will meet?"

"I will only tell you of Gaeldoreg. He is as a gatekeeper. He is the one you must convince to let you pass."

"Is he the one your father referred to?"

"Oh, no. If we convince Gaeldoreg to let us pass, we enter the caves. That is when you meet *him*. You will need to keep your courage and your wits about you with *him*."

"Thank you for the advice. I'll prepare myself. We should get some sleep now."

Lying in the small tent Tirstan had insisted on pitching for her, Alexa thought she might never fall asleep. However, her thick sleeping mat was comfortable and her blanket warm. Quickly drifting into deep slumber, she again listened as that sweet voice returned to visit her dreamtime.

"My dear Alexa, have you remembered me yet?"

Searching her memory, Alexa recalled other nights spent sleeping outside. Sudden recollection prompted a fearful gasp followed by relieved calm. "I do, sweet spirit. You came when I was desperate to save his life. I needed three serving spirits to save him, but only two of us were present. I was able to call you from rest with Val because I carried his son—your grandson—in my womb at the time."

"My spirit gladdens that you remember. We saved him once, Alexa. You and I. We must do so again. We must save him and his son from those who stole my life. You follow the right path, but it may be difficult. Insist, dear one. Use what you have learned without fear. We shall leave you help. Be brave."

"Dear Spirit, I love him too much to give up. I will not fail you. I will never fail him."

When Alexa awoke, she sat with shoulders hunched inside the tight confines of her tent. Despite the odd dream exchange, she felt rested. Pushing aside her blanket to get up, a velvet pouch rolled off to the side.

Picking it up, she puzzled over how it got there. She hadn't brought it with her, and it certainly hadn't been in the tent when she went to bed.

Royal blue velvet was embroidered with the Toscano family crest. Braided silk ties were secured with golden clasps also stamped with the family seal. Opening the fasteners, she loosened the ties and opened the pouch. Pouring the contents onto her lap, she gazed at an engraved platinum ring, a triangular pendant attached to a platinum chain, and the amethyst, diamond, and pearl brooch she had worn to the Celebration of Naming for each of her children. Gregor had shown them to her years ago. They once belonged to his mother.

~

Tirstan Fratino surveyed the site. The day's journey had been every bit as challenging as Samlian had said it would be. The troops had ridden well with few missteps. He had needed to guide Jalisa's horse three times on lead to get past some of the more difficult outcroppings. With pride, the captain watched his queen tend to her horse. Despite the grueling ride, not once had she faltered. The men staying behind were now setting up camp so those leaving tomorrow could eat and take an early rest.

Morning dawned under gray skies. Damp breezes blew from the direction of the sea. Captain Fratino cast a worried glance toward their guide. "The weather is about to change. Perhaps we should wait."

Samlian shook his head. "Rain is still far out to sea. I expect it won't hit until tonight. Have the men staying behind secure the camp for wind and rain. Late spring storms that reach this far inland are rarely more than bluster and long bursts of wet."

"And what if we run into resistance from these giants of yours?"

Samlian shrugged his shoulders. "I suppose we'll have to leave that in the hands of our Lord Val and our Lady Valkana, won't we? Unfortunately, we have little other choice."

Two hours later, Tirstan eased his mount along the ledge ascending the mountain. He still could not believe the approach to Corlozem Pass. Even knowing the general location, he was sure he could have searched for weeks and never located it without the experienced escort now leading them. He looked over his shoulder. His men followed single file, each keeping check on their queen. Not one of them had questioned the sanity of this mission. Each trusted her completely, as did Tirstan.

The captain followed as Samlian guided them to the right when the ledge expanded onto a broad, flat ridge sheltered by spindly pine trees. Raising his arm, Fratino signaled his men into formation around their queen. Just ahead stood five of the tallest, most formidable-looking men he had ever seen in his life.

The man in the center furiously strode forth. His long jacket was made from beige canvas, cinched at the waist with a wide, brown leather belt. Leather boots rose nearly to his knees. Shoulder-length, steel-gray hair fluttered in the breeze. Black eyes glittered threateningly with disgust.

"Samlian Forsay! Come no closer! Why do you break the pledge of your father?"

Samlian dismounted and motioned Tirstan to stay put. "Gaeldoreg, I must speak to you. I bring news of my father. These people will do you no harm."

Gaeldoreg's voice boomed out over the ridge. "Your father pledged to keep our peace. Why does he break his oath and send you here? Who are these people? Take them and leave. Do not return!"

"You must listen. Father has not broken his pledge. Father is dead. Before he died, he had a vision, and these people came. I honor his final request by bringing them here. Would you do less if it were your father's dying request?"

Waving a sheathed sword, the giant eyed him furiously. "Why would your father do such a thing? I cannot understand."

Startling everyone, Alexa's voice rang out as she walked up beside Samlian. "Because I asked him to."

Samlian shot her a shocked glance just as Tirstan looked around at stunned guards whose reactions showed they had never seen her dismount or walk to the spot where the confrontational greeting was taking place. In unison, the soldiers all dismounted, ready to defend their queen.

Gaeldoreg roared an unintelligible response and unsheathed his sword. The other four giants assumed more aggressive stances and also drew swords.

Captain Fratino signaled his men to wait. His heart pounded, but he had discussed this likelihood with her the night before. He would trust her judgment as he always had.

"I assume you are Gaeldoreg?" Alexa said in a maddeningly calm voice.

"And who are you? What do you want here?" he roared back at her, his dark face flushing scarlet as he fiercely glared at her. No wonder Melchan had warned her about them.

"First of all, I am not hard of hearing, so you need not shout at me. I have come to speak with all of you, but most especially *him*, whoever *he* is. I assume *he* must be your leader."

"Woman! Exasperating woman! Who are you that I should let you pass to speak to my lord?" Gaeldoreg bellowed.

"Ah, *he* is your lord. This is progress. Still, you may stop shouting. Now I shall tell you who I am. My name is Alexa. I am High Priestess Valkana and Queen of Turand. Perhaps that is sufficient to grant me an audience with your lord, who resides within my country's boundaries."

Gaeldoreg glared at her. "You cannot be queen and priestess."

"Why not?" Alexa observed the surprise her question evoked, but the recalcitrant giant quickly resumed his foul temper.

"My lord sees no one. Especially not women. He sorrows." Gaeldoreg lifted his bearded chin obstinately in challenge, daring her to continue their verbal duel.

"For seventy years? Yes, I know all about that. I still need to speak with *him*, whatever *his* name is. Now, I tire of your challenges and arguments. I wish to speak to your lord, and I wish to speak to *him* now."

"You may not pass!" he roared.

Alexa glared back at him, her eyes darkening impatiently. Finally, her voice lowered, and her aura began to shimmer, cascading from the top of her head down to her feet. "Gaeldoreg, thousands of lives are in jeopardy. One of those lives belongs to my husband and another to my son. For reasons I do not yet understand, my Lord Val has sent me on a long mission with this as my final stop. Let me pass."

Gaeldoreg stared at her. The sight of her aura sent shivers vibrating along his spine, but he refused to yield. He had sworn to protect the solitude of his lord. "Even with your magic, I cannot."

Alexa sensed an extraordinary desire to protect *him*. "Gaeldoreg, may I ask you a question?"

The man's bushy gray brows knit together. "A question? What sort of question?"

"Does it matter that I know about *her*?"

"About her? Who?"

"*Her*—Mishkla Krisantal."

The giant man's face blanched, and he stumbled backward as if struck a crushing blow. Then, quickly catching his balance, he stared at Alexa with incredulous eyes. "What do you know of Mishkla? Tell me!"

"I will not. I must speak with *him*. That is why I was sent here. I give you my solemn promise as High Priestess Valkana. I will not betray your trust. Nor will I reveal your location without your permission, but I must speak with your lord."

Gaeldoreg grabbed Alexa's hand, still encased in glittering light. A sharp nod of his head brought one of his comrades to him. Abruptly, the man lifted his sword, first slitting Gaeldoreg's hand before cutting Alexa's. As blood flowed, Gaeldoreg held their bloody wounds together. "Your promise is now accepted and binding as a blood bond, Priestess Valkana. You may pass. I must know, though, about these men."

"These men are part of my Royal Guard. My husband personally chose them to protect me whenever I leave our capital city. They are loyal to me, my husband, and Turand. I trust them with my life. My husband trusts them with my life. If you knew my husband, you would understand this is great honor he bestows upon them."

Considering her comment for seconds only, the giant said, "Bad weather approaches. My men will show them where to stable their horses and then settle until my lord decides what to do about you. Samlian, you come with us."

"Gaeldoreg, I respectfully request that Captain Fratino accompany me. My husband would be most displeased with me and the captain if I went alone. The captain will keep a discreet distance."

Gaeldoreg shook his head. This woman perplexed him, but he could not blindly dismiss her reference to Mishkla. "Very well. Your captain may pass, but he must not interfere."

"Captain Fratino's only concern is my safety and welfare. He has spent over twenty years protecting me."

"Protecting you? Or keeping you out of trouble?" The irritable Gaeldoreg's sarcastic smirk earned him no more than raised eyebrows.

Moments later, Alexa observed that only one of the four soldier-guards led her men and horses to safe shelter. Before leaving, he had taken the reins of her horse and Tirstan's. The animals had reacted instantly to the man's voice and touch, his mere presence calming and reassuring the animals. She wondered how men so outwardly fierce and easily provoked could have such a tender effect on Val's more simple creatures.

Entering the yawning opening of an enormous cave, she followed Gaeldoreg and Samlian. Tirstan walked steadfastly by her side, and the two remaining giants walked so close behind she could hear them breathe. One was missing. Alexa concluded he had gone ahead to inform *him* of the arrival of unexpected visitors.

As they proceeded farther into the cave, lanterns and banks of candles lit the way. Unsurprised, Alexa began to recognize the twists and curves as they approached the primary chamber of the cavern. Runners and mats of woven reeds and grasses were rolled aside to reveal thick, colorful, woolen carpets covering the cave's natural stone floors. Reaching the spacious central chamber, she saw that hardware had been pounded into rock walls to hang sconces for lighting and wooden bars for tapestries. Rich trappings indeed for cave dwellers, she thought, and precisely as she remembered from her dreams.

"Gaeldoreg! Have you finally lost your mind?"

Alexa's musings were rudely interrupted by the vibrantly rich voice of a man standing beside a chair and glaring furiously at the gray-haired giant leading their little procession. She knew that voice. How many times had she heard that voice and all its inflections? Her back straightened, and her attention focused on this newest exchange.

"My lord, I beg your forgiveness, but Samlian has come with news. With his tidings, he brings a request from his father. After serious contemplation, I think Melchan's request is one you must decide whether or not to consider."

"Samlian! Come to me!"

Alexa watched as Samlian visibly shuddered before squaring his shoulders and resolutely walking forward. Stopping a safe distance from Gaeldoreg's enraged lord, Samlian executed a respectful bow and waited.

There was no greeting of any kind, only a series of sharp, furious questions. "What news do you bring? What request does your father send? Why does he break his pledge to us? And why do you bring these strange people to our secret place?"

Recalling his father's advice, Samlian mustered every bit of courage he possessed and faced *him* directly. "It is with a sad heart that I carry news of my father's death. I come not to break his pledge but to honor my father's dying request to his son. Before he died, our God Val sent him a dream. These people had arrived and helped ease his passing. Father promised to help them before he died and asked me to keep his promise."

The man raised his head to stare at Alexa. Silver hair fell in waves around his shoulders. His beard framed the dark features of a man who must undoubtedly be in his nineties but whose skin showed few wrinkles despite his age. Eyes the color of obsidian glittered ominously in candlelight as he regarded unwelcome visitors. Tension showed in his posture as his broad chest rose and fell quickly, shoulders squared, and legs spread in an intimidating stance.

"Women are not welcome here. She must leave this place immediately."

Fratino's eyebrows lifted beneath the captain's cap he wore. The gauntlet of challenge had been thrown. She was close enough that he felt the stiffening in her spine. His hand fell to the hilt of his sword. He prayed he would have no need to draw the weapon.

"You dwell in the nation of Turand; therefore, you have no right to order me to leave this cave." Alexa's voice sounded strong and authoritative as she stepped away from her escort and approached the man who had dared banish her from his presence.

Black eyes narrowed. "Gaeldoreg, if you must, carry her out. I want her out of here now."

"No one will touch me. I have spent weeks getting here. Gaeldoreg nor anyone else will remove me until I choose to leave. Furthermore, you have no right to send me away. I am the only one here with the right to send anyone away, so hold your tongue, sir."

The giant's head snapped back, his patience dwindling at her audacity. "Argumentative, aren't you? I command here. What makes you think your rights exceed mine?"

"You are in Turand as a stranger in our nation, sir. I am Alexa, Queen of Turand. That is all the right I need."

"Queen of Turand?" Dubiously, he turned. "Samlian?"

"She speaks the truth, sir. Not only is she Queen, she is our sacred High Priestess Valkana."

Perplexed, the giant returned his attention to the stern-faced woman refusing to be intimidated by the daunting image that had terrified others throughout the decades. Tall compared to Samlian, she certainly possessed the regal bearing of nobility. Despite her dusty appearance, her attire was cut and fashioned from fine fabrics. Although this Queen of Turand appeared tired from long travels, he had to acknowledge both her elegance and her mettle.

"High Priestess and Queen. Quite a combination," he drawled, tempering his inclination toward sarcasm. "Since it seems I owe you a certain amount of respect, why have you come? What do you want? Do you seek taxes for the time I have lived on your soil?"

Alexa almost laughed. "Hardly. What I seek is something of far greater importance. I must know who you are."

"You!" the giant abruptly addressed Fratino. "I have no intention of harming your queen. You may remove your hand from your sword."

Alexa glanced around. "Captain, it's all right. Stay close but do not fear." To the giant, she said, "My husband has assigned Captain Fratino to accompany me whenever I travel. The captain is my primary protector in my husband's absence."

"So Turand has a king?"

"Yes. Now, will you please tell me who you are?"

With a tilt of his head, the man motioned for someone to bring a chair for Alexa. The chair was so high she had to lift herself onto the seat. She could not reach the back even then, but she gladly sat. Curiously, she watched her irascible host sit in the oversized carved chair she recalled from her dreams.

His expression remained suspicious as he assessed her every move. "If it pleases you, my name is Braeklojorn Vosklon. My comrades and I come from a large island nation called Trezvindja. As you probably already know, we are here because of a tragic shipwreck. That is my story. Now, will you explain why you would travel weeks to ask a stranger such a trivial question?"

Growing certainty suffused Alexa's being. Even more so than when she had sat by Mishkla's graveside, she sensed the more profound connection. Her heartbeat quickened as she resisted tears threatening to fill her eyes. His emotions were powerful, making it impossible to predict his reaction. She sensed the need to proceed cautiously.

"How should I address you?" she asked respectfully.

Surprised by her softened tone, he said, "In Trezvindja, I was a prince. Since you are queen in your land, I think we might dispense with formalities. You may call me Braeklojorn."

Carefully pronouncing his name, Alexa began her tale. "Braeklojorn, as High Priestess Valkana, I receive dreams and visions. Many years ago, my dreams showed me this cave. The dreams were infrequent. They recently returned following my recovery from a prolonged, painful ordeal. I saw this place and another. Although I saw no people, I heard voices.

"I started researching the places I saw. Before coming here, I traveled to a place called Zemtoval. What I learned there astonished me. When I see my husband again, I believe I will be able to give him a gift of nearly unparalleled value."

"If he is king, what could you have found that he might value so highly?" Initial cynicism dissolved as the Trezvindjan prince observed her face transform. His heart ached as he recalled another face that often reflected just as much love and adoration as this one. He shook off the painful memory.

"Unlike many with powers to rule, my husband treasures family more than gold and other trappings of wealth. At Zemtoval, I found family ties of which he knows nothing. They are also linked to a tragedy."

Braeklojorn sat quietly. "This is a fine story, but I fail to understand how or why it leads you to me."

Alexa turned and quietly thanked Samlian as he handed her the leather satchel she had asked him to retrieve from her saddlebags. She again gazed up at Braeklojorn. "Some seventy years ago, Zemtoval was destroyed by a tidal wave. That year was marked by unusual storms. It is told that winds and tides shifted directions in ways not seen before or since."

Braeklojorn leaned back in his chair. Something in his stomach began to churn. This woman's story already jarred his nerves. He couldn't bear to think back on those storms. "I have heard enough. I regret the destruction of your Zemtoval. I am glad you found something of value for your husband. Let your story end."

"I cannot. You must hear the rest."

"I will hear no more!" he thundered. "Do you not understand me?"

Unmoved and ignoring his flare of anger, Alexa drew in a deep breath and opened the pouch on her lap. "I found this in Zemtoval in an office— on a high shelf that escaped destructive seawaters."

Finding the page Jalisa had marked with layers of clean toweling, she began reading aloud. "Our mystery patient is very ill. The Healing Graces delivered her from the brink of death, so she must be a woman of faith. She continues to suffer. I believe she fights more for the life of her baby than her own. We do not understand her language, so we make hand signs and draw pictures. With difficulty, we learned her name is Mishkla Krisantal."

Jumping to his feet, Braeklojorn released a series of echoing wails of such unbearable misery and sorrow that everyone present felt them penetrate their very bones. Then, without warning, his enormous hands wrapped around Alexa's waist, and he lifted her high above his head. "What is this terrible torment you bring to me? Why? Why must you torture me?"

"Braeklojorn!" she commanded. "Put me down! Now! I command you as Queen of Turand. Put me down this instant!"

Gaeldoreg's strong hands grasped Braeklojorn's shoulders. "My lord, let her down. She knows what happened to Mishkla! You must listen to her! Please!"

Fratino ran forward, sword drawn. Alexa shook her head. "Tirstan! No! You must not hurt him!"

Slowly, Braeklojorn's vice-like grip around her waist eased, and he lowered her to the floor. Freed, she stepped backward until Fratino placed his arms around her shoulders. She stared at the giant man, hunched and panting like a wounded beast as tears coursed from grieving black eyes.

Trusting her instincts, Alexa pulled free and went to him, grasping his unresisting hands in hers. So large and so powerful, yet they shook helplessly in the wake of his renewed great sorrow. She led him to his chair and then knelt at his knee.

"Dear Braeklojorn, I know your Mishkla was carried overboard in the storm. However, she washed up alive on the shore near Zemtoval. Priestesses from my Order of Val found her there and cared for her."

Incredulous, he stared at her. "My Mishkla lived? The storm was so dreadful! It seems impossible. I believed she surely died. Where is she? I must go to her. Take me."

No longer able to restrain tears, Alexa took a deep breath. "Braeklojorn, Mishkla was very sick for a long time. Later, I can read more of what the priestesses wrote. They nursed her for many months, but Mishkla finally died after her baby was born."

Another sorrowful sob erupted from the giant. "My beautiful Mishkla. Dead?" He stared blankly for long minutes, his mind awash in images from the past. Then, with his attention again focused on the woman who still held his hands, her words crashed through his mind. "The baby. You said she gave birth to the baby. Did our baby live?"

Alexa smiled. "She did. The priestesses took her into their care and left Zemtoval before the tidal wave struck. The Valiria educated her and taught her our faith. Your daughter grew into a fine woman and took vows as a Valiria priestess. She was also quite lovely and caught the eye of a handsome suitor. She eventually married."

Braeklojorn smiled for the first time. "My daughter married? I hope she married well. She doesn't know it, but she carries my wife's Krisantal name. She is the rightful heir to the throne of Trezvindja."

Shock and dread struck Alexa simultaneously. "Braeklojorn, I fear I have more news, some bad and some good." His expression was so achingly familiar. How much did she want to reach out—to touch him and offer some comfort.

"My daughter. Where is my daughter? Can you tell me that?"

Swallowing, Alexa nodded. "Your daughter is also dead, as is her husband."

He sat motionless and saw she was holding back. What was she not saying? Did he dare ask? Could his heart bear more? He had to know. "I hope that was not the good news."

A small smile tugged at Alexa's lips, and she shook her head. "It was not. Your daughter and her husband had a son. They named him Gregor. Although not so much as you, he is unusually tall and dark for a Turandan."

"You have seen this Gregor?" Braeklojorn asked with reviving interest, leaning forward as if life might again hold some promise.

Alexa nodded and risked lifting the giant's hands to her lips for a respectful kiss. "I have. Gregor is my husband."

Long minutes passed in contemplative silence. Braeklojorn Vosklon relived surviving the shipwreck off Turand's shores with eight others. Melchan Forsay and his father had found them and helped salvage belongings and cargo before their vessel floated back to sea and sank. The Forsays then led the Trezvindjans to the hidden caves of Corlozem Pass and helped them establish a safe, dry dwelling.

Blaming himself for being so careless as to let Mishkla go above deck and get swept overboard, he descended into an existence of guilt and grief. His comrades, all distant kinsmen, were sworn to serve him. Unable to find the heart or desire to return to Trezvindja, he chose a secluded life in Turand where he would have few reminders of his beloved wife or the life they once shared.

He had told the others to go—to find a way home if they wanted. Three lay buried beneath green grass at the foot of the mountain. Injuries sustained during the storm had proven fatal. The rest had stayed. Had he wasted their lives?

"Braeklojorn?"

Her voice was so gentle. So kind. And those eyes of hers. Never had he seen eyes like those. "Yes?"

"I have something for you." Alexa unbuttoned her jacket and pulled a small pouch from an inside pocket. She undid clasps and loosened drawstrings. Placing one of his large hands on her lap, she slid the contents onto his open palm.

Reverently, Braeklojorn lifted the precious items close to his face. Tears trickled down his cheeks and caught in the edges of his beard. "My Mishkla's wedding ring," he said, picking up the engraved metal and studying the intricate designs in the light. Sliding the ring onto his little finger, he then touched the pendant. "This is a symbol of our faith. I see you wear something similar. Is it the same for you?"

Alexa nodded. "The three sides represent the three greatest gifts from our Lord Val: love, peace, and fidelity. The gold sun in the center represents our God Val, who is life itself."

"Perhaps I can tell you one day of our faith. I think it may be similar." He then pointed at the brooch. "I gave this to Mishkla when she told me we were to have a child. We were both so happy. You cannot know how happy I was. I loved my Mishkla."

"I think I can appreciate your happiness."

Braeklojorn kissed the brooch and placed it and the pendant back inside the pouch. He kept the ring on his finger, although it only went halfway down. "Where did you find these?"

Glancing at the portfolio now lying on the floor, Alexa said, "According to what the priestesses wrote, Mishkla asked them to give them to your daughter. They did. She left them to my husband, and he has kept them locked up and safe at the palace in Toraval."

"I am ashamed," Braeklojorn murmured. "I haven't even asked. What name did your priestesses give my daughter?"

"I apologize. I didn't tell you. Mishkla asked them to call her Anlía. She was Queen Anlía of Turand."

His breath caught again. "My precious Spirit-Bridge. And a queen as she was meant to be! Shalevkazla!"

"Excuse me?"

Shaking his head, he said, "How tired you must be, and how vile I have been." He called out, "Gaeldoreg, can we offer tea and a meal to our guests?"

"We are preparing a table now, my lord."

"Alexa, tell me before we dine. Do you and my grandson—praise the heavens! I am a grandfather! Gaeldoreg! Did you hear? I am a grandfather!"

"I heard, my lord! Congratulations! I'm also setting out the wine!"

Braeklojorn looked both shocked and pleased. "Do you and my grandson have a child?"

Uncharacteristically, Tirstan's decorum deserted him, and he snorted a short burst of laughter. Samlian glanced at the captain and snickered. Even now, King Gregor's unusually large family elicited good-natured twitters and grins.

Tightly pursing her lips, Alexa barely restrained her own outburst of giggles. "Children. We have children."

"Children! Excellent! It is good to have a sister or brother. Which does yours have?"

"Braeklojorn, Gregor and I have three sons. And three daughters."

Gaeldoreg hurried in and stared down at Alexa in disbelief. "You are mother to six children?"

"I am. I was an only child, and my parents died long ago. Maxim, my husband's father, had no living relatives. As far as Gregor knew, his mother was an orphan with no family. Gregor was an only child. As I said earlier, he treasures family beyond all else. That's why he wanted such a large family of his own——and why we're parents to six children."

Braeklojorn pondered the momentous changes of this woman's revelations to his life and, perhaps, to his nation, should he decide to return to Trezvindja. For now, he wanted to learn more. Was there more written about his Mishkla in the book this Alexa had so gingerly picked up from the floor and carefully closed? What could she tell him about the life and death of his daughter Anlía, the second heartbreak suffered this day? How soon could they arrange to travel to meet this Gregor and all these children?

Six great-grandchildren! For years, he had lamented his alone-ness and the fact that Trezvindjans typically lived long lives—averaging almost a century and a half. He had wanted to die many years ago and had even considered suicide. Now, suddenly, he had his and Mishkla's grandson and great-grandchildren who might accept a grandfather into their midst.

Finishing their dinner of roasted fowl in mushroom gravy, herbed potatoes, and spring vegetables in butter sauce, they heard the first sheets of rain strike the ledges outside the cavern lair. Fratino glanced at Alexa. "Prince Braeklojorn, I thank you for the hospitality of including me at your table. I must excuse myself to check on my men."

Braeklojorn shook his head. "Please, Captain, there is no need. Your men and their horses have been safely accommodated. Everyone was also provided a hot meal. The leading edge of the storm is typically the worst. Wait. Someone will take you later to look in on them."

Noting Alexa's nod, he resumed his seat. "Thank you, Your Highness."

Later, Alexa studied images and costumes woven into one of the larger tapestries hanging on a wall. Some colors had faded, the dyes likely damaged by saltwater during the shipwreck. She felt faint breath stir her hair.

"It is the court in Tarahlaz, our capital."

She turned to acknowledge Gaeldoreg. "It's lovely."

"It was. I pray it still is. When we didn't return, Kaelzron, Mishkla's brother, would have become king upon their father's death. Kaelzron was a decent man but weak and somewhat self-indulgent. He would not have been the leader Mishkla would have been."

"A woman would have been successor to the Crown ahead of a man?"

Braeklojorn joined them. "Is it not so here in Turand?"

Alexa thought back. "I don't know that there has ever been a question of it."

"What about managing the power if the woman is the wiser leader?"

Alexa looked thoughtful. "I don't think we've ever had a situation arise where there was an issue. Our culture does include one form of balance that works well for us. Traditionally, our government has always been led by a king. Men and women participate in advisory positions for government affairs. We also have the Order of Val. Although some branches have priests, the order primarily consists of avowed priestesses headed by the High Priestess Valkana. The priestesses serve as teachers, faith guides, and healers to our people. According to Turand's laws, if ever any priestess has a matter of serious concern, she has the solemn right to appear before Turand's king and claim private council. In any case, the order and the king consult regularly, and the king must heed the order's advice."

"That is a curious arrangement. So the king and the Valkana marry to make this work?" Braeklojorn asked.

Alexa shook her head and smiled. "Gregor and I are the first and only example of such a union. Our marriage occurred under extreme circumstances."

"Come. Sit and tell me. I wish to know more. Your expression indicates there might be quite a story behind those circumstances."

Alexa hesitated, seeking an escape. "I should much prefer to have Gregor with me to share that saga."

"Saga, is it? Am I to understand my grandson is something of a challenge?"

Alexa shut her eyes against the threat of hot tears. When she spoke, her voice was subdued and tremulous. "A challenge he is, but I love him with every breath I take and every beat of my heart." Then, unexpectedly, she began to weep.

Braeklojorn reached for her and drew her into his arms and onto his lap. He could hardly remember the last time he had embraced anyone, but he knew it had been his precious Mishkla. He had forgotten how it felt to comfort another being in pain. "If it's that you've been away, we'll take you home so you can be with him again. It will be a happy time for us all. You will be reunited, and I will know my family for the first time."

Words meant to soothe her reminded her of how far away Gregor was and the extreme dangers he faced. A huge sob racked her body just as her captain returned from his inspection.

Fratino ran toward her, fearful the Trezvindjans had hurt her during his brief absence. "In Val's great name, what have you done to her? Let her go!"

Gaeldoreg grabbed the captain, seizing him from behind. "Quiet! He has not hurt her! She is upset about her husband. Perhaps you know why."

Ceasing to struggle, Fratino nodded. "I do. Let me go to her. Please." He rushed to her side. Unable to see the face hidden against the prince's broad chest, the captain took her hand.

"Milady, I'm here. If you fear for our king, you must remember to trust his safety to Lord Val's care as before. King Gregor is brave and strong. You know how much he hated leaving. What he does is for the good of our people and so those devils will never hurt his family again—especially not you. He made me swear to protect you with my life. No matter what happens, Milady. He will come home. You must believe that. Of all people, you are the one who must keep the strongest faith."

Alexa lifted her tear-streaked face. "Tirstan, I'm trying, but Nikolai is there, too. If something happens, I can't get there the way you and I did all those years ago. I can't let them take him from me. I'd rather die." Again overcome by weeping, she laid her head against the chest of her husband's grandfather.

Braeklojorn's eyes bored into the captain. "I don't understand. I thought we would go to your capital to meet my grandson."

Tirstan continued to hold Alexa's hand. "Milady's five younger children are there. King Gregor and his oldest son, Prince Nikolai, have gone to war."

"War? Why? Where?"

"Why? Because the evil scourge they fight once occupied our nation and nearly destroyed us. They murdered King Maxim and Queen Anlía with poison so that their deaths were long and agonizing. Then, even though we defeated them twenty years ago in a bloody war, they recently began staging raids here. During one raid, they abducted five priestesses, including Queen Alexa. Thankfully, they never discovered her identity. Fortunately, because of her unique persona, they were forced to return the priestesses after a year's captivity. When they did, my beautiful queen was more dead than alive. She had been repeatedly beaten, worked half to death in a labor camp, starved, and then brutally lashed before they finally dumped her into a raging sea. It is a miracle she survived."

Braeklojorn's jaw set. "Who did this, and where is my grandson? I must know."

"A people called Sifiq did this, and King Gregor has sailed to the Sifiq Kingdom to end their violent aggression, once and for all."

Gaeldoreg gasped and uttered several vehement curses. Then, he and Braeklojorn exchanged a string of angry words in their language.

Stern-faced, Braeklojorn said, "Captain, I don't know how long this rain will last. We may have to wait two or three days for the ledges to dry sufficiently to travel safely down the pass, but Gaeldoreg has gone to inform our comrades that we will be leaving with you. We will go with you to your capital of Toraval."

Tirstan stood, somewhat surprised by the prince's abrupt change in mood. Checking on his queen, he was glad to see her calming. To the Trezvindjan, he said, "Your Highness, I am grateful. Your presence should be a balm for her and her children right now. Turand's queen is the strongest person I've ever known, but she has suffered much. She always takes care of her people. Now is our time to help her."

"We shall speak more later, but I assure you. I intend to be more than a simple balm." Once Tirstan left, Braeklojorn tucked his fingers beneath Alexa's chin and lifted her face. "Ma Ishna, are you better?"

When the giant smiled, she suddenly realized how much his smile looked like Gregor's. She wasn't sure if the realization made her want to smile or start crying again. "Ma Ishna?" she murmured thickly, embarrassed by her outburst.

"Ma Ishna," he repeated softly. "My little one."

"Oh. I have a headache. I'm so sorry. I never meant to cry. I don't usually. It's just—I just realized how much my Gregor looks like you. Your eyes. Your smile. Even the way you tilt your head. Maybe that's what happened."

"You do love him, don't you?"

"I sometimes think no woman should love a man as much as I love him. Still, every day I love him more. I physically hurt being separated from him this way."

"I understand. Now, we have a place where you can sleep while you are here. I want you to rest. Would you like something more to eat or drink before you go to bed?"

She shook her head. "No, thank you. After my meditations, I'll try to get some sleep."

She felt silly climbing down from his lap and the tall chair. What would Gregor think to see her now? Pausing, she gave Braeklojorn a wan smile. "A goodnight hug might help."

Lying awake late into the night, Braeklojorn reviewed every moment of a day that had started with him mired in the empty, nearly soulless solitude that had trapped him decades earlier when he had first searched his ship for his missing wife. He remembered struggling to the slick deck of the wildly pitching vessel with the sharp sting of ocean spray against his face that was nothing compared to the daggers stabbing his heart when he realized Mishkla was no longer on board.

Then, Samlian had arrived earlier today with his fellow Turandans. Incensed by the apparent betrayal, he had wanted to snatch Samlian up by the throat and heave him over the side of the mountain. How dare he bring soldiers and a woman to the caves! Braeklojorn wondered how he could have become so easily riled to such murderous fury.

That was when she had stepped forth with those brilliant green eyes and that uncommon air of authority. Never could he have anticipated that she carried news that his precious Mishkla had survived her plunge overboard. He would have searched the world over had he thought even the slightest hope existed that his wife had survived, but the storm had shifted and intensified, wrecking his own sturdy vessel. Lamenting a past impossible to change was useless. He smiled in the dark. As was her way, Mishkla had conquered the storm.

That thought swirled through his mind. Mishkla's father had declared she would be his successor. She had always been brilliant and good with people. When he discovered she was also a mystic, his decision was made easier. Trezvindjans would honor and respect her far more than her brother, the moody, introverted Kaelzron. Knowing that Kaelzron would assume the throne with Mishkla dead, Braeklojorn could not bear to return home. He doubted her brother could maintain the order and values that were Trezvindja's heritage.

Now, Braeklojorn could reconsider. He had briefly discussed the matter with Gaeldoreg. First, they would travel to meet his great-grandchildren and, later, his grandson, who possessed Mishkla's birthright to the royal name and legacy of Krisantal. If Braeklojorn deemed his progeny as worthy as he expected, he would consider returning home to reclaim her crown for her grandson.

Midnight was long past when the giant man's eyes finally closed in slumber. So much had happened in the span of so few hours. As his great heart beat its powerful, regular rhythm and his chest rose and fell with the clean air of this host land, he rested well for the very first time since dragging himself onto Turand's windswept shore after that terrible storm. The vague sensation of fingers floating through the locks of his hair caused him to stir on the fur-covered cushion beneath his head. His mind strained to capture whispers close to his face.

"I always loved watching him as he slept."

"He is beautiful, Mother. My son looks like him."

"I love him so. As I love you."

"I wish we all could have been together."

"Our time will come."

"I must go now, Mother. I love you." Again, the spirit lightly brushed through Braeklojorn's hair. "Farewell, Father."

Braeklojorn turned again, smiling in his sleep with Mishkla's kiss against his temple and the words "I love you, my husband" filling his ears.

⌒

Gaeldoreg inspected horses, bridles, and saddles a final time. "I know you are anxious to rejoin the men you say await you, but it was important to wait for the ledges to dry," he told Fratino. "Lazdrev said the ledges looked fine, but we must still watch for possible rock-falls from above."

The captain nodded understanding. They had arrived four days earlier at the caves. He was indeed anxious to return to his base camp. "My men have been instructed to be watchful and listen for any signs of disturbance on the mountain."

Adjusting the saddle on the horse reserved for Braeklojorn, Gaeldoreg cast Fratino an approving glance. "Wise is the man who knows to listen as well as look for danger on a mountain."

Accepting the compliment without comment, Fratino organized his men for their cautious descent to the camp below. The Trezvindjans knew the pass best. Gaeldoreg and one other would take the lead with Samlian. Turandans and remaining Trezvindjans would alternate, with the queen riding in the middle between her captain and Braeklojorn.

The trip down was much slower than the ascent. The ledge was stable, but rocks had fallen from above, blocking the way in places. Several times, forward riders dismounted perilously close to the precipice's steep edge so they could shove stones over to allow passage. Loose rocks occasionally clattered down the mountainside. Riders gripped their reins while clucking soothing encouragement to nervous horses. Everyone knew a single misstep might prove fatal to rider and beast.

"I'm not certain when I was ever so glad to set my boots on solid ground," Alexa said as Gaeldoreg effortlessly lifted her down from her mount. She stretched and then walked around to her guards, thanking them for their unwavering courage and service that day. Looking around at Gaeldoreg and his men, she said, "No one has told me their names, but I also wish to thank them. It is my way."

He dipped his head respectfully. "They are distant kinsmen but not considered nobility. With your being Queen, we were not sure if we should. Come," he said before leading her to where his men tended their horses.

When they saw her, they immediately formed a line and looked to Gaeldoreg for direction. He spoke quietly in their own language before turning to Alexa. "Braeklojorn and I already knew your language. It is a common one. Melchan helped us teach it to these men. They understand but do not speak it often." He then said, "Queen Alexa, I introduce you to Lazdrev, Talomad, Halnez, and Daelreg."

Alexa proceeded to speak to each, addressing him by name and asking if she was saying his name correctly. She then thanked him for his efforts that day and for joining her journey home to Toraval. They received her attention with sincere appreciation. She could not know how her gesture of genuine gratitude had stirred pride that they could once again serve the Krisantal League.

After a brief rest and time to eat, Samlian suggested continuing on to the base camp. They should be able to complete the short trek before dark. Afterward, they could rest a day or two and plan the remainder of their trip. Concerns had already been discussed about best routes, lodging, and, of course, explanations regarding their enormous travel companions. Captain Fratino agreed with Samlian's logic, so the party mounted and headed toward the waiting camp.

Their arrival sparked a flurry of activity. A very relieved lieutenant was glad he would have no need to send out scouts the following day to search for the opening to the pass. On the other hand, he was unprepared for the fearsome size and appearance of the Trezvindjan travelers who had returned with the queen and his captain. He had thought the stories of mountain giants to be no more than fairy tales. Never was he happier to restore command to a superior officer than that evening.

✑

The day was warm and sunny. Alexa had bathed in the clear waters of a nearby stream and dressed in clean clothes. She now sat on a large rock while Jalisa patiently combed through the tight tangle of golden-brown curls. "Be glad my hair hasn't yet grown back as long as it was," she said humorously.

Captain Fratino laughed. "I do recall watching King Gregor trying to comb through your hair after you washed it when we bivouacked in Garogan Province during the civil war. That was quite a sight."

Too tall to lean against it, Braeklojorn knelt beneath the shade of a nearby tree. "My grandson commands armies and takes time to comb his wife's hair?"

Alexa laughed merrily. "Your grandson, sir, is a man of many talents."

"So it would seem. Now, have you thought more about our route to your capital?"

"I have. The captain and I reviewed our maps earlier. Port Fosan is about three days from here. The roads are good, and there's a garrison along the way where we can stop and spend one night. At Fosan, we will skirt the city and head to the estate of Lord Manaran, an old ally of my husband's and someone whose discretion I can trust.

"I'm certain he'll have valuable suggestions for our trip to Toraval. Safe travel isn't the issue once we leave the coastal region. I just prefer discretion before making a general announcement about your presence until after I introduce you to my children."

"That is understandable," Braeklojorn remarked thoughtfully. "Do you have any ideas about how you might proceed once we depart Fosan?"

Captain Fratino watched Jalisa finish brushing, braiding, and pinning Alexa's hair into place before he walked over and sat on a large tree stump. "The quickest route from Fosan should take only two days to reach Fort Esmeroval. Once there, we can engage a military ferry to carry us most of the way through Zephiria Province. That will shorten the trip considerably."

"That was an excellent suggestion Captain Fratino made this morning. Once we reach the military landing in Zephiria, we're fairly close to the estate of Lord Willem Zephirás. I've known him and his wife most of my life. Gregor and Willem are also close friends. I'm confident they'll help us complete the final leg of the trip, which should only be another two days."

"I dispatched two of my guards this morning to alert the garrison and Lord Manaran to expect us in the coming days," Fratino said. "Another two will depart in the morning ahead of our main party."

"You are an extremely cautious man, Captain Fratino," Braeklojorn observed. "It is fortuitous that you brought such a large contingent of men with you."

"Sir," the captain said as he stood up, "King Gregor left Queen Alexa's safety in my hands. I was away when another captain's lack of vigilance allowed her to be abducted and tormented. I will not be guilty of a similar error in judgment. If you will excuse me."

"I believe you struck a nerve," Gaeldoreg told Braeklojorn as Fratino brushed past him.

Alexa sighed. "When I took up a mission of mercy to another coastal province, he had taken leave for the first time in years to visit his aging parents. I don't know if the captain in charge of that mission could have prevented what happened, but this captain has always blamed himself."

"A man who learns from the mistakes of others is a valuable resource, Ma Ishna, especially when he is as loyal as your Captain Fratino. Always remember that."

A lighter mood prevailed over supper. Throughout the years, the Forsays occasionally went into town and purchased paper, inks, and books for their reclusive friends. The Trezvindjans had always covered purchases with gold and silver pieces. The strangers had also looked forward to visits that included baskets laden with fresh fruits and vegetables, butter, cheese, cooking fat, and homemade soaps. Samlian's grandfather and father had never once asked for anything. Now, although tasked with packing and transporting various Trezvindjan possessions off the mountain for shipment to Toraval, Samlian discussed looking forward to showing his wife many fine items earmarked as gifts for the Forsay family.

Gaeldoreg, who also seemed exceptionally cheerful, continued to be amused by the idea of Alexa's six children. "Dear lady, tell me once again. How do you remember all their names? What are they?"

Alexa rolled her eyes. "Try to remember on your own."

"I cannot."

"I won't tell you again."

"You will." Suddenly, the big man jumped up. Placing his hands at her waist, he lifted her from her seat and started carrying her around. "I now have the advantage. Tell me!"

"Gaeldoreg! Set her down! What are you thinking?"

"I will put her down when she answers me!"

"Gaeldoreg! Release me!" Alexa commanded, trying not to laugh.

"If I release you, you'll fall," he warned teasingly.

"Release me now, I said," she demanded playfully when a sudden, odd sensation rippled through her being.

Gaeldoreg turned, intending to drop her onto a mound of soft grass. Instead of falling when he let her go, Alexa suddenly became enveloped in blue-white light as she rose and hovered above his head. Gaeldoreg's stunned eyes grew wide as he fell to his knees.

As Turandan guards knelt, Braeklojorn swiftly followed Tirstan Fratino and the Valiria priestess to where Alexa had risen just above the treetops. Copying Fratino's lead, the shocked prince also knelt, waiting and watching. He wondered if he imagined the sounds of music carried on the breeze. His one certainty was that he had never witnessed anything quite like the glittering lights accompanying Alexa when she slowly descended to the ground.

Captain Fratino instantly reached out to steady her. "Lady Valkana, praises to our Lord Val. Is all well?"

"Tirstan," Alexa said, her voice quietly insistent, "we must hasten our trip as much as possible. My husband needs my help."

Braeklojorn studied Alexa's solemn features a little later as she sat close to the fire, sipping tea. Then, recovered from his initial shock, he lowered himself onto a mat where he could continue to watch her face. "Ma Ishna," he said tenderly, "tell me. What do you know?"

Heavy eyelids fluttered before Alexa finally met his waiting gaze. "It came to me—a vision. The Sifiq are planning a major offensive. I don't know how soon. Gregor and Nikolai expect something. They're preparing strategies, but I know they need support and reinforcements."

"Why did you not tell me about your mystic capabilities?"

"I told you about my dreams and visions."

"Many have dreams." He reached out, grasping her hand. "The abilities you possess far exceed mere dreams or even visions."

Looking into his eyes, she felt almost as if she were escaping into the comforting refuge of her husband's protection. How much this man resembled Gregor! "We all have similar abilities. I decided to develop and use mine for the good of Val's people. This is how I've helped my husband keep our nation safe and peaceful for years."

"Even though it often frightens and brings you pain?"

Braeklojorn noted the slight quiver of her lips when she nodded yes. He couldn't resist the urge to stroke her cheek. Through this complex woman, the Trezvindjan prince was slowly coming to know, respect, and admire the grandson he had yet to meet. When she remained silent, he said, "Ma Ishna, my grandson is a blessed man to have such a wife. I make you this promise. I will help you give him the support he needs. But, for now, rest so we can start our journey to your city of Toraval."

"Thank you, sir," she murmured appreciatively.

"Perhaps you might consider changing the sir to grandfather," he suggested hopefully.

Sparkling lights chased gloom from her eyes. Intertwining her elegant fingers with those on his strong hands, she whispered words that banished some of the shadows of grief from his soul. "Goodnight, Grandfather."

Chapter 11

"Alexa! Welcome, my dear," the aging nobleman greeted his queen with kisses on her cheeks and an embrace.

"Lord Manaran, how good it is to see you! I do apologize for the late arrival."

"Think nothing of it. A lonely, old widower is glad of company any time. Your messenger said you were bringing guests. Where are they?"

"With my Guard. I wanted to prepare you first," she said, her features simultaneously comical and serious.

"Oh, dear, what have you brought to enliven my boring existence this time?"

"Lord Manaran, I have six of the tallest guests you have ever seen. Ever."

"My dear, you forget how many times I've hosted your dear husband and our Prince Nikolai," Manaran said with a chuckle.

"Not at all," Alexa replied. "I've come to you because I knew I could rely on your hospitality, your confidentiality, and your advice until I could reveal what is nothing less than a miracle."

The lord's forehead crinkled, and his eyebrows knit together as he noted the earnest turn in her mood. "Miracle, you say. What sort of miracle, my dear?"

"A miracle I wish to keep discreet until after I reach Toraval and my children. My lord, the guests in my party include Gregor's grandfather."

"Gregor's grandfather?" he gasped. "Alexa, is that possible? Especially after all these years?"

"A long, tragic story, but a fascinating one. I'll explain later, but I'd like to bring them inside. I only need to be sure that your household staff understands I do not want their presence publicly disclosed yet. My children deserve to be the first to know."

"Of course, my dear. While I inform staff and have quarters prepared, you bring your guests. They are most welcome here."

Despite the late hour and the surprising number of guests, Lord Manaran's kitchen staff succeeded in serving a generous supper. His dining table boasted platters of cold meats, cheeses, olives, freshly sliced vegetables, and baskets of breads accompanied by jugs of wines from the nobleman's own vineyards. While hungry visitors gratefully satisfied appetites whetted by a tedious day of travel, they also deferred all questions concerning their startling appearance to Alexa and Braeklojorn.

With supper consumed, Lord Manaran rose and replenished wine glasses himself. "I am astonished you managed to keep your presence undetected for so long," he told the Trezvindjan prince. "It also saddens me thinking you missed Anlía's life. She was an extraordinary woman."

Braeklojorn's eyes widened with sudden interest. "You knew my daughter?"

"Indeed I did. I introduced her to Maxim. She lived and taught with a community of priestesses here in Fosan Province. I never saw a man so instantly enchanted by a woman in my life, although I understand Gregor reacted much the same to Alexa here."

Alexa blushed uncomfortably. "I think my husband was intrigued by the audacious priestess who walked into the middle of his court filled with Sifiq soldiers who were ready to slit her throat and claim her prized Valiria cloak."

"Is that your explanation?" Manaran chuckled teasingly.

Observing Alexa's attempt to avoid the subject, Braeklojorn rescued her. "Lord Manaran, you are the first person I've met who actually knew my daughter. Might I trouble you to share some of your memories of her?"

The nobleman faced the prince. Those dark, penetrating eyes were insistent—impossible to ignore. "Your Highness, while the others retire to their chambers for the night, let us go where we can be more comfortable. I would be happy to tell you more about your beautiful daughter and another queen Turand loved dearly. Alexa, will you join us?"

Inside a spacious drawing room, Braeklojorn waited for Alexa to sit down before accepting a large snifter of brandy and lowering his tall frame onto a wide sofa upholstered in rose-colored brocade. His long legs stretched beyond the rosewood coffee table finished with touches of burnished gold. Any physical discomfort on the smaller scale furnishings was quickly vanquished by his anticipation of listening to firsthand accounts of his daughter.

"My mother introduced me to Anlía following an outbreak of a fever contagion at the docks. She had come with Valiria to tend to the sick." Manaran grinned. "Mother was enthralled with Anlía's grace and beauty and, being quite honest, was hopeful I would be interested enough to call off my wedding. She never liked my choice for a bride."

Receiving only a hint of a smile from Braeklojorn, the nobleman continued, "Turand's disdain for spiritual matters was reaching a crossroads at the time. Hardships caused some people to look inward. Mother had always maintained faith, which attracted her to Anlía. The two developed a strong bond despite the difference in their ages. Anlía was self-assured, confident, secure in her faith, and compassionate. She was also quite entertaining company. She sang and danced but never lost her essence as Valiria.

"Anyway, with final preparations for my wedding underway, Mother convinced Anlía to spend some time with us. A month later, Maxim arrived as my honored guest. When I introduced the two, their reaction to one another was instantaneous. We all noticed as if time froze in that moment. Yes, in one way, they made an odd-looking couple. Anlía was much taller than Maxim, but the king never lost the regal bearing of his rank. From their first moments together, they moved in synchronous perfection as if destiny meant for them to be together."

〰

"Is Grandfather well this morning?" Alexa asked Gaeldoreg as she gazed through a window and watched Braeklojorn strolling along a gravel path outside.

"His heart is greatly moved," Gaeldoreg replied. "His is a soul of profound emotion, and it has absorbed much of late. Hearing stories last night about the daughter he never even knew was born filled him with joy and sadness. He seeks balance for his heart."

"Have I brought him too much?" Alexa asked, turning concerned eyes to meet the dark eyes of her husband's cousin with whom she now shared a blood bond.

Gentle regard now replaced former ferocity. Gaeldoreg shook his head. "I will not lie and say you haven't opened an unhealed wound. However, you have also given him renewed purpose. Mishkla lives through your Gregor and the children you bore him. That gives Braeklojorn reason to live again."

"We need him." Alexa paused, then smiled. "We need all of you."

Later, Alexa turned grateful eyes to Lord Manaran. "I'm so glad Gregor left his travel coaches here in your care. Your suggestion to use them for Braeklojorn and the others to travel to Toraval is excellent."

"You said you wanted discretion until you introduce them to your children."

"It's clear why my husband values your friendship and your advice so highly. You, sir, are a wonder."

After a flurry of last-minute instructions and farewells, the Trezvindjans settled into the luxurious but somewhat cramped confines of the royal coaches to travel the busy roads around Fosan Port. With their larger mounts now in the care of two soldiers charged as horse masters, Captain Fratino led his party onto the road toward Toraval as Alexa waved a cheery goodbye to Lord Manaran.

~

Early sunrise shone silver and gold ribbons on the ripples formed by currents along the Zephir River. Trees held morning mist captive in their canopy. A veritable symphony of birdsong played to the vibrating rhythms of thousands of crickets. Summer air felt alive with the fragrant blend of wildflowers, soil, and wildlife drifting from the nearby forest.

Closer at hand, the ferry master's sullen expression was no match for Tirstan Fratino's long-practiced ability to command difficult situations. "I have no time for excuses or complaints. Advance notice advised that the queen's party would be arriving. Did the garrison commander advise you, or did he not?"

"He did, but…" the officer began.

"Are both ferries available or not?"

"They are, Captain Fratino, but I didn't expect to have both moving out at the same time."

"Chief Jothan, I am escorting important visitors to the palace in Toraval. Both ferries are to be readied for immediate departure. If they are not, I will advise the garrison commander of your failure to comply with orders."

"Captain, please!"

"Prepare both ferries. Now! Make haste, man, or you will answer to a higher authority than mine!"

Curious about the delay, Alexa decided to investigate. "Captain Fratino, is there a problem?"

"Your Majesty, there was a question about the need for both of the large ferries. I believe that matter is resolved."

The ferry master's eyes widened in shock. Quickly, he bowed low and said, "It is an honor to serve you, Your Majesty. I'm waiting for additional crew to arrive. My men and I will begin supervising the load process now."

Thankfully, early summer weather was hot but clear for the river journey. Conversation was sparse as the ferry master and crew constantly called back and forth about large rocks or fallen trees and branches that might snag the vessels. Passing near shore provided shade from leaf-laden tree branches stretching over the water, offering welcome relief from the sun's blistering afternoon rays. As late afternoon approached, insects buzzed beasts and passengers alike. Despite the trip's miseries, the river route substantially shortened their journey.

Alexa looked up as the transport crew maneuvered the ferries toward their destination. She suddenly smiled and started waving excitedly. With his arm high in the air, Willem waved back at her. Having received Captain Fratino's message, he had checked the military ferry dock twice daily for the past two days, hoping to meet her arrival. The disembarkation ramp had hardly been secured before Alexa raced across its length and threw herself into Willem's arms.

"Greetings, Your Majesty!" he gasped, hugging her before kissing both her cheeks. "Welcome to Zephiria."

"Oh, Willem, I didn't expect you to meet us, but how glad I am you're here. I have so much to tell you."

"Your message said you were bringing important guests to Toraval. Katara has the entire staff in an uproar getting everything ready for something exciting. I hope you're not going to disappoint her."

"I think not," Alexa said, her eyes twinkling mischievously, "but I think you should prepare yourself for a shock. A real one."

"After hearing about your healing and converting your Sifiq tormentor Raf-Zan and then learning that Gregor named him to an official advisory post, I think little could shock me these days." The grin on her face promised otherwise. "Alexa? What now?"

"Have you ever heard of Zemtoval or Corlozem Pass?"

Willem's expression turned thoughtful. "You test my memory. Hmmm. Yes, I do recall reading about a tidal wave destroying Zemtoval years ago. Some say the area is haunted. Corlozem Pass, though. Isn't that somewhere in the Zemfosa Mountains?"

"Yes, it is," Alexa answered in a mysterious voice.

Willem's eyes narrowed. "I seem to remember some sort of mysterious legend connected to it. Don't tell me you solved the mystery."

"Excellent, Willem. And you won't believe what I found."

"Excuse me, Your Majesty, we're ready to disembark," Captain Fratino informed her. He had recognized Lord Zephirás and given her time to prepare him for introductions to the Trezvindjans.

"Please, Captain, you may begin." Then, turning to Willem, she said, "My friend, the legend concerned giants who turned out to be stranded victims of a shipwreck. Because of their leader's tragic heartbreak, they became a group of hermits. I have given him cause to rejoin the world of the living, and now I'm escorting him to Toraval to introduce him to part of his revitalized purpose in life."

At that moment, Willem Zephirás glanced up. Stunned, he stared as Braeklojorn Vosklon and Gaeldoreg strode down the ramp to stand at Alexa's side. The first clear thought to strike Willem was that these men were even taller than Gregor and Nikolai, making their appearance all the more impressive.

"Ma Ishna, may I assume this is the fine friend of whom you spoke so warmly?"

"He is. Grandfather, may I introduce you to Lord Willem Zephirás?" To Willem, she said, "Willem, I am honored to introduce you to Prince Braeklojorn Vosklon of Trezvindja. He is Gregor's grandfather."

Willem's sharp intake of breath was audible. Then, swiftly, he regained his poise, bowed respectfully, and greeted Alexa's surprise guest. "Prince Braeklojorn, I am honored to welcome you to Zephiria. I must admit to being utterly astonished but thrilled to meet you."

Braeklojorn met the kind eyes of the man he knew to be fast friends with his grandson. "I know my presence comes as a shock to you, Lord Zephirás, just as recently learning that I had a grandson shocked me. I'm certain Alexa and I can satisfy your curiosity with quite an interesting story. In the meantime, let me introduce you to my cousin, Gaeldoreg Vosklon."

After Willem greeted the prince's cousin, he took a deep breath as he watched Captain Fratino direct guardsmen and the remaining Trezvindjans from the ferries. With slightly raised eyebrows, he could only imagine how his petite wife would react upon meeting their houseguests. Alexa's message had contained a tone of urgency and confidentiality, but he had never expected anything quite so spectacular.

Taking mercy on Willem's bewilderment, Alexa suggested they avail themselves of one of Gregor's travel coaches. Once horses were harnessed and hitched, Braeklojorn helped her inside before climbing in to sit beside her. Willem and Gaeldoreg then joined them for the ride to Willem's estate.

"So, as I understand, you and your entourage established a refuge inside hidden caves at Corlozem Pass and lived there for seventy years?" Willem asked incredulously, his bright blue eyes carefully studying Braeklojorn.

"Yes. You must understand. I believed my Mishkla had drowned when she washed overboard that night. I lost my wife, who was carrying our baby. She was everything to me, and I blamed myself. I lost all will to live. I had no desire to return home, even had I been able to find the means. What I wanted was to die. Whether by fate or divine providence, I now believe I was meant to survive for this time."

Willem shook his head as if trying to shake the bits and pieces of the story into order inside his mind. "I need only look at you to see how much you and Gregor look alike. The resemblance is uncanny."

"So Alexa tells me," Braeklojorn said with an introspective smile. "I only hope my grandson can forgive me for the time lost and will allow me to be part of his life."

Smiling thoughtfully, Willem nodded. "Once he hears what happened, he will. Gregor and I were boyhood friends. I knew his parents. They instilled in him a deep love of family, and he still grieves their loss. Despite those of us who love him, he always felt a certain aloneness—that is, until Alexa entered his life. I think his greatest fear was returning to that state of aloneness or letting that happen to one of his children."

Gaeldoreg's eyes grew suspiciously misty. "Ishna, is that why you and our Gregor have so many babies?"

Blushing, Alexa stared down at her hands. "Perhaps. Partly, anyway."

Braeklojorn placed an arm around her shoulders. "Ma Ishna, your husband adores you. I think there must be no better reason for you to have so many children."

Willem sat straighter in his seat. "All of Turand will attest to that fact, Your Highness. I knew Gregor and Alexa each long before they met. I know the circumstances of their marriage, and I saw them during the early days of their marriage. When most questioned their union, I remember Alexa fretting over Gregor not getting enough rest and pleading with me to stay loyal to him during extremely trying times. I daresay I've never known two people as devoted to one other as Gregor and Alexa. Our bards even compose ballads about their love. Yes, he adores her, but she also adores him."

Gratitude shone from Braeklojorn's eyes when he looked back at Willem. Although once again noting that haunting reference to an unsettled beginning to his grandson's marriage—something he hoped one day to better comprehend—he also gained further insight into Gregor's commitment to family and the woman who had expended such extraordinary effort discovering her husband's Trezvindjan heritage. The more he learned of his grandson, the more worthy the prince believed Gregor was to wear the sacred Krisantal crest.

By evening, Katara had recovered both speech and humor after her husband's arrival with their old friend and her entourage, who dwarfed their petite hostess. Introductions were quickly followed by refreshments served to weary travelers. As servants guided visitors to their guest chambers, Alexa tarried to explain the origin of the unusual arrivals for Katara's benefit. Later, with Katara's nerves happily restored and a generous supper ready to serve, their hostess made a final check on the kitchen before going to the large parlor, where her husband engaged in intense conversation with their company.

"Willem!" she said more firmly a third time, finally gaining his attention. "Dinner is ready. May we invite our guests to dine?"

"Dear Katara, my apologies. I am beyond fascinated with Prince Braeklojorn's descriptions of Trezvindja. His account of surviving the shipwreck and then living here in Turand all these years is—well—miraculous!"

After Willem and Katara ushered their guests into the dining room, Alexa offered prayer over their meal. Conversation gradually shifted from previously unknown details regarding Gregor's heritage to plans once the party reached Toraval. Braeklojorn expressed elation at the prospect of meeting his great-grandchildren. However, his excitement was tempered by concern about their reaction to his surprise appearance.

The prince then startled his hosts and even Alexa with an open discussion of past conflicts between Trezvindja and the aggressive Sifiq. At one point, following extended bloody campaigns, more powerful Trezvindjan warriors drove Sifiq armies from two neighboring nations, forcing the Sifiq king to agree to end incursions into their territories. Proud of his grandson's bold stand to halt violent Sifiq raids into Turand, Braeklojorn expressed intentions to help stop Bin-Lot from launching further attacks.

As servants cleared remnants of Katara's delicious feast from the table, discussion intensified over dessert. Willem questioned the prince regarding how he might manage such support after his long absence from Trezvindja. Gaeldoreg explained that family leagues in their island nation had developed over millennia. He was confident even a hundred years would be as the blink of an eye when it came to the cooperative nature of the leagues, especially if confronting an enemy threatening one of their own. Further, with Gregor being the rightful heir to the throne of Trezvindja, the family leagues would be called together not only by longstanding charter law but by Trezvindja's Mystic Council to defend their king.

Alexa's eyebrows shot up. "Mystic Council? You never mentioned that before."

"Ma Ishna, we still haven't had time to discuss our spiritual beliefs with you, but our teachings are much the same as yours. Truth, honesty, and love are paramount virtues. We seek peace. Violence and war become our final recourse when no other options remain. You rely on a wide network of priestesses and priests headed by your Valkana to guide your people on spiritual matters. Trezvindjans rely on our Mystic Council."

"In your absence, wouldn't someone else have assumed the throne?" Willem asked, resuming a more definable direction.

Gaeldoreg said, "Assuming Mishkla's father is dead, her brother Kaelzron would have assumed the throne."

"Would he not oppose anyone laying claim to his crown after all these years?" Willem's probing questions were sensible, echoing those Stefan Sidano would surely ask once the group arrived in Toraval.

Braeklojorn nodded. "Perhaps, but it wouldn't matter. Upon presentation of a rightful heir, charter law would defer his reign to historical custodial status. In this case, Gregor is the rightful king, even without an official coronation. If he can't appear to assume his throne, he has children who can act as regent until he can."

"And if this Kaelzron refuses to relinquish the throne?" Willem pressed the issue.

Gaeldoreg smiled grimly. "Time cannot change some things. I know my people, our laws, and our ways. I belong to the Vosklon League—or family. At this moment, Kaelzron likely heads the Krisantal League only because Gregor is unknown to them. Kaelzron may be king now, but any refusal to relinquish his crown would shame their entire league. That is something their league would not tolerate. Once assured of Gregor's right to the throne, their league leaders will make certain that Kaelzron concedes to the proper heir."

"You are doubtful, Lord Zephirás," Braeklojorn said as he watched Willem's countenance settle into its more typically serious expression.

"No, Your Highness," Willem responded, "you know your culture and your laws. I am thinking I might accompany you when you leave for Toraval."

"Willem?"

"Alexa, there's no denying the magnitude of the crisis we face. I've known you too long not to see what you're thinking. If I'm right, Stefan will need all the help he can get."

Alexa sighed. "Gregor needs reinforcements facing the Sifiq in their own lands. I feel it."

Willem nodded solemnly. "More than that, he needs you. I have no idea how you have the courage to even consider this after the way they tortured you, but I see it in your eyes. And I love you for it, dear friend."

"Nothing," she swallowed hard, "not even Bin-Lot himself will stop me from going to Gregor if he needs me."

Alexa rose from her chair and went to Willem. Kneeling beside him at the head of his long dining room table, she gazed up into shining blue eyes. As Willem grasped Alexa's trembling hands, Katara's arms wrapped around her shoulders. Observing the powerful bond the three shared, Braeklojorn began to comprehend their shared commitment as friends and their profound love for Gregor.

⌐

"Your capital city is clean and beautiful," Braeklojorn remarked as he looked out the windows of the coach winding its way toward the royal palace.

A wide grin lit Gaeldoreg's face. "Your people look surprised to see the carriages. I do like the carillon bells. Do they always ring that way?"

Alexa laughed. "They ring daily at noon, on feast days, and when I issue special notices. There are times, though, when our Lord Val sounds them himself. Today is apparently one of those days. The melody is joyful, so I take it you are being welcomed to Toraval."

Gaeldoreg laughed happily. "I accept your Lord Val's welcome with a grateful heart! If only my king were here so I could greet him!"

"All in good time, cousin," Braeklojorn said, his dark face more anxious than his cousin's.

"I believe my lord grows nervous about meeting his family," Gaeldoreg told Alexa, the sparkle in his brown eyes never diminishing.

Taking Braeklojorn's hand. Alexa softly said, "Grandfather, you mustn't worry. Trust me. All will be fine."

Nearly half an hour passed before Alexa successfully guided Braeklojorn and Gaeldoreg into her office suite. At the same time, Willem and Captain Fratino attended the remaining Trezvindjans until the visitors could be introduced to the children. Walking through the corridor toward Stefan's office, she encountered Gregor Maconti.

"Your Majesty, good morning. I wasn't aware you were back. Welcome home."

"Master Maconti, thank you. I've just returned. I need to speak with my daughter. Do you know where she is?"

"Mother! I'm here!" Anlía swept her mother into a welcoming embrace. "When did you return?"

"Not long ago," Alexa said, stretching upward to kiss her daughter's cheeks. "I have brought a fantastic surprise, but I want to start with you before revealing the surprise to your brothers and sisters."

"That should be easy. The little ones are in class. DiMarco and Thikos are with Papino Stefan reviewing the next outbound supply shipment. You will be very proud of the work they're doing."

Pride and relief showed plainly on Alexa's face. Her sons were young, but they were taking their responsibilities seriously. Turning to Gregor Maconti, she said, "Would you kindly arrange to have my other children meet me in the library in forty-five minutes?"

With Maconti dispatched to gather the other children, Alexa linked her arm with Anlía's as they walked to the anteroom outside the office where Braeklojorn nervously waited.

"Mother, are you all right?" Anlía asked, noting her mother's unusual agitation.

Alexa smiled. "I am, my dear. It's just—Anlía, there are two men inside waiting to meet you. We will have to explain all the details of how I came to find them."

"Does it involve all the strange dreams you were having?"

Closing her eyes, Alexa marveled at the depth of her daughter's intuition. "Yes. The dreams led me to them. Anlía, one of the men is extremely nervous about meeting you. And your brothers and sisters. Even more so, he worries about meeting your father."

"Why?"

"Come. First, let me introduce you." Opening the office door, Alexa entered with Anlía following.

When Braeklojorn turned, Gaeldoreg alertly caught him by the arm when he lurched sideways, nearly falling. Alexa also jumped to his aid, steadying him as he stared in disbelief at the beautiful young face gazing back at him with such concern. Waving off his rescuers, Braeklojorn recovered his balance. Then, slowly stepping toward Anlía, he reached out and caressed her smooth cheek.

"Only the eyes are different. Alexa, except for having your eyes, seeing her is exactly like looking at Mishkla."

Empathically sensing their connection, Anlía lifted her hand to cover the large hand resting against her cheek. Shifting her gaze, she whispered, "Mother?"

"Anlía, I want you to meet Prince Braeklojorn Vosklon. He is your father's grandfather."

When Anlía looked back into his face, she instantly felt the familial link and something more. A need to be loved and to give love. Thoughtfully, she lifted both her hands, framing his now-damp face between her palms. "I see my father in your face. Your eyes. The shape of your mouth. My brother Nikolai also looks like you. What a marvelous gift in this terrible time of tumult to receive the gift of a grandfather. May I embrace you?"

For the briefest moment, Braeklojorn thought his heart might explode from his chest with joy greater than he imagined possible in these later years of his life. This child—descended from his great love for Mishkla—calling him a gift when she was the greatest gift of all. Embracing her tightly, he softly chanted a blessing on her in Trezvindjan. Meanwhile, the suddenly serious Gaeldoreg had also grown teary-eyed and translated from where he knelt at their feet.

In the library a little later, while Alexa went to find the other children, the prince contemplated the presence of his great-granddaughter. She had the same beautiful dark complexion as Mishkla. Held away from her face with a padded velvet band, thick black hair fell in lustrous waves to the middle of her back. Tall and graceful, Anlía carried her shoulders back and moved with Mishkla's same air of regal elegance and confidence.

"Grandfather, may I offer you some brandy? This is Father's favorite, especially when he's having a hard day. I know it's early, but today might qualify as an exception." The sparkle in her eye complemented the brilliance of her smile.

"Thank you, Anlía. If it's your father's favorite, we shall make an early exception."

"She is stunning," Gaeldoreg observed quietly as they watched her pour two drinks. "Can you imagine the reactions if she appears at court in Tarahlaz? There will be many who remember Mishkla."

"I expect so," Braeklojorn replied, his thoughts racing. Smiling, he accepted the crystal glass from Anlía. He then waited for her to join him on the first furniture large enough for him to sit on comfortably since departing the Corlozem caves.

While Braeklojorn chatted with his grandson's eldest daughter, Alexa met her middle sons and Stefan in the palace's sun-drenched grand foyer.

"Good morning! I wondered what happened to you two!" she exclaimed as she greeted her sons with affectionate hugs.

Stefan chuckled as he embraced her. "It's my fault. These two young men are proving to be surprisingly apt assistants. DiMarco keeps the Quartermaster Corps on their toes with his reviews, and Thikos is a genius working on ideas with the planners for expanding the shipyards and ports."

"I had the feeling they would make me proud. Now, while they go locate their little sisters, I need a word with you."

As soon as the boys were out of sight, Stefan's gray eyes darkened with concern. "Is everything all right?"

Nodding, she said, "Fine. Willem is here somewhere. He plans to stay to lend you additional support."

"That sounds ominous enough. What are you planning now?"

"Don't always assume the worst. I've actually had quite a momentous journey with results I hope will deliver Gregor some much needed help."

Stefan's gray eyes narrowed suspiciously. "Momentous in what way?"

"Do you recall all of Nikolai's talk about the Protectors after traveling to Coloridia?"

"I do. They refused to meet with Nikolai and advised the Coloridians against providing us further support after Bin-Lot terminated negotiations."

"I believe that situation will change. Soon. I'm planning to sail to the capital city of these Protectors to personally discuss the matter."

Stefan gave a quick shake of his head. "Exactly how do you plan to do that? No one knows where they dwell."

Alexa grinned mysteriously. "It seems some of them were stranded here after a shipwreck years ago. About seventy, as it turns out. One of them is a prince."

"Alexa, am I ready to hear this?"

"No, but I shall tell you anyway. Two days before the shipwreck, the prince's wife was swept overboard and presumed drowned. His wife was heir to the throne of Trezvindja, the homeland of the Protectors. She washed up on shore at a place called Zemtoval and was cared for by Valiria until her baby was born. His wife died, but her baby survived."

Stefan felt his heartbeat quickening. "If you don't tell me soon…"

Shaking her head, Alexa could hardly contain her excitement. "Stefan, if you find Willem, he can tell you more details. Prince Braeklojorn Vosklon is in the library with Anlía and is waiting to meet the other children. The prince is Gregor's grandfather."

Standing with his mouth agape, Stefan found Alexa's announcement impossible to believe. Staring at her, he shook his head in utter disbelief. Stuttering, he finally choked out a response. "How? I cannot believe this! How is that possible?"

Alexa grasped his upper arms. "I comprehend your shock, but it's true. The dreams guided me to Braeklojorn for a purpose. I can only believe that reason was to secure the aid Gregor needs."

Minutes later, Alexa stopped outside the library with her younger children. Kneeling, she smiled into the faces of her twin daughters. "You young ladies, especially, need to mind your manners. Inside are two very distinguished older gentlemen who are quite anxious to meet you. I expect you to behave like the royal princesses you are."

"Mother, who are they, and why are you so serious about them?" Karina asked.

"I'm so serious because I recently gave them a big shock. It will not hurt you to make good impressions after I've told them so much about you."

"Mother," Thikos said, "will you not tell us who they are?"

Looking up into her son's face and thinking how tall he and his brother had grown, she took his hand and stood. "Thikos, I followed those dreams Val showed me. There's so much to tell you, but the dreams led me to these men. One is a prince whose name is Braeklojorn Vosklon. He is your father's grandfather."

DiMarco smiled in astonishment. "Mother, is this a miracle?"

"I believe so. Shall we go in and meet our miracle?"

Opening the library's double doors, Alexa ushered the children inside. Rising from the sofa, Braeklojorn and Gaeldoreg were immediately captivated by four bright, confident faces showing no indication of the disdain or distaste they had feared. Instead, they perceived natural inquisitiveness as Alexa proceeded to introduce her sons, who formally bowed and welcomed their visitors. Presenting two young princesses, however, quickly altered the more formal mood.

Attired in school uniforms of ruffled, light blue blouses and dark blue skirts, the girls looked prim and pretty with thick black hair secured at the back of their heads with large barrettes. However, within moments, their boundless energy and curiosity dispelled the fine impression of demure appearances and decorous curtsies.

"Are you really Father's grandfather?" Marina asked, her brown eyes wide and sparkling.

Sitting down again, Braeklojorn smiled at his young interrogator. "I am."

"This is fantastic! You must tell us the story. You understand that's what grandfathers do. They tell stories. That's how children learn about families and the past and everything," Karina said excitedly.

Gaeldoreg looked up at Alexa, who was trying to stifle laughter. "You did warn him."

"Oh, yes! Stories! You're right, Karina! This is more than amazing! Father will be so excited when he finds out he has a grandfather!" Suddenly, Marina's face turned serious, almost sad. "But..."

"But what, little one?" Braeklojorn asked, concerned by the abrupt change in the girl's expression.

"You are Father's grandfather, not ours."

"Wait. Help me. Which one are you?"

"I'm Marina."

"Yes, of course. Marina, come," Braeklojorn said, pulling the crest-fallen child onto his lap. "I'm your father's grandfather, which makes me your great-grandfather."

The girl's features grew intense as she studied Braeklojorn's face, which reminded her of her father. "Great-grandfather? So you can still tell us stories?"

Karina added, "And maybe give us hugs? Like real grandfathers do?"

Thoroughly charmed, Braeklojorn also drew Karina onto his lap. With an arm snugly around each girl, he relished this precious new connection to a family he had relegated to lost dreams. "If you agree to call me *Grandfather*, I will be more than happy to hug each of you and tell you many stories."

Without the slightest hesitation, Marina extended her arms to encircle Braeklojorn's neck and whispered, "*Grandfather*. That sounds very good. We always wanted a grandfather."

Karina rested her head against his shoulder. "Father has been gone to war a long time, and we miss him so much. It feels especially nice to have a grandfather right now."

Seeing Alexa's tearful reaction, DiMarco and Thikos went to their mother. With loving arms around her, they watched as the elegant, silver-haired stranger, who resembled and sounded like their father, spoke words of encouragement that soothed the worry and fears of children and adults alike.

⌐

"Mother, everyone is waiting in the conference room. Are you ready?"

Alexa cast an upward glance over her shoulder from where she knelt inside the palace chapel. Anlía stood at the entrance. When Alexa rose and faced her daughter, she again admired the young woman before her. Like her mother, Anlía had set aside more fashionable gowns in these austere times for practical attire of blouses and skirts made from fabrics allowing them the flexibility to go from the palace to work on war-related projects in the community whenever needed. Her daughter's height, glossy black hair, and smooth, dark complexion evidenced her father's Trezvindjan heritage. By any standards, she was beautiful to behold.

Anlía exuded fortitude and confidence unusual for her age. Alexa understood that those traits stemmed from values instilled from early childhood, inspiring and impelling her daughter toward imminent assessment and early pronouncement of vows as a Valiria priestess, much like her mother. While the two held differences of opinion on certain issues, mutual respect for essential principles bound them in agreement to accept Val's revelation of his will in all matters. However, for that fleeting moment, all the years of Anlía's life were a treasure filling her mother's heart.

"How was your visit to the gallery with Grandfather?" Alexa asked as the two left the peaceful chapel for what they expected would be a contentious meeting.

"Bittersweet. Grandmother's portraits fascinated him, especially the one of her holding Father when he was little. Tears rolled down his cheeks nearly the whole time. It was hard for him to leave."

"As a parent, I can imagine how he must feel. He missed her entire life when she was relatively close by."

"Despite his sadness, I know his heart is overflowing with happiness that you found him. He constantly spoke of Father and how excited he is to meet him. And us. How well he loves each of us already!"

Alexa nodded as they stopped outside the doors of the conference room. "Let us hope his promises of love for family translate into the help your father needs to defeat the Sifiq, once and for all. That way, we can bring Father, Nikolai, and our people home to live in peace."

Nearly an hour later, Victor hammered away at why the Protectors had only guaranteed the safety of the diplomatic mission when the Coloridian ambassador took Nikolai to meet King Bin-Lot. Moreover, once the diplomatic delegation returned to Coloridia, Protectors had then refused to discuss the failed mission with either the Turandan prince or Ambassador Laritha. If the Protectors were indeed Trezvindjans, then Victor demanded to know why they had appeared to be protecting the Sifiq they supposedly despised.

Impatient with Victor's monopoly of the meeting, Gaeldoreg tossed long, gray hair over his shoulder and finally stood. Brown eyes glittered angrily. Squaring broad shoulders and assuming a menacing stance, he bellowed, "Lord Garogan, we understood your observations and complaints the first five times you expounded them. I believe you can spare us another four repetitions. If you will kindly allow me or my prince to speak."

Glaring furiously at the Trezvindjan but carefully assessing the situation, Victor gave a sarcastic nod and cynical wave of his hand. "Please."

"As Prince Braeklojorn already explained, there is a circumstance that does not correspond with Trezvindjan laws in effect for centuries. Believe me when I say our laws are not easily changed. When we return home, our first task will be to learn why the Council of Protectors did not support Prince Nikolai's mission to Bin-Lot. Even not knowing his heritage, his request for an end to violent raids by the Sifiq should have been sufficient for the Protectors' aid."

"And next on your agenda?" Victor practically snarled the question.

"Excuse me, everyone," Willem interrupted, uncharacteristically grim. "Victor, may I have a moment with you outside?" Those present who had known Willem for years immediately noticed distinct change in his more typical reserved demeanor. His fair complexion was slightly flushed, and bright blue eyes blazed furiously. A mouth accustomed to amiable smiles spread into a thin, stern line.

Victor tapped his heel impatiently. "Say whatever you have to say right here."

"As you wish. Stop acting like an impossible, stubborn ass. These men are willing to set sail as soon as we can assemble vessels and appropriate crews in order to seek critical help for our army. You've wasted valuable time doing little else but rant and rave. I suggest you either listen, offer valuable arguments, and participate with the kind of suggestions I know you're capable of, or leave until you can."

Red-faced, Victor pounded a fist on the conference table, rattling water glasses and nerves. Before he could utter another word, Willem stood and motioned to guards at the doors. "Gentlemen, would you kindly escort Lord Garogan out? I believe he isn't feeling well." Then, looking into Alexa's astounded face, he said, "Your Majesty, if you will allow me a few minutes, I shall see to Lord Garogan's care and then return."

"Of course, Lord Zephirás," Alexa replied, stunned but genuinely pleased by how Willem had stepped in to end Victor's diatribe.

⌒

"Sweetest, why do you think I'm so furious? You can't possibly know these people!"

"Victor, I know them better than you think. I'm convinced Val led me to them because they can help us finish this war with the Sifiq. Gregor needs them if we don't want this war to drag on."

Victor stalked across the elegantly decorated drawing room at Stefan's nearby home. He pushed aside gold damask drapes and stared outside without seeing the finery of a Toravalian summer evening. His voice sounded like a rumbling growl as he resumed his tirade. "Turandans are fully capable of building our ranks and training our soldiers without help from your so-called Protectors! Surely you haven't forgotten all we overcame to evict Sifiq armies from our shores before."

"I also remember the cost in time and lives. My goal is to reduce both. Grandfather is confident he can secure enough assistance to do both."

Releasing the curtain to swing back into place, Victor spun around. His face flushed red. "Listen to yourself, Alexa! Calling this man *Grandfather*! You've known him what? Barely a month? This is insanity!"

"What would you have me call my husband's grandfather?" she asked, her voice maddeningly calm as she sat on the edge of a chair.

"You're being utterly ridiculous! And careless, too. Is it true that you plan to take Anlía with you?"

"What does Anlía have to do with what I call Gregor's grandfather?"

"I want to know if you're dragging my goddaughter off to some country no one ever heard of with some stranger who may have dangerous designs on both of you! It seems to me the only thing you really care about right now is finding a way to that husband of yours! Do you care so much about being with him that you would risk your own daughter's life?"

Alexa's head shot up. Emerald eyes blazed. When she stood, her posture stiffened, and her hands clenched tightly. "Victor Garogan, you know how I abhor violence, but if you ever dare say something like that to me again, I will pick up the nearest thing I can find and hit you as hard as I can."

When he started to interrupt her, she threw up both hands. "Not another word! I came tonight because you asked me to. I've heard one tirade after another from you at the palace and now here. It's your turn to remain silent and listen to me. First of all, yes, Anlía is going with me to Trezvindja. Are there risks? Possibly. We have discussed them. Would I place her life or the lives of any of my children in undue danger? Not if I could avoid it. I am taking precautions. I'm also absolutely sure her grandfather will do everything possible to protect her. Beyond that, she and I are convinced our trip is the will of Val. One more thing. Never again accuse me of needlessly endangering my child, or I will see you rot in Zenox Prison. Remember this. As a priestess in the Order of Val, I dare not lie.

"Now, what I want to understand is why you refuse to offer the wisdom and strategy you're so good at."

Quieted by her shocking threats, he stared. Hazel eyes glazed as he regretted pushing her to such extremes. Swallowing against the choking lump in his throat, he hoarsely said, "Forgive me, Sweetest. Please. I'm terrified for you and Anlía. I don't know these people, and I honestly don't know how you, Stefan, and Willem can all trust them so completely after so little time. It exceeds my comprehension."

When she responded, her voice sounded firm and restrained. "With guidance from Val, I sought the prince where he was living his life in solitude, forever mourning the death of his pregnant wife. I forced myself into his presence with news that she had survived a tragic accident and borne his child. I witnessed the resurrection of a man's soul and his desire to live. His wife and daughter are dead, but the fact that Gregor is alive gives him renewed purpose. Protecting Gregor and Gregor's family gives him more than just a reason to live; it gives him the chance for personal redemption because he always blamed himself for his wife's death.

"That explains what we see in Braeklojorn Vosklon. Your problem is that you see Gregor every time you look at him."

Victor shook his head so hard that his brown hair swept sideways, but before he could deny her observation, she continued, "I see it in your eyes and feel it in your life force. You've never forgiven Gregor. When you look at Braeklojorn, it's impossible not to see my husband's face. You are overcome by thoughts of how different things would have been if the prince's ship had never sailed off course and faltered into Turandan waters—if his wife hadn't gone overboard and washed up on our shores. You blame him for fathering the woman—essentially a foreigner—who charmed Turand's king into marrying her. You blame him for creating the avenue to all your woes."

Victor slowly walked to a burled walnut cabinet and opened elaborately carved doors. Removing a cut crystal bottle and glass, he poured a shot of liquor. Downing a second shot, he turned to face her. "I have nothing against foreigners. I married one who just recently bore me a son. Remember?"

"I haven't forgotten. Exactly why did you marry Oui-lest?"

"What's that supposed to mean?"

"It's a simple question."

"Whether or not you believe me, I love my wife. You know better than anyone how wonderful Oui-lest is."

"If you have nothing against foreigners, why have you done nothing but rail against the Trezvindjans? No matter what they say or what anyone else says, provided you allow someone to speak, you criticize. Viciously so. Why?"

Victor poured a third drink and swallowed its fortifying fire. He was caught in her net. Her ability to read his life force infuriated him because he had no way of stopping her. "I do love Oui-lest, but you're right. I tried, but I never forgave Gregor. I never will. I lost years of my life, all spent in miserable loneliness because of what he stole from me. I won't deny that I hate the fact he was ever born."

"Your perspective surprises me considering your own actions behind what happened, but we won't argue the point. At least I have the truth from you."

Alexa walked toward the doors of the lounge, which stood slightly ajar. She paused before leaving. "I'm at least glad to know you love Oui-lest. I told you before. I would be furious if you would be so careless with her feelings. I also want to remind you that if the Sifiq invade Turand and get their hands on her, the punishment they would inflict is unthinkable."

"I would never let them hurt Oui-lest," he declared defiantly. "I love her far too much. I would die first."

"They would gladly oblige you. No, Victor, the only way to ensure her safety and the safety of every other Turandan is to follow through with Gregor's plan to stop them from ever setting foot in Turand again—a plan you once endorsed. So, to that end and with Grandfather's help, I will pursue my efforts to enlist the Trezvindjans' aid. With Gregor as heir to their throne, we can procure their support and stop this Sifiq scourge at long last. Also, my daughter is not a pawn. As a successor in both royal lines, she willingly accepts responsibility for helping resolve this crisis.

"Victor, I sincerely hope you can accept the beauty of the love you now have with Oui-lest. Unfortunately, I fear it won't happen until you finally purge your hatred for Gregor. That won't happen until you reconcile yourself to the fact that he wasn't solely to blame for my marriage. You postponed our wedding for three years until you got yourself sentenced to death for an assassination plot. Gregor was right all those years ago. Even with my promise to take you home to Garogan, you would have returned to create more havoc. You must also accept that it was always my destiny to love Gregor."

When she left, she saw that Stefan stood solemnly outside. In a low voice, he said, "I didn't want to eavesdrop, but I heard him shouting. I wanted to be close. Just in case."

Alexa smiled and, raising her hand, stroked Stefan's clean-shaven cheek. "Stefan, you are as fine a brother to me as you are to my husband. Thank you. I wish to pray at the temple before returning home. I am exhausted."

As Stefan gave Alexa a comforting embrace, he glanced upward. On the curving marble staircase, he caught sight of the swirl of blue silk skirts as Oui-lest hurried from a landing toward bedchambers on the second floor.

⁀

Braeklojorn sat in the library with his attention riveted on the two men who had asked to speak with Alexa. The older of the two stood quietly near the doors. Although clean and neat, the calloused hands, roughly textured homespun fabrics, and worn boots belonged to a man who worked the land. The prince wondered about the armless sleeve hanging loose and tied near the end with a length of rawhide. The younger man's tall, muscular frame also evidenced a life of physically hard labor that somehow appeared incongruous with the elegant fit of his black trousers, low boots, and fitted blue tunic.

"Milady," the younger man began, "thank you for taking time to hear me out. I know Sir Sidano needs administrative assistance here, but he has many experienced aides on staff. I volunteered to accompany you and the princess on your journey because I'm convinced I can make more than a cursory contribution to your efforts in Trezvindja. I'm certainly not the statesman Sir Sidano is, but I can offer administrative skills. If nothing else, I'm Princess Anlía's friend and can offer her moral support in changing environments."

"Exactly what do you think is going to happen, Master Maconti?" Alexa asked.

Gregor Maconti looked at his father, who nodded for his son to continue, then glanced at the Trezvindjan prince before returning his attention to Alexa. "From everything I've heard over the past few days, I think you and Prince Braeklojorn plan to address the Sifiq crisis with the Protectors who rejected Prince Nikolai's original appeals for assistance. Princess Anlía will go as Turand's only available direct link between our two nations. Hopefully, her strong resemblance to her great-grandmother will stir enough memories to win their help. Then? If all works out, you plan to meet King Gregor in the Sifiq Kingdom to launch a final surge against their capital."

Alexa's eyebrows rose high as she and Braeklojorn looked at one another. Slowly, Alexa blew out a sigh. "Master Maconti, your conclusion is remarkable, although perhaps somewhat underdeveloped. Is there anything you've omitted from your scenario?"

Young Maconti faced the queen confidently. "The princess is ready to confirm her vows as a Valiria priestess, and more Valiria are gathering in Toraval than are necessary for her evaluation. It seems logical they plan to join the others already in the Sifiq Kingdom to provide healing to our soldiers wounded in battle. Once in Sifiq territory, I can be one more soldier fighting for our cause. I've been training with the Royal Guards. I believe it is my duty to protect my friend and my country—just as my father once did."

Braeklojorn stood and faced the elder Maconti. "You, sir, are this young man's father?"

Leondo Maconti respectfully inclined his head. "I am, Your Highness."

"May I assume you lost your arm in Turand's civil war?"

"You assume correctly, sir, if a civil war is what one would call it. It was more a war of deception created as a final act of desperation by Sifiq officers using corrupt Turandans to keep a chokehold on Turand. Our King Gregor refused to allow it. He fought as bravely as any man I ever saw and would have died had it not been for the courage of our Lady Valkana, who delivered Lord Val's Healing Graces to the battlefields."

Braeklojorn frowned at that bit of history he had not yet heard. "Master Maconti, is this young man not your only son?"

Although his face blanched, the man stood firm. "He is, Your Highness. My son respected me enough to send for me and ask my advice on the situation. He knows his mind and the values his mother and I taught him. Our way of life must be defended."

Alexa approached the elder Maconti and placed a reassuring hand on his shoulder. "Your son's conclusions are essentially correct but somewhat incomplete. He has a brilliant mind—one I can ill-afford to waste on a battlefield. Neither would I risk my daughter's life near battlefields. Her grandfather has a somewhat different plan in mind. If you and your Gregor agree, and if Sir Sidano is willing to free him from his present obligations, perhaps we can better use his skills in Trezvindja."

Relief seeped into the father's heart. Gratitude shone from his eyes. "I have always trusted your husband and you, Your Majesty. Thank you for giving my son his chance to serve the good of Turand."

⌣

Alexa nibbled a frosted pastry while gazing over the gardens from the bench where Gregor had first come to comfort her during the more tumultuous days of their marriage. Later, this bench became a favorite place to sit and discuss dreams and events during their marriage. At the moment, she found those memories soothing.

"May I join you?"

An upward glance prompted a faint smile. "Of course."

"I spoke again with Master Maconti and then had a long talk with his son."

"Oh?" Emerald eyes again rested on the jewel tones of blooms in the gardens lining the walks through palace gardens.

"Ma Ishna, more than ever, I am anxious to meet my grandson. Master Maconti explained how he lost his arm and then faced hardships ever since, yet he harbors no bitterness toward the king who led him into battle. Instead, he holds my grandson in highest esteem. Have you any idea how proud that makes me?" She never moved, but he saw the smile that again tugged at her mouth.

"Grandfather, my husband respected his soldiers, and they knew it. Whenever possible, he still demonstrates his high regard."

Braeklojorn nodded and sighed. "I believe you are right in allowing the younger Maconti to accompany us, but you may have a secondary problem."

"How so?"

Something in Alexa's faraway expression concerned him. "The young man is undoubtedly intelligent and as committed to Turand's cause as anyone. However, I think he may be even more committed to our fair princess."

"Meaning?" Alexa asked, her eyes still focused on the gardens.

"Ma Ishna, would you please look at me?" When she finally turned, the sadness in her eyes knifed into his heart. "Alexa, what? Tell me."

"My apologies. When I sit here, I sometimes feel Gregor closer. Right now, he's angry and apprehensive. There was an attack, and he expects another."

"But he is all right? And your Nikolai?"

She closed her eyes and drew in a deep breath, her senses reaching out to that land that had nearly destroyed her. "They are well as we speak." She noted how Braeklojorn's sigh shuddered with relief. "Now, what was your concern about Gregor Maconti?"

Grinning, Braeklojorn said, "I believe the young man might be enamored of our dear Anlía."

"Do you think so?" Alexa asked, a faint gleam appearing in her eyes for the first time that afternoon.

"I'm not so old that I don't recognize the signs of a man in love. That could be trouble."

"Why so?" Alexa asked curiously.

"I imagine her father prefers a noble marriage for her if one has not been arranged already."

Alexa laughed softly. "You would not approve of allowing our daughter to choose a husband based on the direction of her heart?"

"Of course, I would," he replied, "but is it not better to marry…"

"Within one's social class?" Alexa inserted, her eyes glittering with interest. "Is that how it's done in Trezvindja?"

Braeklojorn sat back and cleared his throat. "There are no fast rules, only vague tradition. I imagined it to be clearly defined here in Turand—as it is in other countries, such as Coloridia, for example."

"I'm relieved to learn that, or you might be seriously disappointed in your grandson's choice for a wife. Oh, I was an ordained priestess when we married; however, I was never part of the nobility. My father's family was landed gentry, but my mother was the daughter of a simple farmer just like Master Maconti."

"Really? Fascinating. One would never suspect you weren't reared in a noble family."

"Nobility, dear Grandfather, rises from more than just bloodlines. In the meantime, I plan to leave romance to young hearts."

⌐

Gaeldoreg inspected the seven ships ready to set sail. The past month's hectic activity amazed him with the Turandans' remarkable efficiency at establishing and accomplishing goals. Twelve volunteer Valiria priestesses had arrived from Zinzan and prepared to join their sisters already caring for wounded soldiers in the Sifiq Kingdom. Five had examined Anlía to determine her worthiness before she professed her final vows in a moving ceremony at Toraval's Temple of Val. Crated medical supplies, letters to soldiers, and non-perishable foodstuffs were staged on the dock, awaiting final load approval. Newly cast and tested cannons, secured on sturdy carts, also waited to be rolled onto vessels. Royal Guards and additional troops would make the journey.

"Well? What do you think?"

"My lord, the Turandan vessels are not quite the match to ours, but they are definitely seaworthy. They should be swift and reliable."

Braeklojorn chuckled. "Coming from an island nation, perhaps a thousand years of sailing history gives us a design advantage."

Commanding the mission, Admiral Darandra drily remarked, "With all due respect, gentlemen, such advantages didn't prevent you from being shipwrecked on foreign shores. Now, may I finally give orders to start loading?"

Days later, with fair winds advancing their schedule beyond expectations, Alexa stood at the ship's rail, trying to grasp the expanse of ocean their ships were crossing. Sensing someone approaching, she turned and smiled. "Admiral," she greeted.

"Your Majesty," he replied, "even if we revert to our originally expected pace of travel, we should reach Coloridia three days early. Do you plan to keep to our plan?"

"Unless we see a fleet of Sifiq ships in port, yes. We'll need to secure fresh water and other supplies for vessels sailing on to the Sifiq Kingdom. It depends on whether or not I can secure a meeting with Coloridian officials."

"Prince Braeklojorn will surely be useful in that endeavor."

"If what Nikolai and Stefan told me was correct, I shall rely on that."

Four days later, a port authority escort accompanied Master Maconti and Captain Fratino to the Offices of State Ministry to deliver urgent personal messages to Ambassador Laritha from both Queen Alexa of Turand

and Grand Prince Braeklojorn Vosklon of Trezvindja. Struck by the names on the official dispatches, the receiving aide asked the Turandan messengers to wait while he gave them to the ambassador's Chief of Staff. Within ten minutes, a short, stocky man with wispy brown hair and wire-rimmed glasses on the tip of his nose appeared.

"Gentlemen," he began in an irritated voice, "you delivered these letters?"

"Yes, sir, we did," Maconti answered, sounding very professional.

The Chief of Staff noted Maconti's youthful but immaculate appearance. He then appraised the flawless military presence of the officer beside him. "Ambassador Laritha won't return for at least another hour."

"May we wait, sir? We won't impose on your staff in any way."

The young man was undoubtedly bold enough. The chief huffed a bit. "I suppose there's no reason you can't wait. You're certain this letter is from a Trezvindjan prince?"

"Yes, sir. He placed it in my hand himself this very morning."

"Harrumph," he grunted. "Very well."

More than an hour later, two armed guards opened the door for Ambassador Laritha to enter the meeting room. Laritha carried the opened letters in his hand. "Gentlemen," he demanded without greeting, "what is this all about?"

"Excellency," Master Maconti said, rising and bowing respectfully, "we have delivered the letters at the request of Her Majesty Queen Alexa and His Highness Grand Prince Braeklojorn Vosklon. They are currently on board a vessel docked here in Maraya."

"And you don't know the contents?"

"I have not read them, sir," Maconti replied calmly.

"You?" the ambassador shot at Fratino.

"I am Captain of the Queen's Royal Guard, sir. I am rarely privy to her official correspondence," Fratino replied coolly.

Laritha tapped the dispatches nervously against the palm of his hand. "How am I to believe the man who wrote this dispatch is a Trezvindjan prince?"

"May I offer my advice?" Fratino asked.

"Please," Laritha responded sarcastically.

"I spent many weeks traveling untold miles with Queen Alexa en route to meet this Trezvindjan prince. My best suggestion is to do as we did. Take a ride and meet him yourself."

After over an hour in a small coach traveling along Maraya's crowded streets filled with its typical midday clutch of carriages, street vendors, and wagons and carts transporting cargo, Captain Fratino escorted Ambassador Laritha and Gregor Maconti onto the Turandan vessel *Zephiria Courage*. Alerted to the visitor, Admiral Darandra welcomed the ambassador on board, giving his royal passengers time to prepare to receive their guest. The admiral then guided Laritha to more spacious command quarters and departed.

"Ambassador Laritha, I am Queen Alexa, and this is my daughter, Princess Royal Anlía. Welcome. I am delighted to meet you."

"Your Majesty." Laritha bowed respectfully. Acknowledging Anlía, he said, "Your Highness." Her unusual height and dark beauty made staring almost impossible.

"I have tea and cakes ready. I hope you will join us. Prince Braeklojorn should join us any—ah, here he is."

When Laritha turned, there could be no doubt the man was Trezvindjan. So tall he bent forward to walk inside the admiral's cabin, the elegantly attired prince exuded inbred regal air. His olive-bronze coloring reminded the ambassador of the fearsome, dark-skinned warriors in tales of the Protectors he had heard growing up. Very few Coloridians were ever granted audience with the reclusive race. In his long years of diplomatic service, this was his first personal encounter with a Trezvindjan. Or was it?

"Ambassador Laritha, please, do join us," Braeklojorn said, his voice deep, his words noticeably accented.

"Thank you," Laritha replied slowly. "I—I was surprised to receive your messages today. I was unaware of any Protector collaboration with Turand."

The prince smiled. "To be frank, Trezvindja will also be surprised once I return home. I have important matters to settle there and settle quickly. I have reason to understand you are an honest man who despises war as much as my people are supposed to despise war."

Laritha sat back. "I'm not certain I understand. What is going on here?"

Alexa leaned forward and offered Laritha a cup of tea. "Here, have some tea, Ambassador. I assure you. It contains no poisons or potions." When he cautiously tasted the fine brew, she smiled. "Sir, my son told me of his encounters with you during his two trips to Coloridia. Although he was sorely disappointed with the outcome, he was convinced that you were an honorable man who shared his frustration. He also said he shared confidences with you that, to my knowledge, you have kept."

"Your Majesty, I may live within a life of politics, but if I give a man my word of honor, my word I keep."

"Which is something we both regard with respect," Braeklojorn said, looking to Alexa and Anlía for how they read his life force. Receiving their affirming nods, he continued, "Ambassador, we need your help and your confidence. I must urgently return home to resolve whatever issues resulted in the Protectors refusing to grant assistance when Prince Nikolai requested help in stopping the Sifiq from invading Turand."

"If you know about that, why didn't you help then?"

"I was unaware of the situation at the time. We will explain, but we cannot afford to wait for ordinary protocol. We have come with ships carrying medical supplies, priestesses, and enough soldiers to protect them as they disembark in the Sifiq Kingdom. They need fresh water for the remainder of their journey. Can you arrange that with minimal delay?"

Laritha shrugged. "I think so. We received permission for the armies that already went because Jemini was incensed over the Sifiq ships that violated Turandan territory using Coloridia flags. I can't be sure, though. His adviser from the Protectors seems to be unsympathetic to Turand's plight or perhaps just more cooperative with the Sifiq. Something isn't right—at least not in my opinion."

"Really? Do you know the name of the adviser?"

"I believe her name is Essila."

"Essila? All right." Braeklojorn replied thoughtfully. "The Vosklon League will deal with the issues with the Protectors when I return. We will sail two of our ships to Trezvindja. Is it possible to leave a third anchored offshore here in Coloridia under your nation's sovereign protection?"

"I must obtain official permission. I have no such authority."

"Ambassador, please let us know as soon as you can, one way or another. Many lives hang in the balance—including my son's."

Laritha studied the face of the one woman he knew had faced Bin-Lot in his lair and defeated him. Simply looking at her, he could not imagine how. "Your Majesty, I shall do my best." He paused, his curiosity prickling. "Majesty, if I may, your son seems a fine young man, but I once asked him about his unusual height and coloring compared to other Turandans. Now, suddenly, you appear with a Trezvindjan prince. May I ask why he denied any connection?"

"Ambassador, my son did nothing wrong."

Fending off irritation, Laritha began to protest, "Your Majesty, please."

Braeklojorn interrupted. "Ambassador Laritha, when Prince Nikolai was here in Coloridia, he did not know, nor does he know now that he is second in line to Trezvindja's throne. In fact, he knew nothing at all of

Trezvindja. Neither he nor does his father know that King Gregor is the rightful heir to Trezvindja's Crown. That is why it is so crucial for me to reach home to resolve issues my brother-in-law has created since the deaths of my wife and her heir, our daughter. Do you now comprehend my need for speed and secrecy?"

Part 3

Strength inside them boldly surged
Their souls brightly burned with fire
With abiding faith, they forged ahead
Such courage only love can inspire.

Each man a harbor, a sacred legend
Each heart a story, a mystery untold
As to that evil land, they ventured forth
To the fate their life or death might hold.

Bitter is the wrath of battle and war
Brave souls tattered by cries of dying men
The attacks continue, so wield the swords
Soldier on! Our people, our loves, we shall defend.

Sounds of chaos crash through their minds
The clanging, shouting, moaning, wailing
The bloody fighting goes on and on
Then fate sweeps in, always prevailing.

Bridges of Turand

Quiet settles over blood-soaked lands
The fighting ends; now stop the war
Mend your bleeding, broken men
Walk the battlefields; your dead do gather.

Home again, home again, raise your vict'ry flags
Kiss those you fought to protect and defend
Always sing loud your hymns for the dead
And those broken, now home, let your help never end.

Your homes, your lives, precious treasures are they.
The price was high, this you must always know.
The cost was the sacrifice of time, lives, and blood.
Lift always your voices and praise each brave hero.

Ode to the Heroes

Chapter 12

"Nikolai! Left!" Gregor roared above the bedlam of snorting horses, clanging swords, and shouting men.

Dragging back so hard on the reins of his chestnut gelding that the horse almost fell sideways, Nikolai rolled hard left and caught sight of a splinter group of Sifiq soldiers breaking toward the original target of their attack. Swiftly signaling other nearby officers, he led a mad charge to intercept and route them away from the base camp, where doctors and priestesses tended to a steady influx of wounded soldiers. Then, with swords sweeping wide arcs, cavalry officers engaged their Sifiq counterparts with focused ferocity, allowing Turandan ground troops to follow their king and form a broad barrier of men between their encampment and the attackers.

A company of archers suddenly appeared from the far right side of the camp. They fired a deadly load of arrows into the heart of the oncoming stream of Sifiq soldiers heading toward the wall of defenders. Loading and firing a second round of deadly rain on the attackers, the first group was joined by another band of archers that released arrows in a cross-attack. Sifiq soldiers who didn't fall scattered in confusion as foot soldiers raised ear-splitting battle cries and raced forward with broadswords to route this latest assault.

Hours later, exhausted soldiers hunched over campfires. Many forced themselves to eat following the latest horrors observed during battle. Others talked quietly, glad to have this newest threat behind them. They had fought the enemy in his own land and prevailed yet again.

Each man took heart, encouraged as father and son, King and Prince, walked through their camp and stopped, taking time to speak with them. Their king had not stayed home, safe and protected inside a palace of stone, while his people fought his battles for him. Instead, he had come with his son and fought alongside his men, enduring the same hardships and dangers. Younger men had grown up listening to tales of their king from the times of the Sifiq occupation and civil war. They were now privileged to witness why their grandfathers, fathers, and uncles held King Gregor in such high esteem. Despite the dangers and potential for failure, they believed they must strive to end Sifiq aggression against their homeland. With Gregor leading them, they believed they could succeed.

Inside their tent that night, Nikolai offered prayers for the souls of those lost that day and thanks for the battle's successful outcome. Snuffing out a single candle, he sat cross-legged on a low cot while his father stretched out wearily on his. "As bad as the assault was today, it still seemed ill-conceived."

Gregor stared at the peak of the canvas tent, his mind reviewing every detail of the Sifiq attack. "Either they're desperate to stop us, or they're trying to wear us down. I can't decide which. Whatever the case, I want to establish a safer, more easily defended cantonment now that we've advanced closer to Atuliq. We need to maintain easy access to our ocean supply lines while still moving toward our primary objective."

"Bin-Lot will resist with every bit of military force he can muster," Nikolai replied.

"No doubt. It's more than a game to him now. It's survival. If only I had a better idea of what military reserves are at his disposal."

"For now, the best thing is to rest while we can. Every muscle in my arms and shoulders is screaming at me," Nikolai laughed quietly, hoping to encourage his father to set aside his worries for a while. "We can save our worries for tomorrow after a decent night's rest."

"And you're the young one," Gregor chuckled, unwilling to surrender to the aches in his own body.

Long after Nikolai fell asleep, Gregor forced from his mind the count of dead soldiers and images of wounded ones in hospital tents. For just a little while, he pushed away thoughts of military logistics and battle strategies. With eyes closed, he let his mind drift homeward.

"Alexa." His lips silently formed her name. Shining emerald eyes held him willing hostage. Her fingers laced through the layers of his hair, sending tingling shafts of sensation racing through his body. When she smiled at him, he felt as if his very soul filled with her light. When she kissed him...

⌐

"There." Rafzan Lynmar's index finger forcefully pointed at a spot on the map called Qasalaf. "As I explained earlier, if we position the camp just right, the terrain here will make an attack from behind almost impossible. We can establish the new supply lines with relative ease and maintain them as long as we control either side of the passage through these hills. We'll also have this passage as an emergency escape route if we need it. Our primary concern will be protecting the camp from frontal assaults."

Leaning over the map, Gregor intensely studied areas surrounding Lynmar's suggestion. "Do you know the region, Captain?"

"I was born in Qasalaf, but it has been years since I last went there."

"And you're sure about the accuracy of this map?" Nikolai asked, his dark eyes locked on Rafzan.

"Of course. The Coloridians are famous for their precision when it comes to cartography. Qasalaf lies on higher ground. It should be ideal as our main cantonment and site for initiating direct attacks in our push toward Atuliq."

Lynmar straightened and looked from Nikolai to the king and then to other officers. "I would expect more attacks on the way to Qasalaf. As to how large, I cannot say. My thinking is that Bin-Lot's strategists have been testing us. They also likely need more time to amass their army. Before I last departed Atuliq, I heard that forces were scattered all across the country's northern regions, trying to control insurrections. A glance at the map shows how extensive that territory is."

A lieutenant spoke up. "Captain, what is the potential for resistance in Qasalaf? Are there military installations there?"

Memories caused Lynmar to cringe. "A garrison shut down years ago. It wasn't needed once the surrounding agricultural community started to fail. You can't beat farmers into producing on land that refuses to grow significant crops. I doubt any remaining populace will give us much trouble."

Over a deserted midday table, Lynmar stared into a bowl of stew. When a hand landed on his shoulder, he looked up to see Nikolai standing beside him. "Yes, your company is welcome."

"Thank you for the invitation," Nikolai said, carefully adjusting his long legs to avoid knocking over the planks forming a makeshift table. Setting down his bowl of stew and a large round of flatbread, he paused for quick grace. "Will you tell me why returning to Qasalaf troubles you?"

Lynmar spooned a bite into his mouth and shrugged. "I haven't been there in years. It's just another Sifiq town to manage on the way to Atuliq."

Nikolai dipped a chunk of bread into his stew and then put the saucy bite in his mouth. Gazing thoughtfully across the table, he sighed. Swallowing, he said, "It's more than that, Rafzan. I may be unable to read life forces the way my mother and sister do, but I saw your reaction when Crelino asked you about military installations in Qasalaf."

Both men spent the next few minutes silently eating their food. A cook appeared, bringing mugs of tea and slices of sweetbread. Alone again, Nikolai pursued the issue. "Well?"

"Persistent, aren't you?"

The prince made a face at his bitter-tasting tea and set the mug aside. "You are one of the most valuable officers I have here. If something in our plans troubles you, I need to know."

Lynmar sipped his tea. Swallowing it, he grimaced. "Are you sure that isn't poisoned?"

"Whatever it is, I don't think it's tea. I don't suggest they put it in front of Father. Now, you. What about you?"

Blue eyes stared far past the prince. "Nikolai, the past will not hinder my duties here. If anything, it may provide inspiration. Years ago, my father commanded the garrison here at Qasalaf. Nearby is where I watched him heartlessly slaughter my mother."

Nikolai's eyes fell shut as he sucked in his breath. He knew about Rafzan's mother. Knowing they would be forcing him to spend day and night in a place that represented a child's greatest terror and heartbreak thrust deep into Nikolai's gut. "I don't know what to say. We can reassign you to manage supply line logistics so…"

"No!" Lynmar practically shouted, drawing curious glances from several nearby soldiers. Then, more calmly, he said, "My apologies. Please, Nikolai, I have no desire to be reassigned. While I can't deny the sorrow in my memories, Turand introduced me to faith and hope. I will fulfill my commitments to our nation. If you'll excuse me."

Nikolai watched as Rafzan Lynmar rose, bowed respectfully, and walked away. Contemplating the complexities of a man he might never understand, the prince picked up the mug he had earlier set down. Gazing into its murky depths, he barely avoided laughter upon hearing his father bellow over why he should bother with the Sifiq when his own men were trying to kill him with witch's brew disguised as tea.

⮎

The trek to Qasalaf began as a miserable slog beneath gray, cloud-laden skies and intermittent rain showers. Heat and humidity thickened the air, robbing Gregor's army of energy as it traipsed across barren land. Sparse vegetation allowed rainwater to pool into wide, muddy tracks with few grassy areas to ease passage. Occasional copses of scrub pines and thorny brush broke the monotony of landscape that Lynmar described as once being fertile farmland. Gregor constantly consulted with Lynmar and other officers to ensure they were following the route that lay parallel to Sifiq shores and that they could easily backtrack to their original base camp if necessary.

Three days into the march, with the weather moderating, they encountered the first signs of Sifiq habitation. Several modest homes, all in various stages of disrepair, nestled together to form a small hamlet. The village's few elderly men were both curious and fearful as they stood together beside a post used for general notices. From windows and doors, women peered out at the newest soldiers to pass their humble dwellings.

Dismounting together, Gregor and Nikolai approached the menfolk, unnerved by the sight of the tallest men they had ever seen. "Gentlemen, what is the name of this village?" Gregor asked, his voice even and unthreatening. Receiving no response, he said, "There is no need to fear us. We will not harm you."

"You are the foreigners from Turand. You come to exact revenge for what our king did to your women," offered one of the men in a shaky voice. "If you look for food, we had little to begin with. Now we have almost nothing left. Our soldiers took almost everything."

Dark eyes narrowing, Gregor noted the signs of hunger. Dull eyes and sunken cheeks. Their pallor and apparent weakness. "Dearest Val, they would starve their own people!" he gasped. "Sir, I must ask. Do you know of any soldiers in the area?"

In unison, the men shook their heads. The same old man who had spoken before said, "They raided our barns and cellars more than a week ago and rode off toward the capital. They beat some of our men and women who tried to stop them. They should have killed us all. We will never survive the winter now."

"Sir, how many are you?"

"We are six men standing, three too hurt to stand, plus ten females and three children. What does it matter?" He sounded hopeless.

"It matters, sir, because you are speaking with the King of Turand." Then, turning to Nikolai, he said, "My son, call a halt to today's travel so we can get these people some food and medical care."

"Of course, Father. Immediately."

The remaining three days of their march carried them past several small farms before reaching Qasalaf. Residents were either elderly, children, or female. Their stories were the same. All healthy males over fourteen had been conscripted to serve in the army. Food supplies had been raided. Although many women were either contracted in legal marriages or young daughters promised in marriage, most had been forced to sexually service some of the officers. As a result, bitter dejection, hunger, and hopelessness hung over the countryside like a plague.

The town of Qasalaf had fared little better. Many homes had been boarded up and deserted before people heard of Turand's advancing army. Long accustomed to the abuses of their military and with nowhere to go, the few remaining inhabitants stoically went about the chores necessary for daily survival, taking care to steer clear of the seemingly unending procession of men, horses, and wagons.

Leaving Captain Lynmar and lead officers to guide the army, Gregor, his son, and several aides dismounted in the town's central square. Assuming the lead, Gregor purposefully strode toward the building with a sign identifying it as the official town center. Entering, he called out for assistance. No one responded, but he heard sounds indicating someone was inside.

"Father, take care," Nikolai whispered over his shoulder.

Gregor nodded in acknowledgment and called out, "I know some-one is here. Come out now before I have the place searched. No one will hurt you."

Scuffling sounds and tense, anxious whispers reached his ears. "Come out now! The King of Turand commands you to show yourselves!"

More scuffling sounds were followed by tentative footsteps. Finally, a middle-aged woman wearing a plain gray dress appeared in the sim-ply furnished lobby. Her short, straight hair was neatly combed, but it was impossible to determine her features. Like all other women they had encountered, she stared at the floor.

Shaking his head, Gregor muttered something about the intolerable treatment of Sifiq women. Then, stretching out his long arm, he gently tucked his fingers beneath the woman's chin and lifted her face. "Mistress, I am King Gregor of Turand. Would you kindly tell me your name?"

Her blue eyes opened wide with shock. "I am Kis-mur Han. I am here to serve you, Your Majesty."

"Good, Kis-mur Han. First, I assure you that I have no intention of hurting you in any way. I also heard you talking with someone who is still hiding inside. Whoever it was, I want that person out here. Now."

Her head moved back and forth with quick, nervous shakes. "Your Majesty, I am here alone."

Patiently, Gregor continued, never releasing her chin. "Kis-mur, do not be afraid of whoever is back there. If it is a man threatening to punish you, I will punish him three times as hard if he touches you for obeying my command. Do you understand? The King of Turand does not tolerate the abuse of women."

Tears brimmed in her eyes. Despite his assurances, she was afraid. Reading fear in her eyes, he released her. "Very well. Please sit down." Over his shoulder, he said, "Nikolai?"

"With pleasure, Father."

Within minutes, Nikolai half-dragged a man into the lobby. Appearing to be in his forties, the man's light brown hair was thinning and gray. His slightly heavy build indicated he had lived a physically active life, but his pronounced limp hinted at a debilitating injury. Scowling and with his head tilted back arrogantly, he sneered, "What do you want here?"

"Your name, first of all."

"I am Def-Han, Town Administrator. You are not welcome, Turandan."

"Welcome or not, we are here, Def-Han. I am Gregor, King of Turand. This is my son, Prince Nikolai. He will inform you of the rules to be implemented now that we occupy Qasalaf. You will cooperate with the officers he assigns to manage your town. You will find that we are not a disagreeable people as long as you follow our rules. Direct any questions first to the officers assigned to you. Specific complaints can be escalated to the prince at any time."

Def-Han huffed angrily. "King Bin-Lot will send soldiers to defeat you. You will see."

"I have no doubt he will send more soldiers," Gregor answered. "Who will be defeated remains to be seen." Gregor turned to leave but stopped. "Let me be clear as to my first rule. Be sure to communicate this to all your citizens. Abuse of Sifiq women ends immediately. All offenses will be brought to my personal attention. They will result in severe punishment. Good day, Def-Han."

⤳

Once Gregor's army reached the site, supervisors surveyed the terrain and wholeheartedly agreed with Captain Lynmar's assessment. Quickly laying out plans, they directed the methodical organization of the cantonment while maintaining a sense of urgency. Enormous pavilion tents were raised to use as hospitals and accommodations for doctors and volunteer priestesses. Located near emergency evacuation routes, they were easily accessed when needed. Critical supplies, stacked and organized for easy access, were stored inside large tents at the back of the camp. Enclosures on one side of the supply line held horses and other livestock. In the center of the encampment, food preparation areas were set up and then row after row of tents. Knowing Sifiq attacks could occur without warning, everyone worked diligently with weapons ready.

Skirmishes with roving bands of Sifiq soldiers began almost immediately as the camp settled. While Gregor and his senior officers concentrated on preparing large-scale plans for the advance on Atuliq, Nikolai's scouts and squads fanned out into the countryside. They monitored for the approach of any major strikes by Sifiq forces while routing quick raids against the encampment. Troops staying behind remained on high alert.

⤳

General Kohira stretched his neck above weary shoulders. He had spent hours leaning over maps while plotting potential strategies to advance the final ninety miles to the Sifiq capital. Sighing heavily, he contemplated their progress and the challenges still lying across their path. Since Turandan armies had landed, they had decided on a two-pronged strategy. General Ravendro led his troops in a northward thrust where Sifiq forces had splintered in lightly populated agricultural regions to pursue rebellious farmers led by disillusioned deserters. Ravendro's well-armed soldiers quickly proved themselves as they swept through the northwestern side of the Sifiq Kingdom. Leaving the less strategically important area to Turandan forces, Sifiq military units responded to urgent dispatches to converge and head southeast to defend territories surrounding their capital.

"General, you look dismayed," Gregor said.

"Considering the military fortifications ahead of us and the tenacity of the Sifiq army, I have serious reservations about our numbers and our ability to overcome these butchers in their own arena."

Gregor stared at the loyal officer who had stood by him since the planning stages to oust the Sifiq occupation army from Turand years earlier. "Kohira, I know you're weary, old friend. So am I. You know what they did to Alexa. Your daughter was with her and chose to stay behind. We cannot just turn away and let them do that to another Turandan. I trust the courage and fortitude of our people. We'll find a way. Have faith, Kohira. Val will show us the way."

The sharp, steely ring and clang of broadswords interrupted them as men shouted warnings and curses. Officers and soldiers ran. Gregor shoved Kohira aside as a horse ran past, its rider swinging a sword in passing. Captain Lynmar dragged the general out of the path of marauding Sifiq riders while Nikolai raced by on his horse with cavalry officers following, swords drawn. Gregor snatched his unsheathed sword from the ground where it had fallen and swung around to fend off dismounting Sifiq soldiers. Time warped into a frozen loop as the king and his top advisers fought attacking warriors.

Ignoring the sharp sting when one sword pierced his jacket, Gregor pushed forward harder, plunging his sword into two Sifiq foes with brutal force. Swiftly glancing to his right, the king saw Lynmar at his side, furiously engaged with a Sifiq officer.

"Your Majesty! Kohira! He's hurt! Get him out of here. Nikolai's down now! Go!"

Sparing a quick look around, Gregor saw his son and nearly a dozen cavalry officers engaging the Sifiq. With Lynmar protecting his mad dash to where Kohira lay curled on the ground, the king slid his arms beneath the general's arms and dragged him away from the fighting.

"Kohira! I've got you!" Gregor shouted as he hoisted the general over his shoulder and carried his injured general toward hospital tents. Continuing to place himself between his king and any additional threatening Sifiq soldiers, Captain Lynmar kept his sword at the ready.

Vastly outnumbered, the raiders were quickly routed. Most of the attackers were killed outright in furious combat. A few seriously injured were carried to the hospital tents along with Turandan soldiers. As soon as critical wounds were treated and bound on Turandan soldiers, Valiria priestesses surrounded them and initiated a musical chant. Within minutes, glints of light began dancing through the air above the cots. As the priestesses' chant intensified, the lights grew brighter and stronger until a multi-colored dome of light formed.

From outside, Gregor watched. Kohira had sustained a critical wound and lost a lot of blood. The king's old friend had never failed him. He began reciting the ancient prayer for the sick, beseeching Val's blessing on Kohira and others whose loyalty and bravery had placed them beneath that dome this day.

Beside him, Gregor saw the wide-eyed Rafzan Lynmar. The former Sifiq officer had never before witnessed the marvel of a dome of Val's Healing Graces. Still, he had himself experienced the miracle of Val's healing powers. The captain's immersion into Turand's faith appeared obvious as, in unison with his king, Lynmar also prayed aloud the ancient plea on behalf of those in desperate need of divine healing.

⌇

Gregor sloshed cold tea on the ground by a campfire early the following morning. Four Sifiq soldiers were in critical condition inside the hospital tents. Seventeen had been killed in the raid that had claimed the lives of six Turandan soldiers. Eight other Turandans would require at least a week to recover. The gravely injured General Kohira lay unconscious. Neither doctors nor priestesses offered any hope.

"Father?"

Gregor turned. "Yes?"

"The report you requested?"

"Go ahead," Gregor replied tersely.

"Scouts came the long way around to warn us. They've spotted a large force gathering directly east, about seventy miles from here. I believe we can expect more forays like yesterday. These Sifiq raiders rode in from the northeast and broke through the perimeter. I've ordered extended surveillance boundaries and increased security around the entire camp."

"Very well. We had to expect something like this sooner or later. Are all regimental officers advised?"

"They are. Every officer knows his duty, and every soldier is prepared."

Shaking his head, Gregor turned away and stared at the fire as crumbling logs shifted. "Nikolai, do you see how that fire eats away at the wood, destroying it until the fire dies? What we must not do is allow these Sifiq soldiers and their raids to eat away the resolve of our men. Whatever else, remember that we lead by example. As long as we maintain our confidence, our men will follow."

Chapter 13

A lexa and Anlía stood on deck with Braeklojorn as the captain and crew slowly guided their ship closer toward long, wide piers jutting out into the bay. Dock crews tossed thick, twisted ropes to Turandan sailors, who used them to haul the vessel the final distance to the dock's edge before securing the ship to thick wooden pins from the ship to the pier.

Once the captain ascertained his ship was securely moored alongside the dock, he signaled his crew to stand back at attention. Already, two uniformed officials were boarding the vessel along with ten armed port guards. Dragging in a deep breath, the captain, attired in full dress uniform, walked up beside Prince Braeklojorn Vosklon and Queen Alexa and prepared to explain why his Turandan ship sailed into a Trezvindjan port flying both Turandan and Trezvindjan flags.

Inside the port authority office, the port director paced across his large office. His girth, added to his height, made him appear like a giant roly-poly, but his severe expression allowed no hint of humor. "So, you expect me to arrange an escort to take you to the king's court rather than verify this story you bring about being Prince Braeklojorn Vosklon, the husband of Princess Mishkla Krisantal. According to official port records, their ship sailed some seventy years ago and never returned."

"That ship will never return. It was destroyed during storms you are too young to remember. I have broken no laws, and I make a reasonable request. I've also presented you with documentation bearing official seals. Do you question their authenticity?"

The director returned to his desk and picked up one of Braeklojorn's documents. He could not refute the legitimacy of the gold seal affixed to the elegantly transcribed paper in his hand. Defying a prince of any of the family leagues could prove detrimental to his career. If he refused cooperation and this man was indeed a prince of the Vosklon League and husband or widower of Mishkla Krisantal, the director's career was over.

Recognizing the man's dilemma, Braeklojorn breathed out a frustrated sigh. "I understand my abrupt appearance is more than a surprise and presents you with potential difficulties. Traveling on this ship with me are my cousin, the Queen of Turand, and my great-granddaughter. On the second ship anchored in the bay are the four remaining Vosklon kinsmen who survived the shipwreck. I suggest that perhaps you first summon elders of the Vosklon League. I will write them a message and then wait onboard until they arrive, but I expect your courier to travel with utmost haste."

Relief flooded the beleaguered director's face. "That, Prince Braeklojorn, if that is your true identity, is a satisfactory solution. If you care to sit here, I can provide ink and quill. Write your message while I summon a courier. A fast horseman can reach Tarahlaz in just over an hour. It is good you have arrived early in the day."

Just before twilight, the sounds of pounding hooves echoed from the direction of the port director's office. Within fifteen minutes, boots trod up the ramp from the dock to the *Zephiria Courage's* deck. Gaeldoreg and Braeklojorn joined the captain to greet the port director and two port guards. Behind them followed four men wearing long, dark, elegant tunics.

"Director," Braeklojorn greeted, "on behalf of Captain Norlandro of Turand, I again welcome you to the *Zephiria Courage*."

"Sir, as we discussed earlier, my courier delivered your dispatch. It seems your message has aroused the interest of your kinsmen. Elders of the Vosklon League arrived in a carriage and wait inside my office. They wish to meet with you. Immediately."

"My lord," Gaeldoreg cautioned.

"Excuse me," one of the visitors stepped around the rotund director. Fixing blazing eyes on Braeklojorn, he introduced himself. "I am Drazlor Vosklon, grand-nephew of Princess Elder Sharlia Vosklon. Is this some sort of hoax you try to perpetrate on the Vosklon League?"

Gaeldoreg steadied Braeklojorn with a hand on his arm. "My lord, is it possible?"

Swallowing, the prince nodded. "I seem to be living many miracles these days, Cousin." Addressing the younger Vosklon, he said, "I greet you in peace, Drazlor Vosklon. I would not dream of attempting a hoax against the Vosklon League, which I am sworn to respect in all matters and defend with my life. I am Braeklojorn Vosklon, son of Prince Javlodorn Vosklon and his wife Sharlia."

"My poor aunt heard of your dispatch and insisted on reading it herself. She has undertaken a difficult carriage ride because she is certain the handwriting belongs to her lost son. I warn you now. Your punishment will be swift and harsh if this is some cruel joke."

Braeklojorn's eyes closed. His mother still lived and immediately came upon receiving news that her only son might still be alive. "I will come to my mother and allay your concerns, but please allow me to summon those I must bring with me."

He turned to watch Captain Norlandro escort from a doorway two women dressed in lavender capes with hoods pulled over their heads. To Drazlor Vosklon, the prince said, "We may go now."

"These women are?" Drazlor asked, curiously noting the height of one.

"I will explain to my mother. You may lead the way," Braeklojorn replied imperiously.

Dozens of lanterns cast golden light from the building and posts along the walkways outside the port office. Two enormous carriages, each hitched to teams of four perfectly matched draft horses, were parked in front. In addition to coachmen tending their horses and footmen standing by the coaches, at least a dozen more men milled around outside with the tall, beautiful horses they had ridden to the port city of Najatil in such a rush. Speculative conversation halted as soon as Drazlor appeared with the port director and the strangers for their elders to interview.

Weary after a worrisome, eventful day and unsure what to expect next, the director opened the door and waited for the Vosklon entourage and the new arrivals to pass. Hopeful they could resolve their issues quickly so he could go home, he led them into the reception area, where one of the elders waited.

Staring at a painting of ships with sails unfurled, an older man with hunched shoulders waited alone. Like the others, he wore a long tunic, belted at the waist. His hands were clasped behind his back. He drew in an audible breath and turned. Eyes that were once as bright as polished obsidian had clouded some with age, but his sight had not yet failed. Looking at the familiar face before him, he almost wondered if his mind might be failing. "Is it really you?"

"Uncle Vezjalan, seeing you again brings joy to my heart," Braeklojorn said, his voice catching with emotion. Extending his arms, the returning prince embraced his father's younger brother.

Reluctantly ending their embrace, Vezjalan reached out and affectionately patted his nephew's cheek. "You've grown old since last I saw you."

"Unfortunately so, Uncle," Braeklojorn confirmed with a rueful smile.

"Your letter said you were shipwrecked and stranded in a strange land. You never found a way home in all these years?"

"Oh, Uncle, there is so much to tell. I now believe Espiritus planned everything, but we shall discuss all in detail. I am told Mother is here."

"She is. The second a maid mentioned the letter, she demanded to see it, even though we told her it must be some sort of attempt to extort money. In the end, we decided to show her the dispatch. That's why we've all come."

Braeklojorn chuckled. "Mother has never changed."

Vezjalan laughingly agreed. "Nor will she. Now, you are rude. These ladies with you. Who are they?"

Stately erect between the two women, Gaeldoreg guided them forward to be introduced to Braeklojorn's uncle. Bowing respectfully, he greeted the two princes in Trezvindjan and began to back away but was stopped.

"Gaeldoreg Vosklon? Is that you, you rascal?" Vezjalan asked incredulously.

Not completely successful in suppressing a grin, Gaeldoreg responded, "Yes, Your Highness. True to my pledge, I still serve Milord Braeklojorn."

Shaking his head and laughing, the elder prince exclaimed, "Will wonders never cease! Welcome home, Gaeldoreg!"

Braeklojorn advised his uncle of the need to change from Trezvindjan. "Uncle, if you will indulge me, I prefer to introduce them first to Mother. You must join us, of course."

When Braeklojorn entered the port director's office, he felt his heart throbbing inside his chest. The woman inside had stood upon hearing the door open. How different she looked from his memories of her. Her long black hair was now snow-white and braided into a circular crown atop her head. Her once slender figure had assumed more matronly pro-portions, but her posture remained regal. The years had softened her features and added lines around her eyes and mouth. Still, his mother looked beautiful.

Swiftly crossing the room, the tall prince knelt. "Mother, forgive me."

Trembling hands rested on his silvered locks. "My beautiful son, why do you ask forgiveness for finally coming home to me? Rise. Let me look at you." Tears coursed down his mother's cheeks when he stood and smiled for her. "I surrendered hope years ago, but your father swore you would return. On his deathbed, he made me promise to resume praying and then promised you would come home. That was only months ago. I kept my promise, and here you are."

"Mother, how I regret the grief I've caused you." Then, gathering her in his arms, he held her close, absorbing both her past sorrows and her newfound joy.

When they parted, she asked, "What happened? Where have you been? And Mishkla? What of Mishkla?" The pain that crossed her son's face tore into her heart.

"Mother, we need time for the whole story, but Mishkla perished long ago. She was carried overboard during the storm that drove our ship off course and eventually sank it."

"Oh, Braeklojorn, and her with child. Such tragedy that you should lose them both."

He shook his head. "Mother, by some miracle, she was swept onto the shore of a strange land. There, a group of priestesses found her and took care of her. She survived long enough to give birth to a daughter. Mishkla died soon after, but the priestesses took care of our daughter."

Sharlia smiled. "You have a daughter? My son, such news to rejoice!"

"Mother, please, not so fast. My ship sank far from where I lost Mishkla. I believed Mishkla died, so part of me died. My soul filled with grief and guilt. Very few of us survived the shipwreck. We found a remote place to live in solitude, which suited my distraught state of mind. I only recently learned of my daughter."

"Where is she?" she asked hopefully, glancing behind him. "Have you brought her?"

"No, Mother. Excuse me for switching to the common language. My daughter is also dead. Murdered. For now, I can tell you she had a son—a fine son by all accounts." Turning, he beckoned to Anlía and, with loving hands, lifted the hood of her cape up and away from her face. "I want you to meet my grandson's daughter. Mother, this is Princess Anlía Toscano of Turand."

Sharlia Vosklon gasped as her hand shot out and grabbed her son's arm. "Shalevkazla! Vezjalan! Tell me I am not losing my mind!"

Vezjalan took one look at Anlía and also froze. "Espiritus, bless us! It is as if Mishkla walks among us untouched by the years! Braeklojorn! Explain this!"

Braeklojorn lifted Anlía's hand and tenderly kissed it. "Mother, I reacted the same when first I saw her."

"Wait," Sharlia said, catching her breath and approaching a patiently waiting Anlía. Placing a softly wrinkled hand against Anlía's cheek, the Princess Elder gazed in fascination. "Your eyes are not dark like Mishkla's. No, your eyes burn with flames like the sacred emerald stones of Karzhaman. How utterly unique—and how beautiful you are."

"I thank you, Princess Elder Sharlia," Anlía answered, dropping a low, graceful curtsy before her great-great-grandmother.

"Dear child, do I trust my hearing that you are Princess Anlía?"

"I am, Your Highness. My father is King Gregor of Turand."

Sharlia noted Anlía's flawless, olive-bronze complexion and her tall, statuesque figure. With the exception of those brilliant green eyes, she might easily be taken for any other young Trezvindjan woman of royal birth, and there would be no doubting her nobility. Her elegant carriage, manner of speech, and excellent presence exuded royal upbringing.

"Anlía. An ancient name with hallowed meaning in a land with many rivers and surrounded by angry seas. Welcome, daughter of King Gregor. Your mother?"

Gliding forward as she removed her hood, Alexa performed a respectful genuflect before rising and saying, "I am Alexa Maraná Toscano, High Priestess Valkana and Queen of Turand."

Alexa's mere presence physically impacted both Sharlia and Vezjalan. Although small compared to everyone inside the room, the energy surrounding her was tangible. Each of them bowed, acknowledging her royal status.

"Your Majesty, we are honored to welcome you to Trezvindja on such a joyous occasion for the Vosklon League."

Braeklojorn gave Alexa an affectionate smile before saying, "Mother, you may thank Alexa for this day, but this is not the place for discussion."

"No, the port director will appreciate the return of his office. Vezjalan sent someone to arrange lodging for the night. Will you all join us for supper? Then we can talk, especially considering we must notify the Council of Leagues straightaway."

"Alexa? Anlía?"

"Grandfather, we will be honored to accompany you, but Captain Norlandro must advise the commander of my Guard. Major Fratino will surely insist on coming."

"Of course, Ma Ishna. I shall explain."

The party soon gathered inside a private dining room at a nearby hotel. Servers, wearing bright, multicolored uniforms, laid out a low table, crowding it with platters heaped with delicacies from the sea, steamed vegetables, and whimsical arrangements of fruits exotic to the eyes and palates of the Turandans. Family members ensured their guests were served. Then, eager to learn more about Braeklojorn's time away and his journey home, they quietly consumed their meal. Meanwhile, he and Alexa related the story of her dreams, the expedition to Zemtoval, the resulting trek into the Zemfosa Mountains, and her confrontation with Gaeldoreg.

Amusement over Gaeldoreg transformed into disbelieving laughter when the prince informed his mother that his grandson and Alexa were the proud parents of six children and that he had been privileged to meet all but the eldest. After years of good-natured teases, Alexa blushed only slightly. She stated that she and her husband had both grown up as only children and now appreciated the joys of a large family.

Over drinks after dinner, Braeklojorn broached the subject uppermost on his mind. "Mother, Vezjalan, I have a question that perhaps you can answer. Coloridia recently brought a case before the Council of Protectors on behalf of Turand. Do you know about it?"

"Some," Vezjalan answered. "Drazlor, you sat on that case, did you not?"

"I did. Is there a problem?"

"Yes," Braeklojorn answered definitively. "I am trying to understand why Council denied help when Turand was trying to avoid escalation of hostilities against the Sifiq, especially considering their history with the Sifiq and the recent, documented incursions against Turand's sovereign territory."

"There was no reason for Protector involvement. All indications were that Turand could manage an amicable agreement with Bin-Lot. We guaranteed safe passage for their delegation to and from Atuliq. That was the end of it."

"The end of it? That's all? You just dismissed the case and the people as if they were no more than insects under your feet?"

Drazlor's face reddened, and he bristled angrily. "Are you accusing us of misdeeds?"

"I am asking specifically why no help was provided. The delegation to the Sifiq Kingdom was led by Prince Nikolai, Anlía's older brother—yes, King Gregor's heir. Is that significant to you? He requested an audience with the Protectors after Bin-Lot ordered his delegation to leave Atuliq. Coloridia's Minister Jemini summarily rejected his request. Are you aware of that? Jemini said the Protectors had no further interest in the matter."

Drazlor's expression changed. "The Protectors were never advised that Turand requested an audience with us. Jemini was not authorized to speak on our behalf, although Essila Krisantal may have given him that impression."

"Essila? Essila Krisantal? Ambassador Laritha mentioned her first name only. Who is she?"

"My son, she is Kaelzron's daughter. His only child."

"Milord," Drazlor began, "you mentioned Ambassador Laritha. It was he who sent word that the Turandans could negotiate a resolution with the Sifiq king."

"How? In an official document?"

Drazlor nodded. "According to Essila, she received his report. I assume she provided it to the council secretary."

"Drazlor, Queen Alexa and I personally met with Ambassador Laritha on our way here. We have letters bearing his signature and official seal stating that he submitted a detailed report to Minister Jemini following the failed mission to Atuliq. He advised that Bin-Lot never intended to meet the Turandans in good faith. Furthermore, his report stated that Bin-Lot openly declared his naval officers were free to raid whenever and wherever they had the chance. That is why my grandson and his son felt compelled to lead their armies in an invasion of the Sifiq Kingdom to stop their murderous atrocities."

"Braeklojorn, calm yourself for now," Sharlia said. "We will review your documents tomorrow. I understand your worry for your grandson. This is obviously an issue we must address on multiple levels. However, I am concerned your grandson would go to the extreme of invading a country over what were described as minor incursions involving the theft of livestock and goods. Can you explain why your anger is so fierce?"

Alexa rose from the table and went to stand behind Braeklojorn. Gentle hands rested on his shoulders. "Grandfather, your pain is still too fresh and raw. I have borne mine. I shall help you bear yours."

Lifting her chin in defiance of all she had suffered at the hands of the Sifiq, Alexa shifted fiery emerald eyes from one new family member to the other while Gaeldoreg and Major Fratino proudly watched. Anlía had already perceived her mother's unspoken communication and risen to stand at her back.

"First, may I ask how to properly address you?" she asked Sharlia.

With a slight smile, the woman said, "Your husband will be invited to call me grandmother. You may do the same."

"Grandmother, thank you," Alexa answered, applying tender emphasis to the name. "You ask why your son is so angry and express concern over my husband's decision to deliver war to the Sifiq Kingdom. For years before I met and married Gregor, a Sifiq army occupied Turand. They plundered our nation while torturing and butchering our people. They persecuted the priestesses of my order until only one remained alive—me. The murdered priestesses included the Queen of Turand—Anlía—my husband's mother and your son's only child. Her death was not an easy one. They used poison to exact a prolonged, agonizing death to ensure my husband's father understood what they would do to Gregor if King Maxim didn't cooperate with them. Eventually, they did the same to Maxim.

"If Braeklojorn is furious with the Sifiq, it is because they murdered the daughter Mishkla Krisantal fought death so hard to save. You are a parent, as am I. To lose a child, especially to ruthless, senseless murder, is the most unimaginable nightmare that exists."

Alexa continued, "As far as what you describe as simple incursions for theft, I offer a different perspective. Multiple raids occurred, resulting in the deaths of several Turandan civilians and the rapes of women and young girls. These acts are despicable and unacceptable in our culture.

"One of the worst of these raids occurred almost two years ago. Nine Royal Guards were murdered on a mission of mercy. Five priestesses were abducted and taken to Bin-Lot, with the intention to service his pleasures. What he did not anticipate was the intervention of our Lord Val. Despite warnings from the priestesses regarding their vows of virtue, especially considering several were already married, Bin-Lot made sport of trying to force them into sexual servitude. Failures incited his fury, causing him to initiate brutal beatings. Val countered with punishing natural disasters.

"The Sifiq king failed to break the priestesses despite cruel whippings, starvation, abuse, and even months of unspeakably harsh conditions in a labor camp. Finally, he bowed to our Lord Val's power and sent the priestesses home, but one of them arrived more dead than alive. When Gregor witnessed her condition, he swore never again to allow the Sifiq to harm her."

Vezjalan gazed intently at Alexa. "Still, to go to war for abduction and mistreatment of priestesses?"

"Sir," Alexa answered without yielding, "Gregor learned everything he could about the Sifiq before driving them from our nation some twenty years ago. He understands their mentality probably better than they do.

The Sifiq murdered his mother and his father. They butchered my own parents and everyone in the town where I lived while searching for me. Their king and their military are sadistic. They immensely enjoy inflicting pain on people."

Alexa drew in a deep, sustaining breath. She recognized the serious risk she might be taking but still trusted her instincts. Maintaining eye contact with Vezjalan, she said, "When my husband saw what they did to one of the priestesses they had held captive for a year, he swore he would never again tolerate Sifiq aggression against Turand. I ask you. Were you in his place, would you?"

Without any of them realizing, Anlía had unlaced the back of her mother's gown. Then, without shame or embarrassment, Alexa turned around, revealing to the Vosklon League—including her now-beloved Braeklojorn—the repulsive reminders of her captivity in the Sifiq Kingdom.

⌒

Drazlor tilted a cup of bracing kacha the next morning and drained it. "I do credit the Turandans for pursuing every effort to avoid hostilities despite Sifiq provocations."

"So you do not question the authenticity of the documents?" Braeklojorn asked, accepting a refill of hot kacha from a hotel server. Sipping the rich brew, he savored a favorite flavor from his past.

Shaking his head, the handsome young kinsman scowled. "No. I've conducted prior correspondence with Laritha on other matters. What troubles me most is Essila's deception. Bresklon Krisantal must be advised immediately of this issue. I'm glad Essila is abroad at the moment. It may simplify matters."

"What do you expect from Kaelzron?"

Drazlor shrugged. "He never wanted responsibility for the throne. The Council of Leagues refuses to let him abdicate in favor of Essila. I believe Bresklon has been secretly searching for suitable alternatives, but you know the rules and traditions for succession. Your appearance with news of Mishkla's heir—and an apparently strong and honorable one at that—comes at a particularly opportune moment. That seems almost too coincidental for my blood."

Vezjalan, who had listened quietly, breathed out a sigh. "No doubt we'll be consulting with the Mystic Council on this matter." The elder dipped a piece of pastry into his kacha and popped it into his mouth. "Braeklojorn, I am curious. This Queen Alexa. You've known her such a short time, yet you've developed a very close relationship with her. Even that rascal Gaeldoreg adores her. She is a contradiction. Help me understand."

"Dear Uncle, in the first two minutes I met her, I ordered Gaeldoreg to carry her from the caves where we lived. Alexa faced me squarely and dared me to do it. By that time, she had already confronted Gaeldoreg and drawn him into a blood bond. Since then, what I have personally witnessed from her makes me respect the way she thinks. Beyond that? Let me simply say that she will command great interest from the Mystic Council."

"Many claim mystic gifts," Vezjalan commented drily.

Braeklojorn's silver hair swayed with the shake of his head. "Claim? Uncle, Gaeldoreg and four of our kinsmen personally witnessed her mystic gifts. Along with her Royal Guards and a priestess, we were transfixed, although they weren't surprised. Afterward, I asked Major Fratino, whom you met last night. He said he first witnessed such an incident as a young man. Although he's no longer surprised, he remains awestruck whenever such events occur."

Curious and doubtful, his uncle asked, "Are these incidents really so dramatic?"

"Perhaps you should ask Gaeldoreg how it feels to be carrying a woman who suddenly rises from your arms and levitates above the tree-tops in a cloud of light and heavenly music."

Drazlor leaned across the table. "Seriously?"

"Absolutely. Our Queen Alexa is Turand's high priestess. There, she's beloved by ordinary people. Alexa walks among them as both guide and healer. She is generally soft-spoken and reserved, but we saw last night how bold she can be. How else could a mere woman survive a year of torment as a Sifiq captive and succeed in forcing the Sifiq king to send her home?"

"Braeklojorn, do you think she's why Bin-Lot refused to negotiate?" Drazlor asked.

"Possibly. Alexa told me she avoided revealing her identity as queen. Ambassador Laritha said Bin-Lot never even knew she was high priestess until Nikolai revealed that fact during his trip."

"May I join you?"

All three men rose, with Braeklojorn welcoming Sharlia with a kiss to her hand before guiding her to a chair. "Blessings this day, Mother."

"I am indeed blessed today, my son. Finally, I have you home." She sat and waited for a server to set down a cup of kacha along with a plate of traditional breakfast pastries and fruit. "I see you've already shown Drazlor your documents. Drazlor?"

"Aunt, I have no doubt they're genuine. We've been discussing Turand's original request for assistance against the Sifiq."

"And Turand's visiting queen?" Sharlia's questioning gaze was pointed as she bit into sweet, flaky pastry.

Vezjalan grinned. "My brother once said he always appreciated most your directness, Sharlia. You never played games."

"Games have their time and place. At this moment, they seem most inappropriate." Shifting loving attention to Braeklojorn, she sighed.

"Braeklojorn, you always did exhibit flair for the dramatic. You've outdone yourself this time. This Alexa is fascinating."

"Mother…"

"Do not misunderstand. I admire her. Her approach last night was both self-assured and daring while facing her husband's family. The silent communication between her and her daughter also intrigues me."

Braeklojorn grinned. "As I understand, it is common among Valiria priestesses."

Sipping her kacha, Sharlia considered the previous night's encounter with Alexa and Anlía. Alexa had waited for her daughter to close her gown before forcing a grim smile. After thanking everyone for dinner, she excused herself to return to her ship. Turning to the Turandan officer who had stayed close to her the entire evening, she then slumped into his arms. "Why do you think she collapsed at the end?"

Braeklojorn replied, "Anlía explained that her mother intended to do whatever necessary to help us understand the gravity of Turand's crisis. Alexa's devotion to my grandson is absolute. She feels exceptional pressure knowing he and their son are in the place where she was tortured for a year, especially with their lives in danger daily. What she did last night exacted an emotional toll, but she seemed fine this morning when I left."

"She was awake already?" Drazlor asked in surprise.

"She rises early every day for meditations and prayers. Afterward, she usually works with her priestesses and on various projects. Alexa is resilient and determined to support Gregor."

"I know men who could learn from her example," Vezjalan remarked. "My next question before we leave for Tarahlaz. Your great-granddaughter. Setting aside your emotional attachments, do you believe she can function as a suitable regent?"

Braeklojorn studied the expressions on the faces of his mother and uncle. They must have stayed awake late into the night, much later than he imagined. "You will have little time to know her, but I assure you that she has received the finest education. Education is so important that her mother even engaged tutors to travel with us, and her studies have continued uninterrupted during our journey."

"But how does she respond to education? Is she dull or bright?" Drazlor asked.

"Talk with her yourself. You will find her charming and intelligent. She even demonstrates initiative, having enlisted Gaeldoreg and me to start teaching her to speak Trezvindjan," Braeklojorn said proudly.

"Really?" Sharlia asked, smiling. "And?"

"Her progress surprises me," he replied. Breathing in, Braeklojorn continued, "Mother, Anlía pledged her oath as a priestess only days before we began our journey here. She needed to pass the scrutiny of five priestesses under strict guidelines before pledging her vows. Once you spend time with her, I'm sure you'll sense the tranquility of her spirit as well as her integrity. Decide for yourself before recommending her."

"You are quite taken with these Turandans, aren't you?" Drazlor asked, studying his distant cousin's reaction.

Braeklojorn shrugged. "I did not live among them and develop an affection—if that's what you think. Only three from a single family helped us through the years. Since Alexa barged in on us, with perhaps only one or two exceptions, I have encountered fine people of faith and good intentions. As far as my grandson's family? I freely admit that I'm in love with his children. Gregor's wife has enchanted me. Because of her, I have seen the face of the daughter I never knew and now have purpose restored to my life. And I've finally come home."

Tarahlaz gleamed beneath brilliant sunshine. Buildings were constructed primarily of brick or stucco and roofed in rippled rows of red tiles. Soaring palm trees with feathery fronds lined boulevards crowded with mounted riders and a wide assortment of horse-drawn conveyances. Sidewalks bustled with men and women dressed for a tropical climate very different from Turand's. Alexa smiled indulgently as she watched her daughter and Gregor Maconti looking out the carriage windows. Despite comprehending the critical circumstances bringing them to Tarahlaz, their youth allowed them to exchange excited comments as they observed a world very different from their own.

Leaving busier city streets behind, their carriage traveled a shady lane through a residential quarter. Rambling homes were painted various pastel colors and surrounded by beautifully landscaped grounds peeking out from behind tall iron fences. When their carriage rolled to a stop, they leaned sideways to gaze out as gates twenty feet high were opened by uniformed attendants. Ahead, their mounted escort and the lead carriage rolled beneath a long, multi-arched porte cochere. Household staff appeared from inside to receive their returning mistress and arriving guests, whose appearances garnered more than a few raised eyebrows.

Soon, Braeklojorn walked into a spacious parlor where Alexa and Anlía sat with Master Maconti, sipping refreshing beverages from frosty glasses while waiting to be shown to their rooms. A manservant motioned to Maconti, indicating he should follow him. Setting his drink aside and excusing himself, the aide rose from his chair and quietly left.

The prince sighed. "My dears, it is impossible to express my feelings being in this house again. I grew up here. I imagine you might wish to change. I requested the services of a dressmaker for you, Anlía, so that you might have clothing more comfortable for our climate. I do hope you both will approve of the differences in style."

"I appreciate your thoughtfulness, Grandfather," Alexa responded. Curious, she added, "I haven't seen your mother since we arrived."

"She went up to bed. Traveling so far yesterday and today has caused her much pain." Sadness pinched his features. "Age torments her body, but her heart and mind demanded that she go when she learned she might find me alive."

Anlía's gaze met Alexa's. "Mother?" Receiving an assenting nod, she said, "Grandfather, if she's not asleep, would you consider taking Mother and me to her? Do you think she would see us?"

Braeklojorn looked puzzled. "She was too uncomfortable to sleep. I think she would receive you, but why?" He shivered upon receiving that mysteriously tranquil smile so like the precious one from his past.

"Do you not trust me, Grandfather?" she asked, her voice sweet and gentle.

The Vosklon prince silently questioned when she had risen from her chair and placed those long, elegant fingers on his arm. Suddenly alert again, he looked into those mesmerizing emerald eyes, feeling her voice and another's speaking into his soul. Tingles raced along his spine. He caught his breath. "Of course, I trust you, Ma Levya. Let us go."

Upstairs, he quietly knocked and opened the door to his mother's suite. "Mother? May I enter?"

Her voice, tired and weak, invited him into a room decorated with floral-patterned wallpaper, satin draperies with swagged valances, scroll-topped settees and chaises, matching tables, and an enormous canopied bed where the woman as tall as King Gregor seemed small.

"Mother, I know you don't feel well, but Anlía and Alexa wish to speak with you."

Sharlia looked surprised. Extending her hand to Anlía, she said, "Child, come. Is there something you need?"

Alexa responded to her daughter's glance. "Grandmother, if I may answer. As I understand, you believe in one you call Espiritus. We worship our God Val. I have prayed and meditated and now think they're one and the same divine Creator. We simply know this divine one by different names and worship in different ways."

Anlía further explained, "Val, as we know the Creator, has gifted Mother and me with the ability to channel Val's healing energies. The healing comes in different ways, according to his will. We believe that because you're a woman of faith, we may be able to help. Unfortunately, we cannot heal you completely because of your age, but we can ease the pain—only with your permission, of course."

Sharlia's features were pale and drawn from the persistent pain in her back and joints. The vibrations, bumps, and jolts of two long carriage rides in as many days had worsened her rheumatism. She refused to complain. The joy of her son's return was well worth any physical agony. After careful thought, she decided to allow this child, who was linked to her by blood, to try to alleviate this terrible ache.

She asked Braeklojorn to lock the suite's doors and then wait on a settee. Anlía lovingly caressed her great-great-grandmother's forehead before she and her mother sat on opposite sides of the bed. Joining their voices first in prayer and then in chant, they summoned the Healing Graces. Over Sharlia's bed, multicolored dancing lights appeared, settling above the woman's stately body while Valiria voices hummed melodiously for nearly an hour.

Mesmerized, Braeklojorn kept vigil until the soft, musical tones and lights faded. Finally, Alexa and Anlía emerged from their prayerful trance. He watched Alexa stand first and take his mother's hand, asking, "Grandmother, are you awake?"

Sharlia's brown eyes blinked several times. Her body curled and stretched from side to side until her mouth slowly spread into a smile.

When she spoke, her voice conveyed awe. "You are both mystic healers! I feel no pain! Amazing!"

Anlía smiled. "Grandmother, I feel your desire to get up, but you should rest at least an hour."

Tears glazed Sharlia's eyes. "I know you must change. Will you return and stay with me, child? Your presence lightens my heart."

"Gladly, Grandmother," she replied, bending to kiss Sharlia's forehead. When she turned so her grandfather could guide her to her guest chamber, she saw him wrapped in her mother's arms as the great man wept.

⌒

"Bresklon Krisantal will arrive early tomorrow morning. We need to address this quickly. Speculation has already started regarding the strange ships in port flying Trezvindjan colors. Thankfully, the port director is friendly to the Vosklon League and is securing papers for the military personnel on board. He's doing everything possible to contain details until we meet with Bresklon."

Braeklojorn nodded approval as he drank a glass of liquor. "Drazlor, you are a credit to the family. Thank you for all you've done."

"Milord, it gives me great pleasure serving a Vosklon prince, especially one who delivers a viable solution to King Kaelzron. It would be different if one could hate him. He's not a bad man, but neither is he a leader."

"My brother-in-law was overjoyed when his father declared Mishkla his successor. With his father's best advisers now gone due to old age, our nation suffers Kaelzron's lack of will and judgment. That was what King Bezmaj expected—and feared."

"How right Bezmaj was," Vezjalan said. "What's worse is that Essila is strong but possesses none of the classic perceptions of the Sacred Krisantal.

I must admit that we all see and feel that perception flow from your Anlía. Without doubt, she is Krisantal."

Sharlia, who had been standing in the arched doorway, made her presence known. "Krisantal she is—and likely as great a mystic as any Krisantal who ever lived. I have sent word to Milansa that we have two mystics among us, one of Krisantal descent. We will need urgent input from the Mystic Council, too."

"Aunt, you look remarkably well. I was quite worried when we took you up earlier," Drazlor remarked, having stood to greet Sharlia with a smile and a kiss for her cheek.

"Thank you, Nephew. It has been years since I felt so little discomfort—all thanks to the Turandan priestesses and their—Braeklojorn, what was it they called it?"

"Healing Graces, Mother."

Sharlia smiled. "Ah, yes, beautiful lights and song sweeter than any I've ever heard. I was carried away on a cloud of blessed comfort. When I awoke, my pain was practically gone. Alexa and Anlía said the Healing Graces could help me but not cure me because of my age. I accept that I'm old, just as I accept that I cannot be cured of the maladies of old age. However, I gratefully accept how their Graces eased the pain of those maladies. That will enable me to work to ensure Gregor Toscano receives whatever support he needs to replace Kaelzron Krisantal on Trezvindja's throne."

"Mother, he must first be declared Gregor Krisantal."

Determination shone brightly in obsidian eyes. "My son, the Vosklon League's Grand Prince has come home. That is a miracle unto itself. Anlía Toscano is a mystic who exudes every aspect of the Krisantal Sacred Blood, and there are Krisantal elders who will remember Mishkla, including Mishkla's mother. There will be no doubt that Gregor is Mishkla's proper heir according to the ancient laws of succession. I will not rest until those laws are honored, and your descendants receive their proper due."

Chapter 14

The paper lay open on the table, illuminated by a lantern and leaping flames from the campfire. Thoroughly surprised by the arrival of fresh supplies and extra troops from home, Gregor had also welcomed the small stack of letters from his family. Saving the one from Alexa until last, he read the messages from his twin daughters. Filled with news about their schoolwork and volunteer efforts, the letters conjured up pictures of his dark-haired beauties and their boundless energy as they bounced from one activity to the next. Hearts and flowers drawn in margins and corners reminded him of how young they were, making him long to feel their arms around his neck.

As he opened letters from DiMarco and Thikos, pride burgeoned. He sensed their growing maturity and responsibility. Something in their comments prompted curiosity. Knowing his sons well, he puzzled over the mention of the Quartermaster Corps and infrastructure plans that should exceed their classroom work. He would write and ask about changes in their curriculum.

Anlía's message, as always, encouraged her father. Why did his mind always fall back to that momentous day of her birth? Such a comfort she had been during Alexa's long absence. Now she was reminding him to stay strong. Val was watching over him, Nikolai, and Turand, and their blessed Valkana would bring Val's blessings to save their people in unexpected ways.

"Father, you must trust the guide Val has sent us. She will not fail Turand and never you."

What was it in those words Anlía wrote that shook him to his core? What was it about this daughter that perplexed him? What was it about her mother that had carved such an indelible niche into his very soul?

Folding the letters from his children and setting them safely aside, he reached for a fresh mug of tea brought by an aide. Cautiously sipping the hot brew, he decided it must have been made from fresh Raija leaves from new supplies. Breaking the seal on the letter bearing his wife's flowing script, he unfolded ivory stationery. For a moment, his eyes swam, unable to focus on the lines of elegant handwriting. Regaining his clarity, he began to read.

My beloved Gregor,

How much do I miss you! There are moments when I feel as if my very life may fade away. Being parted from you is like having my life taken. This is the fourth time we are separated because of the Sifiq. I am determined to make it the last. I am quite sure I would not survive a fifth. I need you, my love, if I am to live and breathe. That is my simple truth.

Our children here do us proud. Even the little ones take pride in their studies before they perform volunteer duties. They cheer our people as only children can. DiMarco and Thikos work with their professors and then undertake projects under Stefan's guidance. It gives them valuable experience and the sense of making real contributions to the war effort. According to Stefan, the quartermasters dread DiMarco's reviews because our quiet son possesses his father's keen eye for details and his ability for drilling staff regarding causes for mistakes and inefficiencies. Without meanness, he tolerates no nonsense. Thikos, of course, still loves building and now involves himself with infrastructure projects. You will be surprised, I promise. Anlía is Anlía. She has news, but I will leave that for her to reveal.

As for the rest. Much is happening, but until I can be sure of the progress and its fruition, I hope you will forgive me for not writing about it. It is also best that you receive news when I can see that it is delivered by direct messenger.

On a personal note, trust me when I say that I do have at least one astonishing surprise for you—something you cannot begin to guess, my love.

I must stop for now, or I shall pour bottles of ink onto these pages about how my heart suffers knowing the dangers you and our son confront in that awful place. I want to kiss my son's face again. Gregor, more than anything, I long to feel your arms hold me again. Perhaps it is selfish, but I often doubt my strength to bear my overwhelming need for you when we are separated this way. I just want to lie in our bed—to do naught but cry. But I know that no one can do more than I to help end this separation so we can be together again.

I love you, Gregor. You are my heart and soul, so I will not fail you, nor will I fail our beloved Turand.

Alexa

Gregor read Alexa's letter three times. He better understood comments from his children's letters. Yes, he was more proud than ever and wondered what news Anlía failed to include in hers. She had been more intent on encouraging him to trust in their Valkana. Even Alexa made a shadowy reference to progress of some sort. What was his wife doing? Although not a mystic, he was intuitive enough to sense Alexa was up to something. Knowing her, that could result in quite a shock. What was this astonishing surprise?

"Father?"

"Nikolai, I see you have a sheaf of letters, too."

"Yes, from the family."

"And?"

Nikolai grinned at his father's raised eyebrows. "About a dozen from the lovely ladies of your court. All suitably worried about Turand's Crown Prince."

Gregor laughed heartily. "Have any of them caught his eye?"

Nikolai shook his head, long hair that needed to be cut fluttering. "Not really. They're all pretty. Several are even reasonably pleasant but a little boring."

"So none meet your high standards."

"I've decided I need more than a pretty face."

"Wise decision. Now, did your sister write any news to you?"

"Nothing special. Why?"

"Something your mother wrote. I hope she hasn't accepted some suitor without my approval."

Nikolai snorted. "I doubt that."

"Meaning?"

Evasively, Nikolai replied, "My sister would never accept a suitor's offer of marriage without your approval. She respects you too much. She may have an independent streak but not that independent."

"Anlía? Are we discussing the same sister?"

"We are." Nikolai got up and held his hands over the fire.

"What am I missing?"

"Likely nothing worth catching. I want to get some sleep now. I'm leading troops out early for the next offensive."

Gregor watched his son walk away and wondered what important detail had escaped his usual watchful eye.

⸺

Rafzan Lynmar carefully balanced the lantern, ensuring it wouldn't tip inside his tent. Releasing a frustrated sigh, he twisted his back and legs into a more comfortable position. Military service on land had required more than a few adjustments. Finally satisfied with both his position and privacy, he withdrew the letter he had tucked inside his coat earlier that day. Her handwriting was so distinctive, and the letter had come as such a surprise on a dreary afternoon.

Rafzan gazed several minutes at the script forming his name. She had taken time to write to him. He relished the very idea that, after years of living a life where no one ever cared if he was alive, here was a beautiful princess who considered him worthy enough of her time to send him a letter.

Suddenly, he felt a jolt in the pit of his stomach. What if she had written to tell him she wanted nothing more to do with him? Fear struck, scorching his insides like the lightning bolt tattooed on every Sifiq soldier's shoulder. Never a coward, he flipped the letter over and broke the lavender-colored wax seal.

My dear Rafzan,

How long it has been since we met at our special place in the woods. I sometimes go to gaze at the stars and think of you. I miss you, dear one. I so fear what could happen there. I hold you close to my heart and keep you in prayer. Remember your promise to be careful.

I have news. You may have noticed the lavender seal on my letter. After advancing my studies, I underwent the Scrutiny by the panel of five Valiria. They accepted me, and I have pledged my vows. I am now an anointed priestess in the Order of Val, and Val has blessed me with the gift of the Healing Graces. Mother was not part of the panel, but she administered my vows. Afterward, she cried. I was glad to give her some happiness. I am also happy. Please pray that I will always find strength to fulfill my oath.

So much has happened since you left. How I wish we could sit down to discuss some of the most amazing things that recently occurred. Mother never ceases to astonish me when she pursues her dreams and discovers the meanings. This time is beyond amazing! Just wait until you find out! Oh, Rafzan, I can hardly wait for Father to find out. His life will forever change, and one of his lifelong dreams will be fulfilled in the most spectacular way.

I must go. Odd. I really must leave! A mystery behind that! Rafzan, dearest love, do take care.

Anlía

Rafzan traced his fingertip across his name and the words *dearest love*. He imagined watching those elegant fingers gripping her quill, dipping it into an inkpot, and then writing that graceful script that had crossed the seas to make his heart throb and his eyes brim with hot tears. Anlía was a blessing he didn't deserve, but he honored her request and prayed for Val's blessing on her now that she had achieved her goal of becoming a Valiria priestess.

"Holy Val," he whispered inside the solitude of his tent, "as always, I beg your forgiveness for what I did to her mother. I also thank you for the blessings you've shown me as your servant and for the blessing of someone like Anlía to love."

෴

Two days later, Turandan cavalry officers rode circles around bivouacked Sifiq soldiers. Unlike their enemy, Turandans had little fear of darkness and had risen just after midnight to launch their attack on the sleeping camp. Troops entered the camp and, pitting numbers of alert fighters against unsuspecting soldiers aroused from sleep, scored yet another victory. Surviving Sifiq were marched back to the main Turandan camp near Qasalaf and then imprisoned at the old army garrison.

Turandan forces continued pushing forward. Progress was slow but steady. Fierce fighting had brought them almost halfway from the cantonment to Atuliq. So far, they had successfully protected supply lines behind them, and General Ravendro was squeezing the Sifiq from the north. Nevertheless, Gregor and Nikolai still worried that they did not have enough intelligence about what lay closer to Atuliq. They also questioned if they had enough troops to meet the Sifiq in sustained major battles to take Atuliq.

Gregor and his son lamented General Kohira's continuing battle to recover from his injuries. Kohira was a brilliant military strategist on whom Gregor had relied during the civil war and when his armies first invaded the Sifiq Kingdom. Doctors considered the general's condition too unstable for transport to ships to return him to Turand. Priestesses on-site continued summoning Healing Graces to keep him stable as he slipped in and out of consciousness. In the meantime, Gregor and his advisers worked to compensate for the void left by Kohira.

෴

Bresklon Krisantal whisked through the grand entrance of the Vosklon Royal Residence with his two closest aides. True to his word, he arrived early, with the clock chiming the hour of seven. His expression reflected surprise when he was met by household staff in formal livery and Prince Elder Vezjalan in full royal regalia.

"Your Highness, good morning," Bresklon greeted, bowing respectfully. "I was unaware this was a meeting requiring ceremonial dress."

Vezjalan responded, "On behalf of the Vosklon League, have no concern. Today is a momentous occasion we have chosen to celebrate. Please. Join us."

Following the prince inside a spacious, elaborately decorated salon, the handsome leader of the Krisantal League was surprised by the number of people awaiting him, including Drazlor, whom he knew from the Council of Protectors, and Princess Elder Sharlia. He was unfamiliar with the stranger wearing the regalia of the Vosklon League's Grand Prince, along with the two ladies dressed head-to-toe in lavender capes. Bowing, he waited for an explanation for the urgent summons to this morning's summit.

"Grand Councillor Krisantal, welcome," Sharlia greeted, elegant in her regalia of silver gown and blue sash embroidered with the Vosklon League's official crest and edged with opalescent pearls. "I'm honored by your presence today. It is my great pleasure to introduce you to my son, Grand Prince Braeklojorn Vosklon."

Resplendent in knee-length tunic of royal blue silk, a white silk sash lavishly embroidered with metallic threads and gemstones, gold-fringed epaulets, and gold-trimmed cuffs, Braeklojorn acknowledged Bresklon with a nod and a smile. "Grand Councillor, it is an honor to receive you in our home. I thank you for coming on such short notice. We are celebrating my homecoming after many years away when my family thought I was lost at sea."

After saluting the grand prince with a stately bow, Bresklon regarded him curiously. "Braeklojorn Vosklon? Not the same prince who married our Princess Royal Mishkla Krisantal and later disappeared on a pilgrimage voyage?"

"The same," Braeklojorn responded, his voice catching slightly. "But please, that is partly why we have summoned you. Before further discussion, allow me to introduce you to our guests." Turning, he took Alexa's hand, waiting until a maid ceremoniously removed her lavender cape.

When Alexa stepped forward, Bresklon Krisantal was unprepared for the majestic persona of the woman at the Vosklon prince's side. Golden-brown hair had been braided, its loops secured at the back of her head. She wore a gold filigree tiara and a gown of golden fabric, its silken bodice fitted and the finely woven mesh skirts whispering as she moved. Aside from an unusual pyramid-shaped pendant and a wide, diamond-studded band on one finger, she wore no jewelry. She needed no other adornment. She appeared to gleam as brightly as any jewels he had ever seen.

"Councillor Krisantal, I am honored to present my grandson's wife, the High Priestess Valkana, Queen Alexa Maraná Toscano of Turand."

Bresklon blinked before his eyes widened in surprise. Then, suddenly recovering his wits, he executed a stately bow. "Your Majesty, on behalf of the Krisantal League, I welcome you to Trezvindja."

"Councillor Krisantal, I thank you. I am honored to meet you," Alexa replied before taking Gaeldoreg's hand and stepping aside.

"Councillor Krisantal," Braeklojorn said, "I am now delighted to introduce the last of our party before I invite you to join us for a celebration breakfast. Afterward, we can embark on more serious discussions." Extending his hand once again, he grasped Anlía's hand as a maid unclasped and removed her lavender cape.

The beauty of the young woman impacted Bresklon physically. Her bearing was as noble as anyone he had ever met, yet there existed no hint of arrogance. Instead, her Trezvindjan heritage appeared obvious in her stature and her features. The only exception was her eyes—those startling green eyes—burning with fires promising vitality and accomplishment in all that lay ahead on her life's journey. This he sensed instantly, and she stole his breath away, leaving him slightly dizzy.

"Councillor, I proudly present my great-granddaughter, Valiria Priestess and Princess Royal, Anlía Vosklon Krisantal Toscano."

The initial thought shafting through Bresklon's mind was that his inherited intuitive abilities had not failed. His own great-great-grandmother had led the Council of Mystics for decades. The Grand Councillor of the Krisantal League signaled his aides. In unison, they all knelt with heads reverently bent and arms crossed over their chests.

"Princess of the Sacred Blood, I am honored to offer my pledge of loyalty. I will defend you to the death."

Anlía shook her head. The strange reaction she had first received upon meeting Gaeldoreg and his kinsmen still startled her, but she was learning to accept the ways of her father's previously unknown people. Placing her hands on Bresklon's shoulders, she detected extraordinary waves of energy. The ties of family, perhaps? She closed her eyes and released her own energy flow. "Councillor Krisantal, your pledge honors me. In return, I promise you and the Krisantal League my respect all the days of my life. Please rise. " She then proceeded with the others in like manner.

Over a lavish breakfast where Anlía sat quietly next to Sharlia, Bresklon listened attentively to details of how Braeklojorn had indulged Mishkla's entreaties to embark on a pilgrimage to the island of Lizmadal after dreaming about seeing their child standing in a pool of bubbling waters with a waterfall in the background. She had also seen and smelled sweetly perfumed white and purple flowers surrounding that child, and there had been such a sense of pure joy. She had believed there must be a reason behind the dream. Lizmadal was the only holy site she could think of that might fit the images in her vision and help her discern its meaning. For a matter of seconds, both Bresklon and Anlía watched Alexa's expression shift faraway and freeze before she smiled enigmatically.

Conversation subsided as the Trezvindjans pondered how the hopeful expectation of a pilgrimage transformed into the tragedy of Mishkla's untimely death and Braeklojorn's shipwreck in the distant land of Turand. Compounding the mystery was Alexa's account of dreams decades later. Extensive research had prompted the journey leading her to the abandoned village of Zemtoval and the discovery of Mishkla's arrival on Turand's shores. Immediately afterward, she trekked into the mountains to confront the pugnacious Gaeldoreg as he defended his prince against intrusive outsiders.

"Alexa," Bresklon pronounced her name respectfully, pleased at being included in such familiar intimacy so soon, "I mean no disrespect, but you do not strike me as one so forward. Or so assertive. I am surprised that you would face down the likes of Gaeldoreg in a place he had established as his lair. Even now, parents tell their children stories of Gaeldoreg the Terrible."

Polite laughter erupted around the table. "Tales from five years in the army, after which I decided to watch over my prince here. Stories only."

Vezjalan stared down at his plate. "Not just stories. I was with him on that campaign to oust the Sifiq from Pristalan. He was every bit the terror those stories talk about. Only worse."

Interrupting Gaeldoreg's low growl, Sharlia graciously said, "I think this may be a good time to gather in the salon for kacha. The direction of this conversation merits a change."

Half an hour later, Bresklon held his head low. "My heart aches. Thinking of what you endured at the hands of that despot Bin-Lot sickens me."

"Not just me, Bresklon. Four sister priestesses were with me. With Anlía now a Valiria, she could easily become one of his victims. Bin-Lot and his soldiers commit similar atrocities continuously on any vulnerable women in their path. When he told Nikolai that his officers were free to continue their raids at will, my husband decided their rampages must end."

"Still, how did you survive such abuse? You are so—so..." Searching for words, he finally shrugged and said, "Small."

Alexa smiled. "Perhaps small in size compared to Trezvindjans, but my faith sets me apart." She reached for Anlía's hand. "As you come to know us, you will learn that the faith of every Valiria priestess differentiates her from most you will ever meet. Bresklon, in most ways, we are the same as everyone. We have the same hopes and dreams. We grieve the same. However, truth holds higher significance, as does loyalty. When it comes to love, I think perhaps we love with greater fervor because our Lord Val grants us different perceptions of love."

Holding Bresklon Krisantal captive with her eyes only, she continued, "Faith in Val carried me through my ordeal in the Sifiq Kingdom. Val often revealed his divine presence, especially during my most hopeless moments, until we were finally delivered. Retreat into memories of home, where I knew I was loved and cherished beyond measure, saved me. Val continuously showed me my memories to give me reasons to live and resist the pain and torment. My children didn't need to live without a mother. And Bresklon, my husband—my husband needed me most. My Gregor loves me in ways you can't imagine."

"Councillor," Anlía said, hearing swelling emotion in her mother's voice, "my mother's right. Anyone who has ever seen Father and Mother together is touched forever by the memory. In Turand, they are inspiration and legend. Their love is how she survived."

The Krisantal League's primary leader gazed into Anlía's youthful face. They were cousins, many times removed. Intuition goaded him again, as did guilt. He had failed to support Turand's plea for help with the Sifiq. By ignoring inner voices saying something was amiss, he had helped place the Sacred Blood of two rightful heirs to Trezvindja's throne in serious jeopardy. Thoughts raced through his mind. So much needed to be done—quickly.

Drawing a deep breath, Bresklon tossed his head backward, faint hints of silver at his temples rippling distinctively through the fullness of his black mane. The Trezvindjan Law of Succession was clear.

"Prince Braeklojorn, if you and the Vosklon League agree, when I leave today, I shall call a meeting of the Krisantal Oversight Council to advise what I have learned. I know my stance, but some may not be so certain about this Krisantal connection after literally decades of your absence, especially when the result could be sending troops to war."

Sharlia said, "Councillor, I know that Mishkla's mother and her aunt still live. I suggest that we take Anlía to meet her great-great-grandmother at the earliest possible moment. Also, is not Milansa Krisantal your great-great-grandmother?"

"She is," he answered. "Why do you ask?"

"Circumstances demand that we call together the Mystic Council right away, but I believe Anlía should meet Milansa as soon as possible. Alexa, too. You will understand afterward, I'm certain."

"I believe I can arrange a meeting with Milansa tomorrow morning. Is that too soon?"

"Bresklon," Alexa said softly, "my husband and my son are risking their lives daily in the Sifiq Kingdom. There is little I would not do for their sake, including crawling from this house right now to meet her if it would make a difference."

The ishna's intensity pierced his chest. His breathing quickened as his heart raced. What was it about her that affected him so? Shaking off the reaction, he bowed his head. "Your Majesty," he said, reverting to formal address, "that is not necessary. Trezvindja needs strong leadership after years of Kaelzron's mediocre reign. You present the possibility that we might revitalize the pride long associated with the Protectors. If you will excuse me, I shall take my leave."

⌣

"Rafzan, are you there? I need to talk to you."

Shoving letters and drawings inside his leather binder, Rafzan called out, "I'm here. I'll be right out."

"Not to worry," Nikolai said, lifting the tent's flap and bending far forward to enter. "I noticed a possible alternative route on one of the older maps. I wanted your opinion and to review it before we meet Father for the morning briefing."

Dragging in a nervous breath, Rafzan took the map from Nikolai. "Which route do you mean?"

Nikolai leveled a steady, unnerving gaze at the captain. "The dangerous route that could get you killed. If you only knew how my father once despised you, you might possibly appreciate the value of the trust he now places in you. I just came to suggest you be very careful. I'm not sure he could ever trust you when it comes to my sister."

Rafzan's face blanched. "You know."

Nodding, Nikolai crouched with one knee on the canvas bottom of the tent. "Although she's withholding something important right now that I hope you might share, my sister trusts me to confide many of her secrets. You're one of those secrets."

"I see. Why haven't you commanded me to stay away from her? Or informed your father?" Rafzan was direct but not contentious.

"My sister cares enough about you that she also told our mother. I have no right to override Mother's judgment since she hasn't ended your relationship. Mother must have her reasons."

Nikolai chewed the inside of his cheek. "You've also conducted your-self exceedingly well since father reinstated your rank. You're a valuable officer, Rafzan. I admire and respect you, but be certain of one thing. If you hurt my sister, I will kill you."

Rafzan emitted a slight laugh. "If only you knew the depth of my feelings for her. I would prefer a dagger twisted into my heart rather than hurt her. I am not the same man who…" Stumbling over words he could not utter, he choked. "I pray every day that Val will forgive me for what I did to your mother. Every single day. My worst punishment is living with the knowledge that she has forgiven me and holds no trace of rancor against me. At least that was the worst until I found myself in love with Anlía. A fool caught in a fool's web when I discovered she felt the same."

Nikolai rocked backward until he sat cross-legged across from Rafzan. "How? How did it happen?"

Rafzan looked away, expelling a heavy breath. "I wish I knew. I had talked to her several times at the temple when she explained passages from the Great Book of Val. Then, on the way to Zinzan, she was studying astronomy and asked a question about navigation by stars. That's how it began. Her questions continued in more variety and depth. Our con-versations became more involved. Without my realization, I was soon enchanted."

"That's it?"

Rafzan fixed blue eyes on his prince. "Nikolai, I refused to acknowl-edge my feelings to myself until the night your own nobles caused that fire and shoved your sister into a wall. Never in my life was I so afraid as when I reached the top of those stairs and saw flames threatening Anlía. I only thought of racing through that wall of fire to reach her. The instant I dragged her into my arms was the moment I understood how much I loved her—that there was no danger in this world I would not risk if it meant saving her. Hate me for that, if you will, but that moment gave me the strength to save her life and guide the Maconti boy away from that fire."

Nikolai dropped his face and stared downward. His mind's eye recreated the scene Rafzan's words described. He recalled his mother's description of how the fire had quickly destroyed the top floor of the building, where his own concerns about Maconti not being accepted took a much darker turn than even he had anticipated.

Finally meeting Rafzan's waiting gaze, Nikolai said, "How could I ever hate you? You saved my sister's life."

"You hold in your memory how I came to Turand. For that, I cannot blame you. So here we are. Will you tell your father?"

After a moment, Nikolai shook his head. "I will leave that to Mother. She has her reasons and her ways. If she accepts you, then I must, but my warning stands."

Relieved, Rafzan dared a vague smile. "I swear to you one thing. I will never deliberately hurt Anlía. Never."

"Something I do need to ask. Anlía mentioned in her letters to Father and me about having news. She was unusually mysterious. Do you know what she was talking about?"

Recognizing the need to build Nikolai's trust, Rafzan drew a deep breath. "I assume she mentioned pledging her vows as a Valiria. She was very proud of using the lavender seal on her letter."

Shaking his head in frustration, Nikolai exclaimed, "How in Val's great name did I miss that! She didn't mention it, but you're right! My letter bore the lavender seal! Did she say anything else?"

Shrugging, Rafzan said, "You know your sister's penchant for mystery. She wrote something about a surprise that will change your father's life and about having to go. A real mystery, she said."

"Go? Where?"

"She didn't say, but I had the impression she was taking a journey. She also mentioned dreams. Your mother's dreams and your father's."

Confusion clouded Nikolai's expression. "Dreams? That makes no sense. Well, for Mother, yes, of course. But Father?"

Rafzan shrugged. "A suggestion. Do as I do. Enjoy Anlía's ways, then let time unravel the mystery."

Returning late that night from a reconnaissance mission, Nikolai carried a plate of food to a table where his father sat, rereading the most recent letters from home. "You didn't need to wait up."

"I was ready to lead a party out to see if you needed help."

"Always the father as well as the general?" Nikolai asked as he wearily bit into a piece of flatbread.

"Where you're concerned? Always the father first," Gregor replied.

Hungrily gulping down several bites, Nikolai grinned broadly. "No complaints from your eldest prince, Sire. New letters?"

"No, just still puzzling over comments from your mother and sister."

"Ah, well, I believe I solved one of the mysteries."

"Really? And?"

"Did you check the seal on Anlía's letter?"

Gregor quickly sorted Anlía's last message from his stack and turned it over. Remnants of cracked wax still clung to heavy linen paper and were the same beautiful shade of lavender as Alexa's. He stared for a long moment before the significance penetrated his weary brain. Then, his face becoming undeniably proud, he said, "She planned to wait until we got home to take her vows. I wonder what changed."

"Who knows? I say we pray Val's blessings on her and then try to get some rest. I'm exhausted."

Later, as Gregor waited for sleep, he pondered why neither Alexa nor Anlía had written about his daughter's profession of vows as a Valiria priestess. He recalled his wife's reference to something she didn't want to put in writing. Closing his eyes, he pictured his wife's face and, for just a few seconds, could have sworn he heard her voice murmuring his name. "Beloved, what are you doing now?"

Chapter 15

"Grandfather, we're ready," Alexa announced as she and Anlía entered the formal salon where Braeklojorn waited with Vezjalan, Sharlia, and Gaeldoreg.

Braeklojorn rose from his chair, his smile broad and approving. "Ma Levya, how lovely you look."

Blushing, Anlía asked, "Are you sure, Grandfather? I've never worn anything like this."

Sharlia took Anlía's hands and examined the Trezvindjan-style summer dress she had commissioned eight seamstresses to start early the day before. Lavender silk was trimmed with ribbons in graduated shades of purple on the hems of the sleeves and skirt. Gathered at the waist, crossed pieces formed the bodice and v-shaped neckline while creating fluttering, elbow-length sleeves. The slightly flared skirt stopped above the ankle and opened in front to her knees. Matching shoes that revealed the tips of her toes completed the exotic outfit that, to Trezvindjan eyes, was both beautiful and modest.

"Dear child," Princess Elder Sharlia said, "you look lovely."

Braeklojorn's eyes glittered happily. "Mother is right. I daresay it has been many years since this house has been graced by such elegance or such beauty—with Mother's exception, of course."

"I just feel so—conspicuous."

Alexa hugged her daughter. "You're in a new world, my love. Wear your cape while we're out and observe others. Once you see you're not so different from everyone else, I'm certain you'll feel more confident. Focus on who you are, and you'll be fine."

Anlía gazed doubtfully into her mother's eyes. "You're sure I'm breaking no rules of propriety?"

"Quite certain, although we'd likely have to convince your father if he were here. Fortunately, he's not, and it seems Val has chosen you to be your father's advocate. Are you prepared for the challenge?"

Sighing, Anlía nodded. "Give me three minutes?" Hurrying to the office where Master Maconti was reviewing plans Alexa had asked him to organize, she peeked her head around the door. "Gregor, quick. I need your advice."

Looking up, he smiled, glad for the interruption. "How can I help?"

"They want me to appear as a Trezvindjan. Tell me honestly. Can I do this?" She then walked through the door.

Gregor Maconti's light brown eyes opened wide as his chin dropped. If he had always thought Anlía beautiful, he was positive the princess who just walked into the office must be the most incredible being in Val's entire universe. He wondered for a moment if his heart had stopped beating because he had surely forgotten how to breathe. "In Val's great name, Anlía! Forgive me for saying this, but you must be the most beautiful woman alive. Of course, you can do it! Have faith, my friend."

Tears sprang into her eyes as she rushed forward. Hugging him and kissing his cheek, she whispered in his ear, "Thank you, dear Gregor. Thank you."

Waves of sadness struck Alexa as she walked through the soaring entrance of the Krisantal mansion. Her hand rested formally on the arm of Prince Elder Vezjalan. Braeklojorn followed, escorting Anlía. Closing her eyes, Alexa focused on her daughter's thoughts. For one so new to the order, Anlía's abilities were remarkably well-developed. She, too, sensed the underlying sorrow permeating the home.

Liveried staff escorted the visitors into a formal salon, where they were greeted by a middle-aged woman named Zaranla, a distant relative of the royal family. "The Queen Mother knows of your arrival and is on her way downstairs. May I offer you refreshments in the meantime?" Puzzled, she looked at Alexa and Anlía. "I apologize that no one took your cloaks. May I?"

"Thank you, not yet," Anlía answered in Trezvindjan.

Zaranla excused herself. While Sharlia and Vezjalan sat, Braeklojorn remained with Alexa and Anlía, who went to a bank of windows to gaze at elaborate gardens designed around several enormous fountains. "Are you well?"

"We're both affected by an incredible sense of melancholy permeating this place," Alexa said quietly.

"Mother said Oneshkla never recovered from Mishkla's disappearance. She also has a poor relationship with Essila. She considers her unfit to fulfill the legacy of the Krisantal Sacred Blood."

Zaranla reappeared with an additional visitor. "Grand Councillor Bresklon Krisantal has arrived."

Just as formal greetings were exchanged, a maid entered the salon, advising the Queen Mother had arrived downstairs and would join them shortly. Sharlia turned to her great-great-granddaughter with raised eyebrows. "May I remove your cape when the time comes?"

Abruptly realizing she was almost as tall as the Princess Elder, Anlía leaned forward and kissed the soft cheek. "Of course, Grandmother."

When Queen Mother Oneshkla Krisantal entered the salon, the comparison to Sharlia was dramatic. Both were just past one hundred twenty. Although suffering some health problems, Javlodorn Vosklon had refused to let his wife surrender to grief surrounding their son's disappearance. Instead, believing to the end that Braeklojorn would return home, Javlodorn had inspired his wife to live life as a gift rather than a burden.

Oneshkla and her husband had not borne the tragedy of their daughter's loss so well. The king had died relatively young, leaving his crown to Kaelzron, the son he had declined to name successor because of Kaelzron's indulgent character and lack of interest in official affairs. Ongoing family discord involving Essila, Kaelzron's only child, had taken a toll on Oneshkla emotionally and physically. Her features were drawn and pinched, her skin pale. She looked thin and walked slowly, as if every step pained her. Still, her eyes reflected intense curiosity about the reason for Bresklon's urgent request to meet with the Vosklon League's royal hierarchy.

"Your Majesty," Bresklon greeted, "I appreciate your graciousness in meeting with us today. I have someone who has not seen you for a long time and wishes to pay his respects."

Stepping from behind his uncle, Braeklojorn approached his mother-in-law and knelt. "Mother, how good it is to see you again."

Bresklon alertly braced Oneshkla with an arm at her waist when the former queen wavered. Staring in disbelief at the man kneeling before her, she exclaimed, "No! This cannot be. That voice! Braeklojorn Vosklon disappeared years ago! Who are you? Tell me! Who are you?"

Rising, Braeklojorn wondered if he might be facing a woman unable to accept reality. "Oneshkla, I am indeed Braeklojorn, the same man who was once young and so desperately in love with your daughter that I sent you and her bouquets of rare zhalisal flowers daily for weeks until you allowed me to call on her. Have you forgotten?"

"Where have you been? And where is my daughter? Where is my Mishkla?" Oneshkla demanded, her voice growing shrill.

"Oneshkla, please. Come. Sit beside my mother. Let me explain." With Bresklon's help, Braeklojorn guided the trembling Oneshkla to the wide sofa where Sharlia helped her old friend sit. Then, while his mother placed a comforting arm around the Queen Mother's shoulders, Braeklojorn reminded her of Mishkla's intended pilgrimage before describing the ensuing tragedy.

With tears streaming from her eyes, Oneshkla softly sobbed, "So my beautiful Mishkla really is dead?"

Unable to restrain tears of his own, Braeklojorn nodded. "Long ago, Mother Oneshkla. I cannot describe my guilt or how I punished myself." He paused. "What I can tell you is that our beautiful Mishkla left us a gift."

Barely able to speak, Oneshkla asked, "Gift? What kind of gift?"

"She survived falling overboard and washed onto the beach of the same strange land where our ship wrecked. A group of mystic priestesses found her. Mishkla resisted death until our baby was born."

"She gave birth? What happened to the baby?" Oneshkla asked, suddenly sitting straight and staring at her son-in-law.

"The priestesses cared for the baby. A girl. They honored Mishkla's request and called her Anlía."

Oneshkla aimed a watery smile at Sharlia. "Anlía. Spirit-Bridge. Were the priestesses good to Anlía? Where is my granddaughter now?"

Braeklojorn's voice shook. "The priestesses were very good to her. She grew into a fine woman and became a queen in her own right. Then, tragically, Sifiq invaders who occupied her nation poisoned her."

"Sifiq?" Oneshkla practically spat the word out. "Those filthy devils murdered my granddaughter?"

"Majesty, please, you mustn't distress yourself," Zaranla gasped, instantly rushing to the old queen's side.

"Hush, Zaranla," Oneshkla dismissed her caregiver. "Braeklojorn, you must tell me what happened. Anlía's husband? He could not protect her?"

"He had something more important to do—keeping the promise he made to her. The Sifiq slowly poisoned her to death to control her husband and show what they would do to their son if the king crossed them. Anlía made him swear to protect their son, even if it cost her life."

"Espiritus, deliver us from those devils! Her husband? What happened to him?"

"The Sifiq eventually murdered him with poison, too, but they believed they had conditioned her son well enough to use him as a puppet king. They were wrong. It took him years, but he defeated their occupation army and rebuilt his nation. His people admire and respect him. Everyone from crippled farmers and soldiers who fought beside him to nobles who were friends of his parents. Your great-grandson shines great honor on both the Krisantal and Vosklon legacies."

Oneshkla closed her eyes, attempting to restrain fresh tears. "You have met him, then?"

Braeklojorn shook his head. "The honor has not yet been mine. The Council of Protectors denied his nation's request for assistance in stopping the Sifiq from violently raiding their coastal settlements. Because he holds very personal empathy for the suffering these incursions were causing his citizens, he raised his armies. He declared war on the Sifiq Kingdom and is there now with his eldest son."

Oneshkla sat far back against the sofa, dumbfounded by Braeklojorn's revelation. "He led the army himself?" she asked in dismay. "And took his heir?"

"If you will allow me, Oneshkla," Braeklojorn said, rising and going to the window where Alexa patiently waited. Removing her cape and handing it to a servant, he guided her to the sofa where Oneshkla sat.

Alexa appeared majestic, another Valkana's gown floating over her figure like a golden cloud and her queen's gold tiara gleaming against golden-brown hair.

"Queen Mother Oneshkla, I am honored to present Alexa Maraná Toscano, High Priestess Valkana and Queen of Turand. She is the wife of my grandson, King Gregor."

Acknowledging the elder queen with a bow, Alexa said, "Your Highness, I am honored to meet you. You expressed great concern about my husband's presence in the Sifiq Kingdom. I confess I share not only your concern but the terrible fears of a loving wife and mother. No one knows better than I the vicious nature of the Sifiq. My husband has sworn to end their aggression against our nation or die trying. That terrifies me because Gregor is a man true to his word.

"He went with his armies because he believes it is his responsibility to lead by example. He has taught our sons the same. As hard as this is for me, I respect both his strength and his integrity."

Oneshkla reached out to Bresklon. "Please. Help me stand." Rising, she looked down into Alexa's face. "You are taller than most ishna but still ishna. Gregor?"

Smiling, Alexa answered, "He is much taller than I am, although not as tall as Grandfather."

"You said you have sons. So you have another son who could step in as a suitable heir?"

The very idea disturbed Alexa, but she recognized the reality as a necessary consideration in a monarchy. "Your Highness, I have two more sons. And three daughters."

"Excuse me," Oneshkla said, her voice reflecting disbelief. "Am I to understand that you and my great-grandson have six children?"

"We do. If it pleases you, my oldest daughter is with me today. I would be pleased for you to meet her."

"Really? Of course! Braeklojorn! Why did you not tell me? Where is this child?"

This time, Vezjalan escorted Anlía forward, and Sharlia removed her cape. Alexa said, "Your Highness, I am honored to introduce my eldest daughter, Valiria Priestess and Princess Royal Anlía Vosklon Krisantal Toscano of Turand."

Thankfully, both Bresklon and Braeklojorn alertly reacted, catching the swaying Oneshkla when she fainted. Carefully settling the elderly Queen Mother on the sofa, Bresklon chafed her hands while Braeklojorn called for a glass of water.

"Excuse me, gentlemen," Anlía said, kneeling close to the woman's trembling knees. Lowering her eyelids, she hummed a few notes before passing her hands over Oneshkla's heart and then across her face.

Within moments, the elder queen opened her eyes and fixed her gaze on Bresklon. "Help me sit up."

"Milady, you need…"

"Now! I know what I need. Help me sit up."

With Braeklojorn's assistance, Bresklon helped Oneshkla sit up while Sharlia offered her velvet cushions that the old woman pushed away. "Please! All of you! Just move! Let me see this child!"

With everyone out of her way, Oneshkla took several deep breaths as she stared into the face that had caused her such shock. Then, reaching out with both hands, she took Anlía's. "My beautiful, beautiful child. Looking at you is like turning back time and seeing my precious Mishkla again. Only your eyes are different. You have your mother's eyes. She must have bewitched your father with those eyes. Tell me you are real—that I do not dream."

"I am as real as you are. I came to Trezvindja because this is Grandfather's home, and I wish to study my family's heritage."

Oneshkla stroked bent, arthritic fingers along Anlía's cheek. "No doubt he also told you that your father is Trezvindja's rightful heir. Do you also wish to claim his crown for him?"

Anlía looked her straight in the eye. "Your Highness, if it is for the simple sake of taking a crown? No. My father already has a crown and a nation he loves dearly. In return, his people revere him. He is not a man who seeks power for the sake of power, and he would be sorely ashamed of any of his children who did.

"If it is for the sake of serving a people who will respect him and who will help him stop the evils of the Sifiq—and possibly save the lives of my father and my brother? Then my answer changes to yes. I will seek to claim his crown for him if he is indeed the rightful heir."

Oneshkla smiled. "You are as bold as my Mishkla. You are young, however. Are you willing to stand up to her brother? He is our king now."

"I am not a warrior, but I will face him. I am my mother's daughter and a Valiria priestess. We have our ways."

"A priestess? Yet your mother is married?"

"It is permitted in our order."

"I see. Interesting. Bresklon, have you contacted members of Council?"

"My aides started doing so yesterday, Milady."

"I suggest you hurry. Essila is due to return in a week. It would be wise to resolve this matter before she does," Oneshkla said, color returning to her cheeks and sparkle lighting her eyes. To Anlía, she said, "Child, would you consider calling me Grandmother?"

"I would be honored. Grandmother, may I see your hands?"

Alexa then watched her daughter's transfixed kinsmen as Anlía hummed her connection to the Healing Graces and ran healing hands along Oneshkla's gnarled and bent fingers, leaving them straightened and almost as nimble as they had been in youth.

↜

Bresklon Krisantal smiled as a footman helped Anlía down from the carriage stopped beneath the porte cochere in front of the Grand Hall of Mystics, where his great-great-grandmother waited inside. Although he had hoped to invite everyone to his home for introductions, Grandmother Milansa had been in secluded meditations ever since receiving Sharlia Vosklon's message regarding the arrival of two mystics in Tarahlaz. Intrigued by the mention of one being of Krisantal descent, Milansa had declined Bresklon's invitation. Instead, she had dispatched his messenger with instructions to bring the visitors to her.

Alighting from the carriage, Alexa noticed first the Grand Hall's enormous bronze doors. Panels molded into polished metal captured the beautiful variety of Val's creation: the intricate, delicate geometry of various floral species and the dynamic diversity of magnificent birds in flight. As they passed through the doors, the subtle scent of incense wafted through a corridor illuminated by shafts of sunlight beaming through glass insets in the ceiling, a detail Alexa found amazing.

Painted murals on the walls of the winding corridor depicted the picturesque scenery surrounding Trezvindja's sea-washed shores. Waterfalls tumbled down rocky ridges into rivers feeding seas awaiting fresh water. Rolling tides created ruffled rows hemming in white sandy beaches lined by graceful palms topped with fringed fronds. Swirls of rose and gold swept across the horizon, framing the sun as it kissed the ocean good morning and goodnight. Stormy nights cleared into sunny days with placid seas.

Alexa sensed Trezvindjans' abiding respect for the oceans and nature as she walked through those halls. She also relished an inner peace she hadn't known since departing Toraval for the mission to Kisana. Anticipating all the turmoil ahead of her, she prayed gratitude for this momentary respite.

Two women, wearing knee-length ivory robes with purple sashes at the waist, opened doors at the end of the hallway. Bresklon entered ahead of Braeklojorn, followed by Alexa and Anlía, who had linked arms before entering. They arrived in a spacious, circular room.

Skylights admitted bright sunshine softly diffused by dozens of sheer, shimmering fabric panels in multiple pastel shades secured from ceiling to floor at various angles. Wooden chairs, carved into half-moons, stood at varying heights and boasted plump cushions covered in light-colored silks and satins. What might have appeared opulent to some exuded a sense of exceptional tranquility to Trezvindjans accustomed to their traditions and to the Turandan priestesses whose minds transcended ordinary perceptions.

Waiting for them in the center of the meditation lounge stood an elderly woman dressed in floor-length blue robes accented by a braided belt of silver and gold. Her white hair was pulled away from her face. Secured by a barrette at the back of her head, her hair fell in a straight shaft past her shoulder blades. The expression on her softly wrinkled face transformed from stern to perplexed as she noted the visitors accompanying her great-great-grandson.

In unison, the men knelt as Bresklon greeted, "May the blessings of Espiritus be with you this day, Sacred Shamani Milansa."

"May the blessings of Espiritus be upon all of us this day. Welcome, Bresklon. You bring visitors."

"Shamani, I bring to you one long lost from our shores who has found his way home." Stepping aside so Braeklojorn could advance, Bresklon said, "I present to you Grand Prince Braeklojorn Vosklon."

The Shamani's forehead creased as she studied Braeklojorn's face. "I thought your face was familiar. You were the husband of our beloved Mishkla Krisantal." She reached out, letting her palms create a frame around his face. Faint light appeared in the space, its color fluctuating in shade and intensity before fading.

Milansa stepped back. "I recall the happiness of your wedding day, Prince Braeklojorn. Since then, despair and loneliness have replaced your love and joy. It is a blessing that Espiritus now ends your solitude, but I'm not sure I comprehend this change."

"Sacred Shamani, I come with two who have helped restore my desire to live. At the same time, they require our help. In return, one bears the promise of the return of honor and integrity associated with the tradition of the Krisantal Sacred Blood."

Acknowledging the tilt of the prince's head, Bresklon, as Grand Councillor of the Krisantal League, responded to questions on Milansa's face. "Sacred Shamani, first, I introduce to you Alexa Toscano, High Priestess Valkana and Queen of Turand."

Alexa approached the Shamani, removing her cape and handing it to Braeklojorn. Then, bowing as her blue-white aura shimmered and flowed around her, Alexa said, "Sacred Shamani, I pray many blessings of this day on you and the people of Trezvindja."

Milansa showed no sign of surprise. Instead, she extended her hands and received Alexa's. Holding them for a moment, she gazed into eyes unlike any she had ever seen. Finally, she smiled. "Lady Valkana, I am honored to welcome one such as you to Trezvindja. The mystic voices tell me you are connected to my people, yet you are ishna. How is this so?"

"Respectfully, Sacred Shamani, perhaps it is easiest if I introduce you to my eldest daughter." Alexa extended a hand, drawing Anlía forward. Reaching upward, she undid the clasp, pushed the hood away from her daughter's face, and removed the lavender cloak. Turning around, she said, "Sacred Shamani, this is my daughter, Valiria Priestess and Princess Royal Anlía Lulana Vosklon Krisantal Toscano."

Bresklon instantly grasped Milansa's arm to steady her. She had teetered for several seconds as if she might fall. Then, regaining her balance, Milansa repeated the gesture she had performed with Braeklojorn. This time, the lights appearing in the space between her hands and Anlía's face glittered and sparkled, the colors clinging to hues of lavenders and blues. When she finally—reluctantly—lowered her hands, her smile was brilliant.

"Anlía of the Spirit-Bridge. You nearly stole my breath. You are the very image of one I loved dearly and taught long ago. How is it you bear her likeness?"

"Sacred Shamani, you speak of Princess Royal Mishkla Krisantal. She was my great-grandmother."

Milansa looked toward Braeklojorn. "Her mother is ishna, and they are both accomplished mystics. I feel the Sacred Blood flowing strong in her veins. Is this really so?"

"We will explain, Sacred Shamani," Alexa said. "Then I must beg your support."

Hours later, while Anlía spent time in guided meditations with several members of the Mystic Council, Alexa strolled through a lush garden with Milansa. In one corner, water rose from a spring, trickled over stones, and spread into a shallow pool where tiny pink and yellow flowers floated. Pausing, Alexa gazed at the peaceful scene and let her memory carry her home to Lindaval's hot springs.

"You travel far away," Milansa said.

Alexa breathed in and out. "Home to a place my husband took me many years ago. We still go there. It's our special place—the place where I first began to realize how I loved him."

"Why do I feel your marriage did not begin well?"

"Our marriage began as a catastrophe, at least from my perspective. I only kept my sanity because I knew from the very beginning that Val had changed my plans for marriage and chosen Gregor for my husband. My trust in Val was complete."

"But you were not happy?"

Alexa glanced up into sparkling eyes. "Not for many months, but I gradually came to see Gregor for the man he is. Once I did, I understood Val's reasons and have been profoundly grateful since."

"You have no regrets?" Milansa asked.

"None," Alexa replied. "Not even for the difficult times. Those times taught me lessons about myself and him, both good and bad. We are both stronger as a result."

"And wiser, I believe," Milansa remarked. "We all have lessons to learn in life. Your daughter's names are interesting. Trezvindjans place sacred emphasis on names. Tell me about them."

Alexa shrugged. "Gregor was born into the House of Toscano, an ancient family traditionally revered because of their powerful faith and struggle to bring peace and our way of worship into Turand's daily way of life. The House of Toscano was also originally responsible for sponsoring the Order of Val, providing means for priestesses to teach and heal our people.

"After finding Braeklojorn and learning of the children's Trezvindjan heritage, he wanted nothing more than to add their family league names. I decided to wait for my other children, but Anlía and I discussed her situation. She felt empathic connections to Braeklojorn from the moment they met. She asked to have the names added to hers. Before leaving Turand, I issued a formal decree complying with her request, satisfying her and Braeklojorn.

"As for Anlía, she is named for her grandmother, the daughter of Mishkla and Braeklojorn. Lulana is a name we rarely mention. It was my mother's."

"The name is lovely. Why do you not use it?" Milansa noticed that tears brimmed in Alexa's eyes and darkened them to an evergreen shade.

"My mother was butchered to death by the Sifiq. Not just murdered. Butchered. I helped piece her body and my father's back together before we buried them. It was a warning sign to me."

Milansa frowned. "Because you were a priestess?" Suddenly, she gasped and twisted and stretched her back. "Dear Lady Valkana! Can it be true?"

Alexa swiftly reached out and held the woman's arms, consciously summoning calming energy to flow into her companion's surprised body. "It's all right, Sacred Shamani. Let it go. The pain is gone. Breathe."

Milansa forced herself to breathe in and out, the rhythm calming. "I apologize. I was unprepared for so many revelations. So, after years of dealing with Sifiq atrocities, this became the final incident that forced his hand. Your husband refused further risks with the Sifiq."

"Essentially, yes," Alexa confirmed, her vision distant as she relived that day in Gregor's office when he swore his oath to stop the Sifiq if it was the last thing he ever did. His words continued to haunt her.

"Come, Lady Valkana. I believe we can both use a few moments to recover our serenity." With that, the elder mystic led Alexa to yet another round room containing several tables draped in shimmering purple table-cloths. Each table had two gold-finished chairs and a lantern in the center. Sweeping her hand in invitation, Milansa said, "Choose a table while I request some refreshments."

Over cups of soothing herbal tea, conversation between the two turned to more mundane topics. Especially curious about Alexa's family, Milansa asked what it was like, balancing the demands of her roles as queen and high priestess with those of wife and mother. The Shamani laughed as Alexa shared anecdotes of coping with a house full of bright, spirited children competing for their parents' attention. Milansa blinked back tears in response to the despair and pain the younger mystic described resulting from the Sifiq abduction. Her spirit then rejoiced as she listened to the account of Alexa's reunion with Gregor.

"Lady Valkana," Milansa said as she finished a second cup of tea, "all that you share leaves me with a powerful desire to meet your husband. Your aura is intense, but it brightens noticeably when you speak of him."

A thoughtful smile crossed Alexa's face. "Sacred Shamani, my husband is the greatest gift Val has ever given me. I pray you will one day know him. He is strong in character—a man capable of making difficult decisions and following them to their completion. As king, he dedicates himself to the benefit of his people and his nation. In private, he is a devoted father. Gregor never fails to encourage me to fulfill responsibilities I undertook as a Valiria priestess. Never could I have dreamed of a more loving husband. Now? Our separation and the dangers he faces torment me far worse than anything I suffered at the hands of the Sifiq."

"So I see. I look forward to meeting him." Milansa smiled a serene, reassuring smile and placed a wrinkled hand over one of Alexa's. "After all, Sacred Blood of the Krisantal flows through his veins."

⤷

Nine days, four battles, and maybe seven miles forward progress to show for the effort. Were it not for the tireless presence of Valiria at the base camp, Gregor dreaded to think how many soldiers would be permanently disabled or dead. Thankfully, his losses were minimal. The king praised his soldiers for their courage and determination as wounded men recovered with help from Val's Healing Graces and doggedly prepared to confront their enemy yet again.

Sifiq forces fought tenaciously. Gregor granted them that. What sickened him most was the aftermath of battles. Slightly injured soldiers were helped off battlefields. More seriously wounded fighters were lucky if they were just abandoned. More often, a comrade would strike a fatal blow in passing without considering whether the fallen warrior's wounds might be treatable. Despite the added pressure on his doctors and priestesses,

Sifiq brutality offended Gregor so much that he ordered enemy casualties carried back to the cantonment for medical treatment whenever possible.

"Your Majesty?"

Exhausted after leading an escort back with injured soldiers from the latest skirmish on the way to Atuliq, Gregor looked up. "Lieutenant Zorfeni, tell me."

"Sire, of the fourteen soldiers you brought, I regret to advise we lost three. Another lost two fingers. Otherwise, all have been treated and are responding to the Healing Graces."

Gregor breathed out a long, heavy sigh. "All praises to our Lord Val that so few died, although I grieve for every life lost."

"We are blessed by the perseverance of our priestesses."

"Indeed, Lieutenant. What about the Sifiq wounded?"

"Two died. The others are in serious condition but responding to treatment."

"Very well. Ensure they remain under tight security. Once we know if they will recover, transfer them to the garrison at Qasalaf."

"Yes, Sire." The young officer paused. "Your Majesty, you should get some rest. Tomorrow will likely be another grueling day."

Nodding, Gregor managed what barely passed for a smile. "I will as soon I pray for our dead, Lieutenant. Goodnight."

Zorfeni disappeared before Gregor rose to retire for some much needed sleep. Pausing, he stared into crackling flames as a soldier tossed on another log. His eyelids closed. He prayed for the men who had sacrificed their lives that day and for their families at home who would mourn their passing. Too tired for more, he trudged off to his tent.

Dragging himself from bed the following day, Gregor washed, shaved, and changed into a clean uniform. He stopped long enough to bolt down some toasted flatbread with cheese and fruit and chug a mug of Raija tea sweetened with honey before heading to the hospital tents.

Inside with sick and injured troops, he took time to listen to their battle stories and paused to pray individually with several. Years earlier, he had learned that loyalty was most potent when it traveled in two directions. Most of these soldiers would recover completely. Most would also raise their swords again because they knew their king never took their service or their blood for granted.

He checked on General Kohira. Captain Lynmar's alert lunge had prevented the Sifiq rider's sword from penetrating too far into Kohira's side. However, when the general hit the ground, he suffered a head injury and remained comatose. Field doctors remained fearful of sending him away from the regular care provided by the Valiria. Gregor's ritual remained unchanged each day he was in camp. Taking Kohira's hand, he whispered a prayer and said, "General, you must not die. We need you. I'll be back. Be here. That is your king's royal command."

Leaving the hospital tents, Gregor called camp officers together for a briefing. Maps were strewn across a table as he pointed at scout reports identifying areas where the Sifiq were assembling reinforcements.

"Gentlemen," the king said, "we must address these weak spots before reinforcements arrive. I'm leading a company out now to address this far western flank. You need to get word to the other commanders to report and then assign targets. Questions, anyone?"

With no questions, the officers began clearing maps. Gregor tugged on leather gloves as a soldier led his horse up. He had just lifted his foot into a stirrup when pounding hooves raised clouds of dust as several riders raced toward the hospital tents. All that was clear to Gregor was Captain Lynmar's precarious seat on his horse before reality speared into his consciousness.

"Nikolai!"

Foamy seawater washed over Anlía's bare toes. The warm sensation felt oddly soothing with the grainy, pliable sand beneath her feet. Sunshine also felt warm on her exposed arms and lower legs. Still adjusting to revealing Trezvindjan styles, she occasionally tugged her beach skirt further down past her knees. Laughing to herself, she wondered if she would ever grow accustomed to the differences.

Gregor Maconti grinned. "I think you look beautiful. Even if you send me home to Father's farm for saying it."

"Hush. It's easy for you men. You can just toss away half your clothes and say you're working. I've spent my life being covered up for purposes of modesty. Here? This is modest," she said, sweeping her hand in front of the floral-print beach dress that revealed shapely arms and calves while also dipping low enough to show the cleavage of youthfully full breasts.

"Look on the bright side, Your Highness. This way, you don't have to drag around soggy, heavy, dirty skirts. Only your toes are gritty and sandy. Like mine!"

"Master Maconti!" she shouted, picking up a large shell and hurling it at him.

Maconti dodged the shell and laughed heartily just as Alexa appeared with Prince Braeklojorn, who chuckled and asked, "Is that suitable behavior for a Princess Royal—or a Valiria priestess?"

Anlía tried to pout but couldn't. She surrendered to giggles. "Hardly. We were discussing gritty toes."

Even Alexa laughed. "I don't think I want to know. I was hoping your visit to the shore had been pleasant."

"It has been, Mother. Especially after so many formal meetings. I can hardly believe we've only been here four days."

"I know. That's why I thought you young people might need a break."

Gregor Maconti bowed his head to his queen and the prince. "Milady, your thoughtfulness is appreciated, although I'm not sure Major Fratino appreciated stomping through sea and sand after our princess."

Lifting her head and looking beyond Maconti's shoulder, Alexa met Tirstan's gaze. Rolling his eyes and shaking his head, the major elicited a chuckle from his queen. "My daughter is fortunate that the good major is a patient man. Now, it's time to return home. Grandfather has business to attend."

Dinner had just been served that evening when a servant appeared and delivered a sealed document to Braeklojorn. Vezjalan pushed his chair back, glancing at his sister-in-law. Sharlia focused attention on her son, who glanced at his Turandan family before breaking the seal on the letter and opening it. After reading it slowly, he sat very straight in his chair.

"It seems we will have an early morning tomorrow. The letter is from Bresklon Krisantal. The Council of Leagues, along with the Mystic Council, the Krisantal Oversight Council, and the Krisantal League Council, have reviewed the documents we provided Grand Councillor Krisantal. They also reviewed all details concerning King Gregor Toscano of Turand. The documentation has confirmed the details of Turand's request through Coloridia for assistance to curb Sifiq aggression. As a result, all four councils concur that Kaelzron must abdicate now that they are satisfied Mishkla has living heirs suitable to assume Trezvindja's throne."

Everyone sat quietly except Master Maconti. "Your Highness, may I ask a question?"

Braeklojorn nodded. "Of course."

"This is excellent news, of course, and it implies much. However, my queen, my princess, and your own excellent family league have expended much effort explaining a legitimate claim. Do the councils understand our most pressing issue? King Gregor needs urgent military support since the

Protectors could have used their intimidating influence to stop King Bin-Lot before Turand was forced to conclude war was unavoidable."

Vezjalan stared at Alexa's young aide. The young man's boldness was stunning. Drawing in a sharp breath, the Prince Elder asked, "Young man, are you always so brash?"

Maconti's eyebrows lifted high. "Respectfully, Your Highness, I don't understand what you consider brash about acknowledging everyone's hard work and asking a straightforward question."

"Uncle," Alexa interceded on Maconti's behalf, "Master Maconti has been training under a brilliant man who has been my husband's closest adviser since Queen Anlía brought him to live with them when they were both boys. What Master Maconti just asked is classic Stefan Sidano. Had the question been asked by Sir Stefan, I'm sure you would have perceived it much differently."

Braeklojorn suppressed an admiring smile. "Dinner grows cold. The meeting takes place tomorrow. Perhaps Master Maconti and his well-trained mind should accompany us. If nothing else, Stefan's quick-witted apprentice has already alerted us to a critical issue that may or may not require attention."

Trezvindja's Tarahlaz Royal Palace exceeded Turand's in size only by the necessity of accommodating its citizens. The architectural splendor and interior detail of Toraval's Royal Palace equaled the stately magnificence and sense of permanence projected by the heart of Trezvindjan power. Entering the grandeur of those ancient halls made the Turandans feel no inferiority; their palace was just as impressive.

Inside the gallery reserved for meetings conducted by the Council of Leagues, a throne sat between quarter-circles of tables. Braeklojorn and

Vezjalan, attired formally in league regalia, escorted Princess Elder Sharlia and the Turandans to front rows of velvet-upholstered chairs. Major Fratino and Master Maconti sat directly behind their queen and princess. League councillors filed in and stood behind their chairs. Everyone in the chamber stood respectfully when King Kaelzron entered.

As presider over the Council of Leagues and lead councillor of the Krisantal League, Grand Councillor Bresklon Krisantal met Kaelzron before the king could mount the steps to the throne. "Your Royal Highness, this session concerns a matter that requires your attention on the chamber floor. Please wait here."

Bresklon nodded. Chamber doors were closed, other councillors took their seats, and all attendees sat.

"Grand Councillor Krisantal, I assume a problem has arisen. You know how little patience I have with political games. Will you get on with the process so I can get on with my day?"

Braeklojorn cast his eyes heavenward. He could hardly believe his brother-in-law had matured so little in the decades since he had last seen him. Mishkla always said Kaelzron would forever be their mother's good-natured, spoiled baby boy.

"King Kaelzron, it is partly what the Council of Leagues will refer to as your lack of patience with political games that brings us here. Your inattention to affairs of state cannot continue."

"Grand Councillor, at last, I can agree with Council on an important issue. For years, I have requested the transfer of power to Essila. She is much more suited than I to rule."

Bresklon shook his head in utter frustration. "No, Your Highness, Princess Essila is not. The fact is, her actions are under investigation at this very moment."

"Investigation?" Kaelzron shot back. "For what?"

"Actions contrary to the principles and laws of Trezvindja."

"Are you insinuating my daughter is a traitor?"

A stern-faced Bresklon faced his king. "You used the word traitor. Early results and evidence from the investigation indicate it applies. That aside, I now present to you someone you have not seen in many years."

Braeklojorn walked forward and bowed. "On behalf of the Vosklon League, I bring you greetings, Your Majesty."

Squinting in disbelief, Kaelzron shook his head several times, his crown wobbling. "Braeklojorn? No. That's impossible."

"Hardly impossible since I'm here. Council is aware of my history and how I returned home. I am glad to see you well."

Glancing down, Kaelzron saw Braeklojorn wearing Mishkla's wedding ring. "My sister is dead?"

"She is. It saddens me to see she was right that you would be indifferent to your responsibilities as a king's son."

"I do what I can do. This Council hates me, but I am my father's only heir, and my daughter is my only heir. She would willingly accept the responsibility, but this arrogant Council refuses to let her."

"Considering evidence exists regarding her errant loyalties, they may have had just cause. But, that aside, I've brought someone to meet you. Prince Vezjalan?"

Prince Vezjalan then ceremoniously escorted Anlía forward and placed her hand formally on Bresklon's arm. The Krisantal leader then turned to Kaelzron and announced, "Your Majesty, I present Princess Royal Anlía Lulana Vosklon Krisantal Toscano. She is the great-granddaughter of Grand Prince Braeklojorn Vosklon of the Vosklon League and his late wife, Mishkla Krisantal, Crown Princess of Trezvindja's Sacred Blood of Krisantal."

Kaelzron stared. Features nearly identical to the sister he had last seen leaning over the rail of a ship stunned him. The shocked king swallowed several times before he spoke. "Who are you? I mean Toscano. What is this name?"

Anlía exhibited only confidence in the face of his doubts. "My father is King Gregor of Turand, son of King Maxim of the Royal House of Toscano, and Queen Anlía, daughter of Princess Royal Mishkla Krisantal and Grand Prince Braeklojorn Vosklon."

"And you are his heir?" Kaelzron asked, still visibly shaken by her resemblance to his sister.

"I am second in line to the throne and fully prepared to assume responsibility should my older brother be unable to fulfill his role as my father's heir."

"Espiritus preserve us. You are quite the proud one, aren't you?"

"Not proud, Your Majesty. I have been taught and prepared to serve my people, my family, and our god. That gives me the confidence to face my future and whatever challenges it may bring."

Kaelzron's eyes opened wide as he turned and scanned the full line of seated league councillors. He saw for the first time that members of the Mystic Council were also attending the session. "How long has this conspiracy been going on?"

"It is no conspiracy, Your Majesty," Bresklon said. "You have complained for some time that you wished to be free of the Crown. We finally have a solution acceptable to the Krisantal League and all other governing councils."

Kaelzron smiled sardonically. "You have a mere girl here claiming the Crown. Do you know why? Because her father is off invading the Sifiq Kingdom, that's why! He no doubt wants Trezvindjan Protectors to join him to shed their blood for his wanton quest for power that Essila stopped."

"Enough!" Milansa's voice carried through the chamber with an eerie echo. "Grand Councillor Krisantal, Councillors of the Council of Leagues, may I speak?" No one dared deny her permission and, in unison, pounded silver-clad gavels giving her approval to proceed.

Milansa said, "Kaelzron, you are angry and unreasonable out of parental loyalty, but evidence shows that your daughter has betrayed the tradition and intentions of the Protectors. King Gregor made every effort to avert this war, but your daughter kept underlying, hidden political liaisons linking her to the Sifiq. The war was to her advantage, so beware the nature of your accusations."

Bresklon's eyes blazed furiously. "Do not think the members of these councils are so foolish that we do not comprehend the full scope of our intentions. Essila alone placed our troops in danger. Several argued your very point, but we finally concluded we are honor-bound to protect the Sacred Blood of two heirs to Trezvindja's throne. The decision is already made, Kaelzron."

"You can't be serious!"

"When we leave this chamber, proclamations will be issued here in Tarahlaz and distributed throughout Trezvindja. Espiritus has revealed that a worthy heir of the Krisantal Sacred Blood lives. Unfortunately, his life and the life of his heir have been endangered by your spawn, requiring our action to restore the honorable tradition of the Protectors. Furthermore, Espiritus has sent his heir's daughter, an avowed priestess no less, to act as regent until we set straight our shortcomings that you allowed through your negligence."

Kaelzron stumbled backward, grabbing a handrail in front of risers leading up to the throne. "You're sure my daughter is a traitor? This I cannot believe! Essila may be many things, but she loves Trezvindja!"

Bresklon growled at Kaelzron. "She loves gold and power more. She planned to use our people, including you, to gain more."

Kaelzron clenched his jaw and then stared hard at Braeklojorn. "Mishkla was right. I was never fit or worthy to sit on this throne. I gladly renounce my title as king. It is a mighty responsibility. I hope your great-granddaughter has some idea of the punishment you're inflicting on her."

Anlía approached him and placed her hand on his arm. "Kaelzron Krisantal, you are family, so I tell you this. To live and work for my family and my people is to fill my heart and soul with wealth that one cannot compare to gold or jewels. Why? Metal and stones cannot hold my head when I am ill or love my soul when I am sad. They only coldly shine when they are clean and do nothing more. I must do all, whereas my family and my people will do with me and for me. They can fill my life when I need succor and sing with me when I'm happy. That is why I willingly accept my responsibilities as Princess Royal of Turand and now as Princess of the Krisantal Sacred Blood in Trezvindja."

Late that night, Alexa slumped alone on a downstairs sofa at the Vosklon manor, tears coursing down her face. For brief seconds, she recalled when all the councillors and members of Trezvindja's Mystic Council filed onto the chamber floor and knelt, their arms crossed over their chests. Declarations of unfailing loyalty had raised as almost a single voice. They had pledged fealty to Anlía, who would serve as her father's regent until he and Nikolai could come to Trezvindja to receive personal avowals of allegiance.

Anlía had then made her official pledge as an heir to Trezvindja's throne, amending it slightly to include her responsibilities to Turand. A tiara of white gold with sparkling diamonds and pearls was placed on her head to symbolize her role as King's Regent. Bresklon had then asked how soon she would be prepared to start work on sending troops to the Sifiq Kingdom. She had smiled and answered as soon as he introduced her to each individual councillor. She had begun her regency by putting her new people first.

"Alexa?" Braeklojorn asked, returning with Gaeldoreg from a late meeting with members of the Vosklon League. "Why are you here alone? And why are you crying?"

Gaeldoreg instantly went to her, pulling a handkerchief from his pocket to dry her tears. "Ishna, tell me. Which of these ignorant idiots has upset you?"

Her chin quivered so hard she could barely speak. "Gaeldoreg." Sobbing softly, she murmured, "Nikolai."

Braeklojorn sat beside her instantly, wrapping an arm around her shoulders. "Espiritus, bless us. Ma Ishna, what happened? Tell me."

"Grandfather, I felt the pointed shaft pierce him. An arrow."

"Ma Ishna," Braeklojorn's hushed voice cracked with sorrow, "what do I say? What can I do?"

"Grandfather, I am so tired. It took so much to go to him, but I did. Keeping the connection with him and the Graces was nearly impossible while they were racing to deliver him back to their camp, but I did. Grandfather, I did it. When they got him to the hospital tents, he opened his eyes. Niko knew it was me. He said he loved me.

"Before I came back, I saw Gregor. The terror on his face. I heard a Valiria tell him she sensed the Healing Graces already working. Gregor was crying. Grandfather, I heard him whisper my name. He needed me, but I had to leave him. I had to come back." Her body then shook with uncontrollable sobs as both Braeklojorn and Gaeldoreg held her.

Still unsure of the outcome, Braeklojorn braced himself, knowing he had to ask about Nikolai. He then felt gentle fingers lace through his hair. "Nikolai is resting, Grandfather. Mother's mystical abilities have magnified tremendously since her captivity in the Sifiq Kingdom. What she just did should have been impossible, but add a mother's love to her being Valkana?"

Anlía knelt. Taking Alexa's hands, she softly said, "Mother, it's all right. You've done so much already. Niko is recovering now. You must rest. Father still needs you. No one has your strength or your faith. That's why Val sent you to be our Valkana. Remember?"

Alexa clung to her daughter's words—to the serenity in her voice. She had done that before. Trembling fingers stroked her daughter's cheek. "Your father so wanted you before you were ever conceived," she murmured thickly. "Such a gift you've always been. I'll rest now."

Sure she was too weak to walk, Gaeldoreg stood and lifted her with strong arms. "Ishna, I will carry you up to bed. For tonight, you can be the little girl I never had."

Alexa managed a weak giggle. "Perhaps Grandfather won't mind if I adopt you as my substitute father. I think my own father wouldn't mind if you watch over me in his place."

Gaeldoreg's smile widened. "I warn you. I'll be a very overprotective bibo."

"Bibo?"

"Now she did it," Braeklojorn chuckled in relief. "Off with you. If you're going to be a bibo, you need to learn to put your children to bed."

"As if you've had years of practice," Gaeldoreg taunted, winking as he turned and headed upstairs.

A glaze of tears in Anlía's eyes sparkled in dim candlelight as she wrapped her arms around Braeklojorn. "Grandfather, being with you and Gaeldoreg makes me miss Father more than ever."

Chapter 16

Stefan stopped on the way to his office, beckoned by the sound of his name and the quick rhythm of boots crossing the polished marble floors of the palace's grand entrance. A military courier had just arrived. Stefan quickly signed the receipt for the brown leather pouch of documents and hurried toward his office. Having already noted the seal identifying the packet as originating from Alexa, he was anxious to learn if she had safely arrived in Trezvindja and if Gregor's newfound relatives had offered more than promises.

Stefan opened the pouch with unusually fumbling fingers and paused to pray before breaking the wax seal on the first document marked *Official*. Looking up as he started to read, he saw Willem open the office door.

"I apologize for the interruption. I heard a military courier had arrived."

"News from Alexa. I just sat down to read her report. You're welcome to join me."

"Thank you. These past few weeks have been… Well, you know as well as I."

"Torture? It's a miracle Adrina hasn't banished me to live here at the palace."

Willem chuckled. "You mean you don't already?"

Stefan's gray eyes glinted humorously. "Hmmm, point well taken. Shall we see what Her Majesty has to say about our king's odd new family?"

Dear Stefan and Willem,

(Forgive me if I'm mistaken about Willem still being at the palace, but I trust my instincts about my husband's two finest friends and advisers.)

You should have received my previous letters sent from Coloridia. By now, I hope Ambassador Laritha has discovered reasons behind their Ministry of State's obvious distortion of his report and recommendations following our delegation's failed summit with Bin-Lot. Hopefully, my visit with Coloridia's king afforded the ambassador some measure of safety.

More importantly, Grandfather Braeklojorn and Gaeldoreg accurately described Trezvindja, its laws, and its traditions. Its people do not accept change easily or quickly; however, because their ways are subject to very slow transition, they moved swiftly in the face of evidence Grandfather presented concerning Gregor. I have never seen such organization or quick, methodical analysis and decision-making.

Three primary groups were involved: the Krisantal League independently, which is the official organization representing Gregor's mother's family line; the Council of Leagues, comprised of representatives from Trezvindja's sixteen most prominent families, called leagues, plus five representing alliances of smaller leagues; and the Mystic Council, roughly comparable to the Order of Val. All three groups interviewed Braeklojorn, Gaeldoreg, and survivors from the shipwreck. I was interviewed. You cannot imagine the attention Anlia received. More than a few remembered Gregor's grandmother, and at least three fainted.

Our Anlía has become a shining star. In Trezvindjan, the name means Spirit-Bridge, and I believe it may be prophetic in more ways than one. My daughter is building bridges between Gregor's mother's people and ours. She retains the serenity we always associated with Anlía, but she now demonstrates Gregor's power of thought and character. The results are immediate, thanks be to Val. The Trezvindjan councils have already deposed King Kaelzron, declared Gregor their rightful king through their ancient laws of succession, and named Anlía his Regent.

This all occurred within a week, my friends! Stefan, you especially will appreciate this level of efficiency and cooperation. I have thought on it and believe their ways must be bred into my husband!

As of now, the Trezvindjans are preparing supplies and troops to transport to the Sifiq Kingdom. The first vessels will depart with one of our ships within days. We will carry only seventy-four Trezvindjan soldiers plus Gaeldoreg, but they are fearsome. Additional ships will leave with another five hundred in less than two weeks. We will reassess our needs after that, but I firmly believe we will carry victory with these troops added to the fierce determination of our brave Turandan soldiers. Our armies fight for the sanctity of our home. The Trezvindjans fight for what they refer to as the Sacred Blood of the Krisantal—the very lives of Gregor and Nikolai.

Other notes: I already dispatched one of our ships to Coloridia. It will join Captain Umindri, whose ship is anchored offshore from Maraya, and depart for the Sifiq Kingdom. Master Maconti will remain here for now as Ambassadorial Adviser to Princess Anlía. Please notify his parents. (Separate packets of letters to families have been sent for sorting and delivery.) Our new Major Fratino (much to his dismay and that of the Trezvindjans) will now oversee security for Princess Anlía. I trust no one more than I trust Tirstan, and I have made that abundantly clear. Considering the fact I am now Gregor's queen in two nations, I refused to accept any arguments to the contrary, no matter how large my opponents. I did, however, advise the major he must recruit Trezvindjans into the Royal Guard and train them in his protocol—and to be nice about it. Captain Lisandá will temporarily assume command of the Queen's Royal Guard.

Gentlemen, that is all for now, except your Queen and Valkana requests prayers for your countrymen and our Trezvindjan brothers. Ah, also, please add prayers of gratitude for the life of our Crown Prince Nikolai. He was nearly killed by a Sifiq arrow.

All Praises to Lord Val,
Alexa M. Toscano
Queen of Turand and Trezvindja

Stefan breathed a sigh heavy with shock and relief. Tears swam in his eyes. She had pursued her dreams despite his initial disapproval. Praise be to Val.

"She achieved yet another miracle," Willem said in his typical, understated fashion.

"I sit here and wonder what Gregor will say about all of this."

Willem shrugged. "What can he say? The last time I spoke to him, he said he feared he might need a miracle to defeat the Sifiq in their homeland. His Valkana is delivering two: the military might necessary for victory over Bin-Lot and the extended family of his dreams."

Stefan chuckled as a single teardrop eased from his eye. "I am troubled that she intends to return to that evil place, but how I would love to be there to see his face—and Nikolai's—when she arrives with all those Trezvindjans."

Uncharacteristically, Willem burst into laughter. Stefan joined him just as Adrina and Katara stopped to ask if they were coming for midday. With the prevailing somber mood at the palace, both women worried that their husbands had finally caved under wartime pressures.

⌒

"Poor Gregor. If he survives this war with the Sifiq, he may die of shock seeing Anlía in Trezvindjan attire! What was Alexa thinking to allow such a thing?" Katara exclaimed.

Adrina removed the drawing from her cousin's hands. "She wrote that Anlía is learning the language and immersing herself in their culture. You must remember. It's her heritage as much as ours is. It isn't wrong just because it's so different from Turand's."

Katara's pale blonde features continued to blush bright red even though she was alone with Adrina. "I keep thinking she stood still long enough for that young Maconti to draw this picture! And imagine, Adrina! Our soldiers are seeing her with her legs exposed to her knees! And did you see her shoes? If you can call them shoes!"

Adrina's brown eyes danced with laughter. "And I always thought I was the shy, conservative one!"

"Dear wife, you are shy and conservative," Stefan remarked as he sneaked a kiss to his wife's temple from behind. "It sounds as if your dear cousin is upset. What's wrong?"

"Too many years living with Willem, I believe," Adrina replied, crossing her eyes as she made faces at Katara.

"May I assume you showed her one of Master Maconti's drawings of Anlía?"

"She did," Katara shuddered. "I hope you didn't show Willem."

"Oh, he did," Willem said, entering the room with a bottle of wine in each hand. "I brought my own. I need it. I shall order a case from my cellars—perhaps two—for Gregor when he returns home. He will need them."

"You give him too little credit. Correction. You give Alexa too little credit," Adrina said, ringing for a servant to bring glasses.

"What makes you say that?" Willem asked curiously as he handed the bottles to the servant.

"Alexa understands how important it is for her children to embrace the heritage of both nations that will contribute to their futures. She'll guide Gregor to that realization. Kicking and screaming perhaps, but she will get him there."

"Dear, sweet Adrina," Stefan said with a grin, "you're absolutely right. I almost pity our king. Not quite, though." He sipped his wine. "Willem, this wine is excellent. Shall we toast our king's new crown and hope your cellars are sufficiently stocked for us to enjoy while we watch his tribulations over his daughter's Trezvindjan dishabille?"

⌒

Strong Turandan sailors manned ropes to the sails according to orders called out by skilled officers while captains guided their ships into the harbor captured when Prince Nikolai had commanded the initial invasion of the Sifiq Kingdom. Skeletons of Sifiq warships were still being cleared following the most recent attempt to retake the small port. Deadly cannons now aboard Turandan warships had proven their worth.

"Are you all right?" Gaeldoreg stood beside his adopted daughter, worried about her pale, drawn features as she stared out at the lapping waves and the fast-approaching landfall. As she stretched her arm around his waist and leaned her weight against him, he realized how justified his concern was. "Alexa?"

"Bibo," she murmured, "I'm afraid. I know I must do this, but I'm so afraid."

Accustomed to balancing on the decks of seagoing vessels, Gaeldoreg braced himself and hugged her tightly. "Ma Ishna, stay if it's too much. No one will blame you if you decide to remain on board. If you choose to go, just remember that your bibo goes with you along with thirty-seven members of the Vosklon League who would give their lives protecting you. Better that than face Gaeldoreg the Terrible for letting something happen to you."

Unable to force even the slightest smile, she rested her head against his broad chest. Somehow, it felt good having a flesh-and-blood father again. In her heart, she knew DiMarco Maraná would approve of this huge man's affection. Now, if only her two fathers could help her summon the courage she needed to set foot once again inside the Sifiq Kingdom.

Later, Gaeldoreg stood on the dock and gazed into Alexa's eyes. More than hesitant, she was terrified. A wave of vertigo swept through her. Struggling to keep her balance, she frantically clutched Captain Lisandá's hand. She forced herself to breathe normally. The hubbub around her made everything worse. Finally resting her palm over the crystal pyramid she wore, she turned her thoughts inward.

Two voices rose clearly above the chaotic clamor. Her Lord Val quietly bade her listen. "To this land, you return. I give you strength. You seek courage. Listen, my servant child." Then she heard it, faintly at first, then echoing louder. Gregor's voice calling her name. She drew a deep breath.

Steadying herself, she reached forward to Gaeldoreg. Gripping his hands, she stared at her feet while slowly stepping down the ramp until she triumphantly landed both feet firmly on the dock. Lifting her chin high, Alexa declared, "I return now so King Bin-Lot will know the time has come to end the evils of the Sifiq monarchy."

⌒

"Father, I'm fine. The pain is gone. I have no intention of spending the rest of this campaign reading maps and drawing charts on how to break through those Sifiq fortifications. I will rejoin my regiment on our next sortie."

"Nikolai, listen."

"No, Father, you listen." Nikolai hurled worn leather gloves on top of a stack of maps showing the latest locations of Sifiq camps reported by scouts. "You need my help in the field, and you know it. You were injured in battle years ago. Did you hide from your men then? No! Even when Mother advised against it, you rode back into combat two days later. You've made me sit out more than a week. I'm completely healed. I refuse to look like a coward when some of my soldiers have almost died two or three times. I won't!"

Gregor angrily stalked across the area cleared for briefings. Hospital tents were clear in his line of sight. Dust scattered as he kicked his toes into the dirt. The smells of the encampment were wearing on his nerves. The sounds of horses, crackling fires, blacksmiths at work, axes chopping wood, hammers repairing blockades, cooks wrangling poultry or banging pots and pans, officers drilling subordinates—the entire cacophony of activity necessary to keep his armies fed, protected, armed, and moving was bad enough. He had known the possibility existed that Nikolai might be injured or even killed, but witnessing his son near death had frightened something fundamental deep inside his soul.

"Father," Nikolai's voice gentled, "you know it was Mother who saved me. I felt her with me the minute Rafzan started back to camp. We both smelled the lilacs on my clothes and Rafzan's. She saved me the same way she saved you. Val meant for you to live just as he intends for me to live. You must believe that."

Gregor stopped pacing. "If you only knew how much I love you."

"Perhaps I will one day—when I have children of my own. But, for now, I am Turandan first. Second, I am my father's son. Do not shame me by making me fail the oaths I took at my coronation. I must honor commitments as heir to my father's throne."

Gazing into his son's dark eyes, the king wondered how he had been blessed with such a son. Then, with arms outstretched, he embraced his eldest prince, exchanging fear for confidence and pride in the fine steward who one day would carry forward the legacy of the House of Toscano.

〜

Gregor leaned over revised maps. Ravendro's forces had successfully blocked the influx of Sifiq fighters from northwestern sectors. Enemy troops already in the northeast continued following routes through regions surrounding Atuliq. Large camps between the Sifiq capital and the Turandan strongholds worried Gregor. Time seemed to be as dangerous an enemy as the Sifiq. He desperately needed to devise a strategy to prevent further reinforcements of those camps so he could drive through Bin-Lot's defenses.

"Your Majesty!"

Gregor's head shot up, his attention snared by the excitement in Lieutenant Zorfeni's voice. "Yes, Lieutenant?"

"A guard just advised there's a convoy coming through the pass. A long one. It appears to be bringing supplies and reinforcements. Lots of them!"

Gregor raised his face heavenward. "Praise Val! Our nobles have not failed us!"

Zorfeni grinned and shook his head. "I'm not sure our nobles are the ones to thank. The guards said there are some rather strange riders behind the lead guard, and they're riding under the queen's colors."

Gregor stiffened with dismay. "What?"

"They're flying Queen Alexa's banner and the Valkana's colors, Your Majesty," the lieutenant proudly announced.

In disbelief, Gregor suddenly sprinted toward the receiving area for arriving supply columns. Stopping abruptly, he watched as his beaming wife dismounted, called out his name, and raced toward him. Before he could react, she threw her arms around his neck and, in a rush, said, "Don't scold me! Just hold me!"

Some part of him did want to shout at her. This vile, sordid place didn't deserve being touched by the exquisite beauty that was his Alexa. Still, having her in his arms was like being able to breathe after nearly drowning. His embrace tightened, and he lifted her off the ground. His face buried into the curve where her neck met her shoulder. He chanted her name in that resonant, melodious voice that so often filled his palace with song. Finally setting her down, he beheld the emerald eyes that still enchanted his soul.

"My beloved Alexa, you should not have come to this place," he murmured brokenly as his huge hands framed the face he adored.

"I love you, Gregor. I could stand our separation no longer. Besides, so much has happened. Kiss me, my love, so I can tell you all the amazing news. A real kiss, too. I don't care how many people watch."

Granting her request, he captured her lips in the fiery connection they both needed. The war-weary camp receded from his conscious awareness for precious moments as her kiss restored his waning confidence. With her in his arms, he remembered why he had come. Renewed in spirit and intention, he would find a way to forge ahead to victory.

Reluctantly ending their kiss, Alexa stroked her husband's cheek. "Niko?"

Gregor shook his head. "He's out on reconnaissance. I honestly don't know when to expect him back."

Sandra Valencia

She nodded. "Well, that might ruin Stefan's message. There's so much to tell you. I hardly know where to start." Holding his hand, she glanced around and flinched. "Although I think I might see where."

Following her line of sight, Gregor watched a rider with Alexa's Royal Guards dismount from an enormous horse of a breed he had never seen before. The rider who approached wore a padded blue tunic that fell to mid-thigh over black leggings tucked into knee-high riding boots. His tunic bore a silver crest on the chest. From the wide belt at his waist, he also carried an intricately designed scabbard holding his sword. The man's exceptional height, bold posture, and menacing expression were nothing short of fiercely intimidating.

"Alexa?" Gregor asked, debating if he should whisk his wife out of danger's path.

Long strides rapidly carried the imposing man forward. In a deep, teasing voice, he said, "Ma Ishna? After such a display, I do hope he's the one."

"Dear Bibo," she answered with a glowing smile, "you were supposed to wait. Yes, this is my Gregor."

Gaeldoreg gave Gregor an exaggerated look of assessment. "Just a bit short but a fine specimen, nevertheless." Abruptly, the giant man dropped to one knee with his arms crossed over his chest. "Your Majesty, I am Gaeldoreg Vosklon, and it is my honor to pledge my life and my loyalty to the heir of the Sacred Blood of the Krisantal. I will serve you and your heirs until the end of my days."

Gregor turned confused, questioning eyes to his wife.

"I had hoped to explain before this. First, you must place your hands on his shoulders and express your gratitude for his pledge. When he says he will defend you with his life, he means it."

The insistence in Alexa's eyes gave Gregor little choice. Quickly choosing what he hoped were satisfactory words, he placed his hands on

373

the man's broad shoulders. "Gaeldoreg Vosklon, I accept with gratitude your pledge of loyalty. In return, I offer you a king's oath of duty and respect. Please rise."

Gaeldoreg stood and grinned at Alexa. "Ma Ishna, he did well for that being his first time. I think even Bresklon Krisantal would consider him worthy of his position."

"Alexa? Will you explain what just happened?"

With a sheepish smile, she asked, "Remember my dreams?"

"Your dreams? The ones about Zemtoval and the Zemfosa Mountains? And some caves. I remember that much. Do I really want to know how they connect to—him?" The confused expression on Gregor's face was almost more than Alexa could bear.

"Gregor, my love, after you left with your armies, I journeyed to Zemtoval and then found the caves in my dreams. That's where I met Gaeldoreg and someone else you'll soon meet. Gaeldoreg is one of the famous Protectors."

"Was, Ma Ishna," the Trezvindjan corrected with a twinkle in his eyes. "I still have plenty of fight left in me, but I'm too old now for active ranks of the Protectors."

"So the Protectors really aren't a myth?"

"No, they aren't," Alexa said. "And, my love, Gaeldoreg is your cousin, a couple times removed, I believe."

Gregor choked. "My cousin? Wait! What? How? Alexa!"

"We should find a place to sit down. There's much more, and it gets better. Isn't it about time for midday?"

Stuttering and stammering, Gregor looked at Gaeldoreg and, for the first time, realized the man was even taller than Nikolai. "In Val's great name! Alexa!"

"Ma Ishna, I believe your husband may need more than food."

"Bibo, he needs a clear head to absorb all this," Alexa admonished.

Gregor stared at his wife. "Ma Ishna? Bibo? Alexa, help me. I'm lost."

"Bibo means Papa. Gaeldoreg has become my adopted father. Another long story. Ma Ishna is Trezvindjan for my little one. Trezvindja is the name of the island nation of the Protectors. Learn that well. It's rather obvious why they refer to me as little one."

"Well, at least something is clear. Midday should be ready. We can go if you like."

"Before we do, you should have your people settle the personnel arriving with us. We've brought new cannons for your army, plus twenty-five men trained to use them. Besides my Royal Guard, I've only brought fifty additional Turandan soldiers. The good news is that the Trezvindjans sent seventy of their Protectors plus four commanders, who will report to Gaeldoreg. Believe me, Gregor, when you see them, you'll understand. They are fearsome."

Gregor grimly smiled at Gaeldoreg. "Your men face terrible odds with the Sifiq. Are they aware of the danger?"

Gaeldoreg tilted his head and smiled. "Your Royal Majesty, they are Protectors. Half who came represent the Vosklon League. The others represent the Krisantal League. Trust me. They are aware and will not shirk their sacred duty."

"Gregor," Alexa said gently, "the leagues are family clans in Trezvindja. The other man I met in the caves was Prince Braeklojorn Vosklon. He is your grandfather. There's so much to explain, but his wife was the official heir to Trezvindja's Crown. She died in Zemtoval after giving birth to your mother. No one knew who she was. My dreams helped me connect all the pieces of the puzzle.

"You've now been declared King of Trezvindja. These Protectors, as kinsmen, came as the advance elite. They consider it their sacred duty to protect you and Nikolai. Arrangements were in progress when we departed

Trezvindja, and they expected to dispatch another five hundred Protector troops within two weeks."

Stunned, Gregor stared at his wife. His mind reeled as he struggled to grasp the magnitude of her revelation and its impact. He wasn't sure he was prepared to consider all the implications his connection to Trezvindja would bring to bear on the nation he already ruled. The most immediate consequences were close at hand. This vital new alliance would alter his strategic options as he pushed toward Atuliq.

His dark eyes met those of his kinsman. Eyes like his own. A new experience in his adult lifetime. His mother's family. Alexa said she had met his grandfather. His grandfather! Alive! After all these years he had thought he was alone.

Duty suddenly pierced his mind. "Excuse me," he said and then summoned Lieutenant Zorfeni. "Lieutenant, advise company captains to assign the new Turandan arrivals appropriate campsites. Have Captain Fratino…"

"Captain Lisandá commands my Guard now," Alexa informed her husband.

Gregor shook his head, almost afraid to ask how that happened. "Have Captain Lisandá coordinate camp assignments with company captains for his Guard and our Trezvindjan allies. Make it abundantly clear to everyone that the Trezvindjans are to be treated with utmost respect."

"Yes, Your Majesty. Immediately!"

"Well done, Your Majesty. Your men respect you."

"I do have some practice. Now, if you are indeed a cousin, would you please call me Gregor? And shall we go for midday? I'm starving, and I must understand the complications this beautiful wife of mine just delivered!"

Seasonal changes had made it necessary to erect shelters where Gregor's forces could be protected from inclement weather while taking meals. Inside one and seated at a simple plank table, Gregor offered grace over their food and grinned as Alexa served him and their guest.

"Gaeldoreg, you must admit. My wife is a jewel. I have an army of aides, but my queen rises to fill my plate. A fortunate man am I, would you not agree?"

The Trezvindjan chuckled. "Cousin, I could not agree more. Why else would I claim her as my daughter?"

"That's enough from you two," Alexa said, noting the return of Gregor's confused frown. "We can eat while I try to explain this to my husband."

"You slit her hand with a sword?" Gregor practically shouted minutes later when Alexa described the blood bond incident.

Alexa wrapped his arm with both of hers. "Calm yourself, my love. You had to be there to appreciate the circumstances. It wasn't so terrible, and I would do it again."

Gaeldoreg's gaze remained steady. "You must understand. I had no idea who she was. She refused to say anything other than insisting on talking to Braeklojorn and saying she knew what happened to Mishkla Krisantal. She placed me in a very dangerous and precarious position. I had vowed to protect your grandfather with my life. If she, as a woman of the little people, was willing to swear on her own blood to keep our secret, I was willing to trust her. Foolish on my part? Perhaps, but you must admit, a man is easily bewitched by those emerald eyes of hers."

Somewhat calmer, Gregor turned his head and met his wife's waiting gaze. As always, he was instantly lost the moment he looked into her eyes. Gaeldoreg was right. "She took me captive with those eyes the first time she walked into my court. I've never recovered my freedom."

"Gregor!" Alexa exclaimed softly. "Really? How can you say that to the first relative you've ever met in all the years we've been married?"

"Beloved, it's true, but nothing could entice me to change my life as your prisoner. Now, please continue explaining this adventure. My curiosity is killing me."

Shaking her head, Alexa resumed her saga, with Gaeldoreg offering occasional comments from his perspective. Gregor requested another pot of tea as he tried to absorb how her recurring dreams had led to Zemtoval and, ultimately, Corlozem Pass, where his grandfather had taken refuge after the disastrous sea voyage seventy years earlier. She had then traveled with his newfound family members to Toraval, introducing them to their children and closest friends.

Thoughtfully, Gregor gazed across the table at Gaeldoreg. "So, both Willem and Stefan welcomed you. I have relied on their friendship for many years."

"As you should," Gaeldoreg replied. "They are friends to be trusted. Beyond that, they are both loyal and wise. Your Lord Garogan was quite the different story."

Shifting his attention, he raised his eyebrows. "Alexa?"

Sighing, she said, "Victor was angry for two reasons. First of all, Victor thought I'd taken leave of my senses by trusting Grandfather and Gaeldoreg so soon after meeting them. He argued I couldn't possibly know them well enough to trust them or even be sure of their identities. He grew so vehement that Willem actually escorted him out of a meeting."

"Willem?" Gregor asked incredulously.

"Willem. After calling him an ass."

"Victor must have quite outdone himself if he angered Willem Zephirás."

"I believe Stefan described everything in his letter to you. It was awful, and Victor only got worse when I talked to him later. Much worse."

Distress in her eyes troubled him, causing him to reach out to caress her cheek. "Although he should know you well enough after all these years to trust your intuition and your good sense, I won't fault him for his concerns about how long you had known my grandfather. You mentioned two reasons. The other?" When she hesitated, he gently prompted her. "Alexa?"

Inhaling a deep breath, she said, "He made me so angry I told him if he ever repeated such a thing in my presence that I promised I would see him rot in Zenox Prison."

"You did what? Alexa! What could Victor Garogan have said that would make you, of all people, threaten such a thing?" Gregor was stunned by his wife's admission.

"He accused me of endangering our daughter's life and using her as a pawn so that I could find a way to come here to be with you. He made it sound lewd and revolting. Oh, Gregor, it was so far from the truth, and I was so furious I could have struck him to the ground right there."

Grasping her violently shaking hands, Gregor stared into Alexa's tear-glazed eyes. "Beloved, why would Victor make such a terrible accusation?"

"The second Grandfather saw Anlía, he nearly collapsed from shock. Gaeldoreg and I caught him before he did. It seems, except for her eyes, Anlía is the exact image of your grandmother. We all realized—Stefan and Willem included—the importance of going to Trezvindja to gain Trezvindja's support. Grandfather felt strongly that you should be declared the rightful heir to Mishkla's throne. Although Gaeldoreg can explain the details better, there would be no question of them sending troops to your aid. They were sure there would be people living who would remember Mishkla. If only they could see Anlía…"

"Wait!" Gregor gasped. "Was Victor protesting a plan to take Anlía to Trezvindja?" Seeing his wife nod, he asked, "Did you?"

"Anlía and I both prayed and meditated long and hard. Yes, I did. Three people fainted upon meeting her, including Mishkla's own mother, your great-grandmother. Gregor, you must believe me. I would never carelessly leave our daughter if I thought her life was in peril. You know I love her as much as you. I left her with a full contingent of Royal Guards under Tirstan Fratino's command. Gregor Maconti is her Ambassadorial Aide. Before I left, your daughter was crowned Regent, acting on your behalf until you and Nikolai can visit Trezvindja personally."

"Regent? Are you serious?"

"Gregor, your daughter is maturing into someone as thoughtful and responsible as your eldest son. Her approach may be different, but it is no less effective. She amazed even me with how well she managed leaders of Trezvindja's governing councils."

"If I may," Gaeldoreg interrupted, "Gregor, your daughter moved through our society as if she had been born into it. Braeklojorn was heartbroken that he could not come to meet you, but we insisted he stay to make certain she settles into her current role. The Krisantal League, especially Grand Councillor Bresklon Krisantal, is already devoted to Anlía. They will protect her with their very lives as they teach her our ways. You should be proud. I am proud that Vosklon blood flows through her veins."

Alexa drew her husband's hands to her lips and kissed them. "My love, Val has directed this path ever since he showed me the dreams. I don't understand it completely, but I accept all its mysterious twists and turns. Turn your heart to Val. Have faith."

"My daughter, Alexa. You know how I love Anlía." He swallowed hard, choking back emotion.

"Since the moment I told you we were having a daughter. I remember, but she's not a baby anymore. She's every bit as much your daughter as she is mine—a woman capable of making her own decisions and fulfilling them. When you add the fact she is now a confirmed Valiria priestess, you can be sure she knows her own mind and her path according to Val's will.

"She also told me that her being in Trezvindja is our best chance of bringing her father safely home. We both wept when she said she's not yet prepared to face life without her father if it's in her power to help."

Nearly choking on Alexa's last words, Gregor's eyelids closed. No amount of willpower could prevent the escape of glistening teardrops. Finally regaining his composure, he looked at his wife. "What a terrible struggle this must have been for you, especially returning to this god-forsaken land of misery."

Alexa bent her head, resting her forehead against the large hands she still clasped. When she remained mute, Gaeldoreg spoke in an uncharacteristically subdued voice. "Ma Ishna stayed amazingly strong from the moment I met her. Only three times have I seen her falter. The first was when she revealed how she feared for you and your son. Your Major Fratino had to explain because she could not. The second was when your son almost died."

Gregor leaned forward and kissed her hair. "Beloved, Nikolai insisted you saved his life. I knew he was right when I smelled lilacs." His next kiss lingered when she barely nodded.

Gaeldoreg continued, "The last was the day we arrived. Stepping off the ship onto the dock required the most courage I've ever witnessed from any living being. I know what they did to her. Having seen her scars, I feel immense pride when she calls me Bibo, especially knowing she is now my queen."

⌐

After midday, Gregor escorted Alexa to the hospital pavilions to meet with all the Valiria so he and Gaeldoreg could tour the encampment. Watching the priestesses joyfully receive their Valkana into their midst, the king observed the great need tired volunteers had for their leader's presence. She had done more than bring additional helping hands to relieve the strain of tending to wounded and dying. Their Valkana embodied the renewal and refreshment of the faith and spirituality that sustained them through the best and worst times of their lives.

"She is to them as you are to your armies," Gaeldoreg remarked thoughtfully.

"As we are to one another," Gregor returned with a half-smile.

"Perhaps that's why you dared such a bold undertaking as invading the Sifiq Kingdom. Look at this camp and the site you chose for it. It spreads as far as a small city and is better planned than many towns I've seen. Pathways are clearly aligned and marked. Work areas are organized so your craftsmen can work efficiently. Food is as decent as can be expected. In advance, you provided the best medical care available, knowing there would be casualties. Your camp is clean.

"Officers and soldiers show mutual respect. That reflects leadership from the top and is no easy accomplishment. Cousin, your skills in directing a war are formidable."

Gregor stared at graying skies. "I never wanted another war. Not with anyone, especially not the Sifiq."

"The Sifiq are relentless in their violence. They gave you no choice if you were to protect your people."

"I honor my sworn oath to protect my people and my nation." Stopping abruptly, Gregor turned blazing eyes to his newfound cousin. "A little more than a week passed before I reached her after she washed up on the beach when they brought her back. Gaeldoreg, my beautiful, vital wife was hardly more than skin over bones. Her back. Dearest Val, whenever I think of the infected, shredded skin over her back, I still get physically sick. I live with daily reminders impossible to describe.

"I dared invasion because Bin-Lot stole her wedding ring and tried to rape her. Not for the sake of revenge but for the sake of her peace of mind. I promised myself that, whatever it takes, he will face me—man to man. Bin-Lot will face justice."

Before Gaeldoreg could respond, the sonorous tones of Trezvindjan voices interrupted his thoughts. Assuming his role as senior commander, he addressed the four leaders of warriors sent by the Protectors' High Command. Then, turning to Gregor, he said, "Your Majesty, your kinsmen are keen to offer you their oaths of loyalty."

Still absorbing news his wife had delivered earlier that day, Gregor drew in a deep breath before acknowledging Gaeldoreg and his commanders with a refined tilt of his head. He then watched as, in practiced military synchronicity, the four commanders knelt with heads bowed and arms crossed over their chests. One after the other announced his name and pronounced his vow of loyalty as Gregor ceremoniously repeated his recognition and acceptance to each man.

As Gregor welcomed the commanders with dozens of Turandan soldiers curiously looking on, a hand slid beneath his arm. "How glad I am I didn't miss that. I know how much these gentlemen looked forward to meeting you. It seems Your Majesty needs to issue an announcement about our new alliance."

Chuckling, Gaeldoreg asked, "Cousin, how is it that Ma Ishna appears like magic when we least expect her? Or do I only imagine that?"

Gregor chuckled. "It isn't your imagination. My problem is that when she shows up this way, she usually comes to remind me of important tasks at hand. She's also right about this formal announcement."

⌒

Muted light from the small oil lantern on the table cast shadows throughout Gregor's tent as he concentrated on brushing final tangles from Alexa's hair. "What made you think I would let you stay anywhere else but here with me?"

With her eyes closed, she luxuriated in his touch. "I didn't want to disrupt your routine. Just knowing you were nearby, I would have been satisfied staying with the Valiria."

Laying her brush aside and leaning forward, he drew her from the chair into his arms. Gazing into her eyes, he said, "My love, I hate that you've returned to this dreadful place. Still, with all my heart, I love you more than ever for your courage in coming to me. As much as possible, I will keep you close."

Stroking his cheek, she smiled. "Then you're not angry with me?"

"Angry? You have made a king a king while increasing his chances of winning victory over a loathsome enemy. No, Alexa, I'm not angry with you, but I see how tired you are. Before coming to bed, I need to discuss some matters with Gaeldoreg, his commanders, and my officers. In the meantime, I want you to go to sleep. Promise you'll get some rest. Please?"

"I am tired," she admitted. "When you come back, will you hold me?"

As had been his habit for years, he held her face between loving hands. "Of course, I will. Now, into bed, such as it is."

Alexa giggled. "It's a nice, thick mat, and these are very warm blankets. Poor Nikolai. What a surprise he'll have if he comes dragging in here tonight."

Gregor tucked covers under his wife's chin. "He'll be back soon enough. At least Gaeldoreg's tent is enormous. Let's hope he doesn't snore. Now, off to sleep with you."

"As you wish, Your Majesty."

Gregor stood to leave but paused. Her eyelids had already drifted shut. He grimaced, sure her mention of the mat and blankets had referred to her imprisonment at the labor camp. More than tired, she was exhausted. When he returned, he would keep his promise and hold her close. Even in sleep, he would make her feel safe.

⌒

"Gregor?" Alexa murmured as she rolled over, seeking the strong arms that had held her while she slept. "Gregor, are you there?"

"I'm here. Go back to sleep."

Hearing strain in his voice, Alexa propped herself up on one elbow. "I can't. Not without you. I need you."

The sound he made in response was nearly impossible to describe. Something between a sob and a muffled groan of pain, its resonance vibrated along every nerve of her body. Rising from the warmth of her bed, she saw his dark figure outlined by faint, invading light from the enormous campfires outside their canvas walls. Bent forward with hands gripping the back of a chair, he looked desolate. Feeling the depth of his distress, she went to him, circling his waist from behind and resting her face against his broad back. The instant stiffening in his body—his resistance—would have stung her except for how well she knew her husband.

"Gregor, my love, come to bed. I need you there." There it was—that fleeting, self-deprecating laugh.

"Go back to bed, Alexa."

"I will. When you come with me. Didn't you hear me? I need you."

Her meaning was clear. "Alexa, please! Not here! How selfish can a man be? I will not defile you or our love in this despicable place."

385

"Is that why you left our bed? Because you thought loving me here would be selfish or would somehow taint or desecrate who we are together?"

He stiffened, refusing to turn around, and she refused to release him. "We are in the Sifiq Kingdom, the most damnable place in the world. And the place where that vile despot hurt you. The mere thought of what he tried to do to you torments me."

"Then love me, Gregor Toscano. Love away what happened here and heal me. Val healed me, body and spirit. Now you heal my heart and soul with your love. Please, Gregor. I need you. Don't fail me. Not now when we both need each other so badly."

Tremulous words pierced his heart. Helpless to deny her anything, he turned and cradled her face between shaking hands. "Beloved, I do need you. Perhaps more than ever before, I want you, but I feel so ashamed."

Raising her arms around his neck, she pressed against him and whispered, "No more shame. Ever. Just love me."

Guiding her back to their mat, Gregor carefully knelt with Alexa while showering her face and mouth with kisses. Beneath blankets warding off night's chill, they sought the closeness denied them over the past months. Desperately seeking the tantalizing satisfaction of Gregor's kisses, Alexa's lips welded to his. Responding instantly, his mouth opened. The bond deepened, and they thrilled one another with the sensual teasing and tasting of lovers' kisses.

Seeking further satisfaction, Gregor broke the connection. With marauding lips, he tracked moist lines from her sensitive ear to the base of her neck. He pushed aside the neckline of her nightgown. His mouth then followed the lines of her shoulder before dropping lower to the cleft of her breasts.

Ruing the necessity for clothing, he slipped warm hands beneath her gown and stroked smooth skin, caressing the intimate places he knew gave her the greatest delight. He shuddered when her hands slid under his sleepshirt, sweeping across his back and buttocks. Her lips, hot and damp, found the exact spot at the base of his neck sure to set every nerve in his body on fire.

"Gregor," she begged breathlessly, reaching between them and grasping him firmly, "heal me, my love. Make me whole as only you can."

For the briefest moment, the intimacy of her touch stunned him. He had brought her too far. He had come too far. Banishing his anxieties, he positioned himself so he could support her hips. His possession joined them in a breathtaking surge of rippling sensations.

Liberated from earlier self-incrimination, Gregor loved Alexa. Determined to fulfill her wish, he gave his body freedom not only to love but to receive the love that transcended the violent, hateful land they were in. With every caress, he wanted her to feel the sweetness she was to him. As her hands and lips continued their constant exploration of his body, some part of his mind wondered in amazement that she could still stir him to such excitement after all these years. With each powerful stroke his body made, he reminded her that their love would always be a driving force in their lives.

Her tiny moans grew insistent as she arched against him. Her rapidly building desires matched his until an explosion engulfed them both in rolling waves of pulsating sensation. Every nerve in their bodies vibrated. Breathlessly sobbing, she clung to him. Clutching her close, he felt his pounding heart gradually slow. Finally able to breathe normally, they parted, and he helped her arrange clothing and blankets.

As they lay in pre-dawn darkness, her fingers combed through long locks of his tumbled hair. "Thank you, my husband, for healing me."

"Alexa," he whispered, "who healed whom?"

"Perhaps we both needed healing. That's who we are together, you know." She yawned. "Still, thank you. You chased away my suffering here, leaving naught but shadows." She drew her fingertips across his forehead. "It's been so long since I've known such pure joy. Thank you for giving me this warmth and this joy. I love you, my beloved Gregor."

He listened as her voice faded. She fell asleep with her face nestled against his arm and her hand above his heart. Barely visible, blue-white light shimmered around her face. He had not seen her sleep so peacefully since before she left Toraval for the ill-fated mission to Kisana.

What had she just told him? Yes, she had thanked him for the warmth and joy. He placed a reverent kiss against her forehead. As welcome slumber claimed him, his last thought was that Alexa was his life's greatest joy.

Chapter 17

Sulía Kohira huddled beneath the pile of evergreen branches with Kiralí's head tucked under her elbow. "Do you see anything?" she whispered tensely.

Win-Das held a finger against his lips.

Garbed in a tattered Sifiq officer's uniform, an older man with a patch over his left eye crawled through the underbrush. "Nothing. We should avoid the road, though."

Nodding, Win-Das signaled others hidden nearby. "Everyone, stay alert. We've seen several cavalry units riding toward Atuliq."

Hiding behind a thick stand of scrub pines and tall, brown grasses, the shabby group offered hasty grace over a meager breakfast of dried fruit, jerky, and crisp biscuits they shared from carefully rationed food Sulía carried in a canvas bag. Grateful for what they had, they picked up their journey. Rumors had sprung up about an invasion army from Turand heading toward Atuliq. Insisting she would go alone, Sulía and this small band of volunteer insurgents hoped to find help for their comrades hiding in Talafaq.

Despite their ragged clothing, the rebels ignored brisk autumn temperatures. Cautiously threading their way across rocky terrain and through tangled undergrowth, they kept warm by moving constantly.

Captain Bor-Tan kept his good eye fixed on a landmark where Kiralí had first spotted glittering lights she called the Healing Graces. Another day, Sulía and Kiralí had both seen them at the same time. Confident that Valiria priestesses had come with an army from Turand, the two priestesses insisted that was where they needed to go.

Pausing midmorning to rest, Win-Das took Bor-Tan aside. "How far is it? Even rationing our food, I worry we may not have enough."

The older man shook his head. "Hard to say. At this rate? Perhaps three, four more days. Following the road would be faster, but I fear encountering soldiers."

"What if we walk the edge of the road? I can listen for approaching riders and alert everyone to scatter and hide. The roadsides certainly haven't been cleared in a long time. "

Bor-Tan shook his head. "It is a risk, but perhaps one worth taking."

Rejoining their companions, Win-Das kissed Sulía's hand as she offered him a flask of water. How he prayed that someday he could give her more than the hardship and privations they had known since marrying in the drafty hut at the Talafaq labor hut. She had never once complained.

"Sulía! Look! Is that possible?" Excitement in Kiralí's voice garnered everyone's attention.

Standing, Sulía gasped. "Praise Val! I'm not sure I believe it!" Kiralí stood and threw her arms around her sister-priestess.

Win-Das stared in confusion at the two women, who now both wept. "Sulía, love, what is it?"

"Don't you see? The dome! The Healing Graces really have returned! Oh, praise Val, she lives!"

Win-Das and Bor-Tan spun around. In front of the landmark hill Bor-Tan was using for navigation, a dome of glittering lights settled into a shimmering, blue-white glow.

⌒

Kis-mur Han defiantly ran out her door, her husband behind her, and shouted for help from soldiers on the road. Rushing to her, a lieutenant ordered two men to subdue her cursing husband while he and another soldier took Kis-mur's arms. "Mistress, do not fear. We will help you."

"Not me! Please! My son! He's dying! Inside! Please help him," she begged.

Lieutenant Nalzari glanced at Kis-mur's back. Her sheath was open, revealing fresh, bloody stripes. His face hardened into a furious mask. "Did your husband do this?"

She nodded. "It doesn't matter. My son. Please."

Nalzari barked orders. "Arrest him! You know the king's orders." To Kis-mur, he said, "Take me to your son."

Inside the spotlessly clean house, a boy of about eight lay on a sofa, his face ashen. Despite the heavy blanket covering him, the child shook violently. Nalzari noticed the pool of blood forming on the floor. Going to the child, he lifted the covers and saw the gashes torn into his leg and side.

Kis-mur rushed to the sofa and knelt beside the child, taking his hand and lifting it to her lips. "I was trying to stop the bleeding, but my husband told me to let him die like a man in service to his king. He's just a baby! I struggled with my husband. That's why he beat me."

"Mistress, bandage the wounds as best you can. I'll send for a wagon. We'll take him to our camp for medical treatment. That's the best I can do."

Tears streamed down her face as she rose from the floor and went to bring material for the bloody lacerations on her son's body. "Thank you, sir."

"And, Mistress, cover yourself, too. It's cold outside."

Arriving at the hospital pavilion, Nalzari prayed thanks that the child had survived the trip. Carrying him inside, he was surprised to be greeted by the Valkana. Explaining the situation, he gently placed the child on a cot and watched as Turand's beloved high priestess examined the injuries and gracefully ran her hands over the length of the boy's body.

Looking up, she asked, "The child's mother?"

"I am here. I am Kis-mur Han."

Alexa tilted her head and studied the woman for brief seconds. "You, too, are injured."

"I don't care about me. Please take care of my son."

"Kis-mur, your son is barely alive. We will do what we can, but the healing we deliver comes from our God Val. We are only his instruments. Our people are healed because they believe in him and serve him. Can you understand that?"

Kis-mur's chin quivered. "I'm not sure, but if your god will heal my son, I will serve him however I can. I don't know how this is done, but tell your god I am his if he will save my son. Please."

Alexa stretched out her hand. "Come. Be close to your child. I promise nothing, but the child is an innocent. If Val chooses to heal him and accepts you, you will both be healed. Someone! Please bring General Kohira closer! I prepare to summon the Healing Graces."

As men carried Kohira's cot, Gregor stormed into the tent. "How many?" he demanded.

Alexa's head shot up. "How many what?"

"How many times did he strike her? I want to know now!"

Kis-mur shook, unable to speak in the face of the king's fury. She looked to Alexa. "He—he is the king. I dare not speak to him."

Alexa smiled reassuringly. "Tell me, then. He will not hurt you. How many times did your husband strike you today?"

Fearfully eyeing Gregor, Kis-mur said, "He hit me once in the face and then four times with the strap before I ran from the house."

Trembling with suppressed anger, Gregor ground out, "He was the first I warned here about abusing women. He will be the example that I mean what I say."

Alexa recalled her promise. "Gregor, my love. Please. Not here."

Clenching his jaw, he huffed a furious sigh. "Not here, beloved."

Once Gregor departed and Kohira's cot was in place, Alexa mentally retreated from the commotion and initiated her meditative chant. As the rhythmic notes of her voice increased in volume, so sparked the dancing, prismatic lights of the Healing Graces until a gleaming dome rose above the pavilion, entrancing those who felt privileged to witness the miracle of the Valkana's faith in action.

⮑

In Qasalaf, Def-Han eyed the Turandan king, who had just swung down from the largest horse he had ever seen. Wrath etched itself into every dark feature of the man's face, and the former Sifiq officer suddenly understood the meaning of fear.

"Def-Han! Did I not warn you about abusing women?" Gregor roared as he approached the prisoner restrained by two Turandan soldiers.

Resorting to bravado, the Sifiq answered, "She's my wife! It is my right to punish her when necessary. That's not abuse."

"Rules with descriptions of abuse were distributed. One was placed in your hands. There is no excuse for your actions, so, as you put it, you will be punished."

"You can't punish a man for keeping his wife in her place."

"A real man has no need to beat a woman the way you beat your wife. Neither would a real man send a young child outside alone at

393

night into the wild to perform a spy's mission. Like most Sifiq officers I've ever met, you're a coward. You're only brave when you attack those weaker than yourselves." Gregor practically spat the last sentence at Def-Han.

Sharply jerking his head, Gregor ordered his men to tie Def-Han between two posts and remove his shirt. Then, in a loud, firm voice, he announced to the crowd that had gathered, "Sifiq men have been called here and are required to stay. Sifiq women, you may stay or leave as you choose, although children should go inside. Since we have come, you have all been treated fairly, with respect. My first rule was clearly stated. Sifiq women were not to be subjected to beatings or other abuse. The penalty for violation of that rule was also clear. Def-Han willfully violated that rule and will now stand as an example that the King of Turand is a man of his word."

Lieutenant Nalzari handed the king a bloodstained whip confiscated from Def-Han's house. Staring at the knotted piece of leather, Gregor wondered how many times he had used it against Kis-mur. For several nauseating seconds, he thought back on the times one like it had been used against Alexa.

"Def-Han, my order stated punishment would be three times the strikes against any woman. You hit your wife once in the face and struck her four times with the whip. Therefore, you will bear fifteen strokes of the whip wielded by my own hand."

The crowd released a shocked gasp. Def-Han was a burly man who liked imposing his authority on the local population. His ruddy complexion paled as he faced the wrath of the king, who was a huge man.

"Your Majesty, you wouldn't subject a lame man to such severe punishment, would you?"

Gregor chuckled sarcastically. "So now you plead lameness in a bid for clemency? Lameness did not prevent you from inflicting violence on your wife, Def-Han, nor will it release you from the justice I promised." Drawing back his arm, Gregor delivered the first cracking blow against the man's exposed back.

By the time Gregor completed his bloody task, Def-Han sagged, unable to bear the punishment he had meted out against his wife throughout the years. Turning to face Sifiq men ordered to stay, Gregor grimly stated, "I take no pleasure in this man's punishment. We will take him to our camp for medical attention. Let Def-Han be your example that I will keep my word. I will tolerate no abuse or mistreatment of women. Any man who is truly a man has no need to force himself or his superior strength on any woman."

⌒

"Your Highness! Look!"

Nikolai froze as he turned and stared. From the direction of their camp, glittering, dancing lights had settled into a glowing blue-white dome. "In Val's great name! I don't believe it!" he exclaimed before dropping to one knee and whispering, "Mother."

Concealed by tall grasses, tangled brambles, and heavy undergrowth around a group of evergreens, Sulía whispered, "Win, let go. I'm sure their accents are Turandan. I *feel* they're Turandan."

"And if they're not?"

"Trust me," she said before impatiently tugging free and stubbornly dragging through the clinging, scratching brush. Finally reaching the road, she felt her heart ready to burst. "All praises be to Val!"

Anxious to return to camp, Nikolai glanced around from adjusting his horse's bridle. Then, rushing to the ragged, waif-like figure standing by the edge of the road, he stared at her familiar face in amazement. "Sulía Kohira?"

More shocked than he, she sobbed with joy and started to kneel. "Your Royal Highness!"

Catching and stopping her, he put his arm around her. "Thanks be to Val, you still live! Come. Sit." He then led her to a large rock where she could sit and had someone bring her a blanket and a canteen with water.

Immensely thankful for the blanket's warmth, she gazed into her prince's face. "Your Highness, there are others in the woods. Valiria Kiralí Seraná and Sifiq rebels, including my husband."

Within minutes, Nikolai's men had gathered the others. Blankets were passed around, and welcome food was offered to the hungry travelers.

"You are fortunate we were diverted in our journey and are now returning. Otherwise, we would have missed you." Nikolai hid angry concern behind his smile. "I suggest you eat slowly and a little at a time. We have plenty."

"We heard rumors of an invasion," Sulía said between bites. She glanced toward the still-shimmering dome of light. "That's where we were headed."

Win-Das said, "Our comrades hide in the mountains. Sulía and Kiralí were sure they sensed Turandans, but they aren't as strong as they once were. We volunteered to accompany them."

"We've spotted many soldiers rushing toward the Sifiq capital," Bor-Tan added. "There's little doubt that heavy action is planned."

Captain Lynmar's eyebrows lifted high. "You speak as one with military experience. Am I wrong, or do you wear an officer's uniform?"

Bor-Tan fairly bristled at the question. "I wear what remains of a captain's uniform. And do not think it gives me any sense of pride, young man. I sacrificed my family and my eye for a king who doesn't give a damn about anything except his sordid pleasures. You have no idea how it feels."

"I meant no insult, sir. None at all."

Nikolai smiled grimly. "Bor-Tan, you will find Captain Lynmar remarkably focused on practical matters and most likely empathetic to your plight. Now, why did you choose to travel this direction?"

Bor-Tan again answered. "Our priestesses sensed the presence of other Valiria. Several times, we all saw unusual lights from that direction." He pointed toward Qasalaf. "Both Sulía and Kiralí said those are the Healing Graces and mean Valiria are there. I fixed this good eye on certain landmarks to set our path."

Nikolai's eyelids closed for a moment as emotion threatened to overtake him. "Those lights do belong to the Healing Graces. We turn back because the new blue-white color indicates our Valkana has arrived. I must return to greet my mother."

∽

"Ma Ishna, what magic do you use to tame our king?" Gaeldoreg asked as he handed Alexa a mug of tea.

Seated in front of a blazing campfire while waiting for Gregor to return from his nightly walk through camp, Alexa laughed. "Tame my husband? Whatever do you mean?"

Gaeldoreg's heavy eyebrows raised. "I thought he was ready to rip to shreds everything in his path after he flogged that Sifiq idiot today. Then he stormed into his quarters like some wounded wild animal. I was almost afraid when you followed not long after. Ten minutes later, he carries you out, and both of you are laughing and grinning. He's been fine ever since. I'm just curious how one tames a man like him."

Alexa gazed into the fire. Flames leapt high. Logs occasionally shifted, sending red-hot sparks flying. Vibrant yellows and oranges drew the eye into fiery depths with terrifying power. That had been her husband's anger earlier in the day.

"One does not tame a man like Gregor. His passions are too deep and powerful. Thankfully, his conscience holds him accountable for his actions because he is essentially kind and good. Still, he is not a man to cross. I understand him—his heart and his soul. On days like today, I help him recover his balance."

"But you don't really condone violence. How do you manage?"

Sighing, Alexa drank from her mug, its warmth and sweetness soothing. "Bibo, sometimes it isn't easy, but I also gave Gregor a promise. He told me circumstances forced him to learn to deal with the Sifiq on their terms, in the way they understand things. I promised never to interfere when they force him to deal that way. He promised he would only do so when he believed it absolutely necessary."

"The two of you keep an extraordinary relationship," Gaeldoreg mumbled, wondering about the exceptional connection between two people with such different temperaments.

Alerted by sentries two days later, Alexa hurried to greet Nikolai as he rode into camp ahead of his squad. Watching as he fluidly swung out of his saddle and raced toward her, she laughed as he took her in his arms and lifted her off the ground.

"Mother!" Setting her down, he indulged her as she pulled his face down and kissed both his cheeks multiple times.

"My beautiful son! How glad I am to see you! And how much more you look like your father with that beard! Dearest Val! You look just like him when first I laid eyes on him!"

Nikolai laughed. "I hope that's a good thing."

"You know I consider your father the most handsome man in the world, although you are excellent competition."

Gregor laughed from behind. "Your kind of competition I can stand. Welcome back. I wasn't sure when to expect you. Where are the rest of your men? No problems with the Sifiq, I hope."

"I rode ahead. We saw the dome from the Healing Graces. I knew Mother was here by the color. Besides, we brought some intelligence. It can wait. Mother, why in Val's name have you come?"

Clinging to her son's arm, Alexa grinned. "Your father. You. A message for you from Stefan and an astounding surprise."

Rolling his eyes, Gregor laughed. "A surprise, she calls it. I think you should start slowly with Stefan's message. Then you can move on to your mother's idea of surprises."

Nikolai chuckled. "All right. What message does Papino Stefan send?"

"He says to tell you if you're still confused about your two heads from Coloridia, he knows the solution."

Nikolai's forehead creased in question. "Two heads? All right, I assume this is a joke, right?"

"Ma Ishna! King Gregor! Is this our Crown Prince Nikolai?"

The booming voice and uniquely accented words were more than enough to capture Nikolai's attention. The prince was dumbfounded by the distinctive uniform, dark coloring, muscular build, and towering height. "Mother? Father?"

Grinning ear to ear, the Trezvindjan inspected the newly arrived prince. "Hmmm. Not a bad presentation considering he's just in from reconnaissance. Excellent form for one so young. Good beard. I like that in a young man. Your Majesty, my compliments. You and your queen breed excellent princes and princesses." Abruptly dropping to his knee with arms crossed over his chest, he said, "Prince Nikolai, I am Gaeldoreg Vosklon. It is my honor to pledge my life and my loyalty to you as heir of the Sacred Blood of the Krisantal. I will serve your father, you, and your heirs until the end of my days."

Nikolai's black-brown eyes opened wide as he stared at his father in stark bewilderment.

"My son, place a hand on each of his shoulders and accept his oath of loyalty with your thanks. We'll explain."

Following Gregor's instructions, Nikolai sucked in his breath and said, "Gaeldoreg Vosklon, as Crown Prince Nikolai Toscano, I gratefully accept your oath of loyalty and look forward to a long life of mutual respect for us both."

Standing, Gaeldoreg firmly gripped Nikolai's upper arms. "Very well done, young man! Very well done! I am proud to share bloodlines with one such as you!"

"Father!"

Alexa giggled. "Well, as you now see, Niko, the Protectors are no myth, although Gaeldoreg is no longer an active Protector."

"Oh, no!" Nikolai groaned. "You can't be serious!"

"More than that, Gaeldoreg is your distant cousin. To make things even more interesting, your father is now their king. That makes you the heir to their throne as well as the throne of Turand."

"Mother, seriously?"

Gregor rested a calming hand on his son's shoulder. "My son, she's quite serious. Trezvindja is a heritage nation for us and has already sent reinforcements with more troops coming. There's much to explain. Let's get something to eat while we discuss the details."

Still mentally reeling, Nikolai stopped. "Wait. Mother, I'm sorry. I almost forgot. My squad is bringing in some insurgents we found alongside the road. They should arrive soon. Be happy. Sulía and Kiralí are with them."

"Nikolai? Oh, praise Val! I've had occasional fleeting senses of them, but I didn't realize they were so close! How are they?"

Caressing her cheek, he smiled. "Pathetically thin, Mother, but not nearly as bad as you were when you came home. Joyful when they saw us. Sulía's husband was with her."

"How happy that makes me! Even though Win-Das was an officer, he was never harsh with me inside Bin-Lot's palace. He turned out to be a good man."

"I'm learning there are some good Sifiq men," Nikolai replied.

"Harrumph."

"Bibo, you mustn't be so cynical. I turned your heart, didn't I?"

Gaeldoreg growled. "That's because I have a heart, Ma Ishna."

⤳

That evening, Alexa visited the new arrivals at the hospital pavilion before going to bed. The Valiria had cordoned off a private area where Sulía and Win-Das could stay close to Sulía's father. He had shown subtle signs of responding to her voice, and Alexa believed their emotional connection could rouse him from his comatose state. After bathing and changing into clean clothing, Kiralí had eaten early and fallen fast asleep inside quarters reserved for Valiria. The other men had also bathed and changed into warm clothes quickly altered for their thin frames. Pleased the newcomers appeared to be in surprisingly good condition and in excellent spirits, Alexa called for Captain Lisandá to escort her to the tent she shared with Gregor.

Before leaving, she heard a quiet, slightly gruff voice say her name. Turning around, she met the glittering eye of Bor-Tan. During a day filled with excitement, she was only beginning to notice that something in his life force was thrumming a chord inside her tired mind. "Yes, Bor-Tan? Do you need something else?"

"No, Lady Valkana. This day has been everything Sulía promised. And more. I can't remember the last time I didn't feel hungry. I just wondered if an old man might ask a special favor of you."

She smiled reassuringly. Was it sadness or loneliness that etched such deep lines into his face? "Ask. If I can help, I will."

"The greatest mistake of my life was obeying my father's demands to lead a soldier's life. I lost everything. The eye? That's nothing. My family? I now know I lost everything when I sacrificed my family for life as an officer for a king like Bin-Lot. Ten minutes in your husband's company? Well, that doesn't matter. What I wish to ask is if you would pray for the souls of my family. They..."

Alexa slowly smiled. "Bor-Tan, forgive me for interrupting you."

"I apologize, Lady Valkana. I should not have..." He looked embarrassed.

"No, it isn't that. I never fail to be surprised at our Lord Val's strange manner of working what we often call coincidences."

He looked confused. "I don't understand."

"We will soon send some of our permanently injured home to Turand. I want you to go with them."

"Me? Why me?"

"Because there was a brave woman in Atuliq who helped me and the other priestesses Bin-Lot sent back. She was one of several Sifiq women he exiled. She now lives there under the name Mei-sat Tanna with her son Lortin and his daughter. They live in a lovely Turandan town close to her other son, Vartin, and his family."

Bor-Tan's eye reflected bright moonlight as it moved back and forth, studying her. His mind stalled. Mei-sat had always been more daring than most Sifiq women. How he had admired her spirit! "My wife? She lives in Turand?"

"She does, as do your sons. You even have grandchildren."

"I don't know what to say. My sons. They were such handsome boys. I never wanted them to join the army. I advised them to seek different professions, but my father convinced them when I was assigned to foreign duty. I never spoke to my father again. I thought my boys were dead."

"They're very much alive."

"What if they want nothing to do with me?" he asked, suddenly fearful.

"They are men of faith now, as are you. Trust that Val has prepared this time for all of you.

"Milady? Excuse me, are you ready? His Majesty awaits you."

"In a moment, Captain." Again to Bor-Tan, she said, "I think your biggest challenge may be choosing a new name. Your sons created a fine surname. I'm not sure what to do with Bor."

He tried to smile through his confusion. "I have no idea where to begin."

"A suggestion. Try Captain Lynmar. He's quite good with such matters. Goodnight."

⌒

Dearest Rafzan,

I suppose you know by now all of the impossible and stunning news. How incredibly strange it feels to be living in Trezvindja at the moment and to know that a people I had no idea existed six months ago already accept me as their interim leader. Trezvindja is a beautiful country to behold. It does not have the diversity of plains, mountains, and wind-swept shores like my own Turand. This is primarily a lush, tropical land as far as the eye can see. Oh, there are mountains and broad beaches. It's just so different. I never dreamed there were so many varieties of flowers as I've seen here! The breezes are wonderful, which is delightful because some days are even hotter than Garogan summers. Sunrises and sunsets are exquisite, with colors too varied to describe. How I hope we might walk along a shoreline to share a sunset one evening. You will be enchanted, I promise. You will walk with me, won't you?

Rafzan, I have a great-grandfather now. We grew up with no grandparents, but Mother found Father's grandfather! Such unbelievable circumstances for him to be grieving as a hermit in Turand all these years. Grandfather, as I call him, is very protective but also very indulgent. If his mother sends me one more dressmaker, I think I shall scream! I know I am Regent and need to make proper appearances, but I see no reason to be so extravagant. I am like Mother. A few nice gowns are all I need. I am well satisfied with my practical blouses and split skirts.

Oh! Rafzan, you should see the way Trezvindjan ladies dress. Father will surely faint dead away when he sees. Be very careful because I have enclosed an excellent drawing of me in a day dress. Master Maconti used colored pencils. Whatever you do, don't let Father see this, or we shall both be in trouble! Perhaps you can burn it after you look at it. I am considered overly modest in this dress. There. A good laugh for you.

Dear, dear Rafzan, how I could use your thoughtfulness right now. My responsibilities are many. I want to make sure this new alliance between Trezvindja and Turand enjoys a strong beginning. I seem to have a talent for learning the language, which makes our new people happy. Maconti is extremely diligent in helping me review all of the day-to-day business that Papino Stefan suggested I understand. Council members who advise me are very wise, but they sometimes try to influence me in ways I don't appreciate. I am determined they come to respect me. I do miss your quick mind and easy way of explaining matters.

All right. The truth. I miss you. Are you taking care of yourself? I can't help but worry. Rafzan, we both know the time must be close when Father will be confident to make his move. Help is coming.

I must close. I have a meeting in half an hour. Tonight, I will go to the beach to watch the sunset. I promise to think of you and pray for you. In the meantime, I send you love.

Anlia

Rafzan read the letter once more. Thoughtfully, he considered the changing tone of her words. Circumstances were helping Anlía quickly mature into the woman he always felt she could be. How he wished he could witness her transformation firsthand. Believing she would one day be a force to be heeded, he marveled yet again that she could care one whit about him.

Laying aside the letter, he set about carefully lifting the crimped edges of paper sealing Master Maconti's drawing. Amused by her effort to secure the picture, he could hardly wait to see what she considered so scandalous it would make her father faint. Finally freeing the page, he felt the breath sucked out of his chest.

The sea rolled foamy, rippling waves onto the shore behind her. Wispy, finger-like clouds streaked turquoise skies. Two gulls rode invisible breezes. His own glorious Anlía stood between slender palm trees curved on either side as if bowing and paying homage to her singular majesty. An array of exotic white flowers lavished her lavender dress. The shoulder seams were gathered with the fabric drawn down across the feminine curves of her breasts. Fluttery sleeves ended at her elbows. A wide, ruched inset perfectly defined her narrow waist and accented the slightly flared skirt that stopped well above her ankles. The open center seam revealed a teasing glance of shapely legs up to her knees. Open-toed shoes made her look light and airy—almost unreal.

Gazing at the image, he noticed something different. His lovely Anlía still preferred wearing long tresses down, but a tiara now adorned her head. "Of course," he reminded himself, "she is Princess Regent now." She also wore a pyramid pendant similar to her mother's, the sign of her newfound status as a Valiria priestess. She wore no other jewelry. Nothing ostentatious. That was not her nature.

"Dearest Anlía, how very exquisite you are," he sighed heavily. "As dearly as I love you, how can I ever be the man you need?"

⌐⌐

A week later, Gregor scowled. "What the devil do you think you're doing?"

"What I came here to do. Even if I can only review these plans for an hour, it's an hour closer to victory." Kohira was back and stubborn as ever.

"What did the doctors say?"

"What doctors? I kissed my daughter, prayed with my Valkana, and came directly here. Now, update me on these cursed devils so we can get on with business."

Suddenly grinning, Gregor drew Kohira into a tight embrace. "Welcome back to the world of the living, old friend. Welcome back."

Kohira chuckled. "Let's keep us both among the living, eh?"

While the two discussed recent Sifiq troop movements, Alexa appeared carrying two covered mugs. "Raija, gentlemen. The general needs to guard his energy, and it does no harm for our king, either."

Kohira winked at Gregor. "Better her than Sulía. My daughter has turned domineering among these Sifiq. Drink up."

"General," Alexa said with a smile, "Sulía has always been assertive. I think she may have learned that from someone in Turand."

Collective laughter dissipated as a loud voice called out, "Incoming caravan!"

Alexa closed her eyes briefly and then met Gregor's gaze. "Trezvindjans. True to their word, they're coming to their king."

Kohira quickly drained his Raija. "This still astonishes me. I always wondered why you were so different from the rest of us. I never once imagined something like this, but if they help us defeat this damned Bin-Lot, then praise Val for Trezvindja!"

Gregor and Kohira were rolling up maps and diagrams when Alexa suddenly broke into a run toward a silver-haired Trezvindjan flanked by two younger guards. The older man was richly garbed in a quilted, knee-length gambeson the same blue color Gaeldoreg wore. However, the silver crest on his chest was more prominent and also appeared on armbands. When he saw Alexa, a huge smile lit his face. Handing gloves and a gleaming silver helmet with blue plumes he had carried beneath his arm to a guard, the man opened his arms to receive Alexa's running embrace.

"Braeklojorn Vosklon! You're supposed to be in Tarahlaz looking after my daughter!" she gasped, kissing his cheek.

The grand prince laughed and tightly hugged her. "Grandfather! Have you forgotten so soon? And have no worries for your daughter! All of Tarahlaz clamors to look after her. As for me? I could wait no longer to meet my grandson!" He craned his neck over her shoulder. "Is that him over there?"

Alexa laughed. "Yes, that's our Gregor. Let me take you to him so I can introduce you." Then, linking her arm in his, she guided him toward her obviously curious husband.

Expecting the impact this moment would have on her husband, glad tears glazed Alexa's eyes. "Gregor, my love, I am honored to introduce you to Grand Prince Braeklojorn Vosklon, your grandfather."

Gregor stood transfixed. Gazing into the man's face was akin to looking into his own future. He recalled Alexa's initial description of how much he resembled his grandfather. Finally, after several deep breaths, Gregor discovered the ability to utter a single word. "Grandfather."

The prince dropped to one knee, crossing his arms over his chest, as was the custom of all Trezvindjans. The first words his grandson would hear from him were a heartfelt pledge of loyalty from the Vosklon League's Grand Prince.

Gregor placed his hands on Braeklojorn's shoulders. Touching his grandfather for the first time moved him emotionally in ways he never anticipated. "Beloved Grandfather, accept my gratitude for your loyalty—and the love and respect of your grandson for all you have given to my family in the short time we've known you. Rise and never again kneel before us."

Braeklojorn stood. Tears rolled freely down olive-bronze cheeks as he studied the features of the man who, as Alexa had described, reminded him of himself as a much younger man. "Gregor Maxim Toscano, King of Turand and King of Trezvindja, on behalf of the Krisantal League and the Vosklon League, and with permission from the Council of Leagues, I respectfully request that you add to yours the honored names of Vosklon and Krisantal from Trezvindja. Then, please let me embrace the grandson I have dreamed of meeting since the day your wife told me about you."

Gregor's heart throbbed with emotions new to him. Drawing a steadying breath, he said, "From this day forward, I decree my name shall be Gregor Maxim Vosklon Krisantal Toscano, King of Turand and King of Trezvindja." Reaching out, Gregor then wrapped his grandfather in a powerful embrace.

Later, as the two men held Alexa between them and talked with General Kohira, another group of Trezvindjans appeared. The apparent leader wore a scarlet gambeson and matching cape, its golden crest reflecting sunlight. "May I assume this is the site for the family reunion?" he called out.

Gregor glanced down at Alexa, whose eyes widened in surprise. Before she could respond, the newcomer hurried forward, saying, "Braeklojorn, good job! No doubt your grandson!" The man then dropped to his knees, crossing his arms over his chest. "Your Majesty, I am Prince Kaelzron Krisantal, and I am honored to pledge my life and my loyalty to King Gregor of the Sacred Blood of the Krisantal. I will serve you and your heirs until the end of my days."

Once pledge formalities were completed, the prince stood, momentarily assessing his new king. "Yes, you look much better suited to the role of king than I ever was. I am your mother's uncle, by the way. I hope you'll forgive me for coming, but I decided the time had come for me to perform penance for my lack of action and my daughter's behavior contributing to this disaster."

Shaking his head, Gregor welcomed his uncle before herding everyone to the dining area to discuss the latest updates from Trezvindja. Once everyone had settled with freshly brewed tea or kacha, Kaelzron explained that he had disembarked with three hundred troops and fresh supplies. The remaining two hundred troops should arrive within days. A dispatch had also arrived advising that five Turandan vessels were inbound via Coloridia.

"Five from Turand?" Kohira asked. "Good! Our navy continues to hold its own."

"Most assuredly. Those cannons your people use wreak havoc on Sifiq ships. Whoever devised them is either genius or demon," Kaelzron remarked.

"We can thank the inventive mind of Lord Garogan for those weapons," Kohira said.

"Your friend?" Braeklojorn asked Alexa, accenting the word friend with a hint of malice.

"He is a brilliant tactician and a master at weaponry when he so chooses," she sighed.

Braeklojorn sensed Gregor's gaze. Making eye contact, Gregor gave an almost imperceptible shake of his head. Their bond already allowed them to communicate in silence.

Deciding the split arrivals should facilitate the incorporation of new troops into the cantonment, Gregor left settlement of the camp to company regulars. Meanwhile, he and his command officers would focus on strategy for the advance on Atuliq. With autumn quickly waning, they wanted to avoid prolonging the war through a bitter Sifiq winter. Now assured of his new nation's commitment, Gregor prepared to finish the task begun when Nikolai had declared war against the Sifiq Kingdom.

⁓

"You look very handsome and especially ferocious in these new battle gambesons your grandfather brought," Alexa said as she tugged the hem of the quilted garment into place. "The design is rather ingenious. Silver-gray with the purple, red, and blue stripes representing Turand and the Krisantal and Vosklon Leagues running from your right shoulder to the hem and the row of crests emblazoned on the opposite shoulder. Impressive."

"Trezvindjans do like color, don't they?" he remarked as he tightened the belt and checked his sword.

"They do, but once you go there, you'll understand. Their island is ablaze with color. It is a beautiful land to behold."

"So Anlía wrote in her letter. I could hardly believe my little girl wrote that. For all the world, she sounded very much in control but also aware that there was much yet to learn. Did you meet this Bresklon Krisantal she mentioned?"

"I did. He impressed me as a man of highest integrity and dedication to family and country. Grandfather said Bresklon has undertaken the responsibility of teaching her all she needs to know about Trezvindjan government, laws, procedures, and traditions."

"I can't help but worry about her."

"We'll always worry about her. That's why I promoted Tirstan to major and insisted that he command her security detail and why I left Gregor Maconti with her. Between the two of them and a detail of Turandan guards, I'm confident they'll get her to safety if the need should arise. I also trust my intuition. I believe Bresklon Krisantal would not be a pleasant adversary if forced to defend his regent."

Gregor lifted her chin and dropped a gentle kiss on her lips. "I concede to my wife's judgment and her intuition. Grandfather said much the same, but it feels better coming from you."

He wiggled around. "This works well. I look forward to seeing Nikolai in his."

Just as Gregor lifted the flap to leave the tent, the piercing sound of horns sounded the alarm. Raiders were charging the left side of the camp. Swiftly unsheathing his sword, he grabbed Alexa's arm and simultaneously shouted for his grandfather. "Hurry! Take her to the hospital pavilion! Lisandá! Get your queen to safety!"

Shrieking shrilly, the first turbaned riders jumped their mounts over barriers and engaged soldiers with swords drawn. Braeklojorn clutched Alexa's hand as the two ran while Turandan and Protector troops rushed past them to confront the inbound Sifiq. Alexa stumbled and fell when Lisandá, who had been directly behind her, cried out. Lifting her head, she saw him on the ground, his thigh slit open by a blade. Then, before a Sifiq soldier on foot could ram a sword through his heart, a Royal Guard slashed the enemy's throat.

Another set of arms dragged Alexa to her feet. "Majesty, someone else will see to him! Let's get you to safety!"

"Rafzan!" Alexa gasped. Gulping in a breath, she nodded and started running again. "Grandfather, hurry!"

More Trezvindjans appeared and surrounded them with crest-emblazoned shields, safely escorting them to the hospital pavilion where the parade of bloody soldiers had already begun. Turning, Alexa listened to the jarring sounds of battle she had just escaped. Shrill shrieks as Sifiq raiders attempted to terrorize Turandan and Trezvindjan fighters on the ground. Bellowing shouts and roaring commands from officers directing their soldiers. Loud, agonized cries from men being struck with swords. Echoing, ringing clangs of solid steel against steel generated by soldiers determined to kill one another in the middle of a chilly fall day.

"Your Majesty, are you hurt?" one of her guards worriedly inquired.

"No, Lieutenant, I'm fine. Captain Lynmar helped me up when I fell. Have you seen him?"

"Not since he delivered you and the king's grandfather to the Protectors back there."

"Find him, Lieutenant. He saved my life. I'm sure of it. Find him."

"Don't worry." The officer was leaving when three soldiers, carrying a bloody body, hurried past. As if in slow motion, Alexa turned and followed them.

"Lieutenant, stay the order! He's here!" She ran to Rafzan's side.

With sure fingers, Alexa undid buttons of the captain's coat, but he grasped her hand. Glazed blue eyes sought hers. "Stop, Majesty. This wound will be my end."

"Rafzan, let me tend to you. We'll call the Healing Graces."

"You don't understand," he mumbled. "It is my time. Will you stay with me?"

She closed her eyes and felt the presence of her Lord Val touching her soul. She could not hold back tears. "I won't leave you. Let me at least cover this."

"If it pleases you."

Quickly, she opened his blood-soaked coat and saw the gaping wound that had slashed through the muscles of his abdomen, allowing his intestines to slide outward. Holding them in with her hand, she chanted prayers until lights appeared overhead. If nothing else, she could ease the agony of his passing while energizing the efforts of other Valiria also tending injured soldiers.

"Thank you, Majesty. It hurts less."

"Alexa. You may call me Alexa."

With a weak smile, he spoke haltingly. "Alexa, how do I thank you? I deserved nothing, yet you returned to me my soul. You even forgave me for my atrocity. Then, when you could have destroyed me with a word, you let me experience treasure." His eyes closed, his life ebbing.

Gregor suddenly burst into the pavilion, searching for Alexa. Seeing her on her knees, he started toward her, but Braeklojorn stopped him. "She's safe. That young officer saved her—saved us both, really."

"Rafzan, I only guided you. Val gave you everything you needed. It was your choice to accept his gifts."

"Oh, dear Val! Him! Of all people!" Gregor gasped.

"Rafzan, do you hear me?"

Blue eyes opened again. Teardrops pooled in the corners. "Alexa, she's so beautiful. Tell her—tell her she must use all her talents and intelligence to build a good life. Will you do that?"

"I will. I promise."

"I'm here, Rafzan. I hear you. You were supposed to walk with me on the beach. Did you forget?"

Blue eyes watered more as a smile crossed his face. Alexa also smiled and silently moved her lips while Rafzan quietly spoke aloud, perplexing those watching the poignant scene unfold.

"Anlía? You're here?"

"Yes, I felt what happened. I came to be with you, Rafzan."

"I must stay with him, Anlía. To help him. You go ahead."

"I understand. Rafzan? Can you hear me?"

He released a muffled sob. "I hear you. How?"

"I am a mystic. Like my mother. Dearest Rafzan, I'm losing you, but you know I have loved you."

"My beautiful, sweet love, you finally gave meaning to my life." He coughed and groaned as Alexa pressed her hand more firmly against his abdomen. "Thank you, especially for the drawings. And I did walk the shore with you. Every night since the picture. Me—with you in your lavender dress."

"Don't tell Father."

He struggled for consciousness. "Alexa, in my tent. My portfolio. Bury it with me. Next to my mother. Niko knows where."

"I will."

"Anlía?"

"Rafzan?"

"The song, my love. What was the song I heard you singing that night I found you in the woods?" His words, weakening, came more slowly.

Beneath the blue-white dome of the Valkana, a sweet voice from afar sounded above the quiet rush of people tending their wounded.

Hush, my little one, Soar Free Upon the Breeze

Hush, my little one, hush your tears this night
Dry your eyes and cry no more;
No more to fear, 'Tis time to smile
Like the tiny birds, 'Tis time to take flight

Hush, my little one, Soar Free Upon the Breeze.

By the song's third line, Alexa sang with her daughter. By the second verse, Gregor's resonant voice joined them. As the song ended, Rafzan Lynmar breathed his last breath.

"Mother?" The silent conversation resumed.

"He's gone, dear one."

"I know. Thank you for easing his way."

"Are you all right, love?" Alexa asked, her lips moving soundlessly as everyone looked on in awe.

"I'm fine, Mother. Rafzan was my first love. I shall mourn his death, but he was not to be the love of my life."

"Oh?"

"I have my own Gregor now, although perhaps not the one you anticipated. He's with me now."

"I look forward to your news, but I must go now. Many need my help."

"I know. I love you, Mother."

Alexa leaned forward and closed Rafzan's lifeless eyes. Soldiers assigned as orderlies respectfully attended his body while Gregor helped her stand and led her to where she could wash. "I need to refresh and strengthen myself to renew the Healing Graces. Are you all right? And Nikolai?"

"I'm fine. Nikolai's leading the Trezvindjan cavalry to pursue escaping raiders. You? Are you all right? And was that actually Anlía's voice?"

"It was," Alexa said as she accepted a mug of Raija from a priestess. "She and Captain Lynmar were close."

"How close?"

"Very, but I'll explain later. There was never anything for you to worry about. Trust me."

"Never anything!" He saw familiar fire flash in her eyes and stopped. Exhausted and infuriated by the number of lives ended by his sword that day, Gregor acknowledged her request. "I do expect an explanation."

"You will have one, as you deserve." She stood on tiptoe and kissed him. "If I could only tell you how much I love you for singing with us back there. Why Val gave me such an extraordinary husband, I will never know, but I am thankful every hour of every day. For now, I must help care for your injured warriors. Excuse me, Your Majesty."

"Ma Ishna, you are close to collapse. You must have some rest."

Forcing a shadow of a smile, Alexa nodded. "Bibo, a tall mug of your kacha should keep me going for another hour or two. We're almost finished with all these bandages and medicines. We must always be ready for these surprise attacks."

Gaeldoreg growled. "More Protectors have geared up now. Once they widen the perimeter around this base camp, we can better defend against attacks like this."

"Have I told you today I love you?"

Growling again, he replied sternly, "If you love me, you'll get some sleep. I'm too old to worry about a stubborn daughter."

"Try worrying about a beautiful, stubborn wife," Gregor said, announcing his presence as he walked up behind Gaeldoreg. "Beloved, he's right. We both need rest."

Sighing, she said, "As soon as I finish here. It won't be much longer. Is Niko back yet?"

That's why she was stalling. Their son had not yet returned from his mad chase after Sifiq raiders. Gregor went to her and knelt, removing from her hands the strip of fabric she was rolling for bandages. "No, but I'm sure he'll return soon. Besides, you would know if something was wrong."

"I'm so tired." Emerald eyes clouded. "And I have to tell him."

"Someone will…"

"No. Please. It must be me. Rafzan asked me to have Niko do something for him."

Her sorrowful eyes hurt Gregor. Two of Alexa's guards informed him how Lynmar had helped Alexa after she fell and then guided her and Braeklojorn to Protectors assigned to the hospital pavilion. A group of Sifiq had chased them, and the captain had bodily placed himself between Alexa and the raiders until the Trezvindjans shielded her. Lynmar had valiantly defended his queen, losing his life in the process.

"I'll have Niko sent to our tent the minute he returns. I want you to come with me. Now. I mean it."

She heard the tone of command in his voice and something else—weariness. "All right." Rising in unison with her husband and mindless of her bloodstained clothing, she put her arms around his waist. Listening to the steady beat of his heart, she breathed a brief, thankful prayer that he had survived the attack. "Gregor?"

"Yes?"

"Maybe I'll just sleep standing up. Right here."

Chuckling, he kissed the top of her head. "I'm too tired to carry you."

Sighing, she turned with one arm snugly behind his back. "You shouldn't have spoiled me all these years. Let's go before we both collapse."

Hours later, Alexa woke with a start. Bolting upright, she noticed that the tent's sturdy brazier stand had been replenished with hot coals. The blankets had been tucked snugly around her. Then she heard it again—the sound that had awakened her. Gregor was vehemently cursing. Whatever had happened, he was beyond furious.

Scrambling from beneath the covers, she hurriedly pulled on a clean skirt over warm pantalets, donned a blouse and heavy sweater, and put on low boots over the socks she had worn to bed. Then, smoothing her hair quickly and securing it with a padded headband, she exited the tent to discover the cause of her husband's current outburst of temper.

Following the sound of his voice, she spotted him about twenty yards away with Nikolai beside him. In front stood four Trezvindjan Protectors, one of whom maintained what looked like a powerful, vice-like grip on the shoulders of a Sifiq officer who had been forced to his knees in front of Gregor.

Sensing her presence, Gregor turned. Flushed scarlet, his face reflected sheer, nearly unbridled rage flooding his being. Momentarily, he calmed. "Alexa, I was ready to send for you. A Protector named Eldored just carried a young girl to the hospital tents. This piece of living garbage invaded her mother's farmhouse to hide and decided he needed some recreation. Eldored caught him in the act of raping the child. She's badly hurt. Go to her. See if you can help."

Alexa's eyelids closed against invading images. "Of course." With guards quickly surrounding her, she turned and rushed to the hospital area, dreading what she expected awaited her.

Reaching the tent, a flurry of activity led her directly to the cot where a nine-year-old girl lay sobbing, her legs apart, her clothing torn and bloody. A woman Alexa assumed was her mother sat on the floor, hunched over, her posture one of total demoralization. The child clung desperately to Eldored's hand, terrified to let go of the one man who had rescued her and then clutched her to his chest as he raced back to camp for help.

When Eldored saw Alexa, he bowed his head. "Lady Valkana, she is Lis-kal. She's just a baby. Look what that monster did to her. Help her. Please."

Alexa's heart swelled with sorrow upon seeing tears rolling down the giant man's dark face. "Let me get closer. I will do what I can. I promise."

"No! Don't leave me!" the little girl wailed as Eldored tried to move aside. "He'll come back!"

Eldored cast Alexa a desperate look and then bent over Lis-kal. "Little one, I will stay near. I will not leave you. My Lady Valkana must check you to help you. Trust her. You are badly injured, but I won't let him hurt you again. I swear it."

The child's blue eyes, swollen from crying, fixed on Eldored's face. Theirs was a mysterious bond considering the classic treatment of women in Sifiq society. "It hurts. So much."

"I know, little one. Let our Lady Valkana help. I promise to stay with you."

She continued sobbing, but, releasing his hand, she allowed Alexa closer. Looking up, Alexa blinked back tears. Determined to help, Sulía brought scissors and began cutting away the rest of Lis-kal's sheath that the officer had ripped open. Covering the child with a blanket warmed over a brazier table, they opened her legs further, cringing at her pain-filled cries.

Alexa glanced over her shoulder. "Eldored, perhaps you can stand at her head and rub her shoulders or stroke her hair. Anything to distract her."

He immediately did as requested. Long fingers began stroking short brown curls or tenderly caressing tear-stained cheeks. Softly, his low baritone voice sang a lullaby that captured the suffering child's attention. The seasoned soldier made no attempt to hide his tears. As he tried to comfort that child, Eldored thought of his own daughter, safe at home. He fervently hoped he had not been wrong in obeying orders and trusting his new king would fairly punish the man who committed this atrocity. It had required every shred of Eldored's self-control not to break the Sifiq's neck after dragging him off the girl.

After cleaning the girl and consulting with a physician, Alexa tried to talk with the child's mother, who was in a state of shock. All they could glean was that her husband had been forcibly conscripted, leaving her alone on their farm with her daughter. The Sifiq officer had barged in to hide after the raid, demanding food. He had also carried a flask of liquor. After a few drinks, he grew violent, struck the mother, and attacked the girl. That was when the Protectors had arrived, searching for escaped raiders.

"Will the Healing Graces help her?" Sulía asked.

"I cannot be sure," Alexa replied. "She's severely damaged. If the mother were more engaged, I might feel more positive, but she has given up. She's already lost. Completely."

"Lady Valkana," Eldored spoke up, "the ishna is not my blood, but I saved her. If the mother is lost, then I claim the girl as my own. I have a daughter about her age and a wife who will accept her. We are people who bear faith in Espiritus. Will your Graces heal her with my claim? I swear I will love her as my own."

Surprised, Alexa shook her head. "Eldored, I cannot say. The decision is not mine. It belongs to my Lord Val. However, if you remain here while I summon the Healing Graces, we shall soon know."

Alexa stopped a passing priestess and requested a mug of Raija tea and chairs. She advised her that she would be summoning the Healing Graces, so everyone should prepare to add their energies to hers so all their patients could gain greater benefit from the Graces. Soon, her chants called from the heavens the sparkling lights that delivered comfort and healing to the suffering.

When the blue-white dome finally faded, Alexa lifted her head. She had rested her hands over Lis-kal's slim groin. Bleeding had stopped, and healing had occurred. Sadly, internal damage was severe. Meeting Eldored's hopeful gaze, Alexa managed a bleak smile. "She will never bear children, but she will recover and live a healthy life."

He cast his eyes to the floor. "Her mother no longer lives. Tell me your Lord Val will let me give the girl a new family that will cherish her."

Alexa stood and stretched before walking around the cot to where the Protector remained standing. "You are a fine man, Eldored. I shall speak to my husband and advise him that I believe you should be allowed to adopt this child. Ultimately, it is his decision. Now, return to your duties while the Valiria watch over her. She will sleep for many hours. You can visit later."

Before departing the hospital, Alexa stopped to visit patients, including Captain Lisandá, who already complained about being kept in bed. Meeting Gaeldoreg on her way out, she looked into his concerned eyes.

"Ma Ishna, you are very pale. Have you eaten yet?"

"Actually, no, but I need to find Gregor."

"Eat first," he told her, taking her firmly by the arm. "We talk while you eat. I'll escort you to our king afterward."

Inside the dining tent, Alexa soaked up the last of thick gravy with a chunk of freshly baked bread. "I knew he was livid by the sound of his voice when I woke up. I've rarely heard him sound like that."

"That Sifiq officer behaved like the girl was nothing. His arrogance enraged Gregor to a point almost beyond control. I think you walked up just in time."

"During Turand's occupation, many women and girls were raped. Many younger ones died. Some still suffer from their injuries. Gregor sees our daughters and wonders, what if? I shudder to think what he will do because this child will also suffer this rape for the rest of her life."

Gaeldoreg swallowed hard and cursed under his breath. "He doesn't deserve to live another day."

Outside, Alexa paused to bathe her face in autumn sunshine. The brilliance of the day seemed incongruous with the tragic losses following the Sifiq raid. Alexa reminded herself that Val gave them all different paths to walk. Knowing she might never comprehend the impact some choices would have on innocents, she would always follow her course of service in the hope of easing the suffering inflicted on the helpless.

When Gaeldoreg escorted her into the small structure recently completed for the king to consult with his officers, she saw her husband talking with Braeklojorn and Nikolai. When Gregor looked up, it was clear his anger remained unabated. "Alexa, come. Tell me. How is the girl?"

Going to him, she rested her hand on his arm. "Resting. The Graces have healed her, but she is a small girl. Her internal injuries were severe. She'll never have children of her own, but she should live a normal life otherwise." She paused. "Her mother died. Of a broken heart, I think. The girl has formed an unusual bond with her rescuer, the Protector Eldored. He wishes to adopt the child. I told him I would discuss the matter with you."

"Later," Gregor said. "You will honor your promise?"

His question prompted a sense of dread. "I have always honored my promises, and I always will."

He lifted his hand and stroked her cheek. "I've sent for Sifiq prisoners from the old Qasalaf garrison to witness the sentence alongside some recovering from injuries sustained in yesterday's raid. Since I must set an example they will all understand, I've decided execution is too easy an escape, one they would, in fact, welcome. You must understand."

"Gregor?"

"Beloved, I told you. I would take no extraordinary actions unless I felt I had no other choice. What I plan to do sickens me, but it will deliver the one message these cowardly devils might finally understand."

Lowering her face, she murmured, "I will not question your judgment."

Gregor turned to one of his aides. "Advise Dr. Lorzari to be ready in his surgery in two hours." Everyone in the room exchanged puzzled looks, wondering what the king was planning.

Later, Alexa watched her husband pace in front of the bound Sifiq officer. Too dishonorable even to stand at attention and respectfully face his captor, the Sifiq had snarled insults and spat at Gregor. Earning a black eye and cut lip from the king's fists, the man now knelt on cold, hard ground where Turandan soldiers roughly restrained him.

"So, Captain Fen-Var, I have considered the extent of your hideous behavior."

The Sifiq captain laughed sarcastically. "Come, Your Highness. Females are here for a man's pleasure. I was a man likely about to die. What would you have done?"

"Captain Fen-Var, I do not consider you a man."

Interrupting him and casting a lascivious glance at Alexa, the Sifiq said, "Easy for you. You bring your woman with you. A Sifiq warrior must move fast. He doesn't have such luxuries."

Alexa gently restrained her husband. She gazed down at the audacious officer. Her instincts vibrated. "You are Captain Fen-Var?"

"At your service," he replied with a lewd wink.

"You were married once," she said in a flat voice. "Your wife was Oui-lest?"

Gray eyes narrowed. "How do you know this?"

"I know many things—like the newborn baby whose throat you slit before you threw her body in the river."

Fen-Var spat on the ground. "A useless female child. Oui-lest was beautiful but too delicate to provide suitable male children. I divorced her. So what?"

Alexa's expression was practically a smirk. "Interesting, especially considering she has remarried and just given her new husband a fine son."

"You lie!"

Gregor swung his arm in a wide arc, slamming his hand against the side of Fen-Var's face, knocking him over. "Never speak to my wife that way again!"

Gregor told Alexa, "My decision just became much easier, especially considering everything Oui-lest did for you."

Turning back to where Fen-Var lay sprawled on the ground, the king snarled, "Get up!" Then, when the Sifiq just drunkenly writhed in the dust, he barked orders at his soldiers. "Stand him up!"

Shaking off the effects of Gregor's blow, Fen-Var's arrogance returned. "Protective of your lovely bitch, eh? I'm not worried. Once you execute me, all this pain goes away. I'm ready. Hit me again."

Gregor's laugh was chilling. "I would not give you the satisfaction of an execution. No, Fen-Var, you will live—on my conditions." With a jerk of his head, he instructed the soldiers to follow him with Fen-Var in tow.

Gregor allowed only Nikolai to enter the hospital tent with him while the soldiers held the Sifiq captain outside. They heard Dr. Lorzari shout, "You want me to do *what?*" followed by Gregor bellowing, "If you don't, I'll do it myself, and I'm damned sure I'll be less humane than you will!"

Ten minutes later, a more controlled Gregor reappeared with Nikolai by his side. Alexa stood between Gaeldoreg and Braeklojorn, uncertain what to expect. Finding a sturdy crate to stand on, the king waited as several Protectors appeared, escorting Sifiq prisoners to witness the proceedings.

"I will be as brief as possible. Since our arrival, I've heard multiple accounts of Sifiq soldiers, primarily officers, violating Sifiq regulations regarding the treatment of married and promised women of respectable families. This Sifiq officer in custody is Captain Fen-Var. He was captured in the act of raping a nine-year-old girl who will suffer permanent injury resulting from his sordid behavior. He expresses no remorse and openly attempts to justify actions that, I am told, expressly violate Sifiq law. Such sexual misconduct will not now and never will be tolerated as long as I have breath in my body."

Glaring at the Sifiq prisoner, Gregor said, "Captain Fen-Var, as I told you earlier, I do not consider you a man. To prove my point, a surgeon waits inside. The sentence for your crime is surgical emasculation. That way, no other female will ever again need to worry about being violated by you."

Fen-Var gasped in utter disbelief. "You're out of your mind! You can't do that!"

Staring at him impassively, Gregor answered, "I may very well be out of my mind, but that is your sentence. Let every Sifiq officer and soldier take notice. Prisoners, four of you will witness the surgery. You already know we have treated you humanely and respectfully, but do not cross this line. The violation of women and girls is forbidden and will be so punished."

Stunned Turandan soldiers obeyed orders and dragged their screaming, cursing, and kicking prisoner inside. Eldored, who was off duty, had heard the commotion and appeared. Volunteering to help the others restrain the Sifiq captain so Dr. Lorzari could administer a sedative, the Trezvindjan also stayed to witness the operation.

When the doctor remarked on the drastic nature of the sentence, Eldored stared, asking if he had any daughters. When Lorzari replied he had one, the Trezvindjan said, "I imagine the punishment would not seem so extreme had it been your own little girl torn apart by a grown man seeking a few moments of pleasure. She will pay for the rest of her life. Now? So will he. Fair exchange."

⌁

Alexa leaned back against a post behind a hospital tent. Not quite solitude, she thought, but it was the best she could do under the circumstances. Gregor's sentence to Fen-Var had staggered her. Propping her feet against rising ground, she recalled the sorrowful look in her husband's eyes when he had asked if she would honor her promise. He had already decided on Fen-Var's punishment and fully realized how shocking it would be. Closing her eyes, she tried to clear her mind of the terrible jumble of events that had begun the day before when horns sounded the alarm about the Sifiq raid.

"Mother?"

Raising her head, Alexa blinked several times before her eyes focused in semi-darkness. "Niko," she murmured. "What time is it?"

"Nearly seven. We've been searching everywhere. Father's frantic."

"I'm so sorry. I was trying to meditate. I must have fallen asleep."

"In this cold?" he asked. "I half expected to find you and Rafzan deep in conversation over some passage in the Great Book. I can't find him, either."

"Oh, Niko," she sighed as shadows crossed her face. "This is the first chance I've had to talk to you today. Help me up." Grabbing his hand, she let him haul her up and out from behind the tent. Stretching kinks out of her back, she peered behind the tent. "I almost feel as if I started to put down roots back there."

Chuckling, her son said, "I'm still curious how you wormed your way back there. Anyway, come. We need to go find Father before he turns the whole camp upside down and hangs every one of your guards."

"Desperation for a quiet place to think," she replied, linking her arm with her son's. "Niko, about Rafzan. We lost him in yesterday's raid."

Nikolai abruptly stopped and turned, his face draining of color. "What? I don't believe it!"

"It's true. He helped me up after I fell. He engaged Sifiq warriors until Trezvindjan swordsmen reached Grandfather and me and shielded us. Then, when soldiers brought him to the hospital, I stayed with him until the end."

"Dearest Val," Niko said, hugging his mother close to his side as he turned to escort her to the dining tent. "Poor Anlía. What will she say?"

"You know?"

"My sister shares everything with me."

"She knows. She was with us last night."

"With you? I don't understand."

"Your sister possesses powerful mystical abilities. Rafzan heard her inside his mind, as did I. What was most unusual was that she sang to him at the end. Everyone heard her, even your father. I sang with her. So did he."

"Let me guess. Anlía's favorite song. Soar Free Upon the Breeze?"

Alexa only nodded, then grimaced. "Oh, I hear him."

Hurrying inside the dining tent, she saw Braeklojorn and Gaeldoreg attempting to calm Gregor as he stormed from one side of the tent to the other. "Where can she possibly be?"

"Here, my love! I'm here! I sat down in a corner and fell asleep until Niko found me. I'm so sorry I worried you!" She rushed toward him, side-stepping chairs and people.

"Alexa! Praise Val!" he exclaimed, throwing his arms around her. As he clutched her tightly, his breathing came so fast it made him dizzy. "Dearest Val, I was afraid some Sifiq soldier had abducted you again! Or that you were—nothing matters as long as you're safe."

"I'm so sorry," she repeated, pulling away enough to caress his weary face. "I never expected to fall asleep. Say you forgive me. Please?" She paused. "I know what you're thinking. You must remember what I told you. I love you, and I trust you. I only fell asleep. Gregor, please say you forgive me." Suddenly, she started crying.

Gregor tightened his embrace. How well she understood him. When they couldn't find her, he feared he had gone too far with Fen-Var's sentence. His wife was often too forgiving. Her disappearance gave rise to his greatest dread—the loss of her love and respect.

"Don't cry, beloved. You were tired. That's all. You're safe. There's nothing to forgive." He kissed her hair. He kissed her eyelids, her nose, and her cheeks. Finally, he kissed her trembling lips. "You must be hungry. I know I am. Will you come to eat with Nikolai and me?" he asked tenderly.

Drawing her index finger across his full lower lip, she smiled. "Of course, my love. Of course."

⌒

"You look troubled, Ma Ishna."

Alexa glanced around and smiled. "Grandfather, good morning. I didn't see you at breakfast."

"Kaelzron and I were discussing something. Tell me now. What troubles you? My grandson, perhaps?'

She raised up on tiptoes to kiss his cheek. "Not your grandson. Well, perhaps a little. He heard that someone from Garogan referred to him as Turand's Mad Dark King. It reminded him of something from our past, and he was none too pleased. I promised to ferret out the guilty party later and address the issue."

"I see. Well, if Turand's king isn't your concern, what is?"

"The doctors asked me to check on patients today. Fen-Var hasn't eaten in two days and is showing signs of infection. Gregor is determined to keep him alive as an example to other Sifiq."

"Alexa, before he announced the sentence, I overheard you tell my grandson that you trusted his judgment. I hope that's true. You realize Fen-Var gave Gregor little choice when it came to such extreme punishment, don't you?" Braeklojorn's voice was subdued.

Staring at a bare patch of ground, Alexa considered Gregor's odd behavior in her presence ever since Fen-Var's surgery. His moods changed from gently solicitous to cautiously watchful to shamefully withdrawn. She hadn't been sure what to say or do to reassure him. Finally meeting Braeklojorn's waiting gaze, she replied, "What I understand is this: Two days ago, my husband avoided killing a man while preventing that man from ever harming another little girl like Lis-kal. Grandfather, thank you for helping me finally find the words that might help soothe Gregor's wounded spirit."

Embracing her, Braeklojorn hearkened back to words Anlía had spoken about the love between her parents being legendary. The more he observed their sensitivities to one another and their interactions, the better he understood the foundation that inspired Turand's legend.

Excusing herself, she left to find her husband. Standing at the door of his plain little office and watching him as he highlighted several points on diagrams, she smiled. For the moment, he tended to the business of war. Confident he would concentrate better with their personal issues settled, she held to her resolve. Entering, she excused the interruption and asked to speak with the king.

Gregor's forehead creased with anxiety. Her solemn expression caused his jaw to clench with tension and his heart to beat erratically. Then, catching a deep breath, he took her arm and led her outside. "What is it?"

"Can you spare a few minutes to speak privately in our quarters? I promise I won't take too much of your time."

Her manner was serious, and her eyes, which usually sparkled with such vitality, were dark and grave. Whatever weighed on her mind could not wait. "Of course. Let me advise Nikolai and Kohira."

Minutes later, Alexa drew Gregor down onto their sleeping mat, where she sat cross-legged. Emerald eyes studied features that were drawn and lined following three restless nights. "My husband," she began in a soft voice, "I want you to listen to me very carefully. Hold any questions until after I finish. Agreed?"

He almost rolled his eyes, but her intensity made him think better of it. "Agreed."

"First. Anlía and Captain Lynmar. They had a romantic connection. I didn't tell you because she was afraid for you to know and confided in me inside the temple. My role as Valkana bound me to honor her confidence. As her mother, I told her that you and I had built our marriage on honesty, and if at any time I had even the slightest concern about the relationship, I would go to you immediately. My intuition told me the relationship was never meant to last, although I didn't expect it to end with his death. I can assure you he respected and loved our daughter in a way you would appreciate. He also apologized because he had never expected to find himself in love with her. We can discuss it more another time if that's agreeable."

Staring at her, Gregor had no doubt that Alexa had been vigilant from the outset of their daughter's odd romantic liaison. By adhering to her oaths of service and establishing parameters of parenthood with their daughter, she had also allowed Anlía measured freedoms to make decisions and grow under difficult circumstances.

"My children could have no better mother than you, Alexa. Perhaps we can discuss it further another time." There. Despite wanting to delve into every detail, he let it go.

"Second," she leaned forward and grasped his hands, "Gregor, my beloved husband, listen to me and understand very well what I'm going to say. What happened with Fen-Var weighs heavily on you in different ways. I've been troubled because I had no idea how to ease burdens made worse by your own feelings and doubts. After all the emotional trauma since the Sifiq raid, it took me a while to clarify all that happened.

"What I do know is that you're near exhaustion after the battle and three nights with practically no sleep. We were both terribly worried about Nikolai chasing after fleeing Sifiq. You were stunned by Lynmar's death and the realization that there was more than a casual connection between him and Anlía.

"Then, the matter of Fen-Var presented itself. Gregor, no one knows better than I how painfully difficult that decision had to be for you. I told you I would respect and trust your judgment. I remind you again that is still the case."

Lifting his hands to her mouth, she let her lips linger against his trembling fingers as emerald eyes imprisoned his gaze. "King Gregor, you are responsible for the protection of many people. I want you to consider

Fen-Var's case in this light: When you issued his sentence, you avoided ending a man's life while preventing a future of his defiling an untold number of women and girls the way he did Lis-kal. For that, I love and admire your wisdom and your courage, and I stand by you."

Motionless, Gregor contemplated her words. Finally, his head fell forward, and he felt as if he drew his first full breath since stepping down off that box after announcing the Sifiq officer's sentence. "Alexa," he said, his voice hushed as he grasped her hands and pulled her toward him, "how did you know? Set aside my own inner conflicts. More than anything, I feared losing your respect."

Finding her footing, she slowly stood, helping him up. She put her arms around him and laid her head against his broad chest. "Gregor, I know your heart better than you realize. When I tell you I trust you, always believe me. I am Valkana. I will never lie to you."

"Thank you, Alexa, for a perspective I can live with. Above all else, thank you for your love."

Chapter 18

Gaeldoreg accompanied Alexa when she went with Dr. Lorzari to check Fen-Var. The surgeon complained about the patient's deteriorating condition. Alexa followed the doctor around the partition where Fen-Var was kept under guard. The patient, quiet and pale, lay with his eyes shut.

"Captain Fen-Var, wake up. It's time for breakfast before we check your bandages. Unless you prefer to do it in the opposite order," Dr. Lorzari said.

"Go away," he muttered. "I intend to die in this bed."

Alexa shook her head impatiently. "Captain Fen-Var, like it or not, you will live. Choose your poison. Breakfast first, or have your bandages checked."

Opening his eyes to mere slits, he glared at her. "Go away, woman."

Gaeldoreg growled in a low, threatening voice. "Careful, man, how you address Queen Alexa."

"I'm not a man anymore. Remember?"

Huffing impatiently, Alexa said, "Behaving like a petulant schoolboy won't make matters better. Since it appears bandages are first, I'll call in guards to you tie down so I can inspect your incisions."

"You wouldn't dare."

Within minutes, Royal Guards held the squirming, twisting body while Fen-Var was tied down, and a light sedative took effect. Dr. Lorzari then uncovered the surgical site, cleansed it, and showed Alexa where infection had developed due to Fen-Var's constant efforts to aggravate the wound.

"So you think he's doing it intentionally?" she asked.

"Oh, no doubt."

"And what have you done to stop him?"

Lorzari looked embarrassed. "I asked the other doctors. They suggested securing him, but that seemed…"

"Dr. Lorzari, if you can't manage to tend difficult patients according to the king's commands, then you should return to Turand. You must bear in mind what this man did and how many more women and girls he might have harmed had he not been stopped. Now, if you can continue this patient's care, I'll have the Valiria prepare some poultices containing kirmaya and sirlimian herbs. They will instruct you on their application. When not using the poultices, apply cold compresses to reduce the swelling. For his benefit, keep Fen-Var restrained with his legs apart so he can't continue irritating the wound. Can you do that, or do we change physicians?"

Stung by the queen's tone, Lorzari nodded. "I apologize, Milady. It's so hard."

Her tone gentled. "Doctor, this is easy for none of us. I sincerely understand, but we must deal with the situation he is responsible for creating. Now, as for meals."

"I don't want to eat," Fen-Var mumbled thickly, the sedative wearing off.

"Sir," Alexa said, "want to or not, you will eat. Do it without a fight, and it will be more pleasant than if I have to order guards to force-feed you."

Lifting his head from his pillow, Fen-Var stared at her. "Why? Didn't your husband do enough? Why do you shame me by gloating over the way he mutilated me?"

"Your circumstances give me no joy. There's a little girl in another hospital tent who is recovering from the way you mutilated her. Think about that every time you start whining. You're left with the same choice you gave her: survival. You still look like a man, so act like one. Here's a light breakfast. I will order your hands temporarily released if you agree to sit up and eat. Later, the doctor will treat your incisions."

"You're a heartless woman."

Leaving to escort Alexa to meet with other Valiria, Gaeldoreg scowled at the Sifiq and asked, "How would you know when you have no heart?"

～

On their way for midday, Gaeldoreg and Alexa spun around in response to the announcement of an incoming caravan. Smiling, Gaeldoreg said, "Ma Ishna, the time grows closer to push on to Atuliq and finish this business with Bin-Lot."

"The sooner, the better. I want to take my husband and my son home to be with my other babies."

The big man laughed out loud. "Babies?"

"Even Nikolai is still my baby." She started to smile but turned at the sound of her name. "Oh, dearest Val! I don't believe it."

A string of expletives exploded from Gaeldoreg, prompting Alexa to grab his arm and level a stern look at him. "Say nothing. I'll take care of this."

"Ishna, one word. Just one word. That's all it will take," he said in warning.

"Wait here," she said before heading toward the uniformed figure rapidly striding toward them. "What in Val's name are you doing here?"

Remorse filled the hazel eyes looking back at her. "I knew you'd be upset, but I still expected a better welcome than this. Come, Sweetest, can't you give me some credit for sailing halfway around the world to beg for your forgiveness? Again."

"Victor! Have you lost your mind? You have a small baby at home! How could you leave him and Oui-lest behind?"

"Turand needs every helping hand. I'm not the only man leaving his family behind. Or wives in a family way. Oh, by the way, we have another baby on the way."

"Already?" she exclaimed. "Victor! You have lost your mind!"

"There wasn't much left after you married Gregor." He grinned and started laughing.

The ridiculous expression on his face reminded her of the Victor she had known and loved in her youth. Overtaken by laughter, Alexa was unable to resist when he wrapped her in a snug embrace.

Finally releasing her, he grew serious and said softly, "All I ever do is hurt you, but it's never my intention. I had to apologize. Besides, there was no way I could stay behind in Turand with you and my godson here on danger's doorstep."

She swallowed and forced a smile. "Victor, I appreciate that. In my heart, I do, but Oui-lest and baby Victor need you, too."

"Adrina and Stefan are watching over them. Katara and Willem, too. My coming here is also my way of ensuring these Sifiq devils never have the chance to hurt Oui-lest again. You were also right about that. As usual."

"Ma Ishna, is everything all right?" Gaeldoreg finally interrupted, his voice notably gruff.

Nodding, she smiled and reached for his hand. "Yes, Bibo. You remember Lord Garogan."

Gaeldoreg acknowledged Victor with a sharp tilt of his head. "Lord Garogan. You're a hard man to forget."

Desperately wanting to mend bridges with Alexa, Victor respectfully bowed his head. "Sir. I apologize if I do not know how to address you properly."

"Here, I am a senior commander of the Protectors. You may address me as Commander Vosklon." Gaeldoreg refused to allow the recalcitrant lord any familiarities.

"Commander Vosklon," Victor said graciously, "thank you for keeping to your word and coming to Turand's aid."

Keenly aware that tension still crackled between the two men, Alexa quickly said, "Victor, we were on our way to meet Grandfather for midday. Perhaps you would care to join us."

Appreciating her cheerful rescue, Victor replied, "A wonderful idea. Will Gregor and Nikolai join us?"

"I'm afraid not. Gregor is inspecting a nearby army garrison that was converted to a prison camp. Nikolai is away on a mission."

Concerned by worry drawing lines into her face, he hated that she had returned to this hideous country. Distraction seemed like good medicine. "Well, Sweetest, it looks like you're stuck with a fatigued traveler and your Trezvindjan Protectors for midday. This traveler is also starving."

Attendants placed round loaves of warm bread on the table alongside covered clay pots of hearty soup and roasted meat and vegetables for a substantial meal. Once Alexa prayed grace, she listened attentively as Victor updated the status of arriving vessels to augment the king's forces already on the ground.

"We would have arrived sooner, but there was quite a storm at sea that lasted several days. Our five ships, meaning the Turandan ones, docked first. We brought an additional hundred troops, plus medical and non-perishable food supplies.

"Those ships were setting anchor in the bay to wait for outgoing orders so the Trezvindjan vessels could come in to discharge their troops and cargo." Victor forked a bite of roasted meat into his mouth. "Not bad for field rations. I do admire the wharf management. Excellent organization and execution of procedures."

"Victor, my children. How were they when you left?" Alexa asked anxiously, the food on her plate nearly untouched.

"Ma Ishna, eat," Gaeldoreg told her, his eyes glancing pointedly at her plate.

Like a scolded child, she sheepishly started to eat. "Yes, Bibo. Victor?"

Victor's eyebrows scrunched together curiously, but he replied to her question. "The twins are as vivacious as ever. Those two have completely spoiled baby Victor. Oui-lest suggested you should have another baby so she might have a chance to hold her own."

When Alexa nearly strangled on the bite she had just swallowed, Braeklojorn laughed out loud as he snatched up his napkin to dab her mouth. "Your wife has quite the bright idea there, Lord Garogan."

Casting Braeklojorn an icy glare, Alexa recovered her poise. "Victor, enough of Oui-lest's insanity. And please, tell her not to share her suggestions with Gregor. We know how he feels about babies. Now, my other children?"

Barely controlling snickers, Gaeldoreg reminded Alexa to eat her food. Huffing impatiently, she complied while Victor described ongoing activities keeping DiMarco and Thikos busy in Toraval.

With hazel eyes glittering, Victor smiled at Alexa. "Also, being the excellent godfather I am, I traveled to Tarahlaz to be sure my eldest goddaughter was doing well."

Braeklojorn sat back. "You went to Trezvindja? Why?"

Victor's expression changed. "Prince Braeklojorn, respectfully, I've known Alexa for all but perhaps three months of her life. I assumed responsibility as a godfather for each of her children—a responsibility I've never taken in less than sacred light. I did not know of your country or your people until I met you in Toraval. Please consider it no insult, but I needed to satisfy myself that Anlía was indeed well and safe. I could do that only by seeing and talking to her."

"I see," Braeklojorn replied thoughtfully. "And?"

Meeting Alexa's waiting gaze, Victor sighed. "I can hardly believe how our Anlía has matured. I have put to rest every doubt I had about her being in Trezvindja. She's thriving there. That Grand Councillor—um—Bresklon Krisantal? He watches over her constantly, as do Vezjalan Vosklon and a lady named Milansa. Anlía wins hearts everywhere she goes, but she allows no one to push her against her will or her conscience. Alexa, she is exactly like you always were. She knows her character and has the inner fortitude to live her purpose."

Alexa's eyes glazed. "Anlía helped me survive when I was captive here. She is both joy and mystery."

Victor watched as Gaeldoreg, who had risen from the table, joined Braeklojorn to place comforting arms around Alexa. Their affection was undeniable. Long gone were the days he could freely offer her such solace. Reaching across the table for her hand, he said, "Sweetest, you and your husband have every reason to be proud of her and all your children. As I watch Oui-lest become a fine mother, I can only hope to become such a good father as Gregor to my dear children."

Victor then looked at the Trezvindjans. "Gentlemen, Lord Zephirás called me an ass in your company. In some ways, he was right. I'm known for my temper, but I will never apologize for excessive concern for Alexa or my godchildren. However, I was wrong about you. I offer you both my sincere regrets and my apology. If you'll excuse me."

"It was good for her to hear about her children."

"No doubt reading their letters will cheer us both. I look forward to some quiet time for that." Gregor noted questions in his grandfather's eyes. "I take it something troubles you."

"Perhaps Gaeldoreg is taking this bibo role too seriously. He swears he feels Alexa tense up every time Garogan comes near. I'm sure I don't imagine the tension in you whenever he's around."

Gregor carefully arranged notes and diagrams on the table inside the office. He planned to meet with newly arrived Turandan officers and Trezvindjan commanders to brief them on current intelligence regarding Sifiq troop movements and plans for the final campaign against Atuliq.

"Well?"

"Grandfather, that relationship is far too complicated to discuss tonight. I don't want to leave Alexa waiting too long." Gregor extinguished two oil lanterns, secured the office door, and walked outside into the brisk, clear autumn night. "The sky is beautiful. Who would think it in a place like this? Would you care to join me on my walk through camp?"

Braeklojorn observed his grandson's effective use of nightly rounds to escape a more detailed discussion concerning Victor Garogan. Powerful undercurrents made him wonder what could have happened to make Gregor so reluctant to dredge up memories casting such heavy shadows.

Approaching the heavily guarded area reserved for tents for the king, his family, and top advisers, Braeklojorn saw that a new unit had been erected on the far side. A glance at Gregor revealed fleeting exasperation replaced by mild annoyance.

"Garogan?"

"Garogan."

Braeklojorn stopped, placing his hand on Gregor's forearm. "You no longer need to bear your burdens alone. You now have family. I know Stefan Sidano has stood by you these many years, and I love him for it.

Still, he is not blood. I am, and though I've known you but a short time, I love you most. If ever you feel the need to confide in someone, never hesitate to come to me."

"Grandfather," Gregor replied, "thank you. Believe me when I say it isn't a lack of confidence in you. From the minute we met, I knew I could trust you." He tilted his head toward Alexa, who stood by a campfire, clinging to Gaeldoreg's arm while they and several others chatted with Victor. "When you look there, you don't see what I see. I must go to my wife."

As Gregor lay awaiting slumber, he smiled. How excited she had been as she read aloud her messages from each of their younger children and then prodded him to read his. The letters allowed them to escape their world of canvas tents, bonfires, hitching posts, watering troughs, outdoor latrines, and every other outdoor service. For a little while, they had brought their younger ones close by making gestures that mimicked the typical antics of children left behind in the care of Stefan and Adrina Sidano, both loving godparents to the Toscano brood.

Only one letter had come from Anlía. Addressed to him, it started by telling him that matters of state were contained in a separate letter from the Office of the Council of Leagues. As Council's official head, she had participated in preparing the official report and signed the final document. From that point, she described the story behind her relationship with Captain Lynmar. She apologized for the appearance of deception. She told him she had never lied. She simply had never openly declared the relationship because she needed to explore the true extent of her feelings. She knew she loved Rafzan—the reborn Rafzan—but also knew she needed to seek a love as true and sure as the one between her parents. Then, very slowly, she began to realize that the very love she would need had suddenly appeared right in front of her. She had prayed for guidance because she could not bear to hurt Rafzan, especially with him at war. She had written her father, asking his forgiveness.

Gregor turned over and tucked his arm around his wife. She had known from the very beginning. His lips formed silent words. "My beloved Alexa, how you do amaze me."

⌒

Two days later, a disturbance outside the hospital pavilion caught Alexa's attention. Urgent voices alerted her to incoming injured soldiers. Calling out to priestesses on duty, she hurried to the tent entrance. Nikolai barked orders at men carrying nine litters. When he saw her, he shouted, "Mother! Two Turandans and one Protector! The rest are civilians!"

Quickly assessing the severity of the various injuries, Alexa offered a fleeting, thankful prayer that their soldiers' injuries were serious but not critical. Valiria immediately set about removing field bandages and soiled clothing so they could cleanse and treat wounds. Unfortunately, Sifiq civilians had suffered far more grievous injuries. Summoning physicians, Alexa and her priestesses labored to save the lives of four men and two women.

Gregor came running into the tent, followed by Gaeldoreg, Braeklojorn, and Victor. "Nikolai! Praise Val! You're back! Are you hurt?"

"No, Father. We cleared those three small camps of raiders on the road to Gamaloq. We rode back via the route south of there for additional reconnaissance. A passing Sifiq squad had stopped at a small hamlet. What they couldn't steal, they were burning. I've never witnessed such bloody, vicious brutality. And against their own people!"

Victor shoved past Gaeldoreg and gripped his godson's upper arms. "You, Niko? Are you all right? Are you sure you're all right?"

"Papino! What? Why are you here?"

Gregor firmly took Victor's arm and moved him aside. "Victor, let him finish."

"My son, you obviously engaged."

"We did. Thanks be to Val that none of my men perished, but I have three badly wounded. They're inside. A few Sifiq escaped, but we counted their dead at fifteen. We brought back six injured villagers. Two died before we returned to camp."

"I'm proud of how you executed your mission. Go clean up and rest. We can discuss details afterward."

"I will, Father, after I go inside to check on my men."

Gregor smiled his approval. "Very well. I'll accompany you."

⌣

Gaeldoreg picked up the tall, blue-glazed pot and poured a third steaming mug of kacha.

"You'll never sleep tonight if you keep drinking kacha like that."

"Braeklojorn, did you see him today? You would have thought he was the boy's father instead of our king. The audacity of that man!"

"Calm yourself, Gaeldoreg. Did you not see how well Gregor put him in his place?"

"He should have set him on his famous, hot-tempered…"

"Gaeldoreg! We have enough problems with Lord Garogan's temper. I don't want to risk upsetting Gregor or Alexa more than necessary. My grandson has more than enough resting on his shoulders right now. Tell me. What of these final troop arrivals?"

"The last Trezvindjan warriors are due into camp tomorrow. Do you think Kaelzron's strategic suggestions hold any merit?"

"According to Gregor, he and General Kohira have discussed them thoroughly. It may be the only reasonable value Kaelzron can contribute from his years of playing strategic war games."

Gaeldoreg groaned. "Damn Kaelzron's games! Games are worthless when a man stands against another's steel!"

Braeklojorn smiled thoughtfully. "Therein lies the tragic irony, Cousin. Someone had to imagine where to place those two men for that swordplay. The difference you and I and my grandson must contend with is that Kaelzron's games never drew blood or ended lives. Until now."

⌒

The following day, Alexa walked along the row of cots where new patients were being treated. The Healing Graces had accelerated the healing of the Protector and the two Turandans Nikolai had brought back. Every time she gazed at a recovering Trezvindjan, she gloried in the miracle of Val's reach. Turandans and Trezvindjans were two distinctly different peoples dwelling in the same world. Each had a different language and a different culture, but their faith traditions were powerful and somehow connected. Alexa felt no need to explore the how or why of the connection. There was simple, unadulterated joy in its presence, and she thanked Val for allowing her to partake in it.

The Sifiq villagers, their health already deteriorated by hunger, clung to life. Beneath the dome of Healing Graces, Alexa had pleaded with Val to shed mercy on these humble people of the land. Through Kis-mur and others at Qasalaf, her heart had begun to open again to the sufferings of the good people Oui-lest insisted lived in her nation. Alexa remembered those she had watched beaten and killed during her labors at the Talafaq farm camp.

Hearing that the Turandan occupation force was not unkind, starving farmers and villagers, robbed by Sifiq soldiers, straggled in from miles around to beg for food. Many stayed, offering to work any menial job in exchange for basic necessities for their families. People of the land, Alexa thought, just as she was born of her own land.

Focusing her drifting thoughts, she adjusted the leg of an injured villager. It had slid off the pillow elevating it to reduce swelling. His eyes opened.

"I remember you." His voice was dry and raspy.

She smiled kindly. "I cleaned your wounds yesterday. Would you like some water?" When he nodded, she supported his head and patiently held a cup to his lips while he sipped water. "You have a low fever. I'll have someone check so you can drink more when you feel you can."

"Thank you. I do remember you."

Unusual, she thought, for a Sifiq man to thank a woman for anything. "You are welcome."

"I left work at the palace. What Bin-Lot did to women there made me sick. Not all of us condone such behavior. You were the Turandan priestess. I could do little. I helped Oui-lest Var when she sneaked extra food to you at the prison."

"You helped Oui-lest?"

He nodded. "My leg aches."

"I know. We're doing all we can. What is your name?"

"Dur-Sam."

"Dur-Sam, I am Alexa. Whatever you need, ask for me. I'll leave word that you're under my personal care. I promise to do my best for you and your fellow villagers."

He grasped her hand. "The soldier who led the rescue against our soldiers attacking us. I'm sure he was a Protector. I thought they were myth. He was ferocious, Alexa, and the light around him. Never did I see such a thing!"

Puzzled by the reference to light, Alexa said, "He is Prince Nikolai of Turand and Trezvindja. He is indeed descended from Protectors."

"Mother?" Standing, she smiled as a curious Nikolai placed a large hand behind her waist.

Glancing past her shoulder, Dur-Sam looked stunned. "Your son? That means?"

Alexa straightened blankets and made sure Dur-Sam was as comfortable as possible given the extent of his injuries. "Yes, Dur-Sam. I am Queen of Turand and Trezvindja. Considering your brave help in the past, I'm glad it was my son who came to your aid. I will check on you later."

After leaving instructions to notify her of any changes in Dur-Sam's condition, she went to complete rounds in the second hospital pavilion. Nikolai accompanied her.

"I still can't believe Papino is here. What was he thinking?"

Glancing upward, she observed her son's obvious aggravation. "I wish I could tell you, Niko. Ever since I returned from the Sifiq Kingdom, Victor has gradually become more like he was right after your father and I married—emotional and unpredictable. I can hardly believe he left Oui-lest if she's indeed pregnant again. It makes no sense."

Inside, she listened carefully as doctors reported on patients, mostly Sifiq soldiers. Some were well enough to be transferred to the Qasalaf garrison, freeing valuable hospital resources. Alexa and Nikolai discussed plans for several who remained too ill to leave hospital care.

Finally, they approached their most troublesome patient. Assuming her most daunting expression, Alexa said, "Captain Fen-Var, why are you still in bed?"

In his usual acid tone, the captain replied, "Your Majesty, I find being in this bed a painful ordeal. However, the very idea of standing up and walking terrifies me."

With her patience at an end, Alexa shook her head. "Good. Very good. You can use a little of the terror you've so happily spread around. Get up."

"Excuse me?" Her command held none of the underlying kindness he had tried to manipulate since she began overseeing his care.

"I told you to get up. If you don't, I will personally kick you where it hurts until you do."

"Woman, you wouldn't dare."

"Fen-Var, I grow sick of your pathetic fussing. Get out of bed. Now."

"If I refuse?"

"Nikolai!"

Her son, who had stopped to speak to Dr. Lorzari, hurried over with Lorzari following. "Mother? Do you need help?"

"Indeed I do. Will you help me show the good captain here what one angry Turandan Queen and the Crown Prince of the Protectors can do to an uncooperative Sifiq patient who behaves like an unruly toddler? I want him out of bed and on his feet. Now!"

"Whatever pleases you." Grinning, Nikolai went to the head of Fen-Var's cot, leaned over, and shoved his arms beneath the officer's armpits. Then, heaving the smaller man sideways, he dragged him off the bed as Alexa grabbed the patient's feet and shifted them onto the floor.

Easily holding the man up, Nikolai hissed into his ear, "Either stand on your own, or I let you fall flat on your face. If you fall, I have no doubt Mother will carry through on her threat to kick you where it hurts. From what my father tells me, the first Sifiq officer to suffer a similar fate did so by meeting the heel of her boot."

Fen-Var realized he was helplessly pinned by the taller, much stronger prince. If that weren't enough, the queen standing before him terrified him. Her icy glare was compounded by a sheath of shimmering blue-white light that fully enveloped her body. He shrank backward with no place to go.

"Don't touch me," he said.

"Hush," she commanded, her voice firm and allowing no nonsense. Laying her fingers against his forehead and then his temple, she closed her eyes for several seconds. She glanced around at Dr. Lorzari. "His pulse is only moderately quick, probably due to the unexpected activity. He has no fever." She looked up at her son and stepped aside. "Let him go."

Fen-Var stumbled at the unexpected release before clumsily catching his balance. "Well, Your Majesty, you have your way. I'm out of bed and on my feet. What do you want now? That I should dance? If that's the case, I can't comply. Sifiq officers don't dance."

"She has no need for your sarcasm, Fen-Var. If you persist, we still have surgeons standing by," Nikolai warned. "Father doesn't appreciate anyone who mistreats Mother. You might do well to remember that."

Suppressing a grin at her son's remark, Alexa glared at her patient. "I want you to walk from your bed to that post and back." When he rolled his eyes, she sharply ordered, "Do it!"

Swallowing a curse as he saw Nikolai cock his eyebrows in warning, the captain slowly walked as ordered. Some minor physical discomfort remained, but nothing hindered his ability to walk or move. Instead, his mental state concerned him more. Sheer shock had subsided, replaced by anger and resentment. He feared even those would fade into the more manageable spirit of gelding horses.

"Excellent, Captain," Alexa said. "There's no need for you to continue taking up valuable hospital space here. I think you are well enough for transfer to the Qasalaf prison garrison."

He stumbled to his knees. Her words spawned a wave of terror that had the impact of horse's hooves to the gut. He doubled over as dry heaves racked his body and cold sweat beaded on his forehead. Dr. Lorzari and Nikolai started to help, but Alexa stayed them with a mere glance.

With surprising gentleness, she placed a hand on his shoulder. "Sooner or later, you must return to the world you left. You cannot hide among us forever. You must do something with the life you left."

"What life? I am shamed before man and woman alike. Your husband did this to me, and I must face life with everyone knowing my fate."

"Fen-Var, you did this to yourself. I again remind you that at least one little girl will also pay for your actions for the rest of her life. It is your choice if you make your shame widely known. If you do so, it is more likely you seek pity when you know you'll only be reviled. Feeding your hatred will accomplish nothing. I doubt you've ever been a happy man. My advice is to seek a way to be worthwhile."

"The other prisoners already know who I am. Sifiq law. I'll be worse than an outcast there."

Nikolai gazed at his mother, shaking his head. "Honor among those who don't respect women to begin with." He sighed. "I'll speak to Father."

"Captain, for now, you may stay, but with conditions. You'll be given clean clothing. I expect you to treat those around you respectfully and to cooperate with your physicians. There's no reason you can't help with light chores. The activity will do you good. Remember, this tent and you, especially, are under constant guard. Any misstep will result in your immediate transfer to Qasalaf Prison."

The sudden attack subsided. Fen-Var caught his breath and staggered to his feet. He met her eerie, waiting gaze. "I understand. I will cause no trouble."

Fen-Var felt the invigorating superiority that had always expanded his chest with every breath seep out of his body. He had lived to fight, to draw blood, to revel in the excitement that resulted in his king's rewards. He vaguely recalled the thrill of conquest as he thrust himself on females—the mounting pleasure and explosive releases that fed his hunger for power. He remembered his wife. She had been exquisite, but he had discarded her as useless. Now, he heard she not only had a son but was wed to a wealthy nobleman while he, Fen-Var, courageous Sifiq captain, had been dealt the one blow that broke him. Broken. No more a man, he wondered what direction a eunuch such as he could find in life.

⮑

Despite brilliant sunshine drenching the crushed-grass lanes between rows of tents in the bustling camp, autumn air was yielding to approaching winter. Light breezes nipped cheeks, drawing scarlet blushes as bright as the few leaves clinging to sparse trees around the camp. Brisk air carried aromas from meat smokers and campfires.

Alexa stood before a large blaze, holding gloved hands out to warm them. Gregor stood behind her, his arms wrapped around her waist. "Toraval is colder."

"I know," she agreed, leaning back against his warmth. "It just feels worse here."

Braeklojorn shivered and huddled deeper into his long, heavy cloak. "Ma Ishna, I always wonder how you little people manage the cold so well. I find it terribly disagreeable."

She laughed. "It isn't so terrible with a big fire and someone warm to hold you. Right, my love?"

Grinning mischievously, Gregor tightened his embrace and sought her lips for a quick kiss. Meeting his grandfather's gaze, he said, "She makes a fine point."

"Hmmm," Braeklojorn remarked. "So, is the cold the secret to how the two of you so successfully made so many fine children?"

Laughing out loud, Gregor hugged Alexa. "Only part. A very small part."

Lighthearted banter continued a short while after Victor and Nikolai joined them for a walk to the dining tent for midday. The king's short break would not last. He had left General Kohira and other command officers reviewing plans for the impending offensive.

After offering prayer over their meal, Gregor did his best to maintain a cheerful outlook. He dreaded leaving Alexa in order to lead the assault on Atuliq. His heart ached with fear despite the heavy fortifications and reinforcements now in place to protect her and others staying behind to maintain supply resources and medical services. She reminded him that one hundred fifty heavily armed Protectors, half of the Garogan Guard, and her own Royal Guards would stay to protect the base camp. He needed to let them focus on their base while he focused on Bin-Lot.

"Excuse me?" Gregor's mind had wandered, causing him to miss part of the conversation.

"Grandfather just approved Eldored's adoption of Lis-kal."

Gregor's expression was apologetic. "Grandfather, what prompted your decision?"

Chuckling, Braeklojorn said, "Eldored showed me a letter he just received from his wife. She surprised him with news that she is with child. She also wrote that their agreement was still valid. If he found an orphan he just couldn't leave behind and could lawfully adopt, she still has enough room in her heart and their home to accept that child—but only one more child, not a dozen."

Gregor laughed. "Another woman who drives a hard bargain limiting the size of her family." He snatched up Alexa's hand and kissed it.

"I'm not sure what that means, but I consider the letter to be his wife's written consent to the adoption."

"Alexa?"

Finding it impossible to stay annoyed over his teasing, Alexa grinned. "Lis-kal adores Eldored. She fears her real father should he return. I saw old marks on her mother's body."

Observing Alexa's shrug, Gregor nodded. "Then it's settled. I'll order the adoption decree and sign it tomorrow morning."

"Do you have time to go with me to inform Eldored?" Alexa asked, her face beaming with this bit of light rising from disaster.

Gregor shook his head regretfully as he finished his meal. "I need to get back to Kohira. You advise Eldored. And, Alexa, inform him he won't march on the offensive. He's to stay behind to help defend the cantonment. A warrior protecting his child and his queen should make a doubly fierce Protector." Glancing upward, he said, "Grandfather and Nikolai will be joining me. Gaeldoreg, may I impose on you to escort Alexa to the hospital pavilion to deliver her happy news?"

Grinning broadly, Gaeldoreg rose from his seat and took Alexa's hand. "If you gentlemen will excuse me, Ma Ishna and I have something decidedly pleasant to do in this damnable place, for which I heartily thank you, Your Majesty." He then led Alexa away, leaving Gregor, Nikolai, and Braeklojorn chuckling while Victor broodingly stared after them.

Lost in thought after completing rounds, Alexa exited the hospital tent housing two remaining Sifiq patients and Fen-Var. With the ever-present Captain Lisandá and guards behind her, she started toward the center of camp, running straight into Victor.

"Sweetest," he said gently but accusingly, "you've been avoiding me ever since I arrived."

"Victor," she said, startled by his unexpected appearance, "I have a lot on my mind, plus I've been caring for patients. Time gets away from me."

"Time never got away from you in the past."

"How many times in the past was I working near battlefields?" she countered, hoping to deflect his obvious displeasure.

Sighing, he said, "True. May I walk with you?"

Regretting that Gregor had summoned Gaeldoreg, she somehow felt trapped. "Of course."

"How did things go with your adoption announcement?" Victor asked, walking beside her with his hands clasped behind his back.

Relaxing some, she smiled. "Beautifully. The girl cried, knowing she could finally call Eldored *Bibo*. I think all of us watching also cried. She has suffered so much."

"Is it true a Sifiq officer raped her?"

Alexa paused. He must have been asking questions. "Yes. Eldored saved her and rode in like a madman to get medical treatment."

"The behavior of Sifiq men exceeds my comprehension. Wait. You mentioned her calling him *Bibo*. Isn't that what you call your famous Commander Vosklon?"

Glad to redirect the topic, Alexa softly laughed. "It is. In Trezvindjan, it means Papa. Gaeldoreg and I have developed a father-daughter relationship that's a little hard to describe."

"Sweetest, you had a father, one who loved you very much," Victor said reproachfully.

"I know that. I also have no doubt that my father's spirit approves. Gaeldoreg and I share a blood bond that we both consider sacred. I don't know quite how to explain, and I certainly don't intend to argue with you about it." Alexa tamped down rising impatience.

Victor forced a smile. "It wasn't my intent to start an argument or reprimand you. I don't know what this blood bond thing is, but I do worry about this strange connection you seem to have with these Trezvindjans. It feels unnatural to me."

"You seem to forget. I've been married to Gregor for over twenty years. His mother may have been born in Turand, but she was Trezvindjan. He's part of them. They're part of my children. How can you expect me not to be connected to them?"

Interrupting them, Captain Lisandá handed Alexa a button from her jacket. "Fen-Var found it. He recognized it from your coat and sent an orderly out with it."

Thanking him and mentally noting to thank Fen-Var for returning the lost item, she started walking again. "Now, I hope that puts to rest your concerns about the Trezvindjans. As you see, they proved your concerns in Toraval to be unfounded."

Victor abruptly stopped. "Wait. Did I just hear Lisandá correctly?"

Alexa's heart thudded, and she kept walking. "Victor, I need to get something hot to drink. Let's go."

Reaching out, he grabbed her arm, jerking her to a halt. "You can wait long enough to answer my question. Lisandá just said Fen-Var sent you that button. Fen-Var was Oui-lest's husband's name. In Val's great name, Alexa, don't tell me you've been nursing that reprobate after everything he did to Oui-lest."

"Victor, stop now."

His face started to redden. "Tell me, Alexa. Have you been taking care of that piece of…?"

"Victor! Stop! I do what I must as Valkana and as Queen. Now, release me," she hissed furiously.

"Not until you answer me. Is that Oui-lest's ex-husband, and have you been taking care of him?"

"Victor Garogan, I have been tending a prisoner to meet specific goals determined by your king and mine. Those reasons make perfectly good sense, and if you were less argumentative and more rational, I would explain them. Let me go now."

His bow-shaped mouth that earlier smiled at her sweetly now curled into an ugly snarl. "I don't want your damned explanations." He released her arm. "I'm going back, and I'm going to tear that piece of vermin into a thousand pieces!"

Stunned for only seconds, she watched him turn and break into a dead run. "Captain!" she shouted. "Stop him! Guards! After him! Stop him before he reaches Fen-Var!"

Chasing after them, she was grateful for the long-legged Trezvindjans who had joined her Royal Guard. Swiftly overtaking Victor, they seized and held him until she reached them. Alexa glared furiously at Victor until she caught her breath. Then, livid, she hissed between clenched teeth, "If you ever do something like that again, I will order you put in chains. Do you understand me, Victor Garogan?"

"I want to know what's wrong with you, Alexa! How could you possibly demean yourself to care for a man like that? If you can even call him a man!" Victor retorted bitterly.

"Maybe if you hadn't marched into this camp inside some black cloud, spoiling for trouble, Victor Garogan, you might be willing to give people the chance to talk or explain circumstances instead of blindly hurling innuendos and accusations!" Alexa's patience teetered on a dangerous precipice.

"Then explain to me in terms I can understand! That man doesn't deserve to live! He murdered Oui-lest's baby right in front of her!" Angry tears scorched Victor's face.

Alexa's voice grew uncharacteristically loud. "You think I don't know that? Gregor decreed he should live, and I agree with my husband! Alive, Fen-Var is an example to every Sifiq degenerate around to think twice before abusing another woman or girl. You heard us talking. That little girl was violated!"

"And I assume Fen-Var is guilty!" Victor interrupted, spitting on the ground. "All the more reason to kill him. He's not worthy of being called a man!"

"Oh, Gregor agrees with you on that point, and he felt that was the best reason for keeping him alive! That was also his reason for ordering him castrated—to serve as an example of what would happen to every other Sifiq man guilty of rape!"

"Alexa?" Her husband's strong arm grasped her shoulders, but she wrenched free. "Do you have any other questions regarding the Sifiq for me, Victor?" she demanded, visibly incensed. "Well?"

In a mood bristling for confrontation, Victor tossed his head in absolute disdain. "As a matter of fact, yes! I've been all around this camp since I arrived. I've noticed one person curiously missing—your precious convert, Captain Rafzan Lynmar. What happened to him? I imagine he proved me right by meeting my expectations. What did he do? Take advantage of coming home to desert and rush back into the service of his high and mighty King Bin-Lot?"

Without warning, Alexa emitted a shrill, unintelligible, animal-like cry just before she struck Victor full in the face with her open hand before crumpling into a heap on the ground at her husband's feet. Swiftly kneeling, Gregor realized he couldn't rouse her. Gathering her into his arms and close to his chest, he gratefully accepted his grandfather's help standing.

Enraged, Gregor glowered at Victor, now forcefully restrained by Nikolai and Gaeldoreg. "I will deal with you later, Lord Garogan. Nikolai, do something with him. I don't give a damn what. Just get him out of sight where he cannot upset your mother again."

Back inside their quarters, Gregor removed Alexa's coat and boots with Braeklojorn's help before settling her on the low bed. Covering her, Gregor then lifted her hands to his lips. "Alexa? Beloved, wake up. Alexa! Wake up!"

"Here. For her face." Braeklojorn placed a damp cloth in his grandson's hand.

Gently wiping tear stains from her cheeks, Gregor shoved his fury deep for the time being. That could wait until he knew she was all right. "Grandfather, I'm afraid. I've never seen or heard her so angry. Never. I'm really afraid." His voice cracked on those last words.

Braeklojorn gripped his shoulder reassuringly. "She'll be fine, Gregor. Talk to her. Let her hear you—your voice. She'll come around."

"You're right. I will. Please. Go check on Nikolai."

Braeklojorn gave Gregor a parting, reassuring squeeze on the shoulder. Turning to leave, he stopped and smiled. Deeply anxious, his grandson still managed to convey a precious gift.

"Grandfather, never have I been happier to have you in my life than now."

Lying next to his wife, Gregor stroked Alexa's hair. He lightly kissed her lips. Praying aloud, he begged Val to awaken her from the peculiar blackout. His words transitioned as he pleaded, "Beloved, wake up. Come back to me. Please wake up. I need you back with me. Alexa?"

Tears began to gather at the corners of her eyes, forming rivulets along her delicately sculpted nose. He wiped them away with gentle fingers. "There you are. You hear me, my love. Keep coming. I'm waiting."

Suddenly, a huge burst of sobs racked her body. Crying so hard she shook all over, she curled into his embrace, and he held her tightly. "Gregor," she continued sobbing, "how could he do this? He's done nothing lately except cause trouble. I don't understand. I just don't!"

"Shush, my love, I know. It will be all right," he consoled.

"It can't be all right!" she cried. "I struck him! Do you know how many times in my lifetime I've hit someone in anger?"

"None that I know of."

"Twice, Gregor. Two times! Gor-Dan in self-defense and you by accident! That's it. Until today. I meant to strike him with everything I had in me. Val forgive me, but I meant to hit him and hurt him when I did it!"

"Alexa, shush," he whispered, kissing her forehead. "Val will forgive you. Victor was taunting you. He was pushing you." He kissed her nose. "When did you hit me by mistake?" he asked, trying to divert her attention.

"It doesn't matter," she replied, hiccuping on fresh sobs.

"Yes, it does. I shall go crazy trying to remember if you don't tell me," he soothed.

She hiccuped again. "Years ago. After we first married. When I crumpled up that letter Victor wrote to me. I meant to throw it past you. I was so upset I missed and hit your face. Remember?"

Gregor rolled his eyes. "That led to a night I prefer to forget. Don't remind me." At last, she smiled. Almost. "Alexa, you may be High Priestess Valkana, but I expect Val knows even you have your limits. Victor has been pushing yours for months."

"Gregor, I'm so ashamed," she whimpered.

"No, you're exhausted. I want you to spend the rest of the day here to rest. I'll bring supper later. No arguments, either."

Fresh tears tracked along her cheeks. "No arguments. Victor?"

He shook his head. "Honestly? I have no idea what I'm going to do about Victor. I will not, however, put up with his continued disruptions. I most assuredly will not tolerate him upsetting you this way. Gaeldoreg would have both our heads, his for troubling you and mine for letting him get away with it."

There was that half-smile again. She was slowly returning to him. "My bibo."

He got up, wet the washcloth, and wiped her face again. "Alexa, you should not have come, but see what happened? I rely too much on you. Rest. Please?"

Within minutes, she calmed her mind and spirit and drifted asleep. After praying Val's protection over her, Gregor started to get up but paused. Firmly grasping the heavy chain around his neck, he withdrew the crystal pyramid he had worn constantly since Alexa gave it to him on his way to war. Reverently closing his eyes and kissing the precious symbol of their faith, he whispered, "Mother, I apologize if I disturb your spirit, but Alexa says you watch over us. I miss you, Mother. So much. Your father is here with me. Did you know? A real miracle. For now, since you are Valiria, will you watch over my wife until I come back inside? I won't be long. Her spirit aches, and I need to strengthen mine for all that lies ahead. I love you, Mother. I always have and always will." He then carefully tucked his mother's pendant under the edge of his pillow next to his sleeping wife.

⌐

Instinct had warned Captain Lisandá that the confrontation between Alexa and Lord Garogan was rapidly escalating. He sent a guard to summon the prince, who arrived with his father and great-grandfather at his heels. Gaeldoreg followed close behind. Thoroughly disgusted by what he overheard, Nikolai now paced back and forth in front of his godfather.

"How dare you? How dare you talk to my mother that way?"

"Niko, listen to me! Something is seriously wrong with your mother! Remember! I've known her all her life!" Victor started to rise from the canvas floor of his tent, but Gaeldoreg viciously shoved him back down. "Take your hands off me!"

"Prince Nikolai told you to sit down. You either sit down, or I sit down on top of you," Gaeldoreg growled ferociously.

"Nothing is wrong with Mother except in your imagination. You once sided with her on avoiding executions. Fen-Var's punishment keeps him alive while preventing him from ever violating another woman. An extreme sentence and an effective signal to every other Sifiq now and in the future. Under any circumstances, you had no right to challenge Mother about my father's decisions regarding sentences handed down to Sifiq prisoners. Am I clear?"

"Very. No one seems too keen to answer my question about your father's fine Royal Adviser on Military Affairs. I assume I'm right about him being a fine Royal deserter." Victor ground out sarcastically.

"You bloody fool!" Nikolai barely stopped himself from backhanding his godfather. "You seem to forget Rafzan ran through a wall of fire to rescue my sister and carry her from a burning building!"

"I forgot nothing!" Victor shouted, twisting against Gaeldoreg's fingers digging painfully into his shoulders. "He was just trying to ingratiate himself with Alexa, and a fine job he did! I never thought you could be so easily fooled."

Barely controlling his temper, Nikolai lowered his voice. "A fool who is forever grateful for the Sifiq convert who dragged his prince up on a horse and held onto him for dear life while racing miles back to this base camp after the prince's chest was pierced by a Sifiq arrow. Rafzan held me on that horse while my mother came to me in spirit with the Healing Graces to keep me alive."

Seeing Victor's eyes grow wide with disbelief, Nikolai continued, "That's right. If not for Rafzan's absolute determination to keep me from falling off that horse and get me back here for additional help from the Valiria, I would have been dead weeks ago. I owe my life to him and my mother."

Gaeldoreg dug his fingers deeper into Victor's shoulders. "The boy speaks the truth. I was with Ma Ishna in Tarahlaz when it happened. She was so drained by the effort that I had to carry her to bed. And you, you shameful excuse for a friend and godfather, want to cast aspersions on that man who saved Nikolai?"

"Papino, here's the worst part," Nikolai continued, his voice trembling and his dark eyes glazing over. "I always believed you to be a fair man, willing to listen first before judging any man. Yes, Rafzan committed a terrible act. Of all people, though, you should know Mother well enough to trust her judgment. Just before you arrived, Father and I took her to bury Rafzan Lynmar. No, he's not a deserter. He died fighting off Sifiq raiders while defending Mother and Grandfather until they got to safety."

Victor stared at his godson. "Niko, that can't be true!"

"Papino! In Val's great name! What reason do I have to lie? If Father ever lets you near Mother again, which I doubt, ask her yourself! It may be easier to ask the others here. They all know what happened."

"Niko, I wanted to protect her! I was afraid! I couldn't understand how she could forgive him after the way he hurt her!"

Unable to stop himself, Nikolai blurted out, "You couldn't understand *what*? She forgave you despite all the times you hurt her—even after you almost killed her! And you were supposed to love her! He was at least the damned enemy!"

His godson's words pierced his soul like the honed point of a spear. "Niko, you know? I—I don't know what to say. I'm so sorry. Let me up. I need to fix this."

Nikolai huffed several infuriated breaths. "*Fix it?* From what I understand, you've been saying sorry a lot lately. Then you turn around and stir up new, bigger pots of trouble. No, Papino, goading Mother the way you did today exceeded limits even I'm willing to tolerate. You're confined to quarters. If you dare step outside, I'll have stakes driven into the ground, and you'll be chained to them. And just to be sure you know I mean what I say, guards will be posted all around."

"Niko, there's no need." Victor sounded defeated, his voice conciliatory.

"Someone will bring meals later. Orderlies will attend your brazier and chamber pot. I warn you. Make no more trouble than you already have. That is not a request." With that, Nikolai turned and stormed out of his godfather's quarters. After giving Victor a final, violent shove to the ground, Gaeldoreg followed.

〜

Worried, Braeklojorn waited outside Gregor's quarters. Finally appearing, Gregor rapidly strode off in the direction of a sparse stand of trees. Following, the prince watched his grandson back up against a tree and then sink downward. Gregor wrapped his arms around his shins, tucking his head down on his knees. Braeklojorn's heart lurched inside his chest at the forlorn image. For several moments, he debated disturbing his grandson's solace, but he then remembered his own sense of desolation after losing Mishkla. This, of course, wasn't the same, but he remembered how much he had needed an understanding ear.

Going to Gregor, he stopped a few feet away. "Is she all right?"

"She will be. You were right. She's strong. I left her sleeping." He never looked up.

"Gregor, you've been carrying a dreadful burden for far too many years. I started sensing it right after I met Alexa. I now realize it involves this Lord Garogan. What happened between the two of you?"

Gregor only rolled his head slightly from side to side and quietly groaned.

Braeklojorn approached and ran his fingers through his grandson's hair. "You're my flesh and blood, Gregor, and I love you. Until now, you've had no one but Alexa and friends to help you manage your burdens. Let your grandfather help."

"I don't want to lose your respect."

"I doubt that will happen."

"You might change your mind."

"You could tell me so I might decide for myself."

Without looking up, Gregor rolled his head again. "In some ways, I don't blame Garogan for hating me, although he started everything when he planned to assassinate my advisers and me."

"He did what?" Braeklojorn asked in disbelief.

"That's how this all began. Stefan uncovered his assassination plot, and Victor was sentenced to execution. It happened a year or so before we ended the Sifiq occupation. Enter his bold, brave fiancée—Turand's only surviving Valiria priestess—who walked into my court full of Sifiq officers and demanded private council to plead for Garogan's life."

"Alexa?" his grandfather asked, dumbfounded.

"Alexa," Gregor confirmed. "I was lost the second I looked into those emerald eyes of hers. Telling myself she would never be safe outside the palace and my protection, I finagled circumstances until her only choice to secure his safe return to Garogan Province was to marry me." He straightened his back and stood. Finally facing his grandfather, he said, "Her decision is obvious."

Stunned, Braeklojorn gazed into his grandson's tormented eyes. "Come. Walk with me. This story is not as simple as a broken engagement and a forced marriage. Explain what happened."

Encouraged that his grandfather had not instantly rejected him, Gregor unraveled the events surrounding Alexa's announcement to Victor Garogan that she and Gregor would marry. He related the difficulties she had faced adapting to palace life with Sifiq soldiers constantly around. In the beginning, he had not known her parents were slain in the Zinzan massacre. He had also felt helpless when it came to making her understand his remorse for forcing her into marriage.

Tension was high with secret plans progressing for the revolt against the Sifiq. He often found himself near a breaking point when he felt it necessary to suppress his growing love for Alexa. Then Gregor began noticing changes in her behavior. Subtle at first, he wondered if it was only imagination that she was showing signs of affection.

Braeklojorn listened attentively, only interrupting to clarify when he was unsure of a particular point or prompting Gregor to resume his narrative when his grandson drifted off into memories.

When Gregor described Alexa's forced return to Garogan, his grandfather saw how those memories still disturbed his grandson. First, Gregor had feared losing her to his rival. Then Alexa had then nearly died at Victor's hands. As Gregor's account finally covered the National Council, events of the civil war, and culminated in Nikolai's birth, Braeklojorn felt he finally comprehended the energy infusing his grandson's relationship with Alexa. He also better grasped Lord Garogan's fiery emotions.

"One thing I can say, Gregor. How you have not murdered Garogan with your bare hands is a testament to your personal fortitude."

"I attribute it to faith and Alexa's influence."

"I also tell you this. You must stop berating yourself for the way your marriage began. As I watch the two of you, Espiritus intended for the two of you to be bonded. Accept that, once and for all, and you will find greater peace for your soul than you have ever known. She is matched to you as you are matched to her. I wish you could have heard her when she spoke of you in Trezvindja. In fact, some of her first words to me about you were that you are her heart and her soul. This is what she tells strangers. Let that be something you take away from our confidence today.

"Beyond that, you haven't lost my respect. When you met Alexa, you faced dangerous, complex times with little experience, guidance, or support. You acted based on the dictates of circumstance and likely unrecognized intuition. Yet, you persevered and triumphed over your enemies. Beyond that, you gained a love few in our world have ever commanded. For that, I hold you in high esteem."

Gregor met Braeklojorn's penetrating gaze. Drawing in a deep breath, he embraced him and whispered, "I have missed my father and mother more than I can express in words. Especially now, having you enter my life with your wisdom and perspective means more than you will ever know. Thank you, Grandfather. With all my heart, I thank you."

⌒

Awaking early, Gregor felt refreshed. Such a rare treat, he thought, to awaken with her still snuggled next to him. Sharing his burden of guilt and secret fears with his grandfather had unlocked the last private prison he had built within himself. He felt completely free to enjoy the beautiful wife beside him and the family they had created. His optimism burgeoned. He would finish this war and go home to hold his other children. He would then visit his new nation and his sweet Anlía. Life would be good.

"Gregor?" she murmured, stirring beneath the pile of heavy covers.

"Good morning, beloved," he answered, turning to draw her tightly against him. Kissing her forehead, he felt the frisson of instant desire chase down his spine. His renewed spirit affected his total being. A low, satisfied sigh sounded in his throat as she responded to his body's initial urgings.

Mere seconds passed before they strained against one another. Their need to share touch and pleasure had never lost its power to overtake them. His marauding lips claimed hers and then explored the sensitive expanse of her neck and shoulder while her hands pushed beneath the fabric of his nightshirt to wreak sensual havoc along his back, sides, and hips. When he finally claimed her, their sudden union drew muted cries from each. Surrendering to her pleas, he quickly intensified the pace of his loving until they were both flooded by the throbbing, rapturous sensations that represented their most exclusive gift to one another.

⌒

Letting heavy tent flaps drop, Gregor stood silently before a glum Victor Garogan. "Food is too precious to waste, Lord Garogan. Many in this land are starving," he said, noting the untouched trays holding Victor's supper and breakfast.

Wary of his rival's odd expression, Victor mulishly picked up a stale piece of bread from the night before and bit into it. "Excuse me, Your Majesty. I've had little appetite." He pointed at a chair. "Sit down if you like." He was surprised when Gregor did.

Impatiently sighing several times, Gregor glanced around the relatively comfortable fittings of Garogan's quarters and finally said, "Lord Garogan, we have serious matters to resolve. I won't patronize you by saying I know how you feel. I can scarcely imagine how I'd feel in your place. To be honest, I doubt I would have managed my misery half as well as you."

Victor tilted his head in acknowledgment but only continued nibbling at cold food as he listened to Gregor.

"Yesterday, part of me wanted to pound you to a pulp, especially when Alexa awoke and sobbed about how she had never deliberately struck anyone in anger except a Sifiq soldier in self-defense." He stood and turned around, unable to look at Victor.

"However, I remind myself that, no matter what, in some ways, Alexa will always love you. I'm also forever indebted to you. You saved her first at Zinzan, then on the road to Garogan City." Gregor halted before continuing, "Then in Timeri. For Timeri alone, I cannot begin to thank you."

Victor forced a bite down. "You owe me nothing for Timeri. I went there for her. And my godchildren. And for me."

Gregor turned. "I don't care what your reasons were. I'm telling you mine. Victor, I will never apologize for marrying Alexa. Never. Do I wish circumstances had been different? Being honest again, I won't say yes, although I do regret the grief you suffered.

"What matters right now is the present. When you saved her at Timeri, I made a conscious choice to leave behind the one image that haunted me for years—the image of her with your arrow protruding from her back. I hated you for that, especially when I turned her over and saw her face bruised from a brutal beating. When you found her at Timeri,

I forgave you as fully redeemed. You had given her back to her children, Turand, and me. I would never hate you again."

Victor squeezed his eyes shut. "Anderon is the one who beat her. I wasn't home when that happened. I never would have allowed it."

"I didn't know that at the time, but I doubt it would have mattered. It never would have happened had she been home in Toraval. That's over. Going forward, Victor, what will you do? Will you continue with this recent insolence of yours? If so, pack up and return to Turand. You could offer valuable experience and knowledge, but it isn't worth her peace of mind."

Victor finally stood. "Why? Why do you even offer me the option?"

"You've been a thorn in my side since I married Alexa. Last night, I removed that thorn. You've been an exceptional godfather. My children love you, although Nikolai sees you in much different light today. You've also been an excellent leader throughout Turand's recovery. You now have a lovely wife and a family of your own. Cherish them, Victor, instead of dwelling on a past you can never recover."

"Does it make you mad knowing I still love her?"

"Do you really think I don't know that?"

"Will she let me apologize?" Victor asked, wondering how he would face her again.

"For now, stay away from her. You know Alexa as well as I. Let her signal you when she's ready. Right now, her spirit is wounded. Let her be."

"Very well. I'll avoid her, but I want to stay. As you said, I can contribute to this final stage of your offensive. We must end Bin-Lot's threat against Turand. Once and for all."

"Agreed. Your confinement is ended as long as you leave my wife alone."

Chapter 19

"Forward positions are advancing steadily now that Commander Drozfan's regiment neutralized the Sifiq outpost guarding access to the main road," Nikolai reported.

Kohira nodded. "Reinforcements would have converted that outpost into a bloody stronghold."

Gregor agreed. "Nikolai, we can thank analysis from your new friend Bor-Tan for helping determine where those reinforcements were heading."

Victor swept his index finger across a section on the map. "This area still worries me. I rode out two days ago with Commander Krisantal—one of them, anyway. It doesn't look like much from a distance, but I recall how the Sifiq infiltrators we had in the rebel army advocated using just such areas to hide troops for surprise attacks."

"What are you suggesting?" Gregor asked.

"Just that we not let down our guard because these areas look clear. I see at least four potential routes that could be used to launch assault raids."

Kohira studied the map. "Do you think it would be that easy?"

"Not necessarily easy, but the Sifiq know this territory far better than we do. They're cunning warriors. Don't discount the possibility," Victor said.

Gregor's expression darkened. "Lord Garogan's experience comes from firsthand knowledge of their strategies. Gentlemen, in two days, our main army marches against Atuliq. Let's make sure we leave behind a secure camp while protecting our flank against surprise attacks off that ridge."

After supper that evening, Gaeldoreg and Braeklojorn joined Gregor for his nightly walk through the camp. Since the king had only started learning words in the Trezvindjan language, his family's presence as translators was critical whenever he toured areas reserved for Protector troops. Many warriors spoke little of what they called the common language. Still, all welcomed and admired their new king's demonstrations of respect for those sworn to serve their nation. To a man, they appreciated the differences between their Turandan-born king and Kaelzron.

Gregor made it a point to stop and speak to soldiers here and there. Having already asked counsel from Gaeldoreg as to what might be too intrusive, he learned little was off the table. Among themselves, Trezvindjans were a jolly lot. As their leader, Gregor wanted to establish rapport without sacrificing clear command. With his grandfather and cousin guiding him in culture and tradition, he held his own with the Protectors in camp, little realizing that new arrivals had already heard tales of his battle prowess from those who had witnessed him fighting Sifiq raiders. Braeklojorn's eyes glinted with pride as he often heard comments in passing that they once again had a true Protector King.

↜

"It's cold outside," Alexa warned her husband as she tugged the thin, warm vest into place so he could put on his heavy uniform coat. "Winter is knocking on the door. I hope your trip to Atuliq goes quickly."

"As do I," he replied. "Let's hope all this intelligence about limited food supplies is accurate. It should make siege easier and faster since we've kept our supply lines open."

Alexa's sigh was sad. "I hate thinking of the ordinary people. They always suffer most. Bin-Lot and his soldiers don't care one whit about anyone but themselves."

Gregor kissed her forehead. "True, but Bin-Lot can't keep going without people to run basic services while feeding him and his soldiers. He slits his own throat when he shuts down his people's ability to support his war effort."

"True. That's why you run this war."

"And, unfortunately, why you clean up so much of the mess I'm forced to leave in its wake."

Lifting her arms around his neck, she smiled into the obsidian eyes regarding her with a mix of sadness and adoration. "I love you today more than ever, King Gregor Maxim—Vosklon Krisantal—of the House of Toscano."

He smiled and kissed her. "Brilliant woman I married to remember all that. Now. Breakfast?"

After breakfast, Alexa inspected the hospital pavilion. Priestesses were taking advantage of the time to study or meditate. Kiralí, along with Bor-Tan, had recently departed on a caravan carrying injured Turandans home. Sulía, quickly recovering with proper food and rest, had stayed behind to continue working in the hospital. With all in order, Alexa decided a walk might calm burgeoning nervous energy.

Organized chaos had overtaken the camp. Wagons, carts, and cannons formed rows according to their placement in tomorrow's departure schedule. Last-minute inspections continued in earnest to ensure all wheels and parts were secure and in good working condition. Supplies that had been checked multiple times were being rechecked.

Sighing heavily, Alexa turned and headed toward the center of camp. Near an almost deserted firepot, a lone figure huddled close to low flames. Gathering her cloak and her resolve close, she approached. "Is there room for one more to warm her hands here?"

Glancing upward, light brown eyes registered surprise and relief. "For you? Always." Noticing her uneasy smile as he moved for her to get closer to the fire, Victor lamented his role in the distance once again dividing them.

"That feels good," she said, holding gloved hands over the open fire. "I don't envy our men marching in this weather to Atuliq."

"They'll be marching in close formation. Between body heat and physical activity, they won't notice the cold much. Not until nighttime, anyway."

"Brrrr," she said, giving an exaggerated shiver. "It took me forever to get used to winter cold in Toraval." Then, growing suddenly solemn, she cast her eyes directly at Victor. "We can't go on like this. *I* can't go on like this. Victor, you have meant so much to me over the years, but whenever you lose yourself in the past, the explosions torture me."

Victor wanted to look away, but those emerald eyes refused to release him. "I know, Sweetest. I know. I don't understand what happened this time."

"I do, ever since you admitted at Stefan's how bitterly you still resent Gregor. Unfortunately, only you can fix that. I also know that I can't continue facing your bitterness, nor can I expose my children to it. You've been a beloved godfather to them. I don't want them to lose respect for you. I'm also fighting to keep you from destroying the last vestige of a love that once meant everything to me."

Staring at cloudless blue skies, Victor fought rising emotion. Fumbling for words, he finally mustered breath to say, "I thought there was nothing left of that."

"A love that powerful rarely dies," she said. "I know where it resides, but you're killing it. Perhaps that's best, although I think about what you said when you mentioned each time a person loves, it's different. I don't say this to hurt you, but Gregor is my greatest love. Our love is simply my truth. You must make your peace with that, especially now that you have Oui-lest and children."

He picked up a piece of wood and shoved it into the fire. "When I'm with her, she makes this all go away. I do love her, you know. Not the way I've always loved you, but I love her. I miss her."

"Then go home to her. You have a new baby on the way. You don't need to be here in danger's path. She needs you."

"Alexa, Turand is my country, too. I told you this before, and I meant it. I have a sworn responsibility to protect Turand and Garogan Province—and most assuredly, to keep my wife and babies safe from these Sifiq devils."

"We have support now. You can still help by keeping things organized from Turand. You're masterful at that. Think about it. Gregor doesn't leave until tomorrow. There's time to change your mind. He would never think less of you."

"His Trezvindjan family would. They don't like me one bit."

"No, they don't. With time, though, I can work miracles," she said with a grin.

Try as he might, he couldn't stifle a laugh. "Gregor's right. You are impossible."

"Well?"

"I'll think about it. I miss my boy. And Oui-lest. I wrote her a long, lonely letter last night before I packed up my things."

"Well, I'm heading in for some Trezvindjan kacha to warm my bones. You?"

"For a while. I promised to meet Niko and Kohira. Niko still talks strategy with me."

Alexa gave him a brief hug. "He'll come around. You'll see."

"I hope. I love him more than you know."

Victor had just left her inside the dining tent when alarm bells sounded. Heeding his godfather's warning, Nikolai had sent a unit up the ridge that flushed out Sifiq soldiers in hiding. However, there were more enemy soldiers than expected, and their escape routes were planned well. With the prince's men in swift pursuit, many Sifiq raced directly toward the fortified encampment.

Quickly drawing his sword, Victor rushed back inside the dining tent and grabbed Alexa. "Sweetest! Hurry! Let's go!" Guiding her outside, he handed her off to Captain Lisandá, shouting, "Get your queen to safety! Go, man!"

"Victor! Be careful!" she called out as Lisandá and the guards with him hustled her toward the heavily guarded hospital pavilions.

He paused long enough to give her a hasty, reassuring smile before turning to run toward the initial uproar indicating fighting had already commenced.

With Captain Lisandá's arm firmly at her waist, Alexa started running toward the hospital tents. Her mind was already clicking off practiced procedures when a voice calling her caused her to resist her captain's attempt to move forward. "Stop!" she demanded.

"Majesty! You must get to safety! Now!"

Alexa frantically shifted her gaze and spied a smithy's work booth. She yanked herself free of Lisandá's grasp and ran to the stall where she could be out of sight long enough to catch her breath.

"Your Majesty!" The captain was nearly panicked as he ran to her but grew immediately silent as she threw up her hand. He watched as blue-white light enveloped her body.

"Mother? Do you hear me?"

"Anlía! Yes!"

"I'm here with Bresklon. Is there an attack?"

"Yes, love!" Alexa's heart pounded so hard she felt it might leap from her breast.

"You must be careful, Mother, but we feel you'll be needed. Urgently! We'll help if we can."

"Anlía, all right."

"Do what you must. Bresklon and I will wrap you in our light. Use it! Go!"

Alexa turned emerald eyes to Captain Lisandá. "Whatever you do, don't try to stop me." Then, sliding out from between the booth and Lisandá's protective body, she turned and raced back toward the battle. The captain, unnerved by the haunting, echoing quality of her command, chased after her, sword raised and ready to fight.

Staggering to an abrupt halt, Alexa scanned the bedlam ahead of her as Lisandá and her guards quickly closed ranks around her. Several other Protectors had also seen her mad dash toward the battle and rushed to join them.

Far to her right, Alexa watched Gregor and several Krisantal commanders gallop off to engage a group of Sifiq riders. Ahead, mounted Sifiq screeched their war cries while slashing at soldiers on the ground. Jerking to the left, she tried to make sense of the pandemonium comprised of men shouting or leaping from their mounts, clanging swords, stomping, rearing, snorting horses—all shrouded in rising clouds of dust.

Closing her eyes, she murmured a desperate plea, "Oh, great and holy Val, show me what I must see and help me." Again, she scanned the chaotic scene, and her heart leapt into her throat. Gaeldoreg and Nikolai stood back-to-back, fending off Sifiq swordsmen. Suddenly, two mounted Sifiq warriors let out blood-curdling war cries and raced their horses toward the two.

Alexa screamed out, "No!" just as a bolt of light struck one of the riders, knocking his mount off its feet, accompanied by simultaneous agonized screams of pain as the second horse toppled over where Nikolai and Gaeldoreg had stood.

Paralyzed for mere seconds, Alexa snapped her wits into place and called on every shred of faith she possessed to summon the Healing Graces as she raced directly into the chaos ahead of her. Surrounded by dazzling, impenetrable lights that terrified and stunned Sifiq warriors, Alexa jumped over or shoved her way past bodies of soldiers until she reached the stack of fallen horses and the moaning, groaning bodies beneath.

"Anlía! Are you still with me?" she cried out.

"Yes, Mother!"

"Can you help expand the dome of Graces?"

"We'll try! Hurry, Mother!"

Desperation drove Alexa as she pushed against one dead horse. "Captain! Help me move these animals! Guards! Help us! There are men pinned underneath!"

Alexa jumped over the neck of one horse and saw movement. "Niko!"

"Mother! Help me lift this head aside."

Locking her hands underneath the poor creature's head, she lifted with all her might as Niko freed his legs and helped her push it aside, dragging Gaeldoreg free with him.

"Niko! Bibo! Praise Val! How badly are you hurt?" she asked, tears brimming in her eyes as she hugged them both.

"Mother, I'm fine, but I think Gaeldoreg's arm is broken. Hurry, Mother! Papino is still underneath. He jumped and plunged his sword into the second rider's horse."

"Oh, holy Val! Lisandá! That's Lord Garogan trapped beneath that horse! We've got to free him!" Steadying herself, Alexa closed her eyes, "Anlía? The dome? Victor?"

"Mother," Anlía responded in a calming voice, "the dome is secure for now. You set it well. Papino needs you. Make them hurry!"

"Majesty!" Captain Lisandá called out.

In an instant, Alexa dropped to her knees beside them. "Victor, I'm here," she said, forcing a calm far from what she felt as she examined him.

Nikolai swiftly related how Victor had run full tilt, aiming his sword at the horse to stop it from overrunning him. Its rider had swerved late, causing Victor to plunge his sword deep into the animal's side but giving the Sifiq time to strike Victor. The enemy's sword had lodged in Victor's side, and the horse's weight had caused further injuries.

Barely conscious, Victor opened his eyes. "Sweetest, go. This is—no place for you. Not safe."

"Hush, Victor Garogan. Val watches over me. And you."

"Niko? My Niko?"

"I'm here, Papino. I'm all right. Thanks to you." Nikolai felt more shaken than at any other time since his arrival in the Sifiq Kingdom.

"Praise Val," Victor murmured. "Alexa?"

"Victor, be quiet. You're safe beneath Val's Healing Graces. Anlía is with us. We're going to take care of you."

"Anlía? That's not possible."

"I'm here, Papino."

That sweet voice sounded inside his mind. He managed a smile. "Dear one. I love you."

"I know. I love you, too. I can't stay. Listen to Mother. She'll take care of you now. Pray, Papino, and I'll be praying Val's blessings on you."

"How?" Hazel eyes questioned Alexa.

"Later. The battle is under control. I'm going to take care of you, Victor, but you have to help. Like before. Remember?"

"Not this time, Sweetest."

He clutched her hand as a doctor appeared and skillfully removed the sword. After stanching the bleeding and preparing Victor for the quick trip to the hospital pavilion, the physician stopped Alexa with a firm hand on her shoulder. "Lady Valkana, he's right. I don't think Lord Garogan will survive his injuries. Prepare yourself."

Alexa swallowed hard, fighting tears. "I know, but Val has blessed me with miracles in the past. Perhaps he will again."

Inside the hospital, Alexa quickly assembled with her priestesses. Again, they summoned the Healing Graces. The magnificent domes appeared that provided Val sacred space to heal the injured faithful or gently ease the passing of those whose physical lives were done. She then went to Victor, where a surgeon was already tending the deep wound in his side.

Dr. Lorzari spoke without looking up. "He has a very strong constitution, but he lost a lot of blood. Unfortunately, I can't repair all the damage done here. When the horse fell on him, it crushed part of his chest. Frankly, I'm amazed he's still alive."

"I was there ready with the Healing Graces," Alexa replied. "I—I knew someone would be..." She stuttered to a halt. "I didn't know who."

"I'm finished here. I can't say how long the sedation will last. Majesty, I'm not even sure he'll wake up. You must take care of yourself. Many here rely on you."

She nodded, noting only kindness in his words. "Thank you." Alexa paused to stroke her fingers across Victor's forehead. "Victor Garogan, you listen to me. You've caused me enough grief lately. You will wake up."

A few minutes later, she knelt beside a cot with her arms around Gaeldoreg's waist as a Trezvindjan physician made sure the bones in his arm were correctly aligned. She squeezed him tightly as the doctor set the arm, feeling the involuntary groan erupt from deep inside his gut. "Bibo, I'm so sorry you're hurt," she consoled.

Forcing a grin onto his grimy face, he asked, "And will you not make it better faster?"

"I will as soon as you tell me you really believe in Espiritus, or Val, or?"

"Ma Ishna, have you not figured that out yet? Must I say the words?" he teased.

Tears trickled down her face. "Right now, words would help since you can't hug me the way you usually do, and Gregor isn't here to hold me, either."

Sighing, he said, "Very well, for you only. I've always believed in Espiritus and always will. Good enough?"

Intently, she held her hands above his arm and prayerfully focused healing energies across the injury for several minutes. Finally, she looked up. "How does that feel?"

Puzzled by the odd sensations inside the limb the doctor had just braced, Gaeldoreg met her waiting gaze with uplifted eyebrows. "Exceedingly warm and strangely tingly. Is it supposed to feel that way?"

Alexa closed her eyes again and gracefully floated her hand above his arm. Then, silently thanking Val, she nodded and smiled. "That means the healing is almost done, Bibo. Because it's bone, you should keep your arm in a sling for a few days, but it will be fine."

With his good hand, he cupped her cheek. "I chose a fine daughter, didn't I?"

"I think you're far better being my bibo," she said. "Now, rest. I have work to do."

"I know. As often as Garogan has raised my ire, he might have saved Nikolai's life and mine today. Go."

Returning to Victor's bedside, Alexa found Victor half-awake, fighting sedation. "Victor, calm yourself. You need rest."

He grimaced, pain evident in every breath he took. "Sweetest, I look forward to my eternal rest with Val," he whispered.

"Stop it. We're going to get you home so you can get better," she encouraged while reaching across him to straighten his blankets.

"I do prefer dying at home. I want to see my son once more. My heart breaks that I won't see my new baby. Do you think it will be a girl? I want a baby girl. Very much."

Alexa tried to smile as she held his hands. "I'm not sure. After I rest, I'll try to meditate to see if I can get you an answer. But maybe you should try to live long enough to find out."

"If I could, I would." He shifted his eyes to see if anyone was close. "Alexa, if I don't make it home, the letter I wrote Oui-lest is in my tent. Will you make sure she gets it?"

"Of course."

"Sweetest. Something else." His speech was slow and halting, but his eyes locked on hers. "You must know. As much as I love Oui-lest, and I do, I always loved you more than life and always will. And Niko. I had to save him. I know it's not right, but especially after the march home to Garogan City—when you got so sick—I've always thought of him as my own. Alexa, he should have been ours." Victor's eyes closed again in the sleep of the very sick.

Alexa sat immobilized for a long moment. Then, when Gregor's voice quietly intruded on her weary thoughts, she slowly rose and glided into the refuge of his embrace.

"Beloved, I'm sorry it took so long to come to you. They told me you were safe, so I made sure the camp was secure. Nikolai told me about Victor. How is he?"

When she drew back to gaze into his eyes, his dark features were taut with fatigue and worry. Shaking her head, she said, "Critical. I honestly don't know how long I can keep him alive. He wants to go home to die. Grandfather? Is he safe?"

Gregor nodded. "Yes, but Kaelzron decided to join the fray. He's badly wounded, and I'm going to send him home. I will delay the move on Atuliq."

"I'm so sorry," she said.

"I still have Grandfather and Gaeldoreg here. But, most importantly, you're safe." He kissed her lightly. "Do you know the status of the wounded?"

"The surgeons and priestesses have been busy, but everything was going according to our drills. The last I heard, we had lost three wounded.

All others were recovering. I don't know how many were lost outside."

"Miraculously, only five. If you and the Valiria weren't here, that total would be much higher." He tenderly caressed her cheek with fingers that earlier had gripped a sword swung in deadly arcs against their enemy. "Are you all right?"

Her chin quivered. "I don't know how to answer that."

"I heard everything he just told you."

Alexa once again regretted her inability to read her husband's life force. Still, his expressive eyes reflected turmoil. The man on the cot behind them had created havoc and death in Turand, followed by progress based on foundations of wisdom, innovation, and organization. His intervention had been the difference between her own life and death on three separate occasions. Today, Victor's intervention had possibly saved their son's life.

"Beloved, forgive me if I cannot always find balance with him. I hope you can accept the fact that I don't hate him and that I never wish ill upon him."

Alexa's arms circled his waist once again. "I accept that what you just heard is something no man should have heard. What you have endured where Victor is concerned, no man should have endured. You have done so with incredible forbearance, and I respect and love you more than ever because of it. Gregor, hold me. Please. Just hold me."

Early the next morning, Gregor stopped Alexa when she started to leave the bed. "Wait. I need to talk to you."

So many tasks awaited her, but she could hardly deny him. "What is it?"

"I've been lying here thinking—about Victor."

"Seriously?" she asked. "No matter the circumstances, he's not someone I care to discuss in our bed."

Barely restraining a smile, Gregor rolled onto his side and kissed her forehead. "Thank you for that, Milady; however, it's warm here and cold outside."

"A valid point. I concede. What?"

"Alexa, we're blessed with a dedicated group of Valiria here to manage the hospital. I think you should pack your things and escort Victor back to Turand."

"What? Leave you and Nikolai? Gregor! No!"

He rested a hand against her cheek. "Listen to me. Victor has no chance at all of arriving home alive without your care. You know I'm right. Go with him. Take him home with my blessing. Nikolai and I will be fine. I promise. I'll ask Gaeldoreg to escort you."

"I have no intention of leaving you. You're my husband, Gregor, not Victor. I belong with you. I love you." Tears glazed her eyes.

Resting his bearded chin against her forehead, he felt her body tremble next to his. "I know that, but you also love Victor. It's not the same. That I also know, but he has always been part of your life. He saved your life three times. Beloved, give him this final gift. If nothing else, do this for me. I owe him this for finding you on that beach in Timeri."

Her sob tore into his heart. "Depending on how things go, you can always return. The Valiria here would welcome you back."

Later that afternoon, while Alexa packed Victor's belongings, Gregor visited his old rival. A priestess had just finished feeding Victor some broth and exchanged his blankets for ones warmed over a brazier.

Pallid and weak, Victor still retained his spirit. "You'll soon be rid of the thorn in your side forever."

Gregor sat beside Victor's cot. "No matter what, I could never wish this on you."

482

"Alexa said she's taking me home. Why? Why are you sending her?"

"Your best chance to live long enough to reach home is if Alexa goes with you. If you are indeed going to die, you deserve the peace of dying in Turand, not in this damned land of death and destruction. Despite our personal differences, you proved yourself exemplary in Turand's recovery. You deserve to be remembered as a hero."

Victor emitted a short, sardonic laugh, followed by a painful cough. "Ironic, isn't it? Our personal history comes to this."

Gregor's jaw twitched and then set. "I can do nothing about the past. But, as I said before, I doubt I would change anything were it in my power to do so. I regret your sorrow, but I love her all the more because of what she and I have endured. What you need to understand is that she still cares deeply for you. When you're gone, I'll be left to dry her tears. Have no doubt. She will grieve your death for years to come."

Victor regarded him thoughtfully before gripping his hand with what little strength he had. "I love her, too. My love never changed, but you are her greatest love. Swear to me you'll take care of her—that you'll always love her."

Gregor felt the effort in his grasp. Meeting Victor's intense gaze, he said, "I swear to you. I will love Alexa with my dying breath and beyond."

Satisfied, Victor relaxed and closed his eyes. Seeing that he slept, Gregor stood, said a silent prayer asking Val to deliver Victor Garogan home for a peaceful death, and then left.

⤵

Nearly three weeks later, Alexa inspected the special carriage waiting outside LeAndro Karanan's home in Timeri, where they had spent the night before the final leg of their journey. The trip from camp to the port, followed by the voyage to Turand, had been an ordeal. Alexa had spent most of her time calling on the Healing Graces and caring for Victor during recurring bouts of fever and delirium. Each time, he rallied, insisting he would die at home in Garogan. After arriving with Victor in Turand, fleet couriers were sent ahead to prepare accommodations along the way and to notify Stefan they were en route.

When the carriage finally rolled under a porte cochere one afternoon at the palace in Toraval, Alexa could hardly believe she had arrived that far with Victor still clinging to life. They heard temple bells ringing as soon as they reached the city's outskirts—a poignant, solemn welcome.

Gaeldoreg helped her step down with two good arms, and she hugged him tightly. "Thank you, Bibo. I could not have accomplished this without you."

He smiled proudly. "You could have, Ma Ishna, but sorrowful burdens are always easier when shared with those who love you."

Palace attendants quickly appeared. Following Alexa's instructions, they carefully carried Lord Garogan to a room prepared for him on the palace's main floor. Willem and Katara waited inside the grand foyer to greet Alexa and Gaeldoreg.

"Alexa, how glad I am to see you." Willem welcomed her with a heartfelt hug.

"And I, you. Where is everyone?"

"We weren't exactly sure when you'd arrive. Everyone is at Stefan's. I sent word you've arrived."

"Alexa? How is he?" Katara's blue eyes were wide with concern.

"Deteriorating. My hope is that Victor might improve if we can get him home to Garogan."

"Mother!" A chorus of voices surrounded her, although missing was the exuberance she usually associated with her four youngest children. Caught in their embraces, Alexa relished reconnection to her rapidly maturing brood. Standing back, she smiled through a curtain of tears. "How much you've all grown! How much I've missed you!"

"We missed you, too, Mother," Thikos said. "Karina said you'd be home today when the carillon bells started ringing this morning."

"Do I also get hugs?" Gaeldoreg asked, gladly receiving his own warm greeting from the bevy of Toscano children.

Willem quietly interrupted the family reunion. "Alexa, my apologies. We need help with Victor."

"Of course. Bibo?"

"I'll stay with the children, Ma Ishna."

"Excuse me, my darlings. I'll be back as soon as I can."

"It's all right, Mother. We understand. Go."

Following Willem into Victor's room, Alexa saw Katara supporting Victor's shoulders as he struggled to breathe. Quickly unclasping her cloak and tossing it aside, Alexa asked a servant to boil water for steam. Meanwhile, she passed her arms over Victor's body, summoning healing energy into his battered chest to help draw air into his lungs. Before long, he calmed and lay back against a stack of pillows.

Weak and exhausted, Victor whispered, "Thank you. Where are we?"

"The palace in Toraval. Willem and Katara are here."

He nodded. "I want to go home. I need to see my wife and son."

"Victor, I'm here." Oui-lest, noticeably pregnant, stood in the doorway. Her eyes shone brilliantly blue behind a glaze of tears, but she forced a smile for her husband. "How glad I am to have you back."

"Oui-lest," he whispered, stretching one hand in her direction.

Swiftly crossing the room to his bedside, Oui-lest leaned forward and kissed his forehead, his cheeks, and his lips. "Oh, my husband, what am I to do with you? You leave me plump and healthy and come home pale and thin. I shall be cooking all year long to fatten you up again."

Victor tried to smile, but he had no strength. "Dear one, tell me. How are you? And our son?"

"I am well, even if you have worried me half to death. Our son is napping at the moment and growing too fast to be believed."

"And our new baby?"

"Well. Growing and moving."

He smiled. "Alexa meditated. She says we have a daughter." He struggled for breaths. "A baby girl, Oui-lest. She'll be as beautiful as her mother. Not quite, though. She can't possibly be as beautiful as you."

"Shush," Oui-lest said, stroking his hand. "Rest. You've had a long trip. I'll be here beside you. The nurse will bring baby Victor in once he wakes up and gets fed. All right?"

"Oui-lest?"

"Yes?"

"I missed you. I love you."

"I love you, too. Now rest. I must ask Alexa something. I'll be right back."

Outside the door, Stefan and Adrina waited with Willem, Katara, and Alexa. Oui-lest turned fearful eyes to Alexa. "Please, Alexa, tell me he'll get better. I can't bear to lose him."

Alexa grasped both of Oui-lest's hands. "I wish I could. Just keeping him alive long enough to bring him this far was almost impossible. His injuries are severe, dear one."

"I begged him to stay," she murmured.

"And I begged him to come home," Alexa told her. "He insisted he had to protect Turand and especially you and his family from any further risks. Oui-lest, don't make him feel guilty for that choice. Go to him."

When Oui-lest returned to Victor, Adrina took Alexa by the arm. "Is he really so bad?"

"I've rarely left his side since we left our base camp. It's hard to believe he's still alive."

Hope flared in Adrina's eyes. "That proves my brother's strength. He's fighting to live so he can watch his children grow up."

Alexa faced her old friend squarely. "Adrina, Victor is dying. I cannot maintain the Healing Graces indefinitely."

"Are you just giving up?"

Stefan placed his arm around his wife. "Adrina, please. Alexa has done her best, but she needs rest, too." He looked up. "Alexa, go to your children. Have supper with them and go to bed early. We have a physician for the night."

Stefan watched as Alexa cast him a thankful glance before silently leaving. He then turned his attention to his distraught wife. "Adrina, when Willem and I stopped to speak to Gaeldoreg, he said Alexa stayed at Victor's side day and night since they departed the base camp to come home. Gaeldoreg told us several times he had to insist that she take time to eat and rest. She's near collapse, and he will step in if need be. Willem said he will, too."

"But, Stefan, my brother." Adrina began weeping.

Stefan gripped her shoulders and gazed at her tear-stained face. "I know, love, but I would have to side with Willem. We cannot lose them both."

⌣

Alexa rolled over in bed the following morning. Unable to bear sleeping alone in the suite she shared with Gregor, she had retired to her chambers when she first came to the palace. Smiling into pre-dawn darkness, she listened to soft breathing and snuggled close to her twins, who had fallen fast asleep while talking to her the night before.

Dawdling in the warm bed, Alexa refused to think of the impending tragedy of Victor's death. Instead, she extended her mind far afield, connecting briefly to her husband's spirit. He was focused and determined, but he was safe. So was Nikolai.

Alexa's memory drifted to her last night in the Sifiq Kingdom. With the Valiria maintaining the dome of the Healing Graces she had initiated and doctors watching over Victor, Alexa had spent that final night with Gregor. Tired as they both were, they had still found sufficient energy to make love. She, especially, had sought that intimate connection. As they parted, she felt the distinctive surge of energy she recognized so well after her years of loving him. She had buried her face against his chest, murmuring, "Thank you, my love, for this great gift you bestow on me. I love you."

Sighing, she got up carefully to avoid disturbing her girls, dressed, and left for the sacred Temple of Val for meditations and prayers. By the time she returned to the palace, the sky glowed with dawn's colorful palette of pink, magenta, ruby, and gold banishing deep indigo. Stormy weather ahead, Alexa thought, not boding well for continuing Victor's journey to Garogan Province.

Hurrying inside from the cold, she headed to the kitchens. The perfume of fresh, yeasty breads emerging from wood-fired ovens whetted her appetite. One of the cooks happily obliged her with a thick slice of warm bread slathered with freshly churned yellow butter, jam, and a steaming cup of tea. After enjoying her early morning treat, Alexa thanked the cook and left to check on Victor.

Outside his room, palace physicians had arrived to relieve the doctor who had spent the night with Victor. Joining them, Alexa listened to the report she expected. The patient still suffered violent coughing spells and labored breathing. The night physician expressed utter amazement that the patient had survived the ocean voyage from the Sifiq Kingdom, let alone the overland journey from Timeri. In his opinion, Lord Garogan would need a miracle to survive another day.

Alexa left the doctors to their conference and entered the sickroom. Her heart lurched when she saw Oui-lest, feet tucked beneath her, asleep in a large, padded rocking chair close beside Victor's bed, holding his hand. Adrina had spent the night in another chair in the room's far corner.

Lifting her head upon hearing Alexa enter, Adrina got up and went to her oldest friend. Embracing Alexa, she whispered, "We're losing him, aren't we?"

Alexa swallowed as tears filled her eyes. "I fear it is his time, Adrina. I can do no more."

"Are you sure? I mean—the last time. During the war—in Garogan."

Alexa hated destroying her hope. "That was different, Adrina. His injury was different. This time, the deep organs are too severely damaged. Sometimes, it's just Val's time to call the spirit home."

"Alexa?"

Breathing in deeply, Alexa went to Oui-lest. "Yes, dear one?"

"Thank you for bringing him home."

"You're welcome. Victor and I have been close for as long as I can remember. I could hardly do less. I'll bring it later, but he wrote you a letter before all this happened. He asked me to be sure you get it."

Oui-lest tried to smile but wept softly instead. "How will I live without him? He is everything to me."

A hoarse whisper sounded beside her. "You must love our children for both of us and never let them forget me."

She turned and sat on the bed beside him. "Victor, I love you when I never thought it possible to love any man. I'm so afraid," she said, clasping his hand tightly.

"Of course, you're afraid. My beautiful wife." He paused, gasping in several breaths. "Adrina and Alexa will help you. You have our babies. I leave you a fine home and a legacy to manage for our children's futures. You will be well cared for, Oui-lest. One day—at a time. You're capable—and intelligent. Do this for me. For our family. Promise me."

"Victor, if I can't?"

"You can, Oui-lest. Promise me." His eyes pleaded with her.

Her heart was breaking, and she felt their baby move inside her. Suppressing a sob, she nodded. "I promise."

He smiled and closed his eyes. Adrina and Oui-lest exchanged wildly desperate glances. Alexa instantly went to him. She sighed heavily. "He's only sleeping. Talking tires him so. Both of you. Get some breakfast while I stay with him. Now. Off with you. And tell my children where I am."

When Victor woke again, he saw Alexa holding his hand. "Sweetest, you're here."

"Of course," she answered, noting the increasing effort it took for him to speak.

"Good," he said, wheezing. "I have to tell you."

"You should rest."

"Just listen—while I still have breath. Alexa, I want to remind you. I always loved you more than my own life. Nothing—nothing—ever changed that, but I meant it when I said I love Oui-lest. Promise me." He stopped, laboring to breathe. "Promise you'll watch over her. She's strong but not like you. She is a better wife than I deserve, and I love her very much. Take care of her. And my babies. Make sure they know I loved them and their mother. *They must know that I loved them and their mother.*"

"I will, Victor. I promise."

"Bring Oui-lest. And my son. Please."

Alexa stood, leaned forward to kiss his cheek, and turned to summon Oui-lest. She already stood at the open door with Adrina, both with tears streaming down their faces. Going to them, Alexa said, "He wants you with him, Oui-lest, and the baby."

"Go to him, Oui-lest. Alexa and I will bring the baby for you," Adrina urged.

Chapter 20

B lack bunting draped Garogan Castle and Garogan City for the upcoming state funeral Queen Alexa had declared for Lord Victor Garogan. His death had resulted from an act of heroism. In sacrificing his life, he had saved the lives of his eldest godson, Turand's beloved Prince Nikolai, and Trezvindjan Senior Commander Vosklon, who stood defending the prince. After years of dedicated service to Garogan Province and the Crown, Lord Garogan would be laid to rest with all the pomp and ceremony due a national hero.

True to her promise, Alexa remained close to Oui-lest, staying sensitive to her friend's grief-stricken state and attentive to her mid-term pregnancy. The two women spent hours talking. Sometimes, they shared memories. Other times, they spoke frankly about Victor's divided emotions. In the end, Alexa convinced Oui-lest she had been his last great love and the one he had wanted with him during his final moments.

The day of the funeral dawned cool and overcast. Garogan City's great chapel filled to overflowing. Citizens from around the province lined the streets to glimpse the procession carrying Victor Garogan's coffin inside for services. A priest from the Order of Val opened the moving service. Stefan delivered a heartfelt eulogy, resisting tears before ending his comments. Bravely, DiMarco and Thikos also offered descriptions of their beloved Papino Victor. DiLeno Tarandá, his voice breaking several times, described experiences with the cousin who had been his best friend since the two were in diapers.

A great hush descended on the chapel when Alexa walked behind the podium. Some mourners knew the poignant drama behind her broken romance with Lord Garogan. However, most knew only that the two had been close since childhood and that their Valkana had exerted extraordinary efforts to save Garogan's respected nobleman.

The pyramid suspended above the altar glowed when she began to speak. The High Priestess Valkana's voice echoed throughout the chapel chamber and into the crowded street beyond. Alexa detailed how Lord Garogan's wisdom and courage during Turand's reformation inspired a return to justice in their nation following years of brutal occupation. She also recounted his many talented contributions to the nation's rebuilding. Her closing emphasized his devotion to family and friends, which reflected not only in how he lived but how he died. Final prayers for the peaceful repose of his spirit permeated the mourners with comfort born of their Valkana's faith.

⌐

Late that afternoon, Stefan finally escorted Alexa from the Garogan family cemetery back to the main castle. She had sat and stared at the name a local craftsman had carved into stone. Although she had already commissioned a monument in Victor's honor, she believed even that gesture would be seriously lacking in light of the times he had saved her life and now Nikolai's.

Inside the castle, children lightened the funereal atmosphere where Marina and Karina played with baby Victor. Adrina tried to keep Oui-lest occupied, but neither did well at keeping tears at bay for long at a time.

Katara and Willem engaged in small talk. Everyone coped differently. Gaeldoreg had remained behind in Toraval should important news arrive from the Sifiq front, and Alexa missed him terribly.

"Alexa, are you all right?"

Turning, she met DiLeno's concerned gaze. "I must admit. I am tired." With that, she slumped forward into his arms.

Half an hour later, Katara clucked worriedly as she laid the back of her hand against Alexa's forehead. "Alexa? Can you hear me?"

Blinking several times, Alexa slowly opened her eyes. "Katara," she mumbled. "Gregor. Where's Gregor?"

"He's not here. Don't you remember?"

"Oh," Alexa moaned. "I'm sorry. I must have dreamed I heard him. Did I faint?"

"You did. You scared poor DiLeno half to death. Me, too, if it matters. And your children."

"I'm so sorry."

Alexa started to sit up, but Katara held her down. "I think that's not such a good idea. You need to stay in bed."

"And I think I must get up, or my clothes and the bed may get very wet. Besides, I am feeling better, although I haven't eaten today except for some toast and tea this morning."

"Well, no wonder you're fainting on us! Goodness gracious! I'll help you up. After that, we'll have someone bring you a tray."

Insisting that Alexa eat in bed, Katara sat at Alexa's bedside to make sure her longtime friend ate every bite. "Willem said Gaeldoreg was plenty worried that you were overdoing things. Alexa, I know how close you and Victor were despite your history. You know it isn't good to hold that kind of grief inside."

Appreciative eyes met Katara's concerned gaze. "I can't argue your point. I have much inside right now, but I think only Gregor can help me sort things out. He's the only one who really understands. I can manage with prayer until then."

"Willem and I are always here for you."

Alexa finally smiled. "That I also know. And I shall be asking a great favor of you both in the near future. Fortunately, it will be of a happier nature. This just isn't the time to discuss it."

Gladdened by the return of color to Alexa's cheeks and sparkle to her eyes, Katara grinned. "So, you drop a mysterious note like that and leave me to wallow in a bog of curiosity."

"At least it's not a stinky bog like some I recall."

Katara involuntarily snorted just as Willem poked his head around the door. "It seems Her Majesty is feeling better."

"Willem, yes, thank you. I am," Alexa said, grinning and trying not to laugh as Katara held her hand to her lips to repress giggles. "Your wife is remarkably good tonic on days like today."

⌒

Gaeldoreg Vosklon barely controlled his laughter. Alexa's eyes glittered with anticipation as she breathed in the fresh, perfumed air of multi-hued flowers cascading over white stone retention walls surrounding the magnificent central palace in Tarahlaz. They had arrived in Trezvindja with no fanfare or advance warning, hoping to surprise Anlía.

"Are you sure, Ma Ishna, that you kept your secret from her?"

"I'm hiding many secrets at the moment, Bibo."

"Is that so?"

Grinning brightly, she nodded. "Shall we go? I can hardly wait."

Mounting steps to the palace's stately entrance, sentries stopped them to inquire about their identities and business. Commander Vosklon quickly gained entry, leaving the guards bowing low to their queen.

Leading the way, Gaeldoreg guided Alexa toward the central court, where he expected to find Anlía conducting weekly public hearings.

Before admitting them, a liveried attendant outside a towering arched doorway quietly informed them the session inside would end soon. Alexa proudly observed the way Anlía watched and listened to each presenter and then carefully noted details that Bresklon Krisantal translated. The two conferred. Anlía gave her response, which he translated if necessary, and the decision was rendered.

When the final call sounded, Gaeldoreg winked at Alexa and raised his hand, signaling from the back that there was one final presenter. The crowd parted, allowing space for the presenter to move forward. Anlía, who was leaning sideways to speak to Bresklon, glanced up. A brilliant smile lit her face when she saw her mother's lavender summer cape. Immediately leaving her seat, she stepped down to the main floor and knelt low.

"Your Majesty Queen Alexa, welcome to Trezvindja and the Palace of Tarahlaz."

Surrounded by a sea of suddenly kneeling citizens, Alexa saw only her beloved daughter. Bending to grasp Anlía's hands, she said, "Rise, my love. Let me hold you in my arms again."

"Mother!" Anlía whispered against her mother's ear. "How did I not feel you coming?"

Laughing quietly as she kissed her daughter, Alexa winked and said, "I can still do some things you haven't learned. How are you?"

"Very well! Delighted you're here, but I think we should release the people in court. Then we can talk."

"Of course," Alexa said, turning. "Please rise, everyone, and forgive your queen for her forgetfulness. She was overjoyed seeing her daughter after our separation."

Those gathered rose, receiving Alexa's gracious apology in the spirit it was given. Their queen was already earning widespread respect in

Trezvindja. Warriors writing back from the Sifiq Kingdom shared stories of her tireless labors on behalf of the wounded, Trezvindjan and Turandan alike, and her work to cheer every fighter regardless of his origin. Initial concerns about how their Ishna Queen would accept Trezvindja were swiftly vanishing.

Once the court cleared, Anlía led Alexa to a side office where Grand Councillor Krisantal now instructed Master Maconti and several clerks on finalizing documents related to the day's session. Patiently waiting just inside the door for them to complete their tasks, Anlía finally drew their attention. "Gentlemen, please?"

"Your Majesty!" Gregor Maconti responded, his face turning red as he bowed. "I apologize for not seeing you."

"Master Maconti, how good to see you. I take it you are well."

"Very well, Your Majesty. This opportunity has been far better than I expected. If you'll kindly excuse me, I have another meeting in fifteen minutes. I'm so glad to see you again."

"Thank you," Alexa said. "Go if you must."

Anlía laughed. "He's like that most of the time lately." Linking arms with her mother, she said, "I'm sure you remember Grand Councillor Krisantal."

Bresklon Krisantal. Typically tall Trezvindjan. Alexa remembered meeting him and thinking him impressive. Looking closer this time, she realized his finely chiseled features, wide eyes with lush lashes, and sensually shaped lips gave him the handsome appearance that should leave many young women swooning in his wake. She wondered why he wasn't already betrothed or married. Curious.

"Councillor, how good it is to see you again. I understand my daughter has been quite a drain on your time recently."

Bresklon gazed back at her with those black eyes of his. "Not at all, Your Majesty. I've found the challenge both interesting and enlightening.

I'm surprised that you've returned to Trezvindja just now. Do you bring good news?"

"News, perhaps, but not necessarily good. I must arrange lodging for Bibo and me. And my Guard, of course."

"Your bibo came with you?" Anlía asked delightedly.

"Bibo?" Bresklon echoed, confusion plainly written on his face.

Alexa grinned. "Commander Gaeldoreg Vosklon. Of course, he could take lodgings with the Vosklon family, but I prefer that he stay close to me. He has become very much a father figure to me. I rely heavily on him."

Surprise clearly showed on Bresklon's face. "How interesting. Anlía?"

"Mother, I reside here at the palace now. You and Gaeldoreg will stay here. I'll send word to Major Fratino to make arrangements for your Guard."

"That would be perfect. Thank you."

Later, Anlía showed her mother the spacious apartment reserved for the queen. "This should do for now. I imagine you won't be happy with it once Father comes."

Alexa smiled. "It's beautifully appointed, but you're right. I'm very accustomed to being with your father, even if it means sleeping on a stack of mats inside a canvas tent heated by hot coals in a massive brazier."

"The two of you are not exactly everyone's classic image of two monarchs."

"Perhaps not," Alexa mused thoughtfully, "but few monarchs have ever been as much in love or as happy together. I miss him."

"Mother, how are you right now? Really? I know Papino Victor's death must have been a terrible blow."

Alexa ran sensitive fingertips across the silk tapestry spread on the canopy bed. "The sorrow I feel runs deep, Anlía. That I cannot deny."

"But you haven't cried. You've comforted everyone else, but you haven't shed your own tears. Why not?"

Alexa turned and met her daughter's waiting gaze. "How perceptive you are, dear one. I have shed a few. The truth is, no one would truly understand how I feel except one."

"Father?"

"Your father. And despite his feelings toward Victor, your father is the only one who can hold me and console me without judgment or complaint until I purge the sadness I carry. After that…"

"After that? Your grief will hurt him—not only because of your sorrow but because of his feelings toward Victor. What comes after that?" Anlía wondered if she could ever comprehend the complexities of her parents' relationship.

"I have a gift for your father after that—the one gift I can give him that reminds him that my truest love is his alone."

Anlía looked puzzled. "What sort of gift?"

Smiling, Alexa said, "The gift is your father's. Now, I am a tired and hungry visitor. Does this palace not offer the hospitality of meals to its guests?"

Later that evening, as mother and daughter enjoyed a leisurely walk through delightfully blooming palace gardens, Anlía discussed how Bresklon had cleared her schedule for the next few days so she could spend time with her mother. His one recommendation had been that Alexa attend an event at the end of the week when the Mystic Council would offer prayers for the warriors who had gone to fight in the Sifiq Kingdom. Reacting with surprise when asked if Alexa might have the honor of addressing the gathering, Bresklon graciously agreed to help. He would translate for attendees not proficient in the *common language*.

"Bresklon was thrilled when you offered to speak at the memorial ceremony. He didn't expect that. However, he believes it's an excellent gesture for our people at a time when we are embracing anew the call of the Protectors."

Alexa glanced sideways at her daughter. "You sound as if you've been Trezvindjan all your life."

Anlía blinked her eyes and smiled thoughtfully. "Strange. In some ways, I feel as though I have been, yet my love for Turand is as strong as ever. How can that be, Mother?"

"Something in your blood—even your name—bridges the time and distance that divided our nations and our family." Alexa slowed, walking over to a retention wall to perch on its edge between an overflow of flowering vines. "Now, tell me more about you and Bresklon. He's the one you referred to as your own Gregor, isn't he?"

A rosy blush shone on Anlía's cheeks. "Is it so obvious?"

"From you, not so much, although I am still your mother. However, when he looks in your direction, the energy I perceive is powerful."

"That's a relief. We've been determined to maintain proper decorum."

"Does anyone else know?"

"You know how private I am. I've told no one except Maconti."

"Grandfather was quite certain Master Maconti was sweet on you. Was that not the case?"

Anlía sheepishly smiled. "Yes. For a while. Until we invited Ambassador Laritha. When he arrived with his granddaughter, I think it may have been love at first sight for both of them."

"Ah, what a wide web has been cast across our little part of the world. Look at how people are being caught in it," Alexa mused. "Your first love was a former Sifiq captain, and now?"

"Mother, I know what I said at home about Rafzan. I've thought about that so often. At the time, it was true." Finding a patch of thick grass in front of her mother, Anlía sat down, not caring if anyone thought it unbecoming to her status as regent. "I hope you don't mind my sharing this. I also remember when he kissed me. I felt the warmth and the thrill, but it's completely different whenever Bresklon kisses me.

There was a tentativeness in Rafzan's kisses—as if he were afraid or holding back."

Anlía blushed. "When Bresklon kisses me, he makes me feel like he and I are the only two people in the entire world. I feel his kisses move through my whole body. Sometimes, it almost frightens me. I know how strange it must sound telling you this, but I have no one else I trust. Mother, I'm so glad you're here."

Alexa went to sit with her daughter. Placing her palm against Anlía's face, she smiled. "You're awaking to how it feels to be a woman deeply in love. The question is whether this is only physical. Do you also feel the spiritual love you will need considering your identity as a Valiria priestess?"

Anlía nodded. "Mother, Bresklon and I are well suited despite the considerable difference in our ages. We share so many interests and talk for hours about history, art, music, and poetry. He makes Trezvindja's past come alive for me. He's also very intuitive, which makes my mystical abilities more joyful, and I'm helping him develop his that he ignored for years. Mother, he says loving me is the most powerful thing he has ever felt. I feel the same. How do I explain that in ways that make sense?"

Alexa embraced her daughter. "I believe you just did, dear one, but you must allow me to know him better. As you said, there is a significant difference in your ages. He is a very handsome man, and I would like to hear from him, not you, why such a desirable man with a powerful, influential position like his might be free to seek romance with a younger woman like you."

"You don't trust him?" Anlía asked, worry showing in her eyes.

"I didn't say that. I only said I want to know him better. That is reasonable. One day, I expect you'll have your own children. When that day comes, you'll look back on this conversation and understand exactly what I'm saying. Until then, trust that your mother will do or say nothing to disrupt your relationship if Bresklon's intentions are honorable—with the understanding that if they are honorable, he still must face your father."

Anlía groaned. "That worries me more than facing you."

Alexa chuckled and kissed her daughter. "Facing your father would intimidate any man."

⤸

Two days later, Alexa watched the sun rise over the glistening ocean after leaving the bench where she had said early prayers and lost herself in morning meditations. Softly whispering seas soothed her spirit as she walked along the shore. Seabirds lifted lusty calls on salty air as they embarked on their hunt for breakfast. She grinned as her stomach grumbled, reminding her she needed to eat when she returned to the palace. Glancing downward, she watched a crab scoot along beige sands until frothy tidewaters overtook it and carried it from sight. She sighed, glad for a peaceful morning.

"Your Majesty?"

Turning, she knew her face reflected surprise. "Good morning."

"Please forgive me for disturbing you. I understand you pray and meditate early in the morning. I had hoped I might speak with you—if you would allow."

More than ever, Alexa regretted her inability to read the life forces of Trezvindjans. Black eyes held a complex blend of emotions that reminded her of how Gregor had often looked at her during the early days of their marriage. She felt chills run down her spine. Gregor had described how tormented he had been by his love for her and his fears that she would forever resent him.

"Bresklon, of course, we can speak. It's a lovely morning if you'd like to walk."

"Actually, there's a seaside teashop not far with outside tables where we can sit and speak privately. I know your guards will follow, but the shop is very nice. Anlía assured me you would take no offense if I invited you for kacha and pastries."

At a secluded table beneath a scalloped blue canopy, Alexa and Bresklon waited for a server dressed all in white to place gold-clad porcelain cups of kacha on white saucers on a matching white tablecloth. Flaky, golden-crusted pastries with artistic swirls of frosting tempted diners to choose between ruby, gold, or indigo fruit fillings peeking at them from between buttery layers.

Shaking her head, Alexa chuckled. "Our king will be a lost soul when he arrives here. No one loves sweet pastry more than my Gregor."

"So Anlía says," Bresklon said, glancing around and noting with relief that the hour was too early for many to be about. Those who were had not noticed the queen. "Your Majesty, I do apologize for coming to you so early, but I felt it important to discuss my situation—my relationship—with Anlía. If you have time."

Alexa nodded after drinking from her cup of kacha. "First, when we're in private, especially right now, remember our initial agreement for you to address me as Alexa. It will be more comfortable and less conspicuous. As to the reason you're here, I agree with the importance of the matter. Even if I didn't have time, I would make time."

Nodding his head respectfully, Bresklon said, "Thank you, Alexa." Pausing thoughtfully, he sipped his kacha. "I'm not a man to avoid difficult situations. I prefer being direct. I fully comprehend why you must be concerned about the reasons a man in my position would be so interested in your daughter."

Alexa met his gaze directly. "Do you blame me?"

"Blame you?" he asked. "I would think you a poor mother if you were otherwise. From your standpoint, your daughter is young and inexperienced. On my side, I have never known a more beautiful woman, nor one more charming and intelligent. She is also the daughter of Trezvindja's new king. He is untested and unknown for us, but all signs point to a fair and very powerful monarch. Any Trezvindjan man desiring higher prestige within the realm would be foolish not to seek marriage to Anlía. Believe me. Competition is already fierce among highly placed families to gain introductions for their sons."

"How has Anlía reacted? Or does she know?"

Bresklon glanced away. "She knows. Princess Elder Sharlia has already held various social dinners to introduce Anlía to people, including several desirable suitors."

"Anlía didn't tell me. Knowing my daughter, however, that was likely received graciously but without the results Grandmother planned."

Bresklon almost smiled. "Anlía said she found the young men boring."

"I'm not surprised. She had the same complaint about most potential suitors in Turand. My daughter's mind is far advanced. She also thinks much differently than most people her age. That's partly why she has been such a wonderful challenge for her father and me."

"Alexa, the truth is that I find myself bewildered by Anlía's effect on me. The way she thinks, her many interests, and her compassion are only part of why she captured my heart when I least expected it. When I first saw her, I felt a physical impact that I had never experienced in my life. For several seconds, I literally felt dizzy. Now, I realize it was a mystical reaction to her presence that is synchronous to mine."

"Bresklon, all of that I can understand. What I ask now is not from malice but for my daughter's sake. There are things I simply must know. What about the difference in your ages? And why is it that a man in your position isn't married already?"

Bresklon picked up a pastry and distractedly broke off pieces he slowly ate. "Answering your second question first, I was married. My wife died in childbirth, as did the baby. That was nine years ago. I was already serving on the Council of Protectors. Two years after my wife's death, I was named Councillor of the Krisantal League and three years ago, Grand Councillor of the Council of Leagues, which has provided the opportunity to assist Anlía in learning her duties as regent."

"And tutor her in the language and history of Trezvindja," Alexa added.

"No, the time I devote to her tutoring is my own. Her approach to learning about Trezvindja is a joy and, frankly, has rekindled my appreciation of my own country.

"As for your first question, I am eighteen years older than Anlía. However, those years seem to matter not at all because she is mature far beyond her years. More importantly, we are so alike in our interests and ways of thinking. I never dreamed of meeting someone so well attuned to my character."

Alexa studied the intensity of his features as he spoke. His eyes grew distant as images and memories of moments with Anlía replayed inside his mind. Again regretting her inability for deeper readings, she couldn't shake the feeling there was a missing piece to his story.

"Bresklon, I cannot deny the intensity of Anlía's feelings for you. I also know she was recently in love with someone else."

"Yes, Rafzan Lynmar, the former Sifiq officer. She told me all about him. I was with her when he died, and I consoled her when she grieved his passing."

Alexa bit into her lower lip at the revelation. "That must have been difficult, given your feelings."

"To some extent," he admitted, staring at crumbs on his empty plate. "If Anlía cares, it is real. I don't begrudge Lynmar the love she gave him because it was a sweet, innocent love—for both of them, I believe."

Bresklon finally met her gaze. "There is also a powerful innocence in the love she bears me. She reveres her vows as a Valiria priestess, and I genuinely respect her and those vows in ways I cannot describe. At the same time, we are drawn to one another as powerfully as any man and woman have ever been. I hope to marry her. I want to give her the kind of love she describes so admiringly that you and our king share. Or is that merely her imagination? A story? A myth?"

Alexa shook her head, surprised by his inquiry. "A myth? Hardly." She shifted her gaze out over the ocean, dispatching heart and mind across the vast distance to fleetingly touch her husband's presence. Dearest Val, she thought, how she missed Gregor. Especially now. Returning her attention to Bresklon, she noticed his black eyebrows knitted together in question, almost as if he had felt her rapid journey.

"Bresklon, for now, Anlía's well-being must be my priority. Her inexperience concerns me, but I appreciate your honesty and your sincerity. Please allow me some time to consider our conversation before I leave. Whatever I decide means I must also choose how to present this relationship to my husband. We have three daughters, but Anlía would be the first to leave. From the first seconds of her birth, she has had an especially close relationship with her father."

Bresklon forced a smile. "The first seconds?"

"She hasn't told you?" Seeing his puzzled expression, Alexa continued, "Anlía was in such a hurry to be born that there was no time to get me to the birthing room, let alone for the doctor or attendants to reach our suite. I delivered her straight into her father's waiting hands."

"Are you serious?" Bresklon asked incredulously.

"Quite."

Bresklon's smile was gently reflective. "Her eyes glow when she speaks of him. He is her hero."

"As he should be. Now, I thank you for breakfast and your time. I really must return to the palace."

"Of course." Bresklon stood and pulled her chair out for her. As she stepped away from the table, his voice lowered. "I am grateful for your time, Alexa. I beg you to believe me. I love Anlía with my whole heart. I have every confidence that she feels the same for me. If you but give us the chance, we will never give you cause to regret your decision."

Alexa nodded and smiled. "Good day, Bresklon."

⌐

Citizens crowded the outdoor arena across the broad boulevard from the palace. Families of deceased soldiers filled reserved seats near the front levels of the theater. League councillors and their immediate families, anxious to see their queen, filed into front rows. Many had already watched Princess Royal Anlía perform public engagements as King Gregor's Regent. Alexa's speech would be the first official appearance by one of Trezvindja's newly acknowledged monarchs.

Turquoise skies and golden sunshine contrasted with the solemnity of the event. Red and blue bunting, representing the king's Krisantal and Vosklon family lineage, draped the amphitheater stage. Trezvindja's flag, appearing as a field of light green with a center white orchid and palm trees, stood behind the podium alongside Turand's lavender flag with its broad center stripe of white and gold sun within a pyramid inside three narrow, purple concentric circles. Easels displaying wreaths with elaborate black bows paid tribute to warriors already fallen in the Sifiq War. Urns held tall sprays of blue and white flowers to honor injured Protectors, most of whom had responded to Healing Graces and rejoined their regiments. At Anlía's request, two columns holding vases of white, lavender, and purple flowers had been added to pay silent respect to Turandan soldiers.

A bell signaled for quiet. Bresklon Krisantal escorted his great-great-grandmother to the podium. As leader of Trezvindja's Mystic Council, Shamani Milansa Krisantal conducted the ceremony with traditional chants and prayers. The fine acoustics of the amphitheater carried her words to the far reaches of the crowd despite the weakening tones of her aging voice. Her comments carried the reverence for life demonstrated by each Protector warrior who had marched off to war with intentions to end continuing Sifiq aggression against peaceful peoples. Finally, she asked everyone to turn to prayer to beseech blessings on all, whether they still fought, had been wounded, or had gone to rest in the care of Espiritus. Pausing for a moment of silence, she then went to a chair and waited.

A bell rang twice, indicating the crowd should rise. Bresklon reappeared with Anlía's hand formally resting on his forearm. Escorting her to the podium, he announced, "Our Princess Regent, Anlía Lulana Vosklon Krisantal Toscano." Along with the crowd, he bowed before going to stand beside Milansa.

Anlía honored Trezvindjan customs. Her modest black dress was fashioned with long sleeves gathered at the wrists with golden bands. Black, high-heeled shoes made her look taller than ever. An intricately patterned lace veil, pinned into her hair beneath the edge of her crown, floated around her shoulders and fell to just above her knees. Her image was appropriately solemn and moved the hearts and souls of citizens adapting to foreign-born rulers.

"My dear people," she spoke slowly in carefully rehearsed Trezvindjan, "please be seated. We gather to honor our courageous Protectors and the mission they follow to end aggression against peaceful societies in our part of this world. I will have many opportunities to speak to you in the future. For now, I say only that my soul weeps for each life we have lost. I also pray daily for the recovery of our wounded, the safety of our warriors who continue the brave fight, and a quick conclusion to this war. It is my honor to stand aside so you may hear directly from one who loves them all, as do I. Please welcome my mother, Her Majesty Queen Alexa."

A bell again rang twice, signaling all present to their feet. Escorted by Commander Gaeldoreg Vosklon, who wore black mourning armbands on his formal uniform tunic, Alexa crossed the stage. As the lavender Valiria cape flowed behind her, Alexa's black satin gown created soft swishing sounds almost like the quiet rush of water crossing a mountain stream. She also wore the Turandan Queen's gold filigree crown used for practical occasions, especially a somber occasion like this.

Reaching the podium, Alexa did the unexpected. With her hand still on Gaeldoreg's forearm, she turned to face the waiting crowd and knelt before them. "My people, I come before you, humbled by your presence and appreciative of your kind acceptance of my daughter in your midst. Let us now honor the lives of our brave Protectors who keep us and those around us safe through their willing sacrifice of time, effort, blood, and even life."

According to plan, Bresklon had already arrived at the podium to translate for any who had not mastered the common language. Even his eyes widened with surprise as he paused before translating her initial greeting to the gathering.

Lifting her gaze to Gaeldoreg's shining, approving eyes, she placed both her hands in his and gracefully rose to her feet before stepping behind the podium. When all had quieted after resuming their seats, Alexa looked from side to side at the expectant sea of dark faces so different from those at home.

"I asked Senior Commander Gaeldoreg Vosklon to escort me onstage. Not only is he kinsman to our King Gregor, he and I share what Trezvindjans call a sacred blood bond. He has an esteemed history as a courageous Protector warrior. Most recently, he battled back-to-back with

Crown Prince Nikolai in a vicious attack by Sifiq raiders. His presence today symbolizes my respect for family and the continuity of the Protector legacy, no matter the passage of time.

"As for the present, Turand entered this war against the Sifiq Kingdom alone, never expecting the divine intervention that revealed the blood connection between Trezvindja and Turand. My heart broke seeing my people fight and die in this war. Now, my heart breaks knowing I have two peoples fighting and dying in the Sifiq Kingdom.

"Believe me when I say I consider Trezvindjans my people, too. You see that my daughter does not look like ishna, except for her eyes. She is the only one of my six children who has my eyes. The others all look like their father, who appears far more Trezvindjan than Turandan. Therefore, if my husband and my children are so much Trezvindjan, that makes you my people to honor and care for.

"I've spent much time at the front, and there I prepare to return. Priestesses from my order work with doctors to treat wounded fighters, both Turandan and Trezvindjan. We do all within the scope of our faith to bring healing and comfort to each and every warrior. I am learning that the Creator—Val in our faith and Espiritus in yours—must be the same. The Graces we call upon heal Trezvindjans of true faith the same as Turandans. Those whose time has come to return to the Creator find more peaceful passage.

"What is left? We are. You and I. We remain behind, sorrowing for those we lose. We must never forget that those lost Protectors went with full knowledge of their potential sacrifice. If we must mourn, let us blend our grief with honor because that is what they would want. To do otherwise fails them. For those who return with permanent injuries, as a society, we must resolve to provide them aid and pride as they restore their lives. We must always esteem them and never let them forget that they always remain Protectors in our hearts."

Alexa glanced to the side and nodded. Major Fratino and Captain Lisandá led uniformed Turandan guards onto the stage, each carrying an enormous candlestick holding a tall candle.

"This ceremony honors all warriors, and I understand there have been deaths from every league in Trezvindja. To commemorate each, members of the Queen's Royal Guard, including Captain Lisandá, who was wounded in this war, have just placed a candle representing each league. I would like to invite league councillors to come forward, to state the name of their individual leagues, and light a candle to honor those lives lost."

Surprised council leaders rose from their seats and filed up steps to the stage in a dignified line. They somberly announced their league names and lit candles. Occasional sobs sounded as a league name echoed throughout the theater. Once all candles were lit, Alexa stepped from behind the podium. Once again, she knelt, and everyone else followed suit. When she raised her arms to pray, a collective gasp arose. Blue-white light began to shimmer and surround her figure.

"Dearest Val, or Espiritus as my beloved Trezvindjans know you, bring comfort to those here who mourn lost loved ones and healing to those who suffer. I pray for strength and wisdom as I return to the Sifiq Kingdom. I will tend to those who fight to end the aggression against Turand and other peaceful peoples, as well as the oppression we have discovered against innocent Sifiq. I pray valor, guidance, and strength for our leaders, especially our King Gregor and Prince Nikolai, so that this war might end and the loss of life can stop. I pray for peace so all our warriors can come home."

Seconds passed as heavenly strains of music carried on light summer breezes. The velvety sweet scent of lilac, a flower unknown to Trezvindja, wafted across the theater. Then, slowly, the shimmering light around Turand's high priestess faded.

Anlía approached her mother and extended both hands. Alexa looked up, her expression simultaneously sad and satisfied. Then, hand in hand, the two Valiria slowly departed the stage, leaving even the renowned Milansa Krisantal mystified.

⌐

The following afternoon, Gaeldoreg stared at Alexa. "Escorting you to the podium for the ceremony made sense. And, yes, I will say it again. You were brilliant. Vezjalan and Drazlor have complained to no end about all the requests for introductions and the flood of cards and compliments regarding your presentation. I think you even quite shocked our Grand Councillor Krisantal."

Ignoring his comments about the ceremony, Alexa said, "Why are you so reluctant to escort me to dinner tonight? I don't understand."

"Ma Ishna, the people attending are our society's most respected citizens. Unfortunately, I am not quite their social equal."

"*Pffffthhtt!*"

"What?" Gaeldoreg responded, trying not to laugh.

"You heard me," Alexa complained, plainly aggravated. "Your manners are as fine as anyone's. Better than some I've seen, actually. Bibo, once and for all, you are *my bibo*. I love you, and I'm not ashamed to stand on top of your Mount Shazta—Shazat—well, however you say it, I'm not ashamed to go there and tell all of Trezvindja that you're my bibo. I'm proud of who you are and all you mean to me. Gregor would not have asked you to accompany me if he had any doubts about you, either. So there. Please don't fail me. I know etiquette says Vezjalan should escort me, but let him escort Anlía. After all, she's regent! Isn't that honor enough? Here, you're my rock."

Gaeldoreg couldn't restrain a snicker. "Talking of rocks, it's called Mount Shazatazefforalah. All right, Ma Ishna, if you insist, I shall escort you." Any lingering misgivings instantly disappeared with the watery smile and fervent hug he received when he acquiesced.

That evening, Alexa tucked a stray strand of black hair beneath Anlía's crown. Spinning her around, she looked up into her daughter's youthful features. "All you need is that smile I love so much."

Anlía nodded. "I'm trying, Mother. Bresklon has hardly spoken to me. Did you tell him to avoid me?"

"I did not. We discussed aspects of your relationship and some of his past. I did say I needed time to consider his request. If this is indeed serious, at some point, your father must be informed."

"Mother, I love Bresklon. No matter how hard I work to put him out of my mind, something reminds me of him. I almost feel sick thinking of him here tonight. I don't know what to expect." Her plaintive expression revealed a heart in torment.

For the first time, Alexa felt the full impact of Anlía's devotion to Bresklon and recognized the power of the love feeding that devotion. Her daughter said she had found her own Gregor. Alexa now needed to assure herself that the same love Gregor showered on her was the kind Bresklon prepared to share with Anlía. That assurance would only come if she could satisfy her concerns about Bresklon hiding something.

"Anlía, he told me that he is a widower. What do you know of his marriage?" Alexa asked the question delicately.

Anlía barely smiled. "He said she was beautiful. Their marriage was more of a family alliance than one based on great love, but they were reasonably happy, especially with the baby coming. Bresklon loves children. After she died in childbirth, he focused on his work."

Alexa kissed her daughter's forehead. "I suggest you trust in Val. If Val set your father and me on the right path with the obstacles we faced, you have nothing to worry about. Now, come. I need help to finish dressing, or Bibo will have no one to escort to dinner."

"Of course, Mother, but my lady's maids would gladly help you."

"I know," Alexa said, "but there are times when I tire of sympathetic gasps and comments when strangers see my back."

According to Trezvindjan tradition, dinner guests had been greeted by Princess Elder Sharlia ahead of the appearance of the royals. Refreshments were then served until all party reservation cards were received. At that point, guests formed parallel lines to greet the arrival of their royal hosts.

A butler rang a bell. Attired in colorful regalia, Prince Elder Vezjalan Vosklon proudly escorted his nation's Princess Regent into the marble-walled corridor. Anlía looked breathtaking in an ivory satin gown, Trezvindjan-style, cinched at her waist with a green ruched sash trimmed with twisted gold and silver braid. Drazlor Vosklon, acting as the evening's Conductor of Ceremonies, led them between the lines of guests as Anlía smiled greetings in passing. Guiding Anlía past Bresklon Krisantal and his parents, Vezjalan glanced sideways at the Regent, noticing sudden paleness in her cheeks and trembling in her hands. Patting her hand and receiving a firm nod in response, the two took their places to await Alexa.

The butler rang the bell again, and Drazlor announced, "Please welcome High Priestess Valkana and Queen, Alexa Maraná Toscano."

Again attired in elegant dress uniform complete with mourning armbands, Gaeldoreg presented a stunning figure beside his queen. Alexa wore her gold filigree crown, which perfectly accented the fine, whispering, gold-mesh fabric used only in gowns worn by Valiria high priestesses. Walking through the corridor and stopping beneath an arched doorway, she presented an elegant figure as she graciously welcomed everyone to the palace. Drazlor then began individual introductions as guests filed into the formal drawing room. Departing from ordinary custom, Alexa paused to kiss Milansa's cheek in special welcome. Trezvindja would need to adjust to her ways.

Greeting Bresklon's mother, Alexa was certain she detected a desire to linger. Bresklon's father greeted her with appropriate courtesy. Bresklon, as courtly as ever, returned her greeting respectfully. She immediately noticed shadows around his eyes and tense lines drawing the corners of his mouth.

She formally thanked everyone for their kind welcome and invited her guests to make themselves comfortable in the large, luxuriously decorated parlor. Anlía led her mother around the room, conversing with visitors, discussing various topics of interest with people she knew, and enlisting aid from Drazlor and Vezjalan with those she did not.

Ladies complimented Anlía on her ability to adapt Trezvindjan styles to her more conservative Turandan styles. Everyone was fascinated by the exquisite fabric in Alexa's elaborate gown, a material no one had ever seen. Alexa created much speculation when she explained no one knew its origin because each Valkana received six such gowns immediately following her anointment. Not even the high priestesses themselves knew the source of the fabric or who fashioned the elaborate gowns. Then, throughout the years, the gowns always fit. Upon a Valkana's death, only one dress remained for her burial.

Alexa finally made it a point to cross the room and kneel before Milansa. "My dear Shamani, how are you this evening?"

Milansa smiled her pleasure at being singled out by the queen. "Lady Valkana, I confess the fatigue of an old lady. Otherwise, I am well. And you? There is something different about you. What is it?"

"I carry many concerns, dear Shamani, plus the loss of a dear friend. I long for my husband's shoulder so that I might cry out my sorrow and once again feel the comfort of his arms around me."

"Is that why your ceremony yesterday came so much from the heart that we all felt it in ours?"

"Perhaps, but I've also held many hands of Turandans and Trezvindjans who were wounded or dying. Their suffering never fails to move me. My emotions yesterday were genuine."

"We all felt it and appreciated it, especially the candle tributes to our individual leagues."

Alexa smiled at the woman seated beside Milansa. "You are Amilina Krisantal?"

The woman smiled. "How did you remember with all these people here?"

"I have a talent for remembering names, although Bibo will tell you I can't always pronounce Trezvindjan words yet. However, I will soon begin studying in earnest."

Milansa frowned. "Bibo?"

Alexa blushed and lowered her face. "My apologies. Gaeldoreg. I meant to avoid that slip tonight. I call him Bibo. He has indeed become like a father to me. My parents died years ago in a Sifiq attack during their occupation of Turand."

"Your Majesty, I had no idea," Amilina said, her expression growing sad.

"It happened long ago."

A bell rang, and the butler announced dinner, which turned out to be a cordial, if not jovial, affair. Food was plentiful and excellent. Wines were delicious, perfect accents to the various courses. Conversation focused on satisfying curiosity about their new queen.

"So it is true that you and King Gregor have six children," Councillor Brazjakan stated, a wide grin brightening his dark features.

Alexa tilted her head, smiling back into his sparkling eyes and delighting in his apparent good humor. "Ah, yes, your good king has a great love for children."

"Forgive me for sounding rude, but it seems he may also have a great love for his queen," the venerable councillor replied.

Gaeldoreg barely stifled a guffaw, and Anlía giggled when Alexa blushed bright red. The silver-haired gentleman smiled sheepishly. "I have you at an unfair disadvantage, Milady. I am told that all of Turand is enchanted by the great love between their king and queen."

Gaeldoreg joined the conversation for the first time. "Your sources, Councillor, have not misinformed you. I have visited Turand. Turandans do adore their king and queen. I've also spent time with King Gregor and Queen Alexa. Within the first five minutes of witnessing their reunion in the Sifiq Kingdom, I understood the inspiration behind the love poems I read and the romantic ballads I heard before meeting my illustrious cousin. Seeing the two of them together is quite the unforgettable experience."

Alexa cast an affectionate glance at Gaeldoreg. "My husband and I have had an eventful marriage from the very beginning. The challenges we faced were the kind that either shatter people or build an invincible marriage. As strong as we both are—and with the power of our faith and love—we created a lasting, beautiful union." She gazed back at Councillor Brazjakan with an expression of exaggerated innocence, "My husband also has quite the task of managing a younger wife."

The mix of polite chuckles and outright laughter quickly eased into further questions about her impressions of Trezvindja, how she had discovered her husband's heritage, and his reaction when she told him. Her description of introductions to Gaeldoreg and Prince Braeklojorn captured everyone's rapt attention. Her comments about Gregor's striking resemblance to his grandfather sparked new discussion about initial reactions to Anlía by those who had known Mishkla Krisantal.

Milansa, who listened intently to the conversation, said, "It is as if Espiritus sent them to us with the images of their forebears so we might have no doubts that a new era is upon us. Mishkla was a mystic, but it seems her greater gift was to unfold in the future, which is our present."

"A lovely thought, Grandmother," Bresklon said, his first contribution to the evening.

Alexa said, "Indeed. Now that dessert is regretfully finished, I think we should retire to the drawing room. First, a word of warning. You all must prepare yourselves. When my husband arrives, there will likely be two dessert courses. He's quite famous for his love of sweets, and Trezvindjan dessert selections may ruin both his diet regimen and his trim waistline."

The subsequent round of laughter accompanied them to the drawing room, where light conversation continued. After an hour, Alexa excused herself, smiling brightly and saying she would return shortly. Briskly walking through a corridor toward a small office, she was relieved the evening had gone well, although she lamented the despondency Bresklon and Anlía both struggled to conceal.

Attending her task inside, Alexa looked up when a servant opened the office door. "Your Majesty, Mistress Krisantal wishes to speak with you."

"Of course," Alexa said.

Amilina entered, and the servant closed the door. "I apologize for disturbing you," she said, glancing down at the number of small boxes and tray of tiny, square envelopes Alexa was sorting. "I won't take much of your time, but I hoped I might speak with you."

"Perhaps you can help while we talk. There were last-minute changes to our guest list, so I need to make some changes. White boxes contain token gifts for the ladies, and blue boxes are for the men. The envelopes contain engraved notecards with today's date and my signature. Whenever we host formal dinners in Turand, it is palace tradition to give these to each guest."

"How lovely," Amilina remarked. "A treasured keepsake, especially with this your very first event here."

As they sorted the gifts, Amilina breathed in and said, "Bresklon would not be happy to know I'm speaking with you, but, mother to mother, I must. My son loves Anlía as he has never loved anyone else. I know he told you about his marriage, but his unhappiness was not his fault. My husband and I pressured him into that marriage. In truth, it was more my fault than anyone's. I had no idea the girl was in love with someone else. Her parents did, but we only cared about solidifying family alliances. When her affair went wrong…"

"Wait," Alexa stopped her. "Affair? What affair?"

Amilina looked confused. "He didn't tell you?"

"Bresklon only told me he was married and that his wife died. He never mentioned any affair."

"Oh, my son and his sense of honor." Regretful mist glazed Amilina's eyes. "Bresklon was married five years. His wife maintained an affair the entire time with a man her parents had forbidden her to see because of his lower social rank. He was also disreputable. The girl was a poor match for Bresklon, and they were miserable together. Eventually, she became pregnant, but the baby wasn't Bresklon's."

Alexa sighed as understanding cleared questions from her mind. "That explains everything."

"Your Majesty, my son offered his wife her freedom when he learned the baby wasn't his, but her lover rejected her when he learned she was pregnant. Knowing the girl's parents would also reject her, Bresklon decided not to divorce her. He agreed to accept the child as his own. Life spared him that ordeal, but he was devastated emotionally. He never revealed her secret, feeling there was no reason to shame her further after she begged his forgiveness."

"I can only respect your son's integrity."

"I know you asked Bresklon not to be part of Princess Anlía's life, but the two love one another so much."

"Amilina, I told Bresklon no such thing. I only asked for time to consider the matter. The reason was I sensed something missing in his story that I didn't understand. He never mentioned his wife's affair. I'm glad I know, but I would prefer to hear that from him. You must understand. If I am to trust him with one of the greatest treasures of my life, I must know that he and I can trust one another. Completely."

"Of course."

"Now, please go. I will be out shortly."

The moment Amilina left, Alexa caught her breath. Her estimation of Bresklon Krisantal expanded, and she felt Val's whispers in her soul. Alexa summoned the servant and handed him the tray of envelopes while she carried the tray of gifts. Then, returning to the drawing room with a brilliant smile, she explained Turand's palace tradition that she wanted to start here in Trezvindja.

"Anlía, if you will kindly pass out the gifts," Alexa said.

"Gladly, Mother," her daughter answered. "White for the ladies and blue for the gentlemen?"

"As always, my darling," Alexa said, looking around the room, her gaze dropping to Bresklon, who sat nearby. "Councillor Krisantal, would you be gracious enough to offer your assistance to the Princess by helping her with the envelopes?"

Startled, Bresklon returned Alexa's pointed gaze. Not quite sure how to interpret her expression, he took a deep breath before tilting his head elegantly in response. "It will be my pleasure, Your Majesty."

Alexa then watched as Anlía explained what they would do and started the rounds to deliver the gifts. As Alexa took a seat beside Gaeldoreg, he leaned over and whispered in her ear, "Well done, Ma Ishna, very well done."

"Well done? Whatever do you mean, Bibo?"

"Don't pretend with me, young lady. I am your bibo, remember?" he said with a pleased grin, tilting his head forward.

Alexa shifted her gaze. Bresklon carefully placed an envelope on the open palm of his hand as Anlía set a box on top and then picked up both items to present to each waiting guest. The ploy was ever-so-subtle, but the touch revealed much to Alexa's sensitive eye. With every touch, their individual auras met and brightened.

Days later, Alexa watched towering banks of clouds race northward while she clutched the rail of the frigate's deck. Much like the winds pushing those clouds, rapidly passing time had pushed Bresklon to the realization he needed to act or risk losing his dream. Alexa had received a short, handwritten message requesting a private audience the morning before her departure from Trezvindja. Smiling, she wondered who of several people had been happiest when she granted that audience.

Hardly noticing the chill breeze nipping her cheeks, she recalled his earnest expression and firm stride as he approached and bowed, arms crossed over his chest in formal salute to his queen. "Your Majesty, good morning."

"Good morning, Councillor. Please be seated. May I offer you a cup of kacha before we begin?"

"Afterward, perhaps. Thank you. For now, I must address the way we left matters concerning my relationship with Anlía."

Alexa's attention returned to the sea. Silver-gray waters were choppy. Cold air felt unsettled, portending the onset of stormy weather—a reminder of the tempest of uncertainty that Bresklon had wrestled with after he had first come to Alexa to broach the subject of courtship. With his personal storm still raging that morning, he had reached the storm's fringes. He appeared calmer and more determined.

"Bresklon, tell me." Alexa opened the door.

When he drew breath, he felt the air expand every inch of his great lungs. "I cannot nor will I continue this way. I love your daughter too much to live in this state of uncertainty. When I was married, my life was a pretense. My wife loved another man and died giving birth to his child. I kept some of her letters and her journal, so I have proof of her betrayal and infidelity, but I never saw honor in revealing her shame.

"Your Majesty—Alexa—I wish to build a new life with Anlía at the heart. I realize full well how young she is, but you know, as do I, that her maturity far exceeds many of the older ladies who attended your dinner party. So do her wisdom, her compassion, and her intelligence. She greatly credits her upbringing.

"What I can offer her materially is a fine home and a future with a man who is highly respected in this nation. Most importantly, I intend to love her more than any man in this world possibly could. To protect and care for her—to love and make her happy—that is my most treasured dream.

"I know already how much she and I share in like interests, but what you may not yet recognize is the spiritual connection we share. I think I didn't fully recognize its power until you asked me to help her with those gifts. Every time she touched me, I felt electrical charges race through my skin and then an invasion of her thoughts. Alexa, she and I are connected already, heart and soul. Please, for her sake and mine, I beg your blessing."

The mighty ship heaved upward on a wave. Holding tightly to the rail, Alexa shifted her weight and kept her balance. Trezvindja's sturdy vessel sliced through churning waters, refusing to allow the coming storm to deter it from reaching its destination. Bresklon had been so like the frigate carrying her back to the Sifiq Kingdom. Once his compass had set, he followed the direction without deviation.

"Bresklon, thank you for coming to me with the whole truth. That helps me more than you know. I know my daughter's heart." Alexa sighed. "There is one thing you must understand."

He never wavered, although a flicker of fear showed in his eyes. "That is?"

Her smile was at once reassuring and humorous. "While I give you my blessing, I remind you that you must still earn my husband's blessing. His will be the final word."

The expression of joyful relief on Bresklon's face was as bright as the shafts of sunlight peeking out from a break in the clouds above. Without thinking, he had reached out and taken her hands. "Alexa, with your blessing, I know all will be well. Anlía assures me our king always takes to heart your counsel, so, with all my heart, I thank you."

Chapter 21

"Father! Stop it!" Nikolai scolded as Gregor batted his son's hands away from the profusely bleeding streak across his cheek.

"It's nothing. Leave it!" Gregor growled.

"Be quiet and be still before I sit on you! It needs cleaning to avoid infection. It's deep and likely to scar as it is. Mother will be none too happy. Don't make me explain why you came down with fever, too. Sit still!"

With dead Sifiq soldiers at his feet and sounds of battle raging just beyond the stone fence where Nikolai tended his minor wound, Gregor waited impatiently. "Hurry."

"You know they intended to capture you," Nikolai grumbled as he applied stinging antiseptic to the cut.

"I know they did!" Gregor exclaimed, finally having enough of Nikolai's ministrations and roughly shoving him away. "Where's my sword?"

"Here," Nikolai said, swinging his father's long sword off the ground and into his hand. Then, heaving in a deep breath, he said, "Ready?"

Gregor paused long enough to grasp his son's shoulder. "Not yet. Thank you. Four of them I could handle. I was glad you saw and came to help with the other three."

Nikolai smiled grimly. "Father and son together. It seems we were born to be warriors."

Nikolai's Trezvindjan horse, a gift brought by his grandfather, waited and stomped the ground impatiently. "I don't see yours."

Gregor gave a shrill whistle. Pounding hooves and snorting heralded the arrival of his own mount. He patted the animal's neck appreciatively. "Well-trained and loyal is what Grandfather said." Mounting, he turned a ferocious expression to his son. "Let's go!"

Hours later, Gregor and Nikolai walked the battlefield. Eerie wisps of clouds hovered above the barren landscape with its few gnarled, leafless trees. Strewn about like discarded children's toys were lifeless bodies of men who had fought to their deaths that day. Beside them lay blood-stained swords. Nearly all wore the splash of color that were the turban headpieces favored by Sifiq warriors.

Glad for the biting cold that eased the stench rising from so much death, King and Prince insisted on singling out Turandan and Trezvindjan dead to kneel and pray over as their bodies were gathered for return home. Both men were deeply grateful for relatively few losses, especially considering the magnitude of the battle. Superior training, camaraderie, planning, and conditioning had contributed to their success. The Sifiq had arrived in a horde, but one thing Gregor noticed was that many appeared lean—too lean.

When the last of Gregor's casualties were removed from the field, one of his officers approached with a Protector commander at his side. "Your Majesty, what should we do about dead Sifiq?"

Gregor sighed. "As unlikely as it may seem, at least some of them probably have families who care about them. Have field orderlies organize their bodies in rows close together and cover them. Confiscate all weapons. If anyone comes to claim bodies, make no effort to stop them. Make sure guards are present. I expect claimants may be women who might appreciate assistance but will be afraid to ask for help. Use careful discretion."

"And any that are unclaimed?"

Gregor's gaze swept the battlefield. "I wish I could express how deeply every single death out there, Sifiq included, grieves me." He sighed heavily and turned back to his officers. "Burn them. We can't afford the spread of disease."

The following day, Gregor met with his officers to assess the battle's outcome. They had successfully moved their army within fifteen miles of Atuliq. Their goal was to capture a hillside just outside the city's high walls. The hill's broad crest would be the perfect site to stage large cannons for a final attack on Bin-Lot's capital.

Field Commander Zamtelza reviewed the updated plans. "Your Majesty, may I offer a suggestion?"

Gregor nodded. "Of course, Commander."

"Our enemy has identified you now. I will not suggest you stand down from the battlefield. You are a fierce warrior king who inspires Protector and Turandan fighters alike. I suggest that we assign extra guards to stay near you to avoid incidents such as yesterday's attempted capture. We were fortunate our prince's vigilance brought him to your aid. Our top strategy must be to protect you. You and Prince Nikolai are the pride of both your armies."

Gregor's gaze fixed on the Protector's bold stare. The commander had feigned nothing in his statements. Instead, he had conveyed his assessment of a successfully averted crisis, the kind that must be avoided for the sake of their campaign. He had also combined a complimentary argument with a recommended safeguard impossible for Gregor to summarily reject.

Gregor's head tilted back, his over-long hair feathering across his shoulders. Breathing in and out, he returned his attention to Zamtelza. "I appreciate your assessment, Commander. Since I intend to meet Bin-Lot in his palace to finish this business, I accept your advice. I'll leave arrangements for additional guards to you and the prince. Gentlemen, that's all for today."

Surprised, Nikolai watched his father turn and leave the briefing. Sensing his father's need for time alone, the prince told Zamtelza, "Commander, you have my gratitude and my admiration. What you just accomplished with Father is close to a miracle."

The Trezvindjan almost smiled. "Your Highness, I spoke only the truth. In times of old, Protectors maintained a rich history of defending good under the leadership of brave kings and princes. For the first time in several generations, you and your father have restored that tradition with pride. Like you Turandans, we prefer peace, but if we must fight, let us fight alongside a king and a prince like your father and you."

Nikolai reached out and clasped his officer's shoulder. "Commander, thank you. Although I was born Turandan, never forget. No doubt exists that Trezvindjan blood flows through my veins. I sincerely hope to honor that heritage."

Zamtelza finally smiled, his dark eyes flashing approval. "You, Prince Nikolai, are as fine a Protector Prince as has ever lived."

⌁

Huddled beneath blankets close to a roaring campfire, Gregor sat chewing roasted meat served with buttered chunks of toasted flatbread after discussing final plans for the next day's offensive with his field command officers. Nikolai walked up.

"Not the most satisfying of meals, is it?"

"Hmmm?" Gregor looked up. "My apologies. What did you say?"

Nikolai shook his head. "You've been a million miles away today, Father. Your face is swollen. How do you feel?"

"It's sore, but I had it cleaned and checked. There's no infection."

"Care to share what's on your mind?" Nikolai asked, leaning forward to push extra wood into the fire.

Gregor set aside the metal plate with his unfinished meal. He had no appetite. "Home. Your brothers and sisters."

"You're worried about Mother."

"She resisted leaving, Nikolai, but I insisted. Victor probably wouldn't have lasted long enough to reach the port without her, let alone home. With her, I believe he at least made it back to Turand alive."

"Why, Father? Why did you make her go?"

Gregor's voice faltered. "I had to. Part of your mother never stopped loving him, and I owed him her life after he refused to give up searching for her in Timeri. Think, Nikolai. Had it not been for Victor, I never would have met her in the first place, nor would I have had you children. My whole life would have been an empty shell. Besides..."

When his father trailed off, Nikolai scooted closer and placed a hand on Gregor's knee. "Besides what?"

"Perhaps Turand will inspire him to fight to live. Oui-lest needs him and your mother. Our younger ones need her, too. Maybe she'll stay where it's safe. I want her where she's safe. I felt so torn having her here. For one side, I needed her desperately. She lifted my spirits and made me confident I could see this through. At the same time, I was terrified she'd be hurt again."

Nikolai watched tears form streaks that caught in his father's beard. "Father, the love Mother once felt for Victor died years ago. What replaced it was more a revered memory of the love that was. This place nearly destroyed her, but she came back because you were here. Mother loves us children because of who we are—yes, but even more because we reflect the love you and she have shared through the years. Father, you are her love and her life as much as her faith in Val is. Without you, I doubt Mother would survive even a year."

Gregor smiled. "My son, your mother is strong. Her faith in Val has carried her through terrible trials and tragedies."

"I know that, but during several long talks we had her during her recovery, she told me she almost gave up several times during her captivity. Each time, she felt the strength of your love pulling her—calling her. She told me that's when she realized that, as long as she had you, she had a reason to live. What Mother feared most was losing you because then she would lose her direction and her purpose. She believes Val set you on her path to be her compass—her guidepost. She needs you, Father. Never think otherwise."

"That's exactly how I feel about her. I worry about her, Nikolai. She pushes herself so hard. She always has, but I see her more fragile than before." Gregor stared into flames but saw only images of Alexa.

"In some ways, perhaps. A little. In other ways, I think she has never been stronger. Have faith, Father. Trust in her faith and, more than anything else, trust her love for you. I don't know if any man alive has ever been loved the way she loves you."

A faint smile finally spread Gregor's lips. "Thank you, Nikolai. You are certainly proof of that." His gaze turned to his son. "I have loved you since the moment she told me we were to have a child. Such a gift you've been, especially now. Try to get some sleep. Tomorrow will be another hard day."

As Gregor cleared his mind of concerns related to the coming battle, he ignored the cold and let his mind wander home. So many vivid memories rose to tease him. Her rare flare of temper that once sent coasters flying through the air in the library to break antique statues. The blush on her cheeks as she entered the water that first time they went to Lindaval. His absolute terror before she knocked him off his horse in Garogan. The afternoon they had danced across the meadows outside Garogan Castle when she was so heavily pregnant with Nikolai.

His mind swept through years of recollections tied to Alexa and the children she had borne him. More than ever, he detested war. He had deserted her once before to fight a war. She had come to him to save his life. What had he done? He had sent her away. All these years later, he had once again deserted her to fight a war. Again, she had come to him. What had he done? Again, he sent her away.

He reached beneath his heavy coat and grasped his mother's pyramid pendant Alexa had found for him. Ironically, she had since found the family his mother had never known. His Alexa always gave him everything he needed. She was always everything he needed. Clinging to the crystal, Gregor imagined he heard sweet humming.

"Mother, watch over my wife and our children. Help me stay strong enough to end this terrible fight so I can reunite my family and discover why my two peoples are now joined. And, Mother, please, help me pray hard enough that Val will make it so I never again have to leave Alexa or send her away."

Finally surrendering to exhaustion, Gregor dozed off. Gentle fingers floated through the thick locks of his hair. A gentle lullaby eased lines etched into his brow. "Sleep, my darling, sleep. Mother watches over you. Sleep, my darling, sleep. This night, worry no more. Sleep, my darling, sleep. Soon, you'll be done with war. Sleep, my darling, sleep."

⤶

Horses' hooves pounded cold, hard ground, the percussion carrying through clear winter air. Jangling harnesses, crackling leather, and low snorts and grunts of animals pulling wagons added to the cacophony of an army on the move. With king and prince on opposite sides of the vast force marching toward Atuliq, Turandans and Protectors shared a common goal: End the long Sifiq legacy of deadly aggression. Defeat Bin-Lot.

Protectors prized their history of defending allied nations against Sifiq brutality. Turandans fought for their homeland. Every man among them knew the story of Queen Alexa's abduction and torture at Bin-Lot's hands. Already beloved by Turandans, she had quickly won the hearts of fierce Protector warriors. They claimed the Ishna Queen as their own and would fight to the last breath to achieve justice for what the Sifiq king had inflicted on her and her Valiria companions.

Field Commander Zamtelza had assembled eight elite guards: four Turandans and four Protectors. Under his command, they traveled close to King Gregor, determined to protect him from further personal attacks. Zamtelza had long studied Sifiq tactics and knew they had planned to capture the king and use him to force the Turandan army back. They would have tortured Gregor and likely murdered him in the end. Grateful that Prince Nikolai had rescued the king, thus saving the Sacred Blood of the Krisantal, the Trezvindjan had offered fervent prayers to Espiritus every night since that battle. He also prayed for divine assistance to avoid failing in his mission to shield the Sacred Blood King from further harm.

New resistance suddenly swooped in with shrill shrieks and fringed tassels flying from the sides of colorful turbans. With swords raised, Sifiq fighters aimed their attack with arrow-like precision at one side of Gregor's army, away from mounted officers. Foot soldiers immediately formed circles with reinforced metal shields protecting themselves. Cavalry officers broke marching ranks and swarmed in to defend their ground troops, swinging swords swiftly and effectively. More enemy fighters joined the attack. Gregor's foot soldiers abandoned their circles and met the enemy in a ferocious battle for a few more miles of Sifiq territory.

The clash of swords reverberated, their metallic rings resounding above the melee of squealing horses, urgently shouted commands, Sifiq shrieks, and the grunts, groans, and screams of men fighting yet another ferocious battle for their lives. Protector and Turandan warriors had shed all sense of wariness or resentment. Instead, mutual camaraderie bound them together as they covered one another, availing themselves of the advantages of height and sometimes lack of height. After three hours of brutal combat, Gregor's army beat back the Sifiq marauders.

Nikolai rode up quickly to his father, already kneeling alongside two injured soldiers. Dismounting, the prince passed his reins to a junior officer. Then, striding to his father's side, he said, "Father, senior officers and commanders are securing the perimeter of the battleground. Are you hurt?"

"No. Have you started preparations to transport the injured back to the cantonment?"

"Yes. We're moving the most seriously injured first. Thanks be to Val that Zamtelza's shield strategy worked on the initial Sifiq thrust. Our losses are small compared to theirs. Like you, I still ache at the thought of every death."

Grimacing, Gregor nodded. "Death in combat is a badge of honor for the Sifiq. Let's walk the field and then gather to assess the battle."

That evening, Nikolai warmed his hands in front of the blaze where he, his father, Zamtelza, and his father's guards would spend the night. This day's combat had left him weary and longing for the comforts of home. Today's victory had placed them five miles closer to Atuliq. He shook his head as he considered the toll in lives. So much blood had been spilled simply because of Bin-Lot's obstinate stance that he and his military could take whatever they wanted from whomever they wanted without regard to sovereign borders.

"No matter how long you ponder the subject, you will never make sense of it, my son." Gregor's large hand rested on Nikolai's shoulder.

Nikolai glanced around. "I thought you were still talking with the walking wounded."

"I was. How proud I am of our soldiers. They refuse to surrender this fight." Gregor moved closer to the fire. "You're in a serious frame of mind."

"Just perplexed by Bin-Lot. When I met him, he was exactly as Mother described. Arrogant and irascible. I don't think he possesses a thumbnail's worth of compassion for anyone but himself."

"After seeing what he did to her and now seeing how he allows his people to be treated, I agree. Do you really think we could have progressed this far so quickly if his citizenry felt any real loyalty toward him?"

"I've overheard many of their comments, as have our men. The Sifiq people can hardly believe how we've treated them. There are hold-outs, though."

"All former military accustomed to wielding control over people."

"True. I simply can't comprehend the mentality."

Gregor stretched his arm around his son and hugged him close. "We never will, thank Val for that, but we must always be on guard and ready to defend our way of life against such conduct. It is dangerous and destructive. The worst part is that such lust for power is like weeds growing out of control. They overtake gardens and fertile fields until nothing of genuine value and beauty can grow without determined intervention. Remember that when you become king."

"I won't forget, Father. I promise."

⌐

Braeklojorn Vosklon reviewed the latest reports from the front. Inside the confines of the small field office at the base camp, the Trezvindjan prince appreciated a few moments of privacy. Gregor, who had won both his grandfather's respect and his heart, had sent a personal note along with details of the army's progress toward Atuliq.

My dear Grandfather,

How relieved I am to know I have the support of family like you in such turbulent times as these. I know I told you this, but let it be written forever that I love you as if you had always been part of my life. Abstractly, you always have been part of my life since I never would have drawn my first breath had you not once loved Grandmother Mishkla so well. Ah, the chains of life, mysterious and precious.

You must know how much I have come to respect and rely on your wisdom in such a short time. My very soul tells me I can trust you. Thank you for helping manage the cantonment. The hospital is critical. Our wounded deserve the best care we can provide. Our physicians and Valiria continually demonstrate their courage and dedication. Having you manage general operations frees them to focus on healing.

Grandfather, we soon advance on our target. I pray we succeed. If I survive, I look forward to returning home to Turand to reunite with Alexa and my children. After that, I plan to take my family to Trezvindja, where I expect you to introduce me to the nation and heritage my mother missed. So much to anticipate!

It is late now. I must sleep, but I wanted you to know that your grandson turns loving thoughts to the grandfather he now treasures deep inside his heart.

Gregor

Braeklojorn read the letter twice. Sighing, he carefully folded the sheet and placed it inside the breast pocket of his coat. His memory drifted back to the day Alexa had so stubbornly intruded on his seclusion in Turand. How his life changed that day! Instead of remaining mired in murky, grief-laden clouds, he had resurfaced to live where he was needed and loved. He now carried everywhere a miniature portrait of the daughter he had never known about until Samlian Forsay had guided the Turandan queen to the caves of Corlozem Pass. That day had led him home to his mother and then to this war-torn land to meet and know his grandson.

Gregor Maxim Vosklon Krisantal Toscano. Braeklojorn smiled as he thought how proudly his grandson had assumed his Trezvindjan league names. Facing tragedies and trials, Gregor was a complex man who had confronted complicated circumstances and surmounted nearly impossible odds to achieve peace and prosperity for his people. He treasured integrity and, above all else, family. Acknowledging personal flaws, he showed few qualms seeking wisdom and guidance.

The Trezvindjan prince blinked back tears. "Thank you, Alexa. Wherever you are, thank you, Ma Ishna, for giving me my grandson and restoring meaning to my life."

An hour later, Braeklojorn and General Kohira were visiting recovering soldiers when a bell rang, and a booming voice shouted, "Incoming!" The two men exchanged surprised glances. Departing the hospital tent, both men briskly walked toward lines of wagons and dismounting riders.

"Grandfather!" Alexa, wrapped in a heavy woolen cloak, hurried toward Braeklojorn and embraced him affectionately. "You look well!"

"Ma Ishna! I was just thinking about you! Why have you returned? Gaeldoreg is in serious trouble."

Pulling her hood away from her face, Alexa grinned up at him. "Do you think I could stay away with this business unfinished? Poor Bibo surrendered to the reality that not even the combined Turandan and Protector armies could keep me away. My husband will need me close, so close I am."

Gaeldoreg finally strode up behind her. "Greetings, old friend. She's right. How your grandson manages life with his queen mystifies this old man."

Braeklojorn shook his head in mild dismay, thinking he should have expected her return. "We were getting ready to go for midday. Would you care to join us?"

Gaeldoreg gave Alexa a stern look. "Yes, we would, and you're going to eat well, correct, Ma Ishna?"

With twinkling eyes and pursed lips, Alexa sheepishly replied, "Of course, Bibo, if it will please you."

"It will," Gaeldoreg answered gruffly. "I mean it. I want you to eat a decent meal now that we're here."

Over a hot midday meal of roasted meat with vegetables and fresh bread, Alexa and Gaeldoreg listened as Braeklojorn and General Kohira detailed the progress of joint Turandan and Trezvindjan forces moving on Atuliq. Sulía answered Alexa's questions regarding hospital operations, including ongoing challenges faced by Valiria and doctors treating patients arriving with injuries inflicted days earlier in combat.

Laying her fork on her plate, Alexa shifted her gaze, apparently staring off into the distance. Gaeldoreg looked around, seeing nothing that should have attracted her attention. He often wondered about his ever-increasing sensitivity to her moods as his sense of fatherly protectiveness grew stronger each day. "Ma Ishna, are you well?"

When Alexa continued her mute gaze, the others looked to him with puzzled expressions—all except Sulía, who only smiled thoughtfully. "She's Valkana," she said quietly. "Her mind often wanders into the realm of our Lord Val. She listens when he speaks. Just be patient."

Seconds later, Alexa's eyelids fluttered rapidly, and she shook her head. Glancing down at her plate, she picked up her fork and pushed aside the few remnants of food. Then, grinning wickedly, she looked up at Gaeldoreg as if the moments spent in silence had never happened. "I think I deserve something sweet for dessert. Didn't you bring some tins of those delightful brosha cakes from Trezvindja?"

Surprised at first, Gaeldoreg tossed his head back and laughed out loud. Relief flooded him at seeing her eat properly one of the few times since they had left for Turand. During three voyages and while in Turand, she had eaten small amounts here and there, complaining there was either no time to sit down for a full meal or that she just had no heart to eat. "Ma Ishna, if my brosha cakes will make you happy, then wait here. Your bibo will go fetch some so we can all enjoy them."

Later, while Alexa rested, Braeklojorn studied his cousin. "You look worried."

Gaeldoreg chewed thoughtfully at the inside of his cheek. "You're fortunate to have missed this part of fatherhood. I didn't realize until we left port why Gregor insisted she accompany Victor back to Turand. He wanted her safe at home. I'm sure of it. Besides that, did you know she and Victor once planned to marry?"

Braeklojorn nodded. "Gregor told me. Quite a story, that one. Right before they departed for Turand, Victor also told Gregor he was still in love with Alexa."

"Victor's death hurt her. Deeply. Something else weighs on her mind, though. I can feel it. How is it I feel all this when she is not my own child?"

Braeklojorn shrugged. "Did you two not willingly create a blood bond?"

Gaeldoreg's head tilted to the side. Light glinted from his eyes as he nodded. "Of course! Her mystical tendencies make our blood bond more powerful. That makes perfect sense."

"In reality, it seems she has become your daughter. Perhaps not conceived in the normal way, but your child in blood and spirit, nonetheless. Watch over her, my friend. Trust your instincts with Alexa as I trust mine with my grandson. We both have families to love and protect now."

The following morning, Alexa awoke early for prayers and meditations. Wrapped in blankets she had shared with Gregor, she had fallen asleep more easily since leaving with Victor. Surrounded by possessions her husband left behind in his tent, she felt lingering traces of his presence that calmed her spirit. After centering and rising from bed, she quickly dressed and left for the dining tent, where Gaeldoreg already sat with a heavy mug of hot kacha in hand.

"Bibo, good morning! Please say you've saved some kacha for me. I need to warm my insides and eat something before I start a busy day."

Gaeldoreg stood and opened his arms to embrace her. "Good morning, Ma Ishna! How glad my heart is that you're so bright today."

Easing her Trezvindjan father's concerns, Alexa ate a wholesome breakfast while maintaining a running dialogue regarding options for improving care for battle casualties. Before long, she either huddled with Valiria to listen to their experiences and ideas or ambled along rows of cots, stopping to talk with patients, often praying with Turandans who requested the privilege from their Valkana.

Evening descended on the camp with its usual dark chill. Braeklojorn tugged a wool blanket snugly around the shoulders of his heavy winter cloak and walked over to a huge bonfire where, sitting alone on a split log, Alexa gazed into leaping yellow flames. "My dear girl, may I join you?"

Glancing upward, Alexa sighed. "Grandfather, of course."

Settling down beside her, he asked, "Why are you out here by yourself?"

"Thinking. I'm concerned about upcoming battles and the inevitable casualties."

"You know we're giving the best care possible to our injured soldiers."

She exhaled heavily. "The physicians and Valiria here have worked untiringly. I know. My mind just refuses to settle on the idea that we can't do better." She straightened and stretched. "I heard a late courier ride in. Was there any news?"

"Gregor and Nikolai are organizing for a final advance on Atuliq. They'll probably start marching again tomorrow."

"How long before they reach the city?"

"With all their men and armament? Probably another four or five days, depending on how much resistance they meet along the way." Braeklojorn watched Alexa, but she remained quiet. "What are you thinking, Ma Ishna?"

She shook her head. "I worry about what's sure to come. I desperately want to help Gregor. My thoughts are jumbled. I must settle my mind if I'm to figure out how best to give my husband the help he needs most." She slowly stood and bent forward to kiss his cheek. "I'm going to bed now. I love you. Good night."

Gaeldoreg and Braeklojorn met inside the dining pavilion the following morning, expecting to join Alexa for breakfast. An attendant said she had stopped much earlier, leaving in a rush with tea and slices of toasted flatbread. The Trezvindjans exchanged puzzled glances.

"Let's have breakfast while we're here. We'll find out what she's up to soon enough," Braeklojorn said with a grin.

Gaeldoreg expelled a heavy breath. "This parenting role is a bigger challenge than I expected."

Chuckling as he sat down, Braeklojorn accepted a mug of steaming kacha and took a drink of the bracing brew. "My friend, men and women have said that for centuries, yet children continue to be born. They do have their redeeming graces."

Gaeldoreg paused with his fork over the plate now in front of him. "Redeeming graces indeed. Whenever she smiles at me or hugs me, I wonder what it would have been like to hold a baby of my own and watch that child grow to adulthood. We both missed that. I thank Espiritus daily that your Gregor has given us both such a fine family to enjoy."

"So do I. Let's eat so we can go discover what Alexa is up to now."

Arriving at the hospital pavilion later, both men stopped abruptly. Wagons stood outside the entrance. Orderlies briskly carried crates outside, loading them under Sulía's supervision. A scowling Captain Lisandá barked orders at the queen's Royal Guards, who were assembling for an expedition.

"Alexa! What in the world are you doing?" Braeklojorn called out as he quickly strode toward her.

Glancing up from her tally sheet and handing it to an officer, Alexa smiled. "Grandfather! Good morning! I woke up hours ago and knew exactly how to remedy delays in care for our combat wounded. I've talked to men who were at the last battle and identified a relatively safe spot where we can establish a triage area to provide initial treatment to casualties before transferring them here."

"Wait," Gaeldoreg interrupted, "are you saying you plan to travel close to the front?"

"Absolutely! Six Valiria and two physicians volunteered to accompany me. We can make the trip in three days, quickly set up, and be ready when the fighting starts. We can treat injuries and dispatch the most critical cases here for the surgeons to handle. It will be more efficient and should save more lives. I meditated on it last night, and Val showed me the answer. It's a brilliant solution."

Shaking his head, Braeklojorn's long, silver hair flew side to side. "How can you imagine Gaeldoreg or I would let you travel that close to the fighting?"

Alexa's head snapped back in surprise. "Grandfather, I understand your concern, but my decision is made. Lives are precious, and I'm responsible for preserving them if I can."

"And I've promised our king to protect his queen in his absence!"

"Bibo, I'm taking my Guard. Besides, this excursion will succeed. Trust me."

"Alexa, I cannot let you move ahead with this. The risks are too great. Gregor will have both our heads if something happens to you," Braeklojorn argued.

Alexa's expression stiffened. "First of all, nothing will happen to me. This I know for certain, I assure you. Second, I rarely avail myself of my royal rank, but I'm undertaking this mission as Queen of Turand and Trezvindja. Unless you wish to arrest me and explain that to Gregor, then I'm moving ahead without delay. Now, if you'll excuse me."

As she brusquely turned away, Braeklojorn gently grasped her arm. "Alexa, please reconsider. If you must, send your volunteers, but you stay. Your presence here will bolster the spirits of the medical teams and patients. I'm asking you not to go."

Emerald eyes reflected her determined stance. "Grandfather, I love and respect you, but I cannot change my mind. I must do this. Excuse me."

After she hurried toward her private tent, Gaeldoreg stopped Braeklojorn from following her. "Let me see if I have better luck reasoning with her." Reaching the king's quarters, he heard her moving around inside. "Alexa, may I enter?"

"Yes, Bibo."

Her curt reply didn't stir much optimism, but he pushed aside the door flap and went inside. "Ma Ishna, you mustn't be angry with Milord. He fears for your safety. For that matter, so do I." He watched as she resolutely tightened straps on her travel bags.

"Bibo, I have no choice. I must go because Gregor needs me if he's to finish this business with Bin-Lot without losing self-control. You have no idea how great his fury is or how deep it runs. By setting up the triage camp, I accomplish two goals. First, I prepare to handle casualties while letting Gregor know I'm there if he needs me."

Gaeldoreg's brow furrowed. "How will he know? A courier?"

"No, Bibo, the lights of the Healing Graces. Only a Valkana's are blue. When he's ready to launch his final advance, I'll establish a dome of light to cover the medical operations. He'll see them."

Gaeldoreg held her by her arms. "Alexa, I still don't understand why it's so imperative for you to go. We can dispatch a courier to advise him you're back."

Shaking her head, she looked away. "No, I have to be close enough to get to him. Quickly, Bibo, because he needs inspiration to finish this fight. I can stay here no longer than two months, maybe three. If hostilities continue, I'll have to go home. Gregor needs to vanquish Bin-Lot and confront his desire for retaliation before then. I am the only one who can help him walk off that bed of fire with honor."

Staring intently into her eyes, Gaeldoreg dreaded asking the next question. "Tell me, Ma Ishna, why do you have a departure deadline?"

"Bibo, you must keep my secret if I tell you. Even from Grandfather. And from Gregor, once we meet up with him. Promise me."

"I promise."

"I am with child."

Gaeldoreg's dark eyes grew impossibly wide as he shouted, "What?"

"Shush! I don't want the whole camp to hear."

"Alexa, have you lost your mind?"

"No! I told you. I've meditated and received Val's assurances. I'll be fine. The last thing I expected was to have another baby at this stage in my life, but Val gives me this child as a gift with some special purpose. I would never endanger him unnecessarily. I must help his father."

"Espiritus, deliver me!" Gaeldoreg exclaimed, wrestling with the shock of her revelation. "Ma Ishna, very well. Can you give me time to pack my travel bags? I will not let you go without me."

Tears brimmed in Alexa's eyes, turning them a dark shade of evergreen. "Bibo, you don't have to go, although I love you all the more for offering. And you mustn't worry. I'll come back and give you a grandson of your own to cuddle when this is all over."

"The grandson of my own? I look forward to that day, but I'm still going with you."

Despite all of Gaeldoreg's uncertainties and fears, the journey proved uneventful. As Alexa had predicted, they arrived at a broad field sheltered by tall evergreens near the end of three days' travel. Alexa rapidly surveyed the space and plotted the area for the camp's maximum efficiency. Then, addressing the most immediate matters, meals were cooked over roaring campfires while tents were erected as sleeping quarters for the priestesses, medical volunteers, and military personnel. Somebody found two deserted pens to corral the many horses. Shelters would be set up the following morning for receiving and treating expected battlefield casualties.

Yawning over her trail supper of vegetable stew and flatbread, Alexa grinned at Gaeldoreg's pointed glare. Swallowing her last bite, she said, "Don't worry, Bibo. I have every intention of heading off to bed. I'm utterly exhausted."

"Good. You don't make this parenting business easy."

She chuckled. "You should try parenting six children."

He groaned so loudly that everyone looked around at him. Rising from the crate he sat on, he took her hand, helping her stand. "Go. Sleep while you can."

Alexa wrapped her arms tightly around him. Then, relishing the protective embrace he returned, she said, "Bibo, you mean the world to me. I really do love you. Good night."

⤺

Nikolai's concentrated gaze swept the limits of Bin-Lot's capital city, which stretched out beyond the hill where he and his father stood. Atuliq Bay, the wide harbor essential to Sifiq trade and naval power, lay to his right. Trezvindjan and Turandan vessels had successfully blockaded port operations for months. Shifting his attention to the city itself, the prince noted perimeter reinforcements to the left and directly ahead. Distance made it impossible to discern much about defenses on Atuliq's far side, giving him no choice but to rely on General Ravendro.

"Is everything ready?"

Nikolai turned. "Yes, Father. We moved cannons into place overnight. All troops have reached assigned positions. We await only your command."

Gregor breathed deeply. Casting his eyes toward the ocean, he saw pearl-gray skies streaked with gold as beams of sunshine began to break over the horizon. His heart pounded a quickening rhythm. Gazing at his son, he said, "If I do not survive this battle for any reason, Nikolai, promise you will fulfill my promise to achieve justice for what Bin-Lot did to your mother."

"Father, don't…"

"I have every intention of claiming that justice myself, but there is the possibility I won't. Promise me you will if I fail your mother."

"You won't fail Mother. You can't fail—Mother!"

"Nikolai, promise me! For your mother!"

"No! Father! Mother! Look!" Nikolai exclaimed, tilting his head forward.

Spinning on his heels, Gregor gasped. In the distance behind them, brilliant lights danced and sparkled in the dawning heavens. The two men watched as the lights settled into the glowing blue dome that illuminated the sky. A clear dome then appeared to cap the Valkana's dome of Healing Graces.

Nikolai's face reflected a shocked expression. "Father, what is that?"

Gregor slowly smiled. "Praise Val with all your heart, my son. Your mother has come, and she brings Val's protection to care for our wounded. Signal the cannons."

Chapter 22

From the hill above Atuliq, cannons invented by Victor Garogan fired alternating rounds into the city. Sleeping residents awakened to deafening booms that resounded throughout Bin-Lot's capital. Cannonballs crashed through walls and blasted holes into streets. Fires broke out in swaths of buildings when fireplaces or lanterns were damaged, spreading devastating flames.

Disciplined and well-armed, Turandan troops and Protector warriors advanced into the city. Sifiq soldiers on duty looked to their officers for direction on meeting the massive invasion force. Drowsy reinforcements from local barracks scrambled to defend their capital. Constant, thundering roars from the cannons and subsequent destruction filled early morning air with chaotic reverberations and levels of confusion new to the warlike Sifiq.

Adept in the art of war and vicious command techniques, Sifiq officers swiftly organized waking ranks into the dangerous military expected by Gregor's armies. Fighting grew fierce. Sifiq soldiers navigated their city based on firsthand knowledge rather than studies of maps drawn by defectors. However, Gregor's forces knew where to push Sifiq soldiers to maximize losses caused by the cannons.

Sifiq defenses were most dense near the palace, hinting King Bin-Lot had not fled Atuliq. By midafternoon, Gregor's army had taken possession of almost half the city. Heavy fighting still rocked the port district. General Ravendro's troops engaged in furious combat on the far side of Atuliq.

Suddenly, warehouses in the port district exploded in clouds of flying timbers and debris following several thunderous blasts. Gregor's hilltop position afforded him a vantage point to scan the bay. Two Turandan warships had sailed close enough to fire their cannons. Gregor grimly smiled. "Grandfather. He got word to the warships."

~

Midmorning. Alexa spotted the first carts rolling down the road with casualties. Several guards waited at the edge of the protective dome to receive the injured. Her sister priestesses set to work immediately, assessing injuries and applying the Healing Graces to treat wounds. Physicians and Alexa handled the most severe cases. Shortly after noon, the first wagon departed with patients stable enough for transport but requiring more complex surgery.

As the hours passed, Alexa and Sulía occasionally paused to embrace one another. Both had endured long captivity and suffering in this country. Now, they felt as captive as ever. Each awaited news of husbands who had gone to Atuliq. Knowing Gregor planned to breach the palace and confront Bin-Lot, Win-Das had volunteered to guide them inside the complex where he had served duty for several years.

Wounded fighters arrived in steady streams. Many responded to Val's Graces with near-immediate healing and needed only rest to recuperate. Others required more extensive treatment than the Valiria and physicians provided. Several needed urgent care and stabilization, followed by emergency transport to the base camp for surgery. Because of early assessment and treatment beneath the dome of Healing Graces, Alexa's triage camp would save many lives.

Under Gaeldoreg's watchful eye, Alexa was also bound to honor her pledge to him. He had exacted her promise to listen to him and take care of herself. Twice, he had insisted she take breaks to rest and once to eat. Meekly swallowing protests, she knew how easily she lost track of time when caring for patients. His reminders translated to care for herself and her baby.

Afternoon dragged into evening. The stream of injured soldiers slowed to a trickle, then stopped. According to those transporting the wounded, Gregor's army was securing positions for the night. A concentrated thrust into the heart of Atuliq, including Bin-Lot's palace, was planned for early morning. Their Queen's unexpected presence so close to the battle had bolstered both the courage and spirits of the troops. Leadership from their monarchs inspired Turandan and Trezvindjan troops alike to free this part of their world from savage Sifiq aggression.

Gaeldoreg noticed the effort required for Alexa to smile as she encouraged suffering patients undergoing treatment from Valiria priestesses. Beyond fatigue, her worry was evident. Finally, seeing her stagger, he decided it was time to intervene. Gently taking her arm, he gave her his most stern fatherly frown and said, "You've done enough, Ma Ishna. You need to eat and get some serious rest."

Gazing up into his dark eyes, she had no energy to argue. "Let me wash my hands, and I'll be right with you."

As they sat eating before a campfire, he said, "Alexa, it isn't unusual for a battle of this scope to last days. The Sifiq military is filled with skilled warriors who thrive on fighting. Their culture is to kill or die trying. Taking Atuliq was never an easy prospect. Gregor knew that from the beginning."

Alexa stared into the fire. "I'm certain he did. From the beginning, I also knew convincing him to change his mind would be impossible. Once he decided to come here and confront Bin-Lot, he was determined to let nothing stand in his way."

"Ma Ishna, considering everything I heard, I cannot blame him. Any man whose wife was brutalized the way you were would merit no respect if he did not seek justice for such acts. That is especially true considering Bin-Lot so arrogantly sanctioned continued attacks on Turand. Sifiq kings have long tormented their people and turned their aggression on other parts of our world. Protectors stood against them, but your husband is the first in history with sufficient courage to bring war to Sifiq soil. We must support him however possible."

She turned a woe-filled face to him. "I do support him, Bibo. It's just hard not to be afraid for him. And for Nikolai. I love them so."

Gaeldoreg kissed her forehead. "Rightfully so. Now, finish your supper and try to sleep. I expect tomorrow to be more hectic than today. All right?"

Nodding, she took a bite. Glancing up with tears glistening on her cheeks, Alexa managed a trembling smile. "Bibo, I have no words to express how glad I am that you're my second father. I say again. I do love you."

〜

Eerie chill pervaded Atuliq's streets as darkness slowly yielded to invading dawn's lighter shadows. Huddled close together inside abandoned buildings, squads of Gregor's army stirred and wolfed down breakfast from their knapsacks before making last-minute inspections of weapons and hurriedly reviewing their orders. In the distance, cannon blasts again exploded morning quiet, prompting stealthy glances through windows and doors quickly followed by troops streaming into city streets.

Resolute. Determined. King, Prince, officers, and warriors merged and then surged, swelling into a mighty wave sweeping toward the stone palace that had housed generations of warmongering Sifiq kings. Nearing the sprawling compound, commanders fought hard to assume positions discussed in detailed strategy sessions. Sifiq soldiers stubbornly fought to repel the attack but were worn down in both numbers and physical might. Gregor's stronger army steadily gained ground, forcing dwindling defender ranks to withdraw behind palace walls.

As the morning battle progressed, the artillery corps rolled their deadly cannons closer and started their thunderous storm on outer ramparts surrounding Bin-Lot's palace. Fortifications erected to stand against two-legged marauders soon began to crumble against the onslaught of lead-clad stone cannonballs fired by Lord Garogan's booming beasts. Assault forces swiftly climbed over growing piles of rubble and engaged waiting soldiers while other warriors fiercely fought their way through pockets of defenders to throw open palace gates.

Once inside the walled perimeter, Gregor's astute glance swept the scene from the saddle of his tall Trezvindjan steed. Officers from both armies hoarsely shouted orders. Sifiq soldiers raced in every direction, attempting to reinforce defenses at palace entrances. Shattered glass sparkled on stone and marble steps. Cracks in the walls evidenced the ground-quakes Alexa had described. Turmoil and destruction saturated the very air hanging over Bin-Lot's center of power.

Looking straight ahead and upward, Gregor sneered at the Sifiq coat of arms he had come to detest during his childhood. With ships and crossed swords in each corner, the great serpent coiled around an image of their world. It symbolized the taking of everything the Sifiq lords desired. That crest had once made Turand's young prince want to vomit. He was now king of two allied nations, and that image fed fire into his belly as he watched a squad of Protector and Turandan warriors clear the main entrance and open the towering doors to Bin-Lot's inner sanctum.

"Your Majesty?"

"Win-Das! Commander Zamtelza! Are you ready?"

"We are! Your Guard stands with you, King of the Sacred Blood!" Zamtelza declared. "On foot or on horseback?"

"Gentlemen! Let's make a grand entrance Bin-Lot will never forget!" Urging his magnificent Trezvindjan steed forward, Gregor burst into the Sifiq palace with sword drawn and a resounding cry.

Other soldiers streamed in behind Gregor's leading Guard, initiating a vicious fray with Sifiq palace guards. Meanwhile, according to plan, Win-Das broke to the right, guiding Gregor and his primary Guard toward Bin-Lot's central court. From there, it would be easier to determine where the Sifiq king had gone to seek refuge.

Arriving inside the lavish, expansive hall, only Gregor was unsurprised by the Sifiq monarch's utter arrogance. Attired in full regalia, the man lounged backward on his throne with his feet propped on a velvet-upholstered ottoman. Eight guards stood around him, nervously clutching their swords. Four downcast Sifiq women sat on the floor, two on each side of the elaborate throne.

With a grand flourish, Bin-Lot flipped the dangling tassel of his turban away from his face. "Unless I'm mistaken, I assume the cowardly King Gregor of Turand finally summoned sufficient nerve to meet me in my own house."

Slowly, Gregor dismounted, his guards following in unison. "You are quite mistaken. I am Gregor, yes, and King of Turand. The cowardly part is something you made up, hoping to distress my son. That proved erroneous on your part."

"Of course. My apologies. As men and kings, I'm sure we can agree to forgive my indiscretion on that matter as I forgive your indiscretion on sending a child to do a man's work." Bin-Lot's voice dripped with scathing sarcasm.

Gregor gazed impassively. "If you try to bait me, you fail. Your navy is sunken, and your army is in tatters. Atuliq has fallen. Your palace crumbles around you. The time has come for you to face me."

Bin-Lot chuckled derisively. "Gregor, Gregor. What is this all about? A few pillaged villages and the unfortunate loss of a few peasants? Was this war worth so much effort?"

Zamtelza glanced at his king. The calm facade he observed was remarkable. The tension in the king's body revealed barely contained fury. He nodded to one of his guards in a predetermined signal to summon Prince Nikolai.

"Let me see. Continued violation of my sovereign borders. Murder and rape of citizens under my protection. Abduction, imprisonment, and brutalization of my citizens. I answer yes. Sifiq aggression ends now, and you, Bin-Lot, will personally face justice for what you have done."

The Sifiq king shifted his weight, kicking aside the ottoman without concern that it hit one of the women. Standing, he scowled at Gregor. "Those damned women again. Your son mentioned that when he came with that Coloridian ambassador. What is so important about a bunch of women that I sent home? I lost a valuable ship and crew sending them home, not to mention all the costs I incurred for damages caused by that bitch calling herself Alexa Maraná."

Dark eyes suddenly glittered menacingly. "I suggest you control your tongue, Bin-Lot," Gregor snarled. "You cross lines that bring you perilously close to my breaking point."

Bin-Lot rolled his eyes and shook his head. "I will never understand why you Turandans place such high value on females. They are good for nothing except pleasuring men, bearing children, and working for our comfort. Do you mean to tell me you have invaded my kingdom and fought this war over that damned woman?"

The sharp tap of boots across stone tiles stopped Gregor from responding. "Father! I see you have located our most unworthy enemy."

Turning on his heel, Gregor exhaled heavily. His son's unexpected appearance reminded him of both his purpose and his responsibilities. "I have, and most unworthy he proves to be."

"Ah, Crown Prince Nikolai, welcome back to Atuliq. I apologize that conditions are less inviting than on your last visit."

Nikolai scowled. "As you see, my father accompanied me this time. I also see you are as arrogant and disagreeable as ever."

"Have you no manners, boy? You insult me in my own house."

"Not any longer. This palace now belongs to the King of Turand and Trezvindja." Nikolai announced proudly.

Bin-Lot shook his head. "Wait. What?"

Gregor lifted his bearded chin. "You heard my son. You see me surrounded by both Turandan soldiers and Trezvindjan Protectors. I am king of both nations. We now claim victory over the Sifiq Kingdom and you as our prisoner."

Soldiers who had followed Nikolai quickly disarmed the men guarding the Sifiq king while Win-Das and two of Zamtelza's Protectors roughly took Bin-Lot into custody. The Sifiq king twisted furiously against the painful grip of his captors.

"That is impossible! Kaelzron is King of Trezvindja, and I negotiated an agreement with Princess Essila for the Protectors to stay clear of our business!" Bin-Lot's face flushed scarlet as he spewed a stream of vile curses.

Gregor cocked his brow. "Your bad fortune, I fear. Fate was already intervening in the form of your nemesis, Alexa Maraná, who discovered the trail leading to Trezvindja's rightful heir—me. Also, Essila never had such authority, and Kaelzron has abdicated in my favor."

"Impossible!" Bin-Lot spat on the floor in Gregor's direction. "I don't believe you!"

Noting a nod from Gregor, Commander Zamtelza stepped away from the Sifiq monarch, now restrained by Turandan soldiers. "Protectors, honor your rightful King of the Sacred Blood!" The

Protectors inside the court immediately formed semi-circles in front of Gregor and knelt, arms crossed over their chests.

"My brave and loyal warriors, in turn, I honor you with my gratitude and respect. Please rise."

When the Trezvindjans resumed their positions, Gregor finally approached Bin-Lot. Towering above the Sifiq monarch, he glared down into blue eyes that remained haughty. Gregor seethed with fury regarding every detail Alexa had shared about how this miscreant had ordered and then watched and gloated over her beatings. The thought of how he had attempted to force himself on her sexually made Gregor want to break the man apart, one bone at a time.

"What's the matter, Gregor?" Bin-Lot taunted. "Was I right when I told your son you're a coward?"

Gregor's right hand shot out and clenched tightly around Bin-Lot's throat. Lifting the Sifiq from the floor, he watched with detached curiosity as Bin-Lot's face changed colors. "I have no intention of watching you die of suffocation. Not yet, anyway. As I said before, control your tongue. Otherwise, you might lose it." He then dropped the man to the tiles like a limp ragdoll.

Sprawled on his back with his hands clutching his neck, Bin-Lot hissed, "I will not surrender. My soldiers will continue fighting you."

"There's no reason for them to die. Sign a surrender. Save your people further hardship."

"This is my kingdom. I rule here," Bin-Lot responded caustically. "I will never surrender. My soldiers have sworn to fight to the death as long as I so order."

"You have no concept of the justice you already face. Surrender now. There may be some hope of leniency."

"Hah! You intend to execute me. What kind of leniency am I to expect?"

Gregor's laughter chilled even Bin-Lot's cynical soul. "I have no intention of executing you. That would be far too merciful. No, you will pay in kind for your cruelty—at least part of it."

"Father?"

"Yes, Nikolai?" Gregor stood stark still, coldly glaring at Bin-Lot.

"Father."

Something in the softened tone of his son's voice caused Gregor to turn. Standing at the court's entrance, clad in her hooded lavender cloak with Gaeldoreg by her side, stood Alexa. By all that he held holy, Gregor could hardly believe she had summoned sufficient courage to return to the Sifiq king's lair where she had endured such unbelievable torture and torment, yet there she was. His great heart pounded an uneven rhythm as anguish glazed black-brown eyes. He nearly choked as he swallowed. Of their own volition, his arms stretched out to her.

Slowly, she glided toward him. Sensing her husband would need her, Alexa had already passed the outskirts of Atuliq when she met Nikolai's messenger. Her son's hasty note had not exaggerated her husband's desperate anger. Riding as fast as she dared, she had begged Val to deliver her safely through streets still fraught with violent skirmishes. Reaching Gregor, she raised delicate fingers to caress the scar now marring his cheek. "My love, I have come to stand with you."

He nearly choked again, then whispered, "Beloved, you should not be here. Not after everything that happened."

"Remember. I trust your judgment, and I will keep my promise to let you deal with them on their terms. However, you must manage this with honor—for our children and our two peoples."

Cradling her face between huge hands beneath her hood, he placed a lingering kiss against her forehead. "Thank you, my beloved wife. This will not be easy. I will not allow you to be witness, either, but you must allow me to proceed."

She grimaced, but she nodded her agreement. She felt his inner storms abating. Reason was reasserting itself. He would waste no time.

Gregor turned around. "King Bin-Lot, stand up."

Bin-Lot pushed backward on the floor like a crab, halting when he collided with the unyielding legs of Royal Guards. With turban askew and elegant clothing rumpled, the Sifiq king was hauled unceremoniously to his feet.

"Hmmm. I might venture to ask which king now acts the coward," Gregor mused aloud. "Never mind. For the moment, we shall first clarify something you mentioned earlier. Yes, you're right. Turandans do value women very highly. For that matter, so do Trezvindjans. You already knew that since you were willing to negotiate with Princess Essila.

"Right now, my eldest daughter sits as Regent in Trezvindja. We know women are very talented and intelligent when treated with respect and kindness. They are essential partners in our societies. A lesson you could stand to learn.

"You also referred to the Turandan women who were abducted and imprisoned here for a year. They were beaten multiple times and forced into slave labor when they refused to serve your sexual whims because of their religious convictions and marital status. Your actions were intolerable then and subject to justice now."

"Justice, you say? You just marched across my kingdom, destroyed my army, and blew apart my capital city! How much more justice do you need for a few worthless bitches?" Bin-Lot shouted.

Only Alexa's hand at his back prevented Gregor from leaping forward and squeezing the life out of the Sifiq king. "You were given ample opportunity to avoid this debacle altogether. My son warned you when he came with Coloridia's ambassador. The time has come to pay for your lack of foresight and concern for your own people."

"Why? I just want to know why you have come this far over a few pillaged villages and five abducted women."

"Why?" Gregor repeated furiously. "First, I swore when I ended Sifiq occupation years ago that I would never again allow Sifiq aggression to take hold in Turand and threaten my people. Second, when I saw the condition of the priestesses you returned to Turand, I swore I would exact justice for their abuse. That day has come."

"Do you know what trouble they caused here? Especially the one called Alexa Maraná! She claimed to be a priestess sworn to do good, but she was responsible for immense damage to this city. She claimed to be married with six children, but if that's true, I pity her poor husband."

Smiling, Alexa stepped forward and tucked back her hood. "Perhaps you should ask my husband if he requires your pity."

Bin-Lot gasped, "You!"

"It seems destiny deems we meet again." Emerald eyes locked on his blue ones with unflinching challenge.

As the Sifiq king sputtered senselessly, Gregor took Alexa's hand and said, "Let me introduce you to my wife, Alexa Maraná Toscano, Queen of Turand and Trezvindja, and High Priestess Valkana."

"Your wife?" Bin-Lot finally stammered. "She's *your* wife?"

"My wife and the mother of my children. All six of them, just as she told you."

Bin-Lot's eyes narrowed accusingly at Alexa. "Why did you never tell me who you were?"

"Why would I? You would have used me for ransom or other extortion had you known the true extent of my identity. I never lied about who I was. I just never told you the full truth."

"Bitch!"

Having heard enough, Gaeldoreg backhanded the Sifiq monarch, splitting the man's lip and bruising his pale face. Turning unapologetically to Gregor, he said, "No man speaks to my daughter that way. Do you wish to punish me?"

"No, that was acceptable."

The Sifiq dabbed his sleeve against his bleeding mouth. "I thought you said Sifiq soldiers murdered your parents during the occupation."

"They did," Alexa answered calmly. "Gaeldoreg Vosklon is my adopted father and a noble Protector."

Gregor exhaled impatiently. "As you see, Bin-Lot, I have good reason to demand that you face justice. I will not fritter away time, either. You will be secured as a prisoner until ten o'clock tomorrow morning. That will give us time to assess the battle situation and sort out matters here at the palace. When we meet tomorrow, I will issue the sentence concerning your treatment of my wife and her sister priestesses. After that, we will start deciding on the long-term status related to stabilizing this nation for the future."

Turning to Nikolai, he said, "Can you implement plans for the prisoner?"

"Yes, Father. Win-Das assures me there is a safe and secure location for this so-called king."

⤺

"You stayed in this room with the others?" Gregor asked, studying the plain, almost sterile confines of the room in the women's quarters where he and Alexa would spend the night.

Half-smiling, she nodded. "I'm so glad Lil-Shem Tel is still here and well. I was afraid for her when we left. I hope you don't mind. I just couldn't bear staying at the palace. Not yet, anyway."

Gregor drew her into a protective embrace. "I still can't believe you came today. The way you faced him was a marvel. I intended for you to take Victor home and stay until this was over."

Resting her cheek against his chest, she listened to the comforting sound of his heartbeat. "I know. I had my reasons for returning, one of which was today's initial confrontation. I knew exactly how trying it would be for you."

He exhaled sharply. "I won't lie. I wanted to wring the life right out of him. I'm not ashamed to admit that, but I would have regretted the deed eventually. He must taste justice for what he did to you and your Valiria and then face his people. I promised myself that."

Moving from his arms to adjust pillows and extra blankets the Sifiq women had provided, she smiled at the memory of their shock and joy upon recognizing their king's former prisoner. "Gregor, just promise me that your plans are for justice, not revenge."

Her softly spoken words reflected the soul he adored. Grasping her arms, he turned her toward him. "Alexa, justice and revenge sometimes look alike. It doesn't mean they are intended to be alike. I want you to remember that. If I intended vengeance, my punishment for Bin-Lot would be far more immediate and even more brutal than what I plan. As it is, he'll no doubt require medical treatment, but he will receive compassionate care he never allowed. Give me credit for that."

Her lips formed a slow smile. "I apologize, my husband. Sincerely, I do trust you. I'm just tired. We've been parted too long again. I only wish to lie beside you and sleep with your arm around me."

Noting something delicate and fragile about her, Gregor lifted her chin. "Are you not well, Alexa?"

"I'm very well. Just tired. Too much travel. Victor's death. Too much death and war altogether. I just want my husband to hold me and sing me to sleep."

As they lay in the small, clean bed, Gregor held his wife close. The fresh scent of lilacs floated around her. Drawing in a breath, he began singing a romantic ballad he knew she liked. His resonant voice held a rough edge from so much shouting over the past few days. Still, his song sounded more beautiful than ever to the woman clinging to the husband who had inspired her to survive captivity in this same room three years earlier.

~

Following an early morning briefing with lead officers and commanders, Gregor and Nikolai returned to the women's quarters to share breakfast with Alexa. Her reunion with female Sifiq servants had proven helpful. She had learned many vital details about Bin-Lot's current political crises at home and had recruited willing hands to tend wounded soldiers and ailing citizens alike. Hospital facilities were already being established with the help of doctors and Valiria from the triage camp. Supplies had been ordered from the cantonment.

Five minutes before the hour of ten, King Gregor purposefully walked into the king's court of the Atuliq Royal Palace. Behind him, Prince Nikolai escorted Queen Alexa. Senior Commander Gaeldoreg Vosklon and Gregor's Royal Guard followed, along with the Queen's Royal Guard.

Win-Das had located an antique wooden throne and moved it to the court for Gregor's use instead of Bin-Lot's worn upholstered chair. Gregor glanced around and observed a surly Bin-Lot striking a nonchalant pose in a chair between six guards. Lifting his eyebrows, the Turandan-born monarch said nothing. Instead, he guided his wife to a comfortable seat before sitting on the throne provided for him. After Nikolai stood beside him, Gregor paused and then addressed the gathering, including Turandan and Protector officers, insurgent leaders, and captured Sifiq officers.

"As many here know," Gregor began, "Turand suffered one of several territorial breaches three years ago. During that raid, Sifiq naval and marine forces murdered nine members of the Queen's Royal Guard. Sifiq invaders pushed those guards off a high bridge into a ravine. Queen Alexa and four Valiria priestesses witnessed those murders. Queen Alexa and the Valiria were then transported here to the Sifiq Kingdom. Under direct orders from King Bin-Lot, they were tormented, tortured, and forced into slave labor after refusing to submit to his demands for sexual favors because of their religious convictions and marital status.

"This abuse continued for a year, denying the priestesses all contact with their families, and resulted in severe emotional distress and life-threatening illness. Bin-Lot's sordid treatment grew so dire that our Lord Val finally interceded on behalf of Turand's High Priestess Valkana, forcing the Sifiq king to return the three who returned from the labor camp to their homeland. By then, all were seriously ill. The High Priestess Valkana suffered a final beating on her arrival. Instead of being put off the Sifiq ship in a lifeboat, she was thrown overboard during a storm. Again, only through the merciful intervention of our Lord Val did she survive this last Sifiq atrocity.

"That was not the end of her suffering. Barely alive, she was found on the beach, her back shredded from the last of many floggings. Open wounds were contaminated with saltwater, sand, and broken shells. Despite careful cleansing, severe infection quickly set in, and the fight for her life began. She had been worked to the bone and starved to the point of being little more than a walking skeleton. This was the vital priestess, healer, teacher, queen, wife, and mother King Bin-Lot shamelessly attempted to destroy. As her king and her husband, I claim my right to demand justice. As king for the other priestesses—Sulía Kohira, Kiralí Seraná, Lisana Faradón, and Marlí Gotrano—I also claim proxy rights to demand justice on their behalf."

Ever haughty and arrogant, Bin-Lot sneered. "Justice. Revenge. What you call it doesn't matter. You proved Sifiq philosophy that women are nothing but trouble. You subjected an entire country to ruin for what? Five women? How many good men died when you could have easily found a hundred other females to warm your bed?"

Gregor's features froze, but his eyes blazed. Images of barren farmland, dilapidated farms, half-starved citizens, traumatized girls, and little Lis-kal marched across his field of memory. "You dare to speak to me of ruin in the Sifiq Kingdom after all the neglect, decay, and collapse I observed across your countryside upon my arrival? You dare accuse me of ruining your kingdom, considering how you and your military have stripped your land and your people's ability to provide a decent living for themselves? You blame me after I witnessed the aftermath of your army's sordid abuse of your own citizenry?"

Gregor tossed his head back and laughed a burst of chilling, mirthless laughter. "I would think you funny if not for the tragedy wrapped up in your warped deeds, *King* Bin-Lot." His emphasis on the word king held stinging reproof. "A real king places the interests of his people and his nation ahead of personal pleasures. He does not rape his country and his people to build a military that does the same to other countries to sustain a royal lifestyle of debauchery while his people toil and suffer for minimal survival.

"That's why insurgency grew here. Only your army's unspeakable cruelty kept revolution from your doorstep. Those days are done, Bin-Lot. Your army is defeated, as is your navy. The insurgents joined with us to end your family's reign of destructive neglect, rape of people and lands, and rampant abuse."

Stubborn and egotistic, the Sifiq king held his head high. "I ruled within my rights. You can't tell me you do differently."

Shaking his head in agreement, Gregor answered, "Agreed. I also rule within my rights. I have no need to tell you I do better. I invite you to ask any one of the men or women who are citizens of Turand and know my reign best. Let them speak their peace anonymously. You will hear stories far different from those I've heard since coming here."

Bin-Lot's expression changed. "Coloridia accepts exiles. I demand exile as a political refugee."

Again, Gregor laughed. "You, Bin-Lot, are a criminal. You have committed crimes against your own people and against Turand. As such, justice will be forthcoming. Since I hold the upper hand at this moment, I will exact punishment for your crimes against the Queen of Turand and her sister priestesses while they were captive here in the Sifiq Kingdom. Once I'm satisfied, I will release you into the custody of a new Sifiq governing council that will be organized to help your people recover from the disaster you and your forebears created here."

Standing, Gregor approached the Sifiq king. "We shall see how much a man you really are with all your brave demands. I've spoken to my wife, her sister priestesses, and Sifiq citizens, who were present when you ordered your sadistic beatings. She was flogged in your court seven times and struck at least eight strokes per beating. Then, one of your officers mercilessly beat her at your labor farm in Talafaq before returning her to Atuliq. Finally, there was the last whipping before she was thrown overboard off Turand's shores."

"Your wife caused nothing but trouble while she was here. She deserved the punishment I ordered. What happened in Turand was not my fault. When I sent the prisoners home, I ordered they undergo no further harm," Bin-Lot declared sourly.

Snarling furiously, Gregor retorted, "Every king and commanding officer is responsible for the actions of his subordinates. However, I will grant you reprieve on that one point, although it would never have occurred had the original transgression been immediately rejected by an honorable king! Do I make myself very clear on that point?"

Puffing out his chest, Bin-Lot nodded. "Very."

"Now, your sentence. Alongside Sez-Mil, your favored enforcer, you will be flogged eight times, eight strokes per flogging, as was done to Queen Alexa, at intervals of eight days. Unlike my wife, you will have access to medical management following the events. You will notice the merciful nature of your sentence compared to the whippings you inflicted on my wife."

Bin-Lot's eyes bulged. "You don't dare flog me! I am a king! I demand to meet with a Coloridian ambassador to submit a complaint!"

"Request denied. Coloridia failed to manage its own statesmen and processes concerning your little escapade with Princess Essila. As a result, Princess Regent Anlía and the Trezvindjan governing councils suspended support of Coloridia's diplomatic presence here until remedial actions are drafted, approved, and enacted.

"Your first flogging is scheduled for ten o'clock tomorrow morning and will be performed using the very whip used on my wife. Furthermore, I will be the one wielding the whip tomorrow. Your sentence is issued and final. This session is dismissed."

For the first time, Bin-Lot fought against his captors while shouting a stream of profanity. Incensed upon hearing a derogatory slur against Alexa, Gregor leapt forward, grabbed the Sifiq by his collar, and roared, "Enough! Be glad I am a civilized man who keeps promises to his wife! Otherwise, I would gladly shred you to bits with my bare hands, here and now!" To his guards, he said, "Remove this trash from my sight while some self-control remains to me!"

～

"Father still hasn't returned," Nikolai told Alexa and Gaeldoreg.

"He needs time to purge the fury boiling in his blood," Gaeldoreg said. "His self-restraint today was remarkable. I remain impressed."

"Mother, you're so quiet. Are you all right?"

Alexa met her son's worried gaze. "I will be. Your father warned me he would sentence Bin-Lot in line with Sifiq practices. The fact that he tempered the sentence with measures of mercy doesn't lessen the brutal nature of flogging."

"Ma Ishna," Gaeldoreg said tenderly, "I've heard accounts of the terrible fear and grief your husband experienced when he first saw you in Timeri after Bin-Lot sent you home. That came after spending a year thinking you were dead."

"Gaeldoreg is right, Mother. How Father didn't kill him outright makes me respect him more than ever. His strength of character compares to none. Except yours."

Tears glazed Alexa's eyes, and her chin quivered when she looked at her son. "Niko, this will be one of the hardest tasks he's ever faced. I can't help but worry."

"Alexa, you don't plan to ask him to reduce the sentence, do you?"

"No, Bibo, that I cannot do. I promised not to interfere. I also trust the decisions he makes here. In the end, I'm certain the results will prove to be for the best."

"Now you see why my wife's support is so essential to my life."

Everyone turned to see Gregor standing in the doorway of the palace drawing room. Alexa rose and crossed the lounge to greet him. He took her hands, lifting them to his lips. "Beloved, thank you for believing in me," he murmured.

Unable to respond, Alexa moved into the circle of his arms. Meanwhile, Gregor smiled grimly at his son and Gaeldoreg. "The sentence is not one I pronounced lightly. I learned long ago how critical it is to deal with the Sifiq military on their own terms—beginning at the top. Bin-Lot must experience the punishment he has so generously handed out not only to Alexa and her priestesses but to Sifiq women for years.

Let him taste their pain and suffering to understand exactly what he put them through.

"He has been just as cruel and arrogant toward his own general population. Let them see that he now begins to pay for his misdeeds. They will know the time has come for him to face them for how he allowed and even encouraged his military to devastate their lives for the benefit of an elite few."

Slowly, Gregor guided Alexa back to the elegantly framed sofa. Perching on its edge, he caressed her cheek. "Are you certain you're well?"

"I am. I promise," she replied. "Being back here is just overwhelming."

"Ma Ishna, he needs to know," Gaeldoreg prompted gently.

Gregor looked up. "Know? Know what?"

Alexa dropped her face. "Bibo!" she exclaimed softly.

"You can tell him, or I will. It's for your own good."

"Alexa?" Gregor asked in a demanding tone.

Alexa shot Gaeldoreg a warning look. "Bibo worries too much. I wasn't sleeping or eating well. You can't imagine the effort necessary to keep Victor alive to reach Turand, let alone Toraval. I felt terrible about not getting him to Garogan alive."

Gregor reached out and wiped tears from her face. "Just delivering him alive onto a vessel was a miracle."

"Alexa, tell him the rest."

"Bibo, please. Stop."

"Alexa, what else happened?"

Frustrated, Alexa gave a sharp shake of her head. "The day of Victor's funeral, I was exhausted, but I still spoke at the service. When we returned, I fainted, which upset Katara and Willem. Truthfully, I had also hardly eaten. Afterward, Katara hovered around me like a mother hen, and Bibo assumed that job once we left Toraval. I'm quite recovered now." Her angry glare at Gaeldoreg dared him to utter another word.

Placing his hands on her shoulders, Gregor gazed sternly into her eyes. "You're positive?"

"Gregor, honestly, I'm very well. I would not lie to you. I cannot lie to you. Remember?"

Solemnly nodding, he said, "I believe you, but you should have told me."

"There's been so little time since I arrived. We still have much to discuss once you have some time." The smile she gave him melted his heart.

"I promise to make that time." He sighed impatiently. "First, I'd like Gaeldoreg and Nikolai to accompany me on an assessment of palace grounds. We need to establish a secure headquarters so we can sort out this disaster."

"Of course. While you do that, I'll talk further with Lil-Shem about how best to train more women as nurses who won't be afraid of working with our soldiers."

"As long as you don't overtire yourself. No one knows better than I how hard you push."

She laughed softly. "You mustn't worry. I'm fine. Go." As they turned to leave, she pressed a warning hand against the small of Gaeldoreg's back and hissed, "Not another word, Bibo."

After prayers and meditation the following morning, Alexa helped her husband dress for the day. Tension suffused his tall body, but she said nothing. Instead, she tended to his attire as she had since the early days of their marriage. When they went downstairs for breakfast, she encouraged him to eat, but he only accepted buttered rolls and two large mugs of hot tea. His mind focused on what would be both confrontation and ordeal as he prepared to impose the initial round of Bin-Lot's sentence.

Pensively, Gregor watched as Captain Lisandá escorted Alexa to the palace wing being organized as a hospital facility. He vowed to reserve time later that afternoon to spend with her. Something about yesterday's conversation with Gaeldoreg continued to rattle inside his mind, especially since he had noticed something different about her from the moment of her arrival. He desperately needed to resolve this business with the Sifiq and once again focus on his family and his own national affairs.

Striding into Bin-Lot's court, Gregor presented as fearsome an image as any Trezvindjan Protector there had ever seen, including Prince Braeklojorn Vosklon, who had arrived that morning. Bolstered by his grandfather's encouragement that his victory and the verdict against Bin-Lot honored past generations of Protectors, Gregor signaled for the Sifiq king and his pet enforcer to be escorted into the court.

Stripped of royal finery, Bin-Lot appeared wearing soft slippers and a loose linen shirt over the typical balloon pants favored by Sifiq men. Red-faced and furious, the Sifiq king cursed at guards clutching his arms and lining the way to the columns where he would be tied. The moment he spotted Gregor, he spat in his direction.

"I can't believe you intend to proceed with this charade! She's just a woman! I give her credit that she gave you six children and, judging by your son there, fine ones. Still, no woman is worth all this. Let's stop this nonsense, Gregor, and sit down like reasonable men. Surely we can resolve our differences."

Gregor glanced down and adjusted the black leather gloves on his hands. If he had entertained any doubts about his decision, Bin-Lot had just erased them. He nodded at Turandan guards, who roughly dragged off Bin-Lot's shirt and stretched his arms wide, tying his wrists to the columns and exposing his back.

"You have another option, Bin-Lot. You can lie down across a bench. That's how you made my wife take her whippings. I thought you would consider that an affront to your Sifiq manliness."

"Gregor, you are a filthy…" Before he could finish, the loud, angry snap of the three-tailed whip echoed through the vast chamber. The Sifiq king grunted his shock.

"Two." Gregor began a carefully measured count as he drew back his arm again to release the leather whip. "Three." By the count of five, sweat, mingling with involuntary tears, coursed down the Sifiq's face. On the final two counts, Bin-Lot cried out his agony.

When Turandan guards released the bonds and supported the sagging Sifiq king, Gregor smiled scornfully. "You did well compared to your enforcer. I'm told he passed out by the count of five. As I understand, my beautiful queen never cried out once."

"Make sure the queen sees neither of them on the way back," Gregor cautioned the guards. Then, turning, he exhaled heavily. "I'm glad that's over."

Braeklojorn placed a hand on Gregor's shoulder. "You did well."

"Thank you, but his sentence requires seven more whippings to match what Alexa alone endured. Contrary to what many may think, meting out such punishment, even to one such as Bin-Lot, brings me no pleasure."

"A suggestion, then," his grandfather offered. "Share the responsibility with others who share your anguish. Nikolai is now a man who suffered greatly from his mother's abduction. Gaeldoreg really does see Alexa as his daughter. Sulía Kohira's husband is Sifiq and has double the reason to wield the whip. It's a shame that Major Fratino isn't here. I'm quite certain he would gladly take his turn. Even I'm willing because of the sorrow he inflicted on my family."

"Perhaps you're right," Gregor said after several moments of contemplation. "I will consider it. However, I must find Alexa now. I promised to spend some time with her."

Gaeldoreg, who walked up with Nikolai, overheard and said, "I heard her down the hallway, near the drawing room we were in yesterday."

"Good. I'll go find her." Gregor stopped abruptly before leaving. "Gaeldoreg, did she really faint?"

Gaeldoreg shrugged. "According to Willem, she fell in a dead faint into one of her friend's arms. Scared the lot of them to death."

Gregor's thoughts raced. Through the years, he had seen Alexa face crisis, injury, and illness. Alexa simply did not faint. Unless… "Great and holy Val!" he shouted before spinning on his heel and racing through the open doors of the court with Zamtelza and Royal Guards in rapid pursuit. Braeklojorn and Nikolai looked at each other before exchanging puzzled glances.

"What was that all about?"

Nikolai shrugged his shoulders and shook his head, "Grandfather, when it comes to Father and Mother, one can never tell."

Gaeldoreg only grinned. "I could use a cup of hot kacha about now. Would anyone care to join me?"

Braeklojorn frowned. "Kacha will have to do since it's too early for a stiff jolt of liquor."

~

Alexa sat beside a window reviewing hospital plans when Gregor softly called her name from the lounge doorway. When she looked up and smiled, filtered sunshine created a cloud of natural light around her. He remembered having seen that inner sparkle before that had nothing to do with her role as Valkana. Instead, the glow on her skin and in her eyes rose from a different source, one they had created five times already. How was it possible such a miracle had happened again after all these years?

Quietly, Gregor entered and, making sure his guards were in place, closed carved double doors. "Why did you not tell me when you first came?"

"Tell you what?" she asked, caught off guard by his question. Suddenly, she understood from his expression. "Did Bibo tell you?"

"No, I figured it out on my own because you generally only faint when you're pregnant, but why is it Gaeldoreg knew before I did?"

Alexa stood and went to him. Resting open hands against his chest, she kissed his bearded chin. "Bibo and I had a huge disagreement about my coming to set up the triage camp. I had to tell him."

"Poor Gaeldoreg." Gregor's long fingers tenderly caressed her cheek. "My beloved Alexa, when? I stayed true to my promise never to ask again, but how I wanted more children with you."

She closed her eyes and savored his touch. "Well, you have your wish. He came to us the night before I left with Victor."

"You sound so certain," Gregor murmured.

"I am Valkana. I know these things."

"He? Another son?"

Opening her eyes and gazing into the depths of his, she nodded. "A powerful spirit he possesses. He comes with strength and purpose. I'm not sure why he'll be needed, but his is a Protector soul. We must plan for him to be born in Trezvindja."

"Trezvindja and not Turand?"

"Yes, and don't ask why. I don't know."

Gregor wrapped his arms around her. "Alexa, do you have any idea how much I really love you?"

"Enough to settle things here and take me home so we can be together again with our children?" She felt his body shake with laughter.

"I love you much more than that. I need some weeks. Can you wait that long?"

"Before we left to set up the triage camp, I told Gaeldoreg I could stay no more than three months. Hostilities ended sooner than I expected. I can manage a few weeks."

Gregor grinned broadly before kissing her soundly and lifting her into his arms. Then he called for his guards to open the doors and lead the way so they could join the others for midday.

Inside the banquet hall commandeered for meals, Braeklojorn broke off mid-sentence when Gregor appeared, carrying Alexa. "What in the name of Espiritus!"

"Oh, no, Father's at it again," Nikolai laughed.

"At what?" his great-grandfather asked.

Gaeldoreg laughed heartily as Gregor arrived at their table, carefully setting a blushing Alexa on her feet. "I take it you know!"

"I do! Something good finally happened in this god-awful country!"

"All right," Braeklojorn said as Gregor seated Alexa and then sat beside her. "It appears only Nikolai and I need enlightenment. Will someone kindly correct that situation?"

"Niko," Alexa said, reaching across the table for her son's hand, "don't worry. You can delegate the unpleasant parts to your younger siblings now."

"Unpleasant parts? What unpleasant parts?"

"Don't you remember how you loved holding your baby brothers and sisters until they made smelly messes and the nurses came too slowly to change them?"

"Yes, but." He stopped abruptly. "No. You must be joking."

Gregor laughed happily. "She's not. You have another brother coming in about six months."

"Aren't you two a bit old for this?"

Gaeldoreg affectionately slapped Nikolai on the back. "I daresay you'll not think so when you're your father's age, young man!"

Nikolai's face flushed bright red. "I just meant…"

"Leave it, my boy, and congratulate your parents," Braeklojorn wisely suggested. He then grinned at his grandson. "So I can finally look forward to holding a Vosklon baby?"

"Yes, Grandfather, you can."

Braeklojorn leaned back in the carved banquet chair. "For seventy years, I mourned the loss of Mishkla and our unborn child. I then discovered I never got to hold my own baby girl, nor did I get to hold my baby grandson. This great-grandchild will be the first infant of my own blood I will ever have the chance to hold in my arms." Pure amazement lit his features. "Alexa, I'm not leaving your side for the next six months!"

Everyone at the table burst into laughter as Alexa rose and embraced her husband's grandfather.

Chapter 23

Wanting to see more of what Alexa had faced during her captivity, Gregor asked Win-Das to guide him through the palace. Particularly interested in Bin-Lot's private chambers, Gregor entered with both curiosity and disgust.

Inside, luxurious gold-leafed furnishings stood in stark contrast to the poverty common across the countryside he had crossed to reach Atuliq. However, closer scrutiny revealed fading paint, worn carpets, and threadbare upholstery, indicating that some of the Sifiq king's lavish lifestyle had begun to unravel. Paintings on the walls that should have depicted works of Sifiq artists instead highlighted scenery from Turand's Fosan and Timeri Provinces. Ironically, there was even one of a forested landscape near Zinzan.

"Win-Das, please have these paintings removed and packed for return to Turand. They were most certainly stolen during the occupation. Their presence here is sacrilege."

"Of course."

Against a far wall, Gregor noted a tall, narrow chest with painted drawers. "That is an unusual piece of furniture."

"I believe the king kept his personal jewelry inside."

Gregor tugged at the drawers, which were locked. "I want this opened. If there's no key, bring me a hammer or sword. I'll break it."

"Gladly," Win-Das replied.

"I need assistance from you and Commander Zamtelza," Gregor told Win-Das later as he opened the drawer of a nearby desk to locate paper to use with the quill and inkpot. Then, ten minutes later, Gregor began to place individual pieces of jewelry on the desk and the bed. The king's concentration was intense as he studied the many fine pieces of gold, silver, platinum, and gemstones.

Carefully sorting through gleaming treasure, Gregor recognized several rings and medallions that had belonged to his father. All bore the Toscano family hallmark. He showed those to both Win-Das and Zamtelza and separated them. Continuing through the collection, he also found some pieces that once belonged to his mother and set them aside. "These, gentlemen, were stolen from my family for Bin-Lot's father. I now reclaim them."

"What about the rest? It represents a substantial fortune," Zamtelza said.

"A fortune it is, most of it pillaged and stolen, I'm sure. I've no idea how to identify former owners except for pieces with Turandan family crests. Many pieces are antique and not Turandan in origin. I want the two of you to begin listing items with a brief description. Then wrap and lock them inside a strongbox until we can have them appraised. Selling them should raise a handsome sum toward rebuilding this country."

Win-Das gaped at Gregor in disbelief. "Should you not replenish your own nation's coffers first?"

"You think as a former Sifiq soldier, Win-Das. Begin to think as a new Sifiq citizen. And let's start with a change. The Sifiq Kingdom is too pretentious. Shall we consider something fresh but still bold? Perhaps Sifiqua?"

Win-Das grinned. "I think Sifiqqa will do very well. I'll discuss it with the others. Right now, I need more paper to list all these." Opening the desk drawer with a tug, he heard something roll inside and saw a brilliant sparkle of reflected light. Pulling the item out, he said, "Ah, it seems our good king was hiding something."

Gregor took one glance and gasped, "Praise Val!"

Win-Das immediately passed the ring to him. "What is it?"

With eyes closed, Gregor reverently lifted the diamond-studded circle to his lips. "Alexa's wedding ring—the one thing Bin-Lot took from her that hurt most. We believed it forever lost."

With a brilliant sheen glazing his eyes, Win-Das smiled. "One day, I will give Sulía a real wedding ring. For now, I celebrate the return of this one to our Valkana."

That night, Gregor came late to bed after meeting with Win-Das and rebel leaders about drafting plans for the recovery of the new Sifiqqa. His next priority would be the voyage home to reunite his family. Quietly entering the small bedchamber he shared with Alexa, he was grateful for its warmth and cleanliness compared to field quarters. Quickly shedding clothes and donning the long flannel nightshirt she had left on a chair, he carefully climbed beneath thick blankets to avoid disturbing her. Smiling to himself, he recalled how deep her slumber had always been during earlier pregnancies.

Settling close to her, Gregor kissed her hair. His lips formed silent words. "I love you, my queen. Tomorrow, I have a surprise for you. Sweet dreams, beloved."

When morning sunlight peeked around the edges of the curtains, Gregor sat up in bed to find Alexa sitting on the straight-backed chair with his uniform jacket on her lap. Tears streamed down her face. "Alexa? Dearest Val, what's wrong? Are you sick? Has something happened to the baby?"

Unable to speak, she just shook her head. Swiftly leaving the bed, he went and knelt before her. "Tell me, dear one. What's wrong?"

She produced a wobbly smile before throwing her arms around his neck. "Oh, Gregor, I can't believe it! I just can't."

"Believe what, Alexa? Tell me."

"I was going to take your jacket outside to brush and clean it, so I was making sure nothing was in the pockets that might get lost." She leaned back in the chair and held out a hand, her original wedding ring lying on her palm. "You found it!"

As he so often did, he cradled her face between his palms. "I went on the hunt yesterday, convinced Bin-Lot had kept it as a trophy. He had it tucked away in his desk drawer. I planned to give it to you this morning."

Softly weeping, she said, "I love my new ring and everything it represents. Sincerely, I do, but this ring holds my first sacred vows to you. It woke me to how much I loved you when Victor forced me back to Garogan all those years ago. Oh, Gregor, thank you for finding it for me. Thank you so much."

Taking the ring from her, Gregor once again kissed it. "Let me return it to its rightful place." He then slid the ring into position with the new one he had given her. "I love you, Alexa. Let these two rings proclaim that truth forever."

⤝

"Your Majesty, may I speak with you?"

Alexa looked up from paperwork. "Of course, Doctor. What is it?"

Dr. Lorzari regretted involving her, but he thought her expertise in the use of herbal medicines might benefit his problem case. "Please forgive me. I fear your husband might lash me if he finds out I've come to you."

"I doubt that," Alexa said reassuringly.

"No, I'm quite serious. It concerns Bin-Lot."

"I see. What's the problem?" Alexa asked, color leaving her face.

"After this last—um—session—an infection has developed. I admit he causes most of the problems. He doesn't do well when we cleanse and apply the medicines. If the condition worsens, he could develop a serious fever and die. I don't believe King Gregor wants that to happen."

Alexa sighed. "He definitely does not. You know the Healing Graces will be ineffectual in Bin-Lot's case because he's an active disbeliever."

"Yes, Milady. I thought perhaps you might recommend some useful herbal concoctions or poultice preparations. I hope to stop this infection before it spreads. His pain is severe."

"Doctor, I remember very well how painful floggings are. My husband is compassionate enough to spread Bin-Lot's out by eight days. I, unfortunately, had to endure them only five days apart on two separate occasions."

"Milady, I'm so sorry. I had no idea."

"Of course, you didn't." Relenting, she set aside her reports. "I can't recommend anything without actually seeing the patient. Shall we go?"

"But…"

"Doctor, my husband is visiting troops in the city for the next several hours. If you want my help, the time is now."

Following Dr. Lorzari into the heavily guarded prisoner's quarters, Alexa's sensitive nose instantly detected the faint scent of both infection and fever. On a cot inside the bright, clean room, Bin-Lot lay face-down. In the corner, an iron stove radiated heat and held pots of hot water. A table beneath a barred window was laden with an assortment of medicines and bandages.

Seeing Alexa enter when the door opened, the Sifiq king muttered a curse. "What is she doing here? Get her out!"

Lorzari answered firmly, "I told you I would consult with our most knowledgeable healer regarding your spreading infection. However, she needs to see the problem before making the proper recommendations."

"I said make her go!" he growled hoarsely.

"Bin-Lot, I have no great desire to be here, but neither do I wish to have you die in Turand's custody. Be quiet and be still." She looked up at Lorzari. "I need more light closer to his back."

The king started twisting to keep her from getting a clear view. Some wounds on his back opened as he did, causing pus to run across inflamed flesh. He groaned with pain.

"Bin-Lot, if you don't stop, I'll have my guards come in and tie you to the table like a pig for roasting. The choice is yours. I'm in no mood for your nonsense."

"You enjoy this, don't you, woman?"

"As much as I enjoyed it when you ordered my beatings. Now, what will it be? Do we tie you up, or do you let me examine you?"

Too exhausted from the latest flogging administered by one out-raged Prince Nikolai, he grumbled, "Have it your way, woman. I have no choice."

Alexa huffed a sigh and leaned over his back. Tears flooded her eyes, but she refused to let them fall. His injuries couldn't begin to compare with how her back must have looked when Gregor first arrived in Timeri. No wonder her husband's fury ran so deep.

"Dr. Lorzari, I need tepid rosewater to cleanse these open wounds. Also, this room is much too hot. It only accelerates the infection. Once I clean his back, I'll prepare two Kirmaya-based poultices to draw out the infection. The first must stay on for six hours. Then, cleanse his back again with rosewater and leave to open air for two hours. Leave the second poultice on overnight. Cleanse again in the morning and pat dry."

"Any other instructions?"

"Advise me when you finish without letting my husband know. I'll return as soon as I can get away."

"You talk as if I'm a piece of deadwood," Bin-Lot complained bitterly.

"What a pitiful being you've become for someone who was so smug and supercilious. I'm trying to keep you out of your grave."

"Why? So your husband can execute me?" he snarled from his cot.

"He has no intention of executing you. He thinks you'll make a much better example alive, although your future may be beyond his control. Try to be a little grateful for whatever relief you get."

An hour later, Alexa wiped the last of the rosewater and pus from Bin-Lot's back. With a clean linen cloth, she gently patted the area dry. Glancing up at Lorzari, she said, "I'll wash up and go make the poultices. Remember. Not a word to anyone that I was here. I'll tell Gregor in my own way when I'm ready. He knows my vows as Valkana and healer extend even to our enemies."

Exhausted by what he considered an excruciating ordeal, Bin-Lot later said to Dr. Lorzari, "She could have been rough with me. She was not. Why?"

Aggravated by the king's tone, Lorzari shook his head. "You're a fool who refuses to learn. The High Priestess Valkana is a sworn healer, even to the likes of one such as you."

⌒

"I just introduced Bin-Lot to Gaeldoreg." In response to his wife's questioning glance, Gregor continued, "There are a few pockets of Sifiq resistance further east that we have not yet contained. Bin-Lot has not yet officially surrendered. He's been flogged three times and behaved atrociously with medical staff ever since."

"So?" Alexa asked curiously.

"Even at his age, Gaeldoreg would scare the devil out of me with a whip in his hand. He'll wield it against Bin-Lot this fourth time. I'm considering reducing Bin-Lot's sentence by two floggings in exchange for his unconditional surrender. Otherwise, Gaeldoreg and I will split the remaining floggings."

"Are you asking my opinion or my permission?"

Gregor walked across the drawing room she had claimed and knelt before her. "Both, perhaps."

Reaching out, she laced her fingers into the length of his hair, pushing it back from his dark face. Sighing, she asked, "How could I disagree when lives hang in the balance? Are you certain his army will lay down arms if he agrees to surrender?"

"They continue resisting because he has not. They are sworn to fight to the death until he is no longer in power."

"Then make the offer. The bargain is worthwhile if even one Turandan or Trezvindjan life can be saved."

Gregor's expression darkened. "What about justice for what he did to you?"

"Gregor, I have you and my son safe." She pulled his hands to lay against her abdomen. "We have this new child, conceived here, and your Trezvindjan family. Might he have been the catalyst? I don't have that answer. What I do know is that I'm more than willing to forgo the two floggings to avoid more injuries and lost lives. That will be my justice."

He leaned forward and captured lips as sweet at that moment as they had been at any time during their marriage. "Thank you, my love."

⌐

Gregor cringed as Gaeldoreg struck Bin-Lot the fifth time. As Alexa's adopted father, the gray-haired Protector had walked an intimidating circle around the Sifiq king, growling comments about how a man could fall so low as to beat women for pleasure. Furthermore, Bin-Lot had arrogantly insulted Prince Nikolai and promoted the betrayal of a Trezvindjan princess. The brutality against Gaeldoreg's daughter, however, was unforgivable. Each crack of the whip elicited agonized cries of pain from Bin-Lot, who passed out long before Gaeldoreg completed his task.

When Gregor later entered Bin-Lot's room, the Sifiq hoarsely mumbled, "Come to inspect your Protector's handiwork?"

"Not really, but since you ask. Dr. Lorzari?" When the doctor lifted the white sheet, Gregor grimaced, then shrugged. "That is nothing—and I mean nothing—compared to the condition of my wife's back after she washed ashore in Timeri. Infection and high fevers nearly killed her, and she carries hideous scars to this day. Your whining does not move me."

"Tell me, then, why have you come?"

"You have three regimental strongholds to the east that continue fighting. I want their surrender. I want this war to end."

Bin-Lot sniggered. "What do you want me to do about it?"

"I want you to sign an unconditional surrender and order an end to combat."

"Why should I?"

"Right now, you have four floggings remaining on your sentence. If you sign the surrender, I will reduce your sentence by two."

"Hah! You consider that a bargain?"

"It is when you consider the consequences. If you don't, Gaeldoreg Vosklon and I will share the last four. I'm sure you recall your own history of the last Sifiq War with the Protectors and tales of Gaeldoreg the Terrible. You tasted his wrath yesterday."

"You mean..."

"Protectors live very long lives and have longer memories. He is my distant cousin. You will not fare well if you persist with your obstinate lunacy. Sign the surrender or pay the consequences."

Bin-Lot shifted slightly on the cot and groaned in agony. Accustomed to an easy life, he was convinced he would never survive four more whippings. The torn flesh across his back was more torture than he could bear.

"Very well," he whimpered. "Draw up your damned surrender. Whatever you want. I'll sign."

Surprised by Bin-Lot's easy acquiescence, Gregor said, "If you're certain, I will return this afternoon with surrender documents and witnesses. I warn you, though. Don't waste my time."

Bin-Lot blew out several pained breaths. "Just bring your damned papers so we can be done with this."

As promised, Gregor returned after midday with documents that included the unconditional surrender and transfer of all governing powers to the King of Turand and Trezvindja. He also carried a sheaf of additional documents ordering all field officers of the Sifiq Army to cease every form of military action and to surrender their weapons, effectively ending the war.

Gregor arrived with a company of witnesses, including Prince Nikolai, Braeklojorn Vosklon, Protector commanders, General Kohira, and Queen Alexa. Win-Das and two other insurgent leaders came. Four high-ranking officers represented opposing Sifiq interests. Bin-Lot, accompanied by Turandan physicians, wore a voluminous linen shirt and sat at a table outside his chamber in the corridor.

"Quite a show you have prepared, Gregor," Bin-Lot scathingly remarked.

Holding his temper, Gregor replied, "Witnesses include my people and yours. I want no question that you sign without my holding a sword to your throat."

Grunting, Bin-Lot looked down at the documents neatly laid out on the table. "Explain this mess."

Sitting across the table from his enemy, Gregor picked up a quill. "Here are six copies of the Declaration of Unconditional Surrender. Your officers have read each to ensure they are identical. You are to sign each before I sign my acceptance. The rest are orders to your military to immediately cease all combat hostilities and surrender arms. Designated witnesses will then sign in our presence."

Bin-Lot glanced up at his senior officers. Their eyes reflected shame that they had been captured rather than die fighting. Their king's debilitated state further disgraced them. They knew how he and his enforcer had cried and screamed under the whip when two of them had witnessed the stoic silence with which Gregor's queen had borne her beatings. A Sifiq colonel flatly stated in a gravelly voice, "The documents are consistent and properly executed."

Angry with the officer's disregard for his king's current state of suffering, Bin-Lot muttered a curse. "Very well. Where?"

"You won't read first?" Gregor inquired.

"I still trust my officers," Bin-Lot growled. "I just want this done and over." He then dipped the quill in the inkpot and scrawled a flourishing signature on the first of the surrender documents.

Half an hour later, the deposed Sifiq king leaned forward, elbows on the table and head on his hands. "I always considered paperwork exhausting," he muttered.

"Strange. All you've done is sit on your throne or lie in bed inside your palace. Your people and your military have suffered the worst consequences of your belligerence," Gregor commented drily.

Looking up contemptuously, Bin-Lot retorted, "You think lying in my bed with this back is not suffering?"

Gregor's features were just as contemptuous. "Such suffering passes relatively quickly. You forced my wife, not to mention her priestesses, to suffer more than a year. You also compounded her pain with slave labor. You will not endure such indignity at my hands. Now, go back to your little bed and whine away your afternoon. Good day."

⌒

Alexa gazed up at the masts of the magnificent sailing ship with green eyes alight. The bustle around her on the wharf meant one thing. Gregor was taking her home to reunite with their family. How exhilarating! How joyful! How utterly exciting to anticipate leaving this new Sifiqqa in capable hands so she could depart for her beloved Turand.

"Alexa, I believe you're positively glowing, and it has nothing to do with being Valkana," Gregor observed with a chuckle.

Grinning broadly, she nodded. "This is the third time I leave this country and the first time under happy circumstances. I can hardly wait to reach home."

"Well, pray for decent weather and fair seas. It is still winter, you know."

Again she smiled. "Val has promised me a quick, smooth crossing."

"All praises to our Lord Val," Gregor declared cheerfully. He then escorted his wife up the long ramp to the vessel's deck. King and Queen graciously acknowledged the captain's ceremonious welcome aboard. They then watched as the crew carefully guided the ship away from the pier jutting out into the bay before setting course for Turand.

The vessel would sail together with three other ships. Sulía Kohira and her father traveled on one. Accompanying them were Win-Das and two members of the new Sifiqqa Board of Governors. They would study best governing practices utilized in Turand, leaving General Ravendro to head an interim government in Atuliq. Choosing to return to Toraval, Braeklojorn and Gaeldoreg would travel with Nikolai on another vessel. The fourth was a fully armed battleship serving as escort should the group encounter any Sifiq naval vessels uninformed about the surrender.

A week into the voyage, Gregor found his wife on deck, basking in winter sunshine. "Isn't it too chilly to be out here?"

Turning rosy cheeks to him, she smiled. "I needed some fresh air. I was just getting ready to head below to our cabin to warm up."

"I take it your patient is being as disagreeable as ever."

Her eyebrows lifted comically. "He's none too pleased about being dragged aboard a ship and locked up in the brig. Add the insult of being subjected to my care?"

"Forgive me for asking this of you, but I rather like the idea of him experiencing being uprooted from home and everything familiar as you were. Our people deserve to see him receive his final punishment in Turand."

"He has no close family ties as we do. As I understand, only a half dozen or so former wives since none ever produced sons for him."

Gregor's brow knit together in consternation. "Daughters?"

Alexa shuddered. "That question I feared asking."

"How these men murder their own children exceeds my comprehension," Gregor remarked, shivering.

Alexa took him by the arm. "Let's pray that practice now ends. I think it's time to go below. I'm cold and could use some hot tea and perhaps a bite to eat."

"Whatever your heart desires, Your Majesty."

In the carillon towers of the Great Temple of Val, bells pealed joyfully, welcoming home the High Priestess Valkana and King Gregor. Finally free from threats of Sifiq attack, Turandans spilled into Toraval's streets to celebrate the new alliance with Trezvindja and their shared, hard-earned victory over the savage Sifiq. Turandan soldiers and Protector warriors accompanied their returning monarchs to deafening cheers from people who remembered too well the throes of occupation. They had remained true to their vows to protect their sovereignty, whatever the cost.

In front of Toraval's Royal Palace, King Gregor and Prince Nikolai dismounted in unison from two enormous Trezvindjan horses. Impressively tall, both men stood at attention until a royal carriage rolled forward and stopped. Two liveried footmen opened the carriage door. Braeklojorn and Gaeldoreg, attired in vividly colored Trezvindjan regalia, stepped out and helped Alexa down before escorting her to the king and prince.

Pausing to wave at the crowds, the three walked up marble steps to the top level, where their other children, including Anlía accompanied by Bresklon Krisantal, waited to greet them. Gregor turned back, his dark eyes sweeping the expanse of palace lawns leading to Toraval's broad central square. As if sensing his intentions, the carillons slowed their ringing bells to a halt, and the waiting crowd quieted, knowing the area's acoustics would allow most to hear their king's powerful voice.

"My dear people," he began, "you cannot know the joy filling my heart upon returning home to my beloved Turand with the gift of decisive and final victory over our old enemy, the Sifiq. You worked hard and made many sacrifices to reach this new era of peace. Many fine men sacrificed their lives or will suffer from battle injuries for the remainder of their lives. Forever we must honor our fallen heroes. In Val's great name, let us never forsake our heroes who need our helping hands as they come home to rebuild broken lives. They are as responsible for your newfound peace of mind and freedom as are the brave warriors marching whole.

"As you know, while I was away, our beloved queen gave life to something I thought only a dream. She discovered my mother's blood family and why Mother and I always looked so different from average Turandans. In the process, as you also know, I am now declared the king of a large and powerful island nation called Trezvindja. Coming to know these people is a great honor. Achieving victory over the Sifiq was most certainly faster and less costly in blood and lives because of the valor of their warriors, known as Protectors. I am both grateful and exceedingly proud to share their heritage.

"I look forward to speaking to you again very soon. For now, I have been away from my own family for a long time. A reunion is quite in order, as is a good meal and a rest after a long journey. People of Turand, you have the love, devotion, and loyalty of your King, your Queen, and your Crown Prince. May Val bless us all! Long live Turand! Long live Trezvindja!"

Turandans jubilantly cheered as their beloved king and queen embraced their children. Most now recognized the venerable grandfather and the famous Protector known as Gaeldoreg the Terrible, about whom they had read adventurous stories. Curiosity surrounded the handsome stranger who had arrived two days earlier with Princess Anlía, and good-natured gossip already abounded.

Turand had already embraced these unusual new giants. After all, Turandans had adored Queen Anlía, and it had been her son who delivered them through their darkest days. Now, these tall, dark strangers had helped vanquish the Sifiq. Even more significant was their Valkana's open acceptance. She adored the Trezvindjans, and they loved her in return. Yes, this alliance promised enduring peace.

<hr>

Midday was a noisy affair. After a heartfelt grace, conversation assumed a competitive air. Alexa and Anlía exchanged giggles and grins while watching Gregor ask questions and then field lively, competing responses from DiMarco and Thikos. Marina and Karina piped in whenever possible with sweet, impossibly loud voices, commenting on their own volunteer activities. The four were determined to impress on their father that, while neither had raised a sword or governed an island nation, they had still actively participated in his struggle to defeat the Sifiq.

Finally, Gregor stood, wine glass in hand. "Before our next course, everyone, I believe we should dispense with discussion of the Toscano children's hard work here in Toraval during the war and simply toast their excellent contributions to our victory. I propose awarding a medal to each of them for their efforts and then change conversation for the remainder of our meal."

Every adult stood, agreed with the king, and joined the toast. Afterward, the meal proceeded less competitively but with plenty of discussion as Gregor enjoyed his first meal at home with his family. This midday proved memorable in yet another way. Amid the chaos of excited children, Gregor was sharing the hospitality of his home for the first time with his grandfather, Gaeldoreg, his grandfather's Uncle Vezjalan, who had escorted Anlía from Trezvindja, and Bresklon Krisantal, her very serious suitor. Every drop of wine and every bite that crossed his lips tasted all the better because he was home at last.

A quieter mood settled on the family when they gathered in a spacious drawing room after midday. Walking over to the ornately carved mantelpiece, Gregor relished the warmth of the blazing fire radiating into the room. How tired he had grown of sleeping on hard ground inside cold tents. Glancing around at Alexa, he smiled at the glow on her face as she held Marina's hands. His heart prickled at facing the reality of getting to know the man who gazed so amorously at Anlía. His two younger sons were quickly approaching full manhood, and he wondered how time could have passed so quickly. Nikolai was immersed in discussion with Uncle Vezjalan and Grandfather, while Gaeldoreg looked on everyone with immense affection.

Home. Family. All the discomfort, loss, pain, and terrible decisions had brought him to this. They were safe. Praise Val for giving him the strength, courage, and endurance to carry him through the storm so he could see them secure and protected again. He smiled as his heart skipped a beat. Family. Home.

"Everyone," Gregor said, his voice bright and happy, "I have an announcement—a joyful one that some here already know." He offered his hand to Alexa, who smiled and went to him. He said proudly, "The Toscano family will soon increase by another member. Our Valkana tells me we will be joined by another son. I hope you'll all be as happy as we are."

"Gregor," Braeklojorn said, accepting a glass of brandy, "you earned my deepest respect today at midday. Any man who could settle that chaotic scene with those children of yours deserves every hero's medal in existence."

Vezjalan and Gaeldoreg both laughed while Bresklon attempted to maintain a dignified expression as a grinning servant passed around a tray of brandy snifters. Noting the reaction of the youngest man in the group and understanding the reason behind his attempted self-control, Gregor said, "You may laugh, too, Councillor Krisantal. I've long understood that the Toscano brood is not a typical royal family, but we were behind closed doors with people I'm told we can trust. I hope I wasn't misinformed."

Bresklon's eyes widened with uncertainty as he met Gregor's intimidating gaze. "No, Sire, you weren't misinformed. Ever since I arrived, I have been enlightened on the challenges of such a large family of young people gathered together in such close proximity."

Gregor rolled his eyes heavenward. "In Val's great name! You need to relax, or I shall never get to know you well enough to decide whether you'll make a suitable addition to this family."

For a brief moment, Bresklon feared he might strangle on the brandy he had just swallowed. Surreptitiously drawing a shaky breath, he managed to control his features and his nerves in front of his new king. "Sire, I hope my intentions to speak with you about personal matters so soon after you returned home haven't provoked your ire."

Gregor's eyebrows lifted. "Hmmm," he murmured as he savored the flavor of his brandy. Glancing away from Bresklon, he said, "You know, Grandfather, this is my finest brandy."

"It does have a fine, smooth flavor. The finish is excellent. Anlía thought you wouldn't mind if she offered us a sample to celebrate our arrival the day we first came."

"She has always been such a thoughtful, kind, generous girl. My absolute joy since the moment she was born." Gazing back at Bresklon, he said, "Do you intend to stand over there all evening, or would you care to join us closer to the fire? Contrary to anything you may have heard, I haven't yet struck down any of my daughter's suitors."

Bresklon chuckled, relieved to experience for himself the humor Anlía swore her father possessed. "Thank you, Sire. I'll gladly join you."

"Councillor Krisantal, may I address you as Bresklon?" Gregor asked.

Somewhat surprised by the king's quick directness, Bresklon gave an elegant nod. "Absolutely, Sire."

"Thank you. Bresklon, I'm here with my grandfather and Gaeldoreg Vosklon, family I love and trust. While I've just met Uncle Vezjalan, Grandfather knows him well and trusts him. My daughter is also fond of him, and her instincts are much like her mother's. That prompts me to rely on their advice as I begin to know you.

"Uncle Vezjalan tells me that you are highly respected in Trezvindja. He says you are known for an impeccable sense of integrity and honor. So, if it is true that you have an interest in my daughter, those are but two qualities I would seek in a husband for her."

Bresklon's wide, black eyebrows lifted high. He had heard that King Gregor often addressed situations with forthright directness, but he had not expected this so soon. Grateful for the opening, Bresklon paused to collect his thoughts and responded, "Anlía needed to come to Toraval to welcome you and her mother home after the war. At home in Tarahlaz, she works exceedingly hard to learn Trezvindjan laws and culture. I even expect her to be fluent in our language very soon. Because of that—and her sympathetic character—I imagine you'll find it no surprise to learn she has won the hearts of many Trezvindjans. Mine? I freely admit she conquered my heart before I had the slightest chance to resist.

"Regarding my reputation, Sire, I take pride in living an honorable life. For years, it was a quiet, unhappy life that I filled with work that satisfied but never fulfilled me. The positive aspect is that I established a successful career allowing me to serve the good of my nation, my people, and my league. While I possess no title of nobility, I have earned respected positions in our government and the income that would enable me to provide handsomely for a wife and family. I also have a comfortable home to welcome a bride.

"I won't mislead you. I have failed in some regards. I ignored my mystical heritage. Against my better judgment, I married a woman who proved an unsuitable wife and later died in childbirth. That was all to please my parents, who desired to satisfy social and business considerations.

"With mistakes come wisdom. I learned the value of recognizing the most important matters in life, which is why I joined Anlía on her journey here to Turand. I love your daughter. She awakened my love for life itself. That is why I came to request her hand in marriage."

Gregor sat quietly, studying the man whose countenance had become as serious and forthright as the venerable politician he was. Exhaling heavily, Gregor set aside his glass. "Bresklon, I respect a man brave enough to approach me after such short acquaintance regarding Anlía. I do not exaggerate my love for my daughter. All my children are exceedingly precious, but I often wonder if I would have survived her mother's disappearance had it not been for Anlía's constancy. I'm also quite certain Alexa would not have survived her brutal homecoming if not for Anlía's mystical sensitivities and intervention. My daughter's happiness and well-being will always be of supreme concern to me."

"Without doubt, Sire. She deserves only the best. I may not be nobility, but I vow to do everything possible to care for her if you grant me the honor of her hand. No man could ever love her more than I. Of that, I am sure. I encourage you to talk with her alone and with us together. You will see for yourself how much we love one another."

"Be assured. I intend to do so before I grant my final word. However, in the meantime, I expect you to conduct yourself as a member of my family. I understand we share the Krisantal bloodline from somewhere in the distant past. Let us celebrate that while you're here."

Bresklon finally smiled. "Indeed we do, Sire. May I propose a toast?"

Taking up his glass once again, Gregor nodded assent.

Bresklon met his king's gaze with admiration and respect. "Long live the Sacred Blood of the Krisantal."

Everyone else joined in, "Long live the Sacred Blood of the Krisantal."

"I knew something was different about you, but I never suspected another baby!" Anlía laughed as she and her mother strolled home from the temple after evening prayers and meditation.

"It was neither planned nor expected. A surprise presentation from our Lord Val," Alexa remarked. "Your father could hardly be happier, though, especially in light of your situation."

"Is this baby the gift you mentioned when you were in Tarahlaz?"

"Yes, I thought your father should know first. Now, tell me about Bresklon. I was surprised enough seeing you when we arrived."

Moonlight sparkled in Anlía's green eyes. "I was concerned when Bresklon insisted on coming, but even Uncle Vezjalan and Grandmother Sharlia thought it a good idea. Uncle agreed to come as an escort because he wanted to meet Father. Grandmother Oneshkla sent Zaranla's daughter as a female companion so all would be proper."

Alexa nodded thoughtfully. "So, you're still certain this is your path for your future?"

Anlía stopped beside the Fountain of the Valkana. Carved stone miraculously maintained heat that defied wintry cold temperatures beneath cascading waters. "Mother, I can't begin to imagine my life without Bresklon. As improbable as it may sound, the longer I know him, the better I love him."

Alexa sighed and glanced into the bottom of the fountain, remembering the first time she had seen it and watched people marveling at tiny trickles of water forming in its empty basin. "Truest love is like that, my daughter. It begins as a mere drop and never stops growing or flowing. After all these years, my love for your father still surprises me when I think it impossible but suddenly find I love him more than ever."

"There you ladies are!" Gregor's voice rang out as he and Bresklon strode toward them. "Isn't it rather cold for a midnight stroll?"

"Not if you've come to keep me warm!" Alexa laughed. "Seriously, we were just returning from evening prayers. I stopped to check my fountain."

"It appears to be working just fine despite the frigid temperatures, although I've never figured out how. Perhaps that's a task for Thikos. I suggest we go inside to warm up."

Shivering, Bresklon turned and placed a discreet hand against Anlía's back. "A wise suggestion, Sire. Your ishna impress me with their amazing abilities to withstand these cold temperatures."

Gregor chuckled, glancing down into Alexa's dancing eyes. "You may find my ishna make up for the cold temperatures with their very warm hearts."

⌣

Willem arrived two days later from a brief inspection of new warehouses opened to augment the supply chain supporting Turand's military. He was surprised to learn Stefan and Adrina had not yet returned from Garogan City due to delays caused by a heavy snowstorm.

"Welcome home, my friend, welcome home," Willem greeted Gregor with an unusually effusive embrace. "How glad my heart is that you've returned to us, safe and victorious."

"Willem, I cannot tell you how glad my heart is to be home. How are you?"

"Better now. The news of Bin-Lot's defeat had our people dancing in the streets for two days and nights. I think no one slept for too much merrymaking."

"What a sight that must have been. Well, I've brought you quite a sight for your own eyes. The man himself."

Willem's eyes grew wide. "Bin-Lot? Here? On Turandan soil? In Val's great name, why?"

"Willem! Look at this surprise!" Katara interrupted her husband's inquiry in an excited voice.

When Willem turned, he looked suitably shocked before reaching out to embrace his old friend. "Again?"

Alexa hugged him tightly and kissed his cheek. "Again, my friend. One final gift for my husband."

Releasing her, Willem shook his head and surrendered to laughter. "I thought I heard that with the twins."

Gregor said, "Only that I wouldn't ask her for more children. She surprised me this time."

"Well, congratulations. I know you must be thrilled."

"That I am. My wife says we're having another son. While we haven't yet settled on a first name, we do have a second name—the name of the man we hope will be his godfather—if the friend is willing,"

Willem eyed Gregor suspiciously. "And that man is?"

Alexa grasped her friend's hand. "The name we selected is Willem. We would like you and Katara to be his godparents. With all the changes in our lives, we think his first name should honor Gregor's Trezvindjan heritage."

Gregor's voice softened. "I know this is sudden. Take your time to consider it. We will not be offended if…"

"Gregor," Willem interrupted, "I am beyond honored that you think me worthy. If Katara is willing…"

"Of course, I am!" Katara exclaimed. "I already told Alexa I might not live as close as Adrina, but I'll love this little one as much as Adrina loves your others! He's the real reason you fainted in Garogan, isn't he?"

Alexa nodded and hugged her. "He is."

"Well, now that's settled so quickly, I understand you've already met Grandfather and Gaeldoreg. They're here, so you can renew acquaintances. Anlía has also arrived from Trezvindja—with someone who dares to request her hand in marriage."

"No!" Willem exclaimed. "What did you say?"

"Nothing yet! She's still my baby girl. I'm not ready for this."

Willem laughed. "Gregor, dear friend, you love babies. I just found out I'm to be a grandfather. Babies. Think more babies."

"In Val's great name, Willem! She's my daughter!" Gregor roared with exaggerated horror.

❧

Stefan Sidano returned to Toraval three days later. Braeklojorn Vosklon witnessed firsthand the deep and abiding brotherly love his grandson shared with the loyal friend and adviser Maxim and Anlía Toscano had brought to live in the palace when Stefan was orphaned as a boy. Without shame, tears streamed from Stefan's gray eyes as he held his king in a powerful embrace. Releasing Gregor and pushing him backward, he traced the scar-marked cheek and grimaced as if the injury were a personal affront. Stefan tightly gripped Gregor's arms, assuring him that his palace, his capital, and his homeland had stayed a steady, unyielding course to ensure the triumphant homecoming of their beloved King Gregor and Prince Nikolai.

Unashamed of his emotions, Gregor saluted Stefan with a kiss to his forehead. "You are as my brother, Stefan. I owe you so much. Thank you— and your wife—for caring for my children during my absence. Come. Warm yourself after your journey. My grandfather has also returned. Anlía is home to visit, and an uncle is here."

❧

Stefan knelt before the altar at the Great Temple of Val. Offering intense prayer, he felt strengthened for the ordeal ahead. Whispering final words of devotion, he started to stand but stopped. That familiar, comforting sense of energy swirled around him before penetrating his being. Looking up, he murmured, "Lady Valkana."

Golden veil and gown whispered back as the ethereal figure sat on the altar steps beside him. Her softly melodious voice spoke. "Stefan, you are always with him. Val watches you and blesses you for your unfaltering loyalty."

"Until I met Adrina, Gregor was all I had. He never failed me. Not once."

"I think he would rather die. You do realize how difficult this is for him."

"I know. I also believe that what he does will demonstrate to our people the extent of his dedication to avoiding more death without sacrificing fairness. Turand cries out for justice, and rightfully so. With the Order of Val standing behind him, including those who suffered most, our people receive a valuable lesson that punishment can be tempered with measures of mercy. We must be reminded that death is not always the best solution."

The high priestess rested a hand on Stefan's shoulder. Electricity vibrated throughout his body. "He needs you. Go to him with deepest gratitude from your Lord Val and your Valkana."

Stefan stood to leave, looking up first. The steady hum in the crystal pyramid above him sounded a low note as golden light shimmered around the sun embedded within. Glancing around, the high priestess had disappeared. "Odd," he thought as he turned and walked through the tall doors to leave.

Just outside the temple, he met Alexa and Anlía on their way to pray and meditate during the morning's proceedings. Stefan shook his head and stuttered a surprised greeting. "I was just going to meet Gregor," he added, noting that mysterious, unnerving gleam in Alexa's eyes he had seen many times throughout the years.

"How glad that makes me," Alexa replied softly. "You do realize how difficult this is for him. Go to him. He needs you."

Stefan shivered. Had he not just heard her say those very words inside the temple? "I will see you later?"

"Of course. Stefan?"

"Yes?"

"You go with the gratitude of your Lord Val and your Valkana. And your friend Alexa. Watch over him for me."

Stefan smiled. She had come to him in spirit. "Always."

～

Bin-Lot's fifth round of punishment had been administered by Major Tirstan Fratino, who had returned to Toraval with Princess Regent Anlía. When approached about the possibility, a grim-faced Tirstan immediately accepted the responsibility, claiming it was his duty as the senior officer in the Queen's Royal Guard. When Tirstan faced the Sifiq king, he unleashed the fury and the shame he had felt over the needless deaths of good soldiers, the failure of the Royal Guard to protect their queen during his absence, and the torture inflicted under Bin-Lot's orders. Bin-Lot hung limp after the sixth strike.

Tirstan had represented his Guard, his army, and his people. Like his king, he knew no joy in inflicting pain or injury on any living being. Also like Gregor, he understood that Turandans needed to see their leaders and their defenders would never shirk their duty in protecting them or claiming justice for grievous injuries. The major also comprehended that surviving Sifiq military officers needed to see firsthand that Turandans would never again meekly accept the violent side of Sifiq culture.

This morning, government officials and as many Turandan citizens as practical had been given access to a covered courtyard at Zenox Prison used as a sheltered location for prisoners to exercise during inclement weather. Under heavy guard and secured together with chains, Sifiq Captains Kar-Lan and Bel-Dar stood near two central posts. They wondered if their executions were imminent. The air was charged with electricity—an odd mood of mixed emotions, including anticipation, anxiety, and relief that a conclusion was finally at hand.

This day, true to his promise, Gregor would wield the whip one final time. Walking into the courtyard, he was accompanied by his three sons, his grandfather, Stefan Sidano, Willem Zephirás, Vezjalan Vosklon, Gaeldoreg Vosklon, and Bresklon Krisantal. Leaving his personal entourage in the center area of the courtyard, Gregor walked to posts for a cursory inspection before stopping, hands clasped behind him, eyes closed. Everyone waited in anxious silence.

After more than a minute, Gregor lifted his head and turned a slow circle, meeting the eyes of the many onlookers. His face was solemn. Now wearing his light gray uniform tunic redesigned with brightly colored stripes representing Turand and his Trezvindjan league affiliations on one shoulder and his family crests on the other, he looked more striking than ever. He drew a deep breath.

"We are here today as witnesses to the final term of a sentence imposed for crimes committed against the Queen of Turand and four Valiria priestesses. The initial terms were performed in Atuliq for the benefit of the Sifiq people, who now know that Turand and Trezvindja will stand by our declarations with action whenever necessary. We decided to impose the final two terms here so that our people can see that, however unpleasant, justice will be enforced. Everyone will know my Royal House will apply justice with action, not empty words."

He turned his gaze toward the waiting Sifiq officers. "Captain Kar-Lan and Captain Bel-Dar, although you have lived as prisoners since you arrived in Turand, I believe you have been treated with reasonable respect and courtesy as long as you have followed our rules. Am I correct?"

Although curious and confused, the two responded with affirmative nods.

"Good. You will now see what happens when you cross me. Let this be a lesson if you ever return to your homeland." Gregor then looked at the officer on duty. "Bring the prisoner and prepare him."

Bin-Lot jerked his arms free of his jailer. "I can walk. At least allow me some dignity."

"Still defiant?" Gregor asked, his eyebrows lifted high.

The Sifiq king, his skin pale and his eyes bloodshot, shook his head. "As if defiance would do any good. They drag me and pull on my already battered back when you intend to do even worse. What would you do?"

"You showed no qualms or compassion for my wife when you ordered her whippings. Why should I show you any?"

Bin-Lot glared at him for only a moment. "You are a hard man, Gregor of Turand. I curse the day I ever heard your name—or your wife's."

"As I curse yours, Bin-Lot." He looked at his guards. "Remove his shirt and secure him."

Taking a deep breath, Gregor gripped the handle of the whip and drew back. Then, as before, he began his measured count as he laid each heavy stroke against Bin-Lot's bare back, slicing open flesh and drawing blood with the three-tailed lash that had scarred Alexa.

When the task was finished, the Sifiq king drooped from his bonds. Royal Guards checked him, carefully released the ropes, and carried him to a doctor. Two stunned Sifiq captains were marched away to a conference room. There, Win-Das and his colleagues waited with contracts offering them return to Sifiqqa in exchange for oaths that they would never raise arms against the new Sifiqqa government or against Turand or Trezvindja. Turandan citizens filed out of the prison yard with newfound comprehension of the extremes their king would pursue to obtain justice for their citizens and their nation.

Gregor returned to the palace and took DiMarco and Thikos aside to counsel them. How he had hated including them today, but he recalled his exposure to Sifiq evils during his childhood. He had decided it would be better for them to witness a controlled aftermath than death and destruction as he and Nikolai had. They were, after all, princes of the realm.

Stefan, Willem, and Nikolai discussed the sentence and Gregor's decision to bring the Sifiq king to Turand's shores. They questioned if there was more behind the decision to perform the final floggings in Toraval than just the benefit of Turandan citizens. The Trezvindjans kept together, talking quietly among themselves.

⌣

"Gregor, now that things are settling, there's something I wish to do before we leave for Trezvindja," Alexa said as she lay beside him in bed two nights after Bin-Lot's ordeal.

With arms tucked beneath his head as he stared at the ceiling above, Gregor sighed. "And that is?"

How distant he still sounded, Alexa thought. Hoping he wouldn't resist, she turned toward him and rested her hand on his chest. "It isn't for frivolous reasons. I wish to take Grandfather and Bibo to Lindaval." Silence. She felt a brief, slight quickening in his breathing before he calmed again.

Finally, he asked, "For how long? And what about everyone else?"

"I thought we could leave first. Nikolai and Anlía could then time their departure with everyone else so you and I would have three full days alone there with Grandfather and Bibo. It would be good for all of us."

Prolonged silence again. "Gregor?"

He drew in a deep breath and turned toward her, resting a hand on her growing middle. "Lindaval. What an excellent suggestion. Shall we leave the day after tomorrow?"

When their coach rolled to a stop in front of the favorite Toscano retreat, travelers quickly exchanged weariness for the fragrant, peaceful welcome of the anomalous Lindaval. Met by waiting staff, they mounted steps to the wide, covered veranda and entered the spacious manor house.

Braeklojorn glanced at Gregor with a grin. "I wondered if your wife had lost her senses when she mentioned bringing lightweight clothes. It's warm outside!"

Gregor laughed. "One of the mysterious charms of Lindaval, Grandfather. No matter the season, Lindaval is this way year-round. It's like an isolated little island plopped down in the middle of Turand."

Alexa blinked at her husband's description. She had never heard him describe Lindaval in those words, and her mind drifted back to another description. Convinced she wasn't mistaken, she smiled to herself.

"Ma Ishna," Gaeldoreg said affectionately, "your smile reveals interesting thoughts. Will you not share?"

Green eyes met the glittering obsidian orbs she now adored. "Soon, Bibo. I will soon. I need to go upstairs right now. Gregor can show you and Grandfather around. Supper will be at seven."

Awaking early for prayers and meditation, Alexa paused to kiss her husband's forehead before heading downstairs to the manor's private chapel. Her first prayer was one of gratitude. Gregor had slept peacefully for the first night in more than a week. His spirit was finally calming. Returning to their suite, she slipped beneath the covers and snuggled against him. Before long, she unsuccessfully stifled a giggle.

"My humble apologies, Your Majesty."

Sleep-tumbled hair fell across his forehead, and a groggy smile brightened his face. "Why do you apologize for our son's bad manners?"

She laughed softly. "He's worse than Nikolai."

Gregor caressed her face. "My beautiful wife. Such a challenge after all you've been through already."

"At least this is a happy one. I feel his spirit, Gregor. He's so powerful and capable of so much love. Like you, I would never cross him, but to be loved by him?"

Breathing out a light laugh, Gregor closed his eyes. "All my children are born of love; therefore, they are each capable of great love."

Alexa closed her eyes. "Yes, but my intuition says three will likely exceed what most would call a great love."

Considering her comment for a moment, Gregor finally whispered, "Nikolai, Anlía, and this new baby?"

"Yes," she replied. "It doesn't lessen the beauty of how the others love or will love. I just expect differences I can't explain."

"I think I understand." He sighed and stretched. "I suppose we should get up. Grandfather sleeps late, but your bibo is an early riser."

Alexa giggled again. "He is. I saw light under his door when I came back upstairs from the chapel."

Gaeldoreg rose several times from the outdoor breakfast table to bury his face in perfumed panicles of lavender flowers. "Ma Ishna! These sweet little flowers smell like you!"

"Observant, old friend," Braeklojorn laughed. "That fragrance seems to accompany every Valiria I meet."

Happily smiling, Alexa watched Gaeldoreg with affectionate indulgence. "Lilacs have been the favored flower of Valiria since the inception of our order. Their beauty and fragrance magically affect us all."

Gregor swallowed a bite and dabbed a napkin to his mouth. "The lilacs here are an unusual variety that bloom year-round. My mother developed them with a talented horticulturist and planted them."

Braeklojorn turned fascinated eyes to his grandson before rising to inspect the flowers again. "Amazing. Yet another living testament to my daughter."

Memories carried Gregor back in time. "Grandfather, as I told you, this was my parents' favorite retreat. They started bringing me here when I was little. Mother had a special affinity for Lindaval. I recall Father occasionally teasing her about it. She always hugged him and told him she felt

605

like someone was reaching out to her here, reminding her she had always been loved."

Braeklojorn sat down again, his eyes misty. "An odd thing to say, but she was Mishkla's daughter, too."

"That's partly why we left the others behind when we brought you," Alexa said.

Braeklojorn's eyebrows met together above his nose. "I don't understand."

"I want you to get ready for a short ride. Bring something suitable to wear for bathing. Gregor and I will take towels and lunch." She looked up. "Bibo, would you mind if we go alone today with Grandfather?"

Seeing the serious expression on his daughter's face, Gaeldoreg shook his head. "Of course not, Ma Levya. I saw many books to read. This old man can use the rest."

Ma Levya. My special love. He rarely called her that because he infused *Ma Ishna* with so much affection already. She went to him and fiercely hugged him. Whispering, she said, "You will never know how much I love you, Bibo."

Dismounting later, Gregor carefully lowered Alexa from her horse. Unlike the first time he took her there, a clear path now led down to the hot springs. Arriving at the broad, green perimeter surrounding the pool of bubbling waters, Alexa turned expectant eyes to her husband's grandfather. "This is where I first began to realize how very much I loved Gregor."

Braeklojorn's vision swept the scope of the scene before him. Although still winter beyond Lindaval's boundaries, the temperatures here caressed his face with the same velvety warmth he associated with home. The ground beneath his feet cushioned his steps like thick carpet. Cheerful blurp-blurps rose from the vast pool surrounded by short, dense grasses and ground cover. Clean air blended the fragrances of sturdy trees, high grasses, and the ever-present lilacs. Ahead, tumbling over a tall rock face, the rushing sounds of a waterfall filled the air with soothing sounds and glittering, prismatic sparkles.

"Spectacular!" Braeklojorn murmured, transfixed. What was so haunting about the scene in front of his eyes?

"Don't you remember, Grandfather?"

Both Gregor and Braeklojorn turned questioning eyes to Alexa.

"Remember?" Suddenly, the great man's eyes widened and brimmed with tears. "She saw our child, filled with joy, standing in the center of the pool. She also saw a waterfall. That's why we set out for Lizmadal. It wasn't Lizmadal Mishkla saw in her visions and dreams. It was Turand—Lindaval. We were always destined to come to Turand."

Alexa went to him. Embracing him, she felt the sobs that rose from deep within his great frame. "Dearest Grandfather, I felt the truth the second I heard you tell your story to Bresklon. I was stunned."

"This was always Mother's favorite place," Gregor told him. "She loved relaxing out in the pool. That's why we gave you Mother's bedchamber—so you might feel a closer connection to her."

"I dreamed I felt someone stroking my hair last night. Do you think?" Tears rolled freely down Braeklojorn's face as his words trailed off.

Alexa nodded. "I've never told you. She was a sister Valiria. Because of the connection forged when I was pregnant with Nikolai, I have communicated on several occasions with Anlía's spirit."

Braeklojorn stared at Alexa in near-disbelief. His grandson's wife continued to astonish him with her mystical revelations. "Can you tell me more?"

Although she didn't smile, Alexa's expression reached deeply into both men's hearts. "When Gregor lay dying on the battlefield in Garogan during our civil war, his mother was the one who sustained him until I could arrive to call the Healing Graces. Tirani, another Valiria, and I had summoned her from her sacred rest. We were able to do so only because I carried Gregor's baby.

"Recently, her spirit encouraged me to seek you out. She asked if I would go to you, and I finally agreed. When I still had doubts, she delivered Mishkla's jewelry to me on the road to the caves. How? I don't know. Those jewels were locked away in Toraval when I left on my quest. She retrieved them and placed them in my tent one night as I slept. She knew you would recognize them."

"Beloved, you never told me all this," Gregor murmured.

"The separation of your family and Turand's times of crisis were foreseen. Anlía was destined to bridge time and distance to unite her family and her son's two peoples. Mishkla's fate led her to fulfill her daughter's destiny. And yours."

Braeklojorn shook his head. "I loved my Mishkla. For that matter, I still do. You didn't know her."

Alexa smiled, eyebrows lifting and emerald eyes sparkling.

"No. That is impossible."

"In the realm of mystics, nothing is impossible. Your Mishkla's love has never left you and never will. You will know one another again. That is a promise I can make." She smiled and turned to open a pack Gregor had left on the ground. "You should change and find a place in the water to relax. I've brought a couple of Anlía's old journals I found. You can read them later. Go."

Gregor later thoughtfully watched his Grandfather. "He seems to enjoy the same spots Mother always liked best."

"Not surprising," Alexa commented. "He's probably responding to remnants of her energy. The two of you are much more sensitive than either of you realize."

"Then why did I never sense any of what you just said about Mother?"

"Because you've always been so engrossed in responsibilities for others."

"So have you. Why the difference?"

"Because I practiced from childhood how to manage the responsibilities while allowing my mystical abilities to develop and flourish."

⌒

Cheerful chatter and laughter rose above Lindaval's bubbling pool in a musically happy mist. Alexa watched from the pool's edge with her bare feet dangling in warm water. Her four youngest children monopolized Bibo and Uncle Vezzie, as the twins had dubbed Vezjalan. Grandfather was deeply engrossed in conversation with Nikolai. Glancing around, she noticed Bresklon, Anlía, and Gregor were nowhere to be seen.

The morning had begun humorously enough. Anlía had recognized the importance of actively integrating the customs and traditions of her new people into her daily life. With her mother's support, she decided the time had come to explain to her father how, as regent, she was adapting their fashions into her wardrobe. Bravely, Anlía had knocked on the door of her parents' suite. Entering wearing her long dressing robe, she described differences in clothing styles to Gregor.

Gregor had smiled and agreed—until she removed her robe to reveal her Trezvindjan-styled beach dress. Blood flooded his face as he staggered backward and dropped onto the sofa in the private suite. "Anlía Lulana Toscano! What in Val's name do you think you're wearing?"

Prepared for his reaction, Alexa had immediately gone to him. "Gregor, my love, if you recall, I told you that Trezvindja is an island nation that enjoys a hot tropical climate all year. Its people, women included, spend a great deal of time on its beautiful beaches. Floor-length dresses over heavy petticoats are impractical—and uncomfortable."

"Alexa! In Val's great name! I cannot believe you're saying that...
Oh, Val, preserve me! Nikolai!" While waiting for Nikolai, Gregor looked
askance at Anlía before turning disbelieving eyes back to Alexa. "Do you
mean to say you actually approve of—that? For my daughter? On my
daughter? In front of people?"

Stifling laughter, Nikolai opened the door and peeked in. "Father?
Do you need something?"

"Yes! Brandy! No! No good! Taca! Bring me Taca!"

"Isn't it early for Taca?" Nikolai asked, trying not to laugh. "You
haven't had breakfast yet."

Alexa intervened. "Niko, please send up some toast for your father
and a small glass of brandy. He needs it. He can have Taca later."

"Mother?" Anlía asked with a grimace.

"Go have breakfast, love. I'll take care of your father."

Convincing Gregor that Anlía had already redesigned Trezvindjan
styles to reflect her more conservative Turandan preferences in clothing
had required reassurances from his grandfather, his uncle, and the cousin
sent to attend Anlía. Only Alexa's continued insistence had finally worn
down his open opposition, which he soothed with a second, larger glass of
brandy when Alexa wasn't looking.

Later, on the far side of the pool, out of sight of the family, Bresklon
watched the steady, rushing plunge of water over soaring, craggy rocks.
His beloved Anlía stood by his side, leaning against his side. Surrounded
by her younger siblings, there had been little time for them to be alone
since coming to Toraval. These few moments were precious as she clung to
his arm, and they enjoyed nature's peaceful setting in Lindaval.

"You were right when you told me how beautiful this place is," he
said when they finally turned to walk the long way back.

She stopped him. "I always loved it here. I hoped you would.
Bresklon..."

"No, Ma Mariyeva, he has said nothing more."

"I love when you call me your heart. You say it so beautifully," Anlía said softly.

"Perhaps that's because my heart is so beautiful."

She tilted her face upward and kissed him lightly. "I love Father so. I just wish he would say something and end my misery."

Bresklon smiled patiently. "Anlía, at first, I, too, wanted to press for an immediate answer, but then I reminded myself to be reasonable. Your father just returned from fighting a miserable war. Especially after watching him administer Bin-Lot's sentence at Zenox, I don't even want to imagine what he witnessed in Sifiqqa. He has every right to be careful with your future. He hardly knows me. After considering his perspective, he needs to personally see me and what I have to offer you—in Trezvindja."

"But Bresklon, both Grandfather and Uncle Vezjalan have vouched for you."

"Yes, but in fairness, how long has Prince Braeklojorn really known me?"

"Forgive me, Bresklon. I've never been so impatient as now. I'm not sure why."

He studied her face. Those green eyes he loved so dearly reflected both love and anxiety. "Ma Mariyeva, you are young and full of vitality and desire to build this wonderful new life we dream of sharing. You fear your father may not allow it."

Her voice trembled. "Don't you?"

"Perhaps. A little, but very little. I am coming to see him as a cautious but very wise man. His wisdom rises from the tragedies he experienced and the great sorrows he carried for years. Meeting your mother and then Nikolai's birth made things better, but even that road was paved with grief because, in some small way, his mind connected even those triumphs with the Sifiq and conflict. Unless I'm wrong, our King Gregor is especially protective with you because you are the first absolutely pure joy to enter his life."

Anlía gazed up into pensive black eyes. "I'm not sure I understand."

"The war was over and the Sifiq banished. As I understand, all of Turand was undergoing recovery. He and Alexa were very happy together with their firstborn son. Then along comes this daughter he had wanted, and she is born straight into his hands, sweet and beautiful. His adoring wife decides to name this new baby after his own beloved mother. As I said, you were the first pure joy to enter his life, essentially untouched by war or death.

"My sweet Anlía, I cannot nor will I blame your father for being so cautious with your future. I am confident he will come to see me as a strong, reliable, and honorable man who would face death a thousand times over rather than see his daughter harmed. Your father will see my love for you and yours for me. His love for you and his desire for your happiness will erase any objections he currently has against our marriage. Trust me. Trust him."

Anlía moved into his embrace, feeling safe and comforted. "I never considered it that way. Oh, Bresklon, how I love you. How much more you make me love and appreciate Father when I never thought such a thing possible. Thank you."

Bresklon placed a lingering kiss on top of her head while tamping down his deeper, growing desires for her. Gregor, who had come meaning to speak to the two, quickly turned to rejoin Alexa. He had never intended to eavesdrop, but that single conversation helped him know Bresklon Krisantal better than if they had been stranded together for weeks on some faraway island.

Lowering himself to the blanket beside his wife, Gregor gazed at his family, now lounging restfully in soothing spring waters. He looked down.

Rainbows of light reflected from the stones of Alexa's two wedding rings. Whether it be family to fill aching, empty places in his soul or answers to his most troubling quandaries, she always found ways to guide him to everything he ever needed. Focusing glistening eyes on her questioning face, he smiled and leaned forward to kiss her.

Chapter 24

"Willem, how many cases of this wine did you bring?" Gregor asked, tipping the stemmed glass to his lips for a drink of the rich, red liquid inside.

"Only five, my friend. One case for the voyage and four to help you," Willem paused, "adjust after we arrive."

Alexa leaned over Gregor's shoulder and kissed his cheek. "My husband has never been one to rely on drink for fortitude. I think your excellent wine would be better suited to celebrate his coronation, don't you?"

"Excellent idea. We could also hold a case back to celebrate when my godson makes his arrival," Willem remarked, his eyes twinkling.

"Fine points, both of you. I just tremble when I think of seeing my daughter in such..."

"Stefan used the word dishabille," Willem offered.

Gregor groaned, then chuckled. "Stefan and his extensive vocabulary. That was less than helpful, Willem. On another note, I do hope his voyage will be as smooth as ours when he escorts DiMarco and Thikos. I wanted them to come with us, but they were adamant about completing an important project. How could I not respect such dedication to duty?"

"You made the right decision. Besides, it's always wise for heirs to the throne to travel separately on long voyages like this."

Gregor eyed his wife. "You don't expect problems…"

Sharply shaking her head, she said, "No, all will be well, but it is a consideration for future journeys. Such planning will show our peoples we think of their best interests."

"Well, if you'll excuse me, I must go check Katara. Alexa's attention finally eased her latest bout of ocean sickness. I should be with her."

Alone in their luxurious cabin, Gregor reached for his wife, drawing her onto his lap. Supporting her securely with one arm, he used his free hand to trace circles over the growing mound inside her. He never ceased being fascinated by the idea that a living person could grow inside his wife just because they had loved one another so well.

"I hope sending Nikolai ahead with Anlía was prudent and that the two have made significant progress on plans for the coronation ceremony. I want details organized before he comes."

"What makes you think they might waste time?"

"Not necessarily waste time. Just not use it most effectively. They're both young. As serious and responsible as she is, Anlía is young and completely besotted with Bresklon Krisantal."

"Gregor!"

"I voice no criticism. I'm old and completely besotted with my wife. Neither am I always as efficient as I should be when she's close. There. I confess." He kissed her lightly and continued, "Nikolai won't admit it, but he's exhausted after the Sifiq campaign. He dedicated himself exclusively to resolving the Sifiq issues for so long and then fought an ugly war. I remember how that felt when I was younger. He needs time to relax and be with people his own age."

Stroking her fingers through her husband's hair, Alexa sighed. "Of course. Trezvindja is a perfect place to begin. You'll see."

Suddenly, they felt the ship rise sharply, tilt, and shudder while quickly sliding downward. Gregor clutched Alexa tightly. "Almighty Val, what was that?"

"Nothing to worry about, my love," she soothed. "Just the outer currents that seemingly protect your beautiful island realm. Grandfather taught Captain Norlandro how to navigate them. That was the worst you should feel. Now you understand the heavy glassware and tall rails around tables. Less breakage and chasing things rolling around on the floors."

Her impish grin prompted him to laugh. "Smart folks, these mariners." He looked up when he heard knocking at their cabin door. "Yes?"

Entering excitedly, Marina and Karina bounced over to where Gregor now stood, righting an empty glass that had tipped. "Father! Did you feel it? Gaeldoreg says that big tilt means we're almost there! Wasn't it exciting?"

Closing his eyes to resist rolling them, Gregor grinned and threw his arms around his youngest children in an enthusiastic embrace. "That was definitely heart-stopping! Now, why don't you help Mother get ready for supper? This should be our last night on board. Tomorrow? Najatil and Trezvindja!"

Just before noon the next day, Gregor walked out of the Najatil port director's office after following all of the entry formalities and accepting profuse greetings from the rotund director, who assured him of his discretion. News of His Majesty's arrival would not be released until after the king reached Tarahlaz.

Thankfully, the docks and streets beyond were devoid of crowds. Braeklojorn and Vezjalan waited in front of a long, elegant coach fitted with multiple seats and canopies to shield passengers from the sun. With his jaw trembling and dark eyes glistening, Braeklojorn approached

Gregor with outstretched arms. His voice vibrated with emotion when he said, "Welcome to Trezvindja, King Gregor. Welcome, my beloved grandson."

Gregor looked up, framing that newly loved countenance between his hands. "Thank you, Grandfather, for welcoming me to this second home. How glad I am to see you again."

A flurry of hugs and greetings was followed by the scenic ride in the open coach that carried Gregor toward his royal palace in Tarahlaz for the very first time. Delightedly resuming his Uncle Vezzie role, Vezjalan hugged Marina and Karina close as he pointed out different sights. Gaeldoreg and Willem discussed the changing landscape as they moved inland from the port and laughed good-naturedly as both held Katara on sleek leather seats too high for her short legs to reach the floor, reminding her of her childhood.

Braeklojorn fixed his attention on Gregor. Years of lonely sorrow receded as he proudly introduced his regal grandson to the beautiful realm inherited through Mishkla Krisantal. The venerable prince also cast affectionate glances at Alexa, noting the glow impending motherhood brought to her complexion.

"Grandfather?" For a few brief seconds, she sensed his fleeting lament that he had missed the many special moments of Mishkla's pregnancy and even Anlía's. Then, reaching for his hand, she drew him close and laid his open palm over her stomach.

Watching Braeklojorn's black eyes grow huge, Gregor quietly laughed. "Astonishing, isn't it?"

"Was that really...?" Braeklojorn stuttered to a stop.

Gregor's eyes sparkled merrily. "My seventh child, yet I never tire of feeling a baby move before its birth. A miracle if ever there was one."

"May I?" Gaeldoreg had seen them together and now knelt in front of Alexa.

She chuckled softly. "Yes, but I suggest you not press too hard. You'll make him warm, and he'll just quiet down again."

Gaeldoreg and Braeklojorn both placed hands lightly on her stomach. To their amazement, two strong kicks were followed by a slow, roving slide before the hidden infant grew quiet. Two older Trezvindjans remained utterly mesmerized. Obsidian eyes shone brightly, and smiles quivered.

Braeklojorn finally broke the spell. "Two miracles in my life I missed. I pray thanks that Espiritus granted me this small miracle today."

Alexa reached out and caressed his face. "A greater miracle awaits you, Grandfather. This baby you will hold in your arms. I know it won't be quite the same as having held your Anlía, but he is part of her."

Braeklojorn nodded and smiled. "And part of my Mishkla. And me." He lifted misty eyes to Gregor. "How happy my heart is this day."

Arriving at the palace in Tarahlaz, Gregor hardly noticed the gleaming white walls of his magnificent new home or the many brilliantly colored banners fluttering in the breeze. He missed all of the extensive preparations underway for his upcoming coronation. Instead, his eyes focused on the lovely Princess Regent Anlía, who waited with Crown Prince Nikolai on one side and Grand Councillor Krisantal on the other.

Quickly exiting the carriage once footmen dropped steps and opened the door, Gregor bounded forward. The three awaiting him greeted him according to Trezvindjan custom by kneeling with arms crossed over their chests. "Up! The three of you!" he said unceremoniously.

Gregor grasped his daughter by the shoulders and held her back, appraising her image. She wore the regent's crown of diamonds and pearls set in white gold. Her formal day dress was fashioned according to Trezvindjan styles in white and lavender silk. Sighing, her father said, "I may never grow accustomed to seeing you this way. You have become a strikingly beautiful woman, Anlía."

"Thank you, Father. Welcome to Trezvindja and the Royal Palace of Tarahlaz. I'm so happy I correctly sensed Mother's message about your arrival."

"Now I understand how this works. I should have known." he chuckled as he kissed her cheeks. He then turned and embraced Nikolai. "My son, I hope this trip has fared better than your last two foreign trips."

"Much better, Father. Soon, Trezvindja won't seem foreign at all. You're going to love it here. People can hardly wait to meet their new king."

Meeting Bresklon Krisantal's waiting gaze, Gregor nodded. "Grand Councillor, such a pleasure seeing you again. I trust you are well and have not been too inconvenienced adding my son to your tutoring activities."

Bresklon tilted his head slightly and cocked a black eyebrow. "Not at all, Sire. Prince Nikolai has been as eager a pupil as his sister, although I hope you'll forgive me for saying not quite as delightful."

"Hmmm," Gregor returned. "I've never been asked to forgive a man for an honest admission. Shall we go inside? Grandfather says quite a welcoming committee awaits me."

"Father, it's such a long ride from the port. I'm going to lead everyone up a side staircase first so you can freshen up," Anlía said, taking Gregor firmly by the arm. "Niko, would you escort Mother and the girls? Chesha is waiting to escort Willem and Katara to their suite. This is so exciting! Bresklon, would you kindly let everyone know we'll join them shortly?"

Guiding her father to the luxurious king's suite, Anlía leveled serious green eyes at him that reminded Gregor so much of Alexa he barely subdued laughter.

"Niko only took Mother to the queen's apartment because of the twins. I expect you'll want her to join you here tonight."

"You would be right."

Anlía breathed in deeply. "Father, please try to be more cordial with Bresklon. He spends all his free time helping Niko and me learn and adjust to Trezvindjan ways. He also respects you very much."

Gregor raised his eyebrows. "I wasn't aware I said anything offensive to our venerable Grand Councillor. Now, if you'll kindly excuse me, I see some of my things are arriving. I need a few moments to prepare myself before I go downstairs. Would you send your brother in?"

Concealing disappointment, Anlía opened the door to leave. "Of course, Father."

"Anlía, my darling, calm yourself. I have no intention of insulting your good councillor. Now, your brother?"

Gregor and Nikolai joined Braeklojorn in a sun-dappled, second-floor atrium ten minutes later. Quickly joined by Alexa, his twins, Willem, and Katara, Gregor gave his grandfather an excited smile. "Shall we?"

The afternoon reception delivered Gregor Toscano into the open arms of his two Trezvindjan great-grandmothers. Queen Mother Oneshkla Krisantal appeared more animated than anyone had seen in years as she admired Gregor's regal bearing and praised his outstanding successes as both monarch and father. Princess Elder Sharlia Vosklon insisted Gregor had inherited his handsome looks not just from Braeklojorn but from her own dear husband. Braeklojorn's sister had traveled from the island's far side and agreed wholeheartedly with her mother.

Although an ailing Kaelzron had declined his invitation to attend, other Krisantal relatives arrived to meet the new king and prince so highly acclaimed by Trezvindja's esteemed Protectors. Vosklon League members received Gregor with enormous pride. The sincere good wishes and respect from both leagues carried one vital element Gregor had longed for most of his life—the undeniable connection of family.

"You were remarkable today," Alexa complimented as she untied ribbons on her robe before crawling into bed.

Staring at city lights from a window, Gregor closed the draperies and turned around. "Aunts and uncles. Cousins. Great-grandmothers. Family, Alexa. Real family like I've never had before. Our children have family now, too. I wish I could describe how that feels."

"You don't have to. I'm glad Marina and Karina were so well-behaved with Uncle Vezzie today. They were perfect little princesses."

Gregor laughed. "What magic does he work with them? Do you know how old he is?"

"I know. And Vezzie seems almost disrespectful, but he loves it!"

"He does. And—speaking of love."

"Yes?"

"What am I to do about my daughter?"

"Do you mean *our* daughter?" Alexa asked teasingly. "The one with emerald eyes?"

Gregor nodded. "That one. Yes. Help me. The only time in my life I was ever more lost was when I was so in love with you and thought you would forever hate me."

Alexa reached for him. "Come. Come to bed, my love, and share your thoughts."

Tucked beneath crisp linen sheets and propped up against pillows, Gregor thought for a while. "I see Anlía as mature and very aware of what she wants. I heard so many comments today about how well she has conducted herself as regent—how she surprised a good many people with her wisdom and her diplomacy when dealing with some of the more taciturn league councillors. Marriage is another matter—a huge step requiring lifelong commitment."

"Gregor, may I remind you that she already made one lifelong commitment? I assure you. She was ready. I didn't judge her for that pledge. Five seasoned priestesses did."

Gregor exhaled. "True. What about Bresklon Krisantal? I do respect him. More than you know."

"Really?" Alexa said, sensing an underlying story behind his comment.

"I do, but I don't feel I've had time to know him well enough. I want her to be safe. To be happy and not have to face the trials we faced."

Alexa turned and adjusted her position to gaze at him. "My husband, if she lives here, she will likely be as safe as in Turand—especially now that the Sifiq are defeated. If she marries the man she loves, she can build a happy life, but one can never guarantee how long happiness will last. Look at Oui-lest. Her happiness with Victor was exceptional, but it lasted such a short time. Thinking of how I almost lost you during Turand's civil war still terrifies me, but nearly losing you taught me to cherish every minute we have together, even when we argue. Time is too precious to waste."

"But the difficulties. Do you ever regret all the terrible problems we faced at the beginning of our marriage?"

Alexa inhaled, holding her breath for several seconds before releasing it. Gregor noticed her hands tracing nervous circles over her stomach. "At the time, I was miserable. I was angry and unhappy. I loved and missed Victor and couldn't understand why Val chose you to be my husband. Even knowing you were Val's choice for me, it took quite some time to accept that truth and revert to my trust in Val. When I did, my eyes opened first, then my heart. Slowly, I began to see you for who you really were. I also began to learn myself better than ever.

"The first time you took me to Lindaval, the veils began to lift. When Victor forced me back to Garogan, all the veils fell away. I've never looked back, nor have I since regretted those hardships. Why? Those times taught me who you were, who I was, and how very much I love you. No regrets, Gregor. None."

He got up and extinguished the lights in the room. Returning to bed, he drew her close and kissed her—a slow, deep kiss conveying the multi-faceted feelings she inspired in him. Gently, he tucked the sheets around her shoulders. "Sleep, my beloved wife. You need to rest, but your husband is right here beside you. This is my place now, and I have no intention of ever leaving you again. Sleep sweet, Alexa."

⌒

Reserved for the new arrivals to relax and become familiar with palace routines, the next day began early with changes to plans. A messenger from the Mystic Council arrived bearing a handwritten note from Milansa Krisantal requesting permission to call on Alexa that afternoon. Delighted, Alexa conferred with Gregor and dispatched the messenger with acceptance and time. Late morning produced a welcome surprise. While Gregor's and Alexa's journey had been lengthened by two days while becalmed, favorable winds had advanced Stefan's arrival with DiMarco and Thikos after their earlier-than-planned departure.

Good-natured laughter immediately followed the welcoming hugs when younger brothers started teasing their older sister about her strange new garb. The twins valiantly defended their beautiful big sister. Anlía, unusually stern-faced, reminded her younger brothers that, here in Tarahlaz, she wore the regent's crown, so she could have them arrested. Katara sided with Gregor, saying that Trezvindjan fashions were too revealing. Alexa, Nikolai, and Willem laughingly accused them of being too old and stodgy to adapt to different ways and ideas. Stefan, ever the diplomat, finally suggested they admire the lovely fabric of Anlía's dress and respect all the customs of this new country while they were here—starting by sampling the cuisine.

Midday was served at a long table outside. Joined by Braeklojorn, Gaeldoreg, Uncle Vezzie, and Grandmother Sharlia, Gregor looked fondly at his family and closest friends. Still, some part of him wondered if all this might be a dream. When Grandmother Sharlia leaned sideways to tuck a strand of hair away from Karina's eyes or Grandfather affectionately patted DiMarco's back, Trezvindja seemed the product of an impossible imagination. Drawing in a breath, he felt delicate fingers stroke his scarred cheek.

"My love, are you all right?"

Those eyes. Those captivating emerald eyes. Gregor smiled. "Better than all right. I cannot recall being happier."

⌐

"Lady Valkana, thank you for seeing me on such short notice, especially so soon after your arrival." Milansa Krisantal gazed thoughtfully at Alexa. "So this is the difference I sensed when you were last here."

Alexa's smile beamed. "It is, Sacred Shamani. A gift for my husband."

"A great gift for all of us if my perceptions do not fail me. I met your son Nikolai. He begins to come into his own mystic spirit. He and Anlía descend from two powerful mystic lines. Now? You carry this child— one whose spirit already draws attention from the Mystic Council." She sighed. "How much joy it gives me to live in this time."

"Dear Milansa, these mysteries unfold and amaze me. They are beyond my comprehension, but I thank Val for blessing me to be part of them."

"Have you noticed your Nikolai's aura?"

"Only recently. I often have difficulties viewing the auras of my family, but even a Sifiq villager whose life he saved saw Nikolai's."

"Fascinating. The primary light colors are intriguing. Brilliant white with red. Powerful in one so young, and indicators that he will be a very strong king. I have yet to meet your husband. I am curious to see his."

"He promised to join us before you leave. Nikolai is very much like his father. He even looks like him."

Milansa smiled. "Your son reminds me much of young Braeklojorn when he courted and married our dear Mishkla. Of course, Braeklojorn never wore a beard then."

Alexa chuckled. "Milansa, since you're here, I do wish your counsel on something."

The elder mystic smiled. "I am honored to help if I can."

"When I told Gregor about this baby, I told him we have a son who possesses a Protector soul. After discussing the matter, we believe our baby should be born here, in Trezvindja."

"Indeed? That's an extraordinary decision. It is one that will generate jubilation among my people."

Alexa smiled sweetly. "*Our* people."

"Properly corrected. So, what advice do you seek?"

"Our other decision is a name. We will have a godfather, according to Turandan customs, and the child's second name will be Willem—for his godfather. We want a strong, suitable Trezvindjan name for our son's first name, but one our people in Turand won't struggle to pronounce."

"Your decision is both wise and commendable. Let me ponder this in meditation. I will let you know."

A knock at the door was followed by Gregor's voice. "Alexa?"

Rising from her chair, Alexa opened the door. Milansa's reaction to Gregor was both emotional and inspired. With her hands framing her king's face, brilliant white, red, and gold lights filled the space between her palms and his cheeks. Her mouth slowly spread into a radiant smile as her head moved back and forth in utter amazement.

"Your Majesty," she murmured, "how privileged I am to meet one such as you. The Sacred Blood of the Krisantal flows bright and powerful through your veins, bringing great joy to this woman who serves our people."

Without conscious thought, Gregor raised his own large hands and covered hers, pressing them to his cheeks. "Sacred Shamani, I know you are a devout holy woman serving our people according to the will of Espiritus. May I be so bold as to ask for your blessing?" He abruptly knelt before the ancient mystic.

Tears sprang into Milansa's eyes. Such news to bring before the Mystic Council! Trezvindja's respected Shamani chanted a blessing over King Gregor without realizing his grandfather and eldest son had appeared with Bresklon Krisantal at the open door to look for him.

～

Gregor and Nikolai mounted majestic Trezvindjan stallions and led their first procession through the streets of Tarahlaz. Princes DiMarco and Thikos rode behind their father and older brother. Behind them followed Queen Alexa and Princess Regent Anlía in an open ceremonial carriage. The twin princesses rode with their great-great-grandmothers in another carriage, and an entourage of Gregor's Turandan friends and Trezvindjan family followed. Milansa Krisantal, accompanied by Bresklon Krisantal, represented the Mystic Council.

The event allowed the people of Trezvindja their first opportunity to see their new king in person. With brightly colored flags and pennants fluttering along city avenues, the parade wound along a route crowded with citizens anxious to glimpse the monarch hailed by Protector ranks as the first King of the Krisantal Sacred Blood in generations to satisfy their nation's warrior pride in battle. The Crown Prince had fought just as fiercely and honorably. Excited, roaring cheers from Protector warriors swiftly infused the crowds with their enthusiasm, resulting in resounding ovations along the entire route.

When the procession ended, King Gregor followed Princess Regent Anlía, escorted by Grand Councillor Bresklon Krisantal, into the historic chamber where the king would make his first appearance before the

Council of Leagues. After the traditional pledges of loyalty were given and Gregor delivered a brief address, everyone gathered at a palace reception. Always keen on the value of personal relationships, Gregor kept Anlía busy with introductions to league councillors.

"Your Majesty, I have looked forward to meeting you," Councillor Brazjakan said. "I had the good fortune of dining at a party with your queen when she was last in Tarahlaz. What a delight she is."

Casting his eyes in the direction where Alexa stood with Katara, Stefan, and several other councillors, Gregor's eyes sparkled. "I must agree. She has been my greatest friend and ally for many years."

Feeling her husband's gaze, Alexa glanced across the room and came to him. "Councillor Brazjakan, how lovely to see you again. You look well."

"I am, Your Majesty." He chuckled, recalling their first evening together. "As do you, although somewhat different from our first meeting."

Alexa's eyes glittered with amusement. "Ah, yes. I believe I did mention my husband's challenges coping with a younger wife."

She and the councillor both laughed while Gregor stared and sighed. "Say nothing. I'm sure I'm better off not knowing."

When reception guests finally began to leave, Gregor gained Bresklon's attention. "I wish to speak to you after everyone leaves regarding changes to the coronation ceremony. In private. I don't require much of your time."

Bresklon controlled his expression. With the coronation ceremony only two days away, he hoped any changes wouldn't be too drastic. "Of course, Sire."

When Bresklon later entered the vast library, Gregor stood perusing titles he was able to read on soaring, polished shelves. The king turned and said, "Close the doors and lock them. I wish not to be disturbed." Walking to a large, ornate, wheeled bar, Gregor set out two balloon glasses and looked up. "Brandy?"

"Thank you." Bresklon approached the king and accepted the glass, glad for the fortification considering Gregor's solemn expression.

"My compliments on today's events. Everything went very well."

"Anlía organized most of it. I only advised where fine points of Trezvindjan traditions were involved."

"Then I shall make a point of congratulating my daughter, too. Now, as I mentioned, there are some additions I need to make to the coronation ceremony. Announcements, more precisely. I believe your experience and position as Grand Councillor place you in the best position to advise me."

"I shall do my best, Sire."

"First, only a handful of people know. A Turandan vessel should arrive soon. Our chief palace physician and two experienced Valiria mid-wives will arrive to attend Alexa because we believe this baby should be born here in Trezvindja."

Bresklon's eyebrows shot up. "Indeed, Sire. Such a decision will certainly elicit the public's approval."

"That is likely so, but it isn't the reason behind our decision. Public approval is a bonus only. Alexa strongly feels this is right for our baby, and Milansa Krisantal agrees with her."

"She has consulted Grandmother Milansa?" Bresklon asked in surprise.

"She has, even though we had already decided." Gregor tasted his brandy. "We will also announce that this child is a son who will bear a Trezvindjan first name. He will be called Gaelderon. This way, I can honor Grandfather because that is his second name, and Alexa can honor her bibo since I understand Gaelderon is a form of Gaeldoreg. We serve three purposes with a single name."

Smiling widely, Bresklon chuckled. "Sire, that is absolutely brilliant."

"This is all in confidence, Councillor. Only my wife and I know this."

"Of course. Announcing this during your coronation speech will certainly further endear you and the queen to our people. I look forward to the reaction."

"I've also thought long and hard about other plans for the future. I must look ahead to matters of governance for both Trezvindja and Turand. For the time being, Turand needs my attention most to ensure economic stabilization and growth occur properly now that the damnable Sifiq War is over. I cannot do that from here, and I want Nikolai directly involved.

"Considering she has integrated so well into the Trezvindjan government and society, I intend to announce that Anlía will continue acting as my regent. However, that decision requires your cooperation and agreement."

"Your confidence in Anlía is entirely merited, but I'm not certain I understand, Sire. Such a decision lies entirely in your domain."

"You know her capabilities best. Your position requires that you support her duties. Furthermore, as long as you understand her brother will likely strangle you if you ever hurt her—provided I don't reach you first—the additional announcement of your betrothal and upcoming marriage would also place you in a very unusual position as Grand Councillor and husband to Trezvindja's sitting regent."

Bresklon stared at Gregor. Blinking his eyes in surprise, he set aside his glass. "Sire?"

"You have my permission to marry my daughter, but this remains our secret until I announce it at the coronation. Not even Alexa knows. You must let me know regarding your decision as far as the regency."

Catching his breath, Bresklon silently prayed gratitude to Espiritus for this most wonderful blessing and begged for the ability to keep the king's secret. Finally, he met Gregor's waiting gaze. "To say thank you falls woefully short of the honor you just granted me. I swear by all I hold sacred that I will cherish your daughter and care for her with every breath I take. As for her regency, rely on her. She will have my full assistance and support as a loyal Trezvindjan."

Gregor finally smiled and approached his future son-in-law. Firmly grasping Bresklon's arms, he said, "We may eventually need to change your role to a new royal. Consider that. In the meantime, welcome to my family."

~

As if Alexa hadn't already done so, Braeklojorn inspected every detail of Gregor's silver-gray tunic. Golden epaulets gleamed. Stripes of red, blue, and purple decorated the wide cuffs of his sleeves and repeated in narrow bands from shoulder to hem on his right side. On his left, the crests of both Trezvindja and Turand were arranged vertically, with the Krisantal, Toscano, and Vosklon family insignia horizontally beneath. His black leather belt shone brightly, as did his polished black shoes. Formal black trousers were perfectly cut to enhance the length of his muscular legs.

"You look every inch the warrior king," Braeklojorn said admiringly, handing Gregor the belt with the elaborate scabbard and ceremonial sword used at Trezvindjan coronations for almost a thousand years.

"I pray never again a warrior king," Gregor said. "I trade my fighting sword for Trezvindja's coronation robes, its throne in addition to Turand's, and peace with my family."

Braeklojorn chuckled. "You've certainly earned it."

Inside the queen's apartments, Katara added one more pin to Alexa's hair. "I never did this as well as Adrina, but this should withstand your waves in this humidity."

Alexa gazed into the mirror. "I wish Adrina hadn't felt the need to stay behind with Oui-lest and her new baby, but I do understand. Besides, you always did beautifully with my hair. It's lovely. Now go. Anlía will help me finish dressing."

After Anlía finished tying the final laces of her golden gown, Alexa turned and held her daughter's chin. "What troubles you, dear one? Problems with Bresklon?"

Glancing away, Anlía blinked back tears. "Yes. He seemed so remote after he spoke with Father following the reception. When I asked if something was wrong, he just mumbled something about last-minute changes to coronation plans and said he would explain later. I'm certain he avoided me all day yesterday. I usually have a clear sense of what he's thinking, but I'm sure he's blocking me right now."

"Anlía, Bresklon strikes me as a perfectionist. Especially now, he's trying to earn your father's approval. I'm sure he wants everything to be exactly right today. Don't seek trouble. Trust everything will work out according to Val's plan."

Anlía heaved a sigh. "You have so much more practice doing that than I. I am working on it."

"As I recall, you did an excellent job until you met the good councillor."

Anlía forced a faint smile. "Is this what love does to a person?"

"Sometimes. We lose focus and patience. Nothing matters except being with the object of our affection. You are a Valiria priestess but a young one. Reach deep, my love. Your faith and Val will sustain you."

"You're absolutely right." Anlía bent to kiss her mother. "I love you. I think it's time to go."

The outdoor amphitheater lay beneath azure skies. White clouds skimmed across the heavens as if playing lazy games of catch-me-if-you-can. Flowering trees and blooming gardens filled the air with complex fragrances to tease the senses. Soft breezes dared the summery day to become oppressive. Invited guests followed ushers to assigned seats before the public could enter and claim open seating.

Looking over the arena, Gregor could hardly believe the sheer array of colored banners, pennants, and bunting decorating seats, rails, balconies, poles, literally anything that could hold a flag or streamer. Alexa had not exaggerated when she told him Trezvindjans loved color. In fairness, each league was represented by a different color, adding to the rainbow displays. Smiling to himself, Gregor also considered the lively hues he had seen in plants and animals as he toured the island. All these vivid shades must undoubtedly inspire this joyous radiance.

The ceremony began. Of necessity, key political figures spoke of this new era, highlighting what many now called the Rebirth of the Protectors. Optimism abounded. Braeklojorn quietly translated for the Turandans.

Shamani Milansa Krisantal initiated a chanted prayer, beseeching blessings from Espiritus on Trezvindja and its people. She then summoned Gregor, who solemnly walked down a center aisle, up to the central stage, and knelt. With her hands above his head, the Shamani prayed for divine guidance and blessings on King Gregor and his reign over Trezvindja. When she finished, she invited Alexa to join them. She then requested blessings on the new queen.

Two Protector commanders, each wearing white dress uniforms, escorted Gregor to a gold and white throne. Standing at attention, he listened to the King's Oath in Trezvindjan first, then repeated it slowly, as carefully coached by his grandfather. Then, according to tradition, he extended his right arm. Since Kaelzron again declined familial duty, Grandmother Oneshkla stepped in. With a small, sharp, ceremonial dagger, she made a small cut on Gregor's hand, allowing several drops of his blood to soak into a thick, ancient scroll stained with the blood of all recorded Trezvindjan kings and queens but one.

Gregor then sat while Oneshkla placed a crown of gold studded with diamonds and emeralds on his head. Milansa held the precious scroll up for the onlookers to see and called out, "Hail to our King Gregor. He is now one with all the good kings and queens who have served Trezvindja! Pledge your loyalty now."

Everyone knelt. Their beloved Shamani had accepted him on the Mystic Scroll of the Sacred Blood of the Krisantal. Most onlookers offered their vow of loyalty for the first time to their half-ishna king, who had won the hearts of their Protector warriors. Those who had already pledged renewed their oaths. King Gregor of Turand was now Trezvindja's Sacred Blood King of the Krisantal.

Minutes passed as bells rang out. Citizens chanted an ancient hymn recalling the founding of Trezvindja and how the Krisantal had brought peace and clarity to the people. Braeklojorn had told him parts of the actual events were obscured in the mists of times past, but there was some magic—some powerful mystique—woven into the fiber of every Trezvindjan. Once the mystique took root, it remained a vital, living part of the Trezvindjan psyche. With nearly everyone, it was present from birth.

Gregor had wondered about Grandfather's story and thought he felt an odd stirring afterward. Dismissing it as imagination, he continued with all the coronation plans, especially his speeches. With bells and chants vibrating through his body, frissons traveled down his spine the moment the ancient scroll had pressed against his bleeding hand. He remembered that same tingling sensation after listening to Grandfather's tales. Feeling eyes studying him intently, he suddenly glanced at Alexa. Perhaps the stirring hadn't been imagination after all.

Snapping back to the present, he met the direct gaze of a distinguished elder of the Mystic Council and saluted him with an elegant tilt of his head. The elder pronounced a blessing beyond Gregor's comprehension and placed a second crown in his hands. Gregor stood and waited for Alexa to approach. With the Protectors helping her, Alexa knelt and then chanted her queen's oath, also in carefully practiced Trezvindjan.

Pride plainly showed on Gregor's face as he placed a smaller, identical version of his crown on Alexa's head. Then, offering her his hands to help her up, he said, "Rise, Queen Alexa of Trezvindja. Join your King as we greet our people."

Gregor proudly led Alexa to the far side of the stage and back again for the benefit of applauding, chanting onlookers. He then escorted her to the Queen's throne beside his. Signaling Bresklon, the two men approached podiums at the center front of the stage. The new king waited for the audience to grow quiet.

"My dear Trezvindjans, I beg your forgiveness for delivering this address in the *common language*. As you all know, I was born and grew up in Turand with no knowledge of this exquisite heritage inherited from my mother. To avoid making embarrassing mistakes while learning my new language, Grand Councillor Bresklon Krisantal has kindly offered to translate for those who may not understand my message."

Gregor described briefly how Alexa discovered the romantic tragedy of Princess Royal Mishkla Krisantal and her beloved Grand Prince Braeklojorn Vosklon. He then explained how the courage of Queen Alexa and the determination of long-lost Trezvindjan shipwreck survivors resulted in the voyage to Trezvindja that confirmed his identity as Mishkla's rightful heir.

He then described his reasons for invading the Sifiq Kingdom. By relating recent Sifiq atrocities to historical conflicts forcibly settled in the past by Protectors, Gregor reminded his new people of their purpose stated in Trezvindjan charter documents written millennia earlier. Like the original Krisantal scrolls, his ultimate desire centered on peace. With the Sifiq army and navy now defeated by brave Trezvindjan and Turandan allies, Gregor stated his goal as king of the two nations was to foster lasting peace in this vast region of their world. He ended this part of his speech by describing the newly established government in the renamed nation of Sifiqqa. Both Turandans and Trezvindjans were teaching the new Sifiqqa Board of Governors best governance practices. Turand was providing practical security, construction, and agricultural assistance to help Sifiq civilians recover from decades of abuse, neglect, and corruption. The deposed Bin-Lot waited in a Sifiqqa prison, pending trial for high crimes against his people.

Gregor paused. "Now for lighter commentary." He glanced at Alexa and winked. "I've noticed that Trezvindjans are as observant as Turandans when it comes to what I shall describe as my wife's irresistible charms." The crowd laughed appreciatively as Gregor turned and beckoned to his wife, who blushed admirably.

"For those who don't know, Alexa is Turand's High Priestess Valkana and a mystic whose abilities have astonished me over the years. Many of our own esteemed Protectors owe their lives to her ability to summon our Creator's divine healing. This ability is as amazing to witness in action as it is to experience. I know because I have done both.

"Alexa tells me that this new child she bears me is a son. I have no reason to doubt because she has been right about all our previous six children, although she kept news of our twins a surprise. That's another story altogether." He waited for laughter to subside. "Because of our powerful feelings concerning this new child, we have decided to remain here in Trezvindja for his birth."

Surprised whispers and twitters raced through the crowd. People nodded their heads in approval and quickly quieted, waiting for Gregor's next comments.

"In a short time, the connections with our Trezvindjan family have become solid, loving relationships. If our new baby is to be born in

Trezvindja, then we believe his name should also be Trezvindjan, but one our Turandan people can easily manage. What name, though? A joking comment led us to the perfect decision. My grandfather is now a beacon of light for my soul. Grandfather's second name is derived from the name of someone who shares a unique bond with our queen—a man she loves so dearly she calls him Bibo. Our son will be named Gaelderon."

Gregor spun lightly on his heels, lifted Alexa's hands to his lips for a kiss, and whispered, "Sit down now so I can finish this. I am famished, and Willem promises me wine. Lots of wine."

Alexa grinned and snatched a quick kiss. "You're up to something, Your Majesty. I see it in your eyes." When he gave her a humorous wink signaling her to go, she suppressed laughter and returned to her seat.

"Now, for the future, so I can quickly let you return to yours. I have carefully considered the challenges of ruling two great nations. I plan to spend as much time here as practical. It is vitally important for me to understand issues affecting Trezvindja. Also, from a personal perspective, I want to experience as much as I possibly can of my Trezvindjan heritage. Trezvindja is the piece of my soul that I always knew was missing.

"Realistically, once Alexa recovers sufficiently from the birth of our baby, I must return to help Turand recover from the extreme drain the war effort cost. This is something I have already accomplished once in the past. My son Nikolai needs this experience should he ever face such trials there or here in the future."

He turned and asked a surprised Anlía to join him. "I consulted with Grand Councillor Bresklon Krisantal on a solution to address my responsibilities for Trezvindja since I cannot be here on a constant basis. My daughter, Princess Royal Anlía, has admirably fulfilled her duties as Princess Regent. Because she has been so well received by our good people here, the natural solution seemed for her to continue serving as Princess Regent. I had one pressing concern, but Grand Councillor Krisantal assures me that his betrothal and upcoming marriage to my daughter will not interfere with her duties and should actually ease any pressures resting on her shoulders. As such, I have decided she will remain here in Tarahlaz to represent my Crown.

"I thank you for joining me in this wondrous celebration today. Pray for your King and Queen and your Regent. Pray for your royal family and your country. Long live Trezvindja! Long live Turand!"

Applause and cheers rose in waves and reverberated off the amphitheater's walls. Alexa, teary-eyed, beamed at her husband. Braeklojorn blinked back joyous tears while making faces at Gaeldoreg for the shiny tracks sliding down his face. DiMarco and Thikos exchanged excited comments with Stefan while the twins clung to Uncle Vezzie's hands and basked in his affectionate attention. Willem and Katara watched the king and his daughter with frank amusement where, onstage, Anlía stared dumbfounded at her father.

Gregor gazed back at her. "Dear one, I believe everyone is waiting for us to lead a recessional."

Stirring to her senses, Anlía cried, "Who cares about the recessional?"

She threw her arms around Gregor's neck in an impossibly tight hug. "Oh! Father! Thank you! Thank you so much! You don't know how happy you've made me! Or how much I love you!"

Embracing his daughter tightly, Gregor's memory swiftly swept back to the first time he ever held her. That tiny baby had grown into the beautiful woman he now held in his arms. How and when had that happened? Tears swam in his eyes. "Be happy, my sweet Anlía, with your father's blessings. We must go now."

When she released him and turned, Bresklon held Alexa's hand for Gregor, who immediately placed it formally on his arm and walked with her to lead the recession from the stage. With obsidian eyes glistening, the Grand Councillor then took the hand of his Princess

Regent, saluted it with a kiss, and escorted her into place behind their King and Queen.

That evening, the coronation ball continued the festivities with lavish amounts of food and drink, lively music, dancing, and merry guests. To Gregor's enormous delight, his younger sons and Stefan had engineered a special surprise. Their delayed departure from Turand had concealed the travels of Gregor's godparents so they could attend his second coronation in their lifetime. The king's mood soared as he introduced Lord and Lady Karanan and learned that his future son-in-law had already surreptitiously provided them preferential seating at the banquet table. When Lord Manaran peeked over Lord Karanan's shoulder, Gregor's hearty laughter resounded throughout the ballroom.

Standing aside with Gaeldoreg, Alexa watched. "Bibo, how happy he looks. In all the years we've been together, I don't think I've ever seen him so free and joyful."

Gaeldoreg leaned over and dropped a kiss on his daughter's head. Nowadays, he never thought of her otherwise. "Your Gregor wears the crowns of two nations that admire and respect him. The Sifiq threat is ended, and he achieved justice against the man who hurt you. He has the family he always longed for. He is also loved by the most beautiful wife any man could desire." Gaeldoreg's smile faded. "Forgive me for saying this, Ma Levya—tonight especially—but truth is truth. Your Gregor is also finally free of Victor Garogan's heavy shadow."

Alexa blinked against an amazingly swift, blurred parade of memories. "You're right, Bibo. Truth is truth. Bibo?"

"Yes?"

"I really do love you. Now, will you show me that dance?"

When Alexa finally crawled into bed, she wondered how she had survived the ball. Midnight bells had rung, finding her dancing in Gregor's arms. His eyes had regarded her with such intensity. Gazing back, she

639

smiled. How she loved those dark eyes, heavily lashed and so expressive. Oblivious to their surroundings, she had paused in the middle of the dance. Stretching far up on tiptoe, she sought those lips that stirred her both emotionally and physically.

What had he said when she came to her senses? "Beloved, I believe our guests are applauding. It seems they approve of my happy queen."

She had blushed. He had quickly caught the rhythm of the music and led her back into the romantic dance until its end.

Wriggling into a more comfortable position, she watched Gregor climb into bed beside her. "You don't look tired at all. Unfortunately, your wife is exhausted."

Chuckling, Gregor rolled onto his side and kissed her forehead. "Which is why I excused us from a ball still in full swing. These Trezvindjans do like to party."

"So I see. I do appreciate the reprieve."

"Beloved," Gregor began, caressing her round belly, "I have two precious lives to protect. I'm glad I can do so."

Closing her eyes, she breathed in deeply and sighed. "It was a fantastic celebration." Then, sighing again and smiling, she said, "I will never forget Anlía's expression when you announced the betrothal. She was so distraught earlier thinking Bresklon might be upset with her."

Gregor chuckled. "He and I discussed the announcements I added to my speech the day we met in the library. I made him promise to say nothing."

"Gregor Toscano, that was evil. That poor man."

"I believe he enjoyed the surprise. How many men have their betrothals announced to a nation by his king at the king's coronation?" The exaggerated haughtiness in Gregor's voice prompted his wife to giggles.

"Well, I'm sure you made the right decision. Bresklon is a fine man."

"I know, Alexa. I learned that by accident in Turand. Perhaps I'll tell you about it one day."

Noting very sensitive tones in his comment, she didn't question him. "Did you notice Nikolai?"

"As a matter of fact, I did. As usual, our handsome son was beset by a bevy of beauties, but Grandmother Sharlia introduced him to one young lady who seemed rather reserved. The two then spent most of the evening talking or dancing. I've never seen Nikolai respond to any girl that way."

Alexa felt her eyelids growing heavier. "Nor have I. Recently, I've noticed his aura growing. The more time he spent with that girl, the brighter his aura grew. Hers, too."

"Really? Do you know who she was?"

Yawning, Alexa said, "Yes, and I'm surprised because her father is quite the extrovert. He's Councillor Brazjakan."

"I do remember him. He's the one…" Gregor realized his wife had suddenly grown quiet. A gentle smile softened the lines of his mouth. "Rest, my beloved. Sleep sweet."

↫

Two weeks later, Alexa strolled along a path winding through palace gardens vibrant with colorful flowers of varieties she was only beginning to learn. Restless, she hadn't slept well. Although her baby wasn't due for almost six weeks, she felt huge and uncomfortable. Walking eased some of the ache in her back.

Turning back toward the palace, she paused to gaze at glowing clouds in the sky. Brilliant shafts of sunlight broke through, creating a magical corona shining around the peak of distant Mount Shazatazefforalah. Such a magnificent display of light and golden color. Transfixed, she stood until she felt the familiar, abrupt tug that told her this day would be momentous.

Drawing a deep breath, she laid her hands over her swollen abdomen. "Little one, you come early. Val's light tells me it is your time. Wait for me to get help."

With slow, careful steps, she followed the path back, pausing several times to wait through contractions. Then, still a fair distance from the palace, she heard her name and called out. "Bibo! Here! I need help!"

Quickly rounding a twist in the path, Gaeldoreg appeared, his face drawn into a frown. "Ma Ishna, what's wrong?"

"The baby. He's coming early. Help me inside and send someone for Gregor."

Gaeldoreg wrapped an arm firmly around her and guided her into the palace, where his bold voice announced a string of commands that launched a flurry of activity. Servants raced about to advise everyone that the queen was on her way to the birthing room. A messenger left to notify the king, who had gone with Nikolai to meet with the Council of Leagues. Since the Turandan physician and Valiria had not yet arrived, the palace doctor was summoned. Katara hurried to the birthing room to help Alexa. Braeklojorn, who spent much of his time at the palace, gathered the children to wait.

By the time Gregor arrived in the birthing room with Anlía at his heels, Alexa was livid. "Get that man away from me!"

Gregor hurried to her side. "Beloved, I've come! Whatever is the matter?"

Alexa puffed through another powerful contraction. Katara shook her head in frustration. "The doctor keeps insisting she lie down."

When Alexa could finally speak, she hissed, "No wonder so many older Trezvindjan women suffer pains of the back! Anlía, change clothes and help. You may as well learn."

Gregor shook his head and told the doctor, "My wife is a renowned healer in Turand. Do as she says. We'll help her. Stay and learn our ways."

The Trezvindjan physician stared at him. "You, Your Majesty?"

Managing a stern smile as he positioned pillows behind Alexa's back, Gregor said, "I've attended the births of all my children. I alone delivered this daughter. Yes, doctor, I will help."

With Alexa calming in her husband's presence, Katara and Gregor quickly took the lead. Focusing on her breathing, Alexa could hardly believe the power of contractions driving the babe from her womb. Only faith prevented her from being afraid. She knew Val had willed the life of this child.

While she still could, she instructed Anlía to hold her hand while helping her with the Healing Graces. She expected this delivery to be more difficult than her others.

"Gregor!" She gasped. "Your son! You must be the one!"

Positioning himself to be ready, Gregor carefully grasped the baby's head and then securely held him as he entered the light of day. Katara watched and waited until the doctor separated the infant from his mother. Katara then took the child, now wailing loudly, from his father's hands to a table laid out with warmed toweling, where the doctor checked him. For a premature infant borne by an ishna, he was large indeed. The blonde ishna then cleaned, dressed, and wrapped the baby.

Alexa had collapsed backward against her mountain of pillows. The king gently wiped perspiration from her face while the doctor tended to her and watched sparkling, glittering lights extend from the princess to envelop the exhausted queen. Never had the Trezvindjan physician seen anything like the spectacle before him. He almost wondered if he might be hallucinating.

The lights faded. Gregor bent forward and kissed Alexa's damp forehead. He raised anxious eyes to his daughter's face.

"She'll be fine, Father. Gaelderon is a very big baby despite coming so early."

"Thanks be to Val that you were here to help her."

Katara edged close to Gregor's side. "Are you ready to hold him again?"

Taking his new son into his arms, Gregor once again marveled at the miracle of new life. "He looks just like Nikolai when he was born, only bigger." Gregor held the baby close and kissed his velvety smooth forehead. "Is there anything softer than a newborn babe?"

Anlía stroked her new brother's tiny hands. "Mother will sleep for a while. I think Grandfather and Gaeldoreg were worried when we came upstairs."

Katara chuckled softly. "Braeklojorn was worried. Gaeldoreg was scared out of his wits. That man is as protective a father as yours, Anlía."

"Doctor," Gregor said, "do you think my son is healthy enough for an introduction to his family?"

The physician shook his head. "Ordinarily, I would be terrified about an infant born so far ahead of term. However, this one appears strong and ready to face the world. We shall all keep good care, but I think a brief visit won't hurt."

Hearing Gregor's voice in the corridor outside the large drawing room, Gaeldoreg abruptly stood, his boots landing with a loud thump on carpeted floors. Still, he was frozen in place, fearful of moving if the king bore ill news. By the time Braeklojorn rose from his seat, Gregor had appeared beneath arched doorways, head bent low, carrying a white, blanketed bundle and tenderly cooing. Looking up, he smiled. "As usual, my Alexa was right. We have a son. Grandfather?"

The room's atmosphere brightened. Gregor's unworried smile relieved everyone's fears about problems with the delivery. Braeklojorn quickly approached his grandson and stared down at the tiny face, curiously looking around.

"Espiritus be praised!" Braeklojorn exclaimed softly. "He's beautiful! May I?"

Carefully, Gregor transferred the infant into his grandfather's waiting arms, reminding him to support the baby's head. Braeklojorn slowly moved to a large chair and sat, his attention focused on tiny hands and fingers, bright eyes, and swirls of dark hair covering the baby's head. Glancing upward, the Vosklon prince searched for words, finally asking, "How?"

Puzzled, Gregor asked, "How what, Grandfather?"

"He's but my great-grandson, yet I feel the miracle of his birth as if he were my own. How have you contained such pride and such joy for six other children?"

~

The outskirts of Toraval lay a few miles ahead, but the joyous melodies of temple carillons already carried on summer breezes. Watching Alexa nurse their son, Gregor had laughed at the baby's insatiable appetite and then quietly let his memory delve into images of the day Gaelderon was born.

Grandfather had been completely captivated, and a good-natured squabble had quickly erupted when Gaeldoreg reminded him that Alexa had promised him he could cuddle this grandchild once he was born. Marina and Karina had chimed in, scolding both that they would frighten the baby and telling them they also had plenty of experience tending babies. Nikolai said he was done with war, and he and his brothers would remain spectators for the time being.

Suddenly, Gaelderon had whimpered. Tiny whimpers had then progressed to loud, lusty crying just as Katara showed up. "Alexa is awake."

Gregor had seen the panic on his grandfather's face and laughed out loud. He had lifted Gaelderon into his arms, tucking him close to his heart. "Come, my little one. I think you're hungry, and your mother awaits you."

Gregor couldn't stop thinking of all the people he had met and the lives his family had touched. Grandfather had mused more than once over the name Mishkla had given their daughter. Derived from a much longer Trezvindjan word Gregor had not yet mastered, Anlía meant Spirit-Bridge. He and Alexa had also named their firstborn daughter Anlía. How appropriate the name when they considered how both women were spanning space, time, and distance between Turand and Trezvindja, bonding two peoples along with traditions and faith. How hard it was to avoid asking why. The mystics walking among them accepted the mystery with such patience and grace.

"You're smiling again."

Gregor looked up into those eyes he had long adored. "I have so many reasons to smile."

Alexa finished adjusting her clothes and shifted her now-sleeping baby. "We both do, although there's a lot of work waiting for us when we get home."

"True, but we have help. Nikolai is willing, as long as he keeps his head out of the clouds long enough."

Alexa laughed. "Ah, yes. The kind and sweet Laneshkla Brazjakan. Who would have thought?"

"She's pretty enough but certainly not as beautiful as most young ladies in either of my courts."

"Gregor, shame on you. Just because her teeth aren't perfectly straight, and she has a little bump in her nose from where she broke it as a girl? She's delightful. Admit it."

"Of course, she is. I do like her. Very much. She's bright and a good deal more charming than I first realized. I think she was self-conscious about her very slightly crooked teeth, but Nikolai doesn't mind at all."

"That's because her mind is sharp, and her heart is golden. Once she relaxes, she's like her father—not boring."

Gregor snorted his laughter. "I seem to recall Nikolai mentioning something like that not long ago."

"Well, as far as work, DiMarco and Thikos can arrange their class schedules to help you. In the meantime, I shall be very busy planning Gaelderon's Ceremony of Naming and Anlía's wedding." She looked down as the baby stretched in her arms. "I never expected to have a little one at this stage of our lives."

"Nor did I, but he makes me happy. You make me happiest of all."

Their eyes locked. Gregor drew in the clean air of Turand, the land of his birth, and the sweet fragrance of lilac that always accompanied his wife. Then, with a satisfied sigh, he leaned forward, taking her free hand and kissing it.

"I love you, Alexa. I will love you with my dying breath and beyond."

Epilogue

Song of Turand
(Gregor's Song...Reprise II)

Your gift of grace to me joyfully returned,
From bitter sorrow, my heart is set free.
Into darkness, my soul had drifted alone.
Now your love, your faith are returned to me.

Of Love and of Light, you were born for this land.
I sing the sweet song, the Song of Turand.

Through light, you conquered the pain they inflicted
With strength, you returned to those whom you love
You suffered, you endured, now I must stand the test
Help me keep you safe; I prayed to our God above.

Of Love and of Light, you were born for this land.
I will sing the sweet song, the Song of Turand.

Bridges of Turand

This heart that missed you must face now forward.
I desire home and peace, but my decision is cast
Sail the seas to foreign lands and swing my sword
Heavy my heart, but this threat can no longer last.

Of Love and of Light, you were born for this land.
I sing the sweet song, the Song of Turand.

The trials persist; by faith, we are shielded.
With our son at my side, we will not be conquered.
Through courage sustained, we have never yielded.
Inspired by love, we have neither surrendered.

Of Love and of Light, you were born for this land.
I sing the sweet song, our Song of Turand.

Again, my voice lifts in joyous refrain,
To heaven, my soul soars gloriously free,
Infinite bound'ries extend once again.
For your light, your love come hither to me.

Together again, your hand tightly in mine,
In this land where they threatened your very life,
In this land that tortured you, causing you pain,
To this place, you came to help me face the strife.

Of Love and of Light, you were born for this land.
I sing the sweet song, my Song of Turand.

Sandra Valencia

Strengthened in purpose, in will, and wisdom,
Reminded that darkness can be conquered by light,
Your courage inspired me so I could not fail,
My quest to save you would set other lives to right.

Beloved, you returned to this grieving land of war
To deliver great aid, to make this king a king,
With boundless love, you fulfilled my dreams,
Never can I count all the blessings you bring.

Of Love and of Light, born for more than our land,
Born to bring life to this solitary man.
Again, so sweet this song do I sing,
Two hearts rejoined, eternally one,
United in joy beneath golden sun,
Again, so sweet this song I still sing,
For you, beloved, are my sweet Song of Turand.